About the Editors

ROBERT WEINBERG, one of the foremost authorities on weird fiction pulp magazines, is the author of *The Weird Tales Story,* for which he won the World Fantasy Award.

STEFAN R. DZIEMIANOWICZ is the fiction editor of *Crypt of Cthulhu* and the author of *An Annotated Guide to "Unknown" and "Unknown Worlds."*

MARTIN H. GREENBERG has justly earned the title "King of the Anthologists" with more than 300 books to his credit. Professor of regional analysis and political science at the University of Wisconsin-Green Bay, he also teaches a course in science fiction.

RIVALS OF WEIRD TALES™

**30 GREAT FANTASY & HORROR STORIES
FROM THE WEIRD FICTION PULPS**

•

Introduction by
Stefan R. Dziemianowicz

•

Edited by Robert Weinberg,
Stefan R. Dziemianowicz,
& Martin H. Greenberg

•

BONANZA BOOKS
New York

Copyright © 1990 by Robert Weinberg, Stefan R. Dziemianowicz, and Martin H. Greenberg

Interior illustration "Oscar" by Edd Cartier, copyright 1941 by Street and Smith Publications, Inc. Copyright renewed 1969 by The Condé Nast Publications, Inc. First appeared in *Street and Smith's Unknown*. Reprinted by permission of Edd Cartier and Davis Publications, Inc.

First published in 1990 by Bonanza Books, distributed by Crown Publishers, Inc., 225 Park Avenue South, New York, New York 10003.

Weird Tales® is a registered trademark of Weird Tales, Limited

Printed and bound in the United States of America

Library of Congress Cataloging-in-Publication Data

Rivals of Weird tales : 30 great fantasy and horror stories from the weird fiction pulps / introduction by Stefan R. Dziemianowicz ; edited by Robert Weinberg, Stefan R. Dziemianowicz, and Martin H. Greenberg.
    p. cm.
    ISBN 0-517-69331-3
    1. Fantastic fiction, American. 2. Horror tales, American.
I. Weinberg, Robert E. II. Dziemianowicz, Stefan R.
III. Greenberg, Martin Harry.
PS648.F3R57 1990
813'.0873808—dc20   89-27939
                                                      CIP

8 7 6 5 4 3 2 1

Acknowledgments

Grateful acknowledgment for permission to reprint material is hereby given to the following:

Cool Air by H. P. Lovecraft—Copyright 1928 by Personal Arts Company. Reprinted by permission of the agents for the author's Estate, the Scott Meredith Literary Agency, Inc., 845 Third Avenue, New York, NY 10022.

The Return of the Sorcerer by Clark Ashton Smith—Copyright 1931 by Clayton Magazines, Inc. Reprinted by permission of the agents for the author's Estate, the Scott Meredith Literary Agency, Inc., 845 Third Avenue, New York, NY 10022.

Wolves of Darkness by Jack Williamson—Copyright 1932 by Clayton Magazines, Inc. Renewed © 1960 by Jack Williamson. Reprinted by permission of the Spectrum Literary Agency.

The Cairn on the Headland by Robert E. Howard—Copyright 1932 by Clayton Magazines, Inc. for *Strange Stories*, January 1933. Reprinted by permission of Glenn Lord.

Imp of Satan by Hugh B. Cave—Copyright 1935 by Popular Publications, Inc. Reprinted by permission of Kirby McCauley, Ltd.

Cursed Be the City by Henry Kuttner—Copyright 1939 by Henry Kuttner. Reprinted by permission of Don Congdon Associates, Inc.

Logoda's Heads by August Derleth—Copyright 1939 by Better Publications, Inc. Reprinted by permission of the agents for the author's Estate, the Scott Meredith Literary Agency, Inc., 845 Third Avenue, New York, NY 10022.

Miracle in Three Dimensions by C. L. Moore—Copyright 1939 by Better Publications, Inc. Reprinted by permission of Don Congdon Associates, Inc.

For Fear of Little Men by Manly Wade Wellman—Copyright 1939 by Better Publications, Inc. for *Strange Stories*, June 1939. Reprinted by permission of Karl Edward Wagner, Literary Executor for the Estate of Manly Wade Wellman.

Spawn of Blackness by Carl Jacobi—Copyright 1939 by Better Publications, Inc. for *Strange Stories*, October 1939. Reprinted by arrangement with the author's agent, R. Dixon Smith.

Me and My Shadow by Eric Frank Russell—Copyright 1940 by Better Publications, Inc. Reprinted by permission of the agents for the author's Estate, the Scott Meredith Literary Agency, Inc., 845 Third Avenue, New York, NY 10022.

Strange Stories
(February 1939–February 1941)

Unknown/Unknown Worlds
(March 1939–October 1943)

Fantastic Adventures
(May 1939–March 1953)

Stirring Science Stories
(February 1941–March 1942)

The Magazine of Fantasy and Science Fiction
(Fall 1949–   )

Beyond Fantasy Fiction
(July 1953–March 1955)

Introduction

It may seem curious to define a book by what it is not but, as the title *Rivals of Weird Tales* implies, this is a collection of stories from the weird fiction pulps that did *not* appear in *Weird Tales*. For anyone not familiar with modern horror and fantasy literature or the popular fiction magazines of the 20th century, this may require some explanation.

The pulp magazine era extended roughly from the turn of the century to the early 1950s. Although it was coined originally to describe the crude quality of the paper used in the thousands of popular fiction magazines sold at newsstands, train stations, and drugstores during these years, the term "pulp" eventually came to serve as a description for the kind of fiction those magazines published—accessible "lowbrow" entertainment, meant to be as ephemeral as the paper on which it was printed. The pulp era coincides with the years that saw the publication of the best work of William Faulkner, F. Scott Fitzgerald, Ernest Hemingway, and other literary heavyweights. While those authors were busy creating an enduring 20th-century American tradition for their elite circle of readers, the pulp writers were turning out breathless romances, exotic adventures, action-packed thrillers, and tales of marvels and mystery for the masses. This is not to say that literate and even artistic writing was not being done in the pulps, for it certainly was. However, at the time, pulp fiction stood in relation to "serious" literature much the same way that today's paperback bestseller does to the high-quality hardcover.

Initially, the pulps arose to provide cheap reading for working and immigrant classes. During their heyday in the 1930s and 1940s, though, they served a more important purpose: diversion. In a period marked by the economic deprivations of the Depression and the horrors of World War II, the pulp magazines offered wish fulfillment at bargain prices. Through their pages a reader could temporarily escape from the real world to tramp through the jungle habitat of Amazon warriors, dogfight the Luftwaffe as the co-pilot of America's greatest flying ace, or tag along after supersleuths as they hunted down spies and gangsters who threatened the moral fiber of the country. War stories, love stories, western stories, outer space stories, detective stories, horror stories— the pulps served up all of them for a mere 25 cents or less per issue.

With the exception of several western and detective magazines, most of the early pulps were general fiction magazines that were not limited to a particular genre. Then, in March of 1923, *Weird Tales* made its debut. The first and greatest of the weird fiction magazines, *Weird Tales* was to last for more than thirty-one years and give America a hand in shaping supernatural literature, a body of fiction that hitherto had been almost exclusively the domain of English and European writers. Over the course of 279 issues and three editors—and with offerings from the imaginations of perhaps a thousand writers—*Weird Tales* laid the foundations for modern horror and fantasy fiction.

If one had to choose the single outstanding quality of *Weird Tales,* it would be editorial diversity. In its lifetime, *Weird Tales* published everything from mild science fiction to sword-and-sorcery fiction and anything from Gothic horror to light fantasy. The broad range of tastes catered to not only helped it to survive in spite of perpetual financial difficulties, but also to live up to its subtitle, "The Unique Magazine." As a result, *Weird Tales* was able to accomodate the work of several generations of writers instrumental in the evolution of weird fiction beyond its Gothic primitiveness. A list of the authors whose work helped shaped the character of the magazine reads like a roster of the best fantasists of the 20th century: H. P. Lovecraft, Robert Bloch, Clark Ashton Smith, Ray Bradbury, Robert E. Howard, Fritz Leiber, and Richard Matheson, to name but a few. It's true that the majority of stories these and other authors published in *Weird Tales* were no better than the fiction found in any other pulp magazine, but a good many more have aged remarkably well and are still read today.

What kind of diversion or entertainment did a magazine full of unspeakable monsters, old dark houses, and Gothic nightmares provide for a populace already shocked by the hard times of the Depression years? The answer is very simple: the average *Weird Tales* story seemed to imply that no matter how bad daily life was, *things could always be worse.* Whether it ended happily or horribly, whether it provided an uplifting moral or an insight into the darkness of the human soul, a *Weird Tales* story always let the reader see his worst fears acted out at a safe distance. In this respect, *Weird Tales* provided the same sort of catharsis for weird fiction readers that the western or detective pulps did—but with a bit more imagination.

The demand for the emotional outlet and entertainment *Weird Tales* offered its readers must have been great, for, in time, *Weird Tales* alone wasn't enough to satisfy everyone. Sensing that there was room for more than one weird fiction magazine on the newsstands, a number of enterprising publishers brought out their own titles in an attempt to capture a piece of the market for fantasy and horror fiction established by *Weird Tales.* Some of these magazines were ill-conceived and folded quickly. Others mounted serious competition and enjoyed varying degrees of success. Regardless of their individual merits, all were rivals of *Weird Tales* in the truest sense. In their efforts either to emulate the magazine or distinguish themselves from it, they acknowledged its unique impact on the weird fiction genre.

At first, however, rivalry was slow to develop. Between 1923 and 1931, *Weird Tales* ruled the weird fiction roost and only two magazines tried to steal its thunder: the narrowly focused *Ghost Stories,* and *Tales of Magic and Mystery.* The latter was an unusual combination of "true" occult stories and the occasional weird fiction tale; it lasted for only five issues between 1927 and 1928. However, the magazine could claim one coup: it published a tale by H. P. Lovecraft. Until that time, Lovecraft's work had been almost the exclusive property of *Weird Tales,* a situation that many other weird-fiction authors found themselves trapped in because they had no desire to try their hands at other kinds of fiction. Lovecraft's appearance in *Tales of Magic and Mystery* indicated that *Weird Tales* writers would send their work to other weird fiction markets if they existed.

This point was emphasized with the appearance of *Strange Tales of Mystery and Terror,* or just plain *Strange Tales,* in 1931. Paying two cents a word to *Weird Tales'* one cent (and sometimes less), editor Harry Bates was able to lure Henry S. Whitehead, Hugh Cave, Jack Williamson, Clark Ashton Smith, Robert E. Howard, and some of the best weird fiction writers of the day out from under the wing of *Weird Tales* editor Farnsworth Wright. At times, the contents pages of *Strange Tales* and *Weird Tales* seemed interchangeable, but there was at least one notable difference between the two: *Strange Tales* published slightly longer stories, averaging a novella of perhaps 40,000 words in every issue and a handful of other tales in the 8,000- to 15,000-word range. This gave writers more room to develop their plots and characters— qualities sorely lacking in most pulp fiction. A number of fine stories appeared in the seven issues of *Strange Tales,* and, had the magazine come out at a less precarious time, there's no telling how its success might have affected the fortunes of *Weird Tales.* But in 1931, the Depression was entering its worst years, and by 1933, *Strange Tales* and many other pulps had sunk into oblivion.

The Depression had a mostly destructive effect on the variety and volume of pulp fiction published in the 1930s; it turned the marketplace into a proving ground where survival-of-the-fittest tactics prevailed. But it also ensured that the magazines finding a niche in the public consciousness were likely to survive against incredible odds. It's no coincidence, for example, that the hero pulps flourished during the worst years of the Depression. This was the decade that saw the birth of *The Shadow, Doc Savage, G-8 and His Battle Aces,* and numerous other magazines in which daring do-gooders risked their lives to save their towns, their nations, even the world. Although the stories in these magazines sometimes had a mild fantasy or science fiction element, what really seemed to captivate the reading public was the superhero figure himself. An embodiment of traditional American values, the superhero assured that virtue and goodness would triumph even in the most hopeless circumstances.

The hero pulps were counterbalanced by the infamous weird menace, or "shudder pulps." Starting in 1933, when *Dime Mystery Magazine* shifted from a straight mystery format to stories filled with sadism, soft-core sex, and penny-ante supernaturalism, the shudder pulps supplied escapism of a low (but, apparently necessary) sort. Though they were tame in comparison to contemporary exploitation literature, their garish covers and turgid prose often banished them to a place under the counter. In 1934, Popular Publications launched *Terror Tales* and, in 1935, *Horror Stories,* the two most famous shudder pulps. Tales from these magazines typically involved the hero and heroine in weird events that appeared to have a supernatural basis. By the end of the story, though, all the strange happenings were revealed to be the work of madmen or ordinary criminals with vivid imaginations. Formulaic and ludicrous as most of these stories were, they demanded a certain inventiveness on the writer's part to keep the plot suitably strange without going completely overboard. The bulk of the shudder pulp stories were turned out by a small cadre of pulpsmiths such as Hugh Cave, Paul Ernst, Wayne Rogers, Arthur Burks, Norvell W. Page, and E. Hoffmann Price, many of whom wrote more respectable fiction for other markets. Although it's not likely that the shudder pulps ever threatened to steal away readers, *Weird Tales* felt compelled to retaliate with its own weird menace character, Dr. Satan, in 1935.

It was not until 1939 that *Weird Tales* experienced its first serious sustained rivalry. With the country's economic outlook improving and pulp publishers willing to expand their range of titles, the popular fiction market exploded. A phenomenal number of new titles jostled each other at the newsstands that year, among them *Strange Stories* and *Fantastic Adventures.* The former was a blatant attempt by Standard Magazines to ride *Weird Tales'* coattails, right down to luring some of "the Unique Magazine's" writers into its pages. However, even though occasional contributions from Henry Kuttner, Eric Frank Russell, C. L. Moore, Seabury Quinn, Carl Jacobi, August Derleth, or Manly Wade Wellman read like stories that Farnsworth Wright, in a capricious mood, might have turned down, work by lesser-known authors read like the dregs of the *Weird Tales* rejects. *Strange Stories* lasted only for an unlucky thirteen issues.

Fantastic Adventures, on the other hand, was to live for fourteen years. Brought out as the fantasy companion to *Amazing Stories* (the first science fiction pulp), it offered an uneven mix of fantasy and light science fiction. Although much of its contents had only a juvenile appeal, in later years it published excellent work by Fritz Leiber, John D. MacDonald, William Tenn, and Theodore Sturgeon. Memorable stories from earlier issues included Edgar Rice Burroughs' Carson-on-Venus novels and Robert Bloch's daffy adventures of Lefty Feep. Without a doubt, the major event in weird fiction in 1939 was the premiere of *Unknown* (later retitled *Unknown Worlds*). *Unknown* had been conceived by editor John W. Campbell at about the same time he began publishing the first stories of Robert A. Heinlein, A. E. van Vogt, and Isaac Asimov in *Astounding Science-Fiction*. Just as *Astounding* changed the course of modern science fiction, *Unknown* gave a new direction to fantasy literature. Campbell's one outstanding qualification for editing *Unknown* was his disdain for most of the work then being published in the weird fiction pulps. He found these stories cliched, overwrought, and completely out of touch with the modern world. For this reason, he vowed that *Unknown* would not be simply another *Weird Tales* clone, but would provide readers with a genuine, adult alternative.

"You can't convince a man of normal intelligence of something he knows darn well is cockeyed by any amount of argument," Campbell wrote to one of his authors. "On the other hand he'll accept any premise you want to set up for the sake of the story." It was through this spirit of playful agreement between readers and writers that Campbell hoped to evolve what he called a "new mythology," one that would speak to contemporary interests. He stressed the power of good writing over the cheap theatrics and the purple prose that weighed down other weird-fiction magazines. More importantly, he demanded that his writers make their fantasy as logical as science fiction. There were to be no more fainting narrators, no more last-minute rescues, no more heaping on ridiculous fantastic effects. In *Unknown,* even the incredible had to operate by some sort of rationale. Most *Unknown* stories took place in a world recognizable as the one right outside the reader's own window. Consequently, they tended to play up the incongruity of supernatural phenomena occurring in a rational world hard pressed to accept their existence. This was already a proven formula for horror fiction, and many fine horror stories were to appear in *Unknown*. But the same approach gave rise to an unusual amount of humorous fantasy, a style of fiction all but lacking in the weird fiction magazines up to that time.

Unlike other fantasy editors, Campbell did not try to coax authors away from *Weird Tales*. Rather, he recruited heavily from his science fiction writers, who tended to view fantasy from new and startlingly original perspectives: L. Ron Hubbard and L. Sprague de Camp sent Campbell stories of anti-heroes who possessed powers they could not fully control; Robert Bloch, Fredric Brown, and Theodore Sturgeon wrote of average men and women who tried to incorporate inexplicable experiences into their daily lives; Lester del Rey, H. L. Gold, and Jane Rice told of familiar fantasy creatures trying to adapt to a world that no longer had any use for them; Cleve Cartmill, Fritz Leiber, and Jack Williamson worked out perfectly logical explanations for witchcraft, lycanthropy, and other supernatural phenomena.

Stories from the pages of *Unknown* still rank as some of the best fantasy produced in this century, including Hubbard's *Fear* and *Typewriter in the Sky;* de Camp's *Lest Darkness Fall* and (with Fletcher Pratt) the magical misadventures of Harold Shea; Williamson's *Darker Than You Think;* Leiber's sword and sorcery stories of Fafhrd and the Gray Mouser, and his horror novel, *Conjure Wife;* Sturgeon's "It"; Anthony Boucher's "The Compleat Werewolf"; and Henry Kuttner's "A Gnome There Was" and "The Devil We Know." It is almost impossible to sum up the scope of all the fiction that appeared in *Unknown,* except to say that these stories helped prove that fantasy could flourish outside the confines of the haunted house, the Gothic mansion, and the dark forest. Indeed, it seems the only environment in which *Unknown*'s fantasy could not thrive was a country on the verge of war. When war broke out in Europe in October 1939, *Unknown* muddled through in spite of dwindling foreign markets and evaporating printing supplies. But when America entered the war in 1941, Campbell lost many of his best writers. Finally, in 1943, paper rationing forced him to discontinue the magazine. Despite years of promises, *Unknown* was never revived. The magazine's thirty-nine issues remain notable for an impact on modern fantasy that only *Weird Tales* can match.

Wartime economics had the same adverse effect on the pulps that the Depression had had several years before. Publishers cut their loss leaders, shrank their magazines down to digest size, and shifted from monthly to bi-monthly or quarterly publication. Nevertheless, there were still possibilities for determined editors and writers willing to work for almost nothing. Many such souls could be found in the famous New York science fiction club known as the Futurians, and when club members Frederik Pohl and Donald Wollheim were given editorial positions, they invited fellow members to write for them. The result was a series of short-lived science fiction pulps that launched the careers of esteemed authors such as Robert "Doc" Lowndes, James Blish, Cyril Kornbluth, and Damon Knight. One of these magazines, *Stirring Science Stories,* which ran for only four issues between 1941 and 1942, was built around a unique concept: its contents page was separated into a science fiction *and* a fantasy section, essentially giving the reader two magazines in one. Even so, the majority of the stories in each section was written by Futurians, under their own names and a variety of pen names.

In its own small way, *Stirring Science Stories* helped weird fiction to maintain its tenuous hold on the public's fancy during the 1940s, but its efforts almost went for nought. With the dropping of the atomic bomb, science fiction earned a new respectability that was to help it become the dominant form of imaginative literature in the postwar years. At the same time, the glaring dawn of the nuclear age seemed to dim fantasy's luster and expose the emptiness of horror's dark shadows. A profusion of new science fiction titles flooded the newsstands in the early 1950s and gradually edged weird fiction titles out of the market. Digests like *Fantasy Magazine* (edited by *Unknown* emeritus Lester del Rey) and *Beyond Fantasy Fiction* made valiant efforts to stay afloat, but to no avail. *Beyond's* fate was particularly telling. Begun by *Unknown* alumnus H. L. Gold as a companion to *Galaxy Science Fiction, Beyond* embraced many of the same values as John W. Campbell's magazine. It even printed the work of *Unknown* authors L. Sprague de Camp, Theodore Sturgeon, and Cleve Cartmill, in addition to witty, urbane stories by newcomers Richard Matheson, Philip K. Dick, Jerome Bixby, and Philip Jose Famer. However, *Beyond* failed to find an audience, and even as *Galaxy* skyrocketed to become the most important of the postwar science fiction magazines, it died with the tenth issue in 1954.

Like Gold and del Rey, Anthony Boucher was another *Unknown* writer bitten by the editorial bug, and in 1949 he and J. Francis McComas brought out *The Magazine of Fantasy*, renamed, with the second issue, *The Magazine of Fantasy and Science Fiction*. In its early issues, *F&SF* reprinted classic weird fiction stories—not for lack of original contributions but because the editors hoped to establish a high literary tone for the magazine. *F&SF* studiously avoided the excesses of most pulp fantasy and encouraged writers to experiment and bend (and sometimes blend) genres. Like *Beyond,* it published the work of *Unknown* authors in addition to new work by Ray Bradbury, Kris Neville, Mildred Clingerman, and others. Unlike *Beyond, F&SF* developed a loyal following of readers who liked science fiction with a difference, and so it managed to survive the great shake-out that, by 1954, had killed *Weird Tales* and almost all of the other weird fiction pulps. Gradually, the better writers gravitated to *F&SF*'s pages, where they sowed some of the seeds for the current revival of interest in fantasy and horror fiction. *F&SF* continues to be one of the leading professional markets for fantasy fiction to this day.

No doubt, the average reader who picks up a copy of the most recent horror novel by Stephen King, Dean R. Koontz, or Peter Straub is oblivious to the history of the weird fiction pulps. It was with this thought in mind that the editors of this volume chose the stories you will find here. Though it is by no means the definitive collection of the best horror and fantasy the pulps had to offer, *Rivals of Weird Tales* is a representative anthology of the rich variety of stories and imaginative possibilities readers had to choose from in the formative years of modern weird fiction. Some of these stories have historical importance for their genres, yet none was chosen solely for this reason.

Indeed, our belief that all of these tales are as entertaining today as when they were first published is borne out by the fact that, in recent years, four have been adapted for television. We feel that they have withstood the test of time. Were it not for stories like these, the state of weird fiction would be very different today.

STEFAN R. DZIEMIANOWICZ

New York
1990

Cool Air

H. P. LOVECRAFT

H. P. Lovecraft's "The Call of Cthulhu" is a seminal work of modern weird fiction, one that both expanded the conceptual possibilities of the horror story and officially inaugurated the fantasy subgenre known as "The Cthulhu Mythos." How ironic that only months before he wrote the story in 1926, Lovecraft penned "Cool Air," an homage to the old-fashioned Gothic horrors of Edgar Allan Poe. Lovecraft acknowledged Poe as the most important influence on his writing, and readers familiar with Poe's tales will recognize Lovecraft's story as a rewriting of "The Facts in the Case of M. Valdemar." One of the few stories Lovecraft sold to an outlet other than Weird Tales, *"Cool Air" appeared in the next-to-last issue of the short-lived* Tales of Magic and Mystery.*

YOU ASK me to explain why I am afraid of a draught of cool air; why I shiver more than others upon entering a cold room, and seem nauseated and repelled when the chill of evening creeps through the heat of a mild autumn day. There are those who say I respond to cold as others do to a bad odour, and I am the last to deny the impression. What I will do is to relate the most horrible circumstance I ever encountered, and leave it to you to judge whether or not this forms a suitable explanation of my peculiarity.

It is a mistake to fancy that horror is associated inextricably with darkness, silence, and solitude. I found it in the glare of mid-afternoon, in the clangour of a metropolis, and in the teeming midst of a shabby and commonplace rooming-house with a prosaic landlady and two stalwart men by my side. In the spring of 1923 I had secured some dreary and unprofitable magazine work in the city of New York; and being unable to pay any substantial rent, began drifting from one cheap boarding establishment to another in search of a room which might combine the qualities of decent cleanliness, endurable furnishings, and very reasonable price. It soon developed that I had only a choice between different evils, but after a time I came upon a house in West Fourteenth Street which disgusted me much less than the others I had sampled.

The place was a four-story mansion of brownstone, dating apparently from the late forties, and fitted with woodwork and marble whose stained and sullied splendour argued a descent from high levels of tasteful opulence. In the rooms, large and lofty, and decorated with impossible paper and ridiculously ornate stucco cornices, there lingered a depressing mustiness and hint of obscure cookery; but the floors were clean, the linen tolerably regular, and the hot water not too often cold or turned off, so that I came to regard it as at least a bearable place to hibernate till one might really live again. The landlady, a slatternly, almost bearded Spanish woman named Herrero, did not annoy me with gossip or with criticisms of the late-burning electric light in my third-floor front hall room; and my fellow-lodgers were as quiet and uncommunicative as one might desire, being mostly Spaniards a little above the coarsest and crudest grade. Only the din of street cars in the thoroughfare below proved a serious annoyance.

I had been there about three weeks when the first odd incident occurred. One evening at about eight I heard a spattering on the floor and became suddenly aware that I had been smelling the pungent odour of ammonia for some time. Looking about, I saw that the ceiling was wet and dripping; the soaking apparently proceeding from a corner on the side toward the street. Anxious to stop the matter at its source, I hastened to the basement to tell the landlady; and was assured by her that the trouble would quickly be set right.

"Doctair Muñoz," she cried as she rushed upstairs ahead of me, "he have speel hees chemicals. He ees too seeck for doctair heemself—seecker and seecker all the time—but he weel not have no othair for help. He ees vairy queer in hees seeckness—all day he take funnee-smelling baths, and he cannot get excite or warm. All hees own house-work he do—hees leetle room are full of bottles and machines, and he do not work as doctair. But he was great once—my fathair in Barcelona have hear of heem—and only joost now he feex a arm of the plumber that get hurt of sudden. He nevair go out, only on roof, and my boy Esteban he breeng heem hees food and laundry and mediceens and chemicals. My Gawd, the salammoniac that man use for keep heem cool!"

Mrs. Herrero disappeared up the staircase to the fourth floor, and I returned to my room. The ammonia ceased to drip, and as I cleaned up what had spilled and opened the window for air, I heard the landlady's heavy footsteps above me. Dr. Muñoz I had never heard, save for certain sounds as of some gasoline-driven mechanism; since his step was soft and gentle. I wondered for a moment what the strange affliction of this man might be, and whether his obstinate refusal of outside aid were not the result of a rather baseless eccentricity. There is, I reflected tritely, an infinite deal of pathos in the state of an eminent person who has come down in the world.

I might never have known Dr. Muñoz had it not been for the heart attack that suddenly seized me one forenoon as I sat writing in my room. Physicians had told me of the danger of those spells, and I knew there was no time to be lost; so remembering what the landlady had said about the invalid's help of the injured workman, I dragged myself upstairs and knocked feebly at the door above mine. My knock was answered in good English by a curious voice some distance to the right, asking my name and business; and these things being stated, there came an opening of the door next to the one I had sought.

A rush of cool air greeted me; and though the day was one of the hottest of late June, I shivered as I crossed the threshold into a large apartment whose rich and tasteful decoration surprised me in this nest of squalor and seediness. A folding couch now filled its diurnal role of sofa, and the mahogany furniture, sumptuous hangings, old paintings, and mellow bookshelves all bespoke a gentleman's study rather than a boarding-house bedroom. I now saw that the hall room above mine— the "leetle room" of bottles and machines which Mrs. Herrero had mentioned—was merely the laboratory of the doctor; and that his main living quarters lay in the spacious adjoining room whose convenient alcoves and large contiguous bathroom permitted him to hide all dressers and obtrusively utilitarian devices. Dr. Muñoz, most certainly, was a man of birth, cultivation, and discrimination.

The figure before me was short but exquisitely proportioned, and clad in somewhat formal dress of perfect cut and fit. A high-bred face of masterful though not arrogant expression was adorned by a short iron-grey full beard, and an old-fashioned pince-nez shielded the full, dark eyes and surmounted an aquiline nose which gave a Moorish touch to a physiognomy otherwise dominantly Celtiberian. Thick, well-trimmed hair that argued the punctual calls of a barber was parted gracefully above a high forehead; and the whole picture was one of striking intelligence and superior blood and breeding.

Nevertheless, as I saw Dr. Muñoz in that blast of cool air, I felt a repugnance which nothing in his aspect could justify. Only his lividly inclined complexion and coldness of touch could have afforded a physical basis for this feeling, and even these things should have been excusable considering the man's known invalidism. It might, too, have been the singular cold that alienated me; for such chilliness was abnormal on so hot a day, and the abnormal always excites aversion, distrust, and fear.

But repugnance was soon forgotten in admiration, for the strange physician's extreme skill at once became manifest despite the ice-coldness and shakiness of his bloodless-looking hands. He clearly understood my needs at a glance, and ministered to them with a master's deftness; the while reassuring me in a finely modulated though oddly hollow and timbreless voice that he was the bitterest of sworn enemies to death, and had sunk his fortune and lost all his friends in a lifetime of bizarre experiment devoted to its bafflement and extirpation. Something of the benevolent fanatic seemed to reside in him, and he rambled on almost garrulously as he sounded my chest and mixed a suitable draught of drugs fetched from the smaller laboratory room. Evidently he found the society of a well-born man a rare novelty in this dingy environment, and was moved to unaccustomed speech as memories of better days surged over him.

His voice, if queer, was at least soothing; and I could not even perceive that he breathed as the fluent sentences rolled urbanely out. He sought to distract my mind from my own seizure by speaking of his theories and experiments; and I remember his tactfully consoling me about my weak heart by insisting that will and consciousness are stronger than organic life itself, so that if a bodily frame be but originally healthy and carefully preserved, it may through a scientific enhancement of these qualities retain a kind of nervous animation despite the most serious impairments, defects, or even absences in the battery of specific organs. He might, he half jestingly said, some day teach me to live— or at least to possess some kind of conscious existence—without any heart at all! For his part, he was afflicted with a complication of maladies requiring a very exact regimen which included constant cold. Any marked rise in temperature might, if prolonged, affect him fatally; and the frigidity of his habitation—some 55 or 56 degrees Fahrenheit— was maintained by an absorption system of ammonia cooling, the gasoline engine of whose pumps I had often heard in my own room below.

Relieved of my seizure in a marvellously short while, I left the shivery place a disciple and devotee of the gifted recluse. After that I paid him frequent overcoated calls; listening while he told of secret researches and almost ghastly results, and trembling a bit when I examined the unconventional and astonishingly ancient volumes on his shelves. I was eventually, I may add, almost cured of my disease for all time by his skilful ministrations. It seems that he did not scorn the incantations of the mediaevalists, since he believed these cryptic formulae to contain rare psychological stimuli which might conceivably have singular effects on the substance of a nervous system from which organic pulsations had fled. I was touched by his account of the aged Dr. Torres of Valencia, who had shared his earlier experiments and nursed him through the great illness of eighteen years before, whence his present disorders proceeded. No sooner had the venerable practitioner saved his colleague than he himself succumbed to the grim enemy he had fought. Perhaps the strain had been too great; for Dr. Muñoz made it whisperingly clear—though not in detail—that the methods of healing had been most extraordinary, involving scenes and processes not welcomed by elderly and conservative Galens.

As the weeks passed, I observed with regret that my new friend was indeed slowly but unmistakably losing ground physically, as Mrs. Herrero had suggested. The livid aspect of his countenance was intensified, his voice became more hollow and indistinct, his muscular motions were less perfectly coördinated, and his mind and will displayed less resilience and initiative. Of this sad change he seemed by no means unaware, and little by little his expression and conversation both took on a gruesome irony which restored in me something of the subtle repulsion I had originally felt.

He developed strange caprices, acquiring a fondness for exotic spices and Egyptian incense till his room smelled like the vault of a sepulchred Pharaoh in the Valley of Kings. At the same time his demands for cold air increased, and with my aid he amplified the ammonia piping of his room and modified the pumps and feed of his refrigerating machine till he could keep the temperature as low as 34° or 40°, and finally even 28°; the bathroom and laboratory, of course, being less chilled, in order that water might not freeze, and that chemical processes might not be impeded. The tenant adjoining him complained of the icy air from around the connecting door, so I helped him fit heavy hangings to obviate the difficulty. A kind of growing horror, of outré and morbid cast, seemed to possess him. He talked of death incessantly, but laughed hollowly when such things as burial or funeral arrangements were gently suggested.

All in all, he became a disconcerting and even gruesome companion; yet in my gratitude for his healing I could not well abandon him to the strangers around him, and was careful to dust his room and attend to his needs each day, muffled in a heavy ulster which I bought especially for the purpose. I likewise did much of his shopping, and gasped in bafflement at some of the chemicals he ordered from druggists and laboratory supply houses.

An increasing and unexplained atmosphere of panic seemed to rise around his apartment. The whole house, as I have said, had a musty odour; but the smell in his room was worse—and in spite of all the spices and incense, and the pungent chemicals of the now incessant baths which he insisted on taking unaided. I perceived that it must be connected with his ailment, and shuddered when I reflected on what that ailment might be. Mrs. Herrero crossed herself when she looked at him, and gave him up unreservedly to me; not even letting her son Esteban continue to run errands for him. When I suggested other physicians, the sufferer would fly into as much of a rage as he seemed to dare to entertain. He evidently feared the physical effect of violent emotion, yet his will and driving force waxed rather than waned, and he refused to be confined to his bed. The lassitude of his earlier ill days gave place to a return of his fiery purpose, so that he seemed about to hurl defiance at the death-daemon even as that ancient enemy seized him. The pretence of eating, always curiously like a formality with him, he virtually abandoned; and mental power alone appeared to keep him from total collapse.

He acquired a habit of writing long documents of some sort, which he carefully sealed and filled with injunctions that I transmit them after his death to certain persons whom he named—for the most part lettered East Indians, but including a once celebrated French physician now generally thought dead, and about whom the most inconceivable things had been whispered. As it happened, I burned all these papers undelivered and unopened. His aspect and voice became utterly frightful, and his presence almost unbearable. One September day an unexpected glimpse of him induced an epileptic fit in a man who had come to repair his electric desk lamp; a fit for which he prescribed effectively whilst keeping himself well out of sight. That man, oddly enough, had been through the terrors of the Great War without having incurred any fright so thorough.

Then, in the middle of October, the horror of horrors came with stupefying suddenness. One night about eleven the pump of the refrigerating machine broke down, so that within three hours the process of ammonia cooling became impossible. Dr. Muñoz summoned me by thumping on the floor, and I worked desperately to repair the injury while my host cursed in a tone whose lifeless, rattling hollowness surpassed description. My amateur efforts, however, proved of no use; and when I had brought in a mechanic from a neighbouring all-night garage we learned that nothing could be done till morning, when a new piston would have to be obtained. The moribund hermit's rage and fear, swelling to grotesque proportions, seemed likely to shatter what remained of his failing physique; and once a spasm caused him to clap his hands to his eyes and rush into the bathroom. He groped his way out with face tightly bandaged, and I never saw his eyes again.

The frigidity of the apartment was now sensibly diminishing, and at about 5 a.m. the doctor retired to the bathroom, commanding me to keep him supplied with all the ice I could obtain at all-night drug stores and cafeterias. As I would return from my sometimes discouraging trips and lay my spoils before the closed bathroom door, I could hear a restless splashing within, and a thick voice croaking out the order for "More—more!" At length a warm day broke, and the shops opened one by one. I asked Esteban either to help with the ice-fetching whilst I obtained the pump piston, or to order the piston while I continued with the ice; but instructed by his mother, he absolutely refused.

Finally I hired a seedy-looking loafer whom I encountered on the corner of Eighth Avenue to keep the patient supplied with ice from a little shop where I introduced him, and applied myself diligently to the task of finding a pump piston and engaging workmen competent to install it. The task seemed interminable, and I raged almost as violently as the hermit when I saw the hours slipping by in a breathless, foodless round of vain telephoning, and a hectic quest from place to place, hither and thither by subway and surface car. About noon I encountered a suitable supply house far downtown, and at approximately 1:30 p.m. arrived at my boarding-place with the necessary paraphernalia and two sturdy and intelligent mechanics. I had done all I could, and hoped I was in time.

Black terror, however, had preceded me. The house was in utter turmoil, and above the chatter of awed voices I heard a man praying in a deep basso. Fiendish things were in the air, and lodgers told over the beads of their rosaries as they caught the odour from beneath the doctor's closed door. The lounger I had hired, it seems, had fled screaming and mad-eyed not long after his second delivery of ice; perhaps as a result of excessive curiosity. He could not, of course, have locked the door behind him; yet it was now fastened, presumably from the inside. There was no sound within save a nameless sort of slow, thick dripping.

Briefly consulting with Mrs. Herrero and the workmen despite a fear that gnawed my inmost soul, I advised the breaking down of the door; but the landlady found a way to turn the key from the outside with some wire device. We had previously opened the doors of all the other rooms on that hall, and flung all the windows to the very top. Now, noses protected by handkerchiefs, we tremblingly invaded the accursed south room which blazed with the warm sun of early afternoon.

A kind of dark, slimy trail led from the open bathroom door to the hall door, and thence to the desk, where a terrible little pool had accumulated. Something was scrawled there in pencil in an awful, blind hand on a piece of paper hideously smeared as though by the very claws that traced the hurried last words. Then the trail led to the couch and ended unutterably.

What was, or had been, on the couch I cannot and dare not say here. But this is what I shiveringly puzzled out on the stickily smeared paper before I drew a match and burned it to a crisp; what I puzzled out in terror as the landlady and two mechanics rushed frantically from that hellish place to babble their incoherent stories at the nearest police station. The nauseous words seemed well-nigh incredible in that yellow sunlight, with the clatter of cars and motor trucks ascending clamorously from crowded Fourteenth Street, yet I confess that I believed them then. Whether I believe them now I honestly do not know. There are things about which it is better not to speculate, and all that I can say is that I hate the smell of ammonia, and grow faint at a draught of unusually cool air.

"The end," ran that noisome scrawl, "is here. No more ice—the man looked and ran away. Warmer every minute, and the tissues can't last. I fancy you know—what I said about the will and the nerves and the preserved body after the organs ceased to work. It was good theory, but couldn't keep up indefinitely. There was a gradual deterioration I had not foreseen. Dr. Torres knew, but the shock killed him. He couldn't stand what he had to do—he had to get me in a strange, dark place when he minded my letter and nursed me back. And the organs never would work again. It had to be done my way—artificial preservation—*for you see I died that time eighteen years ago.*"

The Return of the Sorcerer

CLARK ASHTON SMITH

Clark Ashton Smith was not your average pulp writer. A poet and artist, he backed into writing weird fiction only when the exigencies of the Depression forced his hand. Smith tended to set his stories in fantastic locales that called for a vivid imagination to bring them to life, and it was a never-ending source of frustration for him that editors thought his florid vocabulary and baroque style too difficult for readers. In "The Return of the Sorcerer," he kept the exotic flourishes to a minimum, and the story made it into the September 1931 issue of Strange Tales *without a struggle. Smith intentionally loaded the tale with references from the work of H. P. Lovecraft to give the impression that he and his colleague drew from a common mythology.*

I HAD been out of work for several months, and my savings were perilously near the vanishing point. Therefore I was naturally elated when I received from John Carnby a favorable answer inviting me to present my qualifications in person. Carnby had advertised for a secretary, stipulating that all applicants must offer a preliminary statement of their capacities by letter; and I had written in response to the advertisement.

Carnby, no doubt, was a scholarly recluse who felt averse to contact

9

with a long waiting-list of strangers; and he had chosen this manner of weeding out beforehand many, if not all, of those who were ineligible. He had specified his requirements fully and succinctly, and these were of such nature as to bar even the average well-educated person. A knowledge of Arabic was necessary, among other things; and luckily I had acquired a certain degree of scholarship in this unusual tongue.

I found the address, of whose location I had formed only a vague idea, at the end of a hilltop avenue in the suburbs of Oakland. It was a large, two-story house, overshaded by ancient oaks and dark with a mantling of unchecked ivy, among hedges of unpruned privet and shrubbery that had gone wild for many years. It was separated from its neighbors by a vacant, weed-grown lot on one side and a tangle of vines and trees on the other, surrounding the black ruins of a burnt mansion.

Even apart from its air of long neglect, there was something drear and dismal about the place—something that inhered in the ivy-blurred outlines of the house, in the furtive, shadowy windows, and the very forms of the misshapen oaks and oddly sprawling shrubbery. Somehow, my elation became a trifle less exuberant, as I entered the grounds and followed an unswept path to the front door.

When I found myself in the presence of John Carnby, my jubilation was still somewhat further diminished; though I could not have given a tangible reason for the premonitory chill, the dull, sombre feeling of alarm that I experienced, and the leaden sinking of my spirits. Perhaps it was the dark library in which he received me as much as the man himself—a room whose musty shadows could never have been wholly dissipated by sun or lamplight. Indeed, it must have been this; for John Carnby himself was very much the sort of person I had pictured him to be.

He had all the earmarks of the lonely scholar who has devoted patient years to some line of erudite research. He was thin and bent, with a massive forehead and a mane of grizzled hair; and the pallor of the library was on his hollow, clean-shaven cheeks. But coupled with this, there was a nerve-shattered air, a fearful shrinking that was more than the normal shyness of a recluse, and an unceasing apprehensiveness that betrayed itself in every glance of his dark-ringed, feverish eyes and every movement of his bony hands. In all likelihood his health had been seriously impaired by over-application; and I could not help but wonder at the nature of the studies that had made him a tremulous wreck. But there was something about him—perhaps the width of his bowed shoulders and the bold aquilinity of his facial outlines—which gave the impression of great former strength and a vigor not yet wholly exhausted.

His voice was unexpectedly deep and sonorous.

'I think you will do, Mr. Ogden,' he said, after a few formal questions, most of which related to my linguistic knowledge, and in particular my mastery of Arabic. 'Your labors will not be very heavy; but I want someone who can be on hand at any time required. Therefore you must live with me. I can give you a comfortable room, and I guarantee that my cooking will not poison you. I often work at night; and I hope you will not find the irregular hours too disagreeable.'

No doubt I should have been overjoyed at this assurance that the secretarial position was to be mine. Instead, I was aware of a dim, unreasoning reluctance and an obscure forewarning of evil as I thanked John Carnby and told him that I was ready to move in whenever he desired.

He appeared to be greatly pleased; and the queer apprehensiveness went out of his manner for a moment.

'Come immediately—this very afternoon, if you can,' he said. 'I shall be very glad to have you and the sooner the better. I have been living entirely alone for some time; and I must confess that the solitude is beginning to pall upon me. Also, I have been retarded in my labors for lack of the proper help. My brother used to live with me and assist me, but he has gone away on a long trip.'

I returned to my downtown lodgings, paid my rent with the last few dollars that remained to me, packed my belongings and in less than an hour was back at my new employer's home. He assigned me a room on the second floor, which, though unaired and dusty, was more than luxurious in comparison with the hall-bedroom that failing funds had compelled me to inhabit for some time past. Then he took me to his own study, which was on the same floor, at the further end of the hall. Here, he explained to me, most of my future work would be done.

I could hardly restrain an exclamation of surprise as I viewed the interior of this chamber. It was very much as I should have imagined the den of some old sorcerer to be. There were tables strewn with archaic instruments of doubtful use, with astrological charts, with skulls and alembics and crystals, with censers such as are used in the Catholic Church, and volumes bound in worm-eaten leather with verdigris-mottled clasps. In one corner stood the skeleton of a large ape; in another, a human skeleton; and overhead a stuffed crocodile was suspended.

There were cases overpiled with books, and even a cursory glance at the titles showed me that they formed a singularly comprehensive collection of ancient and modern works on demonology and the black arts. There were some weird paintings and etchings on the walls, dealing with kindred themes; and the whole atmosphere of the room exhaled a medley of half-forgotten superstitions. Ordinarily I would have smiled if confronted with such things; but somehow in this lonely, dismal house, beside the neurotic, hag-ridden Carnby, it was difficult for me to repress an actual shudder.

On one of the tables, contrasting incongruously with this mélange of medievalism and Satanism, there stood a typewriter, surrounded with piles of disorderly manuscript. At one end of the room there was a small, curtained alcove with a bed in which Carnby slept. At the end opposite the alcove, between the human and simian skeletons, I perceived a locked cupboard that was set in the wall.

Carnby had noted my surprise, and was watching me with a keen, analytic expression which I found impossible to fathom. He began to speak, in explanatory tones.

'I have made a life-study of demonism and sorcery,' he declared. 'It is a fascinating field, and one that is singularly neglected. I am now preparing a monograph, in which I am trying to correlate the magical practices and demon-worship of every known age and people. Your labors, at least for a while, will consist in typing and arranging the voluminous preliminary notes which I have made, and in helping me to track down other references and correspondences. Your knowledge of Arabic will be invaluable to me for I am none too well-grounded in this language myself, and I am depending for certain essential data on a copy of the Necronomicon in the original Arabic text. I have reason to think that there are certain omissions and erroneous renderings in the Latin version of Olaus Wormius.'

I had heard of this rare, well-nigh fabulous volume, but had never seen it. The book was supposed to contain the ultimate secrets of evil and forbidden knowledge; and, moreover, the original text, written by the mad Arab, Abdul Alhazred, was said to be unprocurable. I wondered how it had come into Carnby's possession.

'I'll show you the volume after dinner,' Carnby went on. 'You will doubtless be able to elucidate one or two passages that have long puzzled me.'

The evening meal, cooked and served by my employer himself, was a welcome change from cheap restaurant fare. Carnby seemed to have lost a good deal of his nervousness. He was very talkative, and even began to exhibit a certain scholarly gaiety after we had shared a bottle of mellow Sauterne. Still, with no manifest reason, I was troubled by intimations and forebodings which I could neither analyze nor trace to their rightful source.

We returned to the study, and Carnby brought out from a locked drawer the volume of which he had spoken. It was enormously old, and was bound in ebony covers arabesqued with silver and set with darkly glowing garnets. When I opened the yellowing pages, I drew back with involuntary revulsion at the odor which arose from them— an odor that was more than suggestive of physical decay, as if the book had lain among corpses in some forgotten graveyard and had taken on the taint of dissolution.

Carnby's eyes were burning with a fevered light as he took the old manuscript from my hands and turned to a page near the middle. He indicated a certain passage with his lean forefinger.

'Tell me what you make of this,' he said, in a tense, excited whisper.

I deciphered the paragraph, slowly and with some difficulty, and wrote down a rough English version with the pad and pencil which Carnby offered me. Then, at his request, I read it aloud:

'It is verily known by few, but is nevertheless an attestable fact, that the will of a dead sorcerer hath power upon his own body and can raise it up from the tomb and perform therewith whatever action was unfulfilled in life. And such resurrections are invariably for the doing of malevolent deeds and for the detriment of others. Most readily can the corpse be animated if all its members have remained intact; and yet there are cases in which the excelling will of the wizard hath reared up from death the sundered pieces of a body hewn in many fragments, and hath caused them to serve his end, either separately or in a temporary reunion. But in every instance, after the action hath been completed, the body lapseth into its former state.'

Of course, all this was errant gibberish. Probably it was the strange, unhealthy look of utter absorption with which my employer listened, more than that damnable passage from the Necronomicon, which caused my nervousness and made me start violently when, toward the end of my reading, I heard an indescribable slithering noise in the hall outside. But when I finished the paragraph and looked up at Carnby, I was more startled by the expression of stark, staring fear which his features had assumed—an expression as of one who is haunted by some hellish phantom. Somehow, I got the feeling that he was listening to that odd noise in the hallway rather than to my translation of Abdul Alhazred.

'The house is full of rats,' he explained, as he caught my inquiring glance. 'I have never been able to get rid of them, with all my efforts.'

The noise, which still continued, was that which a rat might make in dragging some object slowly along the floor. It seemed to draw closer, to approach the door of Carnby's room, and then, after an intermission, it began to move again and receded. My employer's agitation was marked; he listened with fearful intentness and seemed to follow the progress of the sound with a terror that mounted as it drew near and decreased a little with its recession.

'I am very nervous,' he said. 'I have worked too hard lately, and this is the result. Even a little noise upsets me.'

The sound had now died away somewhere in the house. Carnby appeared to recover himself in a measure.

'Will you please re-read your translation?' he requested. 'I want to follow it very carefully, word by word.'

I obeyed. He listened with the same look of unholy absorption as before, and this time we were not interrupted by any noises in the hallway. Carnby's face grew paler, as if the last remnant of blood had been drained from it, when I read the final sentences; and the fire in his hollow eyes was like phosphorescence in a deep vault.

'That is a most remarkable passage,' he commented. 'I was doubtful about its meaning, with my imperfect Arabic; and I have found that the passage is wholly omitted in the Latin of Olaus Wormius. Thank you for your scholarly rendering. You have certainly cleared it up for me.'

His tone was dry and formal, as if he were repressing himself and holding back a world of unsurmisable thoughts and emotions. Somehow I felt that Carnby was more nervous and upset than ever, and also that my rendering from the Necronomicon had in some mysterious manner contributed to his perturbation. He wore a ghastly brooding expression, as if his mind were busy with some unwelcome and forbidden theme.

However, seeming to collect himself, he asked me to translate another passage. This turned out to be a singular incantatory formula for the exorcism of the dead, with a ritual that involved the use of rare Arabian spices and the proper intoning of at least a hundred names of ghouls and demons. I copied it all out for Carnby, who studied it for a long time with a rapt eagerness that was more than scholarly.

'That, too,' he observed, 'is not in Olaus Wormius.' After perusing it again, he folded the paper carefully and put it away in the same drawer from which he had taken the Necronomicon.

That evening was one of the strangest I have ever spent. As we sat for hour after hour discussing renditions from that unhallowed volume, I came to know more and more definitely that my employer was mortally afraid of something that he dreaded being alone and was keeping me with him on this account rather than for any other reason. Always he seemed to be waiting and listening with a painful, tortured expectation, and I saw that he gave only a mechanical awareness to much that was said. Among the weird appurtenances of the room, in that atmosphere of unmanifested evil, of untold horror, the rational part of my mind began to succumb slowly to a recrudescence of dark ancestral fears. A scorner of such things in my normal moments. I was now ready to believe in the most baleful creations of superstitious fancy. No doubt, by some process of mental contagion, I had caught the hidden terror from which Carnby suffered.

By no word or syllable, however, did the man admit the actual feelings that were evident in his demeanor, but he spoke repeatedly of a nervous ailment. More than once, during our discussion, he sought to imply that his interest in the supernatural and the Satanic was wholly intellectual, that he, like myself, was without personal belief in such things. Yet I knew infallibly that his implications were false; that he was driven and obsessed by a real faith in all that he pretended to view with scientific detachment, and had doubtless fallen a victim to some imaginary horror entailed by his occult researches. But my intuition afforded me no clue to the actual nature of this horror.

There was no repetition of the sounds that had been so disturbing to my employer. We must have sat till after midnight with the writings of the mad Arab open before us. At last Carnby seemed to realize the lateness of the hour.

'I fear I have kept you up too long,' he said apologetically. 'You must go and get some sleep. I am selfish, and I forget that such hours are not habitual to others, as they are to me.'

I made the formal denial of his self-impeachment which courtesy required, said good night, and sought my own chamber with a feeling of intense relief. It seemed to me that I would leave behind me in Carnby's room all the shadowy fear and oppression to which I had been subjected.

Only one light was burning in the long passage. It was near Carnby's door; and my own door at the further end, close to the stair-head, was in deep shadow. As I groped for the knob, I heard a noise behind me, and turned to see in the gloom a small, indistinct body that sprang from the hall-landing to the top stair, disappearing from view. I was horribly startled; for even in that vague, fleeting glimpse, the thing was much too pale for a rat and its form was not at all suggestive of an animal. I could not have sworn what it was, but the outlines had seemed unmentionably monstrous. I stood trembling violently in every limb, and heard on the stairs a singular bumping sound like the fall of an object rolling downward from step to step. The sound was repeated at regular intervals, and finally ceased.

If the safety of the soul and body had depended upon it, I could not have turned on the stair-light; nor could I have gone to the top steps to ascertain the agency of that unnatural bumping. Anyone else, it might seem, would have done this. Instead, after a moment of virtual petrification, I entered my room, locked the door, and went to bed in a turmoil of unresolved doubt and equivocal terror. I left the light burning; and I lay awake for hours, expecting momentarily a recurrence of that abominable sound. But the house was as silent as a morgue, and I heard nothing. At length, in spite of my anticipations to the contrary, I fell asleep and did not awaken till after many sodden, dreamless hours.

It was ten o'clock, as my watch informed me. I wondered whether my employer had left me undisturbed through thoughtfulness, or had not arisen himself. I dressed and went downstairs, to find him waiting at the breakfast table. He was paler and more tremulous than ever, as if he had slept badly.

'I hope the rats didn't annoy you too much,' he remarked, after a preliminary greeting. 'Something really must be done about them.'

'I didn't notice them at all,' I replied. Somehow, it was utterly impossible for me to mention the queer, ambiguous thing which I had seen and heard on retiring the night before. Doubtless I had been mistaken; doubtless it had been merely a rat after all, dragging something down the stairs. I tried to forget the hideously repeated noise and the momentary flash of unthinkable outlines in the gloom.

My employer eyed me with uncanny sharpness, as if he sought to penetrate my inmost mind. Breakfast was a dismal affair; and the day that followed was no less dreary. Carnby isolated himself till the middle of the afternoon, and I was left to my own devices in the well-supplied but conventional library downstairs. What Carnby was doing alone in his room I could not surmise; but I thought more than once that I heard the faint, monotonous intonations of a solemn voice. Horror-breeding hints and noisome intuitions invaded my brain. More and more the atmosphere of that house enveloped and stifled me with poisonous, miasmal mystery; and I felt everywhere the invisible brooding of malignant incubi.

It was almost a relief when my employer summoned me to his study. Entering, I noticed that the air was full of a pungent, aromatic smell and was touched by the vanishing coils of a blue vapor, as if from the burning of Oriental gums and spices in the church censors. An Ispahan rug had been moved from its position near the wall to the center of the room, but was not sufficient to cover entirely a curving violet mark that suggested the drawing of a magic circle on the floor. No doubt Carnby had been performing some sort of incantation; and I thought of the awesome formula I had translated at his request.

However, he did not offer any explanation of what he had been doing. His manner had changed remarkably and was more controlled and confident than at any former time. In a fashion almost business-like he laid before me a pile of manuscript which he wanted me to type for him. The familiar click of the keys aided me somewhat in dismissing my apprehensions of vague evil, and I could almost smile at the recherché and terrific information comprised in my employer's notes, which dealt mainly with formulae for the acquisition of unlawful power. But still, beneath my reassurance, there was a vague, lingering disquietude.

Evening came; and after our meal we returned again to the study. There was a tenseness in Carnby's manner now, as if he were eagerly awaiting the result of some hidden test. I went on with my work; but some of his emotion communicated itself to me, and ever and anon I caught myself in an attitude of strained listening.

At last, above the click of the keys, I heard the peculiar slithering in the hall. Carnby had heard it, too, and his confident look utterly vanished, giving place to the most pitiable fear.

The sound drew nearer and was followed by a dull, dragging noise, and then by more sounds of an unidentifiable slithering and scuttling nature that varied in loudness. The hall was seemingly full of them, as if a whole army of rats were hauling some carrion booty along the floor. And yet no rodent or number of rodents could have made such sounds, or could have moved anything so heavy as the object which came behind the rest. There was something in the character of those noises, something without name or definition, which caused a slowly creeping chill to invade my spine.

'Good Lord! What is all that racket?' I cried.

'The rats! I tell you it is only the rats!' Carnby's voice was a high, hysterical shriek.

A moment later, there came an unmistakable knocking on the door, near the sill. At the same time I heard a heavy thudding in the locked cupboard at the further end of the room. Carnby had been standing erect, but now he sank limply into a chair. His features were ashen, and his look was almost maniacal with fright.

The nightmare doubt and tension became unbearable and I ran to the door and flung it open, in spite of a frantic remonstrance from my employer. I had no idea what I should find as I stepped across the sill into the dim-lit hall.

When I looked down and saw the thing on which I had almost trodden, my feeling was one of sick amazement and actual nausea. It was a human hand which had been severed at the wrist—a bony, bluish hand like that of a week-old corpse, with garden-mold on the fingers and under the long nails. *The damnable thing had moved!* It had drawn back to avoid me, and was crawling along the passage somewhat in the manner of a crab! And following it with my gaze, I saw that there were other things beyond it, one of which I recognized as a man's foot and another as a forearm. I dared not look at the rest. All were moving slowly, hideously away in a charnel procession, and I cannot describe the fashion in which they moved. Their individual vitality was horrifying beyond endurance. It was more than the vitality of life, yet the air was laden with a carrion taint. I averted my eyes and stepped back into Carnby's room, closing the door behind me with a shaking hand. Carnby was at my side with the key, which he turned in the lock with palsy-stricken fingers that had become as feeble as those of an old man.

'You saw them?' he asked in a dry, quavering whisper.

'In God's name, what does it all mean?' I cried.

Carnby went back to his chair, tottering a little with weakness. His lineaments were agonized by the gnawing of some inward horror, and he shook visibly like an ague patient. I sat down in a chair beside him, and he began to stammer forth his unbelievable confession, half incoherently, with inconsequential mouthings and many breaks and pauses:

'He is stronger than I am—even in death, even with his body

dismembered by the surgeon's knife and saw that I used. I thought he could not return after that—after I had buried the portions in a dozen different places, in the cellar, beneath the shrubs, at the foot of the ivy-vines. But the Necronomicon is right . . . and Helman Carnby knew it. He warned me before I killed him, he told me he could return—*even in that condition.*

'But I did not believe him. I hated Helman, and he hated me, too. He had attained to higher power and knowledge and was more favored by the Dark Ones than I. That was why I killed him—my own twin-brother, and my brother in the service of Satan and of Those who were before Satan. We had studied together for many years. We had celebrated the Black Mass together and we were attended by the same familiars. But Helman Carnby had gone deeper into the occult, into the forbidden, where I could not follow him. I feared him, and I could not endure his supremacy.

'It is more than a week—it is ten days since I did the deed. But Helman—or some part of him—has returned every night. . . . God! His accursed hands crawling on the floor! His feet, his arms, the segments of his legs, climbing the stairs in some unmentionable way to haunt me! . . . Christ! His awful, bloody torso lying in wait! I tell you, his hands have come even by day to tap and fumble at my door . . . and I have stumbled over his arms in the dark.

'Oh, God! I shall go mad with the awfulness of it. But he wants me to go mad, he wants to torture me till my brain gives way. That is why he haunts me in this piece-meal fashion. He could end it all any time with the demoniacal power that is his. He could re-knit his sundered limbs and body and slay me as I slew him.

'How carefully I buried the parts, with what infinite forethought! And how useless it was! I buried the saw and knife, too, at the farther end of the garden, as far away as possible from his evil, itching hands. But I did not bury the head with the other pieces—I kept it in that cupboard at the end of my room. Sometimes I have heard it moving there as you heard it a little while ago. . . . But he does not need the head, his will is elsewhere, and can work intelligently through all his members.

'Of course, I locked all the doors and windows at night when I found that he was coming back. . . . But it made no difference. And I have tried to exorcize him with the appropriate incantations—with all those that I knew. Today I tried that sovereign formula from the Necronomicon which you translated for me. I got you here to translate it. Also, I could no longer bear to be alone and I though that it might help if there were someone else in the house. That formula was my last hope. I thought it would hold him—it is a most ancient and most dreadful incantation. But, as you have seen, it is useless. . . .'

His voice trailed off in a broken mumble, and he sat staring before him with sightless, intolerable eyes in which I saw the beginning flare of madness. I could say nothing—the confession he had made was so ineffably atrocious. The moral shock, and the ghastly supernatural horror, had almost stupefied me. My sensibilities were stunned; and it was not till I had begun to recover that I felt the irresistible surge of a flood of loathing for the man beside me.

I rose to my feet. The house had grown very silent, as if the macabre and charnel army of beleaguerment had now retired to its various graves. Carnby had left the key in the lock; and I went to the door and turned it quickly.

'Are you leaving? Don't go,' Carnby begged in a voice that was tremulous with alarm, as I stood with my hand on the door-knob.

'Yes, I am going,' I said coldly. 'I am resigning my position right now; and I intend to pack my belongings and leave your house with as little delay as possible.'

I opened the door and went out, refusing to listen to the arguments and pleadings and protestations he had begun to babble. For the nonce, I preferred to face whatever might lurk in the gloomy passage, no matter how loathsome and terrifying, rather than endure any longer the society of John Carnby.

The hall was empty; but I shuddered with repulsion at the memory of what I had seen, as I hastened to my room. I think I should have screamed aloud at the least sound or movement in the shadows.

I began to pack my valise with a feeling of the most frantic urgency and compulsion. It seemed to me that I could not escape soon enough from that house of abominable secrets, over which hung an atmosphere of smothering menace. I made mistakes in my haste, I stumbled over chairs, and my brain and fingers grew numb with a paralyzing dread.

I had almost finished my task, when I heard the sound of slow measured footsteps coming up the stairs. I knew that it was not Carnby, for he had locked himself immediately in his room when I had left; and I felt sure that nothing could have tempted him to emerge. Anyway, he could hardly have gone downstairs without my hearing him.

The footsteps came to the top landing and went past my door along the hall, with that same dead monotonous repetition, regular as the movement of a machine. Certainly it was not the soft, nervous tread of John Carnby.

Who, then, could it be? My blood stood still in my veins; I dared not finish the speculation that arose in my mind.

The steps paused; and I knew that they had reached the door of Carnby's room. There followed an interval in which I could scarcely breathe; and then I heard an awful crashing and shattering noise, and above it the soaring scream of a man in the uttermost extremity of fear.

I was powerless to move, as if an unseen iron hand had reached forth to restrain me; and I have no idea how long I waited and listened. The scream had fallen away in a swift silence; and I heard nothing now, except a low, peculiar, recurrent sound which my brain refused to identify.

It was not my own volition, but a stronger will than mine, which drew me forth at last and impelled me down the hall to Carnby's study. I felt the presence of that will as an overpowering, superhuman thing—a demoniac force, a malign mesmerism.

The door of the study had been broken in and was hanging by one hinge. It was splintered as by the impact of more than mortal strength. A light was still burning in the room, and the unmentionable sound I had been hearing ceased as I neared the threshold. It was followed by an evil, utter stillness.

Again I paused, and could go no further. But, this time, it was something other than the hellish, all-pervading magnetism that petrified my limbs and arrested me before the sill. Peering into the room, in the narrow space that was framed by the doorway and lit by an unseen lamp, I saw one end of the Oriental rug, and the gruesome outlines of a monstrous, unmoving shadow that fell beyond it on the floor. Huge, elongated, misshapen, the shadow was seemingly cast by the arms and torso of a naked man who stooped forward with a surgeon's saw in his hand. Its monstrosity lay in this: though the shoulders, chest, abdomen and arms were all clearly distinguishable, the shadow was headless and appeared to terminate in an abruptly severed neck. It was impossible, considering the relative position, for the head to have been concealed from sight through any manner of foreshortening.

I waited, powerless to enter or withdraw. The blood had flowed back upon my heart in an ice-thick tide, and thought was frozen in my brain. An interval of termless horror, and then, from the hidden end of Carnby's room, from the direction of the locked cupboard, there came a fearsome and violent crash, and the sound of splintering wood and whining hinges, followed by the sinister, dismal thud of an unknown object striking the floor.

Again there was silence—a silence as of consummated Evil brooding above its unnamable triumph. The shadow had not stirred. There was a hideous contemplation in its attitude, and the saw was still held in its poising hand, as if above a completed task.

Another interval, and then, without warning, I witnessed the awful and unexplainable *disintergration* of the shadow which seemed to break gently and easily into many different shadows ere it faded from view. I hesitate to describe the manner, or specify the places, in which this singular disruption, this manifold cleavage, occurred. Simultaneously, I heard the muffled clatter of a metallic implement on the Persian rug, and a sound that was not that of a single body but of many bodies falling.

Once more there was silence—a silence as of some nocturnal cemetery, when grave-diggers and ghouls are done with their macabre toil, and the dead alone remain.

Drawn by that baleful mesmerism, like a somnambulist led by an unseen demon, I entered the room, I knew with a loathly prescience the sight that awaited me beyond the sill—the *double* heap of human segments, some of them fresh and bloody, and others already blue with beginning putrefaction and marked with earth-stains, that were mingled in abhorrent confusion on the rug.

A reddened knife and saw were protruding from the pile; and a little to one side, between the rug and the open cupboard with its shattered door, there reposed a human head that was fronting the other remnants in an upright posture. It was in the same condition of incipient decay as the body to which it had belonged; but I swear that I saw the fading of a malignant exultation from its features as I entered. Even with the marks of corruption upon them, the lineaments bore a manifest likeness of John Carnby, and plainly they could belong only to a twin brother.

The frightful inferences that smothered my brain with their black and clammy cloud are not to be written here. The horror which I beheld—and the greater horror which I surmised—would have put to shame hell's foulest enormities in their frozen pits. There was but one mitigation and one mercy: I was compelled to gaze only for a few instants on that intolerable scene. Then, all at once, I felt that something had withdrawn from the room; the malign spell was broken, the overpowering volition that had held me captive was gone. It had released me now, even as it had released the dismembered corpse of Helman Carnby. I was free to go; and I fled from the ghastly chamber and ran headlong through an unlit house and into the outer darkness of the night.

Wolves of Darkness
JACK WILLIAMSON

There are only so many things a writer can do with a werewolf story before stumbling over the same cliches recycled by countless others. In "Wolves of Darkness," the cover story for the 1932 issue of Strange Tales, *Jack Williamson showed that a writer with a good imagination and room to exercise it could present even the most hackneyed supernatural creature in a new light. Although known today as one of the superstars of modern science fiction, Williamson was one of the few authors who also established a solid reputation in the weird-fiction pulps. In 1940, he combined his skills in both genres and resurrected the werewolf yet again for his classic novel of lycanthropy,* Darker Than You Think.

CHAPTER I

THE TRACKS IN THE SNOW

INVOLUNTARILY I paused, shuddering, on the snow-covered station platform. A strange sound, weird, and somehow appalling, filled the ghostly moonlight of the winter night. A quavering and distant ululation, which prickled my body with chills colder than the piercing bite of the motionless, frozen air.

That unearthly, nerve-shredding sound, I knew, must be the howling of the gray prairie or *lobo* wolves, though I had not heard them since childhood. But it carried a note of elemental terror which even the trembling apprehensions of boyhood had never given the voice of the great wolves. There was something sharp, broken, about that eery clamor, far-off and deeply rhythmic as it was. Something—and the thought brought a numbing chill of fear—which suggested that the dreadful ululation came from straining human throats!

Striving to shake the phantasy from me, I hastened across the icy platform, and burst rather precipitately into the dingy waiting room. It was brilliantly lit with unshaded electric bulbs. A red-hot stove filled it with grateful heat. But I was less thankful for the warmth than for the shutting out of that far-away howling.

Beside the glowing stove a tall man sat tense over greasy cards spread on the end of a packing box which he held between his knees, playing solitaire with strained, feverish attention. He wore an ungainly leather coat, polished slick with wear. One tanned cheek bulged with tobacco, and his lips were amber-stained.

He seemed oddly startled by my abrupt entrance. With a sudden, frightened movement, he pushed aside the box, and sprang to his feet. For a moment his eyes were anxiously upon me; then he seemed to sigh with relief. He opened the stove door, and expectorated into the roaring flames, then sank back into his chair.

"Howdy, Mister," he said, in a drawl that was a little strained and husky. "You sort of scairt me. You was so long comin' in that I figgered nobody got off."

"I stopped to listen to the wolves," I told him. "They sound weird, don't they?"

He searched my face with strange, fearful eyes. For a long time he did not speak. Then he said briskly, "Well, Mister, what kin I do for ye?"

As I advanced toward the stove, he added, "I'm Mike Connell, the station agent."

"My name is Clovis McLaurin," I told him. "I want to find my father, Dr. Ford McLaurin. He lives on a ranch near here."

"So you're Doc McLaurin's boy, eh?" Connell said, warming visibly. He rose, smiling and shifting his wad of tobacco to the other cheek, and took my hand.

"Yes," I said. "Have you seen him lately? Three days ago I had a strange telegram from him. He asked me to come at once. It seems that he's somehow in trouble. Do you know anything about it?"

Connell looked at me queerly.

"No," he said at last. "I ain't seen him lately. None of 'em off the ranch ain't been in to Hebron for two or three weeks. The snow is the deepest in years, you know, and it ain't easy to git around. I dunno how they could have sent a telegram, though, without comin' to town. And they ain't none of us seen 'em!"

"Have you got to know Dad?" I inquired, alarmed more deeply.

"No, not to say real well," the agent admitted. "But I seen him and Jetton and Jetton's gal often enough when they come into Hebron, here. Quite a bit of stuff has come for 'em to the station, here. Crates and boxes, marked like they was scientific apparatus—I dunno what. But a right purty gal, that Stella Jetton. Purty as a picture."

"It's three years since I've seen Dad," I said, confiding in the agent in hope of winning his approval and whatever aid he might be able to give me in reaching the ranch, over the unusual fall of snow that blanketed the West Texas plains. "I've been in medical college in the East. Haven't seen Dad since he came out here to Texas three years ago."

"You're from the East, eh?"

"New York. But I spent a couple of years out here with my uncle when I was a kid. Dad inherited the ranch from him."

"Yeah, old Tom McLaurin was a friend of mine," the agent told me.

It was three years since my father had left the chair of astrophysics at an eastern university, to come here to the lonely ranch to carry on his original experiments. The legacy from his brother Tom, besides the ranch itself, had included a small fortune in money, which had made it possible for him to give up his academic position and to devote his entire time to the abstruse problems upon which he had been working.

Being more interested in medical than in mathematical science, I had not followed Father's work completely, though I used to help him with his experiments, when he had to perform them in a cramped flat, with pitifully limited equipment. I knew, however, that he had worked out an extension of Weyl's non-Euclidian geometry in a direction quite different from those chosen by Eddington and Einstein—and whose implications, as regards the structure of our universe, were stupendous. His new theory of the wave-electron, which completed the wrecking of the Bohr planetary atom, had been as sensational.

The proof his theory required was the exact comparison of the velocity of beams of light at right angles. The experiment required a large, open field, with a clear atmosphere, free from dust or smoke; hence his choosing the ranch as a site upon which to complete the work.

Since I wished to remain in college, and could help him no longer, he had employed as an assistant and collaborator, Dr. Blake Jetton, who was himself well known for his remarkable papers upon the propagation of light, and the recent modifications of the quantum theory.

Dr. Jetton, like my father, was a widower. He had a single child, a daughter named Stella. She had been spending several months of each year with them on the ranch. While I had not seen her many times, I could agree with the station agent that she was pretty. As a matter of face I had thought her singularly attractive.

Three days before, I had received the telegram from my father. A strangely worded and alarming message, imploring me to come to him with all possible haste. It stated that his life was in danger, though no hint had been given as to what the danger might be.

Unable to understand the message, I had hastened to my rooms for a few necessary articles—among them, a little automatic pistol—and had lost no time in boarding a fast train. I had found the Texas Panhandle covered with nearly a foot of snow—the winter was the most severe in several years. And that weird and terrible howling had greeted me ominously when I swung from the train at the lonely village of Hebron.

"The wire was urgent—most urgent," I told Connell. "I must get out to the ranch to-night, if it's at all possible. You know of any way I could go?"

For some time he was silent, watching me, with dread in his eyes.

"No, I don't," he said presently. "Ten mile to the ranch. And they ain't a soul lives on the road. The snow is nigh a foot deep. I doubt a car would make it. Ye might git Sam Judson to haul you over tomorrow in his wagon."

"I wonder if he would take me out to-night?" I inquired.

The agent shook his head uneasily, peered nervously out at the glistening, moonlit desert of snow beyond the windows, and seemed to be listening anxiously. I remembered the weird, distant howling I had heard as I walked across the platform, and could hardly restrain a shiver of my own.

"Naw, I think not!" Connell said abruptly. "It ain't healthy to git out at night around here, lately."

He paused a moment, and then asked suddenly, darting a quick, uneasy glance at my face, "I reckon you heard the howlin'?"

"Yes. Wolves?"

"Yeah—anyhow, I reckon so. Queer. Damn queer! They ain't been any loafers around these parts for ten years, till we heard 'em jest after the last blizzard." ("Loafer" appeared to be a local corruption of the Spanish word *lobo* applied to the gray prairie wolf, which is much larger than the coyote, and was a dreaded enemy of the rancher in the Southwest until its practical extermination.)

"Seems to be a reg'lar pack of the critters rovin' the range," Connell went on. "They've killed quite a few cattle in the last few weeks, and—" he paused, lowering his voice, "and five people!"

"The wolves have killed people!" I exclaimed.

"Yeah," he said slowly. "Josh Wells and his hand were took two weeks ago, come Friday, while they was out ridin' the range. And the

Simms' are gone. The old man and his woman and little Dolly. Took right out of the cow-pen, I reckon, while they was milkin'. It ain't two mile out of town to their place. Rufe Smith was out that way to see 'em Sunday. Cattle dead in the pen, and the smashed milk buckets lying in a drift of snow under the shed. And not a sign of Simms and his family!"

"I never heard of wolves taking people that way!" I was incredulous.

Connell shifted his wad of tobacco again, and whispered, "I didn't neither. But, Mister, these here ain't ordinary wolves!"

"What do you mean?" I demanded.

"Wall, after the Simms' was took, we got up a sort of posse, and went out to hunt the critters. We didn't find no wolves. But we did find tracks in the snow. The wolves is plumb gone in the daytime!

"Tracks in the snow," he repeated slowly, as if his mind were dwelling dazedly upon some remembered horror. "Mister, them wolf tracks was too tarnation far apart to be made by any ordinary beast. The critters must 'a' been jumpin' thirty feet!

"And they warn't all wolf tracks, neither. Mister, part was wolf tracks. And part was tracks of bare human feet!"

With that, Connell fell silent, staring at me strangely, with a queer look of utter terror in his eyes.

I was staggered. There was, of course, some element of incredulity in my feelings. But the agent did not look at all like the man who has just perpetrated a successful wild story, for there was genuine horror in his eyes. And I recalled that I had fancied human tones in the strange, distant howling I had heard.

There was no good reason to believe that I had merely encountered a local superstition. Widespread as the legends of lycanthropy may be, I have yet to hear a whispered tale of werewolves related by a West Texan. And the agent's story had been too definite and concrete for me to imagine it an idle fabrication or an ungrounded fear.

"The message from my father was very urgent," I told Connell presently. "I *must* get out to the ranch to-night. If the man you mentioned won't take me, I'll hire a horse and ride."

"Judson is a damn fool if he'll git out to-night where them wolves is!" the agent said with conviction. "But there's nothing to keep ye from askin' him to go. I reckon he ain't gone to bed yet. He lives in the white house, jest around the corner behind Brice's store."

He stepped out upon the platform behind me to point the way. And as soon as the door was opened, we heard again that rhythmic, deep, far-off ululation, that weirdly mournful howling, from far across the moonlit plain of snow. I could not repress a shudder. And Connell, after pointing out to me Sam Judson's house, among the straggling few that constituted the village of Hebron, got very hastily back inside the depot, and shut the door behind him.

CHAPTER II

THE PACK THAT RAN BY MOONLIGHT

SAM JUDSON owned and cultivated a farm nearly a mile from Hebron, but had moved his house into the village so that his wife could keep the post-office. I hurried toward his house, through the icy streets, very glad that Hebron was able to afford the luxury of electric lights. The distant howling of the wolf-pack filled me with a vague and inexplicable dread. But it did not diminish my determination to reach my father's ranch as soon as possible, to solve the riddle of the strange and alarming telegram he had sent me.

Judson came to the door when I knocked. He was a heavy man, clad in faded, patched blue overalls, and brown flannel shirt. His head was almost completely bald, and his naked scalp was tanned until it resembled brown leather. His wide face was covered with a several week's growth of black beard. Nervously, fearfully, he scanned my face.

He led me to the kitchen, in the rear of the house—a small, dingy room, the walls covered with an untidy array of pots and pans. The cook stove was hot; he had, from appearances, been sitting with his feet in the oven, reading a newspaper, which now lay on the floor.

He had me sit down, and, when I took the creaking chair, I told him my name. He said that he knew my father, Dr. McLaurin, who got his mail at the post-office which was in the front room. But it had been three weeks, he said, since anyone had been to town from the ranch. Perhaps because the snow made traveling difficult, he said. There were five persons now staying out there, he told me. My father and Dr. Jetton, his daughter, Stella, and two hired mechanics from Amarillo.

I told him about the telegram, which I had received three days before. And he suggested that my father, if he had sent it, might have come to town at night, and mailed it to the telegraph office with the money necessary to send it. But he thought it strange that he had not spoken to anyone, or been seen.

Then I told Judson that I wanted him to drive me out to the ranch, at once. At the request his manner changed; he seemed frightened!

"No hurry about starting tonight, is there, Mr. McLaurin?" he asked. "We can put you up in the spare room, and I'll take ye over in the wagon to-morrow. It's a long drive to make at night."

"I'm very anxious to get there," I said. "I'm worried about my father. Something was wrong when he telegraphed. Very much wrong. I'll pay you enough to make it worth while.

"It ain't the money," he told me. "I'd be glad to do it for a son of Doc McLaurin's. But I reckon you heard—the wolves?"

"Yes, I heard them. And Connell, at the station, told me something about them. They've been hunting men?"

27

"Yes." For a little time Judson was silent, staring at me with strange eyes from his hairy face. Then he said, "And that ain't all. Some of us seen the tracks. And they's men runnin' with 'em!"

"But I must get out to see my father," I insisted. "We should be safe enough in a wagon. And I suppose you have a gun?"

"I have a gun, all right," Judson admitted. "But I ain't anxious to face them wolves!"

I insisted, quite ignorant of the peril into which I was dragging him. Finally, when I offered him fifty dollars for the trip, he capitulated. But he was going, he said—and I believed him—more to oblige a friend than for the money.

He went into the bedroom, where his wife was already asleep, roused her, and told her he was going to make the trip. She was rather startled, as I judged from the sound of her voice, but mollified when she learned that there was to be a profit of fifty dollars.

She got up, a tall and most singular figure in a purple flannel nightgown, with nightcap to match, and busied herself making us a pot of coffee on the hot stove, and finding blankets for us to wrap about us in the farm wagon, for the night was very cold. Judson, meanwhile, lit a kerosene lantern, which was hardly necessary in the brilliant moonlight, and went to the barn behind the house to get ready the vehicle.

Half an hour later we were driving out of the little village, in a light wagon, behind two gray horses. Their hoofs broke through the crust of the snow at every step, and the wagon wheels cut into it steadily, with a curious crunching sound. Our progress was slow, and I anticipated a tedious trip of several hours.

We sat together on the spring seat, heavily muffled up, with blankets over our knees. The air was bitterly cold, but there was no wind, and I expected to be comfortable enough. Judson had strapped on an ancient revolver, and we had a repeating rifle and a double barrel shotgun leaning against our knees. But despite our arms, I could not quite succeed in quieting the vague fears raised by the wolf-pack, whose quavering, unearthly wail was never still.

Once outside the village of Hebron, we were surrounded on all sides by a white plain of snow, almost as level as a table-top. It was broken only by the insignificant rows of posts which supported wire fences; these fences seemed to be Judson's only land-marks. The sky was flooded with ghostly opalescence, and a million diamonds of frost glittered on the snow.

For perhaps an hour and a half, nothing remarkable happened. The lights of Hebron grew pale and faded behind us. We passed no habitation upon the illimitable desert of snow. The eery, heart-stilling ululation of the wolves, however, grew continually louder.

And presently the uncanny, wailing sounds changed position. Judson quivered beside me, and spoke nervously to the gray horses, plodding on through the snow. Then he turned to face me, spoke shortly.

"I figger they're sweeping in behind us, Mr. McLaurin."

"Well, if they do, you can haul some of them back, to skin tomorrow," I told him. I had meant it to sound cheerful. But my voice was curiously dry, and its tones rang false in my ears.

For some minutes more we drove on in silence.

Suddenly I noticed a change in the cry of the pack.

The deep, strange rhythm of it was suddenly quickened. Its eery wailing plaintiveness seemed to give place to a quick, eager yelping. But it was still queerly unfamiliar. And there was something weirdly ventriloquial about it, so that we could not tell precisely from which direction it came. The rapid, belling notes seemed to come from a dozen points scattered over the brilliant, moonlit waste behind us.

The horses became alarmed. They pricked up their ears, looked back, and went on more eagerly. I saw that they were trembling. One of them snorted suddenly. The abrupt sound jarred my jangled nerves, and I clutched convulsively at the side of the wagon.

Judson held the reins firmly, with his feet braced against the end of the wagon box. He was speaking softly and soothingly to the quivering grays; but for that, they might already have been running. He turned to me and muttered:

"I've heard wolves. And they don't sound like that. Them ain't ordinary wolves!"

And as I listened fearfully to the terrible baying of the pack, I knew that he was right. Those strange ululations had an unfamiliar, an alien, note. There was a weird, terrible something about the howling that was not of this earth. It is hard to describe it, because it was so utterly foreign. It comes to me that if there are wolves on the ancient, age-dead deserts of Mars, they might cry in just that way, as they run some helpless creature to merciless death.

Malevolent were those belling notes, foul and hateful. Rioting with an infernal power of evil alien to this earth. Strong with the primal wickedness of the cosmic wastes.

"Reckon they are on the trail," Judson said suddenly, in a low, strained voice. "Look behind us."

I turned in the spring seat, peered back over the limitless flat desolation of sparkling, moonlit snow. For a few minutes I strained my eyes in vain, though the terrible belling of the unseen pack grew swiftly louder.

Then I saw leaping gray specks, far behind us across the snow. By rights, a wolf should have floundered rather slowly through the thick snow, for the crust was not strong enough to hold up so heavy an animal. But the things I saw—fleet, formless gray shadows—were coming by great bounds, with astounding speed.

"I see them," I told Judson tremulously.

"Take the lines," he said, pushing the reins at me, and snatching up the repeating rifle.

He twisted in the seat, and began to fire.

The horses were trembling and snorting. Despite the cold, sweat was raining from their heaving bodies. Abruptly, after Judson had begun to shoot, they took the bits in their teeth and bolted, plunging and floundering through the snow, dragging the wagon. Tug and jerk at the reins as I would, I could do nothing with them.

Judson had soon emptied the rifle. I doubt that he had hit any of the howling animals that ran behind us, for accurate shooting from the swaying, jolting wagon would have been impossible. And our wildly bounding pursuers would have been difficult marks, even if the wagon had been still.

Judson dropped the empty rifle into the wagon box, and turned a white, frightened face toward me. His mouth was open, his eyes protruding with terror. He shouted something incoherent, which I did not grasp, and snatched at the reins. Apparently insane with fear, he cursed the leaping grays, and lashed at them, as if thinking to outrun the pack.

For a little time I clung to the side of the rocking wagon. Then the snorting horses turned suddenly, almost breaking the wagon tongue. We were nearly upset. The spring seat was dislodged from its position, and fell into the wagon box. I was thrown half over the side of the wagon. For another agonized moment I tried to scramble back. Then the grays plunged forward again, and I was flung into the snow.

I broke through the thin crust. The thick, soft snow beneath checked the force of my fall. In a few moments I had floundered to my feet, and was clawing madly at my face, to get the white, powdery stuff away from my eyes.

The wagon was already a hundred yards away. The fear-maddened horses were still running, with Judson standing erect in the wagon, sawing wildly at the reins, but powerless to curb them. They had been turning abruptly when I was thrown out.

Now they were plunging back toward the weirdly baying pack!

Judson, screaming and cursing, crazed with terror, was being carried back toward the dimly seen, gray, leaping shapes whose uncanny howling sobbed so dreadfully through the moonlight.

Horror came over me, like a great, soul-chilling wave. I felt an insane desire to run across the snow, to run and run until I could not hear the wailing of the strange pack. With an effort I controlled myself, schooled my trembling limbs, swallowed to wet my dry throat.

I knew that my poor, floundering run could never distance the amazingly fleet gray shapes that bounded through the silver haze of moonlight toward the wagon. And I reminded myself that I had a weapon, a .25 caliber automatic pistol, slung beneath my shoulder. Something about the strange message from my father had made me fasten on the deadly little weapon, and slip a few extra clips of ammunition into my pockets.

With trembling hands, I pulled off a glove and fumbled inside my garments for the little weapon.

At last I drew out the heavy little automatic, gratefully warm with the heat of my body, and snapped back the slide to be sure that a cartridge was in the chamber. Then I stood there, in a bank of powdery snow that came nearly to my knees, and waited.

The dismal, alien howling of the pack froze me into a queer paralysis of fear. And then I was the horrified spectator of a ghastly tragedy.

The wagon must have been four hundred yards from me, across the level, glistening snow, when the dim gray shapes of the baying pack left the trail and ran straight across toward it. I saw little stabs of yellow flame, heard sharp reports of guns, and the thin, whistling screams of bullets. Judson, I suppose, had dropped the reins and was trying to defend himself with the rifle and shotgun, and his old-fashioned revolver.

The vague gray shapes surrounded the wagon. I heard the scream of an agonized horse—except for the unearthly howling of that pack, the most terrible, nerve-wracking sound I know. A struggling mass of faintly seen figures seemed to surround the wagon. There were a few more shots, then a shriek, which rang fearfully over the snow, bearing an agony of pain and terror that is inconceivable. . . . I knew it came from Judson.

After that, the only sound was the strange, blood-congealing belling of the pack—an awful outcry that had not been stilled.

Soon—fearfully soon—that alien ululation seemed to be drawing nearer. And I saw gray shapes come bounding down the trail, away from the grim scene of the tragedy—toward me!

CHAPTER III

THE WOLF AND THE WOMAN

ICAN give no conception of the stark, maddened terror that seized me when I knew that the gray animals were running on my trail. My heart seemed to pause, until I thought I would grow dizzy and fall. Then it was thumping loudly in my throat. My body was suddenly cold with sweat. My muscles knotted until I was gripping the automatic with painful force.

I had determined not to run, for it was madness to try to escape the pack. But my resolution to stand my ground was nothing in the face of the fear that obsessed me.

I plunged across the level waste of snow. My feet broke through the thin crust. I floundered along, with laboring lungs. The snow seemed tripping me like a malevolent demon. Many times I stumbled, it seemed. And twice I sprawled in the snow, and scrambled desperately to my feet, and struggled on again, sobbing with terror, gasping in the cold air.

But my flight was cut short. The things that ran behind me could travel many times faster than I. Turning, when I must have gone less than a hundred yards, I saw them drawing near behind me, still vague gray shapes in the moonlight. I now perceived that only two had followed.

Abruptly I recalled the little automatic in my hand. I raised it, and emptied it, firing as rapidly as I could. But if I hit either of those bounding gray figures, they certainly were invulnerable to my bullets.

I had sought in my pocket for another clip, and was trying with quivering fingers to slip it into the gun, when those things came near enough, in a milky haze of moonlight, to be seen distinctly. Then my hands closed in rigid paralysis upon the gun—I was too astounded and unstrung to complete the operation of loading.

One of those two gray shapes was a wolf. A gaunt prairie wolf, covered with long, shaggy hair. A huge beast, he must have stood three feet high at the shoulder. He was not standing now, however, but coming toward me with great leaps that covered many yards. His great eyes glowed with a weird, greenish, unnatural light—terrible and strange and somehow hypnotic.

And the other was a girl.

It was incredible. It numbed and staggered my terror-dazed mind. At first I thought it must be a hallucination. But as she came nearer, advancing with long, bounding steps, as rapidly as the gray wolf, I could no longer discredit my eyes. I recalled the weird suggestion of a human voice I had caught in the unearthly cry of the pack; recalled what Connell and Judson had told me of human footprints mingled with those of wolves in the trail the pack had left.

She was clad very lightly, to be abroad in the bitter cold of the winter night. Apparently, she wore only a torn, flimsy slip, of thin white silk, which hung from one shoulder, and same not quite to her knees. Her head was bare, and her hair, seeming in the moonlight to be an odd, pale yellow, was short and tangled. Her smooth arms and small hands, her legs, and even her flashing feet, were bare. Her skin was white, with a cold, leprous, bloodless whiteness. Almost as white as the snow.

And her eyes shone green.

They were like the gray wolf's eyes, blazing with a terrible emerald flame, with the fire of an alien, unearthly life. They were malevolent, merciless, hideous. They were cold as the cosmic wastes beyond the light of stars. They burned with an evil light, with a malicious intelligence, stronger and more fearful than that of any being on earth.

Across her lips, and her cheeks of alabaster whiteness, was a darkly red and dripping smear, almost black by moonlight.

I stood like a wooden man, nerveless with incredulous horror.

On came the girl and the wolf, springing side by side through the snow. They seemed to have preternatural strength, an agility beyond that of nature.

As they came nearer, I received another shock of terror.

The woman's face was familiar, for all its dreadful pallor and the infernal evil of the green, luminous eyes, and the red stain on her lips and cheeks. She was a girl whom I had known. A girl whom I had admired, whom I had even dreamed that I might come to love.

She was Stella Jetton!

This girl was the lovely daughter of Dr. Blake Jetton, whom, as I have said, my father had brought with him to his Texas ranch, to assist with his revolutionary experiments.

It came to me that she had been changed in some fearful way. For this could be no sane, ordinary human girl—this strange, green-eyed being, half-clad, white-skinned, who ran over the moonlit snow beside a gaunt gray wolf, with dripping red upon her fearfully pallid skin!

"Stella!" I cried.

More a scream of frightened, anguished unbelief, than a human voice, the name came from my fear-parched throat. I was startled at my own call, hoarse, inchoate, gasping.

The huge gray wolf came directly at me, as if it were going to spring at my throat. But it stopped a dozen feet before me, crouching in the snow, watching me with alert and strange intelligence in its dreadful green eyes.

And the woman came even nearer, before she paused, standing with bare feet in the snow, and stared at me with terrible eyes like those of the wolf—luminous and green and filled with an evil, alien will.

The face, ghastly white, and fearfully red-stained as it was, was the face of Stella Jetton. But the eyes were not hers! No, the eyes were not Stella's!

They were the eyes of some hideous monstrosity. The eyes of some inconceivable, malevolent entity, from some frozen hell of the far-off, night-black cosmic void!

Then she spoke. The voice had some little of its old, familiar ring. But there was a new, strange note in it. A note that bore the foreign, menacing mystery of the eyes and the leprous skin. A note that had a suggestion of the dismal, wailing ululation of the pack that had followed us.

"Yes, Stella Jetton," the dreadful voice said. "What are you called? Are you Clovis McLaurin? Did you receive a telegram?"

She did not know me, apparently. Even the wording of her sentences was a little strange, as if she were speaking a language with which she was not very familiar. The delightful, human girl I had known was fearly changed: it was as if her fair body had been seized by some demoniac entity.

It occurred to me that she must be afflicted with some form of insanity, which had given her the almost preternatural strength which she had displayed in running with the wolf-pack. Cases of lycanthropy, in which the suffered imagines himself a wolf—or sometimes a tiger or some other animal—and imitates its actions, have been common enough in the annals of the insane. But if this is lycanthropy, I thought, it must indeed be a singular case.

"Yes, I'm Clovis McLaurin," I said, in a shaken voice. "I got Dad's telegram three days ago. Tell me what's wrong—why he worded the message as he did!"

"Nothing is wrong, my friend," this strange woman said. "We merely desired your assistance with certain experiments, of a great strangeness, which we are undertaking to perform. Your father now waits at the ranch, and I came to conduct you to him."

This singular speech was almost incredible. I could accept it only on the assumption that the speaker suffered from some dreadful derangement of the mind.

"You came to meet me?" I exclaimed, fighting the horror that almost overwhelmed me. "Stella, you mustn't be out in the cold without more wraps. You must take my coat."

I began to strip off the garment. But, as I had somehow expected, she refused to accept it.

"No, I do not need it," her strange voice told me. "The cold does not harm this body. And you must come with us, now. Your father waits for us at the house, to perform the great experiment."

She said *us!* It gave me new horror to notice that she thus classed the huge gaunt wolf with herself.

Then she sprang forward with an incredible agility, leaping through the snow in the direction in which Judson and I had been traveling. With a naked, dead-white arm, she beckoned me to follow. And the great, gray wolf sprang behind me.

Nerved to sudden action, I recalled the half-loaded automatic in my hand. I snapped the fresh clip into position, jerked back the slide mechanism to get a cartridge into the breech, and then emptied the gun into that green-orbed wolf.

A strange composure had come over me. My motions were calm enough, almost deliberate. I know that my hand did not shake. The wolf was standing still, only a few yards away. It is unlikely that I missed him at all, impossible that I missed him with every shot.

I know that I hit him several times, for I heard the bullets drive into his gaunt body, saw the animal jerk beneath their impact, and noticed gray hairs float from it in the moonlight.

But he did not fall. His terrible green eyes never wavered in their sinister stare of infernal evil.

Just as the gun was empty—it had taken me only a few seconds to fire the seven shots—I heard an angry, wolfish snarl from the woman, from the strange monster that Stella Jetton had become. I had half turned when her white body came hurtling at me like a projectile.

I went down beneath her, instinctively raising an arm to guard my throat. It is well that I did, for I felt her teeth sinking into my arm and shoulder, as we fell together into the snow.

I am sure that I screamed with the horror of it.

I fought at her madly, until I heard her strange, non-human voice again.

"You need not be afraid," it said. "We are not going to kill you. We wish you to aid with a greatly remarkable experiment. For that reason, you must come with us. Your father waits. The wolf is our friend, and will not harm you. And your weapon will not hurt it."

A curious, half-articulate yelp came from the throat of the great wolf, which had not moved since I shot at it, as if it had understood her words and gave affirmation.

The woman was still upon me, holding me flat in the snow, her bared, bloody teeth above my face, her fingers sunk claw-like into my body with almost preternatural strength. A low, bestial, growling sound came from her throat, and then she spoke again.

"You will now come with us, to the house where your father waits, to perform the experiment?" she demanded in that terrible voice, with its suggestion of the wolf-pack's weird cry.

"I'll come," I agreed, relieved somewhat to discover that the strange pair of beasts did not propose to devour me on the spot.

The woman—I cannot call her Stella, for except in body, she was not Stella!—helped me to my feet. She made no objection when I bent, and picked up the automatic, which lay in the snow, and slipped it into my coat pocket.

She and the gaunt gray wolf, which my bullets had so strangely failed to kill, leaped away together over the moonlit snow. I followed, floundering along as rapidly as I could, my mind filled with confused and terror-numbed conjecture.

There was now no doubt remaining in my mind that the woman thought herself a member of the wolf-pack, no doubt that she actually was a member. A curious sympathy certainly seemed to exist between her and the great gaunt wolf beside her.

It must be some strange form of lunacy, I thought, though I had never read of a lycanthrope whose symptoms were exaggerated to the terrible extent that hers appeared to be. It is well known that maniacs

have unnatural strength, but her feats of running and leaping across
the snow were almost beyond reason.

But there was that about her which even the theory of insanity did
not explain. The corpse-like pallor of her skin; the terrible green
luminosity of her eyes; the way she spoke—as if English were an
unfamiliar tongue to her, but half mastered. And there was something
even more indefinite: a strangeness that smacked of the alien life of
forbidden universes!

The pace set for me by the woman and the wolf was mercilessly
rapid. Stumble along as best I could, I was unable to move as fast as
they wished. Nor was I allowed to fall behind, for when I lagged, the
wolf came back, and snarled at me menacingly.

Before I had floundered along many miles, my lungs were aching,
and I was half blind with fatigue. I stumbled and sprawled in the soft
snow a last time. My tortured muscles refused to respond when I tried
to rise. I lay there, ready to endure whatever the wolf might do, rather
than undergo the agony of further effort.

But this time the woman came back. I was half unconscious, but I
realized vaguely that she was lifting me, raising me to her shoulders.
After that, my eyes were closed; I was too weary to watch my surroundings. But I knew dimly, from my sensations of swaying, that I
was being carried.

Presently the toxins of exhaustion overcame my best efforts to keep
my senses. I fell into the deep sleep of utter fatigue, forgetting that my
limbs were growing very cold, and that I was being borne upon the
back of a woman endowed with the instincts of a wolf and the strength
of a demon; a woman who, when I had last seen her, had been all
human and lovable!

CHAPTER IV

A STRANGE HOMECOMING

NEVER CAN I forget the sensations of my awakening. I opened
my eyes upon gloom relieved but faintly by dim red light. I lay
upon a bed or couch, swathed in blankets. Hands that even to my
chilled body seemed ice-cold were chafing my arms and legs. And
terrible greenish orbs were swimming above in the terrible crimson
darkness, staring down at me, horribly.

Alarmed, recalling what had happened in the moonlight as a vague,
hideous nightmare, I collected my scattered senses, and struggled to a
sitting position among the blankets.

It is odd, but the first definite thing that came to my confused brain
was an impression of the ugly green flowers in monotonous rows across
the dingy, brown-stained wall paper. In the red light that filled the

room they appeared unpleasantly black, but still they awakened an ancient memory. I knew that I was in the dining room of the old ranch house, where I had come to spend two years with my uncle, Tom McLaurin, many years before.

The weirdly illuminated chamber was sparsely furnished. The couch upon which I lay stood against one wall. Opposite was a long table, with half a dozen chairs pushed under it. Near the end of the room was a large heating stove, with a full scuttle of coal and a box of split pine kindling behind it.

There was no fire in the stove, and the room was very cold. My breath was a white cloud in that frosty atmosphere. The dim crimson light came from a small electric lantern standing on the long table. It had been fitted with a red bulb, probably for use in a photographer's dark room.

All those impressions I must have gathered almost subconsciously, for my horrified mind was absorbed with the persons in the room.

My father was bending over me, rubbing my hands. And Stella was chafing my feet, which stuck out beneath the blankets.

And my father was changed as weirdly, as dreadfully, as the girl, Stella!

His skin was a cold, bloodless white—white with the pallor of death. His hands, against my own, felt fearfully cold—as cold as those of a frozen corpse. And his eyes, watching me with a strange, terrible alertness, shone with a greenish light.

His eyes were like Stella's—and like those of the great gray wolf. They were agleam with the fire of cosmic evil, with the light of an alien, hellish intelligence!

And the woman—the dread thing that had been lovely Stella—was unchanged. Her skin was still fearfully pallid, and her eyes strange and luminously green. The stain was still on her pale face, appearing black in the somber crimson light.

There was no fire in the stove. But, despite the bitter cold of the room, the woman was still clad as she had been before, in a sheer slip of white silk, half torn from her white body. My father—or that which had once been my father—wore only a light cotton shirt, with the sleeves torn off, and a pair of ragged trousers. His feet and arms were bare.

Another fearful thing I noticed. My breath, as I said, condensed in white clouds of frozen crystals, in the frigid air. But no white mists came from Stella's nostrils, or from my father's.

From outside, I could hear the dismal, uncanny keening of the running pack. And from time to time the two looked uneasily toward the door, as if anxious to go to join them.

I had been sitting up, staring confusedly and incredulously about, before my father spoke.

"We are glad to see you, Clovis," he said, rather stiffly, and without emotion, not at all in his usual jovial, affectionate manner. "You seem to be cold. But you will presently be normal again. We have surprising need of you, in the performance of an experiment, which we cannot accomplish without your assistance."

He spoke slowly, uncertainly, as a foreigner might who has attempted to learn English from a dictionary. I was at a loss to understand it, even if I assumed that he and Stella both suffered from a mental derangement.

And his voice was somehow whining; it carried a note weirdly suggestive of the howling of the pack.

"You will help us?" Stella demanded in the same dreadful tones.

"Explain it! Please explain everything!" I burst out. "Or I'll go crazy! Why were you running with the wolves? Why are your eyes so bright and green, your skins so deathly white? Why are you both so cold? Why the red light? Why don't you have a fire?"

I babbled my questions, while they stood there in the strange room, and silently stared at me with their horrible eyes.

For minutes, perhaps, they were silent. Then an expression of crafty intelligence came into my father's eyes, and he spoke again in those fearful tones, with their ring of the baying pack.

"Clovis," he said, "you know we came here for purposes of studying science. And a great discovery has been ours to make; a huge discovery relating to the means of life. Our bodies, they are changed, as you appear to see. Better machines they have become; stronger they are. Cold harms them not, as it does yours. Even our sight is better, so bright lights we no longer need.

"But we are yet lacking of perfect success. Our minds were changed, so that we do not remember all that once it had been ours to accomplish. And it is you whom we desire to be our assistant in replacing a machine of ours, that has been broken. It is you that we wish to aid us, so that to all humanity we may bring the gift of the new life, that is ever strong, and knows not death. All people we would change with the new science that it has been ours to discover."

"You mean you want to make the human race into monsters like yourselves?" I cried.

My father snarled ferociously, like a beast of prey.

"All men will receive the gift of life like ours," his strange voice said. "Death will be no more. And your aid is required by us—and it we will have!" There was intense, malefic menace in his tones. "It is yours to be our aid. You will refuse not!"

He stood before me with bared teeth and with white fingers hooked like talons.

"Sure, I'll help you," I contrived to utter, in a shaken voice. "I'm not a very brilliant experimenter, however." It appeared that to refuse would be a means of committing very unpleasant suicide.

Triumphant cunning shone in those menacing green eyes, the evil cunning of the maniac who has just perpetrated a clever trick. But it was even more than that; it was the crafty look of supreme evil in contemplation of further victory.

"You can come now, in order to see the machine?" Stella demanded.

"No," I said hastily, and sought reasons for delay. "I am cold. I must light a fire and warm myself. Then I am hungry, and very tired. I must eat and sleep." All of which was very true. My body had been chilled through, during my hours on the snow. My limbs were trembling with cold.

The two looked at each other. Unearthly sounds passed between them, incoherent, animal whinings. Such, instead of words, seemed to be their natural speech; the English they spoke seemed only an inaccurately and recently learned tongue.

"True," my father said to me again, in a moment. He looked at the stove. "Start a fire if you must. What you need is there?" He pointed inquiringly toward coal and kindling, as if fire were something new and unfamiliar to him.

"We must go without," he added. "Light of fire is hurtful to us, as cold is to you. And in other room, called—" he hesitated perceptibly, "kitchen, will be food. There we will wait."

He and the white girl glided silently from the room.

Shivering with cold, I hurried to the stove. All the coals in it were dead; there had been no fire in it for many hours, none, perhaps, for several days. I shook down the ashes, lit a ball of crumpled newspaper with a match I found in my pocket, dropped it on the grate, and filled the stove with pine and coal. In a few minutes I had a roaring fire, before which I crouched gratefully.

In a few minutes the door was opened slowly. Stella, first peering carefully, apparently to see if these was light in the room, stepped cautiously inside. The stove was tightly closed, no light escaped from it.

The pallid, green-eyed woman had her arms full of food, a curious assortment that had evidently been collected in the kitchen in a haphazard manner. There were two loaves of bread, a slab of raw bacon, an unopened can of coffee, a large sack of salt, a carton of oatmeal, a can of baking powder, a dozen tins of canned foods, and even a bottle of stove polish.

"You eat this?" she inquired, in her strangely animal voice, dropping the articles on the table.

It was almost ludicrous; and too, it was somehow terrible. She seemed to have no conception of human alimentary needs.

Comfortably warm again, and feeling very hungry, I went over to the table, and examined the odd assortment. I selected a loaf of bread, a tin of salmon, and one of apricots, for my immediate use.

"Some of these things are to be eaten as they are," I ventured, wondering what her response would be. "And some of them have to be cooked."

"Cooked?" she demanded quickly. "What is that?"

Then, while I was silent, dazed with astonishment, she added a terrible question.

"Does it convey that they must be hot and bleeding from the animal?"

"No!" I cried. "No. To cook a food one heats it. Usually adding seasonings, such as salt. A rather complicated process, requiring considerable skill."

"I see," she said. "And you must consume such articles, to keep your body whole?"

I admitted that I did, and then remarked that I needed a can cutter, to get at the food in the tins. First inquiring about the appearance of the implement, she hurried to the kitchen, and soon returned with one.

Presently my father came back into the room. Both of them watched me with their strange green eyes as I ate. My appetite failed somewhat, but I drew the meal out as long as possible, in order to defer whatever they might intend for me after I had finished.

Both of them asked many questions. Questions similar to Stella's query about cooking, touching subjects with which an ordinary child is familiar. But they were not stupid questions—no, indeed! Both of them evinced a cleverness that was almost preternatural. They never forgot, and I was astounded at their skill in piecing together the facts I gave them, to form others.

Their green eyes watched me very curiously when, unable to drag out the pretense of eating any longer, I produced a cigarette and sought a match to light it. Both of them howled, as if in agony, when the feeble yellow flame of the match flared up. They covered their strange green eyes, and leaped back, cowering and trembling.

"Kill it!" my father snarled ferociously.

I flicked out the tiny flame, startled at its results.

They uncovered their terrible green eyes, blinking. It was several minutes before they seemed completely recovered from their amazing fear of the light.

"Make light no more when we are near," my father growled at me. "We will tear your body if you forget!" His teeth were bared; his lips curled like those of a wolf; he snarled at me frightfully.

Stella ran to an east window, raised the blind, peered nervously out. I saw that the dawn was coming. She whined strangely at my father. He seemed uneasy, like an animal at bay. His huge green eyes rolled from side to side. He turned anxiously to me.

"Come," he said. "The machine which we with your aid will repair is in the cellar beneath the house. The day comes. We must go."

"I can't go," I said. "I'm dog tired; been up all night. I've got to rest, before I work on any machine. I'm so sleepy I can't think."

He whined curiously at Stella again, as if he were speaking in some strange wolf-tongue. She replied in kind, then spoke to me.

"If rest is needful to the working of your body, you may sleep till the light is gone. Follow."

She opened the door at the end of the room, led me into a dark hall, and from it into a small bedroom. It contained a narrow bed, two chairs, a dresser, and wardrobe trunk.

"Try not to go," she snarled warningly, at the door, "or we will follow you over the snow!"

The door closed and I was alone. A key grated ominously in the lock. The little room was cold and dark. I scrambled hastily into the bed, and for a time I lay there, listening.

The dreadful howling of the wolf-pack, which had never stilled through all the night, seemed to be growing louder, drawing nearer. Presently it ceased, with a few sharp, whining yelps, apparently just outside the window. The pack had come here, with the dawn!

As the increasing light of day filled the little room, I raised myself in the bed to scrutinize its contents again. It was a neat chamber, freshly papered. The dresser was covered with a gay silk scarf, and on it, in orderly array, were articles of the feminine toilet. A few dresses, a vivid beret, and a bright sweater were hanging under a curtain in the corner of the room. On the wall was a picture—of myself!

It came to me that this must be Stella's room, into which I had been locked to sleep until night had come again. But what weird and horrible thing had happened to the girl since I had seen her last?

Presently I examined the windows with a view to escape. There were two of them, facing the east. Heavy wooden bars had been fastened across them, on the outside, so close together that I could not hope to squeeze between them. And a survey of the room revealed no object with which they could be easily sawed.

But I was too sleepy and exhausted to attempt escape. At thought of the ten weary miles to Hebron, through the thick, soft snow, I abandoned the idea. I knew that, tired as I already was, I could never cover the distance in the short winter day. And I shuddered at the thought of being caught on the snow by the pack.

I lay down again in Stella's clean bed, about which a slight fragrance of perfume still lingered, and was soon asleep. My slumber, though deep, was troubled. But no nightmare could be as hideous as the reality from which I had found a few hours' escape.

CHAPTER V

THE MACHINE IN THE CELLAR

ISLEPT through most of the short winter day. When I woke it was sunset. Gray light fell athwart the illimitable flat desert of snow outside my barred windows, and the pale disk of the moon, near the full, was rising in the darkening eastern sky. No human habitation was in view, in all the stretching miles of that white waste. I felt a sharp sense of utter loneliness.

I could look for no outside aid in coping with the strange and alarming situation into which I had stumbled. If I were to escape from these dread monsters who wore the bodies of those dearest to me, it must be by my own efforts. And in my hands alone rested the task of finding from what evil malady they suffered, and how to restore them to their old, dear selves.

Once more I examined the stout wooden bars across the windows. They seemed strongly nailed to the wall on either side. I found no tool that looked adequate to cutting them. My matches were still in my pocket, however, and it occurred to me that I might burn the bars. But there was no time for such an undertaking before the darkness would bring back my captors, nor did I relish the thought of attempting to escape with the pack on my trail.

I was hungry again, and quite thirsty also.

Darkness fell, as I lay there on the bed, among the intimate belongings of a lovely girl for whom I had owned tender feelings—waiting for her to come with the night, amid her terrible allies, to drag me to I knew not what dread fate.

The gray light of day faded imperceptibly into pale silvery moonlight.

Abruptly, without warning, the key turned in the lock.

Stella—or the alien entity that ruled the girl's fair body—glided with sinister grace into the room. Her green eyes were shining, and her skin was ghastly white.

"Immediately you will follow," came her wolfish voice. "The machine below awaits the aid for you to give in the great experiment. Quickly come. Your weak body, it is rested?"

"All right," I said. "I've slept, of course. But now I'm hungry and thirsty again. I've got to have water and something to eat before I tinker with any machine."

I was determined to postpone whatever ordeal lay before me as long as possible.

"Your body you may satisfy again," the woman said. "But take not too long!" she snarled warningly.

I followed her back to the dining room.

"Get water," she said, and glided out the door.

42

The stove was still faintly warm. I opened it, stirred the coals, dropped in more fuel. Soon the fire was roaring again. I turned my attention to the food I had left. The remainder of the salmon and apricots had frozen on the plates, and I set them over the stove to warm.

Soon Stella was back with a water bucket containing a bulging mass of ice. Apparently surprised that I could not consume water in a solid form, she allowed me to set it on the stove to thaw.

While I waited, standing by the stove, she asked innumerable questions, many of them so simple they would have been laughable under less strange conditions, some of them concerning the latest and most recondite of scientific theories, her mastery of which seemed to exceed my own.

My father appeared suddenly, his corpse-white arms full of books. He spread them on the table, curtly bid me come look with him. He had Einstein's "The Meaning of Relativity," Weyl's "Gravitation und Elektricität," and two of his own privately printed works. The latter were "Space-Time Tensors" and the volume of mathematical speculation entitled "Interlocking Universes" whose bizarre implications created such a sensation among those savants to whom he sent copies.

My father began opening these books, and bombarding me with questions about them, questions which I was often unable to answer. But the greater part of his queries related merely to grammar, or the meaning of words. The involved thought seemed easy for him to understand; it was the language which caused him difficulty.

His questions were exactly such as might be asked by a super-intellectual being from Mars, if he were attempting to read a scientific library without having completely mastered the language in which its books were written.

And his own books seemed as unfamiliar to him as those of the other scientists. But he ran through the pages with amazing speed, pausing only to ask an occasional question, and appeared to gain a complete mastery of the volume as he went.

When he released me, the food and water were warm. I drank, and then ate bread and salmon and apricots, as deliberately as I dared. I invited the two to share the food with me, but they declined abruptly. The volley of questions continued.

Then suddenly, evidently concluding that I had eaten enough, they started toward the door, commanding me to follow. I dared not do otherwise. My father paused at the end of the table and picked up the electric lantern, whose dimly glowing red bulb supplied the only light in the room.

Again we traversed the dark hall, and went out through a door in the rear of the frame building. As we stepped out upon the moonlit snow, I shuddered to hear once more the distant, wailing ululation of the pack, still with that terrible note which suggested strained human vocal organs.

A few feet from us was the door of a cellar. The basement had evidently been considerably enlarged, quite recently, for huge mounds of earth lay about us, filling the back yard. Some of them were covered with snow, some of them black and bare.

The two led the way down the steps into the cellar, my father still carrying the electric lantern, which faintly illuminated the midnight space with its feeble, crimson glow.

The cellar was large, neatly plastered. It had not been itself enlarged, but a dark passage sloped down beside the door, to deeper excavations.

In the center of the floor stood the wreck of an intricate and unfamiliar mechanism. It had evidently been deliberately smashed—I saw an ax lying beside it, which must have been the means of the havoc. The concrete floor was littered with the broken glass of shattered electron tubes. The machine itself was a mass of tangled wires and twisted coils and bent magnets, oddly arranged outside a great copper ring, perhaps four feet in diameter.

The huge copper ring was mounted on its edge, in a metal frame. Before it was a stone step, placed as if to be used by one climbing through the ring. But, I saw, it had been impossible for one actually to climb through, for on the opposite side was a mass of twisted apparatus—a great parabolic mirror of polished metal, with what appeared to be a broken cathode tube screwed into its center.

A most puzzling machine. And it had been very thoroughly wrecked. Save for the huge copper ring, and the heavy stone step before it, there was hardly a part that was not twisted or shattered.

In the end of the cellar was a small motor-generator—a little gasoline engine connected to a dynamo—such as is sometimes used for supplying isolated homes with electric light and power. I saw that it had not been injured.

From a bench beside the wall, my father picked up a brief case, from which he took a roll of blue prints, and a sheaf of papers bound in a manila cover. He spread them on the bench and set the red lantern beside them.

"This machine, as you see, has been, most unfortunately for us, wrecked," he said. "These papers tell the method of construction to be followed in the erection of such machines. Your aid we must have in deciphering what they convey. And the new machine will bring such great, strong life as we have to all your world."

"You say 'your world'!" I cried. "Then you don't belong to this earth? You are a monster, who has stolen the body of my father!"

Both of them snarled like beasts. They bared their teeth and glowered at me with their terrible green eyes. Then a crafty look came again into the man's sinister orbs.

"No, my son," came his whining, animal tones. "A new secret of life have we discovered. Great strength it gives to our bodies. Death we fear no longer. But our minds are changed. Many things we do not remember. We must require your aid in reading this which we once wrote—"

"That's the bunk!" I exclaimed, perhaps not very wisely. "I don't believe it. And I'll be damned if I'll help repair the infernal machine, to make more human beings into monsters like you!"

Together they sprang toward me. Their eyes glowed dreadfully against their pallid skins. Their fingers were hooked like claws. Saliva drooled from their snarling lips, and naked teeth gleamed in the dim crimson radiance.

"Aid us you will!" cried my father. "Or your body will we most painfully destroy. We will eat it slowly, while you live!"

The horror of it broke down my reason. With a wild, terror-shaken scream, I dashed for the door.

It was hopeless, of course, for me to attempt escape from beings possessing such preternatural strength.

With startling, soul-blasting howls, they sprang after me together. They swept me to the cellar's floor, sinking their teeth savagely into my arms and body. For a few moments I struggled desperately, writhing and kicking, guarding my throat with one arm and striking blindly with the other.

Then they held me helpless. I could only curse, and scream a vain appeal for aid.

The woman, holding my arms pinioned against my sides, lifted me easily, flung me over her shoulder. Her body, where it touched mine, was as cold as ice. I struggled fiercely but uselessly as she started with me down the black, inclined passage, into the recent excavations beneath the cellar's floor.

Behind us, my father picked up the little red lantern, and the blue prints and sheets of specifications, and followed down the dark, slanting passage.

CHAPTER VI

THE TEMPLE OF CRIMSON GLOOM

HELPLESS IN those preternaturally strong, corpse-cold and corpse-white arms, I was carried down narrow steps, to a high, subterranean hall. It was filled with a dim blood-red light, which came from no visible source, its angry, forbidding radiance seeming to spring from the very air. The walls of the underground hall were smooth and black, of some unfamiliar ebon substance.

Several yards down that black, strangely illuminated passage I was carried. Then we came into a larger space. Its black roof, many yards above, was groined and vaulted, supported by a double row of massive dead-black pillars. Many dark, arched niches were cut into its walls. This greater hall, too, was sullenly illuminated by a ghastly scarlet light, which seemed to come from nowhere.

A strange, silent, awful place. A sort of cathedral of darkness, of evil and death. A sinister atmosphere of nameless terror seemed breathed from its very midnight walls, like the stifling fumes of incense offered to some formless god of horror. The dusky red light might have come from unseen tapers burned in forbidden rites of blood and death. The dead silence itself seemed a tangible, evil thing, creeping upon me from ebon walls.

I was given little time to speculate upon the questions that it raised. What was the dead-black material of the walls? Whence came the lurid, bloody radiance? How recently had this strange temple of terror been made? And to what demoniac god was it consecrated? No opportunity had I to seek answers to those questions, nor time even to recover from my natural astonishment at finding such a place beneath the soil of a Texas ranch.

The emerald-eyed woman who bore me dropped me to the black floor, against the side of a jet pillar, which was round and two feet thick. She whined shrilly, like a hungry dog. It was evidently a call, for two men appeared in the broad central aisle of the temple, which I faced.

Two men—or, rather, malevolent monstrosities in the bodies of men. Their eyes shone with green fires alien to our world, and their bodies, beneath their tattered rags of clothing, were fearfully white. One of them came toward me with a piece of frayed manila rope, which must have been a lasso they had found above.

Later it came to me that these two must be the mechanics from the city of Amarilo, who, Judson had told me on the evening of our fatal drive, had been employed here by my father. I had not yet seen Dr. Blake Jetton, Stella's father, who had been the chief assistant of my own parent in various scientific investigations—investigations which, I now began to fear, must have borne dreadful fruit!

While the woman held me against the black pillar, the men seized my arms, stretched them behind it, and tied them with the rope. I kicked out, struggled, cursed them, in vain. My body seemed but putty to their fearful strength. When my hands were tied behind the pillar, another length of the rope was dropped about my ankles and drawn tight about the ebon shaft.

I was helpless in this weird, subterranean temple, at the mercy of these four creatures who seemed to combine infernal super-intelligence with the strength and the nature of wolves.

"See the instrument which we are to build!" came the snarling voice of my father. Standing before me, with the roll of blue prints in his livid hands, he pointed at an object that I had not yet distinguished in the sullen, bloody gloom.

In the center of the lofty, central hall of this red-lit temple, between the twin rows of looming, dead-black pillars, was a long, low platform of ebon stone. From it rose a metal frame—wrought like the frame of the wrecked machine I had seen in the cellar, above.

The frame supported a huge copper ring in a vertical position. It was far huger than the ring in the ruined mechanism; its diameter was a dozen feet or more. Its upper curve reached far toward the black, vaulted roof of the hall, glistening queerly in the ghastly red light. Behind the ring, a huge, parabolic mirror of silvery, polished metal had been set up.

But the device was obviously unfinished.

The complex electron tubes, the delicate helixes and coils, the magnets, and the complicated array of wires, whose smashed and tangled remains I had observed about the wreck of the other machine, had not been installed.

"Look at that!" cried my father again. "The instrument that comes to let upon your earth the great life that is ours. The plan on this paper, we made. From the plan, we made the small machine, and brought to ourselves the life, the strength, the love of blood—"

"The love of blood!" My startled, anguished outcry must have been a shriek, for I was already nearly overcome with the brooding terror of my strange surroundings. I collapsed against the ropes, shaken and trembling with fear.

The light of strange cunning came once more into the glaring green eyes of the thing that had been my father.

"No, fear not!" he whined on. "Your language it is new to me, and I speak what I do not intend. Be not fearing—if you will do our wish. If you do not, then we will taste your blood.

"But the new life came only to few. Then the machine broke, because of one man. And our brains are changed, so that we remember not to read the plans that we made. Your aid is ours, to restore a new machine. To you and all your world, then, comes the great new life!"

He stepped close to me, his green eyes burning malevolently. Before my eyes he unrolled one of the sheets which bore plans and specifications for the strange electron tubes, to be mounted outside the copper ring. From his lips came the curious, wolfish whine with which these monsters communicated with one another. One of the weirdly transformed mechanics stepped up beside him, carrying in dead-white hands the parts of such a tube—filaments, plate, grid, screens, auxiliary electrodes, and the glass tube in which they were to be sealed. The parts evidently had been made to fit the specifications—as nearly as these entities could comprehend those specifications with their imperfect knowledge of English.

"We make fit plans for these parts," my father whined. "If wrong, you must say where wrong. Describe how to put together. Speak quick, or die slowly!" He snarled menacingly.

Though I am by no means a brilliant physicist, I saw easily enough that most of the parts were useless, though they had been made with amazing accuracy. These beings seemed to have no knowledge of the fundamental principles underlying the operation of the machine they were attempting to build, yet, in making these parts, they had accomplished feats that would have been beyond the power of our science.

The filament was made of metal, well enough—but was far too thick to be lit by any current, without that current wrecking the tube in which it were used. The grid was nicely made—of metallic radium! It was worth a small fortune, but quite useless in the electron tube. And the plate was evidently of pure fused quartz, shaped with an accuracy that astounded me; but that, too was quite useless.

"Parts wrong?" my father barked excitedly in wolfish tones, his glowing green eyes evidently having read something in my face. "Indicate how wrong. Describe to make correct!"

I closed my lips firmly, determined to reveal nothing. I knew that it was through the wrecked machine that my father and Stella had been so dreadfully altered. I resolved that I would not aid in changing other humans into such hellish monsters. I was sure that this strange mechanism, if completed, would be a threat against all humanity—though, at the time, I was far from conceiving the full, diabolic significance of it.

My father snarled toward the woman.

She dropped upon all fours, and sprang at me like a wolf, her beastly eyes gleaming green, her bare teeth glistening in the sullen red light, and she was hideously howling!

Her teeth caught my trousers, tore them from my leg from the middle of the right thigh downward. Then they closed into my flesh, and I could feel her teeth gnawing . . . gnawing . . .

She did not make a deep wound, though blood, black in the terrible red light, trickled from it down my leg toward the shoe—blood which, from time to time, she ceased the gnawing to lick up appreciatively. The purpose of it was evidently to cause me the maximum amount of agony and horror.

For minutes, perhaps, I endured it—for minutes that seemed ages.

The pain itself was agonizing: the steady gnawing of teeth into the flesh of my leg, toward the bone.

But that agony was less than the terror of my surroundings. The strange temple of black, with its black floor, black walls, black pillars, vaulted black ceiling. The dim, sourceless, blood-red light that filled it. The dreadful stillness—broken only by my groans and shrieks, and by the slight sound of the gnawing teeth. The demoniac monster standing before me in the body of my father, staring at me with shining green eyes, holding the plans and the parts that the mechanic had brought, waiting for me to speak. But the most horrible thing was the fact that the gnawing demon was the body of dear, lovely Stella!

She was now digging her teeth in with a crunching sound.

I writhed and screamed with agony. Sweat rolled from my body. I tugged madly against my bonds, strove to burst the rope that held my tortured leg.

Fierce, eager growls came wolflike from the throat of the gnawing woman. Her leprously pallid face was once more smeared with blood, as it had been when I first saw her. Occasionally she stopped the unendurable gnawing, to lick her lips with a dreadful satisfaction.

Finally I could stand it no longer. Even if the fate of all the earth depended upon me—as I thought it did—I could endure it no longer.

"Stop! Stop!" I screamed. "I'll tell you!"

Rather reluctantly, the woman rose, licking her crimson lips.

My father—I find myself continually calling the monster by that name, but it was *not* my father—again held the plans before my face, and displayed upon his palm the tiny parts for the electron tube.

It took all my will to draw my mind from the throbbing pain of the fresh wound in my leg. But I explained that the filament wire would have to be drawn much finer, that the radium would not do for the grid, that the plate must be of a conducting metal, instead of quartz.

He did not easily understand my scientific terms. The name tungsten, for instance, meant nothing to him until I had explained the qualities and the atomic number of the metal. That identified it for him, and he appeared really to know more about the metal than I did.

For long hours I answered his questions, and made explanations. A few times I thought of refusing to answer, again. But the memory of that unendurable gnawing always made me speak.

The scientific knowledge and skill displayed in the construction of the machine's parts, once the specifications were properly understood, astounded me. The monsters that had stolen these human bodies seemed to have remarkable scientific knowledge of their own, particularly in chemistry and certain branches of physics—though electricity and magnetism, and the modern theories of relativity and equivalence, seemed new to them, probably because they came from a world whose natural phenomena are not the same as ours.

They brought, from one of the chambers opening into the great hall, an odd, glistening device, consisting of connected bulbs and spheres of some bright, transparent crystal. First, a lump of limestone rock, which must have been dug up in the making of this underground temple, was dropped into a large lower globe. Slowly it seemed to dissolve, forming a heavy, iridescent, violet-colored gas.

Then, whenever my father or one of the others wished to make any object—a metal plate or grid, a coil of wire, an insulating button, anything needed in building the machine—a tiny pattern of it was skilfully formed of a white, soft, wax-like substance.

The white pattern was placed in one of the crystal bulbs, and the heavy violet gas—which must have been disassociated protons and electrons from the disrupted limestone—was allowed to fill the bulb through one of the numerous transparent tubes.

The operator watched a little gauge, and at the right instant, removed from the bulb—not the pattern, but the finished object, formed of any desired element!

The process was not explained to me. But I am sure that it was one of building up atoms from the constituent positive and negative electrons. A process just the reverse of disintegration, by which radium decomposes into lead. First such simple atoms as those of hydrogen and helium. Then carbon, or silicon, or iron. Then silver, if one desired it, or gold! Finally radium, or uranium, the heaviest of metals. The object was removed whenever the atoms had reached the proper number to form the element required.

With this marvelous device, whose accomplishments exceeded the wildest dreams of the alchemist, the construction of the huge machine in the center of the hall proceeded with amazing speed, with a speed that filled me with nothing less than terror.

It occurred to me that I might delay the execution of the monsters' dreadful plan by a trick of some kind. Racking my weary and pain-clouded brain, I sought for some ruse that might mislead my clever opponents. The best idea that came to me was to give a false interpretation of the word "vacuum." If I could keep its true meaning from my father, he would leave the air in the tubes, and they would burn out when the current was turned on. When he finally asked the meaning of the word, I said that it signified a sealed or enclosed space.

But he had been consulting scientific works, as well as my meager knowledge. When the words left my lips, he sprang at me with a hideous snarl. His teeth sought my throat. But for a very hurried pretense of alarmed stupidity, my part in the dreadful adventure might have come to a sudden end. I protested that I had been sincere, that my mind was weary and I could not remember scientific facts, that I must eat and sleep again.

Then I sagged forward against the ropes, head hanging. I refused to respond, even to threats of further torture. And my exhaustion was scarcely feigned, for I had never undergone a more trying day—a day in which one horror followed close upon another.

Finally they cut me loose. The woman carried me out of the sullen crimson light of the temple, up the narrow passage, and into the house again; I was almost too weak to walk alone. As we came out upon the snow, the distant, keening cry of the weird pack broke once more upon my startled ears.

The pale disk of the moon was rising, cold and silvery, in the east, over the illimitable plain of snow. It was night again!

I had been in the subterranean temple for more than twenty-four hours.

CHAPTER VII

WHEN I RAN FROM THE PACK

AGAIN I was in the little room that had been Stella's, among her intimate possessions, catching an occasional suggestion of her perfume. It was a small room, clean and chaste, and I had a feeling that I was invading a sacred place. But I had not choice in the matter, for the windows were barred, and the door locked behind me.

Stella—or, I should say, the werewoman—had let me stop in the other room to eat and drink again. She had even let me find the medicine cabinet and get a bottle of antiseptic to use in the wound on my leg.

Now, sitting on the bed in a shaft of cold, argent moonlight, I applied the stinging liquid, and then bound the place with a bandage torn from a clean sheet.

Then I got to my feet and went to the window: I was determined to escape if escape were possible, or end my life if it were not. I had no intention of going back alive to the hellish red-lit temple.

But the quavering, dismal, howling of the pack came faintly to my ears, as I reached the window, setting me trembling with horror. I gazed fearfully across the fantastic desert of silvery snow, bright in the opalescent haze of moonlight.

Then I glimpsed moving green eyes, and I cried out.

Below the window was a huge, lean gray wolf, pacing deliberately up and down, across the glistening snow. From time to time he lifted his head, stared straight at my windows with huge, malevolent eyes.

A sentinel set to watch me!

With my hopeless despair came a leaden weight of weariness. I felt suddenly exhausted, physically and mentally. I stumbled to the bed, crept under the covers without troubling to remove my clothing, and fell almost instantly asleep.

I awoke upon a gray, cold day. A chill wind was whistling eerily about the old house, and the sky was gloomy with steel-blue clouds. I sprang out of bed, feeling much refreshed by my long sleep. For a moment, despite the dreary day, I was conscious of an extraordinary sense of relief; it seemed, for the merest instant, as if all that had happened to me was a horrible nightmare, from which I was waking. Then recollection came, with a dull pain in my wounded leg.

I wondered why I had not been carried back into the terrible temple of blood-red gloom before the coming of day; perhaps I must have been sleeping too soundly to be roused.

Recalling the gray wolf, I looked nervously out at the window. It was gone, of course; the monsters seemed unable to endure the light of day, or any other save the terrible crimson dusk of the temple.

I wrapped a blanket about my shoulders, for it was extremely cold, and I set about at once to escape from the room. I was determined to win my liberty or die in the attempt.

First I examined the windows again. The bars outside them, though of wood, were quite strong. My utmost strength failed to break any one of them. I could find nothing in the room with which they might be cut or worn in twain, without hours of labor.

Finally I turned to the door. My kicks and blows failed to make any impression upon its sturdy panels. The lock seemed strong, and I had neither skill nor tools for picking it.

But, while I stood gazing at the lock, an idea came to me.

I still had the little automatic, and two extra clips of ammunition. My captors had shown only disdain for the little weapon, and I had rather lost faith in it after its puzzling failure to kill the gray wolf.

Now I backed to the other side of the room, drew it, and deliberately fired three shots into the lock. When I first tried the door again, it seemed as impassable as ever. I worked upon it, twisting the knob, again and again. There was a sudden snap, and the door swung open.

I was free. If only I could reach a place of safety before darkness brought out the weird pack!

In the old dining room I paused to drink, and to eat scantily. Then I left the house by the front door, for I dared not go near the mouth of that hell-burrow behind the house, even by day. In fearful, desperate haste, I set out across the snow.

The little town of Hebron, I knew, lay ten miles away, directly north. Few landmarks were visible above the thick snow, and the gray clouds hid the sun. But I plodded along beside a barbed wire fence, which I knew would guide me.

Slowly the time-yellowed ranch house, an ugly, rambling structure with a gray shingle roof, dwindled upon the white waste behind me. The outbuildings, resembling the house, though looking smaller, more ancient and more dilapidated, drew toward it to form a single brown speck upon the endless desolation of the snow-covered plain.

The crust upon the snow, though frozen harder than upon the ill-fated night of my coming, was still too thin to support my weight. It broke beneath my feet at every step, and I sank ankle-deep in the soft snow beneath.

My progress was a grim, heartbreaking struggle. My strength had been drained by the nerve-racking horrors and exhausting exertions of the past few days. Soon I was gasping for breath, and my feet felt leaden-heavy. There was a dull, intolerable ache in the wound on my leg.

If the snow had been hard enough to support my weight, so that I could run, I might have reached Hebron before dark. But, sinking deep into it at every step, it was impossible for me to move rapidly.

I must not have covered over half the distance to Hebron, when the gloom of the gray, cheerless day seemed to settle upon me. I realized, with a chill of fatal horror, that it had not been early morning when I set out; my watch had stopped, and since the leaden clouds had obscured the sun, I had no gauge of time.

I must have slept through half the day or more, exhausted as I had been by the day and night of torture in the dark temple. Night was upon me, when I was still far short of my destination.

Nearly dead with fatigue, I had more than once been almost on the point of stopping to rest. But terror lent me fresh strength. I plodded on as fast as I could, but forcing myself to keep from running, which would burn up my energy too soon.

Another mile, perhaps, I had covered, when I heard the weird, blood-congealing voice of the pack.

The darkness, for a time, had been intense, very faintly relieved by the ghostly gleam of the snow. But the clouds had lightened somewhat, and the light of the rising moon shone through them, casting eldritch shadows of silver on the level snow.

At first the dreadful baying was very distant, low and moaning and hideous with the human vocal note it carried. But it grew louder. And there was something in it of sharp, eager yelping.

I knew that the pack which had run down Judson and me had been set upon my trail.

The terror, the stark, maddening, soul-searing horror that seized me, is beyond imagination. I shrieked uncontrollably. My hands and body felt alternately hot and fevered, and chilled with a cold sweat. A harsh dryness roughened my throat. I reeled dizzily, and felt the pounding of my pulse in all my body.

And I ran.

Madly, wildly. Ran with all my strength. Ran through the thick snow faster than I had thought possible. But in a few moments, it seemed I had used up all my strength.

I was suddenly sick with fatigue, swaying, almost unable to stand. Red mists, shot with white fire, danced in front of my eyes. The vast plain of snow whirled about me fantastically.

And on and on I staggered. When each step took all my will. When I felt that I must collapse in the snow, and fought with all my mind for the strength to raise my foot again.

All the time, the fearful baying was drawing nearer, until the wailing, throbbing sound of it drummed and rang in my brain.

Finally, unable to take another step, I turned and looked back.

For a few moments I stood there, swaying, gasping for breath. The weird, nerve-blasting cry of the pack sounded very near, but I could see nothing. Then, through the clouds, a broad, ghostly shaft of moonlight fell athwart the snow behind me. And I saw the pack.

I saw them! The pinnacle of horror!

Gray wolves, leaping, green-eyed and gaunt. And strange human figures among them, racing with them. Chill, soulless emerald orbs staring. Bodies ghastly pallid, clad only in tattered rags. Stella, bounding at the head of the pack.

My father, following. And other men. All green-orbed, leprously white. Some of them frightfully mutilated.

Some so torn they should have been dead!

Judson, the man who had brought me out from Hebron, was among them. His livid flesh hung in ribbons. One eye was gone, and a green fire seemed to sear the empty socket. His chest was fearfully lacerated. And the man was—eviscerated!

Yet his hideous body leaped beside the wolves.

And others were as dreadful. One had no head. A black mist seemed gathered above the jutting, lividly white stump of his neck, and in it glowed malevolently—two green eyes!

A woman ran with them. One arm was torn off, her naked breasts were in ribbons. She ran with the rest, green eyes glowing, mouth wide open, baying with other members of the pack.

And now I saw a horse in that grotesque company. A powerful, gray animal, he was, and he came with tremendous leaps. Its eyes, too, were glowing green—glowing with the malignant fire of an evil intelligence not normally of this earth. This was one of Judson's animals, changed as dreadfully as he and all the others had been. Its mouth yawned open, with yellow teeth glistening, and it howled madly with the pack.

Swiftly, hideously, they closed in upon me. The weird host sprang toward me from all directions—gray wolves, men, and horse. Eyes glaring, teeth bared, snarling, the hellish horde came closer.

The horror of it was too much for my mind. A merciful wave of darkness overcame me as I felt myself reeling to fall upon the snow.

Chapter VIII

THROUGH THE DISK OF DARKNESS

I AWOKE within the utter stillness of a tomb. For a little time I lay with eyes closed, analyzing the sensations of my chilled, aching body, conscious of the dull, throbbing pain from my wounded leg. I shuddered at recollection of the fearful experiences of the past few days, endured again the overwhelming horror of the moment when the pack—wolves and men and horse, frightfully mutilated, eyes demoniacally green—had closed in upon me on the moonlit snow. For some time I did not dare to open my eyes.

At last, nerving myself against the new horrors that might surround me, I raised my lids.

I looked into the somber, crimson radiance of the ebon-pillared temple. Beside a dull jet wall I lay, upon a pile of rags, with a blanket thrown carelessly over me. Beyond the row of massive, black, cylindrical pillars, I saw the great, strange machine, with the huge copper ring glistening queerly in the dim, bloody light. The polished mirror behind it seemed flushed with a living glow of molten rubies, and the many electron tubes, now mounted in their sockets, gleamed redly. The mechanism appeared to be near completion; livid, green-orbed figures were busy about it, moving with a swift, mechanical efficiency. It struck me abruptly that they moved more like machines than like living beings. My father, Stella, the two mechanics.

For many minutes I lay very still, watching them covertly. Evidently they had brought me down into this subterranean chamber, so that I would have no chance to repeat my escape. I speculated upon the possibility of creeping along the wall to the ascending passage, dashing through it. But there was little hope that I could do it unseen. And I had no way of knowing whether it might be night or day; it would be folly to run out into the darkness. I felt the little automatic still under my arm; they had not troubled to remove a weapon which they did not fear.

Suddenly, before I had dared to move, I saw my father coming across the black floor toward me. I could not repress a tremor, at closer sight of his deathly pallid body and sinister, baleful greenish eyes. I lay still, trying to pretend sleep.

I felt his ice-cold fingers close upon my shoulder; roughly I was drawn to my feet.

"Further assistance from you must be ours," whined his wolfish voice. "And not again will you be brought back living, should you be the fool to run!" His whine ended with an ugly snarl.

He dragged me across toward the fantastic mechanism that glistened in the grim, bloody radiance.

I quailed at the thought of being bound to the black pillar again. "I'll help!" I cried. "Do anything you want. Don't tie me up, for God's sake! Don't let her gnaw me!" My voice must have become a hysterical scream. I fought to calm it, cudgeled my brain for arguments.

"It would kill me to be tied again," I pleaded wildly. "And if you leave me free, I can help you with my hands!"

"Be free of bonds, then," my father whined. "But also remember! You go, and we bring you back not alive!"

He led me up beside the great machine. One of the mechanics, at a shrill, wolfish whine from him, unrolled a blue print before me. He began to ask questions regarding the wiring to connect the many electron tubes, the coils and helixes and magnets, all ranged about the huge copper ring.

His strange brain seemed to have no conception of the nature of electricity; I had to explain the fundamentals. But he grasped each new fact with astounding quickness, seemed to see the applications instinctively.

It soon developed that the great mechanism was practically finished; in an hour, perhaps, the wiring was completed.

"Now what yet is to be constructed?" my father whined.

I realized that no provision had been made for electricity to light the tubes and energize the magnets. These beings apparently did not even know that a source of power was necessary. This, I thought, was another chance to stop the execution of their hellish plan.

"I don't know," I said. "So far as I can see, the machine now fits the specifications. I know nothing else to do."

He snarled something to one of the mechanics, who produced the bloody rope with which I had previously been bound. Stella sprang toward me, her lips curled in a leering animal snarl, her white teeth gleaming.

Uncontrollable terror shook me, weakened my knees until I reeled. "Wait! Stop!" I screamed. "I'll tell if you won't tie me!"

They halted.

"Speak!" my father barked. "Quickly describe!"

"The machine must have power. Electricity?"

"From what place comes electricity."

"There is a motor generator up in the cellar, where the other machine is. That might do."

He and the monster that had been Stella hurried me down the black-pillared hall, and up the inclined passage to the old cellar. He carried the red-glowing electric lantern. In the cellar I showed them the generator and attempted a rough explanation of its operation.

Then he and the woman bent and caught the metal base of the unit. With their incredible strength, they lifted it quite easily and carried it toward the passage. They made me walk ahead of them as we returned to the machine in the black hall—blasting another hope for a chance to make a dash for the open.

Just as they were placing the heavy machine—gasoline engine and dynamo, which together weighted several hundred pounds—on the black platform beside the strange, gigantic mechanism, there came an interruption that, to me, was terrifying.

From the passage came the rustle of feet, and mingled whining, snarling sounds such as the monsters seemed to use for communication. And in the vague, blood-red light, between the tall rows of great black pillars, appeared the pack!

Huge, gaunt wolves there were. Frightfully mutilated men—Judson, and the others that I had seen. The gray horse. All their eyes were luminously green—alight with a dreadful, malevolent fire.

Human lips were crimsoned. Scarlet smeared the gray wolves' muzzles, and even the long nose and gray jaws of the horse. And they carried—the catch!

Over Judson's livid, lacerated shoulders was hung the torn, limp, bleeding body of a woman—his wife! One of the gaunt gray wolves had the hideously mangled body of a man across his back, holding it in place with jaws turned sidewise. Another had the body of a spotted calf. Two more carried in red-dripping jaws the lax gray bodies of coyotes. And one of the men bore upon his shoulder the remains of a huge gray wolf.

The dead, torn, mutilated specimens were dropped in a horrible heap in the wide central aisle of the jet-pillared temple, near the strange machine, like an altar of death. Dark blood flowed from it over the black floor, congealing in thick, viscid clots.

"To these we bring life," my father snarled at me, jerking his head toward the dreadful, mangled heap.

Shuddering and dazed with horror, I sank on the floor, covering my eyes. I was nauseated, sick. My brain was reeling, fogged, confused. It refused to dwell upon the meaning of this dreadful scene.

The mad, fearful, demoniac thing that had been my father jerked me roughly to my feet, dragged me toward the motor generator, and began plying me with questions about its operation, about how to connect it with the strange mechanism of the copper ring.

I struggled to answer his questions, trying vainly to forget my horror in the work.

Soon the connection was completed. Under my father's directions, I examined the gasoline engine, saw that it was supplied with fuel and oil. Then he attempted to start it, but failed to master the technique of choking the carburetor. Under constant threat of the blood-darkened rope and the were-woman's gnawing fangs, I labored with the little motor until it coughed a few times, and fell to firing steadily.

Then my father made me close the switch, connecting the strange machine with the current from the generator. A faint, shrill humming came from the coils. The electron tubes glowed dimly.

And a curtain of darkness seemed suddenly drawn across the copper ring. Blackness seemed to flow from the queer tube behind it, to be reflected into it by the polished mirror. A disk of dense, utter darkness filled the ring.

For a few moments I stared at it in puzzled wonder.

Then, as my eyes became slowly sensitized, I found that I could see through it—see into a dread, nightmare world.

The ring had become an opening into another world of horror and darkness.

The sky of that alien world was unutterably, inconceivably black; blacker than the darkest midnight. It had no stars, no luminary; no faintest gleam relieved its terrible, oppressive intensity.

A vast reach of that other world's surface lay in view, beyond the copper ring. Low, worn, and desolate hills, that seemed black as the somber sky. Between them flowed a broad and stagnant river, whose dull and sullen waters shone with a vague and ghostly luminosity, with a pale glow that was somehow unclean and noisome, like that of decaying foul corruption.

And upon those low and ancient hills, that were rounded like the bloated breasts of corpses, was a loathsome vegetation. Hideous, obscene travesties of normal plants, whose leaves were long, narrow, snake-like, with the suggestion of ugly heads. With a dreadful, unnatural life, they seemed to writhe, lying in rotting tangles upon the black hills, and dragging in the foul, lurid waters of the stagnant river. Their thin reptilian, tentacular vines and creepers glowed with a pale and ghastly light, lividly greenish.

And upon a low black hill, above the evil river, and the rotting, writhing, obscene jungle, was what must have been a city. A sprawled and hideous mass of red corruption. A foul splash of dull crimson pollution.

This was no city, perhaps, in our sense of the word. It seemed to be a sort of cloud of foul, blood-hued darkness, trailing repulsive tentacles across the low black hill; a smear of evil crimson mist. Mad and repulsive knobs and warts rose about it, in grotesque mockery of spires and towers. It was motionless. And I knew instinctively that unclean and abdominable life, sentience, reigned within its hideous scarlet contamination.

My father mounted to the black stone step between the copper ring, and stood there howling weirdly and hideously, into that world of darkness—voicing an unclean call!

In answer, the sprawled, nightmare city seemed to stir. Dark things— masses of fetid, reeking blackness—seemed to creep from its ugly protuberances, to swarm toward us through the tainted filth of the writhing, evilly glowing vegetation.

The darkness of evil concentrate, creeping from that nightmare world into ours!

For long moments the utter, insane horror of it held me paralyzed and helpless. Then something nerved me with the abrupt, desperate determination to revolt against my fearful masters, despite the threat of the bloody rope.

I tore my eyes from the dreadful attraction that seemed to draw them toward the foul, sprawled city of bloody darkness, in that hideous world of unthinkable evil.

Realization came to me that I stood alone, unguarded. The green eyes of the monsters about me were fixed in avid fascination upon the ring through which that nightmare world was visible. None of them seemed aware of me.

If only I could wreck the machine, before those creeping horrors of darkness came through into our world! I started forward instinctively, then paused, realizing that it might be difficult to do great damage to it with my bare hands, before the monsters saw me and attacked.

Then I thought of the little automatic in my pocket, which I had been permitted to keep with me. Even though its bullets could not harm the monsters, they might do considerable damage to the machine.

I snatched it out and began firing deliberately at the dimly glowing electron tubes. As the first one was shattered, the image of that hideous, nightmare world flickered and vanished. The huge, polished mirror was once more visible beyond the copper ring.

For the time being, at least, those rankling shapes of black and utter evil were shut out of our world!

As I continued to fire, shattering the electron tubes and the other most delicate and most complicated parts of the great mechanism, a fearful, soul-chilling cry came from the startled monsters in human and animal bodies.

Suddenly the creatures sprang toward me, over the black floor, howling hideously.

CHAPTER IX

THE HYPNOTIC REVELATION

IT WAS the yellow, stabbing spurts of flame from the automatic that saved me. At first the fearfully transformed beasts and men had leaped at me, howling with the agony that light seemed to cause them. I kept on firing, determined to do all the damage possible before they bore me down.

And abruptly they fell back away from me, wailing dreadfully, hiding their unearthly green eyes, slinking behind the massive black pillars.

When the gun was empty, some of them came toward me again. But still they seemed shaken, weakened, uncertain of movement. In nervous haste, I fumbled in my pockets for matches—I had not realized before how they were crippled by light.

I found only three, all, apparently, that I had left.

The weird monsters, recovered from the effect of the gun flashes, were leaping across toward me, through the sullen, blood-red gloom, as I struggled desperately to make a light.

The first match broke in my fingers.

But the second flared into yellow flame. The monsters, almost upon me, sprang back, wailing in agony again. As I held the tiny, feeble flame aloft, they cowered, howling, in the flickering shadows cast by the huge, ebon pillars.

My confused, horror-dazed mind was abruptly cleared and sharpened by hope of escape. With the light to hold them back, I might reach the open air.

And to my quickened mind it came abruptly that it must be day above. It was morning, and the pack had been driven back to the burrow by the light of the coming sun!

As swiftly as I could, without extinguishing the feeble flame of the match with the wind of my motion, I advanced down the great hall. I kept in the middle of the wide central aisle, afraid that my enemies were slinking along after me in the shadows of the pillars.

Before I reached the passage which lead to the surface, a stronger breath of air caught the feeble orange flame. It flickered out. Dusky crimson gloom fell about me once more, with baleful green eyes moving in it, in the farther end of the temple. The howling rose again, angrily. I heard swiftly padding feet.

Only one of the three matches was left.

I bent, scratched it very carefully on the black floor and held it above my head.

A new wailing of pain came from the monsters; they fell back again.

I found the end of the passage, rushed through it, guarding the precious flame in a cupped hand.

In the great hall behind me, the blood-chilling wail of the pack rose again. I heard the monsters surging toward the passage.

By the time I had reached the old cellar, from whose wall the slanting tunnel had been dug, the match was almost consumed. I turned, let its last dying rays shine down the passage. Dreadful cries of agony and terror came again; I heard the monsters retreating from the tunnel.

The match suddenly went out.

In mad haste I dashed across the cellar's floor and blundered heavily into the wall. I found the steps that led to the surface and rushed up them desperately.

I heard the howling pack running up the passage, moving far swifter than I was able to do.

At last my hand touched the under surface of the wooden door, above the steps. Beyond, I knew, was the golden light of day.

And at the same instant, corpse-cold fingers closed about my ankle, in a crushing, powerful grasp.

Convulsively, I thrust upward with my hand.

The door flew up, slammed crashingly beside the opening. Above was soft, brilliant azure sky. In it the white morning sun blazed blindingly. Its hot radiance brought tears to my eyes, accustomed as they were to the dim crimson light of the temple.

Fearful, agonized animal wailing sounds came again from behind me.

The grasp on my ankle tightened convulsively, then relaxed.

Looking back, I saw Stella on the steps at my feet, cowering, writhing as if in unbearable agony, animal screams of pain coming from her lips. It seemed that the burning sunlight had struck her down, that she had been too much weakened to retreat as those behind her had done.

Abruptly she seemed to me a lovely, suffering girl—not a strange demoniac monster. Pity for her—even, perhaps, love—came over me in a tender wave. If I could save her, restore her to her true, dear self!

I ran back down the steps, seized her by the shoulders, started to carry her up into the light. Deathly cold and deathly white her body still was. And still it had a vestige of that unnatural strength.

She writhed in my arms, snarling, slashing at my body with her teeth. For a moment her green eyes smoldered malevolently at me. But as the sunlight struck them she closed them, howling with agony, and tried to shield them with her arm.

I carried her up the steps, into the brilliant sunlight.

First I thought of closing the cellar door, and trying to fasten it. Then I realized that the light of day, shining down the passage, would hold back the monsters more effectually than any locked door.

It was still early morning. The sun had been up no more than an hour. The sky was clear, and the sunshine glittered with blinding, prismatic brilliance on the snow. The air, however, was still cold; there had been no thawing, nor would there be until the temperature had moderated considerably.

As I stood there in the blaze of sunlight, holding Stella, a strange change came over her. The fierce snarling and whining sounds that came from her throat slowly died away. Her writhing, convulsive struggles weakened, as though a tide of alien life were ebbing from her body.

There was a sudden last convulsion. Then her body was lax, limp.

Almost immediately, I noticed a change in color. The fearful, corpse-like pallor slowly gave place to the normal pinkish flush of healthy life. The strange, unearthly chill was gone; I felt a glow of warmth where her body was against mine.

Then her breast heaved. She breathed. I felt the slow throbbing of her heart. Her eyes were still closed as she lay inert in my arms, like one sleeping. I freed one of my hands and gently lifted a long-lashed lid.

The eye was clear and blue—normal again. The baleful, greenish fire was gone!

In some way, which I did not then understand, the light of day had purified the girl, had driven from her the fierce, unclean life that had possessed her body.

"Stella! Dear Stella! Wake up!" I cried. I shook her a little. But she did not rouse. Still she seemed sleeping heavily.

Realizing that she would soon be chilled, in the cold air, I carried her into the house, into her own room, where I had been imprisoned, and laid her on the bed, covering her with blankets. Still she appeared to be sleeping.

For an hour, perhaps, I tried to rouse her from the profound syncope or coma in which she lay. I tried everything that experience and the means at hand made available. And still she lay insensible.

A most puzzling situation, and a surprising one. It was almost as if Stella—the real Stella—had been dispossessed of her body by some foul, alien being. The alien, evil life had been killed by the light, and still she had not returned.

At last it occurred to me to try hypnotic influence—I am a fair hypnotist, and have made a deep study of hypnotism and allied mental phenomena. A forlorn hope, perhaps, since her coma appeared so deep. But I was driven to clutch at any straw.

Exerting all my will to recall her mind, placing my hand upon her smooth brow, or making slow passes over her still, pale, lovely face, I commanded her again and again to open her eyes.

And suddenly, when I was almost on the point of new despair, her eyelids flickered, lifted. Of course, it may have been a natural awakening, though a most unusual one, instead of the result of my efforts. But her blue eyes opened and stared up at me.

But still she was not normally awake. No life or feeling was revealed in the azure depths of her eyes. They were clouded, shadowed with sleep. Their opening seemed to have been a mechanical answer to my commands.

"Speak. Stella, my Stella, speak to me!" I cried.

Her pale lips parted. From them came low, sleep-drugged tones.

"Clovis." She spoke my name in that small, colorless voice.

"Stella, what has happened to you and my father?" I cried.

And here is what she told me, in that tiny, toneless voice. I have condensed it somewhat, for many times her voice wandered wearily, died away, and I had to prompt her, question her, almost force her to continue.

"My father came here to help Dr. McLaurin with his experiment," she began, slowly, in a low monotone. "I did not understand all of it, but they sought for other worlds besides ours. Other dimensions, interlocking with our own. Dr. McLaurin had been working out his theory for many years, basing his work upon the new mathematics of Weyl and Einstein.

"Not simple is our universe. Worlds upon worlds lie side by side, like the pages of a book—and each world unknown to all the others. Strange worlds touching, spinning side by side, yet separated by walls not easily broken down.

In vibration is the secret. For all matter, all light, all sound, all our universe, is of vibration. All material things are formed of vibrating particles of electricity—electrons. And each world, each universe, has its own order of vibration. And through each, all unknown and unseen, are the myriad other worlds and universes vibrating, each with an order of its own.

"Dr. McLaurin knew by mathematics that these other worlds must exist. It was his wish to explore them. Here he came, to be alone, with none to pry into his secrets. Aided by my father, and other men, he toiled through years to build his machine.

"A machine, if successful, would change the vibration rate of matter and of light. To change it from the order of our dimension, to those of others. With it, he might see into those myriad other worlds in space beside our own, might visit them.

"The machine was finished. And through its great copper ring, we saw another world. A world of darkness, with midnight sky. Loathsome, lividly green plants writhed like reptilian monstrosities upon its black hills. Evil, alien life teemed upon it.

"Dr. McLaurin went through into that dark world. The horror of it broke down his mind. A strange madman, he came back. His eyes were green and shining, and his skin was very white.

"And things he brought back with him—clinging, creeping things of foul blackness, that stole the bodies of men and beasts. Evil, living things, that are the masters of the black dimension. One crept into me, and took my body. It ruled me, and I know only like a dim dream what it made my body do. To it, my body was but a machine.

"Dim dreams. Terrible dreams. Dreaming of running over the snow, hunting for wolves. Dreams of bringing them back, for the black things to flow into, and make live again. Dreams of torturing my father, whom no black thing took, at first.

Father was tortured, gnawed. My body did it. But I did not do it.

I was far away. I saw it only dimly, like a bad dream. One of the black creatures had come into my body, taken it from me.

"New to our world were the black things. Light slays them, for it is a force strange to their world, against which they have no armor. And so they dug a deep place, to slink into by day.

"The ways of our world they knew not; nor the language; nor the machines. They made Father teach them; teach them to speak; to read books; to run the machine through which they came. They plan to bring many of their evil kind through the machine, to conquer our world. They plan to make black clouds to hide the sun forever, so our world will be as dark as their own. They plan to seize the bodies of all men and animals, to use as machines to do that thing.

"When Father knew the plan, he would not tell them more. So my body gnawed him—while I looked on from afar, and could not help. Then he pretended to be in accord with them. They let him loose. He smashed the machine with an ax, so no more evil things could come through. Then he blew off his head with a gun, so they could not torture him, and make him aid them again.

"The black things could not themselves repair the machine. But in letters they learned of Clovis McLaurin, son of Dr. McLaurin. He, too, knew of machines. They sent for him, to torture him as Father had been tortured. Again my mind was filled with grief, for he was dear to me. But my body gnawed him, while he aided the black things to build a new machine.

"Then he broke it. And then . . . then. . . ."

Her tiny, toneless voice died wearily away. Her blue eyes, still clouded with shadowed sleep, stared up unseeingly. Deep indeed was her strange trance.

She had even forgotten that it was I to whom she spoke!

CHAPTER X

THE CREEPING DARKNESS

A N AMAZING and terrible story, was Stella's. In part, it was almost incredible. Yet, much as I wished to doubt it, and much as I wished to discount the horror that it promised our fair earth, I knew that it must be true.

Prominent scientists have speculated often enough of the possibility of other worlds, other planes, side by side with our own. For there is nothing solid or impenetrable about the matter of our universe. The electron is thought to be only a vibration in the ether. And in all probability, there are vibrating fields of force, forming other electrons, other atoms, other suns and planets, existing beside our world, yet not making their existence known. Only a tiny band of the vibrations in the spectrum is visible to our eyes as light. If our eyes were tuned to other bands, above the ultra-violet, or below the infrared, what new, strange worlds might burst upon our vision?

No, I could not doubt that part of Stella's story. My father had studied the evidence upon the existence of such worlds invisible to us, more deeply than any other man, had published his findings, with complete mathematical proof, in his startling work, "Interlocking Universes." If those parallel worlds were to be discovered, he was the logical man to make the discovery. And I could not doubt that he had made it—for I had seen that world of dread nightmare, beyond the copper ring!

And I had seen, in that dark, alien world, the city of the creeping things of blackness. I could well believe the part of the story about those strangely malignant entities stealing the bodies of men and animals. It offered the first rational solution of all the astounding facts I had observed, since the night of my coming to Hebron.

And it came to me suddenly that soon the monstrous beings would have the machine repaired; they could need no further aid from me. Then other hordes of the black shapes would come through. Come to seize our world, Stella had said, to enslave humanity, to aid them in making our world a planet of darkness like the grim sphere they left. It seemed mad, incredible—yet I knew it was true!

I must do something against them! Fight them—fight them with light! Light was the one force that destroyed them. That had freed Stella from her dread bondage. But I must obtain better means of making light than a few matches. Lamps would do; a searchlight, perhaps.

And I was determined to take Stella to Hebron, if she were able to go. I must go there to find the supplies I needed, and yet I could not bear the thought of leaving her for the monstrosities to find when night fell again, to seize her fair body again for their foul ends.

I found that at my command she would move, stand, and walk, though slowly and stiffly, like a person walking in sleep. It was still early morning, and I thought there might be time for her to walk to Hebron, with me to support her steps, before the fall of darkness.

I investigated her possessions in the room, found clothing for her: woolen stockings, strong shoes, knickers, sweater, gloves, cap. Her efforts to dress herself were slow and clumsy, like those of a weary child, trying to pull off his clothing when half asleep, and I had to aid her.

She seemed not to be hungry. But when we stopped in the dining room, where the remainder of the food still lay on the table, I made her drink a tin of milk. She did it mechanically. As for myself, I ate heartily, despite ill-omened recollections of how I had eaten at this table on the eve of my first attempt to escape.

We set out across the snow, following along by the wire fence as I had done before. I could distinguish my old footprints and the mingled tracks of wolf, man, and horse, in the trail the pursuing pack had left. We followed that trail with greater ease now, for the soft snow had been packed by the running feet.

I walked with an arm about Stella's waist, sometimes half-carrying her, speaking to her encouragingly. She responded with slow, dull mechanical efforts. Her mind seemed far away; her blue eyes were misty with strange dreams.

As the hours of weary struggle went by, with her warm body against mine, it came to me that I loved her very much, and that I would give my life to save her from the dread fate that menaced us.

Once I stopped, and drew her unresisting body fiercely to me, and brought my mouth close to her pale lips, that were composed, and a little parted, and perfumed with sleep. Her blue eyes stared at me blankly, still clouded with sleep, devoid of feeling or understanding. Suddenly I knew that it would be wrong to kiss her so. I pushed her pliant body back, and led her on across the snow.

The sun reached the zenith, and began declining slowly westward.

As the evening wore on, Stella seemed to tire—or perhaps it was only that her trance-like state became deeper. She responded more slowly to my urgings that we must hurry. When, for a few moments, my encouraging voice was silent, she stood motionless, rigid, as if lost in strange vision.

I hurried her on desperately, commanding her steadily to keep up her efforts. My eyes were anxiously on the setting sun. I knew that we would have scant time to reach the village before the fall of night; haste was imperative.

At last, when the sun was still some distance above the white horizon, we came within sight of the town of Hebron. A cluster of dark specks, upon the limitless plain of glittering snow. Three miles away, they must have been.

Still the girl seemed to sink deeper into the strange sea of sleep from which only hypnotic influence had lifted her. By the time we had covered another mile, she refused to respond to my words. She was breathing slowly, regularly; her body was limp, flaccid; her eyes had closed. I could do nothing to rouse her.

The sun had touched the snow, coloring the western world with pale rose and purple fires. Darkness was not far away.

Desperately, I took the limp, relaxed body of the girl upon my shoulders and staggered on beneath the burden. It was no more than two miles to Hebron; I had hopes of getting there with her before dark.

But the snow was so deep as to make the effort of even unburdened walking exhausting. And my body was worn out, after the terrible experiences I had lately undergone. Before I had tottered on half a mile, I realized that my effort was hopeless.

Dusk had fallen. The moon had not yet risen, but the snow gleamed silvery under the ghostly twilight that still flooded the sky. My ears were straining fearfully for the voice of the dreadful pack. But a shroud of utter silence hung about me. I was still plodding wearily along, carrying Stella.

Abruptly I noticed that her body, against my hands, was becoming strangely cold. Anxiously, I laid her down upon the snow, to examine her—trembling with a premonition of the approaching horror.

Her body was icy cold. And it had again become ghastly, deathly white. White as when I had seen her running over the snow with the gaunt gray wolf!

But her limbs, strangely, did not stiffen; they were still pliant, relaxed. It was not the chill of death coming over her; it was the cold of that alien life, which the sunlight had driven from her, returning with the darkness!

I knew that she would soon be a human girl no longer, but a weird wolf-woman, and the knowledge chilled my soul with horror! For a few moments I crouched beside her inert body, pleading wildly with her to come back to me, crying out to her almost insanely.

Then I saw the hopelessness of it, and the danger. The monstrous life would flow into her again. And she would carry me back to hateful captivity in the subterannean temple, to be a slave of the monsters— or perhaps a member of their malefic society.

I must escape! For her sake. For the world's. It would be better to abandon her now, and go on alone, than have her carry me back. Perhaps I would have another chance to save her.

And I must somehow render her helpless, so that she could not pursue me, when the dread life returned to her body.

I snatched off my coat, and then my shirt. In anxious haste, I tore the shirt into strips, which I twisted rapidly into cords. I drew her ankles together, passed the improvised bonds about them, knotted them tightly. I turned the frightfully pallid, corpse-cold girl upon her face, crossed the lax arms behind her back, and fastened her wrists together with another rope of twisted cloth. Then, by way of extra precaution, I slipped the belt from my trousers and buckled it firmly about her waist, over the crossed wrists, pinioning them.

Finally I spread on the snow the coat I had taken off, and laid her upon it, for I wanted her to be as comfortable as possible.

Then I started off toward Hebron, where a little cluster of white lights shone across the snow, through the gray, gathering dusk. I had gone but a few steps when something made me pause, look back, fearfully.

The inert, deathly pallid body of the girl still lay upon the coat. Beyond it, I glimpsed a strange and dreadful thing, moving swiftly through the ghostly, gray twilight.

Incredible and hideous was the thing I gazed upon. I can hardly find words to describe it; I can give the reader no idea of the weird, icy horror that grasped my heart with dread fingers as I saw it.

It was a mass of darkness, flowing over the snow. A creeping cloud of foul *blackness,* shapeless and many-tentacled. Its form changed continually as it moved. It had no limbs, no features—only the inky, snake-like, clinging extensions of its blackness, that it thrust out to move itself along. But deep within it were two bright green points—like eyes. Green baleful orbs, aflame with fiendish malevolence!

It was alive, this living darkness. It was unlike any higher form of life. But it has since come to me that it resembled the amoeba—a single-cell animal, a flowing mass of protoplasmic slime. Like the amoeba this darkness moved by extended narrow pseudopods from its mass. And the green eyes of horror, in which its unearthly life appeared to be concentrated, perhaps correspond to the vacuoles or nuclei of the protozoan animals.

I realized, with a paralyzing sensation of horror unutterable, that it was one of the monsters from that world of black nightmare, beyond the copper ring. And that it was coming to claim again Stella's body, to which it was still connected by some tainted bond.

Though it seemed only to creep or flow, it moved with a terrible swiftness—far faster, even, than the wolves.

In a moment after I saw it, it had reached Stella's body. It paused, hung over her, a thick, viscid, clinging cloud of unclean blackness with those greenish, fearful eyes staring from its foul mass. For a moment it hid her body, with its creeping, sprawling, ink-black and shapeless masses, crawling over her like horrid tentacles.

Then it *flowed* into her body.

It seemed to stream through her nostrils, into her mouth. The black cloud hanging over her steadily diminished. The infernal green orbs remained above, in the writhing darkness, until the last. And then they seemed to sink into her eyes.

Abruptly, her pallid body came to terrible life.

She writhed, straining at her bonds with preternatural strength, rolling from the coat into the snow, hideously convulsed. Her eyes were open again—and they shone, not with their own life, but with the dreadful fire of the green, malevolent orbs that had sunk into them.

Her eyes were the eyes of the creeping blackness.

From her throat came the soul-numbing, wolfish baying, that I had already heard under such frightful circumstances. It was an animal cry, yet it had an uncanny human note that was terrifying.

She was calling to the pack!

That sound nerved my paralyzed limbs. For the few moments that it had taken the monstrous thing of blackness to flow into Stella's body, I had stood motionless, transfixed with the horror of it.

Now I turned and ran madly across the snow toward the dancing lights of Hebron. Behind me the werewoman still writhed in the snow, trying to break her bonds, howling weirdly—summoning the pack!

Those twinkling lights seemed to mock me. They looked very near across the ghostly, gleaming plain of snow. They seemed to dance away from me as I ran. They seemed to move like fireflies, pausing until I was almost upon them, then retreating, to scintillate far across the snow.

I forgot my weariness, forgot the dull, throbbing pain of the unhealed wound in my leg. I ran desperately, as I had never run before. Not only was my life at stake, but Stella's and my father's. Even, I had good reason to fear, the lives of all humanity.

Before I had covered half the distance, I heard behind me the voice of the pack. A weird, wailing, far-off cry which grew swiftly louder. The werewoman had called, and the pack was coming to free her.

On I ran. My steps seemed so pitifully short, despite my agony of effort, so pitifully slow. My feet sank deep into the snow which seemed to cling to them with maleficent demon-fingers. And the lights that seemed so near appeared to be dancing mockingly away before me.

Sweat poured from my body. My lungs throbbed with pain. My breath came in quick, agonized gasps. My heart seemed to hammer against the base of my brain. My mind seemed drowning in a sea of pain. And on I ran.

The lights of Hebron became unreal ghost-fires, false will-o'-the-wisps. They quivered before me in a blank world of gray darkness. And I labored on toward them, through a dull haze of agony. I saw nothing else. And nothing did I hear, but the moaning of the pack.

I was so weary that I could not think. But I suddenly became aware that the pack was very near. I think I turned my head and glanced back for a moment. Or it may be that I remember the pack only as I saw it in imagination. But I have a very vivid picture of gaunt gray wolves leaping and baying hideously, and pallid, green-eyed men running with them, howling with them.

Yet on I ran, fighting the black mists of exhaustion that closed about my brain. Heartbreaking inertia seemed to oppose every effort, as if I were swimming against a resisting tide. On and on I ran, with eyes for nothing, thought for nothing, except the lights before me, the dancing, mocking lights of Hebron, that seemed very near, and always fled before me.

Then suddenly I was lying in the soft snow with my eyes closed. The yielding couch was very comfortable to my exhausted body. I lay there, relaxed. I did not even try to rise; my strength was utterly gone. Blackness came upon me—unconsciousness that even the howling of the pack could not keep away. The weird ululation seemed to grow fainter and I knew no more.

CHAPTER XI

A BATTLE OF LIGHT AND DARKNESS

PRETTY NEAR all in, ain't you, Mister?" a rough voice penetrated to my fatigue-drugged mind. Strong hands were helping me to my feet. I opened my eyes and stared confusedly about me. Two roughly clad men were supporting me. And another, whom I recognized as the station agent, Connell, held a gasoline lantern.

Before me, almost at hand, were the lights of Hebron, which had seemed to dance away so mockingly. I saw that I had collapsed in the outskirts of the straggling village—so near the few street lights that the pack had been unable to approach me.

"That you, McLaurin?" Connell demanded in surprise, recognizing my face. "We figgered they got you and Judson."

"They did," I found voice to say. "But they carried me off alive. I got away."

I was too nearly dead with exhaustion to answer their questions. Only vaguely do I recall how they carried me into a house, and undressed me. I went to sleep while they were examining the wound on my leg, exclaiming with horror at the marks of teeth. After I was sleeping they dressed it again, and then put me to bed.

It was noon of the following day when I awoke. A nervous boy of perhaps ten years was sitting by the bed. His name, he said, was Marvin Potts, son of Joel Potts, owner of a general store in Hebron. His father had been one of the men who had found me when their attention was attracted by the howling of the pack. I had been carried into the Potts home.

The boy called his mother. She, finding that I was hungry, soon brought me coffee, biscuits, bacon, and fried potatoes. I ate with good appetite, though I was far from recovered from my desperate run to escape the pack. While I was eating, still lying in bed, raised on an elbow, my host came in. Connell, the station agent, and two other men were with him.

All were anxious to hear my story. I told it to them briefly, or as much of it as I thought they would believe.

From them I learned that the weird pack had found several more human victims. A lone ranch house had been raided on the night before and three men carried from it. They told me, too, that Mrs. Judson, frantic with grief over the loss of her husband, had gone out across the snow to seek him and had not come back. How well I recalled now that she had found him! Bitterly I reproached myself for having urged the man to risk the night trip with me.

I inquired if any steps had been made to hunt the wolves.

The sheriff, I learned, had organized a posse, which had ventured

70

out from Hebron several times. Abundant tracks of men and wolves, running side by side, had been found. There had been no difficulty in following the trail. But, I gathered, the hunters had not been very eager for success. The snow was deep; they could not travel rapidly, and they had owned no intention of meeting the pack by night. The trails had never been followed more than six or seven miles from Hebron. The sheriff had returned to the county seat, twelve miles down the railroad, promising to return when the snow had melted enough to make traveling easier. And the few score inhabitants of Hebron, though deeply disturbed by the fate of their neighbors who had been taken by the pack, had been too much terrorized to undertake any determined expedition on their own account.

When I spoke of getting someone to return with me to the ranch, quick evasions met me. The example of Judson's fate was very strongly in the minds of all present. None cared to risk being caught away from the town by night. I realized that I must act alone, unaided.

Most of that day I remained in bed, recuperating. I knew that I would need my full strength for the trial that lay before me. I investigated the available resources, however, and made plans for my mad attempt to strike at the menace that overhung humanity.

With the boy, Marvin, acting as my agent, I purchased an ancient buggy, with a brown nag and harness, to carry me back to the ranch house; my efforts to rent a vehicle, or to hire someone to take me back, had proved signal failures. I had him also to arrange to procure for me other equipment.

I had him buy a dozen gasoline lanterns, with an abundant supply of mantles, and two five-gallon tins, full of gasoline. Finding that the Hebron High School boasted a meager supply of laboratory equipment, I sent the boy in search of magnesium ribbon, and sulphur. He returned with a good bundle of the thin, metallic strips, cut in various lengths. I dipped the ends of each strip in molten sulphur, to facilitate lighting.

He bought me two powerful electric flashlights, with a supply of spare bulbs and batteries, extra ammunition for my automatic, and two dozen sticks of dynamite, with caps and fuses.

Next morning I woke early, feeling much recovered. The shallow, gnawed wound in my leg was fast healing, and had ceased to pain me greatly. As I sat down to a simple breakfast with the Potts family, I assured them confidently that, on this day, I was going to return to the den of the strange pack, from which I had escaped, and put an end to it.

Before we had finished eating, I heard the hail of the man from whom the buggy had been bought, driving up to deliver it and collect the ample price that Marvin Potts had agreed that I would pay. The boy went out with me. We took the vehicle, and together made the rounds of Hebron's few stores, collecting the articles he had bought for me on the day before—the lanterns, the supply of gasoline, the electric searchlights, and the dynamite.

It was still early morning when I left the boy at the end of the street, rewarding him with a bill, and drove alone through the snow, back toward the lonely ranch house where I had experienced such horrors.

The day, though bright, was cold. The snow had never begun to thaw; it was still as thick as ever. My brown nag plodded along slowly, his feet and the buggy's tires crunching through the crusted snow.

As Hebron vanished behind me, and I was surrounded only by the vast, glittering sea of unbroken snow, fear and dread came upon me— a violent longing to hurry to some crowded haunt of men. My imagination pictured the terrors of the night, when the weird pack would run again upon the snow.

How easy would it be to return, take the train for New York, and forget the terrors of this place! No, I knew that I could never forget. I could never forget the threat of that dread, night-black world beyond the copper ring, the fact that its evil spawn planned to seize our world and make it a sphere of rotting gloom like their own.

And Stella! Never could I forget her. I knew now that I loved her, that I must save her or perish with her.

I urged the pony on, across the lonely and illimitable desert of sunlit snow.

It was somewhat past noon when I reached the ranch house. But I still had a safe margin of daylight. Immediately I set about my preparations.

There was much to do: unpacking the boxes piled on the buggy; filling the dozen gasoline lanterns, pumping them up with air, burning their mantles, and seeing that they operated satisfactorily; attaching caps and fuses to the sticks of dynamite, testing my powerful flashlights; loading the little automatic and filling the extra clips; stowing conveniently in my pockets an abundance of matches, ammunition, extra batteries for the electric torches, the strips of magnesium ribbon.

The sun was still high when the preparations were completed. I took time then to put the pony in the stable behind the old house. I locked the door, and barricaded the building, so that, if any dread change converted the animal into a green-eyed monster, it would find itself imprisoned.

Then I went through the old house, carrying a lighted lantern. It was silent, deserted. All the monsters were evidently below. The door of the cellar was closed, all crevices chinked against light.

I lit my dozen powerful lanterns and arranged them in a circle about it.

Then I threw back the door.

A weird and fearful howl came from the dark passage below it! I heard the rush of feet, as the howling thing retreated down the tunnel. From below came angry growls, shrill feral whines.

A physical wave of nauseating horror broke chillingly over me, at the thought of invading that red-lit temple-burrow, where I had endured such unnamable atrocities of horror. I shrank back, trembling. But at the thought of my own father and lovely, blue-eyed Stella, down in that temple of terror, ruled by foul monsters, I recovered my courage.

I stepped back toward the yawning black mouth of the den that these monsters had built.

The lanterns I had first intended to leave in a ring about the mouth of the burrow, except one to carry with me. Now it occurred to me that they would prevent the escape of the monsters more effectively if scattered along the passage. I gathered up six of them, three in each hand, and started down the steps.

Their powerful white rays illuminated the old cellar with welcome brilliance. I left one of them there, in the center of the cellar's floor. And three more of them I set along the slanting passage that led down into the deeper excavation.

I intended to set the two that remained on the floor of the temple, and perhaps return to the surface for others. I hoped that the light would drive the alien life from all of the pack, as it had from Stella. When they were unconscious, I could carry out Stella and my father, and any of the others that seemed whole enough for normal life. The great machine, and the temple itself, I intended to destroy with the dynamite.

I stepped from the end of the passage, into the vast, black, many-pillared hall. The intense white radiance of the faintly humming lanterns dispelled the terrible, blood-red gloom. I heard an appalling chorus of agonized animal cries; weird, feral whines and howls of pain. In the farther end of the long hall, beyond the massive ebon pillars, I saw slinking, green-orbed forms, crowding into the shadows.

I set the two lanterns down on the black floor and drew one of the powerful flashlights from my pocket. Its intense, penetrating beam probed the shadows beyond the huge columns of jet. The cowering, howling shapes of men and wolves shrieked when it touched them, and fell to the black floor.

Confidently I stepped forward, to search out new corners with the brilliant finger of light.

Fatal confidence! I had underestimated the cunning and the science of my enemies. When I first saw the black globe, my foot was already poised above it. A perfect sphere of utter blackness, a foot-thick globe that looked as if it had been turned from midnight crystal.

I could not avoid touching it. And it seemed to explode at my touch. There was a dull, ominous *plop*. And billowing darkness rushed from it. A black gas swirled up about me and shrouded me in smothering gloom.

Wildly I turned, dashed back toward the passage that led up to open air and daylight. I was utterly blinded. The blazing lanterns were completely invisible. I heard one of them dashed over by my blundering feet.

Then I stumbled against the cold temple wall. In feverish haste I felt along it. In either direction, as far as I could reach, the wall was smooth. Where was the passage? A dozen feet I blundered along, feeling the wall. No, the passage must be in the other direction.

I turned. The triumphant, unearthly baying of the pack reached my ears; the padding of feet down the length of the temple. I rushed along the wall, stumbled and fell over a hot lantern.

And they were upon me. . . .

The strange, sourceless, blood-hued radiance of the temple was about me once more. The thick, black pillars thrust up beside me, to support the ebon roof. I was bound, helpless, to one of those cold, massive columns, as I had once been before, with the same bloody rope.

Before me was the strange mechanism that opened the way to that other plane—the Black Dimension—by changing the vibration frequencies of the matter of one world, to those of the other, interlocking universe. The red light gleamed like blood on the copper ring, and the huge mirror behind it. I saw with relief that the electron tubes were dead, the gasoline engine silent, the blackness gone from the ring.

And before the ring had been erected a fearful altar, upon which reposed the torn, mangled, and bleeding bodies of men and women, of gaunt gray wolves, and little coyotes, and other animals. The pack had found good hunting, on the two nights that I had been gone!

The corpse-white, green-orbed, monstrous things, the frightfully changed bodies of Stella and my father and the others, were about me.

"Your coming back is good," the whining, feral tones of the thing in my father's body rang dreadfully in my ears. "The manufacturer of electricity will not run. You return to make it turn again. The way must be opened again, for new life to come to these that wait." He pointed a deathly white arm to the pile of weltering bodies on the black floor.

"Then the new life to you also we will bring. Too many times you run away. You become one with us. And we seek a man who will act as we say. But first must the way be opened again.

"From our world will the life come. To take the bodies of men as machines. To make gas of darkness like that you found within this hall, to hide all the light of your world, and make it fit for us."

My mind reeled with horror at thought of the inconceivable, unthinkable menace risen like a dread specter to face humanity. At the thought that soon I, too, would be a mere machine. My body, cold and white as a corpse, doing unnamable deeds at the command of the thing of darkness whose green eyes would blaze in my sockets!

"Quickly tell the method to turn the maker of electricity," came the maleficent snarl, menacing, gloating, "or we gnaw the flesh from your bones, and seek another who will do our will!"

Chapter XII

SPAWN OF THE BLACK DIMENSION

I AGREED to attempt to start the little gasoline engine, hoping for some opportunity to turn the tables again. I was certain that I could do nothing so long as I was bound to the pillar. And the threat to find another normal man to take my place as teacher of these monsters from that alien world brought realization that I must strike soon.

Presently they were convinced that they required more than verbal aid in starting the little motor. One of the mechanics unbound me, and led me over to the machine, keeping a painful grip upon my arm with ice-cold fingers.

Unobtrusively, I dropped a hand to feel my pockets. They were empty!

"Make not light!" my father snarled warningly, having seen the movement.

They had awakened to the necessity of searching my person. Glancing about the red-lit temple, I saw the articles they had taken from me, in a little pile against the base of a huge black pillar. The automatic, spare clips of ammunition, flashlights, batteries, boxes of matches, strips of magnesium ribbon. The two gasoline lanterns that I had brought into the great hall were there too, having evidently been extinguished by the black gas which had blinded me.

Two gray wolves stood alertly beside the articles, which must have been taken from me before I recovered consciousness after the onrush of the pack. Their strange green eyes stared at me balefully, through the crimson gloom.

After fussing with the engine for a few moments, while my father kept his cold, cruelly firm grip upon my shoulder, and scores of hideous green orbs in the bodies of wolves and men watched my every move, I discovered that it had stopped for lack of fuel. They had let it run on after I wrecked the machine, until the gasoline was exhausted.

I explained to my father that it would not run without more gasoline.

"Make it turn to cause electricity," he said, repeating his menacing, wolfish snarl, "or we gnaw the flesh from your bones, and find another man."

At first I insisted that I could not get gasoline without visiting some inhabited place. Under the threat of torture however—when they dragged me back toward the bloody rope—I confessed that the fuel in the gasoline lanterns might be used.

They were suspicious. They searched me again, to be certain that I had upon my person no means of making a light. And the lanterns were examined very carefully for any means of lighting without matches.

Finally they brought me the lanterns. With my father grasping my arm, I poured the gasoline from them into the engine's fuel tank. Under any circumstances it would have been difficult to avoid spilling the liquid. I took pains to spill as much as seemed possible without rousing suspicion—contriving to pour a little pool of it under the exhaust, where a spark might ignite the fumes.

Then they made me start the engine. Coils hummed once more; the electron tubes lit. Blackness seemed to pour from the strange central tube, to be reflected into the great copper ring by the wide, polished mirror.

Again, I looked through the vast ring into the Black Dimension!

Before me lay a sky of gloom, of darkness unutterable and unbroken, stagnant, lurid waters, dimly aglow with the luminosity of foul decay; worn black hills, covered with obscene, writhing, reptilian vegetation that glowed vaguely and lividly green. And on one of those hills was the city.

A sprawled smear of red evil, it was, a splash of crimson darkness, of red corruption. It spread over the hill like a many-tentacled monster of dark red mist. Ugly masses rose from it, wart-like knobs and projections—ghastly travesties of minarets and towers.

It was motionless. And within its reeking, fetid scarlet darkness, lurked things of creeping gloom—nameless hordes of things like that unthinkable monstrosity that I had seen flow into Stella's body. Green-eyed, living horrors of flowing blackness.

The monsters about me howled through the ring, into that black world—calling!

And soon, through the copper ring, came flowing a river of shapeless, inconceivable horror! Formless monsters of an alien universe. Foul beings of the darkness—spawn of the Black Dimension!

Fearful green eyes were swimming in clotted, creeping masses of evil darkness. They swarmed over the pile of dead things on the floor. And the dead rose to forbidden, nameless life!

Mutilated corpses, and the torn bodies of wolves sprang up, whining, snarling. And the eyes of each were the malevolent, glaring green eyes of the things that had flowed into them.

I was still beside the rhythmically throbbing little engine. As I shrank back in numbed horror from the fearful spectacle of the dead rising to unhallowed life, my eyes fell despairingly upon the little pool of gasoline I had spilled upon the black floor. It was not yet ignited.

I had some fleeting idea of trying to saturate my hand with gasoline and hold it in front of the exhaust, to make of it a living torch. But it was too late for that, and the ruthless, ice-cold fingers still clutched my arm painfully.

Then my father whined wolfishly.

A creepy, formless, obscene mass of blackness, with twin green orbs in it, glowing with mad, alien fires, left the river of them that poured through the ring and crept across to me.

"Now you become one like us!" came the whining voice.

The thing was coming to flow into my body, to make me its slave, its machine!

I screamed, struggled in the cruel hands that held me. In an insanity of terror, I cursed and pleaded—promised to give the monsters the world. And the creeping blackness came on. I collapsed, drenched with icy sweat, quivering, nauseated with horror.

Then, as I had prayed it would do, the little engine coughed. A stream of pale red sparks shot from the exhaust. There was a sudden, dull, explosive sound of igniting vapor. A yellow flash lit the black-pillared temple.

A flickering column of blue and yellow flame rose from the pool of gasoline beside the engine.

The things of blackness were *consumed* by the light—they vanished!

The temple became a bedlam of shrill, agonized howls, of confused, rushing, panic-stricken bodies. The fierce grasp upon my arm was relaxed. My father fell upon the floor, writhing across the room toward the shelter of a black pillar, hiding his green eyes with an arm flung across them.

I saw that the gray wolves had deserted their post beside the articles of mine they had been guarding, at the foot of the massive black column. I left the flickering pillar of fire and dashed across to them.

In a moment my shaking hands had clutched upon one of the powerful electric flashlights. In desperate haste I found the switch and flicked it on. With the intense, dazzling beam, I swept the vast columned hall. The hellish chorus of animal cries of pain rose to a higher pitch. I saw gray wolves and ghastly white men cowering in the shadows of the massive pillars.

I snatched up the other searchlight and turned it on. Then, hastily gathering up pistol, ammunition, matches, and strips of magnesium ribbon, I retreated to a position beside the flaring gasoline.

This time I moved very cautiously, flashing the light before me to avoid stumbling into another bomb of darkness, like that which had been my undoing before. But I think my precaution was useless; I am sure, from what I afterward saw, that only one had been prepared.

As I got back to the engine, I noticed that it was still running, that the way to the Black Dimension, through the copper ring, was still open. I cut off the fuel, at the carburetor. The little engine coughed, panted, slowed down. The wall of darkness faded from the copper ring, breaking our connection with that hideous world of another interpenetrating universe.

Then I hastily laid the flashlights on the floor, laying them so they cast their broad, bright beams in opposite directions. I fumbled for matches, struck one to the end of a strip of magnesium ribbon, to which I had applied sulphur to make it easier to light.

It burst into sudden blinding, dazzling, white radiance, bright as a miniature sun. I flung it across the great black hall. It outlined a white parabola. Its intense light cut the shadows from behind the ebon pillars.

The cowering, hiding things howled in new agony. They lay on the black floor, trembling, writhing, fearfully contorted. Low, agonized whinings came from them.

Again and again I ignited the thin ribbons of metal and flung them flaming toward the corners of the room, to banish all shadow with their brilliant white fire.

The howling grew weaker, the whines died away. The wolves and the corpse-white men moved no more. Their fierce, twisting struggles of agony were stilled.

When the last strip of magnesium was gone, I drew the automatic, put a bullet through the little engine's gasoline tank, and lit a match to the thin stream of clear liquid that trickled out. As a new flaring pillar of light rushed upward, I hurried toward the passage that led to the surface, watching for another of those black spheres that erupted darkness.

I found the gasoline lanterns I had left in the tunnel still burning; the monsters had evidently found no way of putting them out.

On to the surface I ran. I gathered up the six lanterns I had left there—still burning brilliantly in the gathering dusk—and plunged with them back down the passage, into the huge, pillared temple.

The monsters were still inert, unconscious.

I arranged the powerful lanterns about the floor, so placed that every part of the strange temple was brilliantly illuminated. In the penetrating radiance, the monsters lay motionless.

Returning to the surface, I brought one of my full cans of gasoline, and two more of the lighted lanterns. I filled, pumped up, and lit the two lanterns from which I had drawn the gasoline.

Then I went about the black-walled temple, always keeping two lanterns close beside me, and dragged the lax, ice-cold bodies from their crouching postures, turning them so the faces would be toward the light. I found Stella, her lovely body still unharmed, except for its deathly pallor and its strange cold. And then I came upon my father. There was also the mangled thing that had been Judson, and the headless body that had been Blake Jetton, Stella's father. I gazed at many more lacerated human bodies and at the chill carcasses of wolves, of coyotes, of the gray horse, of a few other animals.

In half an hour, perhaps, the change was complete.

The unearthly chill of that alien life was gone from the bodies. Most of them quickly stiffened—with belated *rigor mortis*. Even my father was quite evidently dead. His body remained stiff and cold—though the strange chill had departed.

But Stella's exquisite form grew warm again; the soft flush of life came to it. She breathed and her heard beat slowly. *HEART?*

I carried her up to the old cellar, and laid her on its floor, with two lanterns blazing near her, to prevent any return of that forbidden life, while I finished the ghastly work left for me below.

I need not go into details. . . . But when I had used half my supply of dynamite, no recognizable fragments were left, either of the accursed machine, or of the dead bodies that had been animated with such monstrous life. I planted the other dozen sticks of dynamite beside the great black pillars, and in the walls of the tunnel. . . .

The subterranean hall that I have called a temple will never be entered again.

When that work was done, I carried Stella up to her room, and put her very gently to bed. Through the night I watched her anxiously, keeping a bright light in the room. But there was no sign of what I feared. She slept deeply, but normally, apparently free from any taint of the monstrous life that had possessed her.

Dawn came after a weary night, and there was a rosy gleam upon the snow.

The sleeping girl stirred. Fathomless blue eyes opened, stared into mine. Startled eyes, eager, questioning. Not clouded with dream as when she had awakened before.

"Clovis!" Stella cried, in her natural, softly golden voice. "Clovis, what are you doing here? Where's Father? Dr. McLaurin?"

"You are all right?" I demanded eagerly. "You are well?"

"Well?" she asked, raising her exquisite head in surprise. "Of course I'm well. What could be the matter with me? Dr. McLaurin is going to try his great experiment today. Did you come to help?"

Then I knew—and a great gladness came with the knowledge—that all memory of the horror had been swept from her mind. She recalled nothing that had happened since the eve of the experiment that had brought such a train of terrors.

She looked suddenly past me—at the picture of myself upon the wall. These was a curious expression on her face; she flushed a little, looking very beautiful with heightened color.

"I didn't give you that picture," I accused her. I wished to avoid answering any questions, for the time being, about her father or mine, or any experiments.

"I got it from your father," she confessed.

I have written this narrative in the home of Dr. Friedrichs, the noted New York psychiatrist, who is a close friend of mine. I came to him as soon as Stella and I reached New York, and he has since had me stay at his home, under his constant observation.

He assures me that, within a few weeks, I shall be completely recovered. But sometimes I doubt that I will ever be entirely sane. The horrors of that invasion from another universe are graven too deeply upon my mind. I cannot bear to be alone in darkness, or even in moonlight. And I tremble when I hear the howling of a dog, and hastily seek bright lights and the company of human beings.

I have told Dr. Friedrichs my story, and he believes. It is because of his urging that I have written it down. It is an historical truism, my friend says, that all legend, myth, and folklore has a basis in fact. And no legends are wider spread than those of lycanthropy. It is remarkable that not only wolves are subjects of these legends, but the most ferocious wild animals of each country. In Scandinavia, for instance, the legends concern bears; on the continent of Europe, wolves; in South America, jaguars; in Asia and Africa, leopards and tigers. It is also remarkable that belief in possession by evil spirits, and belief in vampires, is associated with the widespread belief in werewolves.

Dr. Friedrichs thinks that through some cosmic accident, these monsters of the Black Dimension have been let into our world before; and that those curiously widespread legends and beliefs are folk-memories of horrors visited upon earth when those unthinkable monstrosities stole the bodies of men and of savage beasts, and hunted through the darkness.

Much might be said in support of the theory, but I shall let my experience speak for itself.

Stella comes often to see me, and she is more exquisitely lovely than I had ever realized. My friend assures me that her mind is quite normal. Her lapse of memory is quite natural, he says, since her mind was sleeping while the alien entity ruled her body. And he says there is no possibility that she will be possessed again.

We are planning to be married within a few weeks, as soon as Dr. Friedrichs says that my horror-seared mind is sufficiently healed.

The Cairn on the Headland
ROBERT E. HOWARD

The writer who creates a popular hero risks being identified with that character for life, often to the exclusion of his other achievements. For proof, one need look no further than Sir Arthur Conan Doyle, who is remembered primarily as the author of the Sherlock Holmes stories, and Edgar Rice Burroughs, who has gone down in history as the man who created Tarzan. A similar fate has befallen Robert E. Howard, whose tales of Conan the Barbarian were published in the 1930s. Howard's stories of the rock-solid, iron-willed Conan are a showcase for some of his best writing, but they tend to overshadow fine pre-Conan efforts like "The Cairn on the Headland," published in the last issue of Strange Tales *in 1932.*

"And the next instant this great red loon was shaking me like a dog shaking a rat. 'Where is Meve MacDonnal?' he was screaming. By the saints, it's a grisly thing to hear a madman in a lonely place at midnight screaming the name of a woman dead three hundred years."
—The Longshoreman's Tale

THIS IS the cairn you seek," I said, laying my hand gingerly on one of the rough stones which composed the strangely symmetrical heap.

An avid interest burned in Ortali's dark eyes. His gaze swept the landscape and came back to rest on the great pile of massive weatherworn boulders.

"What a wild, weird, desolate place!" he said. "Who would have thought to find such a spot in this vicinity? Except for the smoke rising yonder, one would scarcely dream that beyond that headland lies a great city! Here there is scarcely even a fisherman's hut within sight."

"The people shun the cairn as they have shunned it for centuries," I replied.

"Why?"

"You've asked me that before," I replied impatiently. "I can only answer that they now avoid by habit what their ancestors avoided through knowledge."

"Knowledge!" he laughed derisively. "Superstition!"

I looked at him somberly with unveiled hate. Two men could scarcely have been of more opposite types. He was slender, self-possessed, unmistakably Latin with his dark eyes and sophisticated air. I am massive, clumsy and bearlike, with cold blue eyes and touseled red hair. We were countrymen in that we were born in the same land; but the homelands of our ancestors were as far apart as South from North.

"Nordic superstition," he repeated. "I cannot imagine a Latin people allowing such a mystery as this to go unexplored all these years. The Latins are too practical—too prosaic, if you will. Are you sure of the date of this pile?"

"I find no mention of it in any manuscript prior to 1014 A. D.," I growled, "and I've read all such manuscripts extant, in the original. MacLiag, King Brian Boru's poet speaks of the rearing of the cairn immediately after the battle, and there can be little doubt that this is the pile referred to. It is mentioned briefly in the later chronicles of the Four Masters, also in the Book of Leinster, compiled in the late 1150's, and again in the Book of Lecan, compiled by the MacFirbis about 1416. All connect it with the battle of Clontarf, without mentioning why it was built."

"Well, what is the mystery about it?" he queried. "What more natural than that the defeated Norseman should rear a cairn above the body of some great chief who had fallen in the battle?"

"In the first place," I answered, "there is a mystery concerning the existence of it. The building of cairns above the dead was a Norse, not an Irish, custom. Yet according to the chroniclers, it was not Norsemen who reared this heap. How could they have built it immediately after the battle, in which they had been cut to pieces and driven in headlong flight through the gates of Dublin? Their chieftains lay where they had fallen and the ravens picked their bones. It was Irish hands that heaped these stones."

"Well, was that so strange?" persisted Ortali. "In old times the Irish heaped up stones before they went into battle, each man putting a stone in place; after the battle the living removed their stones, leaving in that manner a simple tally of the slain for any who wished to count the remaining stones."

I shook my head.

"That was in more ancient times; not in the battle of Clontarf. In the first place, there were more than twenty thousand warriors, and four thousand fell here; this cairn is not large enough to have served as a tally of the men killed in battle. And it is too symmetrically built. Hardly a stone has fallen away in all these centuries. No, it was reared to cover something."

"Nordic superstitions!" the man sneered again.

"Aye, superstitions if you will!" fired by his scorn, I exclaimed so savagely that he involuntarily stepped back, his hand slipping inside his coat. "We of North Europe had gods and demons before which the pallid mythologies of the South fade to childishness. At a time when your ancestors were lolling on silken cushions among the crumbling marble pillars of a decaying civilization, my ancestors were building their own civilization in hardships and gigantic battles against foes human and inhuman.

"Here on this very plain the Dark Ages came to an end and the light of a new era dawned on a world of hate and anarchy. Here, as even you know, in the year 1014, Brian Boru and his Dalcassian ax wielders broke the power of the heathen Norsemen forever—those grim anarchistic plunderers who had held back the progress of civilization for centuries.

"It was more than a struggle between Gael and Dane for the crown of Ireland. It was a war between the White Christ and Odin, between Christian and pagan. It was the last stand of the heathen—of the people of the old, grim ways. For three hundred years the world had writhed beneath the heel of the Viking, and here on Clontarf that scourge was lifted forever.

"Then, as now, the importance of that battle was underestimated by polite Latin and Latinized writers and historians. The polished sophisticates of the civilized cities of the South were not interested in the battles of barbarians in the remote northwestern corner of the world—a place and peoples of whose very names they were only vaguely aware. They only knew that suddenly the terrible raids of the sea kings ceased to sweep along their coasts, and in another century the wild age of plunder and slaughter had almost been forgotten—all because a rude, half-civilized people who scantily covered their nakedness with wolf hides rose up against the conquerors.

"Here was Ragnarok, the fall of the Gods! Here in very truth Odin fell, for his religion was given its death blow. He was last of all the heathen gods to stand before Christianity, and it looked for a time as if his children might prevail and plunge the world back into darkness and savagery. Before Clontarf, legends say, he often appeared on earth to his worshipers, dimly seen in the smoke of the sacrifices where naked human victims died screaming, or riding the wind-torn clouds, his wild locks flying in the gale, or, appareled like a Norse warrior, dealing thunderous blows in the forefront of nameless battles. But after Clontarf he was seen no more; his worshipers called on him in vain with wild chants and grim sacrifices. They lost faith in him, who had failed them in their wildest hour; his altars crumbled, his priests turned gray and died, and men turned to his conqueror, the White Christ. The reign of blood and iron was forgotten; the age of the red-handed sea kings passed. The rising sun slowly, dimly, lighted the night of the Dark Ages, and men forgot Odin, who came no more on earth.

"Aye, laugh if you will! But who knows what shapes of horror have had birth in the darkness, the cold gloom, and the whistling black gulfs of the North? In the southern lands the sun shines and flowers blow; under the soft skies men laugh at demons. But in the North who can say what elemental spirits of evil dwell in the fierce storms and the darkness? Well may it be that from such fiends of the night men evolved the worship of the grim ones, Odin and Thor, and their terrible kin."

Ortali was silent for an instant, as if taken aback by my vehemence; then he laughed. "Well said, my Northern philosopher! We will argue these questions another time. I could hardly expect a descendant of Nordic barbarians to escape some trace of the dreams and mysticism of his race. But you cannot expect me to be moved by your imaginings, either. I still believe that this cairn covers no grimmer secret than a Norse chief who fell in the battle—and really your ravings concerning Nordic devils have no bearing on the matter. Will you help me tear into this cairn?"

"No," I answered shortly.

"A few hours' work will suffice to lay bare whatever it may hide," he continued as if he had not heard. "By the way, speaking of superstitions, is there not some wild tale concerning holly connected with this heap?"

"An old legend says that all trees bearing holly were cut down for a league in all directions, for some mysterious reason," I answered sullenly. "That's another mystery. Holly was an important part of Norse magic-making. The Four Masters tell of a Norseman—a white-bearded ancient of wild aspect, and apparently a priest of Odin—who was slain by the natives while attempting to lay a branch of holly on the cairn, a year after the battle."

"Well," he laughed, "I have procured a sprig of holly—see?—and shall wear it in my lapel; perhaps it will protect me against your Nordic devils. I feel more certain than ever that the cairn covers a sea king— and they were always laid to rest with all their riches: golden cups and jewel-set sword hilts and silver corselets. I feel that this cairn holds wealth, wealth over which clumsy-footed Irish peasants have been stumbling for centuries, living in want and dying in hunger. Bah! We shall return here at about midnight, when we may be fairly certain that we will not be interrupted—and you will aid me at the excavations."

The last sentence was rapped out in a tone that sent a red surge of bloodlust through my brain. Ortali turned and began examining the cairn as he spoke, and almost involuntarily my hand reached out stealthily and closed on a wicked bit of jagged stone that had become detached from one of the boulders. In that instant I was a potential murderer if ever one walked the earth. One blow, quick, silent and savage, and I would be free forever from a slavery bitter as my Celtic ancestors knew beneath the heels of the Vikings.

As if sensing my thoughts, Ortali wheeled to face me. I quickly slipped the stone into my pocket, not knowing whether he noted the action. But he must have seen the red killing instinct burning in my eyes, for again he recoiled and again his hand sought the hidden revolver.

But he only said: "I've changed my mind. We will not uncover the cairn tonight. Tomorrow night perhaps. We may be spied upon. Just now I am going back to the hotel."

I made no reply, but turned my back upon him and stalked moodily away in the direction of the shore. He started up the slope of the headland beyond which lay the city, and when I turned to look at him, he was just crossing the ridge, etched clearly against the hazy sky. If hate could kill, he would have dropped dead. I saw him in a red-tinged haze, and the pulses in my temples throbbed like hammers.

I turned back toward the shore, and stopped suddenly. Engrossed with my own dark thoughts, I had approached within a few feet of a woman before seeing her. She was tall and strongly made, with a strong stern face, deeply lined and weather-worn as the hills. She was dressed in a manner strange to me, but I thought little of it, knowing the curious styles of clothing worn by certain backward types of our people.

"What would you be doing at the cairn?" she asked in a deep, powerful voice. I looked at her in surprise; she spoke in Gaelic, which was not strange of itself, but the Gaelic she used I had supposed was extinct as a spoken language: it was the Gaelic of scholars, pure, and with a distinctly archaic flavor. A woman from some secluded hill country, I thought, where the people still spoke the unadulterated tongue of their ancestors.

"We were speculating on its mystery," I answered in the same tongue, hesitantly, however, for though skilled in the more modern form taught in the schools, to match her use of the language was a strain on my knowledge of it. She shook her head slowly. "I like not the dark man who was with you," she said somberly. "Who are you?"

"I am an American, though born and raised here," I answered. "My name is James O'Brien."

A strange light gleamed in her cold eyes.

"O'Brien? You are of my clan. I was born an O'Brien. I married a man of the MacDonnals, but my heart was ever with the folk of my blood."

"You live hereabouts?" I queried, my mind on her unusual accent.

"Aye, I lived here upon a time," she answered, "but I have been far away for a long time. All is changed—changed. I would not have returned, but I was drawn back by a call you would not understand. Tell me, would you open the cairn?"

I started and gazed at her closely, deciding that she had somehow overheard our conversation.

"It is not mine to say," I answered bitterly. "Ortali—my companion— he will doubtless open it and I am constrained to aid him. Of my own will I would not molest it."

Her cold eyes bored into my soul.

"Fools rush blind to their doom," she said somberly. "What does this man know of the mysteries of this ancient land? Deeds have been done here whereof the world reëchoed. Yonder, in the long ago, when Tomar's Wood rose dark and rustling against the plain of Clontarf, and the Danish walls of Dublin loomed south of the river Liffey, the ravens fed on the slain and the setting sun lighted lakes of crimson. There King Brian, your ancestor and mine, broke the spears of the North. From all lands they came, and from the isles of the sea; they came in gleaming mail and their horned helmets cast long shadows across the land. Their dragon-prows thronged the waves and the sound of their oars was as the beat of a storm.

"On yonder plain the heroes fell like ripe wheat before the reaper. There fell Jarl Sigurd of the Orkneys, and Brodir of Man, last of the sea kings, and all their chiefs. There fell, too, Prince Murrough and his son Turlogh, and many chieftains of the Gael, and King Brian Boru himself, Erin's mightiest monarch."

"True!" My imagination was always fired by the epic tales of the land of my birth. "Blood of mine was spilled here, and, though I have passed the best part of my life in a far land, there are ties of blood to bind my soul to this shore."

She nodded slowly, and from beneath her robes drew forth something that sparkled dully in the setting sun.

"Take this," she said. "As a token of blood tie, I give it to you. I feel the weird of strange and monstrous happenings—but this will keep you safe from evil and the people of the night. Beyond reckoning of man, it is holy."

I took it, wonderingly. It was a crucifix of curiously worked gold, set with tiny jewels. The workmanship was extremely archaic and unmistakably Celtic. And vaguely within me stirred a memory of a long-lost relic described by forgotten monks in dim manuscripts.

"Great heavens!" I exclaimed. "This is—this must be—this *can* be nothing less than the lost crucifix of Saint Brandon the Blessed!"

"Aye." She inclined her grim head. "Saint Brandon's cross, fashioned by the hands of the holy man in long ago, before the Norse barbarians made Erin a red hell—in the days when a golden peace and holiness ruled the land."

"But, woman!" I exclaimed wildly, "I cannot accept this as a gift from you! You cannot know its value! Its intrinsic worth alone is equal to a fortune; as a relic it is priceless—"

"Enough!" Her deep voice struck me suddenly silent. "Have done with such talk, which is sacrilege. The cross of Saint Brandon is beyond price. It was never stained with gold; only as a free gift has it ever changed hands. I give it to you to shield you against the powers of evil. Say no more."

"But it has been lost for three hundred years!" I exclaimed. "How—where. . . .?"

"A holy man gave it to me long ago," she answered. "I hid it in my bosom—long it lay in my bosom. But now I give it to you; I have come from a far country to give it to you, for there are monstrous happenings in the wind, and it is sword and shield against the people of the night. An ancient evil stirs in its prison, which blind hands of folly may break open; but stronger than any evil is the cross of Saint Brandon which has gathered power and strength through the long, long ages since that forgotten evil fell to the earth."

"But who are you?" I exclaimed.

"I am Meve MacDonnal," she answered.

Then, turning without a word, she strode away in the deepening twilight while I stood bewildered and watched her cross the headland and pass from sight, turning inland as she topped the ridge. Then I, too, shaking myself like a man waking from a dream, went slowly up the slope and across the headland. When I crossed the ridge it was as if I had passed out of one world into another: behind me lay the wilderness and desolation of a weird medieval age; before me pulsed the lights and the roar of modern Dublin. Only one archaic touch was lent to the scene before me: some distance inland loomed the straggling and broken lines of an ancient graveyard, long deserted and grown up in weeds, barely discernible in the dusk. As I looked I saw a tall figure moving ghostily among the crumbling tombs, and I shook my head bewilderedly. Surely Meve MacDonnal was touched with madness,

living in the past, like one seeking to stir to flame the ashes of dead
yesterdays. I set out toward where, in the near distance, began the
straggling window-gleams that grew into the swarming ocean of lights
that was Dublin.

Back at the suburban hotel where Ortali and I had our rooms, I did
not speak to him of the cross the woman had given me. In that at
least he should not share. I intended keeping it until she requested its
return, which I felt sure she would do. Now as I recalled her appearance,
the strangeness of her costume returned to me, with one item which
had impressed itself on my subconscious mind at the time, but which
I had not consciously realized. Meve MacDonnal had been wearing
sandals of a type not worn in Ireland for centuries. Well, it was perhaps
natural that with her retrospective nature she should imitate the apparel
of the past ages which seemed to claim all her thoughts.

I turned the cross reverently in my hands. There was no doubt that
it was the very cross for which antiquarians had searched so long in
vain, and at last in despair had denied the existence of. The priestly
scholar, Michael O'Rourke, in a treatise written about 1690, described
the relic at length, chronicled its history exhaustively and maintained
that it was last heard of in the possession of Bishop Liam O'Brien,
who, dying in 1595, gave it into the keeping of a kinswoman; but who
this woman was, it was never known, and O'Rourke maintained that
she kept her possession of the cross a secret, and that it was laid away
with her in her tomb.

At another time my elation at discovering this relic would have been
extreme, but, at the time, my mind was too filled with hate and
smoldering fury. Replacing the cross in my pocket, I fell moodily to
reviewing my connections with Ortali, connections which puzzled my
friends, but which were simple enough.

Some years before I had been connected with a certain large university
in a humble way. One of the professors with whom I worked—a man
named Reynolds—was of intolerably overbearing disposition toward
those whom he considered his inferiors. I was a poverty-ridden student
striving for life in a system which makes the very existence of a scholar
precarious. I bore Professor Reynolds' abuse as long as I could, but
one day we clashed. The reason does not matter; it was trivial enough
in itself. Because I dared reply to his insults, Reynolds struck me and
I knocked him senseless.

That very day he caused my dismissal from the university. Facing
not only an abrupt termination of my work and studies, but actual
starvation, I was reduced to desperation, and I went to Reynolds' study
late that night intending to thrash him within an inch of his life. I
found him alone in his study, but the moment I entered, he sprang
up and rushed at me like a wild beast, with a dagger he used for a
paperweight. I did not strike him; I did not even touch him. As I

stepped aside to avoid his rush, a small rug slipped beneath his charging feet. He fell headlong and, to my horror, in his fall the dagger in his hand was driven into his heart. He died instantly. I was at once aware of my position. I was known to have quarreled, and even exchanged blows with the man. I had every reason to hate him. If I were found in the study with the dead man, no jury in the world would not believe that I had murdered him. I hurriedly left by the way I had come, thinking that I had been unobserved. But Ortali, the dead man's secretary, had seen me. Returning from a dance, he had observed me entering the premises, and, following me, had seen the whole affair through the window. But this I did not know until later.

The body was found by the professor's housekeeper, and naturally there was a great stir. Suspicion pointed to me, but lack of evidence kept me from being indicted, and this same lack of evidence brought about a verdict of suicide. All this time Ortali had kept quiet. Now he came to me and disclosed what he knew. He knew, of course, that I had not killed Reynolds, but he could prove that I was in the study when the professor met his death, and I knew Ortali was capable of carrying out his threat of swearing that he had seen me murder Reynolds in cold blood. And thus began a systematic blackmail.

I venture to say that a stranger blackmail was never levied. I had no money then; Ortali was gambling on my future, for he was assured of my abilities. He advanced me money, and, by clever wire-pulling, got me an appointment in a large college. Then he sat back to reap the benefits of his scheming, and he reaped full fold of the seed he sowed. In my line I became eminently successful, I soon commanded an enormous salary in my regular work, and I received rich prizes and awards for researches of various difficult nature, and of these Ortali took the lion's share—in money at least. I seemed to have the Midas touch. Yet of the wine of my success I tasted only the dregs.

I scarcely had a cent to my name. The money that had flowed through my hands had gone to enrich my slaver, unknown to the world. A man of remarkable gifts, he could have gone to the heights in any line, but for a queer streak in him, which, coupled with an inordinately avaricious nature, made him a parasite, a blood-sucking leech.

This trip to Dublin had been in the nature of a vacation for me. I was worn out with study and labor. But he had somehow heard of Grimmin's Cairn, as it was called, and, like a vulture that scents dead flesh, he conceived himself on the track of hidden gold. A golden wine cup would have been, to him, sufficient reward for the labor of tearing into the pile, and reason enough for desecrating or even destroying the ancient landmark. He was a swine whose only god was gold.

Well, I thought grimly, as I disrobed for bed, all things end, both good and bad. Such a life as I had lived was unbearable. Ortali had

dangled the gallows before my eyes until it had lost its terrors. I had
staggered beneath the load I carried because of my love for my work.
But all human endurance has its limits. My hands turned to iron as
I thought of Ortali, working beside me at midnight at the lonely cairn.
One stroke, with such a stone as I had caught up that day, and my
agony would be ended. That life and hopes and career and ambitions
would be ended as well, could not be helped. Ah, what a sorry, sorry
end to all my high dreams! When a rope and the long drop through
the black trap should cut short an honorable career and a useful life!
And all because of a human vampire who feasted his rotten lust on
my soul, and drove me to murder and ruin.

But I knew my fate was written in the iron books of doom. Sooner
or later I would turn on Ortali and kill him, be the consequences what
they might. And I had reached the end of my road. Continual torture
had rendered me, I believe, partly insane. I knew that at Grimmin's
Cairn, when we toiled at midnight, Ortali's life would end beneath my
hands, and my own life be cast away.

Something fell out of my pocket and I picked it up. It was the piece
of sharp stone I had caught up off the cairn. Looking at it moodily, I
wondered what strange hands had touched it in old times, and what
grim secret it helped to hide on the bare headland of Grimmin. I
switched out the light and lay in the darkness, the stone still in my
hand, forgotten, occupied with my own dark broodings. And I glided
gradually into deep slumber.

At first I was aware that I was dreaming, as people often are. All
was dim and vague, and connected in some strange way, I realized,
with the bit of stone still grasped in my sleeping hand. Gigantic, chaotic
scenes and landscapes and events shifted before me, like clouds that
rolled and tumbled before a gale. Slowly these settled and crystallized
into one distinct landscape, familiar and yet wildly strange. I saw a
broad bare plain, fringed by the gray sea on one side, and a dark,
rustling forest on the other; this plain was cut by a winding river, and
beyond this river I saw a city—such a city as my waking eyes had
never seen: bare, stark, massive, with the grim architecture of an earlier,
wilder age. On the plain I saw, as in a mist, a mighty battle. Serried
ranks rolled backward and forward, steel flashed like a sunlit sea, and
men fell like ripe wheat beneath the blades. I saw men in wolfskins,
wild and shock-headed, wielding dripping axes, and tall men in horned
helmets and glittering mail, whose eyes were cold and blue as the sea.
And I saw myself.

Yes, in my dream I saw and recognized, in a semi-detached way,
myself. I was tall and rangily powerful; I was shock-headed and naked
but for a wolf hide girt about my loins. I ran among the ranks yelling
and smiting with a red ax, and blood ran down my flanks from wounds

I scarcely felt. My eyes were cold blue and my shaggy hair and beard were red.

Now for an instant I was cognizant of my dual personality, aware that I was at once the wild man who ran and smote with the gory ax, and the man who slumbered and dreamed across the centuries. But this sensation quickly faded. I was no longer aware of any personality other than that of the barbarian who ran and smote. James O'Brien had no existence; I was Red Cumal, kern of Brian Boru, and my ax was dripping with the blood of my foes.

The roar of conflict was dying away, though here and there struggling clumps of warriors still dotted the plain. Down along the river half-naked tribesmen, waist-deep in reddening water, tore and slashed with helmeted warriors whose mail could not save them from the stroke of the Dalcassian ax. Across the river a bloody, disorderly horde was staggering through the gates of Dublin.

The sun was sinking low toward the horizon. All day I had fought beside the chiefs. I had seen Jarl Sigurd fall beneath Prince Murrough's sword. I had seen Murrogh himself die in the moment of victory, by the hand of a grim mailed giant whose name none knew. I had seen, in the flight of the enemy, Brodir and King Brian fall together at the door of the great king's tent.

Aye, it had been a feasting of ravens, a red flood of slaughter, and I knew that no more would the dragon-prowed fleets sweep from the blue North with torch and destruction. Far and wide the Vikings lay in their glittering mail, as the ripe wheat lies after the reaping. Among them lay thousands of bodies clad in the wolf hides of the tribes, but the dead of the Northern people far outnumbered the dead of Erin. I was weary and sick of the stench of raw blood. I had glutted my soul with slaughter; now I sought plunder. And I found it—on the corpse of a richly-clad Norse chief which lay close to the seashore. I tore off the silver-scaled corselet, the horned helmet. They fitted as if made for me, and I swaggered among the dead, calling on my wild comrades to admire my appearance, though the harness felt strange to me, for the Gaels scorned armor and fought half-naked.

In my search for loot I had wandered far out on the plain, away from the river, but still the mail-clad bodies lay thickly strewn, for the bursting of the ranks had scattered fugitives and pursuers all over the countryside, from the dark waving Wood of Tomar, to the river and the seashore. And on the seaward slope of Drumna's headland, out of sight of the city and the plain of Clontarf, I came suddenly upon a dying warrior. He was tall and massive, clad in gray mail. He lay partly in the folds of a great dark cloak, and his sword lay broken near his mighty right hand. His horned helmet had fallen from his head and his elf-locks blew in the wind that swept out of the west.

Where one eye should have been was an empty socket and the other

eye glittered cold and grim as the North Sea, though it was glazing
with approach of death. Blood oozed from a rent in his corselet. I
approached him warily, a strange cold fear, that I could not understand,
gripping me. Ax ready to dash out his brains, I bent over him, and
recognized him as the chief who had slain Prince Murrogh, and who
had mown down the warriors of the Gael like a harvest. Wherever he
had fought, the Norsemen had prevailed, but in all other parts of the
field, the Gaels had been irresistible.

And now he spoke to me in Norse and I understood, for had I not
toiled as slave among the sea people for long bitter years?

"The Christians have overcome," he gasped in a voice whose timbre,
though low-pitched, sent a curious shiver of fear through me; there
was in it an undertone as of icy waves sweeping along a Northern
shore, as of freezing winds whispering among the pine trees. "Doom
and shadows stalk on Asgaard and here has fallen Ragnarok. I could
not be in all parts of the field at once, and now I am wounded unto
death. A spear—a spear with a cross carved in the blade; no other
weapon could wound me."

I realized that the chief, seeing mistily my red beard and the Norse
armor I wore, supposed me to be one of his own race. But crawling
horror surged darkly in the depths of my soul.

"White Christ, thou hast not yet conquered," he muttered deliriously.
"Lift me up, man, and let me speak to you."

Now for some reason I complied, and as I lifted him to a sitting
posture, I shuddered and my flesh crawled at the feel of him, for his
flesh was like ivory—smoother and harder than is natural for human
flesh, and colder than even a dying man should be.

"I die as men die," he muttered. "Fool, to assume the attributes of
mankind, even though it was to aid the people who deify me. The
gods are immortal, but flesh can perish, even when it clothes a god.
Haste and bring a sprig of the magic plant—even holly—and lay it on
my bosom. Aye, though it be no larger than a dagger point, it will free
me from this fleshly prison I put on when I came to war with men
with their own weapons. And I will shake off this flesh and stalk once
more among the thundering clouds. Woe, then, to all men who bend
not the knee to me! Haste; I will await your coming."

His lionlike head fell back, and feeling shudderingly under his corselet,
I could distinguish no heartbeat. He was dead, as men die, but I knew
that locked in that semblance of a human body, there but slumbered
the spirit of a fiend of the frost and darkness.

Aye, I knew him: Odin, the Gray Man, the One-eyed, the god of
the North who had taken the form of a warrior to fight for his people.
Assuming the form of a human he was subject to many of the limitations
of humanity. All men knew this of the gods, who often walked the
earth in the guise of men. Odin, clothed in human semblance, could

be wounded by certain weapons, and even slain, but a touch of the mysterious holly would rouse him in grisly resurrection. This task he had set me, not knowing me for an enemy; in human form he could only use human faculties, and these had been impaired by onstriding death.

My hair stood up and my flesh crawled. I tore from my body the Norse armor, and fought a wild panic that prompted me to run blind and screaming with terror across the plain. Nauseated with fear, I gathered boulders and heaped them for a rude couch, and on it, shaking with horror, I lifted the body of the Norse god. And as the sun set and the stars came silently out, I was working with fierce energy, piling huge rocks above the corpse. Other tribesmen came up and I told them of what I was sealing up—I hoped forever. And they, shivering with horror, fell to aiding me. No sprig of magic holly should be laid on Odin's terrible bosom. Beneath these rude stones the Northern demon should slumber until the thunder of Judgment Day, forgotten by the world which had once cried out beneath his iron heel. Yet not wholly forgot, for, as we labored, one of my comrades said: "This shall be no longer Drumna's Headland, but the Headland of the Gray Man."

That phrase established a connection between my dream-self and my sleeping self. I started up from sleep exclaiming: "Gray Man's Headland!"

I looked about dazedly, the furnishings of the room, faintly lighted by the starlight in the windows, seeming strange and unfamiliar until I slowly oriented myself with time and space.

"Gray Man's Headland," I repeated, "Gray Man—Graymin—Grimmin—*Grimmin's Headland!* Great God, the thing under the cairn!"

Shaken, I sprang up, and realized that I still gripped the piece of stone from the cairn. It is well known that inanimate objects retain psychic associations. A round stone from the plain of Jericho has been placed in the hand of a hypnotized medium, and she has at once reconstructed in her mind the battle and siege of the city, and the shattering fall of the walls. I did not doubt that this bit of stone had acted as a magnet to drag my modern mind through the mists of the centuries into a life I had known before.

I was more shaken than I can describe, for the whole fantastic affair fitted in too well with certain formless vague sensations concerning the cairn which had already lingered at the back of my mind, to be dismissed as an unusually vivid dream. I felt the need of a glass of wine, and remembered that Ortali always had wine in his room. I hurriedly donned my clothes, opened my door, crossed the corridor and was about to knock at Ortali's door, when I noticed that it was partly open, as if some one had neglected to close it carefully. I entered, switching on a light. The room was empty.

I realized what had occurred. Ortali mistrusted me; he feared to risk

himself alone with me in a lonely spot at midnight. He had postponed
the visit to the cairn, merely to trick me, to give him a chance to slip
away alone.

My hatred for Ortali was for the moment completely submerged by
a wild panic of horror at the thought of what the opening of the cairn
might result in. For I did not doubt the authenticity of my dream. It
was no dream; it was a fragmentary bit of memory, in which I had
relived that other life of mine. Gray Man's Headland—Grimmin's
Headland, and under those rough stones that grisly corpse in its semblance of humanity—I could not hope that, imbued with the imper-
ishable essence of an elemental spirit, that corpse had crumbled to dust
in the ages.

Of my race out of the city and across those semi-desolate reaches,
I remember little. The night was a cloak of horror through which peered
red stars like the gloating eyes of uncanny beasts, and my footfalls
echoed hollowly so that repeatedly I thought some monster loped at
my heels.

The straggling lights fell away behind me and I entered the region
of mystery and horror. No wonder that progress had passed to the
right and to the left of this spot, leaving it untouched, a blind back-
eddy given over to goblin-dreams and nightmare memories. Well that
so few suspected its very existence.

Dimly I saw the headland, but fear gripped me and held me aloof.
I had a vague, incoherent idea of finding the ancient woman, Meve
MacDonnal. She was grown old in the mysteries and traditions of the
mysterious land. She could aid me, if indeed the blind fool Ortali
loosed on the world the forgotten demon men once worshiped in the
North.

A figure loomed suddenly in the starlight and I caromed against him,
almost upsetting him. A stammering voice in a thick brogue protested
with the petulancy of intoxication. It was a burly longshoreman returning to his cottage, no doubt, from some late revel in a tavern. I
seized him and shook him, my eyes glaring wildly in the starlight.

"I am looking for Meve MacDonnal! Do you know her? Tell me,
you fool! Do you know old Meve MacDonnal?"

It was as if my words sobered him as suddenly as a dash of icy
water in his face. In the starlight I saw his face glimmer whitely and
a catch of fear was at his throat. He sought to cross himself with an
uncertain hand.

"Meve MacDonnal? Are ye mad? What would ye be doin' with *her*?"

"Tell me!" I shrieked, shaking him savagely. "Where is Meve
MacDonnal?"

"There!" he gasped, pointing with a shaking hand where dimly in
the night something loomed against the shadows. "In the name of the
holy saints, begone, be ye madman or devil, and l'ave an honest man

alone! There—there ye'll find Meve MacDonnal—where they laid her, full three hundred years ago!"

Half heeding his words I flung him aside with a fierce exclamation, and, as I raced across the weed-grown plain, I heard the sounds of his lumbering flight. Half blind with panic, I came to the low structure the man had pointed out. And floundering deep in weeds, my feet sinking into musty mold, I realized with a shock that I was in the ancient graveyard on the inland side of Grimmin's Headland, into which I had seen Meve MacDonnal disappear the evening before. I was close by the door of the largest tomb, and with an eery premonition I leaned close, seeking to make out the deeply-carven inscription. And partly by the dim light of the stars and partly by the touch of my tracing fingers, I made out the words and figures, in the half-forgotten Gaelic of three centuries ago: "Meve MacDonnal—1565–1640."

With a cry of horror I recoiled and, snatching out the crucifix she had given me, made to hurl it into the darkness—but it was as if an invisible hand caught my wrist. Madness and insanity—but I could not doubt: Meve MacDonnal had come to me from the tomb wherein she had rested for three hundred years to give me the ancient, ancient relic entrusted to her so long ago by her priestly kin. The memory of her words came to me, and the memory of Ortali and the Gray Man. From a lesser horror I turned squarely to a greater, and ran swiftly toward the headland which loomed dimly against the stars toward the sea.

As I crossed the ridge I saw, in the starlight, the cairn, and the figure that toiled gnomelike above it. Ortali, with his accustomed, almost superhuman energy, had dislodged many of the boulders; and as I approached, shaking with horrified anticipation, I saw him tear aside the last layer, and I heard his savage cry of triumph, that froze me in my tracks some yards behind him, looking down from the slope. An unholy radiance rose from the cairn, and I saw, in the north, the aurora flame up suddenly with terrible beauty, paling the starlight. All about the cairn pulsed a weird light, turning the rough stones to a cold shimmering silver, and in this glow I saw Ortali, all heedless, cast aside his pick and lean gloatingly over the aperture he had made—and I saw there the helmeted head, reposing on the couch of stones where I, Red Cumal, placed it so long ago. I saw the inhuman terror and beauty of that awesome carven face, in which was neither human weakness, pity nor mercy. I saw the soul-freezing glitter of the one eye, which stared wide open in a fearful semblance of life. All up and down the tall mailed figure shimmered and sparkled cold darts and gleams of icy light, like the northern lights that blazed in the shuddering skies. Aye, the Gray Man lay as I had left him more than nine hundred years before, without a trace of rust or rot or decay.

And now as Ortali leaned forward to examine his find, a gasping cry broke from my lips—for the sprig of holly worn in his lapel in defiance of "Nordic superstition," slipped from its place, and in the weird glow I plainly saw it fall upon the mighty mailed breast of the figure, where it blazed suddenly with a brightness too dazzling for human eyes. My cry was echoed by Ortali. The figure moved; the mighty limbs flexed, tumbling the shining stones aside. A new gleam lighted the terrible eye and a tide of life flooded and animated the carven features.

Out of the cairn he rose, and the northern lights played terribly about him. And the Gray Man changed and altered in horrific transmutation. The human features faded like a fading mask; the armor fell from his body and crumbled to dust as it fell; and the fiendish spirit of ice and frost and darkness that the sons of the North deified as Odin, stood nakedly and terribly in the stars. About his grisly head played lightnings and the shuddering gleams of the aurora. His towering anthropomorphic form was dark as shadow and gleaming as ice; his horrible crest reared colossally against the vaulting arch of the sky.

Ortali cowered, screaming wordlessly, as the taloned malformed hands reached for him. In the shadowy indescribable features of the Thing there was no tinge of gratitude toward the man who had released it— only a demoniac gloating and a demoniac hate for all the sons of men. I saw the shadowy arms shoot out and strike. I heard Ortali scream once—a single unbearable screech that broke short at the shrillest pitch. A single instant a blinding blue glare burst about him, lighting his convulsed features and his upward-rolling eyes; then his body was dashed earthward as by an electric shock, so savagely that I distinctly heard the splintering of his bones. But Ortali was dead before he touched the ground—dead, shriveled and blackened, exactly like a man blasted by a thunderbolt, to which cause, indeed, men later ascribed his death.

The slavering monster that had slain him lumbered now toward me, shadowy tentacle-like arms outspread, the pale starlight making a luminous pool of his great inhuman eye, his frightful talons dripping with I know not what elemental forces to blast the bodies and souls of men.

But I flinched not, and in that instant I feared him not, neither the horror of his countenance nor the threat of his thunderbolt dooms. For in a blinding white flame had come to me the realization of why Meve MacDonnal had come from her tomb to bring me the ancient cross which had lain in her bosom for three hundred years, gathering unto itself unseen forces of good and light, which war forever against the shapes of lunacy and shadow.

As I plucked from my garments the ancient cross, I felt the play of gigantic unseen forces in the air about me. I was but a pawn in the game—merely the hand that held the relic of holiness, that was the symbol of the powers opposed forever against the fiends of darkness. As I held it high, from it shot a single shaft of white light, unbearably pure, unbearably white, as if all the awesome forces of Light were combined in the symbol and loosed in one concentrated arrow of wrath against the monster of darkness. And with a hideous shriek the demon reeled back, shriveling before my eyes. Then with a great rush of vulture-like wings, he soared into the stars, dwindling, dwindling among the play of the flaming fires and the lights of the haunted skies, fleeing back into the dark limbo which gave him birth, God only knows how many grisly eons ago.

Imp of Satan

HUGH B. CAVE

Hugh Cave was that rare writer who produced solid work on a regular basis for a number of different pulp markets. Although he wrote several excellent stories for the regular weird fiction magazines (in particular "Murgunstrumm," a memorable vampire tale that appeared in Strange Tales*), more of his work appeared in the weird menace and shudder pulps. It took a lot of imagination to make a story stand out in such formulaic magazines, but "Imp of Satan," from the March 1935* Horror Stories*, shows that Cave knew a trick or two for getting around editorial limitations.*

THE STORM caught me while I was fishing for bullheads near the deserted shack which leaned there in weeds and scum-covered water on the far shore of Painter's Pit—that black, bottomless well of murk buried in the heart of the deep woods near Norvale, a mile or so from the house of Philias Arns.

"Well, it's certainly gloomy enough," I had been thinking. "It harmonizes nicely with all the hellish things that have happened since my marriage to Lenore."

The first few drops of rain splashed unnoticed in the black water around me. Then I realized with alarm that the gloom had suddenly deepened. Hurriedly I hauled in my line, gathered up the oars. The storm, with its accompanying darkness, had caught me on the side of the pond farthest from the trail that led through the woods to Philias Arns' house.

I thought of seeking shelter in the forlorn shack leaning there on shore, but the idea sent a shudder through me. That shack had been abandoned for years, its cellar inundated, its timbers warped by severe rains. And there were strange, dark tales whispered. . . . I bent my back to the oars and made for the opposite shore.

Abruptly I stopped rowing, for through the roar of the storm shrieked a sound that sucked my bent body forward. I heard laughter—heard a mad ululation of mirth laden with all things evil! It came again, eating its way into my soul, as I hunched forward.

I was peering in the direction from which its eerie crescendoes rose into air—peering at the spectral hulk of that abandoned shack on shore. Terror crawled within me and pushed my eyes from their sockets. Suddenly something small and dark whined past my arm, struck with a dull thud in the side of the boat.

I gaped at the thing, saw it quivering there within inches of my stiff body. Stifling a cry of alarm, I shrank back. That trembling missile was a feathered dart—the kind of poison-tipped dart used in jungle blow-guns!

Fear put strength in my corded arms as I drove the boat away from that place of hell. Whispered tales of the Pit's nameless evils went screaming through my mind. I thought of the crawling shadows in old Philias Arn's eyes, the fear which for days haunted the face of my wife.

I thought of my marriage to Lenore, the dark-eyed, quietly lovely girl whom I had met only a few months ago. A strange marriage, perhaps a hasty one, our few short days of wedded life had been a peculiar admixture of heaven and hell.

I heard again the shrill, childish voice which had shrieked down from the empty balcony of Hampton's "Little Church on Main Street" and had thrown the marriage ceremony into turmoil. *"Make them man and wife, and then—God help them! For the curse of Kawalo will follow them to the ends of the earth and destroy them!"*

The curse of Kawalo! Strange words without meaning! From the depths of the church balcony those words had wailed forth—but when it was searched the balcony had been found empty of anything human!

I thought of the dark suspicions which had festered in my soul after Lenore and I had come to live in the huge, gloomy home of old Philias Arns, who was Lenore's guardian. "Philias needs us," my wife had said. "He has only a few months more of life, John. We must watch over him and care for him." But I had never liked the man, and from the beginning I had hated the house of shadows which was to be our home until his death.

Dark suspicions had plagued me, and I had realized, from the beginning, that my wife and Philias Arns shared some evil secret. Only last night, at midnight, she had crept downstairs and kept a surreptious rendezvous with him, behind the locked door of his study. And I had heard words, ominous words, from Philias Arns' thin lips.

"My dear, you must be silent. There are things your husband must never know. . . ."

I thought of all those things as I labored to get the rain-filled rowboat across the storm-lashed water of Painer's Pit. With every passing second I expected one of those infernal death-darts to needle my flesh. But no more came.

After an eternity, the boat hissed through slimy weeds on shore and I clambered out, went wallowing along the inundated path that snaked through the woods to the house.

I knew that I would say nothing to Philias, or to my wife, or to the ferret-eyed Mrs. Sargy whose official title was that of housekeeper. I knew that I would keep this latest threat to myself, just as I had kept the others. I could trust no one, not even Lenore. God!

It was after supper that night when I first noticed the change in my wife's guardian. My wife was curled in the big fireside chair, a magazine in her lap, her face flushed and lovely in the glow of the fire. Philias sat at an ancient desk, where he had been hunched for over an hour, laboriously writing in some sort of ledger. Suddenly I noticed that he was ill.

I stared at him—at his short, stumpy, woodenish body and over-sized head. I had never liked him anyway. I hated his arrogance and feared the glitter of his near-sighted eyes. I sometimes hated Lenore for defending him, for so loyally maintaining that the old man really had a heart of gold.

But this was something more. A decided change had crept over him, subtly altering his appearance. He seemed older, more wizened. His face had taken on a yellowish tinge that did not come from the glow of the lamp at his elbow. "Dr. Giblin gave him six months," I thought. "It will not be that long. . . ."

An alien sound in the room's silence made me grow rigid. The storm outside had abated. This new sound was a tread of stealthy footsteps *above* me. I stared wonderingly at the ceiling.

Old Philias stopped writing in his book. My wife put down her magazine.

I say it was the sound of *stealthy* footsteps. It *might* have been the muffled thumping of a loose shutter somewhere in the upper reaches of the house. The room above us was Philias Arns' bedchamber.

The sound came again—this time followed by the fearful clamor of a peal of mad mirth which wailed down into the room. And then— silence.

It was Lenore who reacted first. A sob burst from her lips. She was suddenly in my arms, clinging to me, her face white with terror.

"It's up there!" she screamed. "It's in father's room!"

I stared at Philias. He was erect, striding grimly to the door, and was muttering to himself as he hurried into the corridor. I heard him go thumping up the stairs.

I knew suddenly that he was walking into some monstrous peril, but when I turned to lurch after him, my wife clung to me. We stood there, she and I, waiting fearfully for him to return.

We heard his dragging feet as he went along the upstairs corridor. A door creaked open, closed with a dull thud. The scuffling feet whispered directly above us—and stopped.

Five minutes later Philias came downstairs and paced back to his desk. "There was nothing up there," he said dully. "Nothing at all."

It was about ten o'clock when I again noticed the sinister change in the man. He was poring over his ledger, his face full in the glow of the lamp. That face was a wrinkled grey mask which might have been a death's head. I stared, felt a ghastly sensation of horror creeping through me.

He seemed to have grown smaller. His twisted body was hunched down in the chair, his feet curled on the chair-rungs. His shrivelled head was thrust forward, the cords of his thin neck bulging amid shadowed pits of taut flesh. He *had* grown smaller! But how, in the name of God. . . .?

I leaned toward him, murmured that he looked tired and asked if he were ill, but he jerked his head curtly in negative response. He was in an ugly mood. I shrugged, got up and went to the bookcase.

I found a photograph album, took it back to the chair. It was dusty, dog-eared. I stared at a picture of my wife.

Perhaps the glowing radiance of her face in that photograph should have filled me with delight, but it did not. The radiance was not for me, but for the young man who stood close to her. A lean, good-looking young man, his face was handsome except for a deep-cut, triangular scar which disfigured one cheek. Worms of dark jealousy were spawned in the gloom of my heart. I looked at my wife and she was staring at me, her face ghastly white.

"Who—is he?" I said heavily.

Lenore came slowly toward me and took the album from my hands. "I should have told you before." Her words were barely audible. "But I didn't think it was that important, after three years. He was an engineer. His name—it doesn't matter now, does it? When I said goodbye, that was the end."

I shrugged, said nothing. Old Philias Arns glanced at us queerly as he got up from the desk and paced out of the room on his way to bed. An hour later Lenore and I went upstairs to our room. As we reached the head of the stairs, the door of Philias Arns' room creaked open; Mrs. Sargy stood staring at us.

Mrs. Sargy—the strange, silent woman who had been Philias Arns' housekeeper for years! I knew she hated me. Only yesterday Lenore had said to me: "Philias thinks a lot of Mrs. Sargy. He planned to divide his money between her and me when he died, but when you and I were married he changed his plans. Philias *has* a lot of money, you know, even if this old house doesn't look it."

Yes—my marriage to Lenore had caused the housekeeper to become a grim, sinister being whose hatred toward me I could feel in the very air. For Mrs. Sargy would no longer come into a large part of the old man's fortune.

She stared at us now. "Good-night, my children," she said acidly. "Pleasant dreams to you both." Without answering her, I pushed open the door of our room and drew Lenore over the threshold.

I hesitated before walking in farther. Last night, when I had entered this same room, a sudden scratching, scraping sound had stiffened me. I had lurched forward in time to see a dark, contorted shape on the sill of the open window. The thing had vanished with astonishing quickness.

A prowling animal, perhaps, from the woods outside—but I had not been sure. I peered into the room's darkness now before entering, but this time no lurking evil was there to greet me.

I snapped the light-switch, strode forward. Too late I tried to hide from my wife's gaze the sinister words which leered there on the smooth surface of the bureau mirror!

Lenore saw that evil message almost as soon as I did. A moan of terror filled her throat as she stood swaying. Scrawled there in a handwriting childishly crude, was that damnable message.

"Soon the curse of Kawalo will destroy you both!"

Had I encountered that evil message earlier in the evening, before witnessing the almost unbelievable transformation in Philias Arns— and seeing the strange glint of hatred in Mrs. Sargy's eyes—I might have been less terrified. But I had endured so much that this last threat was unbearable.

I gripped my wife's trembling shoulders. "Tomorrow morning," I cried hoarsely, "you and I are leaving this damned house and not coming back! Do you hear? I've had enough!"

"I—I can't leave Philias," she moaned. "He needs me."

"He's got Mrs. Sargy. Look here, Lenore." I drew her closer to me and stared into her wide eyes. "Can't you see what's behind all this? Some scheming fiend is bent on driving us out of here. When we became man and wife we disturbed the plans of several people. Don't you see that?"

She seemed to be listening without hearing what I was saying.

"Well, we're getting out of here!" I raged. "Tomorrow morning we're leaving!"

"Yes," Lenore whispered listlessly. "We'll go—tomorrow morning. . . "

But we didn't go. When we went downstairs together the next morning, we found Mrs. Sargy in the kitchen, preparing breakfast. The woman's haggard face told us that she had spent a sleepless night.

"Philias is worse," she said hoarsely. "All night long he's been suffering. Someone's got to go for Dr. Giblin."

Giblin was the physician who had given Philias only six months to live. He had attended Philias for years. He was a close friend of Mrs. Sargy herself. But I had never liked the man, never trusted him.

"You mean—Philias is dying?" I said huskily.

Mrs. Sargy nodded.

I knew then that my wife could not keep her promise to go away with me. I could not decently hold her to it. Lenore went upstairs alone. I strode out of the house, got into my car and went for the doctor. With a vision of that ghastly look on Mrs. Sargy's face riding with me, I knew that I was racing with death.

When I returned with Giblin to that house of death and blundered into the room where my wife and Mrs. Sargy were anxiously awaiting our arrival, I knew the meaning of horror.

I stared at the thing on the bed, knew that I was looking at Philias Arns. But, merciful God, this contorted shape no longer even resembled anything human! It was a wrinkled, shrivelled mockery!

I looked frantically at my wife, at Mrs. Sargy. They, too, were terrified by the ghastly thing that had happened. "What in God's name is wrong with him?" I croaked, as Dr. Giblin bent over the bed.

He spat terse, clipped commands at Mrs. Sargy. I thought I saw worms of dark suspicion crawling in his eyes. "You were right," he said grimly. "Philias is dying," he said so venomously that I stepped abruptly away from him.

I had never trusted him. Like Mrs. Sargy, he had good reason for hating me.

On the very day of our arrival in this huge house of shadows, Giblin had come here to give Philias Arns his monthly examination. I had been present during the ritual, and old Philias had said suddenly: "You kind of figured on getting this place after my death, didn't you, Giblin? Kind of figured on turning it into a sanatorium, eh? Well, you'll have to forget that, now. It goes to John and Lenore."

Giblin's face had darkened for a moment. Then he had shrugged, smiled queerly and said: "We won't worry about that, Philias. Not yet."

And now he was glaring at me, saying ominously: "You were right. Philias is dying."

But Philias did not want to die! Throughout that dreary, nerve-racking day he clung tenaciously to life. And at eleven o'clock that night, when Giblin finally quit the sick-room, old Philias was neither better nor worse.

"I've told Mrs. Sargy what to do in case of emergency," Giblin said wearily. "I'll return first thing in the morning."

Two hours later Mrs. Sargy said, peering at Lenore and me: "There's no use for all of us sitting up with him. Go on to bed, you two."

Lenore and I did go to bed. We needed sleep, at least needed a relief from the ghastly atmosphere of the sick-room.

My wife slept. For a while I lay listening to the savage sweep of storm-wind that had come up again. Then I, too, slept.

When I awoke, Lenore was gone. The door was open, the threshold yellow with a glow of gaslight from the corridor. I sat up in bed, remembering. Philias Arns! Had the crisis come at last?

I slid my feet into slippers and strode into the hall, angry with Lenore for having failed to arouse me.

The door of Philias Arns' room refused to open!

I stood stiff, became suddenly a slave of evil suspicions. But when I hammered on the barrier and shouted my wife's name, I got no answer. The jangling echoes of my voice lived and died in the corridor's depths.

I was bewildered, suddenly terrified. I seized the knob and strove feverishly to force the door open. My clamoring voice rose to a hysterical wail.

"Open the door!" I raged.

Then I saw a dull gleam on the floor at my feet. I stooped, reached down a palsied hand. My fingers dipped into wet, sticky stuff that snaked from under the door.

Blood! *Good God!*

And suddenly a thin, sobbing voice, barely audible, moaned through the corridor's gloom behind me!

"John! Oh, God, help—! Come quick!"

I lurched around, followed the echoes of that wail as one might follow a guiding length of string through some black labyrinth. I stumbled past the head of the stairs. At the end of the hall, a door hung half open and the moaning voice came to me from the murk of the room beyond.

I did not stop to think, in my terror, that the voice might belong to someone other than the woman I was seeking. I went blindly over the sill, faltered to a stop and muttered my wife's name. There was no answer. Straining to see what lay before me, I walked slowly into the room.

Behind me the door creaked ominously. Screaming a lurid oath, I flung myself toward the closing barrier. A key turned raspingly in the lock.

Rage and fear fumed within me. I hurled myself at the door, fought it with the fury of a caged madman. I was locked in—a prisoner. And from the corridor outside came an evil chuckling sound that stiffened me.

"There is no escape, John Barrett! It's a heavy door, too heavy for you to break down, and there are no windows. There are matches on a table near the wall. Strike one, light the lamp on the table and see what I have prepared for you!"

I pawed slowly along the wall, collided with a table. My groping hands found matches, a lamp. My face must have been ghastly grey in the lamp-glow as I straightened, peered around me.

The room was a musty, L-shaped chamber of gloom. My gaze focused on a table which loomed against the wall. I took slow steps forward.

Yes, I was to be a prisoner—and for some time. The stuff on the table was food—a huge jug of water, a platter of cooked meat, vegetables, a bowl of figs and dates and nuts. Evidently I was not to be allowed to starve. . . .

But, good God, why was I being held here? Where was my wife?"

The hideous truth struck home. I was to be kept here while that fiend of darkness carried out his evil designs on Lenore! Unless I found some way out. . . .

I lurched again to the door. Again that shrill voice came from the depths of the corridor to drive me back.

"There is no way out, Barrett. In a little while I shall leave you, taking your wife with me. Then you will be alone in this huge house— alone with the shrivelled corpse of Philias Arns and the murdered body of Mrs. Sargy, whose blood you saw creeping beneath the door of the sickroom.

"I destroyed Mrs. Sargy so that you *would* be alone, Barrett—so that none will hear your screams as the hours drag by. You will grow hungry, and the food on the table will tempt you. But you will not touch it, unless you wish to contract the same disease which brought death to old Philias. *Taste it, and you taste the curse of Kawalo. . . .!*"

The sound of receding footsteps died away—and I thought I heard those stealthy feet whispering down the big staircase, but I could not be sure.

Terror seethed in my soul, rushed devouringly through every part of me. Something jarred loose in my mind. I hurled myself at the barrier, snarled frightful curses and sobbed out piteous pleas.

Then I realized what a mindless idiot I had become. That shrill-voice fiend had spoken truth: the barrier between me and freedom was too heavy. Already my fists were red with blood.

But that door must be opened! It had to be!

I strode to the table where that array of poisoned food had been spread out to taunt me. A sweep of my arm sent the dishes crashing against the wall. I swung the table to my shoulders.

My bloody hands clamped around two of the heavy legs. I braced myself, hurtled forward. The door bent back a trifle under the impact of the blow.

I lunged again and again. The barrier shuddered, groaned its protests. Then the lock gave way and I went headlong over the threshold.

Moments passed while I lay retching, sobbing, my body racked with agonies. But then Lenore's name shrieked through my brain, gave me strength to stagger erect. Lenore! I had to find her!

I went stumbling down the corridor to Philias Arns' room, and the pool of blood under the door made a carpet for my feet as I lurched against the barrier. I groaned Lenore's name. No answer.

I stared back at the shattered table. Should I smash this door down, too? Merciful God where *was* Lenore? What had the monster said about leaving me alone here and taking my wife away to some isolated place of torment. . . .?

Suddenly I knew. I heard again the mad peal of laughter which had shrilled across Painer's Pit. I saw again the ancient shack leaning on the farther shore. There could be no other answer!

The fiend's monstrous threat clamored in my soul as I raced out of the house. *"I shall bring your wife back to you. Then you will go mad . . .!"*

Clad only in pajamas, I rushed out into the storm, became a frantic scarecrow in a hell of moaning wind and rain. Somehow I found the trail that led through the woods to Painer's Pit. Somehow I blundered along it. Again and again I lurched erect in sloughs of stagnant water when treacherous bull-briars flung me headlong.

I got to the edge of the pond, found the battered rowboat which I had abandoned there—dragged it on shore, dumped it, heaved it forward again and clambered in. I seized the oars. . . .

Eternities later, when that wallowing tub scraped through mud and weeds on the far shore of Painer's Pit, the abandoned house loomed above me, and I saw a light glowing dully through the cracks of a boarded window.

It was a weird place. God alone knows who had been mad enough to erect a house on such a site. The porous ground had slowly sunk; the building had leaned forward in an attitude of supplication. The Pit's black waters had crept ever higher. . . .

But the light lured me on, filled me with a mad hope! I splashed forward, my hands outthrust to clutch a flight of wooden steps that poked up out of weeds and muck.

I blundered onto the veranda, went over a dim threshold, and groped forward. The floor under my feet was treacherous, filled with pitfalls.

Twice I stumbled. Once Lenore's name welled to my lips, died there. Ahead of me a light glowed murkily, and I groped toward it. This was the only thing in the evil gloom around me that suggested the presence of anything human. No alien sound rose above the din of the storm. I heard only the sibilant hiss of my own breathing, the scrape of my own groping feet.

Had I come *too late?*

That question was answered! Before me the ocher glow suddenly vanished, left me groping in darkness. I jerked to a stop, clawed the wall with ice-cold and trembling fingers. But nothing came at me in the gloom. Nothing threatened me.

I moved forward again, reached the open doorway from which that ghastly glow had emanated. I stared, saw only undulating darkness. Reluctantly I took a step forward, and another.

From the black depths before me a voice shrilled my name. *"Look out, John! Oh, God, look out—!"*

I lurched backward, but something above me had already come to life. I heard an evil chuckle from the darkness. At the same instant a huge, writhing mass fell from the ceiling, crashed down upon me and enveloped me.

I stumbled drunkenly in an effort to extricate myself. For fully half a minute I battled insanely before realizing that my assailant was neither man nor monster but an inanimate mass of ropes.

While I fought, the room around me was full of sounds that chilled the blood in my heaving body. Somewhere in the gloom my wife was hysterically moaning my name, and very close to me came a vile outburst of mirth that croaked an accompaniment to her sobs.

When at last I had sense enough to stop threshing about, my arms and legs were hopelessly entangled in the great net which had dropped upon me. I stood swaying, drenched with sweat. I was hopelessly, hellishly trapped.

I heard footsteps receding in the room's darkness, heard someone clambering as though onto a chair. A match sputtered; the yellow glare of an oil-lamp spread out.

At one time that room had been a kitchen. Its humped floor crawled into crooked walls. Its ceiling hung low at one end over an iron sink, a sloping sinkboard.

My wife—*my* wife lay there, half-naked, her wrists and ankles bound, her head lolling horribly, her hair cascading into the sink's rusty depths. Oh, God . . .!

I sobbed her name but she did not look toward me. Yet she was not dead. Her uncovered breasts were gently rising, falling. The muscles of one leg twitched spasmodically against the ropes that held her.

I lurched toward her, spilled to my knees as something jerked cruelly on the huge web that held me prisoner. I swayed there, and twisted my head around at a chuckling sound behind me. Then—I saw.

I went rigid, gaping.

Master-cords snaked away from my web prison, curled across the floor and ended in the gnarled hands of a thing that squatted there on the chair. I saw then how the fiend had trapped me. The net had hung suspended from the ceiling, awaiting a new victim. The monster had jerked those two master-cords, releasing it. Now he was studying me with tiny eyes of evil, and chuckling at my helplessness.

Monster? My God, the thing was no bigger than a doll! The creature I stared at was a shrivelled, hideous mockery of something that had once been human! It crouched there on stumpy, hairless legs, its naked body leprous-white in the glare of the lamp. It had clambered onto the chair in order to lean over the table and light the lamp.

Now it leaped down, looped the mastercords around a leg of the table and made them fast. Slowly it advanced toward me.

Merciful God, what *was* this thing? I shrank from the glare of its evil eyes as it came closer. Was it human? Its hairless body was stark naked except for a leather thong that held a knife. Its face was a horror of wrinkled flesh from which the color had been sucked by some frightful disease. And that gargoyle countenance was no mask. It was real!

Suddenly I knew that this stunted monster had been prowling around Philias Arns' house. It was he who had shrilled those words of evil from the balcony of the church in Hampton. He could easily come and go without being seen. . . .

The creature stood glaring at me, its gnarled hands gently stroking its hideous body. A scarlet lump of tongue bulged from its curled lips, licked noisily at the corners of its mouth in anticipation of some promised delight.

Then a shrill, childish voice—a voice hellishly familiar—whined toward me.

"You came just in time, Barrett!" an evil grin writhed over the little man's face. "It's a good thing I heard you stumbling down the hall and was prepared to receive you."

I strained forward, gasped out the questions that were twisting my soul. "In the name of God, *who are you?* What do you mean to do to us?"

His answer was a vile snicker. He jerked around, peered at the nearly naked form of my wife. Again his gnarled hands caressed his own horrible body, stroked the knife in his belt—the weapon which had left blood in the upstairs corridor of Philias Arns' home.

"So you don't know who I am?" the creature shrilled. "No, it isn't likely you would. I've changed a lot in the past few years." His stumpy legs carried him forward in a sudden rush, and he leered at me, made hideous faces. I knew that the brain in that doll-sized body was diseased. "I was big enough a few years ago!" he screamed. "Now look at me! That's what comes of wallowing for twelve months in the slime and filth of South American jungles, and contracting a vile disease that lurks there. That's what comes of trusting a band of treacherous natives, Guapelos, led by Kawalo, the cunning one—and eating the poisonous fruit they gave me. *Look at me!"*

The shrill voice died to a growl. "Yes, I'm horrible, Barrett. But soon I won't be the only horrible one. When I came back from the jungles of Brazil I brought some of Kawalo's filthy poison back with me. I had shrunk only a few inches then; I thought that by analyzing the poison I could find a cure. . . .

"But I was wrong, Barrett. There is no cure! Once that hellish virus runs in your blood you are doomed to a slow lingering death that takes years; that is, unless you devour as much of the stuff as I fed to Philias Arns, in his medicine. Then it takes only a few hours."

His lips curled in a frightful grin, and he stabbed a shrivelled forefinger at my bulging eyes. "When *I* was poisoned, Barrett, the stuff was fed to me in its native element—in the harmless-looking red fruit of the aoya bush. But when I escaped from Kawalo's clutches I brought back a canteen full of the extracted juice of that same devilish fruit. Now I have a use for it! I'll show you what two ounces of the stuff can do to the woman you married."

He jerked away from me, spun on crooked legs and waddled across the room. As I watched him, a shriek of terror gathered in my throat. I used hands and feet and teeth in a mad effort to escape the clutching coils of the net.

The little monster chuckled with savage delight at my futile efforts. With amazing dexterity he clambered onto the sink, walked like an ugly, animated puppet toward the bound form of my wife. That end of the room lay in shadows. But I saw the glitter of his eyes, the gleam of his teeth as he grinned across at me.

Merciful God, what *was* this thing? *Who* was he? Why was his shrivelled heart so black with hate for Lenore and me?

"Your wife has fainted, Barrett," he croaked. "But the poison will work just the same. In a little while—maybe an hour or so after I pour the stuff down her throat—the virus will begin to take effect. You saw what it did to Philias Arns."

He stared at Lenore's body. "You'll enjoy watching the transformation, Barrett. And you can blame yourself for it. You were warned not to marry this woman!"

I sobbed words of supplication to which he paid no attention. He stood on tiptoes, reached for a long-necked flask that sat on the window-ledge. Seating himself, he crossed his legs and put the container between his knees, caressed it with his shrivelled hands.

"The curse of Kawalo," he grinned. "I call it that because Kawalo, the cunning one, first introduced me to its hellish powers, by feeding it to me." Indifferently he raised his head, blinked at me. "Don't be impatient, Barrett. We have plenty of time. No one will come here to interrupt us. . . ."

Time! From the moment of my entrance into this room every instant had dragged to an eternity! My heart had become a relentless, grinding sledge. But I could do nothing but stare and hope. Yes, hope! Despite the soul-eating terror that numbed me, I had devised a mad scheme of action!

If only those glittering eyes would cease watching me. . . .

The little man leered at me for a long time before pushing himself erect. Then he moved sluggishly across the sink-board and bent above my wife. I choked a scream of anguish in my throat. He was like a hungry jackal daring to sniff at the body of a dying human being—working up courage to pounce and begin feeding.

But his was not that kind of hunger. He sat on the edge of the sink with his bare feet swinging above Lenore's face. He leaned forward, pried her mouth open. Then he grinned at me.

"Watch!" he croaked. "She'll come to life soon enough! Watch carefully, so you'll know what to expect when I attend to you!"

He thrust the slender neck of the flask into his own drooling mouth, pulled the cork with his teeth. Again he leaned forward. The flask tipped in his outthrust hand, hung poised above Lenore's parted lips. Slowly it descended. Slowly. . . .

Then I hurled forward! Stark terror gave me courage!

The fiend had looped the master-cords of the net around a leg of the table. On that table squatted the lamp. When I hurled myself in a headlong lunge, the master-cords jerked tight. With a splintering crash the table spilled over; the lamp shot through space.

The room was suddenly plunged into darkness!

I lay in a sprawled heap, hopelessly entangled in ropes. Breath sobbed in my throat, strangled me, as I worked to force my hands and wrists through the net.

From the darkness came a sputtering screech of rage. I heard the tiny monster scramble erect on the sink-board. I braced myself, prayed for courage.

Out of the darkness came a hurtling, twisting shadow that leaped with horrible speed through space. I saw the dull gleam of a knife.

God! It is one thing to stand erect and trade blows with a grown man—another thing to be imprisoned in a huge spiderweb of ropes while a shrivelled demon of hell leaps to the attack with murder in his soul!

The monster shrieked vile curses as he slashed at me with the blade. Had those glittering eyes been able to see clearly, the knife would have reached a vital part of my writhing body. But darkness gave me a fighting chance for life!

I had one arm free, used it to ward off the knife that leaped toward my throat. Again and again the blade, and the gnarled monkey-like hand that held it, made vicious contact with my heaving body. Hot, wet blood drooled into my face, smeared my bloated chest.

It was a strange, unholy combat . . . and the evil spirits who rule over South American jungles must have leered with delight to know that here, in a house of horror thousands of miles away, was being enacted the climax to a horror which they had begun, years ago, in the black depths of their own domain.

A full-grown man, trapped in the kind of net used to snare savage beasts of the jungle . . . sobbing now, half mad with pain, fighting for his life against a shrieking, cursing pygmy who fumed over him, seeking to destroy him. God!

Then my other arm worked itself free! I had something to fight with!

I do not like to remember the final moments of that hideous battle. They were moments of darkest horror.

My assailant backed away from me and stood crouching in darkness, gathering strength and fury for another assault. He did not know I was waiting for him with both arms outstretched.

His last attack had hurled me backward. I lay with my knees humped, my bare feet braced. Blood was in my throat; agony seethed in my brain. I waited. . . .

With an ear-splitting shriek he leaped. I saw his shrivelled body hurtling toward me, saw the gleam of the blade in his unflung fist.

I stabbed out both arms and caught that hurtling, doll-sized monstrosity in the grip of my clutching fingers. And I lay there, holding him aloft, my left hand clamped in his throat, my other curled around one of his crooked legs.

Breath soughed in my throat. I felt the white-hot agony of gouged flesh as the knife raked at my wrists. Then, slamming my upthrust knees together, I crashed that shrivelled shape down upon them as a man might smash a piece of box-wood.

The monster's shriek of terror was accompanied by a sudden sickening snap of bone. The thing in my hands went limp, its back broken, its tiny legs beating a tattoo of agony. The scream ended in a gurgling, bloody sob of agony. The knife fell from paralyzed fingers.

I flung the broken body away from me and used the knife to free myself from the prison of tangled nets. Unsteadily I groped erect, kicked my legs clear of the tangle of ropes and lurched forward. My dragging feet kicked the lamp which had spilled from the table.

I carried the broken lamp with me, and found matches on the sink-

board. In the feeble glow that filtered through the room's darkness, I
stared down at myself and shuddered.

My wife was moaning with returning consciousness. Beside her, still
full, lay the glass bottle whose contents would have made a horror of
her lovely body. . . .

I do not remember much of what I did then. I think I found water
in a bucket under the sink, used it to arouse Lenore from her stupor.
Then I helped my wife down from the death-platform and walked
toward the limp, broken thing which lay dead against the wall.

I remembered leaning above that thing, with the lamp clutched in
my hand. I remember peering into the shrivelled mask of agony which
had been its face—and seeing there a thin, triangular scar, half hidden
by folds of wrinkled flesh. It was a scar such as I had seen on a face
in a photograph—in a musty album. . . .

"This," I mumbled, staring at my wife, "is the man you—you
were—?"

She nodded, and when I limped toward a pile of refuse in a corner
of the room, and poured oil from the lamp, and struck a match—she
did not protest. There were things in this house which were better
destroyed. Their discovery by the police would cause dark doubts and
disbeliefs.

We stood in the doorway until the room was a roaring inferno. Then,
together, we went out into darkness and drizzling rain. Together we
found the boat in which the fiend had carried Lenore across the lake
to the abode of horror. As I sent the boat crawling through the evil
waters of Painer's Pit, my wife told me how the monster had seized
her.

Lying awake in our room she had heard the voice of Philias Arns
moaning her name from the corridor. Quietly she had tiptoed from
the room, not knowing the voice had come from the lips of a fiend
who lay in wait.

In the gaslit gloom of the corridor the little monster had hurtled
down upon her from a ledge above the door. He had locked his flailing
legs around her neck, twisted a strangling-cord around her throat. . . .

When she told me that, I stared bitterly back at the crimson pyre
on the far shore. And I clenched my fists.

Together we made our way back to Philias Arns' house . . . and
there I took my wife in my arms, thanked God for giving her back to
me.

Lenore said to me: "I thought I loved him once, John. He was an
engineer, young and strong, just as you saw him in the photographs.
Then he went to South America, and for two years I had no word.
When he returned, that horrible poison had made a monster of him,
just begun to shrivel him, and warp his mind. . . .

"He wanted me to marry him. He said I had promised. But I couldn't!

I felt sorry, and tried to help him, but he wanted more. Then—I had to send him away."

Her hands clung to mine, and I drew her closer to still the trembling of her slender body. "For three years," she told me, "I did not know what had become of him, except that people told of seeing a strange dwarf in the woods near Painer's Pit. Then I met you, John. We announced our engagement. Then he came to me, told me he would kill us both if I married you. I went to Philias, and Philias knew that I loved you. He told me to marry you, made me promise to bring you here to this house to live, so he could watch over us and protect us.

"He told me not to be afraid. 'If you love John,' he told me, 'marry him. Then the other one will go away, leaving you in peace.' But Philias was wrong. . . . I knew he was wrong when that horrible voice screamed in the church. That was the beginning, John. I wanted to tell you, but Philias made me keep silent. He said you would never understand. . . ."

"It is over now," I said softly. "All over. We can leave this house forever. There will be just you and I—and our love for each other."

But I wonder if there is not something else. Sometimes, even now, a mist of memory forms in my mind, and I see shadows which only time and a merciful God will erase. . . .

Cursed Be the City

HENRY KUTTNER

Robert E. Howard all but invented sword-and-sorcery fiction, a type of fantasy in which a warrior hero pits his strength, cunning, and instinct against the supernatural. Howard's death in 1936 left a void in this subgenre that many tried to fill, among them the versatile Henry Kuttner. Kuttner's tales of "Elak of Atlantis," clearly patterned on Howard's Conan stories, appeared in Weird Tales *between 1938 and 1941. In the April 1939 issue of* Strange Stories, *he began another heroic fantasy series with "Cursed Be the City," the first of two adventures of Prince Raynor of Sardopolis. It's fitting that Kuttner had another story in the same issue of the magazine under a pen name—in time, his science fiction writing as the pseudonymous Lewis Padgett and Lawrence O'Donnell (both in collaboration with his wife, C. L. Moore) would win greater acclaim than stories bearing his own name.*

This is the tale they tell, O King: that ere the royal banners were lifted upon the tall towers of Chaldean Ur, before the Winged Pharaohs reigned in secret Aegyptus, there were mighty empires far to the east. There in that vast desert known as the Cradle of Mankind—aye, even in the heart of the measureless Gobi—great wars were fought and high palaces thrust their minarets up to the purple Asian sky. But this, O King, was

114

long ago, beyond the memory of the oldest sage; the splendor of Imperial Gobi lives now only in the dreams of minstrels and poets . . .
—The Tale of Sakhmet the Damned

CHAPTER I

THE GATES OF WAR

IN THE gray light of the false dawn the prophet had climbed to the outer wall of Sardopolis, his beard streaming in the chill wind. Before him, stretching across the broad plain, were the gay tents and pavilions of the besieging army, emblazoned with the scarlet symbol of the wyvern, the winged dragon beneath which King Cyaxares of the north waged his wars.

Already soldiers were grouped about the catapults and scaling-towers, and a knot of them gathered beneath the wall where the prophet stood. Mocking, rough taunts were voices, but for a time the white-bearded oldster paid no heed to the gibes. His sunken eyes, beneath their snowy penthouse brows, dwelt on the far distance, where a forest swept up into the mountain slopes and faded into a blue haze.

His voice came, thin piercing.

"Wo, wo, unto Sardopolis! Fallen is the Jewel of Gobi, fallen and lost forever, and all its glory gone! Desecration shall come to the altars, and the streets shall run red with blood. I see death for the king and shame for his people. . . ."

For a time the soldiers beneath the wall had been silent, but now, spears lifted, they interrupted with a torrent of half-amused mockery. A bearded giant roared:

"Come down to us, old goat! We'll welcome you indeed!"

The prophet's eyes dropped, and the shouting of the soldiers faded into stillness. Very softly the ancient spoke, yet each word was clear and distinct as a sword-blade.

"Ye shall ride through the streets of the city in triumph. And your king shall mount the silver throne. Yet from the forest shall come your doom; an old doom shall come down upon you, and none shall escape. He shall return—HE—the mighty one who dwelt here once. . . ."

The prophet lifted his arms, staring straight into the red eye of the rising sun. "Evohe! Evohe!"

Then he stepped forward two steps and plunged. Straight down, his beard and robe streaming up, till the upthrust spears caught him, and he died.

And that day the gates of Sardopolis were burst in by giant battering-rams, and like an unleashed flood the men of Cyaxares poured into the city, wolves who slew and plundered and tortured mercilessly. Terror walked that day, and a haze of battle hung upon the roofs. The defenders were hunted down and slaughtered in the streets without mercy. Women were outraged, their children impaled, and the glory of Sardopolis faded in a smoke of shame and horror. The last glow of the setting sun touched the scarlet wyvern of Cyaxares floating from the tallest tower of the king's palace.

Flambeaux were lighted in their sockets, till the great hall blazed with a red fire, reflected from the silver throne where the invader sat. His black beard was all bespattered with blood and grime, and slaves groomed him as he sat among his men, gnawing on a mutton-bone. Yet, despite the man's gashed and broken armor and the filth that besmeared him, there was something unmistakably regal about his bearing. A king's son was Cyaxares, the last of a line that had sprung from the dawn ages of Gobi when the feudal barons had reigned.

But his face was a tragic ruin.

Strength and power and nobility had once dwelt there, and traces of them still could be seen, as though in muddy water, through the mask of cruelty and vice that lay heavy upon Cyaxares. His gray eyes held a cold and passionless stare that vanished only in the crimson blaze of battle, and now those deadly eyes dwelt on the bound form of the conquered king of Sardopolis, Chalem.

In contrast with the huge figure of Cyaxares, Chalem seemed slight; yet, despite his wounds, he stood stiffly upright, no trace of expression on his pale face.

A strange contrast! The marbled, tapestried throne-room of the palace was more suitable to gay pageantry than this grim scene. The only man who did not seem incongruously out of place stood beside the throne, a slim, dark youth, clad in silks and velvets that had apparently not been marred by the battle. This was Necho, the king's confidant, and, some said, his familiar demon. Whence he had come no one knew but of his evil power over Cyaxares there was no doubt.

A little smile grew on the youth's handsome face. Smoothing his curled dark hair, he leaned close and whispered to the king. The latter nodded, waved away a maiden who was oiling his beard, and said shortly:

"Your power is broken, Chalem. Yet we are merciful. Render homage, and you may have your life."

For answer Chalem spat upon the marble flags at his feet.

A curious gleam came into Cyaxares' eyes. Half inaudibly he murmured, "A brave man. Too brave to die. . . ."

Some impulse seemed to pull his head around until he met Necho's gaze. A message passed in that silent staring. For Cyaxares took from his side a long, bloodstained sword; he rose, stepped down from his dais—and swung the brand.

Chalem made no move to evade the blow. The steel cut through bone and brain. As the dead man fell, Cyaxares stood looking down without a trace of expression. He wrenched his sword free.

"Fling this carrion to the vultures," he commanded.

From the group of prisoners near by came an angry oath. The king turned to face the man who had dared to speak. He gestured.

A pair of guards pushed forward a tall, well-muscled figure, yellow-haired, with a face strong despite its youth, now darkened with rage. The man wore no armor, and his torso was criss-crossed with wounds.

"Who are you?" Cyaxares asked with ominous restraint, the sword bare in his hand.

"King Chalem's son—Prince Raynor."

"You seek death?"

Raynor shrugged. "Death has come close to me today. Slay me if you will. I've butchered about a dozen of your wolves, anyway, and that's some satisfaction."

Behind Cyaxares came a rustle of silks as Necho moved slightly. The king's lips twitched beneath the shaggy beard. His face was suddenly hard and cruel again.

"So! Well, you will crawl to my feet before the next sun sets." He gestured. "No doubt there are torture vaults beneath the palace. Sudrach!"

A brawny, leather-clad man stepped forward and saluted. "You have heard my will. See to it."

"If I crawl to your feet," Raynor said quietly, "It'll be to hamstring you, bloated toad."

The king drew in his breath with an angry sound. Without another word he nodded to Sudrach, and the torturer followed Raynor as he was conducted out. Then Cyaxares went back to his throne and mused for a time, till a slave brought him wine in a gilded chalice.

But the liquor had no power to break his dark mood. At last he rose and went to the dead king's apartments, which the invaders had not dared to plunder for fear of Cyaxares' wrath. Above the silken couch a gleaming image hung from its standard—the scarlet wyvern, wings spread, barbed tail stiffly upright. Cyaxares stood silently staring at it for a space.

He did not turn when he heard Necho's soft voice. The youth said, "The wyvern has conquered once again."

"Aye," Cyaxares said dully. "Once again, through vileness and black shame. It was an evil day when we met, Necho."

Low laughter came. "Yet you summoned me, as I remember. I was content enough in my own place, till you sent your summons."

Involuntarily the king shuddered. "I would Ishtar had sent down her lightnings upon me that night."

"Ishtar? You worship another god now."

Cyaxares swung about, snarling. "Necho, do not push me too far! I still have some power—"

"You have all the power," the low voice said. "As you wished."

For a dozen heart-beats the king made no answer. Then he whispered, "I am the first to bring shame upon our royal blood. When I was crowned I swore many a vow on the tombs of my fathers—and for a time I kept those vows. I ruled with truth and chivalry—"

"And you sought wisdom."

"Aye. I was not content. I sought to make my name great, and to that end I talked with sorcerers—with Bleys of the Dark Pool."

"Bleys," Necho murmured. "He was learned, in his way. Yet—he died."

The king's breathing was unsteady. "I know. I slew him—at your command. And you showed me what happened thereafter."

"Bleys is not happy now," Necho said softly. "He served the same master as you. Wherefore—" The quiet voice grew imperious. "Wherefore live! For by our bargain I shall give you all power on earth, fair women and treasure beyond imagination. But when you die—you shall serve me!"

The other stood silent, while veins swelled on his swarthy forehead. Suddenly, with a bellowing, inarticulate oath, he snatched up his sword. Bright steel flamed through the air—and rebounded, clashing. Up the king's arm and through all his body raced a tingling shock, and simultaneously the regal apartment seemed to darken around him. The fires of the flambeaux darkened. The air was chill—and it whispered.

Steadily the room grew blacker. Now all was midnight black, save for a shining figure that stood immobile, blazing with weird and unearthly radiance. Little murmurs rustled through the deadly stillness. The body of Necho shone brighter, blindingly. And he stood without moving or speaking, till the king shrank with a shuddering cry, his blade clattering on the marble.

"No!" he half sobbed. "For *His* mercy—no!"

"*He* has no mercy," the low voice came, bleak and chill. "Therefore worship me, dog whom men call king. Worship me!"

And Cyaxares worshipped. . . .

CHAPTER II

BLOOD IN THE CITY

PRINCE RAYNOR was acutely uncomfortable. He was stretched upon a rack, staring up at the dripping stones of the vault's roof, and Sudrach, the torturer, was heating iron bars on the hearth. A great cup of wine stood nearby, and occasionally Sudrach, humming under his breath, would reach for it and gulp noisily.

"A thousand pieces of gold if you help me escape," Raynor repeated without much hope.

"What good is gold to a flayed man?" Sudrach asked. "That would be my fate if you escaped. Also, where would you get a thousand golden pieces?"

"In my apartment," Raynor said. "Safely hidden."

"You may be lying. At any rate, you'll tell me where this hiding place is when I burn out your eyes. Thus I'll have the gold—if it exists—without danger to myself."

Raynor made no answer, but instead tugged at the cords that bound him. They did not give. Yet Raynor strained until blood throbbed in his temples, and was no closer to freedom when he relaxed at last.

"You'll but wear yourself out," Sudrach said over his shoulder. "Best save your strength. You'll need it for screaming." He took an iron bar from the fire. Its end glowed red, and Raynor watched the implement with fascinated horror. An unpleasant way to die——

But as the glowing bar approached Raynor's chest there came an interruption. The iron door was flung open, and a tall, huge-muscled black entered. Sudrach turned, involuntarily lifting the bar as a weapon. Then he relaxed, his eyes questioning.

"Who the devil are you?" he grunted.

"Eblik, the Nubian," said the black, bowing. "I bear a message from the king. I lost my way in this damned palace, and just now blundered to my goal. The king has two more prisoners for your hands."

"Good!" Sudrach rubbed his hands. "Where are they?"

"In the—" The other stepped closer. He fumbled in his belt.

Then, abruptly, a blood-reddened dagger flashed up and sheathed itself in flesh. Sudrach bellowed, thrust out clawing hands. He doubled up slowly, while his attacker leaped free, and then he collapsed upon the dark stones and lay silent, twitching a little.

"The gods be praised!" Raynor grunted. "Eblik, faithful servant, you come in time!"

Eblik's dark, gargoylish face was worried. "Let me—" He slashed the cords that bound the prisoner. "It wasn't easy. When we were separated in the battle, master, I knew Sardopolis would fall. I changed clothes with one of Cyaxares' men—whom I slew—and waited my chance to escape. It was by the merest luck that I heard you had offended the king and were to be tortured. So—" He shrugged.

Raynor, free at last, sprang up from the rack, stretching his stiffened muscles. "Will it be easy to escape?"

"Perhaps. Many are drunk or asleep. At any rate, we can't stay here."

The two slipped cautiously out into the corridor. A guard lay dead, weltering in his blood, not far away. They hurried past him, and silently threaded their way through the palace, more than once dodging into passages to evade detection.

"If I knew where Cyaxares slept, I'd take my chances on slitting his throat," Raynor said. "Wait! This way!"

At the end of a narrow hall was a door which, pushed open, showed a moonlit expanse of garden. Eblik said, "I remember—I entered this way. Here—" He dived into a bush and presently emerged with a sword and a heavy battle-ax; the latter he thrust in his girdle. What now?"

"Over the wall," Raynor said, and led the way. The high rampart was not easy to scale, but a spreading tree grew close to it, and eventually the two had surmounted the barrier. As Raynor dropped lightly to the ground he heard a sudden cry, and, glancing around, saw a group of men, armor gleaming in the moonlight, racing toward him. He cursed softly.

Eblik was already fleeing, his long legs covering the yards with amazing speed. Raynor followed, though his first impulse was to wait and give battle. But in the stronghold of Cyaxares such an action would have been suicidal.

Behind the pair the pursuers bayed menace. Swords came out flashing. Raynor clutched his comrade's arm, dragged him into a side alley, and the two sped on, frantically searching for a hiding place. It was Eblik who found sanctuary five minutes later. Passing the blood-smeared, corpse-littered courtyard of a temple, he gasped a hasty word, and in a moment both Raynor and Eblik were across the moonlit stretch and fleeing into the interior of the temple.

From a high roof hung a golden ball, dim in the gloom. This was the sacred house of the Sun, the dwelling place of the primal god Ahmon. Eblik had been here before, and knew the way. He guided Raynor past torn tapestries and overthrown censers, and then, halting before a golden curtain, he listened. There was no sound of pursuit.

"Good!" The Nubian warrior said. "I've heard of a secret way out of here, though where it is I don't know. Maybe we can find it."

He drew the curtain aside, and the two entered the sanctuary of the god. Involuntarily Raynor whispered a curse, and his brown fingers tightened on his rapier hilt.

A small chamber faced them, with walls and floor and ceiling blue as the summer sky. It was empty, save for a single huge sphere of gold in the center.

Broken upon the gleaming ball was a man.

From the wall a single flambeau cast a flickering radiance on the twisted, bloodstained body, on the white beard that was dappled with blood. The man lay stretched across the globe, his hands and feet impaled with iron spikes that had been driven deeply into the gold.

Froth bubbled on his lips. His hoary head rolled; eyes stared unseeingly. He gasped. "Water! For the love of Ahmon, a drop of water!"

Raynor's lips were a hard white line as he sprang forward. Eblik helped him as he pried the spikes free. The tortured priest moaned and bit at his mangled lips, but made no outcry. Presently he lay prostrate on the blue floor. With a muttered word, Eblik disappeared, and came back bearing a cup which he held to the dying man's mouth.

The priest drank deeply. He whispered, "Prince Raynor! Is the king safe?"

Swiftly Raynor answered. The other's white head rolled.

"Lift me up—swiftly!"

Raynor obeyed. The priest ran his hands over the golden sphere, and suddenly, beneath his probing fingers, it split in half like a cloven fruit, and in its center a gap widened. A steep staircase led down into hidden depths.

"This altar is open? I cannot see well. Take me down there. They cannot find us in the hidden chamber."

Raynor swung the priest to his shoulders and without hesitation started down the steps, Eblik behind him. There was a low grating as the altar swung back, a gleaming sphere that would halt and baffle pursuit. They were in utter darkness. The prince moved cautiously, testing each step before he shifted his weight. At last he felt the floor level beneath his feet.

Slowly, a dim light began to grow, like the first glow of dawn. It revealed a bare stone vault, roughly constructed of mortised stones, strangely at variance with the palatial city above. In one wall a dark hole showed. On the floor was a circular disk of metal, its center hollowed out into a cup. Within this cup lay a broken shard of some rock that resembled gold-shot marble, half as large as Raynor's hand. On the shard were carved certain symbols the prince did not recognize, and one that he did—the ancient looped cross, sacred to the sun-god.

He put the priest down gently, but nevertheless the man moaned in agony. The maimed hands clutched at air.

"Ahmon! Great Ahmon . . . give me more water!"

Eblik obeyed. Strengthened, the priest fumbled for and gripped Raynor's arm.

"You are strong. Good! Strength is needed for the mission you must undertake."

"Mission?"

The priest's fingers tightened. "Aye; Ahmon guided your steps hither. You must be the messenger of vengeance. Not I. I have not long to live. My strength ebbs. . . ."

He was silent for a time, and then resumed, "I have a tale to tell you. Do you know the legend of the founding of Sardopolis? How, long ago, a very terrible god had his altar in this spot, and was served by all the forest dwellers . . . till those who served Ahmon came? They fought and prisoned the forest god, drove him hence to the Valley of Silence, and he lies bound there by strong magic and the seal of

Ahmon. Yet there was a prophecy that one day Ahmon would be overthrown, and the bound god would break his fetters and return to his first dwelling place, to the ruin of Sardopolis. The day of the prophecy is at hand!"

The priest pointed. "All is dark. Yet the seal should be there—is it not?"

Raynor said, "A bit of marble—"

"Aye—the talisman. Lift it up!" The voice was now preemptory. Raynor obeyed.

"I have it."

"Good. Guard it well. Lift the disk now."

Almost apprehensively the prince tugged the disk up, finding it curiously light. Beneath was nothing but a jagged stone, crudely carved with archaic figures and symbols. A stone—yet Raynor knew, somehow, that the thing was horribly old, that it had existed from the dawn ages of Gobi.

"The altar of the forest god," said the priest. "He will return to this spot when he is freed. You must go to the Reaver of the Rock, and give him the talisman. He will know its meaning. So shall Ahmon be avenged upon the tyrant. . . ."

Suddenly the priest surged upright, his arms lifted, tears streaming from the blind eyes. He cried, Ohe—ohe! Fallen forever is the House of Ahmon! Fallen to the dust. . . ."

He fell, as a tree falls, crashing down upon the stones, his arms still extended as though in worship. So died the last priest of Ahmon in Gobi.

Raynor did not move for a while. Then he bent over the lax body. A hasty examination showed him that the man was dead, and shrugging, he thrust the marble shard into his belt.

"I suppose that's the way out," he said, pointing to the gap in the wall. "though I don't like the look of it. Well—come on."

He squeezed himself into the narrow hole, cursing softly, and Eblik followed.

CHAPTER III

THE REAVER OF THE ROCK

WITH SLOW steps Cyaxares paced his apartment, his shaggy brows drawn together in a frown. Once or twice his hand closed convulsively on his sword-hilt, and again the secret agony within him made him groan aloud. But not once did he glance at the scarlet symbol of the wyvern that hung above his couch.

Going to a window, he looked down over the city, and then his gaze went out to the plain and the distant, forested mountains. He sighed heavily.

A voice said, "You may well look there, Cyaxares. For there is your doom, unless you act swiftly."

"Is it you, Necho?" the king asked heavily. "What new shamefulness must I work now?"

"Two men go south to the Valley of Silence. They must be slain ere they reach it."

"Why? What aid can they get there?"

Necho did not answer at first. His voice was hesitant when he said, "The gods have their own secrets. There is something in the Valley of Silence that can send all your glory and power crashing down about your head. Nor can I aid you then. I can only advise you now and if you follow my advice—well. But act I cannot and must not, for a reason which you need not know. Send out your men therefore, with orders to overtake those two and slay them—swiftly!"

"As you will," the king said, and turned to summon a servitor.

"Soldiers follow us," Eblik said, shading his eyes with a calloused hand. He was astride a rangy dun mare, and beside him Raynor rode on a great gray charger, red of nostril and fiery of eye. The latter turned in the saddle and looked back.

"By the gods!" he observed. "Cyaxares has sent half an army after us. It's lucky we managed to steal these mounts."

The two had reined their horses at the summit of a low rise in the forest. Back of them the ground sloped to the great plain and the gutted city of Sardopolis; before them jagged mountains rose, covered with oak and pine and fir. The Nubian licked dry lips, said thirstily, "The fires of all hells are in my belly. Let's get out of this wilderness, where there's nothing to drink but water."

"The Reaver may feed you wine—or blood," Raynor said, "Nevertheless, our best chance is to find this Reaver and seek his aid. A mercenary once told me of the road."

He clapped his heels against the charger's flanks, and the steed bounded forward. In a moment the ridge had hidden them from the men of Cyaxares. So the two penetrated deeper and deeper into the craggy, desolate wilderness, a place haunted by wolves and great bears and, men whispered, monstrous, snake-like cockadrills.

They went by snow-peaked mountains that lifted white cones to the blue sky, and they fled along the brink of deep gorges from which the low thunder of cataracts rose tumultuously. And always behind them rode the pursuers, a grim and warlike company, following slowly but relentlessly.

But Raynor used more than one stratagem. Thrice he guided his charger up streams along which the wise animal picked its way carefully; again he dislodged an avalanche to block the trail. So it came about

that when the two rode down into a great, grassy basin, the men of
Cyaxares were far behind.

On all sides the mountains rose. Ahead was a broad, meadow-like
valley, strewn with thickets and green groves. Far ahead the precipice
rose in a tall rampart, split in one place into a narrow canyon.

To the right of the gorge lifted a great gray rock, mountain-huge,
bare save for a winding trail that twisted up its surface to a castle
upon the summit. Dwarfed by distance, the size of the huge structure
could yet be appreciated—a castle of stone, incongruously bedecked
with fluttering, bright banners and pennons.

Raynor pointed. "He dwells there. The Reaver of the Rock."

"And here comes danger," Eblik said, whipping out his battle-ax.
"Look!"

From a grove of nearby trees burst a company of horsemen, glittering
in the afternoon sunlight, spears lifted, casques and helms agleam.
Shouting, they rode down upon the waiting pair. Raynor fingered his
sword-hilt, hesitating.

"Put up your blade," he directed Eblik. "We come in friendship
here."

The Nubian was doubtful. "But do they know that?"

Nevertheless he sheathed his sword and waited till the dozen riders
reined in a few paces away. One spurred forward, a tall man astride
a wiry black.

"Are you tired of life, that you seek the Reaver's stronghold?" he
demanded. "Or do you mean to enter in his service?"

"We bear a message," Raynor countered. "A message from a priest
of Ahmon."

"We know no gods here," the other grunted.

"Well, you know warfare, or I've misread the dents in your armor,"
Raynor snapped. "Sardopolis is fallen! Cyaxares has taken the city and
slain the king, my father, Chalem of Sardopolis."

To his amazement a bellow of laughter burst from the troop. The
spokesman said, "What has that to do with us? We own no king but
the Reaver. Yet you shall come safely before him, if that is your will.
It were shameful to battle a dozen to two, and the rags you wear aren't
worth the taking."

Eblik started like a ruffled peacock. "By the gods, you have little
courtesy here! For a coin I'd slit you where you stand!"

The other rubbed his throat reflectively, grinning. "You may have
a trial at that later, if you wish, my ragged gargoyle. But come, now,
for the Reaver is in hall, and tonight he rides forth on a raid."

With a nod Raynor spurred his horse forward, the Nubian at his
side, and, surrounded by the men of the Reaver, they fled across the
valley to the castle. Thence they mounted the steep, dangerous path

up the craggy ramp, till at last they crossed a drawbridge and dismounted in a courtyard.

So they took Raynor before the Reaver of the Rock.

A great, shining, red-cheeked man he was, with grizzled gray beard and a crown set rakishly askew on tangled locks. He sat before a blazing fire in a high-roofed stone hall, an iron chest open at his feet. From this he was taking jewels and golden chains and ornaments that might have graced a king's treasury, examining them carefully, and making notes with a quill pen upon a parchment on his lap.

He looked up; merry eyes dwelt on Raynor's flushed face and touseled yellow hair.

"Well, Samar, what is it now?"

"Two strangers. They have a message for you—or so they say."

Suddenly the Reaver's face changed. He leaned forward, spilling treasure from his lap. "A message? Now there is only one message that can ever come to me . . . speak, you! Who sent you?"

Raynor stepped forward confidently. From his belt he drew the broken shard of marble, and extended it.

"A priest of Ahmon bade me give you this," he said. "Sardopolis is fallen."

For a heartbeat there was silence. Then the Reaver took the shard, examining it carefully. He murmured, "Aye. So my rule passes. For long and long my fathers held the Rock, waiting for the summons that never came. And now it has come."

He looked up. "Go, all of you, save you two. And you, Samar—wait, for you should know of this."

The others departed. The Reaver shouted after them, "Summon Delphia!"

He turned to stare into the fire. "So I, Kialeh, must fulfill the ancient pledge of my ancestors. And invaders are on my marches. Well—"

There came an interuption. A girl strode in, dark head proudly erect, slim figure corseted in dinted armor. She went to the Reaver, flung a blazing jewel in his lap.

"Is this my guerdon?" she snarled. "Faith o' the gods, I took Ossan's castle almost single-handed. And my share is less than the share of Samar here!"

"You are my daughter," the Reaver said quietly. "Shall I give you more honor, then, in our free brotherhood? Be silent. Listen."

Raynor was examining the girl's face with approval. There was beauty there, wild dark lawless beauty, and strength that showed in the firm set of the jaw and the latent fire of the jet eyes. Ebony hair, unbound, fell in ringlets about steel-corseleted shoulders.

The girl said, "Well? Have you had your fill of staring?"

"Let be," the Reaver grunted. "I have a tale for all of you . . . listen."

His deep voice grew stronger. "Ages on ages ago this was a barbarous land. The people worshipped a forest-god called—" his hand moved in a queer quick sign—" called Pan. Then from the north came two kings, brothers, bringing with them the power of the sun-god, Ahmon. There was battle in the land then, and blood and reddened steel. Yet Ahmon conquered.

"The forest-god was bound within the Valley of Silence, which lies beyond my castle. The two kings made an agreement. One was to rule Sardopolis, and the other, the younger, was to rear a great castle at the gateway of the Valley of Silence, and guard the fettered god. Until a certain word should come. . . ."

The Reaver weighed a glittering stone in his hand. "For there was a prophecy that one day the rule of Ahmon should be broken. Then it was foretold that the forest-god should be freed, and should bring vengeance upon the destroyers of Sardopolis. For long and long my ancestors have guarded the Rock—and I, Kialeh, am the last. Ah," he sighed. "The great days are over indeed. Never again will the Reaver ride to rob and plunder and mock at gods. Never—what's this?"

A man-at-arms had burst into the hall, eyes alight, face fierce as a wolf's. "Kialeh! An army is in the valley!"

"By Shaitan!" Raynor cursed. "Cyaxares' men! They pursued us—"

The girl, Delphia, swung about. "Gather the men! I'll take command—"

Suddenly the Reaver let out a roaring shout. "No! By all the gods I've flouted—no! Would you grudge me my last battle, girl? Gather your men, Samar—but I command!"

Samar sprang to obey. Delphia gripped her father's arm. "I fight with you, then."

"I have another task for you. Guide these two through the Valley of Silence, to the place you know. Here—" he thrust the marble shared at the prince. "Take this. You'll know how to use it when the time comes."

Then he was gone, and curtains of black samite swayed into place behind him.

Raynor was curiously eyeing the girl. Her face was pale beneath its tan, and her eyes betrayed fear. Red battle she could face unflinchingly, but the thought of entering the Valley of Silence meant to her something far more terrible. Yet she said, "Come. We have little time."

Eblik followed Raynor and Delphia from the hall. They went through the harsh splendor of the castle, till at last the girl halted before a blank stone wall. She pressed a hidden spring. A section of the rock swung away, revealing the dimlit depths of a passage.

Delphia paused on the threshold. Her dark eyes fliskered over the two.

"Hold fast to your courage," she whispered—and her lips were trembling. "For now we go down into Hell. . . ."

CHAPTER IV

THE VALLEY OF SILENCE

YET AT first there seemed nothing terrible about the valley. They entered it from a cavern that opened on a thick forest, and, glancing around, Raynor saw tall mountainous ramparts that made the place a prison indeed. It was past sunset, yet already a full moon was rising over the eastern cliffs, outlining the Reaver's castle in black silhouette.

They entered the forest.

Moss underfoot deadened their footsteps. They walked in the dim gloom, broken by moonlit traceries filtered through the leaves. And now Raynor noted the curious stillness that hung over all.

There was no sound. The noise of birds and beasts did not exist here, nor did the breath of wind rustle the silent trees. But, queerly, the prince thought there was a sound whispering through the forest, a sound below the threshold of hearing, which nevertheless played on his taut nerves.

"I don't like this," Eblik said, his ugly face set and strained. His voice seemed to die away with uncanny swiftness.

"Pan is fettered here," Delphia whispered. "Yet is his power manifest. . . ."

Soundlessly they went through the soundless forest. And now Raynor realized that, slowly and imperceptibly, the shadowy whisper he had sensed was growing louder—or else his ears were becoming more attuned to it. A very dim murmur, faint and far away, which yet seemed to have within it a multitude of voices. . . .

The voices of the winds . . . the murmur of the forests . . . the goblin laughter of shadowed brooks. . . .

It was louder now, and Raynor found himself thinking of all the innumerable sounds of the primeval wilderness. Bird-notes, and the call of beasts. . . .

And under all, a dim, powerful motif, beat a wordless shrilling, a faint piping that set the prince's skin to crawling as he heard it.

"It is the tide of life," Delphia said softly. "The heart-beat of the first god. The pulse of earth."

For the first time Raynor felt something of the primal secrets of the world. Often he had walked alone in the forest, but never yet had the hidden heart of the wilderness reached fingers into his soul. He sensed a mighty and very terrible power stirring latent in the soil beneath him, a thing bound inextricably to the brain of man by the cords of flesh which came up, by slow degrees, from the seething oceans which

once rolled unchecked over a young planet. Unimaginable eons ago
man had come from the earth, and the brand of his mother-world was
burned deep within his soul.

Afraid, yet strangely happy, as men are sometimes happy in their
dreams, the prince motioned for his companions to increase their pace.

The forest gave place to a wide clearing, with shattered white stones
rearing to the sky. Broken plinths and peristyles gleamed in the moonlight. A temple had once existed here. Now all was overgrown with
moss and the slow-creeping lichen.

"Here," the girl said in a low whisper. "Here. . . ."

In the center of a ring of fallen pillars they halted. Delphia pointed
to a block of marble, on which a metal disk was inset. In a cuplike
depression in the metal lay a broken bit of marble.

"The talisman," Delphia said. "Touch it to the other."

Silence . . . and the unearthly tide of hidden life swelling and ebbing
all about them. Raynor took the amulet from his belt, stepped forward,
fighting down his fear. He bent above the disk—touched marble shard
to marble—

As iron to lodestone, the two fragments drew together. They coalesced
into one. The jagged line of breakage faded and vanished.

Raynor held the talisman—complete, unbroken!

Now, quite suddenly, the vague murmurings mounted into a roar—
gay, jubilant, triumphant! The metal disk shattered into fragments.
Beneath it the prince glimpsed a small carved stone, the twin of the
one beneath the temple of Ahmon.

Above the unceasing roar sounded a penetrating shrill piping.

Delphia clutched at Raynor's arm, pulled him back. Her face was
chalk-white.

"The pipes!" she gasped. "Back—quickly! To see Pan is to die!"

Louder the roar mounted, and louder. In its bellow was a deep shout
of alien laughter, a thunder of goblin merriment. The chuckle of the
shadowed brooks was the crash of cataracts and waterfalls.

The forest stirred to a breath of gusty wind.

"Back!" the girl said urgently. "Back! We have freed Pan!"

Without conscious thought Raynor thrust the talisman into his belt,
turned, and, with Delphia and Eblik beside him, fled into the moonlit
shadows. Above him branches tossed in a mounting wind. The wild
shrieking of the pipes grew louder.

Tide of earth life—rising to a mad paean of triumph!

The wind exulted:

"Free . . . FREE!"

And the unseen rivers shouted:

"Great Pan is Free!"

A clattering of hoofs came from the distance. Bleating calls sounded
from afar.

The girl stumbled, almost fell. Raynor gripped at her arm, pulling her upright, fighting the unreasoning terror mounting within him. The Nubian's grim face was glistening with sweat.

"Pan, Pan is free!"

"Evohe!"

The black mouth of the cavern loomed before them. At its threshold Raynor cast a glance behind him, saw all the great forest swaying and tossing. His breath coming unevenly, he turned, following his companions into the cave.

"Shaitan!" he whispered. "What demon have I loosed on the land?"

Then it was race, sprint, pound up the winding passage, up an unending flight of stone steps, through a wall that lifted at Delphia's touch—and into a castle shaking with battle. Raynor stopped short, whipping out his sword, staring at shadows flickering in the distance.

"Cyaxares' men," he said. "They've entered."

In the face of flesh-and-blood antagonists the prince was suddenly himself again. Delphia was already running down the corridor, blade out. Raynor and the Nubian followed.

They burst into the great hall. A ring of armed men surrounded a little group who were making their last stand before the hearth. Towering above the others Raynor saw the tangled locks and bristling beard of Kialeh, the Reaver, and beside him his lieutenant Samar. Corpses littered the floor.

"Ho!" roared the Reaver, as he caught sight of the newcomers. "You come in time! In time—to die with us!"

CHAPTER V

CURSED BE THE CITY

GRIM LAUGHTER touched Raynor's lips. He drove in, sheathing his sword in a brawny throat, whipped it out, steel singing. Nor were Eblik and Delphia far behind. Her blade and the Nubian's ax wreaked deadly havoc among Cyaxares' soldiers, who, not expecting attack from the rear, were confused.

The hall became filled with a milling, yelling throng, from which one soldier, a burly giant, emerged, shouting down the others.

"Cut them down! They're but three!"

Then all semblance of sanity was lost in a blaze of crimson battle, swinging brands, and huge maces that crashed down, splitting skulls and spattering gray brain-stuff. Delphia kept shoulder to shoulder with Raynor, seemingly heedless of danger, her blade flickering wasplike through the air. And the prince guarded her as best he could, the sword weaving a bright maze of deadly lightnings as it whirled.

The Reaver swung, and his sword crushed a helm and bit deep into bone. He strained to tug it free—and a soldier thrust up at his throat. Samar deflected the blade with his own weapon, and that cost him his life. In that moment of inattention a driven spear smashed through corselet and jerkin and drank deep of the man's life-blood.

Silent, he fell.

The Reaver went beserk. Yelling, he sprang over his lieutenant's corpse and swung. For a few moments he held back his enemies—and then someone flung a shield. Instinctively Kialeh lifted his blade to parry.

The wolves leaped in for the kill.

Roaring, the Reaver went down, blood gushing through his shaggy beard, staining its iron-gray with red. When Raynor had time to look again, Kialeh lay a corpse on his own hearth, his head amid bright jewels that had spilled from the overturned treasure-chest.

The three stood together now, the last of the defenders—Raynor and Eblik and Delphia. The soldiers ringed them, panting for their death, yet hesitating before the menace of cold steel. None wished to be the first to die.

And, as they waited, a little silence fell. The prince heard a sound he remembered.

Dim and far away, a low roaring drifted to his ears. And the eerie shrilling of pipes. . . .

It grew louder. The soldiers heard it now. They glanced at one another askance. There was something about that sound that chilled the blood.

It swelled to a gleeful shouting, filling all the castle. A breeze blew through the hall, tugging with elfin fingers at sweat-moist skin. It rose to a gusty blast.

In its murmur voices whispered.

"Evohe! Evohe!"

They grew louder, mad and unchecked. They exulted.

"Pan, Pan is free!"

"Gods!" a soldier cursed. "What devil's work is this?" He swung about, sword ready.

The curtains of samite were ripped away by the shrieking wind. Deafeningly the voices exulted:

"Pan is free!"

The piping shrilled out. There came the clatter of ringing little hoofs. The castle rocked and shuddered.

Some vague, indefinable impulse made Raynor snatch at his belt, gripping the sun-god's talisman in bronzed fingers. From it a grateful warmth seemed to flow into his flesh—and the roaring faded.

He dragged Delphia and the Nubian behind him. "Close to me! Stay close!"

The room was darkening. No—it seemed as though a cloudy veil of mist dropped before the three, guarding them. Raynor lifted the seal of Ahmon.

The fog-veils swirled. Dimly through them Raynor could see the soldiers moving swiftly, frantically, like rats caught in a trap. He tightened one arm about Delphia's steel-armored waste.

Suddenly the hall was ice-cold. The castle shook as though gripped by Titan hands. The floor swayed beneath the prince's feet.

The mists darkened. Through rifts he saw half-guessed figures that leaped and bounded . . . . heard elfin hoofs clicking. Horned and shaggy-furred beings that cried jubilantly as they danced to the pipes of Pan. . . .

Faun and dryad and satyr swung in a mad saraband beyond the shrouding mists. Faintly there came the screaming of men, half drowned in the loud shrilling.

"Evohe!" the demoniac roar thundered. "Evohe! All hail, O Pan!"

With a queer certainty Raynor knew that it was time to leave the castle—and swiftly. Already the great stone structure was shaking like a tree in a hurricane. With a word to his companions he stepped forward hesitantly, the talisman held high.

The walls of mist moved with him. Outside the fog-walls the monstrous figures gamboled. But the soldiers of Cyaxares screamed no more.

Through a castle toppling into ruin the three sped, into the courtyard, across the drawbridge, and down the face of the Rock. Nor did they pause till they were safely in the broad plain of the valley.

"The castle!" Eblik barked. pointing. "See? It falls."

And it was true. Down it came thundering, while clouds of ruin spurted up. Then there was only a shattered wreck on the summit of the Rock. . . .

Delphia caught her breath in a little sob. She murmured, "The end of the Reavers for all time. I—I lived in the castle for more than twenty years. And now it's gone like a puff of dust before the wind."

The walls of fog had vanished. Raynor returned the talisman to his belt. Eblik, staring up at the Rock, swallowed uneasily.

"Well, what now?" he asked.

"Back along the way we came," the prince said. "It's the only way out of this wilderness that I know of."

The girl nodded. "Yes. Beyond the mountains lie deserts, save toward Sardopolis. But we have no mounts."

"Then we'll walk," Eblik observed, but Raynor caught his arm and pointed.

"There! Horses—probably stampeded from the castle. And—Shaitan! There's my gray charger. Good!"

So, presently, the three rode toward Sardopolis, conscious of a weird dim throbbing that seemed to pulse in the air all about them.

At dawn they topped a ridge and saw before them the plain. All three reined in their mounts, staring. Beneath them lay the city—but changed!

It was a ruin.

Doom had come to Sardopolis in the night. The mighty towers and battlements had fallen, and huge gaps were opened in the walls. Of the king's palace nothing was left but a single tower, from which, ironically, the wyvern banner flew. As they watched, that pinnacle, too, swayed and tottered and fell, and the scarlet wyvern drifted down into the dust of Sardopolis.

On fallen towers and peristyles distant figures moved, with odd, ungainly boundings. Quickly Raynor turned his eyes away. But he could not shut his ears to the distant crying of pipes, gay and pagan, yet with a faintly mournful undertone.

"Pan has returned to his first altar," Delphia said quietly. "We had best not loiter here."

"By all hell, I agree," the Nubian grunted, digging his heels into his steed's flanks. "Where now, Raynor?"

"Westward, I think, to the Sea of Shadows. There are cities on its shore, and galleys to take us to haven. Unless—" He turned questioning eyes on Delphia.

She laughed, a little bitterly. "I cannot stay here. The land is sunk back into the pit. Pan rules. I go with you."

The three rode to the west. They skirted, but did not enter, a small grove where a man lay in agony. It was Cyaxares, a figure so dreadfully mangled that only sheer will kept him alive. His face was a bloody mask. The once-rich garments were tattered and filthy. He saw the three riders, and raised his voice in a weak cry which the wind drowned.

Beside the king a slim, youthful figure lounged, leaning idly against an oak-trunk. It was Necho.

"Call louder, Cyaxares," he said. "With a horse under you, you can reach the Sea of Shadows. And if you succeed in doing that, you will yet live for many years."

Again the king cried out. The wind took his voice and shredded it to impotent fragments.

Necho laughed softly. "Too late, now. They are gone."

Cyaxares let his battered head drop, his beard trailing in the dirt. Through shredded lips he muttered, "If I reach the Sea of Shadows . . . I live."

"True. But if you do not, you die. And then—" Low laughter shook the other.

Groaning, the king dragged himself forward. Necho followed.

"A good horse can reach the Sea of Shadows in three days. If you walk swiftly, you may reach it in six. But you best hurry. Why do you not rise, my Cyaxares?"

The king spat out bitter oaths. In agony he pulled himself forward, leaving a trail of blood on the grass . . . blood that dripped unceasingly from the twin raw stumps just above his ankles.

"The stone that fell upon you was sharp. Cyaxares, was it not?" Necho mocked. "But hurry! You have little time. There are mountains to climb and rivers to cross. . . ."

So, in the trail of Raynor and Eblik and Delphia, crept the dying king, hearing fainter and ever fainter the triumphant pipes of Pan from Sardopolis. And presently, patient as the silent Necho, a vulture dipped against the blue and took up the pursuit, the beat of its wings distinctly audible in the heavy, stagnant silence. . . .

And Raynor and Delphia and Eblik rode onward toward the sea. . . .

Logoda's Heads

AUGUST DERLETH

Were it not for the efforts of August Derleth, many authors represented in this book would not be as well known as they are. Derleth foresaw the value of preserving the work of his colleagues between book covers, and, in 1939, he founded Arkham House, a specialty press for fantasy and science fiction that is still publishing today. As fate would have it, Arkham House collections of the stories of H. P. Lovecraft, Frank Belknap Long, Robert Bloch, Clark Ashton Smith, and other pulp authors are now more sought after than the hundreds of fantasy and horror stories written by Derleth himself. Admittedly, many of Derleth's tales were routine pulp fiction that served to fill up the back pages of magazines, but "Logoda's Heads," published in the April 1939 issue of Strange Tales, *shows that now and then he was capable of producing a story with bite.*

A LL RIGHT, here we are," said Major Crosby, halting. He glanced briefly at the four men who formed his bodyguard, and then turned to young Henley.

"Now, Henley," he said, "I don't want any interruption from you. I'm going to handle this thing myself, understand? You know how much influence these native witch-doctors have, and it's no go angering them needlessly. And Logoda's a bad one—he and his filthy heads."

Henley flushed beneath his bronze. "One of those heads may be all that's left of my brother," he said shortly.

"Logoda knows too much to bother an Englishman," returned the major.

"My brother knew his magic. He knew too much of his magic," said Henley, staring through the bushes toward the squat hut of the witch-doctor, Logoda.

"Well, for God's sake, don't start anything."

The major started forward, but Henley caught his arm.

"Wait, Major," he said.

"What is it?" Crosby snapped.

"Talk to him in his own language," said Henley.

"I haven't mastered the native tongue yet," returned the major crossly.

"I didn't mean that," said Henley significantly.

"Oh," said the major, startled for a moment. Then he shook his head moodily and strode on across the clearing, with Henley at his heels.

A few natives scattered warily as they came on, leaving the door to Logoda's hut clear. There was a collection of trophies about the entrance; some of them were not pleasant to look at. Major Crosby reflected briefly upon England's inability to stamp out certain practices. Then he turned and curtly ordered his men to stay outside.

Major Crosby lifted the matted doorway and went inside, followed by Henley. It took them a minute to get used to the darkness. Then he saw Logoda—the ugly, stained heads dried and strung along on poles above the witch-doctor's head.

Major Crosby had been in the hut once before, not so very long ago. There were ten heads then; now there were eleven. The additional one, in the light of Bob Henley's disappearance, made him uneasy.

Logoda, an ungainly hulking man, sat on his haunches in a corner. He wore an odd head-dress, apparently hastily put on at the intimation of visitors, but apart from this and a few streaks of none too fresh paint, he looked very little different from his fellow natives. Yet the man was a very tangible and irritating power to the English stationed at the nearby post.

"Logoda, a white man is missing," said the major, coming directly to the point of his visit. "He was known to have come in your direction. A week ago, seven days. Seven times the sun he came this way. Where is he?"

"No white man," said Logoda serenely.

He moved the upper half of his body slightly forward, so that his outflung arms came to rest on palms pressed flat against the ground. "No white man," he said again.

"Logoda," Crosby replied sternly, "many men will come to search.

They will burn your village, they will put you in a room with many bars."

Surprisingly, Henley interrupted. "You're wasting our time, Major. I told you to talk to him in his own language. Will you let me talk to him?"

"No," snapped the major angrily. "I'm convinced you're needlessly worried. We've no actual proof that your brother's dead, and there's—"

Once again Henley interrupted him "I'm going to look at those heads," he said, and before Crosby could stop him, he stepped forward.

Instantly Logoda pointed furiously at Henley and shouted, "You go 'way!"

But Henley paid no attention. He stood under the dried heads, gazing at them imperturbably mid Logoda's furious mouthings and Major Crosby's nervous scrutiny.

Suddenly Henley caught his breath, and expelled it again with a sharp, hissing sound.

"Bob!" he muttered.

Major Crosby expostulated. "Now, look here, Henley—Logoda's not had time to dry a head. Only a week, hardly that."

Henley looked at him. "You are too new here, Major Crosby," he said. "I know how quickly they can dry them."

There was something about Henley's cold stare that stayed Crosby's angry words on his lips.

Abruptly Logoda crossed his hands before his face, bowed his head quickly to the ground, and turned toward the dried heads, flinging out his arms as if in entreaty to them, his palms turned upward toward them. From his mouth issued a stream of weird gibberings.

"He is talking to the heads," said Henley softly. "Do not be surprised if they answer."

"You don't actually believe in this tomfoolery, Henley?" demanded the major incredulously.

"Yes," said Henley simply. "I do. Bob and I have studied it a long time. There is more in it than you think."

Logoda's gibbering quickly ceased. For a moment there was complete silence. The major was about to stalk out, disgusted—

Then there sounded, as if from far away, a shrill, strange tittering— it grew—it mounted—until it sounded all about them . . . and then it subsided into a subdued whispering, which was gradually lost in silence again.

Above them, Logoda's heads were swaying back and forth, though no one had touched them.

"Good God," whispered the major.

"Major," said Henley in a strong voice, "will you take Logoda out of the hut for a minute or two. I want to be alone here."

Logoda sat smiling to himself, his eyes half-closed, rocking back and forth a little, like a drowsy joss.

"But I thought you promised—," stammered the major.

"Nothing will be disturbed, I promise you. Logoda will have no cause for complaint."

"But then why must he go out?" The major's skepticism was shaken and he was trying not to show it.

"Will you do me this favor, Major? I will not bother you again, on my honor. I want to talk to Logoda's heads, and I do not want him to hear what I say to them."

The simplicity with which this request was uttered was in strange contrast to the weirdness of its content.

The major swallowed with some difficulty and asked in a thick voice, "Will you go after that?"

"Yes, I'll go then," replied Henley.

"Very well."

The major stepped to the doorway and signalled to two of his men, knowing they would be needed to move Logoda, who would certainly not go of his own volition. Despite his furious protests, Logoda was dragged to the doorway, where he rose and walked, so that his natives might not see this indignity being visited on him.

Henley was left alone in the hut, and his whispering voice drifted eerily to Major Crosby and his men, who looked questioningly at each other. Henley was speaking in a native tongue.

Only a few minutes elapsed. Then Henley stepped from the hut, his eyes glittering strangely, and Logoda, after glaring at him in murderous fury, entered his home again. "I'm ready now, Major," said Henley.

"Very well," said the major in a low voice.

The five men made their long way back to the English post, where they arrived just in time for supper.

For a long time Henley and the major did not speak to each other, but over coffee at last, Henley spoke.

"How much would you people give to be rid of Logoda?" he asked softly.

Major Crosby was startled, but resolved not to show it. "A good deal, I think. But if you're planning to go back there to get him, stop now. We could have potted him a long time ago, but for an Englishman to be seen anywhere around when a witch-doctor dies suspiciously is certain to cause an insurrection—and a nasty one."

"Will you guarantee me passage to the coast?" pursued Henley.

"I told you it was impossible, Henley. I need all my men here, anyway."

"I didn't mean protection—I meant money. I have money waiting for me in Cairo—but that's a hellish long way off. I want to get there, and I haven't enough money."

"Oh," said the major, softening. "I had no idea. Well, you don't have to earn it," he went on, smiling now. "I'm glad to be able to help you out."

"And get rid of me," murmured Henley, smiling, too. "But there's one more favor I want to ask of you before I leave."

"I want you to tie me to my cot tonight, and set a guard over me," said Henley grimly.

"What an extraordinary request!" exclaimed Major Crosby.

"Nevertheless an earnestly meant one. Will you, Major?"

"Well . . . if you insist. And will you go then, in the morning?"

"Yes."

"I feel very odd about this," said the major some hours later, as he sat beside the cot to which Henley had been tied.

"You needn't," said Henley shortly. "I'm just protecting myself. Logoda's afraid of me. He isn't afraid of you, if you'll forgive my saying it. He knows I know too much. Bob did, too, and Bob's a dried head now. I have decided I don't want to die, and there are so many ways of bringing about my death for a man like Logoda. He could call me, and I would have to follow. Or he could come himself—maybe a little white dog, or a snake—almost anything. That's the why of all this, you see."

"Really, Henley," said the major somewhat stiffly, "you're talking like the most impossible madman. I find it difficult to believe that you're the same man who has been so sane in my company the previous weeks."

"Yes, I understand that," said Henley. "I know how you feel. I am sorry to disturb the waters like that. Most of us like them smooth. But there *are* things like this, and they *do* happen. Bob and I have studied them too long to deny them. You don't have to believe them—you'd probably be better off without knowing anything about them."

"Who made the laughter this afternoon, and who made those heads sway like that?" asked the major curiously, and obviously against his will.

"I told you—Logoda spoke to them, and they answered."

"That's not telling me a thing," replied the major.

"Perhaps not. That's the only answer, though. Now—forgive me—I've got a long journey ahead of me, and I've got to get some sleep."

In the morning Henley awoke to find the major bending over him, untying the ropes that bound him.

"Good morning," Henley said. "Hope you slept well."

"Thanks," said the major, smiling. "I didn't."

"Did anyone call for me in the night?" asked Henley, his voice grim.

"No one. I watched for dogs and snakes and things, and even considered potting a couple of birds that got lost in the clearing."

"Good old major. Thanks. I think it was too late for Logoda to send for me."

"I suppose you'll be leaving directly after breakfast?" asked the major then.

"I am expecting a message—and as soon as it comes, I'll be on my way."

"From whom?" asked Major Crosby bluntly.

"That I can't say. But you have scouts out, haven't you?"

"Of course," said Crosby shortly. Henley smiled.

They were at breakfast when one of the major's scouts came dodging out into the clearing. He was excited and breathless from the exertion of running.

"There's my message, I think," said Henley calmly. "How about my passage money, Major?"

The scout came up to them. "Logoda's dead," he said jerkily. "He's been killed!"

"Killed!" echoed the major. "Good God! I hope there weren't any Englishmen around. How'd it happen?"

"The natives say his magic killed him. It's a queer business, sir. His guards didn't see anyone enter the hut or anyone come out. They heard Logoda talking to his heads and they heard the heads answer. Then they heard him cough once or twice, and finally he slept. That was all. This morning he was found in his hut with his throat torn out— terribly mutilated, cut and torn as by thousands of rats."

"Go back and find out whatever else you can," ordered Major Crosby.

The scout disappeared at once into the jungle.

Crosby turned to Henley. "You were on the bed all night, Henley. I know. And you guessed Logoda would be killed. Who did it?" the question came angrily.

"I did," said Henley simply.

Major Crosby flushed. "Nonsense," he snapped.

Henley stood up, smiling. Yet his voice was grim.

"I told you it wasn't good to know about forbidden things. But I'll tell you. You heard Logoda and those heads and you will recall my insistence on being left alone with them. Logoda knew how to make them talk and sway back and forth. *I knew how to make them rend and tear!*"

Miracle in Three Dimensions

C. L. MOORE

Movies, like the pulp magazines, were important diversions during the Depression years—a form of entertainment that allowed people to put aside the concerns of daily life and lose themselves in someone else's adventures. C. L. Moore clearly was intrigued by the technological magic that Hollywood used to transport the filmgoer into its illusory worlds when she wrote "Miracle in Three Dimensions" for the April 1939 issue of Strange Stories. *Curiously enough, the same year that Moore's story was published saw the release of* The Wizard of Oz, Gone with the Wind, The Grapes of Wrath *and so many other film classics, that most experts consider it the greatest year ever in motion picture history—probably just a coincidence.*

I'VE GOT it, Abe! It's as near to life itself as the movies will ever come. I've done it!" Blair O'Byrne's haunted black eyes were bright with triumph.

Abe Silvers, gaunt and dark and weary-eyed, shifted the cigar to the other side of his mouth and stepped in under the doorway that made sharp division between the glare of California sunlight outside and the lofty shadows of O'Byrne's long, dim studio.

"I hope you're right," he said around the cigar. "I've waited a long time for it. And God knows you've spent more years than you ought, and more money than even you could afford. Why have you done it, Blair? A man with your money, your background, shutting yourself up here in the dark, sweating over shadows?"

"I haven't been shut up away from life—I've been shut in with it!" O'Byrne's smile spread across the pallor of his delicate face. "It's life itself I've been groping after all these years, and I've found it, Abe. I've got it!"

"Got the illusion of it, maybe. A little better than Metro-Cosmic has been filming for the last few years. And if it's as good as you say we'll buy it—and so what?"

O'Byrne turned to him fiercely, his dream-haunted eyes suddenly blazing.

"I tell you this *is* life! As near as shadows can come—too near, perhaps. 'Moving pictures'! They'll have to find a new name for what I've got. It isn't pictures—it's breathing, living reality. I've worked over it until nothing else seemed to matter, nothing else seemed real. I've got it, Abe. It's—life."

Abe Silvers shifted the cigar back across his mouth, and if his eyes were understanding, his voice was only patient. He had heard such words before, from many fiercely sincere inventors. That he had known O'Byrne for many years did not alter his accustomed attitude toward such things.

"All right," he murmured. "Show me. Where's the projection room, Blair?"

"Here." O'Byrne waved a thin, unsteady hand toward the center of the big studio where under a battery of high-hung lights a U-shaped bar of dull silver rose from a low platform to the height of a man's waist. Beyond it against the wall bulked a big rectangular arrangement of chromium and glass, behind whose face bulbs were dimly visible. Silvers snorted.

"There? That thing looks like a radio—that doubled-over pipe? But the screen, man—the seats—the—"

"I'm telling you this is utterly new, Abe. You'll have to clear your mind of all your preconceived ideas of what a moving picture should be. All that is obsolete, from this minute on. The 'moving picture' is as dead as the magic lantern. This is the new thing. These batteries of lights, that 'radio' as you call it, the platform and bar, one for each individual spectator—"

"But what is it? What happens?"

"I can't explain it to you now," said O'Byrne impatiently. "For one thing, you wouldn't believe me until after you've seen it. And it would take weeks to give you enough ground-work to understand the principles. The thing's too complex for anyone to explain in words. I can't even explain the appearance except in metaphors—there's never been anything like it before.

"Roughly, though, it's the projection of the illusion of life on a three-dimensional screen composed of fogged light. Other men are just beginning to fumble around with the principles of three-dimensional movies projected on a flat screen, giving the appearance of a stage with depth. That's going at it clumsily. I've approached the problem from a much newer angle. My screen itself is three-dimensional—the light that bathes you when the batteries of arcs are on. You're in the midst of it, the action is projected on the light all around you from double films taken from slightly different angles, on the stereoscopic principle. I'll show you later.

"And there is in that bar you're to hold on to, sufficient current to stimulate very selectively the nerves which carry tactile impression to the brain. You'll feel, as well as hear and see. You'll even smell. On occasion you may actually taste—it's close enough to the sensations of smelling to work out. Only that doesn't figure so much in this case, for you as a spectator will not enter into the action. You'll simply witness it from closer quarters than any audience has ever dreamed of doing before.

"Here, step up on the platform and take hold of the rod there, at the curve. That's it. Now hold tight, and don't be surprised. Remember, nothing like this has ever been done before. Ready?"

Abruptly the great banks of lights blazed into radiance that closed the dazzled Silvers about in soft, pouring brightness. There was a quality of mistiness about it that made even his own hands invisible before him on the bar. It was as if the light poured upon innumerable motes in the air, so refracting from their infinitesimal surfaces that nothing was visible but that shimmer of bright blindness. Silvers gripped the bar and waited.

Through the bright fog a voice as smooth as cream spoke in vast, clear echoes, rolling in from all around him at once, filling the little artificial world of mist wherein he stood lost. Mellowly the deep tones said:

"You are about to enter an enchanted wood outside Athens on a midsummer night, to share in a dream that Shakespeare dreamed over three hundred years ago. Titania, Queen of Faeryland, will be played by Anne Acton. Oberon, the King, is Philip Graves—"

Abe Silvers clutched the bar in amazement as that unctuous voice rolled on. Anne Acton and Philip Graves were under contract to his own Metro-Cosmic, and every one of the other names were stars of the first magnitude. The greatest actors of the day were playing in this incredible fragment of a Midsummer Night's Dream. What it had cost O'Byrne he shuddered to think.

The creamy voice died away. The mist began to clear. Silvers' hands closed hard on the bar and he stared in blankest incredulity about the dim blue glades of forest stretching around him, silvery in the light of a high-riding moon. A breeze whispered through the leaves, blowing cool on his face. Save that it did not stir a hair of his head he could have believed it an actual breeze sighing through the moonlit dark.

He looked down. He was himself invisible, disembodied, no longer standing on a bare floor but in the midst of a flowering meadow whose grasses were faintly fragrant at his feet. There was no flicker, no visible light-and-shadow composition of the projection upon this incredible three-dimensional screen that surrounded him. The glade stretched away into actual distances much deeper than the studio's walls could possible contain; the illusion of deep, starry sky overhead was perfect; the flowers in the grass were so real he thought he could have knelt and gathered them in his hands.

Then, under the trees, the mists parted like a curtain and the Queen of Faeryland came splendidly into the moonlit glade. Anne Acton had never looked so lovely. The long veil of her silver-pale hair streamed like gossamer behind her, and every curve and shadowy roundness was as real as life itself. Yet there hovered about her a hint of unreality, so that she blended perfectly the illusion of fantasy and reality as she moved over the unbending grass, the bright wings streaming from her shoulders.

There was a blast of silvery challenge from elfin horns and into the moonlight strode Oberon, his lean features wrathful. The famous deep tones of Philip Graves resounded angrily through the moonlight. Titania answered in silvery defiance.

Then came full, rich human voices ringing through the wood. Phoebe Templeton in Hernia's rustling satin came radiantly into the glade, brushing so close by the watching Silvers that he caught a whiff of her perfume, felt the touch of her satin skirts. And he knew—almost he *knew*—that he could put out a hand and stop her, so warmly real was she at that close range. Her lovely throaty voice called to Lysander behind her.

And then somehow the forest was slipping away past Abe Silvers' face—somehow he had the illusion of walking as if in a dream down an enchanted forest aisle, the dim air quivering with starlight, and Helena came running and weeping through the trees, stumbling, sobbing the name of Demetrius.

She passed. Silvers started involuntarily as from a swaying branch above him pealed the wild, half-human laughter of Puck, delicate as the chatter of a squirrel, and down through the air over his very shoulder, the breeze of his passing fanning Silvers' face, the lithe little goblin sprang.

The scene clouded over as if a mist had been drawn across the moon. Silvers blinked involuntarily, and when he looked again Titania lay exquisitely asleep on the dew-spangled bank where the wild thyme grew.

Then through the magic-haunted wood suddenly shrilled a bell. Insistently, metallically it rang. Silvers glanced about the glades of the forest, trying to locate among the dew-shimmering leaves the source of that irritating noise. And suddenly the Athenian woods melted like smoke about him. Incredulously he stared around a big bare studio. It was like waking in bewilderment from a dream so vivid that reality itself paled beside its memory.

"The studio wants you on the telephone, Abe," said O'Byrne's voice. "Here, wake up! Didn't you hear the bell?"

Silvers shook himself, laughed sheepishly.

"I'm still in Athens," he admitted, blinking. "That's the damnedest thing I ever—studio, did you say? Where's the phone?"

Thinly over the wire came a worried voice.

"Hate to bother you, chief, but I think you ought to know. Anne Acton's been mumbling around in a sort of daze for half an hour. The doctor can't do a thing with her. And Philip Graves passed out on set and is just kind of whispering to himself—poetry, it sounds like."

Silvers blinked. "D-don't let the papers get it. I'll be right over."

He slammed the telephone back on its cradle and turned blankly to O'Byrne.

"Something's gone wrong with a couple of our actors you stole," he said. "I've got to get back right away. But listen, Blair—you've got something! How long will it take you to have some more of these bar and platform arrangements rigged up? Say a dozen for a starter. I'd like to have our board see it as soon as possible. This is going to be the most tremendous thing that ever happened in motion pictures. When can you have things ready to show the board?"

"I—I don't know, Abe. Somehow—I'm a little afraid of it."

"Afraid? Good God, man, what do you mean?"

"I don't know, exactly—but did you have a feeling, as you watched the action, that somehow it came—too near—to life?"

"Blair—I'm afraid you've been working too hard on this. Let me handle it from now on, will you? And stop thinking about it. I've got to get back to the studio now and see what's happened to my actors— attack of temperament, probably—but I'll see you tonight about quantity production. Until then, you won't let anyone else in on this, will you?"

"You know I won't, Abe. It's yours if you want it."

All the way back to the studio Silvers' mind was spinning with the magnitude of what lay before him. He had dared to let the inventor know how enormously impressed he was, how anxious to have the new process, because he knew O'Byrne so well. The man was wealthy in his own right, indifferent to fame, to everything but the deep need to create which had driven him so hard for so many years toward the completion of his miracle. Miracle in three dimension! It seemed like a dream, what he had just seen, but behind it lay the prospect for a fortune vaster than any movie magnate had ever dared to hope for. To control this was to control the whole world. Silvers clenched his cigar tighter and dreamed magnificent dreams.

Anne Acton lay on a low couch in her lavish little dressing bungalow, staring up with conscious pathos into the doctor's face as Silvers came into the room. Somehow, illogically, it was a shock to him to see her here when he had so short a time before left that perfect illusion of herself in the enchanted wood outside Athens, asleep on the bank of wild thyme.

"How are you, Anne?" he demanded anxiously, for she represented a fabulous sum to the company and an illness now, in the midst of her latest picture, would be ruinous. "Is she all right, Doc? When did she come out of it?"

"While they were phoning you, Abe," said Acton herself in a faint, pathetic voice, moving her head uneasily so that the great slipping rope of silver-pale hair moved across the brocade. "It—it was all so queer. Suddenly I felt too tired to move, as if all the strength had drained right out of me. And I must have fainted, but I wasn't really out. Kept having sort of dreams—I don't remember now—woods, somewhere, and music. And suddenly it all ended and I opened my eyes here. I'm all right now, only I feel as weak as a kitten. Look." She held up an exquisite hand to show it quivering.

"What is it, Doc?" demanded Silvers anxiously.

"Um-m-m—overwork, perhaps, general exhaustion—it's impossible to say definitely without further examination."

"Will she be okay now?"

"I see no reason why, with rest and care, she shouldn't be."

"I'll send for your car, Anne," said Silvers authoritatively. "You're going home to bed. I'll see you later."

Philip Graves, in the braid-bedecked finery of a movie caballero, was sitting up on his couch and holding a cigarette in unsteady fingers when Silvers pushed through the little knot of attendants that surrounded him.

"Feeling better, Phil?" he demanded. "What was it?"

"Nothing—nothing," said the actor impatiently. "I'm okay now. Just passed out for a few minutes. I'll be all right."

Abe Silvers lost no time in calling a meeting of the board. The twelve members of Metro-Cosmic stood about in twos and threes, murmuring incredulously in the shadows of the O'Byrne studio on the night when the first dozen bar-platforms were erected. Silvers had not dared to describe fully this modern miracle.

"It's like nothing you ever saw before," he warned them as rather sheepishly they allowed themselves to be herded forward to the platforms. When they were all at their stations and Silvers signaled O'Byrne to begin, he glanced once around the little company before the lights blazed on. Doubtfully they returned his stare with a murmur or two of protest rising.

"Feel so damn silly," an official said, "standing here. Mean to say there isn't any screen? What are we supposed to look at?"

And then like a wall of brilliant blindness the foggy light closed down upon them and every man was cut off from his fellows so that he stood alone and disembodied in the heart of that soft, misty blaze. Startled exclamations sounded through the mist, murmurs that died away as Silvers heard for the second time the creamy smoothness of the announcer's voice rolling through the dimming brightness.

"You are now about to enter an enchanted wood outside Athens on a midsummer night, to share in a dream that Shakespeare dreamed. . . ."

Somehow, as the play went on, Abe Silvers began to wonder a little uneasily at the violence of the quarrel between Titania and Oberon that flamed almost tangibly through the clear dim air. Had they fought before so fiercely? Had they—

A gibber of wild inhuman laughter, the long leap of Puck over his shoulder, broke the queer thought half-formed, just as a bell began to shrill through the forest. He knew a moment of unreality. He remembered that in the previous performance the bell had not rung until Titania lay down to sleep on the bank where the wild thyme grew. But with shocking completeness the forest vanished. Silvers stared blankly around the studio's reaches that had so suddenly replaced the glades of faeryland, blinking at the circle of dazed men in amazement.

"Telephone for you, Abe," O'Byrne's voice called through the fading mists of the dream that had so strongly gripped him. He grinned sheepishly and stepped down from the platform.

"Listen, chief," babbled a distressed voice over the wire, shrill above the rising babble of delight behind Silvers, "Acton's out like a light at the Grove!"

"Is she plastered?"

"I don't think so—but try to tell the papers that! She—wait—oh, she's just coming out of it. What'll we do?"

"Send her home," sighed Silvers. "I'll get onto the papers right away. What a life!"

He turned back to O'Byrne with a shrug. "Acton's passed out again," he murmured unhappily. "I wonder if she—well, if she folds now in the middle of 'Never Tomorrow' we'll lose our shirts on it. I'm going to get a doctor to—"

"Abe," said O'Byrne in a voice so quiet that the other man turned to him in surprise. "Abe, do you realize that every time we run this picture Anne Acton faints? I wonder if the other actors feel the same reaction?"

"Why—what do you mean? Why should they? Blair, are you going crazy?"

Silvers' voice was stoutly confident, but despite himself an uneasy little flicker woke in his mind. Philip Graves, who played Oberon, had been dazed and out of his head too that other time. And—yes, hadn't he noticed an item in a gossip column saying that Phoebe Templeton had collapsed at a tea in New York? Was it the same day? Rather terrifyingly, he thought it was. But of course all this was the most flagrant nonsense. His job now was to keep Acton out of the papers. She had not endeared herself to reporters, and he knew they would make the story sound as bad as possible. They—the phone rang again.

"A wire from Philip Graves' man has just come in, Abe," his wife's voice told him worriedly. "Philip's been taken terribly sick on shipboard. His man says it will be in all the papers tomorrow, and he wants your advice."

Silvers ran a hand distractedly through his hair. "Thanks," he said a little blankly. "I'll take care of it. Be home later."

He turned to the men still grouped around the bar-platforms in their babble of amazed delight. They had not heard his low-voiced conversations at the desk.

"We've got this fellow under contract, haven't we?" said someone anxiously at his elbow. "Ought to get going on production right away. This is the most tremendous thing that ever happened."

"Yes—he'll let us have it," Silvers told him abstractedly. "Blair, how's the production on the first hundred bar-platforms coming? We've got to give a larger showing right away."

"A hundred and fifty will be ready in about a week," O'Byrne admitted reluctantly. "But Abe—Abe, do you think we ought to do it?"

Silvers pulled him aside. "Look, Blair," he said gently, "you mustn't let your imagination run away with you. What possible connection can there be between the showing of this picture and the fact that a few overworked, nervous people have fainting spells? I'll admit it's a coincidence, but we've got to be sensible. We can't let the biggest thing that ever happened in pictures slip through our fingers just because some dizzy actress passes out once or twice."

O'Byrne shrugged a little. "I wonder," he murmured, as if thinking aloud, "how long people have been trying to create life? Something's always prevented it—no one's been allowed to succeed. This thing of mine isn't life, but it's too near it to leave me at peace with myself. I think there's a penalty for usurping the powers of godhead—for coming too close to success. I'm afraid, Abe."

"Blair, will you do me a favor?" demanded Silvers. "Will you go to bed and forget all about this until morning? I'll see you tomorrow. Right now I'm up to my neck in trouble."

O'Byrne smiled ghostily. "All right," he said. . . .

TEMPLETON-FREDERICKS
ELOPEMENT!

That was the headline the newsboys were yelling when Silvers stepped out of his car the next day. He looked twice at the headline to be sure, for the romance of Phoebe Templeton, not with Bill Fredericks but with Manfield Drake, had kept screen magazines in ecstasies for the past six months. The wedding was to have been this week, but—he bought a paper hastily, a wild thought flashing through his mind. Templeton and Fredericks had played the *lovers* in O'Byrne's photoplay!

"Bill and I have known one another for about six months," Phoebe Templeton was quoted as saying, "but we never realized until last night how much we meant to each other. It happened rather miraculously. I was on my way west and Bill was here in Hollywood. And suddenly in Denver it came over me that I simply must talk to him. I phoned long distance and—well, it's all pretty hazy to look back on, but I chartered a plane and met him in Yuma, and we were married this morning. Of course I feel badly about Manfield, but really, this was too big to fight against. We've known since ten o'clock last night that we were meant for each other."

Silvers tucked the paper under his arm and bit down hard on his cigar. It was at ten last night that they had watched Hermia and Lysander, in the actual, breathing presences of Templeton and Fredericks, murmuring passionate love under a high-floating moon. For a moment a fantastic wonder crossed his mind. "I must be going nuts," he murmured to himself.

A week later an audience of a hundred and fifty people gathered for the real preview of O'Byrne's "Midsummer Night's Dream." The bar-platforms had been set up in the big studio that had seen the first running of the miraculous illusion. It was crowded now with murmurous and skeptical people—officers and directors of Metro-Cosmic, a sprinkling of wives. Silvers conquered an inexplicable uneasiness as he sought O'Byrne in a corner near the controls. Blair was sitting on a heavy stool before the machine, and the face he turned to his friend was full of a queer, strained tension. He said, his voice a thread of sound:

"Abe—I've had the maddest notion that every time I show this the figures come back realer than before into the scenes they play. Maybe they don't always hold to the action we photographed—maybe the plot carries them on beyond what Shakespeare wrote—more violently than—"

Silvers' fingers gripped the other man's shoulders hard. Sharply he shook him, an absurd uneasiness darkening his memory of that impression of fiercer violence in the quarrel between Oberon and Titania the last time he saw the play, even as he said firmly:

"Snap out of it, Blair! You've been working too hard. Maybe someone else could run the picture tonight—you need rest."

O'Byrne looked up at him apathetically, his alarm gone suddenly flat.

"No, I'll do it. If you're really determined to run the thing, maybe I'd better. Maybe I can control them better than an assistant could. After all, I created them. . . ."

Silvers looked down at him for a moment in frowning silence. Then he shrugged and turned toward the last empty bar-platform where the audience waited the beginning of the show. O'Byrne was dangerously overworked, he told himself. After this was over he must go to a sanatorium for a long rest. His mind was cracking. . . .

Misty radiance closed down about him, veiling the hundred and fifty from his vision. There was a moment of murmurous wonder, punctuated by small, half-frightened screams from a few of the women as each spectator was shut off into a little world of silence and solitude.

Into the silvery mist that familiar rich voice rolled smoothly. For the third time Silvers saw the broad gray glades of faeryland, hedged with immemorial forest, opening magically up about him. For the third time Titania trailed her streaming wings into the moonlight. Oberon strode with a jingle of mail from among the trees, and they met in fury halfway down the glade, their feet pressing the bending grass with elfin lightness. But there was no lightness in their anger. That ancient quarrel flared up in violence between them, and the breezes shivered with their wrath.

Again Hermia and Lysander came half laughing, half fearful into the woods. Again Helena sobbed Demetrius' name among the unanswering trees. Puck flitted in goblin glee about his business of enchantment and Titania lay down to sleep on the spangled grass among the wild thyme.

This time no telephone bell broke into the magic of the dream.

And again these were living people who moved so tangibly before the audience, the wind of their passing brushing them, the sound of their breathing in their ears when they stood near, going about their magic-haunted ways as obliviously as if the spectators were the phantoms, not they. Their loves and hates and heartbreak were vividly real under that incredibly real moon.

Once or twice Silvers thought vaguely that here and there in the action things happened not exactly as he remembered them. Had Titania actually slapped Oberon's dark, angry face before she swept out of the glade? Had Hermia and Lysander kissed quite so lingeringly under that deep-shadowed oak? But as the play went on Silvers lost all thought of times that had gone before, and sank fathoms deep in the reality of the scene before him.

Puck lured the spell-bewildered lovers into the fastnesses of the forest.

They went stumbling through the fog, quarreling, blinded by mist and
magic and their own troubled hearts. Swords flashed in the moonlight.
Lysander and Demetrius were fighting among the veiled trees. Puck
laughed, shrill and high and inhuman, and swept his brown arm down.
And from Lysander came a choked gasp, the clatter of a fallen sword.
    Demetrius bent fiercely above him. Silvers watched the bright blood
bubbling from his side, saw the blade drip darkly, smelled the acrid
sharpness of that spreading stain. The illusion was marvelous. Lysander's death was a miracle of artistry from the first choked gasp of
pain to the last bubbling of blood in his throat, the last twist of
handsome silk-sheathed limbs. Lysander's death—
    Something troubled Silvers' memory, but before he could capture it
a woman's voice cried hysterically somewhere in the misty forest, "He's
dead—he's dead!" and suddenly, blankly, the forest was gone from
about them and he was staring into dazed, half-dreaming faces where
an instant before faeryland had stretched depth upon depth of moonlit
dimness, where Lysander had lain dying on the moss. Somewhere in
the crowd a woman was sobbing hysterically.
    "He's dead, I tell you! Lysander's dead, and he doesn't really die in
the play! Someone's killed him! That was real blood—I smelled it! Oh,
get me out of this awful place!"
    Silvers brushed the fog of dreamland from his eyes and was halfway
across the floor to the projection machine before the scream had ended,
for he remembered now that tug of memory as Lysander fell. Shakespeare's play was romance, not tragedy. Lysander should not have died.
    O'Byrne clung to his high stool, his fingers white-knuckled as he
stared into Silvers' eyes.
    "You see?" he said in a strained monotone. "You see what mass
hypnotism will do? They couldn't help it—poor things—they must be
half alive—wandering in the fog. . . ."
    "Blair!" Silvers' voice rang sharply. "Blair, snap out of it! What are
you raving about? Are you mad?"
    The staring eyes turned to his almost apathetically.
    "I was afraid," said O'Byrne, in that whispering monotone as if he
spoke in a dream. "I was afraid to run it before this many people—I
should have guessed what would happen when Acton and Graves
and—"
    "Are you still harping on that coincidence?" demanded Silvers in a
fierce undertone. "Can't you see how foolish it is, Blair? What earthly
connection can there be between pictures on a screen and living people,
some of them half the world away? I'll admit what happened tonight
was—"
    "Did you ever hear—" broke in Blair softly, as if he were following
some private train of thought and had not heeded a word of Silvers'
harangue—"of savages covering their faces when explorers bring out

their cameras? They think a photograph will steal their souls. It's an idea so widespread that it can't have originated in mere local superstition. Tribes all over the world have it. African savages, Tibetan nomads, Chinese peasants, South American Indians. Even the ancient Egyptians, highly civilized as they were, deliberately made their drawings angular and unlifelike. All of them declared and believed that too good a likeness would draw the soul out into the picture."

"Well, yes—everybody's heard of such things—but you're not suggesting—"

"After the Templeton elopement—after Anne Acton's fainting-spells and Philip Graves' illness—yes, after what happened tonight, how can you deny it, Abe? No, the Egyptians, the modern savages, were closer to the truth than we. Only before now no likeness has been perfect enough to absorb sufficient personality so that people could notice it. But these illusions of mine—they're real, living, breathing. While you watch you can't believe the actual men and women aren't standing in front of you.

"It had an effect on Acton and Graves when only you were watching—enough of their personality was drained out of them into the illusion by your own temporary conviction that they were there, so that they went into vague dreams of woodland and music. I don't know how the other actors were affected—I do know that several of them were sick and dizzy that day. I haven't checked—maybe I've been afraid to. . . .

"When the twelve board-members were watching, the drain was stronger; so that Graves was really ill on shipboard and Acton couldn't be roused from her faint until the telephone call to you broke the illusion here. It affected Templeton and Bill Fredericks another way—hypnotized them into believing what the audience was believing, that they were really in love—"

Recollection flooded into Silvers' mind. He remembered what he had felt when he read the headlines of the elopement. He said:

"*Could* it happen that way, Blair? How greatly could a mass mind affect the reactions of the people it concentrates on? I thought of it before—if twelve individuals, each convinced for a time that he saw two people desperately in love, might really work a sort of persuasion on those two—No, that's crazy! It couldn't happen!"

"You saw it happen," murmured Blair quietly. "You saw what happened when a hundred and fifty people joined in that fierce concentration—that utter conviction that they saw a man's sword poised, aimed, descending—mass hypnotism, it was! For a majority of them that sword really struck—their imagination outran the actual fact and they thought they saw Lysander spitted on Demetrius' blade. They thought they saw him die."

"Well, he didn't, did he? I mean, nothing happened this time or they'd have called me."

A thin smile twisted up O'Byrne's strained mouth. He reached behind him. Silvers heard a click and realized that the telephone had been lying out of its cradle on the desk ever since he reached Blair's side.

"I wanted you to understand before they broke the news to you," O'Byrne was explaining gently. "And I knew the telephone would interrupt me unless I—"

Shrill buzzing whirred from the desk. With a little spurt of terror for what he had yet to learn, Silvers snatched it up. A voice shouted thinly in his ear:

"Silvers? Is that you, chief? My God, I've been trying to get you all evening! Acton's been in a coma for over an hour—doctor can't rouse her. And a call just came in from London that Phil Graves is out too—can't be waked! And—what's that? *What?* Chief! Word's just come in that Templeton's passed out too, and Bill Fredericks has dropped dead! What's the matter with this town? It's like the end of the world—"

"Abe—" O'Byrne's voice behind him twisted Silvers around like a hand on his shoulder. The receiver shrilled unnoticed as their eyes met. O'Byrne's face was almost serene—knowledge of what the telephone was crying showed in his eyes. He said:

"Do you believe me now? Do you understand? Do you realize how much of life itself I've woven into this damnable thing I've made? Yes—it's like two-dimensional pictures that carry a shadow of the third—enough dark to give a feeling of depth. In my three-dimensional picture I've somehow got a shadow of the fourth—life, maybe, or something too near it. Maybe that's what the fourth dimension is—life itself. But it won't kill men again—not again!"

The crash of glass shattered into the hysterical buzz of the crowd. Silence like death fell over the confusion of the murmurous throng among the bar-platforms as they turned white faces toward the corner. O'Byrne's frail arms swung his heavy stool with desperate strength, crunching and smashing and crashing among the delicate intricacies of his projector. Silvers clutched the still shrilling telephone and watched him, not moving.

For Fear of Little Men

MANLY WADE WELLMAN

While other writers for the weird fiction pulps summoned the monsters of Gothic horror or conjured unspeakable creatures out of extradimensional protoplasm, Manly Wade Wellman found his inspiration in a rich and underexplored source, regional folklore. As a result, whether he was writing about the antebellum South, the mountains of Appalachia, or the rural towns inhabited by psychic detectives John Thunstone and Judge Keith Pursuivant, Wellman's stories were always notable for a homely simplicity and honesty that contrasted sharply with the purple embellishments of most pulp fiction. In "For Fear of Little Men," which appeared in the June 1939 Strange Stories, *Wellman focuses on the legends of the Chippewa and Sioux Indians.*

> *Up the airy mountain,*
> *Down the rushy glen,*
> *We daren't go a-hunting,*
> *For fear of little men. . . .*
> William Allingham

I

A RUSTLE IN THE GRASS

THE HIAWATHA MEMORIAL, a magnificent colossus, looms on a great hill among Minnesota's ten thousand lakes. It can be seen for miles above the treetops, from any one of three great highways. As soon as you cross its horizon you see it, as though a shout had brought your eyes around. There stands Hiawatha, huge and noble, one hand lifted to rule and bless the land. And you wonder silently how the eye and finger of the sculptor caught such grandeur of pose and spirit.

In the days before the statue was done, the hill might have been called dark, even gloomy. Its sides were clothed in close, rank pine and cedar brush, and rose steeply from a thickly grown forest of mixed evergreen, birch, oak and hemlock. In contrast, the flat acre at the top grew only turf, like a meadow. Here was built a little shack of rough planking, for the sculptor and his model. On a certain clear July afternoon they stood together outside the door.

They were bronzed young men, with the blue-black hair and the bold features of the American Indian. David Return, of rugged medium size, wore a clay-blotched polo shirt, corduroy slacks and canvas sneakers. Stacey Brant, longer and leaner but powerfully muscled, was stripped to the waist for posing, with his abundant straight locks combed back and adorned with a fillet and single feather. He wore fringed leggins and beaded moccasins.

On a stand at Return's right elbow was the almost-finished study of Brant's figure, a cubit-high warrior in clay. But Brant did not pose, and Return did not ply his sculptor's tools. They were on the verge of a quarrel.

"You haven't anything to get wrathy about," Return said. "I only remarked that a statue of Sitting Bull would be as appropriate here as one of Hiawatha. Minnesota used to be Sioux country, you know; and Sitting Bull was a real person, not a myth, like Hiawatha."

Brant's fine, strong face did not furrow in anger. Plainly he fought to keep a calm brow and mouth, but his eyes glowed like signal fires before a war raid and the muscles in his bronzed arms flexed.

"It's not what you said, it's the superior way you said it," he replied. His college-smoothed English was slow and precise, itself a sign of his mounting fierceness. "You're like all the Sioux nation, dead sure that you're an original grand duke of the Western hemisphere. Well, I'm a Chippewa, one of Hiawatha's people. He was no myth, and the Chippewa are every ounce as fine a race as the Sioux ever dared to be."

This was the sort of discussion that the Hiawatha Memorial Foundation, made up of white men and women, had not bargained on, not

154

understanding that young men of the different tribes among which the foundation was fostering artistic expression, were apt to be steadfast and even intolerant about their diverse heritages. True, tribal independence was now but a brave memory, but spiritual allegiance to the tribe still lived on in the hearts of young men like Return and Brant.

David Return could never forget that he was the great-grandson of an Ogalallah Sioux war chief, a man who had helped obliterate Custer, who had defied Miles and Carr, who had refused ten thousand dollars to join Buffalo Bill's wild west show, who had been first to fight and last to subside on the reservation. Perhaps it might have been wiser if a Chippewa student sculptor—there were several passable ones at Nebraska University—had been chosen as an interpreter in bronze of Hiawatha, the Chippewa demigod, instead of a descendant of the Sioux.

"What you mean," Return said, his own voice fallen to dangerous depth, "is that your sister—what's her funny name—should have this job. Remember that the foundation chose me, not her, in regular competition. My only mistake was in picking you for a model."

"I didn't ask you to pick me," Brant flung back. "While we're on the subject of our tribes, I want to say that the Chippewa never had to ask the Sioux for anything." His nostrils broadened contemptuously. "The Sioux—a race of wild men, teepee-dwellers! They never learned to build a house or scratch a furrow or dig a well!"

That was an old scorn of the Chippewa, whose native arts included corn-growing and permanent settlement.

But Return was ready with a slur of his own "There's another tribal difference. Until the white men took over, the Chippewa never dared cross the Mississippi for fear of the Sioux. The north woods are still full of old Chippewa uncles who, whenever someone says 'Dakota' to them, feel to see if their scalps are still fastened on."

Brant seemed to swell. His naked shoulder-muscles bunched, his fists clenched into clublike lumps, he rose on his moccasined toes as if to spring. Return's hand dropped to the side of the clay figure and closed on the haft of a mallet.

"If you get violent," he warned, "I'll beat that handsome Chippewa head down between your collarbones."

The bigger Indian's eyes grew hatefully narrow. He turned quickly to one side, and entered the shack. Return waited, motionless, ready for a possible surprise assault. Half a minute passed, then the Chippewa emerged. He had drawn a jacket over his naked torso, and his arms were full of his clothes and other possessions.

"What's the idea?" demanded Return, but Brant strode past him without word or look. At the brush-lined rim of the slope, he found the narrow trail and fairly plunged down it. Indianlike, he made no noise in the descent.

David Return, left alone, tried to justify himself. He could hardly have backed down—that would have been weak, especially when the Sioux were insulted. Old men at home on the Rosebud Agency would have scowled and turned their proud backs on him. . . .

A sudden rustle of movement made him face quickly in the direction of the trail-head. But nothing emerged. Yet there was a stealthy stir in the ground-hugging branches of some dark juniper scrub. Somehow it bespoke menace. Return walked across the clearing, mallet still in hand, and there was a scuttle as of tiny retreat. A squirrel? A bird? He bent to look beneath the bushes. Tiny marks showed in the moist black mold, two and two, where a biped had hurried downhill.

But what thing so small went on two feet? Birds have spreading tracks and these were narrow and compact. A jumping rat, then, the Sioux judged though jumping rats are plains animals. In any case, it had not been Brant; Brant would not have made noise in his spying.

Return went back to his own doorstep. He narrowed his eyelids to study, artisan-fashion, his miniature figure of Hiawatha. It stood straight, head proudly raised, right hand aloft in a gesture of peace and benediction.

Well, the break-up with Brant would not stop the work. He would go on with it in town. A tremendous enlargement of this small-scale Hiawatha, then a painstaking moulding of the bronze giant. Quite a job getting it back here and setting it up, but that would be the responsibility of the foundation's transport committee. . . .

Again that rustling noise, this time beside his foot!

A tussock of tall grass grew there. Return bent down quickly and spied, or imagined, something tiny and dull-colored, drawing back out of sight. Patently it had been watching him, and now withdrew when it felt the impact of his gaze.

He struck swiftly and accurately with the mallet, squashing down the clump of grass, but could not be sure that he had found a living mark. He knelt, dropped the tool, and with his hands parted the grassy ambush.

In its heart was a small hole, perfectly round and full of darkness oddly smooth and hard around its rim. Return fancied it might even be lined with something, baked clay or enamel or glaze. He half thrust his face close to peer in, but checked himself. A snake might nest there, and David Return disliked snakes as much as the next Indian. He contented himself with grubbing up a bit of turfy loam and plugging the hole with it.

There was still plenty of daylight and he decided to work. He fingered the clay experimentally. It remained quite soft; the slowness of drying was due to his own secret process. He wiped it carefully over with an oily mixture, then attempted to re-fashion some of the more delicate parts with a tiny steel-pointed pick.

Thus he worked for an hour, and another. The daylight began to modify itself into gray evening. Finally Return drew back, rubbing his big skilful hands to rest them, and surveying with critical eyes his preliminary figure. It looked better, though it still lacked something. Again, he comforted himself with thought of the complete large figure. The whole Indian race could be proud of that, and proud of David Return as well. His chest broadened at the fancy. The true red man is not often modest, though he seldom boasts of what he cannot and does not perform.

It was near supper time. He washed his hands, took up a bucket and, leaving the shack, descended the trail. At its foot, just where the path joined a double-rutted stretch that might be called a road, there purled a spring, cool and encircled with moss.

By now, Return judged, Brant would be miles away, perhaps at the cottage where, so Return had heard him say, some Chippewa relatives were staying for the summer. Among them would be the sister, who had unsuccessfully competed for the memorial commission. A sober lump, he imagined her, one of the dull pseudo-scholars so often found among modern young Indians.

II

THE LITTLE ARROW

DRAWING HIS pail full of water, he mounted again to the top of the hill. As he did so, he had a sense—perhaps he saw a quick, shy shadow—that something, or several things, very small and swift, had darted away from in front of his very door.

Return's brown face grew hard and intent. Three times in one afternoon he had felt the presence of wee spies or raiders. Odd that this had never happened while Brant was around—had Brant something to do with it?

Return brushed aside the disturbing fancies, entered the shack, and began to prepare his meal.

Over a small fire in the stove, he fried ham and potatoes, and heated coffee he had made at lunch time. With cold corn-bread and a small tin of cherries, this made his supper. Dusk had fallen by the time he finished, and he lighted a kerosene lamp, then produced his pipe.

It was a real Sioux relic, with a bowl of traditional red stone and a stubby stem of ancient dark wood. His great-grandfather, the war chief, had smoked it ceremonially, in the old free days when the stem was longer and wore two enemy scalps for decoration. Return carefully packed it with coarse burley tobacco, struck a match, and drew a great fragrant lungful of the smoke.

At that instant, the tail of his eye caught movement on the split-log threshold of the front door. He swung abruptly around on his chair, at the same time blowing out a mighty cloud of smoke in the direction of the doorway.

Once again, there was retreat. But this time he saw the thing, for only a second, and obscured by the blue fog of tobacco. Not a mouse, nor a squirrel—it sprang away on two legs that were shorter and thinner than his pipestem, and it flashed a gaze backward with a little nut of a head upon a tiny shoulder.

"Frog," he breathed, half-aloud; but it was no frog either. No frog is pale pink-brown, no frog comes voluntarily close to watch a man, no frog stands and runs erect on its hind feet. . . .

He took the lamp, and gazed out into the new-fallen dusk. The flickering flame showed him only the turfy flat, but he was not reassured. He closed and locked the door, and sat smoking in silence. Finally he rose and tapped the ashes from his red stone pipe.

He found himself suddenly thinking of that sculptress sister of Stacey Brant, the girl whose odd name he could not remember, and whom he had nosed out in the competition. What sort of Hiawatha did she imagine, how close had she come to the ideal? Except for the day's quarrel, he might even ask her advice on how to improve his own attempt. But at this moment she was probably helping her brother curse the name of David Return. He shrugged, grimaced, and went into his bedroom.

Sleep did not come readily in spite of his day's work. Once he dreamed, of the little statuette in the front room coming to life and clattering about its stand. At dawn he awoke, rose, washed hurriedly, drew on his clothes, and went out to resume his labors.

He paused a pace beyond the bedroom door, and cursed hotly in guttural Sioux.

His clay study had been thrown from the stand, and lay shattered to bits upon the floor!

His leap carried him almost across the room. He knelt and seized some of the larger fragments. No, there was no hope of mending the thing, it had been too cunningly broken.

The torso remained a single large lump, but the face, on which he had wrought so carefully an arresting expression of savage dignity, had been chipped to tiny morsels. The carefully articulated arms were broken in a dozen places, the painstakingly-fashioned fingers were torn from the hands. The legs, rent from the body, had been broken again and again.

This was no accident, no gust of wind, no jostling of a rat. Malicious intelligence had arrayed itself against his work.

Let any artist tell how David Return felt at that moment, and let every fair-minded man sympathize with his grief and rage.

"Stacey Brant sneaked back and did this to me," he muttered darkly. "He thinks that the scalp-lifting days are over. But—"

Rising again, he took from the pile of kindling wood a hand-ax. He balanced it knowingly. A harsh scowl locked his black brows. He strode to the front door, and with his free left hand seized the knob.

The door was locked, and on the inside. He himself had locked it, the night before. His tense muscles relaxed, mystification softening his rage. If Brant had done this cowardly trick, how had Brant come in?

He examined the front window, nearest the stand. The sash was up, but the screen was tightly in place. Nobody had tampered with that. He went to the other windows and found them, too, properly screened.

Baffled, he searched for loose boards in the walls, in the floor, or sprung shingles on the roof. The shack had no such weaknesses. The one opening he found was a hole in the corner behind the stove—a scant inch across. Its wooden rim was smooth and shiny, as with a finishing agent, and Return thought of the burrow he had blocked in his front yard.

Return threw his ax back upon the kindling. Gathering up the broken pieces of his study, he pored over them intently. They could not be restored, but they might guide him in remodelling.

From the bedroom he fetched his mirror, a sizable rectangle. This he hung on the wall opposite the position he would occupy while working. It gave back a clear image of his own face, shoulders and arms. Nodding in approval, he stripped off his shirt. His bared muscles showed fine and symmetrical, worth any sculptor's attention. His Sioux face was as noble as Brant's. Quickly he bound back his hair with the fillet Brant had worn, and set a feather in it. His mirror showed him a very adequate Hiawatha. He emitted an honest Indian "Wagh!" of satisfaction and began mixing a fresh supply of clay.

He twisted wires into a sketchy skeleton of a manikin with head up and right hand lifted. Then, wetting his hands, he whisked well kneaded clay upon and around this framework. Within minutes he had the figure blocked roughly into proper proportion—eighteen inches tall, head and torso lumpy but well indicated, arms and legs already half-tapered and muscles smoothly swept into view.

For full sixty minutes he toiled, then stepped back, drew a deep relaxing breath, and produced his red stone pipe. Tamping in tobacco with a clay-clotted thumb, he struck a match.

Chock!

Return jumped nervously, and stared. What had struck with that abrupt little sound, and where? His eyes found the clay figure, and widened in half-stupid amazement. In the breast of his new Hiawatha was stuck a needle—no, a straight sliver of wood. Its free end was winged with tiny feathers, like a toy arrow.

That was what it was, an arrow. Somebody, or something, had sped it, and struck his statue.

Return's eyes seized the line along which that almost-microscopic missile must have traveled. He followed its course backward to the corner by the stove.

By the leg of the stove lurked something, in a little blot of shadow. It was motionless, as though it hoped to escape Return's search; but he saw it, plainly enough to catch the attitude of an archer.

A wee, malevolent doll of an archer, not as high as his shoetop— toy-sized; misshapenly human, staring back at him with pallid-bright points of eyes!

The sculptor ran at it. The wee thing retreated, slowly and coolly. To its bow, a bent twig, it was fitting a second tiny arrow. Return's foot made a lunging kick, but his puny antagonist dodged as nimbly as an insect. Stooping with bent knees, Return curved his hands for a sudden clutch and capture. His pipe, still in his mouth, drove out a wide wreath of smoke.

And, even as it prepared to face him, the little archer scuttled away. The tobacco, of course—Return had seen the same thing happen the night before, when the stealthy mite on the door-sill had fled from a similar cloud of vapor.

Return emitted a grunt of perplexity. He was finding time to wonder if his eyes deceived him. Crouching lower, he peeped around the corner of the stove, and found only the smooth-edged hole in the floor. Into this he thrust an exploring finger.

Chock!

His pipe fell from between his teeth as he flinched in surprised pain. Drawing his finger back into view, he stared at it. An arrow, that second tiny arrow like the one that had struck his clay image, was driven deep into the fleshy tip.

Standing up, he tugged at the shaft. It had gone full half of its length into his finger, and seemed loath to come out again; it hurt fiercely, too. Probably it was barbed. Better cut it out, he decided at once, then rip the floor away, and see what made those attacks upon him. He went to the door, unlocked it, and stepped out into the bright light of morning.

His wounded finger had begun to throb as though with a pulse of its own. His whole hand took up that throbbing, and the pain with it. Reaching across his body with his left hand, he managed to draw his penknife out of the right-hand pocket of his trousers, and with the aid of his teeth he opened it. His right hand and wrist were puffing up rapidly, like a pudding in boiling water. Boiling hot, too, was the blood that raced in his veins.

With the point of the knife he touched the flesh beside the imbedded arrow. It had turned quite black and mortified-looking, and even his Indian stoicism shook at the great wave of agony that shot along his finger and hand, up his elbow and shoulder, an agony greater than that of an ulcerated tooth. Cutting the thing out wouldn't do. He dropped his head, as if to tear at the feathered shaft with his teeth. Then his mind whirled. He staggered, as though his knees had become unhinged, and he had to plant his feet wide to hold himself erect.

"Are you David Return?"

It was a voice he did not know, and near him floated a face he had never seen before. A woman's voice, a woman's face. Indian woman . . . young . . . amber skin, bright black wings of hair . . . he liked her face, her voice . . .

"I came to ask if you wouldn't forget that quarrel with my brother. I'm Lohaie Brant, Stacey Brant's sister—why, you're sick!"

"Sick," he repeated, through lips like wet, swollen leather. "Poisoned. See." He lifted his arm, crushingly heavy, its joints creaking with fiery pain.

He heard her sharp gasp of alarm, but she seemed to know what must be done.

"Come at once," she said to him, as though through a muffling blanket. "Can you get down the hill? I've a car on the road below, and about six miles from here my grandfather—he knows a lot about remedies—"

Return's sight failed, and his wits, but still he felt her trying to guide him. Lohaie Brant, the Chippewa girl with the funny name was offering help. Still staggering, his consciousness almost gone, he remained on his weakening feet.

III

MOKWA

HE AWOKE slowly, timidly. David Return felt that he had lain silent and stupid for hours. He cleared his throat, shook his head to banish the buzzing from his ears, the blur from his sight. He tried to sit up in bed.

For he was in bed, a sturdy wooden bunk just under a big double window. Over him hung a great square face, brown as buffalo-hide and as tough, with strong knowing wrinkles, and braided black-gray hair.

"Lie still, *Lakota*," a drum-deep voice cautioned. "You have been like dead for a day and a night. It is morning again. My medicine is good."

The words were English, but the inflection and manner bespoke the old-fashioned Indian. "Who are you?" asked Return, sleepily hoarse.

"Mokwa," boomed back the reply. "*Wabeno*—medicine—magic man. Grandfather of Stacey and Lohaie."

Mokwa signifies "bear" in Chippewa. Return, who made out the great clifflike shoulders and giant chest in the old flannel shirt, thought the name appropriate. Vaguely he remembered what had happened to him. "I was hurt somehow," he hazarded slowly.

"*Huh!*" assented Mokwa. "The *pukwitchee* poisoned you."

"Puk—puk—" The new word was strange. "What's that?"

"Little people." A massive thumb and finger indicated small size. "Wild things, bad." Thumb and finger snapped, the Indian sign of disapproval. "Hate Hiawatha. Hate you."

Return was strong enough to shake his head. That memory of a tiny, deadly archer could only be a sick dream. "I can't believe it," he demurred.

"Take it easy, old man!" called a cheery voice. Stacey Brant stepped into view beside the bed. He looked slender, almost fragile, compared to his immense grandfather. "You look healthy again," he continued. "Lohaie, Return's awake."

Beside Brant appeared the figure of a girl, tall and graceful. If it was a dream Return remembered, she had been part of that dream.

"You got me out of a bad scrape," he addressed her. "Thanks, but what happened?"

Grandfather's telling you," she smiled, and again he thought her face gentle and golden and lovely.

"The *pukwitchee,*" boomed old Mokwa. "Mighty bad. Hate men. Hate the *Lakota*—the Sioux."

Lohaie had brought an earthen bowl of hot soup. Return drank it, and felt strong enough to sit up on the edge of the bed. He was able to see a comfortable room, its walls hung with Indian blankets and beadwork, the furniture plain and modern. "Did I take your bed?" he asked Stacey Brant. "Thanks. I'm glad we're friends again."

"Me, too," said Brant. "Now to decide about how to fight these *pukwitchee.*"

"*Huh!*" grunted Mokwa. "I make medicine."

He rose from the stool on which he sat, and immediately became grotesque. His size was all in head, chest and arms; his legs were short and bowed, as in the bear for which he was named and he measured no taller than his grandson's shoulder-point.

He tramped austerely into another room.

"Won't you tell me what he means?" Return begged.

Lohaie sat down on Mokwa's stool. "Gladly. Stacey, will you fetch that little arrow we dug out of Mr. Return's hand?" When her brother had gone, she asked a question: "Do you read Longfellow?"

Return shrugged. "Yes, in school. And some just recently, when the foundation announced the memorial competition."

"Remember 'The Song of Hiawatha'? And Kwasind, the strong man? And his enemies?"

Return thought, then nodded. "Yes. Kwasind was killed by—by a race of little wild dwarfs."

"Exactly." She quoted from memory:

> *No man could compete with Kwasind,*
> *But the mischievous Puk-wudjies,*
> *They, the envious Little People,*
> *They, the fairies and the pygmies,*
> *Plotted and conspired against him—"*

"I remember that," Return assured her. "And there's another part of the poem, about their origin. A family of wicked people, transformed and shrunken up, enemies of mankind—but you don't tell me that this is the truth."

"You find it hard to grasp, Mr. Return?"

"Please," he smiled, "you've been too good a friend to stand on formality. My first name's David."

"Don't change the subject, David," and Lohaie Brant smiled back, very prettily. "You're an Indian like us. You must understand."

"My tribe has its own mysteries and folklores," he said, "and our *Wakonda* is probably the same Great Spirit as your *Manitou*. But I'm a college man. So is your brother. You went to school, too, I judge. And how can rational, civilized people accept this *pukwitchee* belief?"

Stacey Brant, coming back into the room, heard this question. "Seeing is believing," he reminded. "Even if you were having hallucinations yesterday, you're sane today. Take a look at this."

He held it out on a china saucer—something the length of a needle, shaped like a tiny arrow.

"Don't touch it," warned Lohaie quickly. "Grandfather's herb-medicine, or his magic, or both, sweated the poison out of you once; but don't tempt fate."

Return took the dish and gazed closely. "It's a toy," he demurred.

Brant handed him a small, powerful magnifying glass. "Look again."

Return did so. He made out beautiful shaping of the cut feather, from some small bird, and delicate lashing with cord thinner than gossamer.

"Amazing," he conceded, "but a skilful workman might have done it."

"Look at the head of the arrow," urged Brant. "What do you see?"

"A perfect barbed point of stone."

"And how are stone arrowheads made?"

Return set down the dish and the glass. "They aren't made any more," he replied, "but the old-timers used to chip a flake of flint with a stone—"

"Look at the thing again," urged Brant, and, as Return did so, "See how the thing is chipped? Perfect orthodox arrow-maker's technique—

but almost too tiny for the naked eye. It needed hands small enough to handle and judge and strike."

Silence, triumphant on the part of the two young Chippewa, doubtful on the part of David Return, the Sioux.

"If these things are true," said the Sioux at last, "why did they come hunting me—attacking me and spoiling my work?"

"They didn't come to you," Lohaie made answer. "You came to them."

Return stared in his surprise. She went on:

"Grandfather offered the clue. That high, flat hill couldn't have been anything but a *waakan*—a place set apart for spirits and wild things, Medicine men used to put leavings of food there for good luck. And so, from before the white men's time until the day the foundation selected it as a memorial site, that hill was a *pukwitchee* stronghold—"

"That could very well be!" cried Return. "There was a *waakan* at home on the Rosebud Agency. It was a high rock, with painted figures. My father used to get up early to watch the sun rise over it." His enthusiasm grew. "Like fairy hills in England, and the Elfburg in Norway, isn't it?"

The girl's gleaming dark head nodded. "Very much the same. Well, these little wild things feel a right to the place. And you're invading it, to work on an image of their great enemy, Hiawatha?"

"They didn't bother Stacey," reminded Return suddenly.

"Grandfather explained that, too," chimed in Brant. "We're a family of *wabenos,* medicine men, from 'way back. Even I have done simple magic. Perhaps my presence slowed them up for a few days."

From a front room came the muffled thudding rhythm of a drum. After a moment, the voice of Mokwa began to sing in deep minors.

"That's his strongest song to kill evil magic," whispered Lohaie. "Let's go and listen."

The three turned to the door. Return's mind was busy. The word *pukwitchee* suggested two English terms—"puck" and "witch." Another less apparent but possible, was "pixie." And what was that name in Michael Drayton's "Nymphidia," the fierce warlike elf? Pigwiggen—a coincidence almost startling. How universal was the *pukwitchee* belief?

They had come into the front room of the cottage. Before a central table stood the savage old Mokwa. In a polished bowl of black stone, in the middle of the table, rose the smoke of pungent, burning leaves. The medicine man pounded softly with a muffled stick upon a little drum of rawhide stretched across a wooden hoop.

As the three came into his presence, he made an end of his chant. Laying down the drum, he drew from the bosom of his shirt a buckskin pouch and scattered more dried herbs on the fire in the bowl.

"Medicine to kill poison," he announced. "You, my son," and his mighty hand beckoned Return, "come close. Breathe the smoke."

"Very well, old man," agreed Return. He addressed Mokwa thus, not familiarly but in the Indian tradition of respect for age. Approaching the table, the young Sioux let dark, semi-opaque clouds rise around his face, stinging the inner membranes of eyes and nose; but he did not choke. After a moment, he felt definitely stronger. And his right hand, the wounded one, was not even sore.

"Come close, my grandchildren," urged Mokwa. "Breathe smoke. It protects from *pukwitchee* poison."

All of them drew their lungs full of the vapors, and again and again as long as the fire remained alive. Return at least felt a great swelling of nerves and veins. The fumigation-medicine was definitely stimulating.

"But the *pukwitchee* can do other harm," pronounced Mokwa. "They will fight to keep Hiawatha's image from their hill."

Return examined his right forefinger, wondering how flesh could heal so suddenly and completely. Mokwa spoke yet again:

"By magic, we drive away the *pukwitchee* tonight."

"Tonight!" repeated Stacey Brant, as though in formal response, and, "Tonight!" breathed his sister Lohaie.

They had come up on either side of Mokwa. The old man's huge forefinger scooped up ash from the bowl of burnt herbs, and this he smeared on Brant's forehead, then on Lohaie's.

The massive, leathery face did not smile, but its deep ridges softened a little, as though in affectionate welcome. "I have made you *wabenos*, like me."

"We will help tonight," promised Brant, and Lohaie nodded.

"I'll help, too, old man," offered Return, but the big gray head shook. "You are a *Lakota*, a stranger. Let the Chippewa fight the *pukwitchee*."

And Mokwa turned and stalked majestically out. Return gazed after him, in some chagrin.

"Don't feel hurt," Stacey Brant admonished. "The responsibility is ours."

"And meanwhile," added Lohaie, "it's time for me to fix lunch."

IV

THE SPELL OF THE CHIPPEWA

ONCE AGAIN the dusk thickened and fell, and then midnight and finally the dark hour that foretells the dawn. Along the ill-used dirt road to the *pukwitchee* hill moved a procession of four.

At the head tramped old Mokwa, setting a fast pace for all his squat body and considerable age. Bleakly he had waved aside Lohaie's car, though it was fully half a dozen miles from cottage to hill.

His flannel shirt and khaki trousers had been discarded, and he wore instead a leather breechclout and fringed moccasins. His naked chest and arms, ridged with thews like oak roots, he had painted in strange barred color-combinations, significant of prayer and magic. Around his brows clung a broad fur band, set with a pair of horns and three feathers in a rear tuft. He carried a drum, several pouches and a gourd rattle.

Probably no such figure had walked those woods in three-quarters of a century.

One pace behind strode Stacey Brant. He too was naked to the waist, and wore the leggins and moccasins in which he had posed for Return. His face bore the ash-smear with which Mokwa had consecrated him to the Chippewa priesthood, and a red-edged star of black blazed on his chest.

Half a dozen yards behind him walked Lohaie, in a white buckskin frock and moccasins. Her lustrous black hair, when the moonlight struck it through the roadside foliage, gave off blue radiance. She wore no paint, and kept her eyes demurely down.

With her came David Return, still in white men's clothing and strongly aware of his own exclusion from the ceremonial that was to come.

"I still think this is heathen," he muttered. "Barbarous."

"You say that because it's Chippewa," she whispered back.

"No offense," he apologized quickly, "but it's still not straight and clear in my mind. You and your grandfather expect to drive away these little imps—"

"You still don't believe," she chided him patiently.

"Oh, there's something mysterious and dangerous," he admitted, "and your arguments are pretty striking. But I want to go up and have another look for myself."

"Wait until grandfather says to go." Her eyes lifted. "And here we are, at the very foot of the hill."

Their march was completed. The road broadened here and the branches opened above to a clear patch of star studded sky. Mokwa was pausing beside the spring, where the trail turned off and up the hill.

"We build a fire," he decreed deeply. "Then magic."

His two grandchildren went to gather wood. Mokwa moved to pry flakes of tinderlike bark from a fallen birch, and to pick up a single stubby branch that lay almost at his feet. Return would have helped to fetch kindling, but the old man dissuaded him with a gesture. Plainly, the ceremony was to be pure Chippewa, down to the last and humblest detail.

Stacey Brant fetched a great armful of thick, dead boughs and Lohaie gleaned two handfuls of straw-thin dry twigs. Mokwa accepted their offerings with grunts of approval, and arranged them carefully on the margin of the spring.

Once again Return offered help, in the form of a match. Once again Mokwa shook his head in majestic refusal, and from one of his pouches drew a great notched chip of white pine. He next produced a spindle-like rod of darker, harder wood, as thick as a pencil and longer. The moonlight showed its whittled point to be charred, as though by former fires.

Mokwa knelt, laid his pine chip flat, and under the notch thrust a doubled sheet of bark. Into the notch he slid the point of his spindle and began to twirl it between his palms, swiftly and skilfully.

Return knew rubbing-sticks when he saw them; yet this ancient Indian mode of making fire seemed strangely impressive now, an important and appropriate part of magic to come. A tiny curl of smoke mounted upward, barely perceptible in the dim red glow of a little fire beneath.

Mokwa carefully added the splinters Lohaie had brought. They blazed up, and ate the larger wood from Stacey Brant's pile. The light was strong. Mokwa added the billet of wood he himself had picked up, a piece of hemlock. It burst out in a shower of sparks.

"Now," intoned Mokwa, "we sing—pray—call Hiawatha. When morning comes, he will drive the *pukwitchee* away."

He gave Brant the gourd rattle, and the young Chippewa shook it abruptly. The pebbles inside sang sharply, and Mokwa responded with three cadenced taps on his drum. Again Stacey Brant jerked the rattle, again the three taps. Again—again—

Whoosh—tap, tap, tap—
Whoosh—tap, tap, tap—
Whoosh—tap, tap, tap—

Mokwa burst into song, apparently making it up as he went along. It was in Chippewa, which Return understood but slightly. Yet he caught the name of Manitou, the Algonquin Great Spirit, then that of Hiawatha.

"Hiawatha, Hiawatha!" echoed Brant and Lohaie.

A new rhythm of the song fitted itself into the swish and tap of drum and rattle. Return, standing apart, heard the word *pukwitchee*. A moment later, *Lakota*—that meant a Sioux, himself.

His adventures were being told. His eyes studied Lohaie. The firelight made her coppery-gold face, rosy and fine. It came to his mind that Sioux and Chippewa had loved ere this, that Hiawatha himself had taken a Sioux bride. And Lohaie was beautiful, and good.

She sang, repeating the words her grandfather chanted. Again the word *pukwitchee* bobbed up, and another word partially recognizable— *pagak*. Wasn't that the word for death? Was death being invoked, or warded away?

David Return was increasingly respectful and interested, but he would prefer a real Sioux ally to Hiawatha—Sitting Bull, or Crazy Horse, or his own war-wise great grandfather.

Mokwa was casting herb-dust on the fire. It made the flames burn white and hot as a blast furnace, and throw off a pale smoke that seemed to shine with its own radiance against the dark sky. A pungency filled the air, faintly akin to tobacco.

That brought a memory to Return. Tobacco had driven away certain shadowy little enemies on the hill above—why not add a smoke-column of his own to the ceremonial? He felt that he had stood static long enough.

Return still doubted the true existence of the *pukwitchee,* but, even if there were such things, must a Sioux be completely in debt to Chippewa defense-magic? His mind rapidly rehearsed a half-remembered prayer against enchantment. That, with ceremonial tobacco-smoking, would suffice. He groped in his pocket for the red stone pipe.

It was gone.

At once he remembered—the pipe had fallen from his mouth just as he had poked a forefinger into a certain mysterious floor-hole and received a wound. It must be lying there now. Meanwhile, the stars above the treetops grew pale. If he was to make a move in his own behalf, it would have to be now.

Quickly he turned and, unnoticed by the raptly chanting trio, climbed the hillside trail, his knowing feet finding their way in the dark. Up above was already gray light, and he could see the oblong hunch of his shack, the open door. He could no longer hear the singing in the woods.

He hurried indoors, groped to the shelf, found and lighted the lamp. Before looking for his pipe, he glanced toward the stand where he had left the newly-begun study for the Hiawatha memorial.

Like the first,it was broken in pieces, a clutter of clay chips and a bent wire skeleton. He cursed, and then he saw his pipe, where it had fallen. He made two strides and bent to pick it up.

With a sharp patter, as of hail on a hard dirt road, a volley of tiny arrows struck his hand.

He straightened quickly, shaking his hand. Some of the little shafts fell away, and with his free hand he plucked out others. There was no barbed clinging this time, and his hand did not smart—only felt numb, awkward. Mokwa's remedy for strange wounds had some efficacy, apparently.

But there was no time to ponder on that—his ambushers were grouped behind and among the legs of the stove. They were venturing out into the open light.

So tiny, and so evil—this much Return saw and absorbed in a moment. Perhaps it was later that he realized their gargoyle grotesquerie of shape, their squatness of head with greenglow eyes and lizard mouths and no noses at all, their pinky-drab nakedness, their apish disproportion of arms and bandy legs. Later, yes. For, in that first single moment of their advance into fair view, they rushed.

V

HIAWATHA'S COMING

MORE ARROWS struck him, one deep in his cheek, several in the folds of his clothing. His ears roared, but he was not agonized or stunned, as before. He kicked at the little monsters, savagely but ineffectually. They scattered warily around his big, unsure feet, dancing to bemuse him. Then, winning past him, they formed up in a group between him and the open door. They flourished their bows, and other things that might have been match-length warclubs.

Return, wagging his head to keep it clear against that modified attack of the arrow-venom, saw that there were fully a dozen—no, a score. From other hidings, reenforcements had stolen out. And Return saw, too, with dreamy disgust, that they had hairy pointed ears like bats, and that their paunches swelled grossly, indicative of greedy natures. He must not let them live and shame the normal, natural earth.

To his lips came the shrill war-whoop of the Sioux, and he sprang forward, stamping. Again the atomies judged the danger, fled from under his driving shoe-soles and over the split-log threshold. One or two lagged back, dancing derisively.

Again he moved in savage pursuit, summoning his strength against the drowsiness that afflicted him. As he reached the door, he saw a brighter gray in the dawn sky. The smoke of Mokwa's medicine fire rose, darkly now, above the bush-fringe and the treetops.

He saw, too, his tormentors, capering among the little tufts of grass. He would have thrown himself bodily at them, but he tripped and fell, clumsily headlong, to lie for the instant in stupid silence.

Something had clutched and tightened around his ankles. A noose of cord, a snare, laid by the imps for his feet!

He kicked and strove, but the cord held, and his strength seemed to ebb from him like water from a leaky kettle. Probably the other end of his tether was made fast to something inside the shack. Meanwhile, the *pukwitchee* that had fled before him now came stealing back, to his very face. He could see them in the growing dawn-light magnified by their nearness.

One came within inches of his nose, its grotesque semi-humanity partaking of ape, bear, and toad. Its mouth gaped at him like a fierce lizard's, he could see a narrow, whip-like tongue inside. Its eyes, white as pearl buttons with a central speck of evil blackness, challenged and hated him. Wickedness was distilled a hundredfold to pack itself into that loathsome dwarfed body.

He clutched at this leader, but his arms moved slowly. Pain attacked from the side, far-away pain such as one feels through local anaesthesia. Sharp points were prodding there, spears or hooks in vile little hands.

Return thrashed around, like a stranded whale among scavenger birds trying to bring both arms to his defense. But he could move the left only—a ligature had whipped itself unnoticed around his right wrist. Now he was held prone, unable to retreat or creep forward, like a steer caught by two lariats.

The turf around the door now swarmed with his foes. They burst out of the higher grass, like warriors charging from a forest ambush. There were scores, hundreds of them—and he could hear their voices, squeaking and shrilling and twittering like bats or locusts. His face was pulled so close to earth that he could see the flourished weapons of the horde between himself and the sky, a whole thicket of lances and clubs and hooks.

With a desperate rolling heave, he flung himself upon his back, flailing with his free arm at an advancing wave of assailants. His veins must be teeming with *pukwitchee*-poison, stunning but not slaying him. His left fist lay wearily in the grass for a moment, and that moment was enough.

For they had bound him there, too, at wrist and elbow. He was a helpless prisoner, gazing up into the gray sky, across which drifted a great tumbling wreath of smoke. He remembered the Chippewa. Would they come if he called?

He opened his mouth to shout, but the imps were ready for that, too. A great wad of grass was crammed violently upon his tongue, gagging him effectively. This would be the end of him—these wee conquerors that now swarmed upon him unafraid, like ants upon a dead mouse, would grant no truce, no mercy—

"David Return!"

It was Lohaie Brant, coming up the trail, speaking to him again at the door of his shack. He tried to splutter a warning, but he could not get words past the gag.

"We missed—" she began to say, from a point closer, and then she must have seen what had befallen him. She screamed sharply and wordlessly, and he heard the thud of her running feet. Her face came within range of his vision, close down, as though she was on her knees beside him. Her hands moved in quick, empty jerks, as though to frighten something away.

"Hiawatha!" she cried out, clearly and in mortal terror. "Hiawatha, behold what is happening here! We call for you!"

From his spread-eagled position on the grass, Return saw a thin loop of cord rise up, settle around Lohaie's shoulders. The *pukwitchee* were snaring her, too.

"Hiawatha!" she cried, "hear us!"

Return lifted his head. Somehow he got a grip on his remaining strength, and managed to spit out some of the clogging rubbish. He spoke, appealing to one whom the Sioux had never sought as an ally.

"Hiawatha . . . I, a *Lakota,* turn to you . . ."

Was it the smoke of Mokwa's fire that thickened and ascended above them then? Or was it a cloud, floating across the dawn-sky that had been clear and increasingly bright?

Return smelt a strengthening pungency, the same vapor that had once before given him healing strength. He stared up as there formed above the hill a—something.

The strange cloud, that had been a formless blob, was molding itself. It took form, far more swiftly and surely and gigantically than ever sculptor had imagined possible. It towered like a pillar into the upper abyss, a pillar with shoulders and arms; a pillar with a head, and on that head a great thicketlike bonnet of brave plumes.

A human figure, a war chief, but unthinkably vast. Return, his vision clear, his wits come back, saw that the presence was one with the bright dawn, the boundless sky. An arm lifted, a hand gestured in command. A face bent, as full of immortal wisdom and nobility as Egypt's sphinx—but more vast, infinitely more vast.

Hiawatha spoke a word from the sky. Return did not understand. Perhaps Lohaie did not understand.

But the *pukwitchee* understood. They feared. They fled.

They vanished, like dew before the rising sun.

When Mokwa and Stacey Brant came up the trail, they found Lohaie and David Return seated on the threshold log of the shack. On Lohaie's neck, on Return's wrists, were the thin dark wales of their cast-off bonds. They were earnestly in conversation.

"Strangest of all," Return was saying, "I know now how I want to fashion the memorial. I don't even need a model—only the memory of what I saw."

"You can work in peace," replied Lohaie. "The spirit of Hiawatha has spoken. The *pukwitchee* will never dare come back, nor any other danger."

"But you will come back," the young Sioux pleaded.

"Of course," said Lohaie; and then they were both aware of the arrival of Brant and Mokwa, and were filled with un-Indian confusion.

Spawn of Blackness

CARL JACOBI

Although most of the journeymen pulp authors have been forgotten today, the pulps could never have existed without them. The competent, accessible work these writers turned out month after month helped to fill a variety of genre pulps and balance out the work of better-known authors who tended to write exclusively in one genre or for a particular magazine. Carl Jacobi wrote many stories for the detective, western, weird menace, and science fiction magazines, but his best work appeared in Weird Tales *and the other weird fiction pulps. "Spawn of Blackness," from the October 1939* Strange Stories, *is one of his better journeyman efforts.*

IT LACKED twenty minutes of midnight when I locked the door of my apartment and raced down the steps to the waiting cab. A heavy rain, driven by a howling wind, swirled across the pavement.

"Sixteen Monroe Street," I snapped to the driver. "Oak Square. And drive like hell!"

The cab jerked forward, roared north into Monte Curve and turned east toward Carter. I leaned back then and prayed for a clear way through the night traffic. But even with the best of luck I knew I was treading on counted time.

Only a scant few minutes before, I had been in bed asleep. Then had come that urgent telephone call with that familiar voice over the wire.

"Dr. Haxton? Dr. James Haxton? This is your old friend, Stephen Fay. Can you come immediately? Something terrible has happened, and I'm in need of medical help. Hurry, man!"

The voice had ended in a gasp and a moan, and the connection had been severed with a crash.

Fay—Stephen Fay. I had known the man for a matter of ten years. We had worked side by side, in fact, as struggling students with adjoining laboratories. A huge man with a frank, open face, an engaging smile and an uncontrollable desire to probe deeper into the mysteries of science.

Down Carter we sped, windshield gray with drooling rain, across St. Clair, and into Monroe. Stephen Fay's residence was a forlorn pile of red brick, three stories in height, with a narrow, uninviting doorway.

A girl answered my ring, and as I hesitated, staring at her, she grasped my arm and drew me quickly inside.

"Thank God, you've come, Doctor," she said. "My uncle—Mr. Fay— is in the library. He's bleeding badly."

Even in the excitement of the moment I found myself noting the exquisite beauty of the white-faced girl as we paced silently down the corridor. Then she thrust a connecting door open, and I found myself face to face with my old friend.

He lay stretched full length on a divan, face contorted in agony. His coat and shirt had been ripped to shreds, as if by the repeated slashes of a razor-edged knife, and the exposed flesh was striped and cross-striped with deep gashes and incisions. A bath towel, red with blood, had been pressed against his throat. Removing it, I saw that he was bleeding profusely from a wound a scant inch from the jugular.

Fay rose up as I slid out of my coat.

"Leave the room, Jane," he gasped. "Dr. Haxton will take care of me."

It was a hospital job, one that required four stitches and possibly a local anesthetic, but I knew Fay's wonderful strength and his hatred for any undue commotion. So without further word I set to work.

Half an hour later he was resting easily, weak from loss of blood, but still amazingly calm and composed.

"Haxton," he said as I tried to keep him from talking, "Haxton, I want you to stay here tonight. Can you arrange it? I—I need someone to help me protect that girl. It—it may come again."

I started to give him a bromide, thought better of it, and closed my case with a snap.

"What may come again?" I asked. "In heaven's name, what's wrong here?"

Fay swallowed painfully. "I'll tell you," he said. "I'll tell you what was wrong. It's a rat!"

I saw that he was in deadly earnest and that he was awaiting my reaction with almost feverish anxiety. His hands opened and closed convulsively, and his eyes regarded me with set pupils.

"A *what?*" I stammered.

He rose from the divan and lurched across to the great flat-topped desk and stood in the center of the room. He seized something like a paper weight from its surface and handed it to me.

"Look at it. I don't think you've ever seen anything quite like it before."

The thing was made of wood, mounted on a flat base, and from top to bottom measured no more than six inches. A small carving it was, with agate eyes, protruding teeth, and a long, curved tail, crudely fashioned to resemble a life-size rat.

Placed on the desk where it belonged, it would hardly have attracted a second glance, but leering up at me as it was now from my cupped hands, it was a thing of inanimate horror. There was something repulsive in that squat gray form, something utterly loathsome in the way it crouched there on its black mounting, poised as though ready to leap at my throat.

I shuddered slightly. "Not very pretty."

Fay sat down in a chair and closed his eyes.

"I found that in an Arab shop," he began, "in the native quarter of Macassar, in the Celebes. Bought it for a few pennies simply because it caught my eye. I didn't find out what it was until I came back to the States and showed it to my friend, Henderson, of the Chicago School of Anthropology. That carving is not a fetish or an ornament, but an image, a native object of worship."

I said nothing. There was a story coming, but I had associated with Fay long enough to know that he would start at the beginning, reserving any climax there might be for the last.

"North of New Guinea, almost on the equator, in longitude one hundred and forty-two degrees," he continued, "there is an island known as Wuvulu, a tiny pinpoint of land near the Moluccas. Henderson tells me the aborigines of this island have one of the lowest forms of religion in the Indies. They worship the rat! This image is one of the few that has found its way into the outside world.

"When Jane, my niece, came to live with me, she refused to let the ugly thing repose on my desk openly and insisted that I cover it. I dropped an old piece of black cloth over it, and it has remained there in that manner until tonight—until five minutes before I telephoned you. Then"—Fay braced himself and leaned far forward—"then it came alive!"

The man sat there, scrutinizing me intently, watching my every facial move. He must have seen the incredulity in my eyes, for he rose slowly like a figure on clockwork.

"You don't believe, Haxton? You think I'm joking? Come, and I'll show you the proof!"

He moved to the door, still weak from loss of blood, and I followed a few steps behind. At the threshold two people entered the room to meet us—the girl who had admitted me to this house, and a tall, thin man clad in a rubberized raincoat.

Fay waved his hand in introduction.

"My niece, Jane Barron, Haxton. I've already explained to her that my accident was caused by the breaking of a glass acid vat in the laboratory."

He nodded significantly, and I understood at once that he desired to keep the truth from the girl for the present.

"And this," he went on, "is Corelli, my laboratory assistant and helper."

The Italian bowed low. Apparently he had been out and had returned to the house only a few moments before the accident, whatever it was, had occurred.

"Are you all right, Uncle?" the girl cried. "You look so weak and pale." Then to me: "You must tell him to be more careful with his experiments, Doctor."

Fay patted her gently. "I'll be all right, child, but it's so late I've asked Dr. Haxton to stay the rest of the night. Will you arrange the guest room?"

Corelli looked at his employer with concern. "I trust the wounds are not too painful, Signor," he said. "If you wish, I will—"

Fay nodded absently. "Go to bed, Corelli. Dr. Haxton and I are going to stay up awhile. I'm going to show him my color-music machine."

The Italian bowed once more and left the room. Jane disappeared up a staircase that led to the floor above, and a moment later I found myself pacing down an ill-lighted corridor by the side of the wounded man.

We came at length to a large high-ceilinged room, lined with racks of apparatus.

"My laboratory," Fay said.

My attention was attracted to a ponderous machine in the center, which at the moment seemed only a confusing mass of wheels, tubes, reflectors and dials.

Fay led the way past this instrument, and stopped abruptly, pointing to a spot near the floor. There was a large ragged hole there, reaching from the bottom of the baseboard to a point some distance up the wall. From the hole, leading across the parquet floor, were a series of sharp scratches, marks that had penetrated the varnish.

To the left a small zinc-covered table was overturned on its side, with a mass of apparatus thrown in wild confusion. Still wet and dripping over the latter was a large clot of blood and a tuft of what I saw on closer inspection to be short gray fur.

I rose to my feet slowly. Fay moved across the room to one of several chairs.

"I told you that rat image came to life tonight. You thought I was crazy when I said it. Believe me, Haxton, I never was more sane in my life.

"I've been working hard the last month or so, perfecting an experiment with what is known as color-music. Tonight Jane insisted I take the evening off and go with her to a movie. Accordingly I told Corelli, my assistant, to get everything ready for a final test in the morning before he left for the evening. We returned early. Jane went to her room, and I went immediately to the laboratory.

"All the way I was conscious of some kind of danger ahead. Then I pushed open the laboratory door and stepped inside. It happened before I could move. By the light of the night lamp in the corridor I had a glimpse of a gray shape and a head with red eyes and white gleaming teeth. The thing was utterly huge, large as a dog, and it threw itself straight at my throat, clawing like mad.

"I screamed, I believe. Then I managed to twist free, reach out and switch on the light.

"With the room lit, I saw it. It stood there a moment, eyes blinking in the sudden glare. Then as if the light were its only fear, it turned, raced across the floor, upset that table and made for that hole which it had gnawed in the wall. But before it reached it, I had sufficiently collected my wits to seize a heavy knife from the stand by the door, hurl it and catch the thing a full blow on the back. It let out a terrible shriek, then disappeared through the wall."

Fay paused, gripped the chair arm tightly.

"And unquestionably that rat was a gigantic incarnation of the image on my desk in the library!"

I sat there stupidly. "It all sounds impossible," I said. "Mad—insane in every detail. But why do you say that the rat was an incarnation of that wooden image?"

Fay leaned back. "Because," he said huskily, "the thing was no real rat, no natural creature of a living order. I know that. It was a hideous caricature, a deformed monstrosity with the same exaggerated lines and detail of that wooden god. The head was rectangular rather than round. The eyes were far out of proportion, and the teeth—were long white fangs. God, it was horrible!"

For a long time after that, while a clock high up on the wall ticked off the passing seconds, we sat in silence. At length I voiced my thoughts.

"Whatever the thing is, supernatural or otherwise, it's real enough to cause flesh-and-blood wounds and to be wounded itself. We can't stand by and let it come and go as it wills. Where does that hole in the wall lead?"

Fay shook his head. "This is an old house," he said, "and there are unusually large spaces between the walls. I found that out when I tapped them for several of my experiments. That rat has the run of the entire structure. It must have been only chance that led it to choose the laboratory for a point to gnaw its way to freedom."

We used two heavy boards and a piece of sheet-iron to cover the opening. Along the baseboard on each of the four walls we ran an uncovered piece of copper wire, electrically charged with a high voltage from Fay's laboratory current. It meant that a second attempt on the part of the horror to enter the room would result in its instant electrocution. It meant that—if the thing were not invulnerable to such a mundane defense.

"No one knows about what happened tonight, save me?" I asked then.

Fay shook his head. "No one. I didn't choose to frighten my niece, and Corelli was out at the time."

"Corelli has been with you long?"

"About a year. He's an odd sort of person but harmless, I think. Never says much except when he talks about his color theory. Then he babbles incessantly. The man has a mad way of mixing spiritualism with science. Believes that white is the essence of all that is good and black is the lair of evil, or some such rot. He even showed me a thesis on this which he had written. Aside from that however, he's really a capable laboratory assistant. . . ."

A strange bed to me, whatever the surroundings, is always the same. Tonight, with my mind milling over the story that had been related to me, I found sleep almost impossible. Hours passed before I dozed off.

But at three o'clock by the radium clock on the dresser, I found myself sitting upright in bed. Something, some foreign noise had wakened me.

I got up, crossed to the door and looked out into the corridor. Blackness met my eyes. Then a sound reached me from the far end of the hall, and I stole stealthily forward. The sound came louder. It was *swish-swish* of liquid being brushed on a hard surface, the sound of a man painting.

I pressed my body close to the wall, muffling the noise of my breathing through the cloth of my pajama tops. Footsteps then, receding footsteps. Carefully keeping my distance I moved on, and at the turn of the hall stopped abruptly.

The door of the bedchamber there—Jane's bedchamber—stood out in the blackness like a panel of silver fire. It had been painted with some kind of luminous paint. The brush marks were still wet and sticky.

I twisted the latch and peered into the room. The faint glow from the window revealed the girl sleeping peacefully in the bed.

Nodding with relief, I moved on again down the corridor. At the staircase I heard the library door on the floor below click shut. I descended slowly and waited at the foot of the stairs for an eternity, listening.

At length I pushed boldly into the library. Corelli was sitting at the desk, a trail of smoke rising from his cigarette, an open book before him. He looked up as if in surprise.

"Couldn't sleep," I said shortly. "Thought I'd come down here and read a spell. You seem to have had the same idea."

He stared at me, then broke into a short laugh.

"I do more than read, Signor. I study. I am busy days, so I have only nights to work on my theory."

"Ah, yes," I replied. "Mr. Fay spoke to me about it. Something about color, isn't it, and the qualities of black and white?"

A gleam of interest sprang into his eyes.

"The Signor is interested in color, yes?"

"Some. Stephen Fay is my friend, and I have worked with him on many of his experiments."

The Italian nodded and pointed a finger toward his book.

"I am reading LaFlarge," he said. "A brilliant mind, but a fool. They are all fools, these scientists. They see only the physical facts. They see only things which exist materially before their eyes. They claim there is nothing psychic."

I crossed to a chair and sat down.

"Tell me," I said, "what has the psychic to do with color?"

"Everything, Signor. Fay—all scientists—will tell you that color is a phenomenon that occurs when daylight passes through a quartz prism. The rays from the sun are decomposed and form what the eyes see as the spectrum band, red at one end, violet at the other. That is elementary, of course.

"A body, a piece of blue cloth, for example, illuminated by daylight, appears colored because it absorbs red and yellow and throws back blue. In other words color in an object is produced by absorption. Is that clear?"

"I know all that," I said.

"Black, which of course is the absence of all color, is seen as black because it is the absorption of all and the reflection of none. One might liken it to a lake of pitch in the midst of the jungle. It takes everything into itself and allows nothing to escape. It is iniquity, the essence of all evil.

"Has it never occurred to you that even the ancients recognized this fact? We have Satan as the prince of blackness; the worshipping ceremonial to him is the black mass; we have black art and black magic. Throughout the ages black has always been synonymous for everything that is evil."

"I see," I said slowly.

"My theory then," Corelli went on, "lies in the exploration of black, not only physically but psychically. Let us say we have a room entirely painted black. Those walls are then the absorption of all wave lengths of light. Any photographer will tell you that an object—a book, a chair, a table—is seen only as a result of that object refracting wave lengths of light into the retina of the human eye.

"Is it not reasonable to suppose, therefore, that in this room of which I speak, any object or the refracted psychic equivalent of it will find itself likewise absorbed into the black walls?

"You begin to perceive, Signor? Where there is blackness, there is always fear. A child cries out when it enters a dark room. We reason with the child, tell it there is nothing there. Might we not be wrong? Might not the child's clean mind sense something which we in our more complex lives do not see nor understand?"

Corelli leaned back in his chair and lit another cigarette.

"Granting all that," I said slowly, "why would it necessarily follow that in black we would find only evil. Since black, as you say, is the absorption of everything, it must absorb the good as well, and the former has always been acknowledged to be the stronger of the two."

The Italian's eyes did not change.

"Think a moment, Signor," he said, "and you will see that only evil can live where there is utter blackness. Anything else would be smothered like a flower away from its precious sunlight. I—"

His voice clipped off, and I stiffened in my chair. From the floor above had come a girl's scream. Hollow and muffled by the intervening walls, the cry filtered through the house, filled with fear and stark terror.

With a single leap I was across the room and racing up the stairs. In the corridor above I switched on the lights as Stephen Fay emerged from his room and, white-faced, began to run toward me.

I reached the freshly-painted door of Jane's room, ripped it open and burst inside. The girl was huddled on the bed, eyes wide with terror.

"Miss Barron, are you hurt?"

She gave a low moan and buried her head in her hands, sobbing.

"It was horrible!" she gasped. "A monster! A rat! A rat twenty times the ordinary size! It came out of that hole in the wall next to my dressing table and—and leaped onto the bed. Then it crouched, staring at me. Then—"

The girl sobbed hysterically. . . .

It was a grim group that stood in the gray light of the library next morning. Jane Barron was still white and trembling, though I had administered a slight sedative a few minutes before. Corelli smoked nervously, throwing away cigarettes and lighting fresh ones before they were half consumed.

"I'm warning each of you," Fay said, "to move about the house with the greatest of caution. Something is loose in these walls, something we can't understand. Besides that, during the night the door of Jane's room was for some unexplainable reason coated with a paint containing calcium sulphide, making it appear luminous in the dark. Also someone entered my laboratory and tampered with my color-music machine.

"Haxton"—Fay nodded toward me—"I'm placing my niece's protection in your hands. Later perhaps it may be necessary to call the police."

After that I was alone in the library.

For some reason I had chosen not to reveal to Fay that it was the Italian who had smeared paint on the girl's room. Until further developments I meant to keep that fact to myself.

I picked up the thing then, which Fay claimed was at the bottom of the whole affair; the wooden carving of the rat. Again as I stared down upon its ugly body and curiously deformed head, an inner sense of horror welled over me.

Yet I told myself that was absurd. The image was only a manufactured god, representing a fanatic religion.

But an instant later I sat quite still as an insane idea began to clamor for recognition far back in a corner of my brain! An insane idea, yes, and yet one which fitted the conditions and which offered a method of combat! I leaped to my feet and headed for the laboratory.

Fay was there, as I had expected, and his composed manner quieted me for a moment.

"I can't understand it," he was saying. "The instrument was quite all right yesterday evening when I left for the movie. Corelli claims not to have touched it, and anyway he would have no reason at all for doing so. Yet the entire slide containing the color plates has been removed and this wooden frame inserted in its place."

I stared at the device. "It looks like a projection machine," I said.

Fay nodded. "It is. The instrument is constructed to throw upon a screen a rapidly changing circle of colors. It will be synchronized with an organ in such a way that when a piece of music is played, each note of sound will be accompanied by a corresponding color on the screen. There are seven notes, and there are seven primary colors. Thus in a rendition of a sonata we will both see and hear the composition. I—"

He broke off as the door burst open and Corelli lurched into the room.

"The rat, Signors!" he whispered. "It has come again! I saw it in the corridor."

But the corridor was empty. We traversed its length from one end to the other. Then we continued our search through the entire house. Deep into the many shadows of that ancient structure we probed. The rooms were silent and empty. Those on the third floor were closed off and barren of furniture. We found nothing.

At the foot of the stairs I suddenly whirled upon Fay.

"This new machine of yours," I said. "It uses artificial light to produce its colors?"

"Of course," he replied. "A carbon arc at present. Later an incandescent of some kind."

"And with the color plates removed as they are, the only thing that would appear on the screen would be a circle of white light. Is that right?"

"Not exactly," Fay explained. "Artificial light differs from daylight in that there is a deficiency of blue. Strictly speaking, the instrument would throw a shaft of yellow light."

"But could it be made pure white light?" I persisted.

He thought a moment. "Yes," he said, "it could. I have a Sheringham improved daylight lamp. Its light is the nearest man-made parallel to the rays of the sun. What are you driving at?"

"Fay," I said, "if you value your life, if you value the life of your niece, listen to me! Insert that lamp in your machine and arrange the projector so that it can be moved in a complete arc. Do you understand? In a complete arc!"

At half-past ten that night I stood once again before the frowing door of 16 Monroe Street. The intervening hours I had spent in a hurried trip to my own rooms and a brief but necessary visit to my patients in St. Mary's Hospital.

Nothing had happened during my absence. Fay led me to the library, poured two glasses of brandy and then nervously packed his pipe.

"The machine is ready," he said. "What you've got in mind, I don't know, but the daylight lamp has been substituted for the carbon arc, and the projector is mounted on a swivel. What now?"

I set down my glass. "Let's have a look," I said.

In the laboratory a moment later Fay adjusted several controls and pointed the instrument toward a screen. Then, motioning me to extinguish the lights, he switched on the current.

A dazzling shaft of light leaped from the narrow tube and spread a glaring circle of effulgence on the screen. Fay moved the projector, and the light traveled slowly, stabbing each article in the room in sharp relief.

"You have casters you could mount on the instrument, making it moveable?" I asked.

Fay thought a moment. "Yes," he slowly replied.

"Use them then and add an extension of at least twenty-five feet to the current wire."

He glared at me, but I swung about and left the room before he could voice protestations.

From eleven o'clock until eleven-thirty I prowled aimlessly about the house, glancing from time to time to time at the wall baseboards, nervously sucking a cold cigar. Finally in the library I picked up the desk phone and called Police Headquarters.

"McFee?" I said. "Dr. Haxton speaking. Yes, that's right—of St. Mary's. McFee, I'm at Mr. Stephen Fay's residence, Sixteen Monroe Street, just across from Oak Square. Can you send a man out here right away? No, no trouble yet, but I'm afraid there might be. . . . Yes, in a hurry. I'll explain later."

I forked the phone and waited. A quarter of an hour passed, and then, answering the ring at the street door, I found a lanky, hawk-faced policeman.

"Listen," I said before he could ask any questions, "I'm the physician in charge here. Your job is simply to look on, remember anything you see and prepare to sign a written report as a witness."

At ten minutes past twelve the five of us—Fay, Jane, Corelli, the patrolman and I entered the laboratory. We took positions according to my directions, the girl between Fay and me, the Italian in a chair slightly to the side.

Five feet in front of the door a connecting drop-cord was let down from the ceiling with a red-frosted electric light. Fay had wheeled the heavy color machine forward, facing the door.

"Ready, Fay?" I said, trying hard to keep my voice steady.

He nodded, and I stepped to the door, closed it halfway and extinguished the lights. We were in deep gloom now with the dim glow of the red light gleaming like an evil eye before us. And silence broken only by the hollow rumble of a far-away street car.

Suddenly Corelli leaped to his feet.

"Signors," he cried, "I refuse to sit here like a cat in the dark!"

"You'll stay where you are!" Fay snapped.

And so we waited. I could hear the ticking of my wristwatch. The Italian's breathing grew louder and more hurried, and I could feel Jane's hands open and close convulsively around the chair arm.

A quarter of an hour snailed by. I wiped a bead of perspiration from my forehead. Ten minutes more. And then we heard it!

From the outer corridor came the padding of approaching feet. Toward the laboratory door they came. I placed a warning hand on Fay's arm.

The door opened wide. A scream of horror mounted unsounded to my lips. What I saw I will never forget. A shapeless gray body with a rectangular head crouched there, eyes gleaming hellishly.

For a split second the five of us remained motionless with horror. Then riving the silence came Jane's shriek followed by a deafening roar from the policeman's revolver. The rat braced itself and leaped into the room.

"The light!" I cried. "Fay, the white light, do you hear?"

There was a snap and a hum, and a shaft of glaring blue-white radiance shot from the mouth of the projector. But even as it formed a circle on the far wall, the horror singled out one of our number for its attack. Corelli!

The Italian went down with a scream as the rat threw itself upon him.

I heard the dull crunch and the snap of breaking bone.

Then that beam of light swept across the room under Fay's guiding hand and centered full on the thing; livid under the ghastly ray, its head twisted around, eyes twin globules of hate. With a mewling cry of rage it made for the door.

"After it!" I shouted.

Together Fay and I rolled the projector into the outer corridor. It was blind, that corridor. It ended in a blank wall, and the doors on either side beyond the laboratory were closed.

Straight down the hall we pushed the color machine. The rat was uttering queer rasping sounds now, shambling wildly from side to side as it sought to escape the hated light.

Trapped, the thing stopped, whirled, then plunged straight at Fay. Even as the scientist's cry rose up I rushed forward to aid him. A raking claw gashed its way to the bone in my left shoulder. A nauseating animal stench choked my nostrils.

Then I seized the machine's projector tube and swung it. The white glare swept upon the rat squarely, centered on the head. An instant the horror poised motionless. Then slowly it began to disintegrate. The features ran together like heated clay. The eyes and mouth fell away. Before me a lump of gray fur diminished to a thin slime, to a darkish mist that rose slowly upward. Then that, too, wavered under my gaze and disappeared. . . .

I came back to consciousness on the divan in the library with Jane Barron chafing my wrists and Stephen Fay looking on nervously.

"It's all over, Haxton," he was saying. "Corelli's dead. The rat killed him. But—but I don't understand—"

I struggled to my feet, dazedly.

"Come to the laboratory, Fay," I said, "and I'll show you."

We made our silent way to that room of apparatus where the Italian's body still lay motionless on the floor. Bending over it I searched the pockets and at length drew forth two objects. A small leather-covered notebook and a piece of black cloth, about the size of a napkin.

"Recognize it?" I asked, holding up the cloth.

Fay nodded. "Yes. It's the covering Jane gave me for the rat image on the library desk. But—"

I opened the notebook, glanced at it, then handed it to Fay. For a long time he remained silent as he scanned the pages.

When he looked up at length a strange light was in his eyes.

"You see," I said, "Corelli was in love with your niece. Didn't he at some time ask if he could marry her?"

"Yes," Fay replied. "But that was absurd, of course. I told him he was crazy and let it go at that."

"Exactly," I nodded. "And in doing so you injured his Latin pride. He became mad with secret rage, and he swore revenge against you. You know the man's color theory—that black being the absorption of everything in the lair of all evil. He saw that rat image on the library desk, and he recognized it as an artifact of devil-worship, the essence of everything satanic.

"Over the image you had draped a black cloth. According to Corelli's theory then, that cloth was the psychic equivalent of all that the image in its carved form represented. Do you understand?

"He stole the cloth, mounted it on a wooden frame and inserted it in your color-music machine. Then he reversed the mechanism, and by casting a beam of black light upon the screen caused that horrible monster to be freed from its black cloth imprisonment and endowed with physical life.

"If we accept that reasoning, then Corelli's intention was to find a way of destroying you and at the same time prove the truth of his theory. That is why he smeared the luminous paint on Jane's bedroom door. White, being the antithesis of black, was a counter-defense, and he had no desire to see your niece harmed.

"For the same reason I asked you to insert the daylight lamp in the color machine. It was the only way of fighting the thing."

Fay had listened to me in silence. A queer, bewildered look crossed his face.

"But—but you can't expect me to believe all that," he objected. "It isn't scientific. It's mad from beginning to end! The whole thing has no foundation in fact. Black—white—Good Lord, man, no scientist in the world would believe—"

"Perhaps not," I agreed. "Perhaps I'm wrong. If I am, we'll never know. Corelli is dead. But one thing I do know. I'm going to take this cloth and notebook and that image in the library, throw them into the fire and burn them."

And I did.

Me and My Shadow
ERIC FRANK RUSSELL

Many British authors cracked the American pulp market, but few were to achieve the fame of Eric Frank Russell. Although remembered mostly for his work in the science fiction magazine Astounding, *Russell earned a permanent niche in pulp history as the author of* Sinister Barrier, *the novel John W. Campbell featured as the cover story for the first issue of* Unknown. *The serious and somewhat paranoid mood of that novel might have fooled readers into thinking that Russell lacked a sense of humor, but "Me and My Shadow," which appeared the following year, revealed his whimsical side and offered a sharp contrast to the usual gruesome fare served up in* Strange Stories.

L ITTLE TRIMBLE lowered a shaking spoon, blinked his weak, apologetic eyes.

"Now, now, Martha! Don't be like that!" he quavered.

Resting a beefy arm athwart her end of the breakfast table, Martha spoke slowly and viciously. Her voice was harsh with emotion, her features red with wrath, her expression venomous.

"For fifteen years I've lectured you, instructed you, commanded you. For seven hundred and eighty weeks of seven days each I've tried to do my duty as a wife by knocking some spark of manhood into your

185

miserable body." She slammed a huge, horny hand upon the table, made the milk jump in its jug. "And what've I got?"

"Aw, Martha!"

"What I've got," she bellowed, "is exactly what I had right at the start—a crawling, quivering, undersized, cowardly, spineless and gutless little worm!"

"I ain't as bad as that," he protested feebly.

"Prove it!" she shouted. "Prove it! Go and do what you haven't found the nerve to do in fifteen shivering years. Go and tell that boss of yours you've got to have a raise."

"Tell him?" Trimble blinked at her, aghast. "You mean ask him?"

"I said to tell him." Her voice was bitingly sarcastic, and still loud.

"He'll fire me."

"Of course, you would think of that!" Down came the hand again. The milk went over the top with fixed bayonets, flopped, made a spatter in No Man's Land. "Let him fire you. It'll be your chance. Tell him you've waited for it fifteen years, then hand him a poke in the gizzard. Find another job."

"What if there ain't another job?" he asked, almost tearfully.

"There're plenty. Dozens of them." She stood up, her mighty bulk still awing him despite years of familiarity. "Unfortunately, they're for men!"

He flinched, reached for his hat.

"I'll see," he murmured.

"You'll see! You were going to see a year back. And the year before that."

Her voice followed him out the front door and a hundred yards down the street. "And the year before that, and the one before that. Pfah!"

He mirrored himself in a window farther down. There he was, well under average height, paunchy, flabby, insignificant. Guess everybody was pretty well right about him. Just a fat little slob.

A downtown bus came along. He reached the door, got boosted in by a brawny hustler behind. The hustler rough-housed past him while he stood dumbly tendering the driver a quarter.

Trimble didn't say anything when a hard, heavy elbow dented the flabbiness over his ribs. He was used to it.

The driver slapped five nickels into his hand, scowled, shoved his machine into gear. Dropping a coin into the box, Trimble wandered to the back.

There was a vacant seat blocked by a blue-jowled individual. The sitter undressed Trimble with one contemptuous rip of his eyes, made no attempt to move.

Stretching himself, Trimble inserted pudgy fingers in a swinging handle, hung on without remark.

Dismounting ten blocks down, he crossed the road, his path including a deep safety curve around the backside of a policeman's horse. Trotting along the sidewalk, he reached the office.

Watson was already in. Trimble said, "Good morning!" and Watson growled, "Humph!" Every day their exchange was the same—good morning, and humph.

The others came in later. One replied to Trimble's greeting with what might have been, "Marn!" or "Garn!" The rest grunted, snorted, or grinned as if at a secret joke.

At ten, the boss made his advent. He never just turned up, or arrived, or landed. He always made an advent. This time was the same. The boss entered with the air of one about to lay a foundation-stone, or launch a battleship, or something. Nobody greeted him. They tried to look extremely respectful and very busy at one and the same time. Except Trimble, who managed to depict servile idleness.

He gave the boss an hour to get through the morning mail, then prayed for strength, knocked, went in.

"Excuse me, sir."

"Hey?" The bison head came up, savage eyes transfixed the petitioner. "Well, what d'you want?"

"Nothing, sir, nothing," assured Trimble, his blood turning to water. "It wasn't important, and I've forgotten it."

"Then get out!"

Trimble got out. Twelve o'clock came, and he tried to steel himself once more. There seemed to be a shortage of steel. He sat down again wearily.

At ten minutes to one, he tried for the third time, stood outside the boss' door, lifted his knuckles, and then changed his mind. He'd leave it until after lunch. The food would fortify him.

There was a bar on the way to the cafeteria. He'd passed it a thousand times, but had never gone inside. This time, it struck him that a shot of whiskey might help. He'd heard it called Dutch courage, and any sort of courage—Dutch or Zulu—was something he could do with aplenty.

Warily, his gaze went up and down the street. If Martha caught him in this sink of iniquity she'd fell him in his tracks. Yes, another Indian would bite the dust. But there wasn't any Martha. Greatly daring, he entered the bar.

The clients, or inmates, or whatever they're called, stared at him with open suspicion. Six of them were propped against the lengthy counter, their eyes summing him up as a barley-water addict. He'd have gone back if it hadn't been too late.

A bartender came along, said curtly, "What's yours?"

"A drink."

Somebody's snicker brought home to Trimble that one couldn't very well ask for a drink. One had to be more specific. For the life of him, he couldn't think of anything but beer. He didn't want beer.

"What's good?" he asked, brightly.

"It depends."

"Depends on what?"

"Whether you've got a thirst, a yen, or a woe."

"I have," said Trimble fervently, "got a woe!"

"Leave it to me." With an assured flick of his cloth, the bartender went away. He did things with bottles, came back, placed before the customer a glass of cloudy, yellow liquid. "That'll be forty."

Trimble paid, sat and stared at the glass. It fascinated him. It frightened him. It was as full of invitation and terror as an uncoiled cobra. He was still looking at it five minutes later when his neighbor, a hefty six-footer, casually put out a hairy hand, took the glass, drained it at a gulp. On no one but Trimble could such a breach of saloon etiquette be perpetrated.

"Always glad to help a pal," jeered the speaker's mouth, while his eyes said, "Well, d'ya want to make anything out of it?"

Offering no retort, no protest, Trimble went out. The contempt on the bartender's face was a hurtful thing. The others' raucous laughter was a dancing flame that scorched his neck and ears.

Safely outside, he communed with himself. What was the matter with him that he should be at the receiving end of all the kicks and butts? Could he help it that he was not a rip-roaring tough? Wasn't it the way he was made? Most important of all, what could he do about it—if anything?

There were these something-analysts to whom one could appeal. But they were doctors of a sort. He was terrified of doctors with their background of hospitals and operations. Besides, he feared appealing to anyone lest his reward be ridicule. He'd had plenty of ridicule ever since he was a kid. Was there a thing he didn't fear—just one, single thing of which he wasn't scared?

Somebody spoke close by him.

"Now don't be frightened. Maybe I can help you."

Turning, Trimble saw a little, white-haired man with a shriveled form topped by a parchment face from which peered eyes of the clearest blue. The clothes this man wore were old-fashioned, curious, but his general appearance served to strengthen his expression of amiable understanding.

"I saw what happened in there." The little man nodded toward the bar. "I appreciate your position."

"Why should it interest you?" asked Trimble, at once on his guard.

"I'm always interested in people." His friendly hand took Trimble's arm and they walked along side by side. "People are infinitely more interesting than things." The blue eyes twinkled gently. "It is an iron rule that everybody has one outstanding fault, or, if you prefer, one fundamental weakness. The commonest one is fear. The man who fears no man may yet fear cancer. The dictator fears hidden thoughts. Many people fear death, and those who don't, fear life."

"True," conceded Trimble, thawing in spite of himself.

"You are a slave of fear," went on the ancient. "Your case is made malignant by your own consciousness of it. You are too aware."

"Don't I know it!"

"That's exactly what I'm telling you! You know it. And it is always with you. You cannot forget it."

"I wish I could," said Trimble. "Maybe someday I shall. Maybe I'll get guts. Heavens knows I've tried!"

"I'm sure you have." The wizened one smiled happily. "All a trier needs is the support of an ever-present friend. He craves encouragement, and, if need be, assistance. Every man has a friend of his own."

"Show me mine," challenged Trimble lugubriously. "I'm a hell of a pal to myself."

"You shall have the support gained only by a favored few," promised the other.

He looked around very cautiously, then felt in the depths of a pocket. "You shall quaff from a fountain in nethermost Tibet."

He produced a long, thin vial filled with liquid of iridescent green.

"This," he whispered, "will give you ears to hear the voice of darkness, a tongue to talk in tones of a ghost."

"It'll what?"

"Take it," urged the other. "I give it because it is the law of Shan that grace shall beget grace, and strength shall father strength." Another gentle smile. "You have now only one fear to conquer—the fear to drink!"

He was gone. How he went was a mystery to the astonished Trimble. First, the little man was there, the next instant his wraithlike form had merged with distant pedestrians. Trimble stood, stared up the street, then at the vial clenched in plump fingers. He put the thing in his pocket.

Ten minutes to spare outside the time required to get back to the office. Trimble exited from the cafeteria, his stomach only half filled, his soul troubled. The choice lay between a scene with the boss or a scene with Martha. He was between the devil and the deep sea and the fact had spoiled his appetite.

Detouring around a block, he found a vacant lot free from scurrying people. Seeking the comparative privacy of the space's farthest corner, he took out the shining vial, had another look at it.

The contents were brilliantly green and looked oily. The stuff might be a drug, or even poison. If a drug could make gangsters hold up banks, what could it make him do? Or, if it was a poison, would it

make him die peacefully and without pain? Would Martha weep when
she saw him lying stiff and cold, a saintlike expression upon his waxen
face?

Uncapping the vial, he put his nose to it, got a whiff of dreamy,
elusive odors. He stuck in the tip of his tongue, licked it around his
mouth, absorbed the flavor. Strong, aromatic, enticing. Putting the vial
to his lips, he swigged the contents to the last drop. It was the first
chance he had ever taken, the most reckless thing he had ever done.

"And about time, too!" commented an eerie voice.

Trimble looked around. There wasn't anybody near him. He threw
away the empty vial, decided he'd been deluded.

"Down here," hinted the voice.

"Uhn?" Trimble stared in a circle. Nobody! Gosh, that must have
been a potent brew—he was imagining things already.

"Down here," urged the voice with sudden impatience. "On the floor,
you barrel-shaped lump of stupidity!" A pause, then complainingly:
"I'm your shadow."

"Oh, suffering snakes!" mouthed Trimble, covering his face with
quivering hands. "I'm talking to my shadow! I've got the rats on one
drink!"

"Don't be such a damned dope!" reproved the shadow. "Every man's
got his black ghost, but not every guy can use or understand shady
language." Silence, while the shade pondered, then the blunt command:
"Come on—we're going places."

"Where?"

"We're going to beat up that bum in the bar."

"What?" yelled Trimble, at the top of his voice. A couple of pedestrians stopped dead on the sidewalk, gaped across the lot. Trimble
took no notice. His mind was a whirl of wild confusion, his whole
being tormented by fear of the strait-jacket and the padded cell.

"Don't be so all-fired noisy."

The ghost faded slightly as a cloud crossed the sun, then came back
at full strength. "Now that we can pow-wow, I reckon I'd better have
a name. You can call me Clarence."

"Cl . . . Cl . . . Cl. . . ."

"Sure! Anything wrong with it?" demanded the other aggressively.
"Shut up! Get over here, nearer the wall—that's right! See me sitting
up? See me big—bigger'n you? Now bend that right arm. Okay, take
a look at mine. A humdinger, huh? What wouldn't Dempsey give for
a limb like this!"

"God!" groaned Trimble pitifully, his arm bent, his eyes turned
appealingly to the sky.

"You'n me," went on Clarence, "can now cooperate. You do the
aiming, and I'll hand the wallops. You've got to make sure you get
the right side of the light to make me big and strong, then we'll lash

out together. Just take good aim, remembering that I'm with you. Every time you hand a guy a prod, I'll paste him one that'll hang him on a ledge twelve floors up. D'you understand?"

"Y-yes," admitted Trimble, his voice almost inaudible. He cast a leery glance at his rear, saw that the number of onlookers had increased to ten.

"Turn around so's I'll be behind you," ordered the shadow. "Take a swipe by yourself, then another one with me. You'll be surprised at the difference."

Obediently, Trimble turned, faced the grinning audience, plunged his pudgy fist into thin air. It was a futile effort, and he knew it. Drawing back, he swung again, using all his strength and weight. His arm shot out like a piston, dragging his body off balance. He stumbled forward. The spectators laughed.

"See? What did I tell you? Not one guy in ten knows his own strength." Clarence permitted himself a ghostly chuckle. "Now we're all set. How about laying those kibitzers in a row, just to get our hand in?"

"No!" shouted Trimble. He wiped perspiration from a crimson, half-crazed face. The audience went up to fifteen.

"Okay, have it your own way. Now let's get back to the bar, and remember I'm always with you!"

With his feet dragging more and more reluctantly, Trimble reached the bar. He stood outside, knees knocking, while his bellicose shade gave quick instructions.

"Nobody can hear me but you. You're one of the favored few who can hear and speak the language of the dark. We'll go in there together, and you'll do what I tell you to do, say what I tell you to say. Whatever happens, don't get scared—I'll be with you, and I could flop a bull elephant."

"You b-bet," agreed Trimble with total lack of enthusiasm.

"All right. What in hell are you waiting for?"

Like a condemned criminal pacing the thirteen fateful steps, Trimble moved through the doors and into the bar. The same gang was still there, the same beefy hijacker lounging at the nearer end.

The bartender took one look at the entrant, smirked, then jerked an informative thumb. The hijacker sat pat and scowled. Still smirking, the bartender came up.

"What can I do for you?"

"Switch on the lights," gasped Trimble in an unearthly voice, "and I'll show you something."

Now he'd done it! He'd committed himself beyond withdrawal. He'd have to go through with the whole whacky affair right until the internes came and bore him away.

The bartender considered. Whatever was going to be shown, it could be twisted into something that would add to the day's fun. He decided to oblige.

"Sure!" he said, and switched them on.

Trimble looked around, absorbed a sudden dose of confidence. It was the sight at his side. There was Clarence, towering up the wall like a mighty djinn.

"Go on," commanded the tremendous shadow. "Do your stuff!"

Taking one step forward, Trimble snatched up the hijacker's glass, flung its contents into the fellow's face.

The recipient arose like one in a dream, gasped, mopped his streaming features, gasped again. Then he removed his jacket, folded it carefully, placed it on the counter. He spoke to his opponent very slowly, very deliberately, and very politely.

"I ain't rolling in money, but my heart is bursting with charity. I'll see that you get a decent burial!" With that, he released a pile-driver.

"Duck!" yelped Clarence.

Trimble pulled his head into his boots, felt an express locomotive rush across his hair.

"Now!" screamed Clarence frantically.

Popping up, Trimble slammed out a fist, concentrating on his aim, but putting all his weight and strength behind the blow. He tried for the Adam's apple, got it, and for a moment thought he was going to stick his arm through the bum's neck. It was something like walloping the sixtieth floor of the Empire State, and the effect was just as spectacular. The fellow went down like a poled ox. Oh, boy, had he got power!

"Again!" raved Clarence. "Lemme soak him another as he gets up."

The smitten one was struggling to rise, an expression of absolute incredulity upon his face. He got halfway, making uncertain motions with his arms and legs.

Trimble wound up his right arm until he could almost hear it whiz. Then he let his fist fly, this time trying for the other's smeller. He got it with a loud swack like the sound of a skied baseball. The victim tried to throw his head clean off his shoulders, then collapsed and slid a foot along the floor.

"G-g-gosh!" stuttered an awed voice.

Shaking with excitement, Trimble turned his back on his supine opponent, went to the counter. The bartender came up, his features wearing an expression of deep respect. Trimble licked his own forefinger, drew a spit face inside a beer-ring on the counter.

"Put curls on that!"

The bartender hesitated, looked around with a beseeching air, swallowed hard. Meekly, he licked his finger, added the curls.

Reaching across the counter, Trimble snatched the fellow's cloth.

"This is what'll happen next time you pull faces at me." He rubbed out the face.

"Now, mister, don't get tough," pleaded the bartender.

"Nuts!" It was the first time Trimble had used the word as a retort. He shied the cloth back, had a look at his snoring victim, walked out.

As his plump little form passed through the doors, a customer said, "That guy sure is dynamite! Looks to me like he's full of dope, and ripe for a killing."

"I dunno." The bartender was both subdued and sheepish. "You can't never tell from the looks of them. Take Slugs McKeefe, he's a world-beater at his weight, but he's only a fat little guy. I didn't like that feller's looks from the first—he might be Slugs' brother."

"He might," conceded the critic thoughtfully.

Down on the floor, the stricken one's bubbling snore ended in a gasp, a gulp, and an oath. He stirred, tried to sit up.

"Now for the boss," said Clarence, delight in his voice.

"No, no, not that!" Trimble's apologetic face was crimson from the strain of his recent adventure. His eyes kept flickering back, searching for the murderous pursuit that he thought was inevitable. It was hard to believe that he'd actually done what he had done, and he couldn't understand how he'd escaped alive.

"I said now for the boss, you animated pumpkin!" repeated the shadow, with much asperity.

"But I daren't batter the boss." Trimble's voice grew to a loud, protesting wail. "It'll get me in stir."

"What'll get you in stir?" demanded a passer-by, stopping and staring at the distracted speaker.

"Nothing—I was talking to myself." Trimble stopped as his irritated shadow snarled an interruption. He was reluctant to take the offered advice, but it looked as if he had to. "Hey!" he called. His questioner came back.

"Mind your own damn business," said Trimble, rudely.

"Okay, okay, keep your hair on!" The other was startled, hurried away.

"See?" chortled Clarence. "Now for the boss. We won't get hard unless we hafta."

"Have to," corrected Trimble.

"Hafta," Clarence persisted. "We'll talk first. If he won't appease us, we'll resort to force." He was quiet for a moment, then added: "And don't forget the lights—I like to grow powerful before I slap 'em."

"Oh, all right." Trimble began to feel resigned to a course of events that eventually was going to dump him in a cell, if not in the morgue. With a sigh of martyrdom, he entered the building, went upstairs to the office.

"Afternoon!"

"Humph!" said Watson.

Switching on the office lights, Trimble looked around, located his
shady partner, then walked up close to Watson, and spoke in a very
loud voice.

"I don't expect anything from a pig but a grunt. Might I remind
you that I bade you good afternoon?"

"Eh? . . . ah! . . . huh?" Watson was both scared and thunderstruck.

"Ah! . . . very well . . . good afternoon!"

"That's right! Remember it in future." With numb feet and a whirling
brain, Trimble went across to the boss' door. He raised his knuckles
to knock.

"Don't!" swore Clarence.

Trimble shuddered, grasped the door-knob, turned it gently. Taking
a deep breath, he gave the door a tremendous thrust that sent it back
with a crash. The thing almost flew off its hinges. As the boss shot up
from behind his desk, Trimble walked in.

"You," roared the boss, vibrating with rage, "you're fired!"

Turning, Trimble went back, closing the maltreated door behind him.
He didn't say a word.

"Trimble," bellowed the boss, his voice reverberating behind the
door, "come here."

Trimble entered for the second time. Closing the door on extended
ears in the outer office, he scowled at the boss, then went to the wall,
switched on the lights. After that, he fooled around until he got a
position that made Clarence ceiling-high. The boss squatted and watched
all this, his face purple, his eyes popping.

They stared at each other awhile, their silence broken only by the
boss' heavy, asthmatic breathing. Finally, the latter spoke.

"Have you been drinking, Trimble?"

"My taste in liquid refreshment is not a matter for discussion," said
Trimble, flatly. "I came in to tell you that I've resigned."

Stark horror filled his soul as the fateful words fell from his lips.
He'd done it now! Which menace was the worse, Clarence or Martha?
He didn't know—but he sure had burned his boats!

"Resigned?" parroted the boss, mouthing it as if it was some new,
outlandish word.

"Sure! I'm fed up. I'm going to offer my services to Rubinstein and
Flanagan." The boss shied like a frightened horse, and he went desperately on: "They'll pay me well for what I know. I'm sick and tired
of my lousy salary."

"Now Trimble," said the boss, gasping for breath, "I've no desire
to part with you after your many years of service. I would not like to
see your undoubted talents wasted on a gang of pikers like Rubinstein
and Flanagan. I'll give you another two dollars a week."

"Lemme wipe his face off his neck," suggested Clarence, eagerly.

"No!" shouted Trimble.

"Three dollars," said the boss.

"Come on—just one crack," Clarence persisted.

"No!" yelled Trimble, sweating at every pore.

"All right. I'll give you five." The boss' face contorted. "And that's final."

Mopping his brow, Trimble felt as if he was nearing the end of an hour upon the rack. Perspiration trickled down his spine, and his legs felt weak.

"I've been grossly underpaid the last ten years, and I wouldn't stay with you for a raise of less than twelve bucks. I'm worth an extra twenty to you, but I'm willing to take twelve, and let you have eight for cigars."

"C-c-cigars."

"Rubinstein and Flanagan'll raise me twelve. You can do it—or do without."

"Twelve!" The boss was dumbfounded, then annoyed, then thoughtful. Eventually, he reached a decision.

"It seems, Trimble, that I have been guilty of underestimating your abilities. I'll give you the increase for which you ask"—he bent forward and glared—"in exchange for a fidelity bond."

"Okay, I'll stay." Making for the door, he opened it, said, "Thanks!"

"See?" said Clarence.

Without answering his nagging shade, Trimble took his seat at his desk.

In tones audible all over the room, he spoke to Watson.

"Nice weather we're having."

"Humph!"

"Eh?" Trimble bawled.

"Very nice," replied Watson, meekly.

His heart sang like a nest of nightingales while he worked through the afternoon. Somehow, the story of his affair with the boss leaked around the office. People spoke to him in manner different from that of yore. It was almost incredible, but he was getting something he'd never had before—respect.

Rain was hammering down when he closed his books and left for home. What did it matter? The stinging drops felt good on his plump, beaming face, and the air was like old wine. Disdaining the bus, he walked along the wet, shining avenue, whistling to himself as he trotted along. He'd got news that would paralyze Martha!

A noise came from around the next corner, an explosive sound like that of a burst tire. Then another and another and another. Running feet pounded somewhere around the angle of the corner building. He came level, saw two figures racing toward him. One was six jumps behind the other, and both had guns. The nearest of the sprinting pair was twenty yards away. It was his opponent in the bar!

Spears of fear jabbed themselves into Trimble's brain. There was an uproar further down that street, and it looked like the running pair were making a frantic getaway. If the leader recognized Trimble, he'd seize the chance to blot him out in full flight. There was nowhere to hide in those split-seconds, no place in which to bury himself until the danger had passed. Even worse, the sky was heavily clouded, and his precious shadow was gone.

"Clarence!" he screamed, fearfully.

No reply. His shout drew the leading fugitive's attention. The fellow knew him immediately, sucked back thin lips in a deathy grin, raised his weapon. He was almost upon his quaking victim, the range was less than one yard, and it was impossible to miss.

Trimble kicked him on the kneecap.

He didn't do it on the impulse of the moment, nor with the desperation of a cornered rat. He was driven to it by the inevitable conclusion that his only hope lay in behaving exactly as if his missing shadow was still in support. So he lashed out with his foot, striving to connect accurately, using every ounce of his strength.

The other promptly plunged onto his face as if determined to poke his head through the sidewalk and have a look at the subway. It was a heartening sight that made Trimble suspect his efficient shade might still be hanging around even though unseen. The thought lent him courage.

With the startled expression of one who has seen an ant miraculously change into a lion, the second runner pulled up almost chest to chest with Trimble. He was a tall, lanky specimen whose Adam's apple seemed beyond reach.

Trimble batted his stomach against his spine. The fellow gagged, bent his upper half to a convenient angle, and Trimble bashed the apple. The victim did not assume the expected horizontal position. His sallow features suffused with a mixture of hatred and agony, he straightened, swiped at Trimble with the barrel of his weapon.

The blow failed to connect. Following former practice, Trimble sucked his head into his shoulders, blew it up again, stabbed another one into the stomach. The face came down once more and he smacked it up with considerable vim.

A crash sounded behind him, and a red-hot wasp bit off the lobe of his left ear. He took no notice, and he concentrated upon the face to the complete exclusion of everything else. Foul oaths were pouring from somewhere near the source of the crash, heavy feet were thumping the sidewalk toward him, people were shouting and whooping all around.

He heard none of it. His mind had no knowledge of his first assailant's resurrection. That snarling pan opposite his own was his sole object in life, the one purpose of his being.

With aim and weight and strength, he bashed the face up, socked it down, clouted it backward. Something hard and knobbly exploded out of nothingness, seemed to tear the left cheekbone from his own head. Another one appeared to tear his ribs apart. But Trimble kept working on that face, battering it into a bloody mask and pounding in the gore.

His heart was a jitterbug, and his breath was coming in whistling sobs when a long, black object sailed over the hateful face, descended, pushing it down to the floor. He made a couple more automatic swiping motions, then stood shuddering and blinking. His vision cleared slowly.

The cop said, "Mister, for a feller your size you sure are sudden death!"

Looking around, Trimble saw that half a dozen cops had arrived, and were bundling up his recent opponents.

"That first guy," went on the other, "was Ham Carlotti, and we've wanted him for months." He clothed Trimble in admiration. "We owe you one for this. Any time we can do something for you, just ask."

Getting out a handkerchief, Trimble dabbed his ear, looked at the handkerchief. There was blood on it. God, he was bleeding like a stuck pig! And his left eye was swelling up, his cheekbone felt like hell, his ribs were a torment. He was in a devil of a mess!

"You can do something for me right now," he told the cop. "Ever since I was a kid I've wanted to ride home in a police car. How about it?"

"You bet!" the cop enthused. "It'll be a pleasure." He called to the driver of a car that had just swung in. "This gent's been a help. The ride's on us."

"Where d'ya live?"

Clambering in, Trimble sat back and enjoyed himself. Off they went, hell-for-leather, the siren yelling like a banshee, traffic scuttling madly from their path. This was the life!

The sun came out, beaming at full strength. He became aware of his shadow riding by his side.

"Clarence."

"Yes, Master," he said very humbly.

"In future, you can leave it to me."

"Yes, Master. But—"

"Shut up!" bawled Trimble.

"Shut up who?" inquired the driver, glancing surprisedly over his shoulder.

"The missus," Trimble answered glibly. "I'm ready for war."

Smiling broadly, the driver whirled his car into the curb, followed his passenger to the door. When Martha opened it, he touched his cap, said: "Ma'am, your husband's a hero." Then he went.

"Hero!" snorted Martha, crossing brawny arms on her ample bosom, she braced herself for an informative speech. Then her eyes found her partner's war-scarred face. She let the eyes protrude. "Where've you been to get a mug like that?"

Vouchsafing no reply, Trimble pushed past her, went into the hall. He waited until she had closed the door, then put skinned knuckles on his hips, faced her squarely. He had a kindly nature, and he had no desire to hurt her unduly, but it was now necessary to impress this woman that she had to deal with a man.

"Martha, I've slapped down a couple of gangsters, and I've soaked the boss another twelve bucks." He blinked as she clutched at the wall for support. "I've been very patient with you for many years, but I've reached the end of my tether. I wish you to understand that from now on I want no more of your lip."

"Lip," she echoed dazedly, not believing her ears.

"Otherwise, I'll paste you one that'll make you wish you'd brought your parachute."

"Horatio!" She staggered forward, her face a picture of utter stupefaction. "You wouldn't strike a woman, would you?"

"Wouldn't I!" He spat on his sore knuckles.

"Oh, Horatio!" In one wild swoop she had embraced his neck and found his protesting lips.

Heck, aren't women peculiar critters? They liked 'em gentle, but a few—like Martha—preferred 'em tough. Might as well give her more of the same.

Grabbing her hair, he pulled her face over to a comfortable slant. Then he kissed her. He concentrated on aim, weight, and strength. It was a pouting, juicy, emphatic osculation that finished in a loud report.

Grinning triumphantly, he peeked over her shoulder to see what his subdued shadow thought of that. But Clarence was too busy to bother. Didn't Martha have a shadow too?

Doomed

SEABURY QUINN

Seabury Quinn's fiction appeared almost exclusively in Weird Tales, *and for good reason—his tales of the psychic sleuth, Jules de Grandin, proved so popular with readers that Quinn turned them out on an average of one every three issues during his long tenure with the magazine. Jules de Grandin never appeared outside of* Weird Tales, *but on occasion, other efforts by his creator did. "Doomed," from the December 1940 issue of* Strange Stories, *is a simple tale of the supernatural, something of a departure from the complex plots Quinn usually worked out for his Gallic ghostbuster.*

McCUMBER FOLDED his newspaper and choked back a yawn as the subway train slid into Borough Hall station. He was dog-tired. But the item he had just read in the paper disturbed him. He almost forgot that it was nearly midnight and that he'd been working like a horse since eight that morning.

GOVERNOR REFUSES
COMMUTATION

Central City, June 13—Gov. Chas. B. Oglesby today refused to commute Olga Wheatley's death sentence to life imprisonment.

Women's clubs in all sections of the country have forwarded petitions for clemency to the capital, but the chief executive stood firm in his expressed determination to let the law take its course.

On the night of January 22, the twenty-year-old blond factory operative, who had "never had a date," went to dinner with a girl friend and two traveling salesmen who picked the girls up near the factory entrance. When she returned home after ten o'clock, after having taken in a movie with her friend and the young men, her stepfather, Fred Hatton, forty-eight and a widower, gave her a lashing with his belt. According to her testimony at her trial, he "called her bad names."

Still smarting from the flogging and harboring resentment, the girl crept into his room after her stepfather had gone to sleep. She beat him to death with a hammer as he lay in bed. Then she walked to police headquarters and gave herself up.

She admitted the killing in court and repeatedly declared she would do the same thing again under like circumstances. The jury, composed for the most part of factory workers with daughters of their own, brought in a verdict of murder in the first degree after deliberating less than half an hour. Such verdicts make the death sentence mandatory.

Why, he wondered, should the obscure item buried on page six among the white sale ads, affect him so strongly? Murder was no rare occurrence in present-day America, nor were sentences and executions, if the guilty parties were obscure and poor. He shrugged his shoulders in slight irritation. Probably exhaustion. Little things get you down when you're tired, and, Lord, but he was tired!

The schedule had been heavy at the office with Burks and Jamison away on vacation. But now his turn had come. He had two blessed weeks of laziness before him. No fool vacation trips, no hiking, fishing or exhausting exercise—just a good old-fashioned loaf. He would sleep as late as he wanted to, swim in the St. George pool or at Jones Beach, drive around Long Island and Westchester. That would be living!

A fog had blown in from the bay since he left Times Square. As he crossed Court Street, the traffic lights showed blurs of red and green against the gathering mist. The cold of it struck through his clothes and seemed to chill him to the marrow. Moisture gathered on the sills and cornices until the cold drops spattered on the sidewalk with a sound like autumn rain.

Joralemon Street was empty, lifeless, blurred with slowly drifting fog. The buildings facing it were formless and obscure as objects in a painting, on which the second color had been brushed while the first was still wet. High above the rooftops and the mist, the moon was

not yet quite obscured. A hazy halo trailed around it like a blown
scarf. A snatch from Oscar Wilde's "Salome" came to him as he looked
up.

> The moon . . . she is like a dead
> woman;
> A dead woman who covers herself with
> a veil and goes looking for lovers—

"I beg your pardon!" He broke off the half mumbled quotation.
Moon gazing, he had run full-tilt into a woman. Even as he voiced
his quick apology, he saw her reel, clutch at the railing of an areaway.
She swayed for a moment, and fell.

"I'm so sorry!" He knelt by her, slipping an arm underneath her
shoulders. "Are you badly hurt? I wasn't looking where I walked—"
But while he spoke contritely, he was arguing with a backwash of
thought. "The street was empty as a blown eggshell just now. There's
no doorway here, no cross street, no area. . . . Where in hell did she
come from?"

A broken moan, half trembling sigh and half stifled groan, came
from her. Through the light cloth of her raincoat he could feel her
warmth. It was incredible. The sleek silk felt hot to his touch, as if it
had lain in the sun, or on a heated radiator. His hand brushed her
cheek. It was almost scalding to his fingers. She seemed scorching,
parched with fever.

"Good heavens, you're ill!" he cried. "Let me help you!"

"I—I'm just faint," she broke in. Despite his apprehension, he was
aware of the throatiness, the deep, mellow quality of her voice. "If
you'll only help me home. . . ."

He raised her, and she seemed to gain strength from his touch. For
the first few faltering steps she leaned against him heavily. But when
they reached the cross street, her shoulder was barely brushing his.
When they were halfway down the block, her hand was resting on his
arm more in formality than for assistance.

"I'm sorry if I made you feel uneasy," she told him. "You really
didn't hurt me, only took me off my balance. I also wasn't looking
where I walked, and when we bumped into each other—" Her voice
trailed off and she fell silent for a dozen steps. "I'd come out for a
breath of air. The cool, sweet fog seemed so good— And the next
thing I knew—"

"But you're ill," he insisted. "You're burning." The tightening of her
fingers on his arm was like the sudden clamping of a vise. He could
hear the breath rasp sharply through her teeth. "You're feverish."

"Ah!" She let the exclamation out slowly, like a sigh of relief. "It's nothing, really. I often run a temperature. That's why the fog felt so good. But I'm quite all right now—see!"

She stripped a glove off and laid bared fingers on his cheek. He started with surprise. Three minutes ago she had been feverish enough to burst a thermometer. Now her hand was cool and smooth, faintly moist—as normal as his own. It was soft, too, and beautifully formed, he knew by its feel. He caught from it the vestige of faint scent— mingled musk and sandalwood and wild carnation, provocative as half heard Oriental music.

For a moment he had an impulse to turn his head and press a kiss against the fingers resting softly on his cheek. But he fought down the blind urge.

Three-quarters of the long block was taken up with brownstone fronts, dear to the *haut monde* of New York in the late seventies and early eighties. Now they had been remodeled into small, dark flats, some with "Vacancy" cards in their front windows. At the corner reared a tall apartment building.

Between the older houses and the new apartment, set back from the sidewalk by a grass plot fenced in with an ornamental iron railing, was a little red-brick residence. It was two stories high, with a low, white stoop and long twin windows, through whose drawn curtains a gleam of cozy lamplight glowed against the coldness of the fog.

"I live here," she told him. "Thank you so much for—"

"May I come in—to see that you're all right?" he asked diffidently. To presume upon the service he had done her was unfair, he realized. But she had seemed gravely ill when he crashed into her and—Why beat about the bush? In all his thirty years, he'd never been so attracted to a woman as he was to her.

Her laugh bore out the promise of her voice. Beginning with a low, soft chuckle, it ended in a gay, infectious bell-tone.

"Why not?" she countered as she handed him her key. "I know you're dying for a drink and a cigarette. I could do nicely with them, myself."

The little house was only one room wide. They stepped from a small entrance into a combination living room and parlor.

Bokhara scatter-rugs lay on the polished floor. Old-fashioned chintz, patterned with bouquets of roses, hung at the low windows. Deep chairs and sofas were slip-covered in a warm rose linen that went well with the gray goodwork and walls. A low coffee table of pear wood, waxed to a satin finish, stood before the nearest couch. A baby grand piano with the score of *Der Fliegende Hollander* open on its music rack was by the windows. Over all, the shaded lamplight cast a glow like mellow, antique gold.

She slipped her shrouding raincoat off and doffed her felt storm hat. Her knitted dress of coral rayon molded her slim figure as revealingly

as if it had been cased in plastic cellulose. McCumber felt his heart
beat quicker. She had long, violet eyes, a long mouth. Her light hair
was warmer than ash blond, but still too pale to be called yellow. It
was drawn back in smooth soft waves from her forehead. Her small,
straight nose and small, pointed chin made his eyes go soft. Every line
of her was long, but definitely feminine.

She waved him to a seat and left him. But she returned in an
incredibly short time with a tall, sweat-beaded shaker and two glasses.
The Martinis were just right, with vermouth cutting the sharp flavor
of the gin without destroying its dryness. He had never tasted better
cigarettes. The more he looked at her, the lovelier she seemed. The
more he listened to the throaty pizzicato of her voice, the more his
fascination grew.

He had no idea what they talked about. He knew only that one
spoke and the other listened alternately. He was happier in that lamplit
room, with the chintz curtains drawn against the outside fog, than he
had ever been before.

"I'm Frank McCumber, an accountant by profession. But now, thank
goodness, I'm on a two-weeks' vacation."

She smiled acknowledgment of the self-introduction. Then she replied
when he waited for an exchange of confidence.

"Real names are so prosaic. You found me in distress and rescued
me like a true knight. I'll be Niume to you, and call you
Pellinore."

So they were Niume and Pellinore to each other.

When finally he rose to leave, she came to the door with him. His
farewell glance took in the lovely contours of her face, the gleam of
lamplight on her silken, pale gold hair, the softness of her half closed
eyes.

"May I come to see how you are in the morning?" he begged.

"I know I'll be quite well, but please don't let that keep you away,"
she laughed.

"If you're well—Do you ride?" he asked.

"Of course."

"Then shall we say we have a date for half-past six, if the weather's
fine?"

She nodded, smiling. He turned away, begrudging even the few hours
of sleep that lay between their first farewell and their next meeting.

Morning came, sweet and cool, with limpid, fog-washed air and bright
June sunshine sparkling on wet trees and grass. The little brick house
looked even more inviting in daylight. Its white woodwork had been
freshly painted. Geraniums blossomed in green window boxes. Its three-
stepped stoop was scrubbed to almost dazzling brightness.

She was waiting, dressed for riding in white Bedford cord breeches,
and a shirt of soft white silk open at the throat. About her almost

incredibly slim waist, a scarf of pistachio green was wound and rewound like a cummerbund. A length of silk of the same shade was twisted turbanwise about her bright, fair hair. Black, high boots cased her narrow, high-arched feet and slender legs.

All morning they rode through the park while a light breeze played among the white birch trees. The fresh turned earth of flower beds beside the bridle paths smelled rich and warm.

By the time they stopped for hamburgers and beer at the zoo lunch-room, he knew he was in love with her—deeply, tremulously; wonderingly.

The tempo of their relationship quickened with each sun-bright summer day. Women had never meant much to him. One does not get a C.P.A. certificate at twenty-six without hard study, and he had never had the time or inclination for romance.

But this girl— She was like someone he might have read about, or dreamed of when he made up stories to himself. She seemed too wonderful and beautifully perfect for anyone like him to meet and know. He treasured every moment of her company, drawing each one out as long as he could, counting it as misers count their gold.

Every waking moment he was with her. She had a sort of eagerness, a questing, ardent love of life and a vitality that was almost startling. Besides, she fairly reveled in the things they did together. She might have been some schoolgirl brought up in a convent and just given freedom, judging by the way she plunged into activity.

They visited the shore. Lovely as a Greek statue in yellow halter-neck swim suit, long limbed and graceful as a second Atalanta, she ran along the gleaming beach. With the sunlight frothing in her hair, she plunged through the breakers to swim out into the deep blue water with fearless, beautiful vitality. Emerging presently, dripping and lovely as a naiad from the foam, she was ready to lead him to some fresh activity.

Yet there was a mysterious timidity, or fearfulness about her which clashed oddly with her physical daring. She would be laughing, fairly bubbling with the joy of living. Suddenly her mood would change. The laugh-lights would vanish from her eyes. Her pupils would swell and spread until they seemed almost to hide the irises, like those of a frightened cat. Sometimes, in the midst of a laugh, she would halt abruptly and look round her with an apprehensive glance. Then he'd see the tremor of horripilation ripple through her glowing skin as if a chilling wind blew over her.

Once, as they sat at luncheon in a midtown restaurant, a man at the next table raised his voice angrily.

"I'll be damned if I do!" he shouted.

At the mild oath, her face went as white as parchment. The breath hissed softly through her teeth. Her lower lip began to quiver. Her eyes darkened, and he saw fear staring from them—fear that came from heart and soul. It looked out from her eyes as from the windows of a torture chamber.

"Please, Pellinore," she begged. "Take me out—out into the sunshine."

Five minutes later she was chatting gayly as if she had never known a thought of fear. They strolled down Fifth Avenue, admiring the displays in the shop windows.

Two weeks passed, fourteen drifting days when time hung suspended. To him it had been like a view of fairyland with Niume as its Titania. . . . Niume in backless, strapless evening gown, dancing with him on the roofs or at the supper clubs. Niume in smart crepe print with doeskin gloves and a hat that would have made any other woman look ridiculous, smiling at him across luncheon tables. Niume on the tennis court in shorts and halter, the sunlight like a halo on her misty golden hair. Niume in a swim suit of molded lastex. Her teeth were as white as ocean foam, her red lips startling against the green spume of water as she swam beside him with long, easy strokes. . . .

They were driving back from Asbury. A light rain had come up as they neared Jersey City, a soft summer rain darkening the pavements and bringing surcease from the sultry summer heat. Drifting in between the curtains of the car, it fell delicately against their cheeks. It seemed to him that the drops fell gayly past the butter-yellow of the street lamps' glow. He sensed that the entire universe shared his elation. For in her eyes that afternoon he'd surely read the answer to the question he hadn't been able to make his lips ask.

"Niume." He took his hand off of the steering wheel and laid it on hers when a red light signaled a stop. "Tonight ends it."

"Yes, Pellinore, it ends tonight."

She had answered so softly that he hardly heard. Yet something in the quality of her tone drew his eyes to her face.

In the faint reflection of the dashboard light, her features were expressionless as a dead woman's. Her eyes were set, fixed, fearful, as though they looked at something just beyond her vision, something nameless, dreadful, horrible.

"You're not well?" he asked in quick apprehension. Through the soft suede of her glove he felt the mounting fever, as he'd felt it through her raincoat on the night he met her in the fog.

"Not very . . . Please, dear, take me back quickly. I can't stand it—"

Her voice was flat, expressionless, almost mechanical. When he looked at her again, he felt a shiver light as air go through him. It was as if he sat beside the suffering ghost of a girl in the flesh. He shoved the automatic gear-shift forward when the red light changed to green. They drove the rest of the way in silence.

"May I call tomorrow, on my way to office?" he pleaded as they stopped at her door. "I'd like to ask—"

"Don't—don't say it, Pellinore," she begged him in a breaking voice. "I couldn't bear it, now."

He swung the car around and looked back. She was standing on the threshold with her head thrown back. Her hands were clasped upon her breast and her body leaned toward him in agonized and blind embrace. Her lips were parted lightly and her eyes tight closed. Then she turned slowly, shoulders drooping. The darkness of the doorway swallowed her.

He went home, but not to bed. For hours he paced his living room, walking a frustrated diamond-shaped figure on the rug. Finally the sky turned tawny gray, steel, then pale blue. A rose glow quickened in the east, like blood that comes back in the face of one reviving from a faint.

By the time he reached her corner, he was almost running. If she were ill, she needed him. Sick or well, he needed her—needed her with passionate longing.

"Niume! Niume!" His hurrying footsteps beat the rhythm of her name against the sidewalk. The last old brownstone house was passed. He was at her gate.

Hand on the iron, he came to a halt. His heart gave a cold, nauseating lurch. The world seemed spinning crazily on a loose axis. Time stopped, and breathing with it. He licked his dry lips with a tongue that had suddenly gone arid. He clutched the rusty iron gate as if he clung to the cornice of a high building.

This was not the little freshly painted house with spotless white woodwork and red geraniums abloom in long, green window boxes! This place reeked with decay. The window casings sagged awry. The paint was blistered on them, peeling off like sunburned skin. The steps of the stoop had warped until they could hold small puddles of rain in their troughs. The little yard was bare of grass and littered with old bottles, bits of soiled newspaper and the rusting wreck of a discarded bedspring. Window panes were cracked and broken. In one of them leaned a "For Rent" sign, tattered and stained with age and dust.

Plainly, the house had not been occupied in years.

Next door, a colored boy laid out the rubber vestibule mats of the apartment house, before hosing them on the sidewalk. McCumber half walked, half lurched toward him.

"The young lady who lived here"—he waved a shaking hand at the ruinous little house—"when did she move—"

The Negro eyed him askance.

"Young lady, suh?" he countered. "Ain't no young lady lived there. Ain't no one lived there since ah come to work here, an' that's five years ago. No, suh. That place always been fo' rent."

McCumber turned away. He was finding it hard to breathe. There was a curious, stifled feeling in his breast. The blood churned in his ears.

How could he trace her. How was he to find her? Inside him rose a silent, hopeless cry.

"I don't even know her name!"

The drugstore near his house was just opening as he went past.

"Some aromatic ammonia, please," he told the young man at the soda counter. He drained the stimulant at a gulp.

"Want your films, now, Mr. McCumber?" asked the drug clerk. "They come in late last night."

He thrust the envelope into his pocket and hurried to his apartment. He couldn't go to the office today. He couldn't bear to face them. . . .

Had he dreamed it all? Had he imagined it? Quick fear traced icy fingers down his spine. Was he going mad?

The pictures! They'd reassure him. He had taken several of her. She had taken one or two of him. They had asked a passing stranger at the beach to photograph them together.

As if it held reprief from the gallows, he tore the envelope open, spilled its contents on the desk. Six bewildering pictures showed nothing but views of sea and sand and sky. He recognized them after awhile.

Niume had posed against those backgrounds, but there was no human being in the scenes! His own face smiled at him from several bright, glossy prints.

Here was the one the stranger had taken of them. How silly he looked, standing there against the background of the curling waves. With an inane smirk upon his face, he held his left arm horizontal from his body, as if it clasped invisible shoulders. . . .

Mad! Over and over, the drums of his mind beat the dreadful word, pounded it into a terrifying rhythm. Mad. Mad. Mad-mad-mad! In every corner of the chamber, shadows seemed to hunch and rear and pant, waiting to pounce on him—drag him down into the plumbless abyss of insanity.

To and fro across the rug he paced, like a caged beast counting its bars. Ten steps this way, ten steps back, then turn and pace ten more. His throat was tight. His lips were dry. There was a burning, scratching feeling, as of hot sand, on his eyelids.

Knuckles pounded on his door.

"McCumber?" the expressman asked. "Sign here, please. Parcel of books from Cincinnati."

Mechanically he hunted for the hammer. Opening the box would occupy his hands. Anything was better than that everlasting pacing back and forth. The books were wrapped in newspaper, several layers of it. As he peeled off the padding, a two-week-old headline caught his eye.

BLOND HAMMER SLAYER
WALKS LAST MILE

Central City, June 14—Olga Wheatley, the girl who "never had a date" until the night she was picked up by a small-time traveling salesman and came home to a beating and to kill her stepfather for administering it, paid the final penalty tonight at 11:49.

Disdaining prison matrons' arms or spiritual help from prison chaplains, she walked unaided to the death chamber. She maintained that iron silence which had marked her ever since the jury found her guilty of the hammer slaying of Fred Hatton.

The prison has its own grim lexicon. Prisoners call the death house "the dance hall." The strain of waiting for the call to the electric chair affects even the most hardened convict's nerves. It produces involuntary jerkings and twitchings, like St. Vitus dance.

But Olga Wheatley remained calm throughout the long ordeal of waiting. Even when the warden came to tell her yesterday that Gov. Chas. B. Oglesby had refused a commutation of the death sentence, she showed no more emotion than if he had merely called to pass the time of day.

Not until they strapped her in the chair did she break the sullen, brooding silence. Then the cankering resentment that had festered inside her burst forth in a sharp, blazing statement.

"I killed him, and I'm not sorry. I'm glad of it. I'd do it again, I never had a good time in my life—never had a date, never went to a party, never had a party dress. If I could have just two weeks of the kind of life girls in big cities have, I'd be willing to go to hell. I'd call the bargain square."

Then the guards clamped down the death-cap on her shaven blond head. Warden Thompson raised his hand and the executioner applied the current.

Two minutes and six seconds later, Prison Doctor Edward Earnshaw stepped back with his stethoscope.

"I pronounce this woman dead," he declared.

"Picture on Page Four," the cutline read. With an urgency he could not explain McCumber ruffled through the sheets of crumpled paper.

His heart, just a moment ago, had seemed wrung dry of misery. Now it refilled itself from memories. He began to sob, the hard, dry, ugly sobs of a man unused to tears.

Smiling at him from the rumpled sheet of two-weeks-old newspaper were the lovely features of "Niume." Underneath the picture was the caption:

Would trade hell for two weeks' good time. Olga Wheatley, the blond hammer murderess who "never had a date," died in the electric chair last night. She stated that if she could have two weeks of life and love she'd burn in hell for all eternity and "call it square."

The Coppersmith

LESTER DEL REY

Most weird fiction pulps published stories of modern men and women terrorized by the same supernatural creatures that had scared their grandparents and great-grandparents. Unknown stood that tradition on its head. Many of its stories described the plight of mythical creatures who found themselves forced to change their ways and seek untraditional livelihoods in a modern age that didn't find them at all frightening. Lester del Rey proved himself one of the magazine's most capable writers on this theme. In "The Pipes of Pan," he transformed the god of the shepherds into a jazz clarinetist. In "Anything," he told of a selfless brownie whose good deeds meet with nothing but skepticism and distrust in the average American town. "The Coppersmith" (along with its sequel, "Doubled in Brass") is about one of the little people, and the difficulty he has finding work in the modern industrial era.

IN THE slanting rays of the morning sun, the figure trudging along the path seemed out of place so near the foothills of the Adirondacks. His scant three feet of stocky height was covered by a tattered jerkin of brown leather that fell to his knees, and above was a russet cap with turned-back brim and high, pointed crown. Below, the dusty sandals were tipped up at the toes and tied back to the ankles, and on each a little copper bell tinkled lightly as he walked.

Ellowan Coppersmith moved slowly under the weight of the bag he bore on his shoulders, combing out his beard with a stubby brown hand and humming in time with the jingling bells. It was early still and a whole day lay before him in which to work. After the long sleep, back in the hills where his people lay dormant, work would be good again.

The path came to an end where it joined a well-kept highway, and the elf eased the bag from his shoulder while he studied the signpost. There was little meaning for him in the cryptic marker that bore the cabalistic *30*, but the arrow below indicated that Wells lay half a mile beyond. That must be the village he had spied from the path; a very nice little village, Ellowan judged, and not unprosperous. Work should be found in plenty there.

But first, the berries he had picked in the fields would refresh him after the long walk. His kindly brown eyes lighted with pleasure as he pulled them from his bag and sat back against the signpost. Surely even these few so late in the season were an omen of good fortune to come. The elf munched them slowly, savoring their wild sweetness gratefully.

When they were finished, he reached into his bag again and brought forth a handful of thin sticks, which he tossed on the ground and studied carefully. "Sixscore years in sleep," he muttered. "Eh, well, though the runes forecast the future but poorly, they seldom lie of the past. Sixscore years it must be."

He tossed the runes back into the bag and turned toward a growing noise that had been creeping up on him from behind. The source of the sound seemed to be a long, low vehicle that came sweeping up the road and flashed by him so rapidly that there was only time to catch a glimpse of the men inside.

"These men!" Ellowan picked up his bag and headed toward the village, shaking his head doubtfully. "Now they have engines inside their carriages, and strange engines at that, from the odor. Even the air of the highway must be polluted with the foul smell of machines. Next it's flying they'll be. Methinks 'twere best to go through the fields to the village."

He pulled out his clay pipe and sucked on it, but the flavor had dried out while he had lain sleeping, and the tobacco in his pouch had molded away. Well, there'd be tobacco in the village, and coppers to buy it with. He was humming again as he neared the town and studied its group of houses, among which the people were just beginning to stir. It would be best to go from house to house rather than disturb them by crying his services from the street. With an expectant smile on his weathered old face, Ellowan rapped lightly and waited for a response.

"Whatta you want?" The woman brushed back her stringy hair with one hand while holding the door firmly with the other, and her eyes were hard as she caught sight of the elf's bag. "We don't want no magazines. You're just wastin' your time!"

From the kitchen came the nauseating odor of scorching eggs, and the door was slammed shut before Ellowan could state his wants. Eh, well, a town without a shrew was a town without a house. A bad start and a good ending, perchance. But no one answered his second knock, and he drew no further response than faces pressed to the window at the third.

A young woman came to the next door, eying him curiously, but answering his smile. "Good morning," she said doubtfully, and the elf's hopes rose.

"A good morning to you, mistress. And have you pots to mend, pans or odds that you wish repaired?" It was good to speak the words again. "I'm a wonderful tinker, none better, mistress. Like new they'll be, and the better for the knack that I have and that which I bring in my bag."

"I'm sorry, but I haven't anything; I've just been married a few weeks." She smiled again, hesitantly. "If you're hungry, though . . . well, we don't usually feed men who come to the door, but I guess it'd be all right this time."

"No, mistress, but thank'ee. It's only honest labor I want." Ellowan heaved the bag up again and moved down the steps. The girl turned to go in, glancing back at him with a feeling of guilt that there was no work for the strange little fellow. On impulse, she called after him. "Wait!" At her cry, he faced her again. "I just thought; mother might have something for you. She lives down the street—the fifth house on the right. Her name's Mrs. Franklin."

Ellowan's face creased in a twinkling smile. "My thanks again, mistress, and good fortune attend you."

Eh, so, his luck had changed again. Once his skill was known, there'd be no lack of work for him. "A few coppers here and a farthing there, from many a kettle to mend; with solder and flux and skill to combine, there's many a copper to spend."

He was still humming as he rounded the house and found Mrs. Franklin hanging out dish towels on the back porch to dry. She was a somewhat stout woman, with the expression of fatigue that grows habitual in some cases, but her smile was as kindly as her daughter's when she spied the elf.

"Are you the little man my daughter said mended things?" she asked. "Susan phoned me that you'd be here—she took quite a fancy to you. Well, come up here on the porch and I'll bring out what I want fixed. I hope your rates aren't too high?"

"It's very reasonable you'll find them, mistress." He sank down on a three-legged stool he pulled from his bag and brought out a little table, while she went inside for the articles that needed repairs. There were knicknacks, a skillet, various pans, a copper wash boiler, and odds and ends of all sorts; enough to keep him busy till midday.

She set them down beside him. "Well, that's the lot of them. I've been meaning to throw most of them away, since nobody around here can fix them, but it seems a shame to see things wasted for some little hole. You just call me when you're through."

Ellowan nodded briskly and dug down into his seemingly bottomless bag. Out came his wonderful fluxes that could clean the thickest tarnish away in a twinkling, the polish that even the hardest grease and oldest soot couldn't defy, the bars of solder that became one with the metal, so that the sharpest eye would fail to note the difference; and out came the clever little tools that worked and smoothed the repair into unity with the original. Last of all, he drew forth a tiny anvil and a little charcoal brazier whose coals began to burn as he set it down. There was no fan or bellows, yet the coals in the center glowed fiercely at white heat.

The little elf reached out for the copper boiler, so badly dented that the seam had sprung open all the way down. A few light taps on his anvil straightened it back into smoothness. He spread on his polish, blew on it vigorously, and watched the dirt and dullness disappear, then applied his flux, and drew some of the solder onto it with a hot iron, chuckling as the seams became waterproof again. Surely now, even the long sleep had cost him none of his skill. As he laid it down, there was no sign to show that the boiler had not come freshly from some shop, or new out of the maker's hands.

The skillet was bright and shiny, except for a brown circle on the bottom, and gleamed with a silvery luster. Some magic craftsman must have made it, the elf thought, and it should receive special pains to make sure that the spell holding it so bright was not broken. He rubbed a few drops of polish over it carefully, inspected the loose handle, and applied his purple flux, swabbing off the small excess. Tenderly he ran the hot iron over the solder and began working the metal against the handle.

But something was very wrong. Instead of drawing firmly to the skillet, the solder ran down the side in little drops. Such as remained was loose and refused to stick. With a puzzled frown, Ellowan smelled his materials and tried again; there was nothing wrong with the solder or flux, but they still refused to work. He muttered softly and reached out for a pan with a pin hole in it.

Mrs. Franklin found him sitting there later, his tools neatly before him, the pots and pans stacked at the side, and the brazier glowing brightly. "All finished?" she asked cheerfully. "I brought you some coffee and a cinnamon bun I just baked; I thought you might like them." She set them down before the elf and glanced at the pile of utensils again. Only the boiler was fixed. "What—" she began sharply, but softened her question somewhat as she saw the bewildered frustration on his face. "I thought you said you could fix them?"

Ellowan nodded glumly. "That I did, mistress, and that I tried to do. But my solder and flux refuse all but the honest copper yonder, and there's never a thing I can make of them. Either these must be wondrous metals indeed, or my art has been bewitched."

"There's nothing very wonderful about aluminum and enamelware—nor stainless steel, either, except the prices they charge." She picked up the wash boiler and inspected his work. "Well, you did do this nicely, and you're not the only one who can't solder aluminum, I guess, so cheer up. And eat your roll before it's cold!"

"Thank'ee, mistress." The savory aroma of the bun had been tantalizing his stomach, but he had been waiting to make certain that he was still welcome to it. "It's sorry I am to have troubled you, but it's a long time ago that I tinkered for my living, and this is new to me."

Mrs. Franklin nodded sympathetically; the poor little man must have been living with a son, or maybe working in a side show—he was short enough, and his costume was certainly theatrical. Well, hard times were hard times. "You didn't trouble me much, I guess. Besides, I needed the boiler tomorrow for wash day, so that's a big help, anyway. What do I owe you for it?"

"Tu'pence ha'penny," Ellowan said, taking out for the bun. Her look was uncertain, and he changed it quickly. "Five pence American, that is, mistress."

"Five cents! But it's worth ten times that!"

"It's but an honest price for the labor, mistress." Ellowan was putting the tools and materials back in his bag. "That's all I can take for the small bit I could do."

"Well—" She shrugged. "All right, if that's all you'll take, here it is." The coin she handed him seemed strange, but that was to be expected. He pocketed it with a quick smile and another "thank'ee," and went in search of a store he had noticed before.

The shop was confusing in the wide variety of articles it carried, but Ellowan spied tobacco and cigars on display and walked in. Now that he had eaten the bun, the tobacco was a more pressing need than food.

"Two pennies of tobacco, if it please you," he told the clerk, holding out the little leather pouch he carried.

"You crazy?" The clerk was a boy, much more interested in his oiled hair than in the customers who might come in. "Cheapest thing I can give you is Duke's Mixture, and it'll cost you five cents, cash."

Ellowan watched the nickel vanish over the counter regretfully; tobacco was indeed a luxury at the price. He picked up the small cloth bag, and the pasteboard folder the boy thrust at him. "What might this be?" he asked, holding up the folder.

"Matches." The boy grinned in fine superiority. "Where you been all your life? O. K., you do this . . . see? Course, if you don't want 'em—"

"Thank'ee." The elf pocketed the book of matches quickly and hurried toward the street, vastly pleased with his purchase. Such a great marvel as the matches alone surely was worth the price. He filled his clay pipe and struck one of them curiously, chuckling in delight as it flamed up. When he dropped the flame regretfully, he noticed that the tobacco, too, was imbued with magic, else surely it could never have been cured to such a mild and satisfying flavor. It scarcely bit his tongue.

But there was no time to be loitering around admiring his new treasures. Without work there could be no food, and supper was still to be taken care of. Those aluminum and enamelware pans were still in his mind, reminding him that coppers might be hard to get. But then, Mrs. Franklin had mentioned stainless steel, and only a mighty wizard could prevent iron from rusting; perhaps her husband was a worker in enchantments, and the rest of the village might be served in honest copper and hammered pewter. He shook his shoulders in forced optimism and marched down the street toward the other houses, noting the prices marked in a store window as he passed. Eh, the woman was right; he'd have to charge more for his services to eat at those rates.

The road was filled with the strange carriages driven by engines, and Ellowan stayed cautiously off the paving. But the stench from their exhausts and the dust they stirred up were still thick in his nostrils. The elf switched the bag from his left shoulder to his right and plodded on grimly, but there was no longer a tune on his lips, and the little bells refused to tinkle as he walked.

The sun had set, and it was already growing darker, bringing the long slow day to a close. His last call would be at the house ahead, already showing lights burning, and it was still some distance off. Ellowan pulled his belt tighter and marched toward it, muttering in slow time to his steps.

"Al-u-mi-num and en-am-el-ware and stain-*less* STEEL!" A row of green pans, red pots and ivory bowls ran before his eyes, and everywhere there was the glint of silvery skillets and dull white kettles. Even the handles used were no longer honest wood, but smelled faintly resinous.

Not one proper kettle in the whole village had he found. The housewives came out and looked at him, answered his smile, and brought forth their work for him in an oddly hesitant manner, as if they were unused to giving out such jobs at the door. It spoke more of pity than of any desire to have their wares mended.

"No, mistress, only copper. These new metals refuse my solder, and them I cannot mend." Over and again he'd repeated the words until they were as wooden as his knocks had grown; and always, there was no copper. It was almost a kindness when they refused to answer his knock.

He had been glad to quit the village and turn out on the road to the country, even though the houses were farther apart. Surely among the farming people, the older methods would still be in use. But the results were no different. They greeted him kindly and brought out their wares to him with less hesitancy than in the village—but the utensils were enamelware and aluminum and stainless steel!

Ellowan groped for his pipe and sank down on the ground to rest, noting that eight miles still lay between him and Northville. He measured out the tobacco carefully, and hesitated before using one of the new matches. Then, as he lit it, he watched the flame dully and tossed it listlessly aside. Even the tobacco tasted flat now, and the emptiness of his stomach refused to be fooled by the smoke, though it helped to take his mind away from his troubles. Eh, well, there was always that one last house to be seen, where fortune might smile on him long enough to furnish a supper. He shouldered the bag with a grunt and moved on.

A large German shepherd came bounding out at the elf as he turned in the gate to the farmhouse. The dog's bark was gruff and threatening, but Ellowan clucked softly and the animal quieted, walking beside him toward the house, its tail wagging slowly. The farmer watched the performance and grinned.

"Prinz seems to like you," he called out. " 'Tain't everyone he takes to like that. What can I do for you, lad?" Then, as Ellowan drew nearer, he looked more sharply. "Sorry—my mistake. For a minute there, I thought you was a boy."

"I'm a tinker, sir. A coppersmith, that is." The elf stroked the dog's head and looked up at the farmer wistfully. "Have you copper pots or pans, or odds of any kind, to be mended? I do very good work on copper, sir, and I'll be glad to work for only my supper."

The farmer opened the door and motioned him in. "Come on inside, and we'll see. I don't reckon we have, but the wife knows better." He raised his voice. "Hey, Louisa, where are you? In the kitchen?"

"In here, Henry." The voice came from the kitchen, and Ellowan followed the man back, the dog nuzzling his hand companionably. The woman was washing the last few dishes and putting the supper away as they entered, and the sight of food awoke the hunger that the elf had temporarily suppressed.

"This fellow says he's good at fixin' copper dishes, Louisa," Henry told his wife. "You got anything like that for him?" He bent over her ear and spoke in an undertone, but Ellowan caught the words. "If you got anything copper, he looks like he needs it, Lou. Nice little midget, seems to be, and Prinz took quite a shine to him."

Louisa shook her head slowly. "I had a couple of old copper kettles, only I threw them away when we got the aluminum cooking set. But if you're hungry, there's plenty of food still left. Won't you sit down while I fix it for you?"

Ellowan looked eagerly at the remains of the supper, and his mouth watered hotly, but he managed a smile, and his voice was determined. "Thank'ee, mistress, but I ain't. It's one of the rules I have to live by not to beg or take what I cannot earn. But I'll be thanking you both kindly for the thought, and wishing you a very good night."

They followed him to the door, and the dog trotted behind him until its master's whistle called it back. Then the elf was alone on the road again, hunting a place to sleep. There was a haystack back off the road that would make a good bed, and he headed for that. Well, hay was hardly nourishing, but chewing on it was better than nothing.

Ellowan was up with the sun again, brushing the dirt off his jerkin. As an experiment, he shook the runes out on the ground and studied them for a few minutes. "Eh, well," he muttered, tossing them back in the bag, "they speak well, but it's little faith I'd have in them for what is to come. It's too easy to shake them out the way I'd want them to be. But perchance there'll be a berry or so in the woods yonder."

There were no berries, and the acorns were still green. Ellowan struck the highway again, drawing faint pleasure from the fact that few cars were on the road at that hour. He wondered again why their fumes, though unpleasant, bothered him as little as they did. His brothers, up in the grotto hidden in the Adirondacks, found even the smoke from the factories a deadening poison.

The smell of a good wood fire, or the fumes from alcohol in the glass-blower's lamp were pleasant to them. But with the coming of coal, a slow lethargy had crept over them, driving them back one by one into the hills to sleep. It had been bad enough when coal was burned in the hearths, but that Scotchman, Watts, had found that power could be drawn from steam, and the factories began spewing forth the murky fumes of acrid coal smoke. And the Little Folk had fled hopelessly from the poison, until Ellowan Coppersmith alone was left. In time, even he had joined his brothers up in the hills.

Now he had awakened again, without rhyme or reason, when the stench of the liquid called gasoline was added to that of coal. All along the highway were pumps that supplied it to the endless cars, and the taint of it in the air was omnipresent.

"Eh, well," he thought. "My brothers were ever filled with foolish pranks instead of honest work, while I found my pleasure in labor. Methinks the pranks weakened them against the poison, and the work gives strength; it was only after I hexed that factory owner that the sleep crept into my head, and sixscore years must surely pay the price of one such trick. Yet, when I first awakened, it's thinking I was that there was some good purpose that drew me forth."

The sight of an orchard near the road caught his attention, and the elf searched carefully along the strip of grass outside the fence in the hope that an apple might have been blown outside. But only inside was there fruit, and to cross the fence would be stealing. He left the orchard reluctantly and started to turn in at the road leading to the farmhouse. Then he paused.

After all, the farms were equipped exactly as the city now, and such faint luck as he'd had yesterday had been in the village. There was little sense in wasting his effort among the scattered houses of the country, in the unlikely chance that he might find copper. In the city, at least, there was little time wasted, and it was only by covering as many places as he could that he might hope to find work. Ellowan shrugged, and turned back on the highway; he'd save his time and energy until he reached Northville.

It was nearly an hour later when he came on the boy, sitting beside the road and fussing over some machine. Ellowan stopped as he saw the scattered parts and the worried frown on the lad's face. Little troubles seemed great to twelve-year-olds.

"Eh, now, lad," he asked, "is it trouble you're having there? And what might be that contrivance of bars and wheels?"

"It's a bicycle; ever'body knows that." From the sound of the boy's voice, tragedy had reared a large and ugly head. "And I've only had it since last Christmas. Now it's broke and I can't fix it."

He held up a piece that had come from the hub of the rear wheel. "See? That's the part that swells up when I brake it. It's all broken, and a new coaster brake costs five dollars."

Ellowan took the pieces and smelled them; his eyes had not been deceived. It was brass. "So?" he asked. "Now that's a shame, indeed. And a very pretty machine it was. But perchance I can fix it."

The boy looked up hopefully as he watched the elf draw out the brazier and tools. Then his face fell. "Naw, mister. I ain't got the money. All I got's a quarter, and I can't get it, 'cause it's in my bank, and mom won't let me open it."

The elf's reviving hopes of breakfast faded away, but he smiled casually. "Eh, so? Well, lad, there are other things than money. Let's see what we'll be making of this."

His eyes picked out the relation of the various parts, and his admiration for the creator of the machine rose. That hub was meant to drive the machine, to roll free, or to brake as the user desired. The broken piece was a split cylinder of brass that was arranged to expand against the inside of the hub when braking. How it could have been damaged was a mystery, but the destructive ability of boys was no novelty to Ellowan.

Under his hands, the rough edges were smoothed down in a twinkling, and he ran his strongest solder into the break, filling and drawing it together, then scraping and abrading the metal smooth again. The boy's eyes widened.

"Say, mister, you're good! Them fellers in the city can't do it like that, and they've got all kinds of tools, too." He took the repaired piece and began threading the parts back on the spindle. "Gosh, you're little. D'you come out of a circus?"

Ellowan shook his head, faintly smiling. The questions of children had always been candid, and honest replies could be given them. "That I did not, lad, and I'm not a midget, if that's what you'd be thinking. Now didn't your grandmother tell you the old tales of the elves?"

"An elf!" The boy stopped twisting the nut back on. "Go on! There ain't such things—I don't guess." His voice grew doubtful, though, as he studied the little brown figure. "Say, you do look like the pi'tures I seen, at that, and it sure looked like magic the way you fixed my brake. Can you really do magic?"

"It's never much use I had for magic, lad. I had no time for learning it, when business was better. The honest tricks of my trade were enough for me, with a certain skill that was ever mine. And I wouldn't be mentioning this to your parents if I were you."

"Don't you worry, I won't; they'd say I was nuts." The boy climbed on the saddle, and tested the brake with obvious satisfaction. "You goin' to town? Hop on and put your bag in the basket here. I'm goin' down within a mile of there—if you can ride the handlebars."

"It would be a heavy load for you, lad, I'm thinking." Ellowan was none too sure of the security of such a vehicle, but the ride would be most welcome.

"Naw. Hop on. I've carried my brother, and he's heavier than you. Anyway, that's a Mussimer two-speed brake. Dad got it special for Christmas." He reached over for Ellowan's bag, and was surprised by its lightness. Those who helped an elf usually found things easier than they expected. "Anyway, I owe you sumpin' for fixin' it."

Ellowan climbed on the luggage rack at the rear and clutched the boy tightly at first. The rack was hard, but the paving smoothed out the ride, and it was far easier than walking. He relaxed and watched the road go by in a quarter of the time he could have traveled it on foot. If fortune smiled on him, breakfast might be earned sooner than he had hoped.

"Well, here's where I stop," the boy finally told him. "The town's down there about a mile. Thanks for fixing my bike."

Ellowan dismounted cautiously and lifted out his bag. "Thank'ee, lad, for helping me so far. And I'm thinking the brake will be giving you little trouble hereafter." He watched the boy ride off on a side road, and started toward the town, the serious business of breakfast uppermost in his mind.

It was still in his mind when midday had passed, but there was no sign that it was nearer his stomach. He came out of an alley and stopped for a few draws on his pipe and a chance to rest his shoulders. He'd have to stop smoking soon; on an empty stomach, too much tobacco is nauseating. Over the smell of the smoke, another odor struck his nose; and he turned around slowly.

It was the clean odor of hot metal in a charcoal fire, and came from a sprawling old building a few yards away. The sign above was faded, but he made out the words: MICHAEL DONAHUE—HORSE-SHOEING AND AUTO REPAIRS. The sight of a blacksmith shop aroused memories of pleasanter days, and Ellowan drew nearer.

The man inside was in his fifties, but his body spoke of strength and clean living, and the face under the mop of red hair was open and friendly. At the moment, he was sitting on a stool, finishing a sandwich. The odor of the food reached out and stirred the elf's stomach again, and he scuffed his sandals against the ground uneasily. The man looked up.

"Saints presarve us!" Donahue's generous mouth opened to its widest. "Sure, and it's one o' the Little Folk, the loike as me feyther tolt me. Now fwhat—Och, now, but it's hungry ye'd be from the look that ye have, and me eatin' before ye! Here now, my hearty, its yerself as shud have this bread."

"Thank'ee." Ellowan shook his head with an effort, but it came harder this time. "I'm an honest worker, sir, and it's one of the rules that I can't be taking what I cannot earn. But there's never a piece of copper to be found in all the city for me to mend." He laid his hands on a blackened bench to ease the ache in his legs.

"Now that's a shame." The brogue dropped from Donahue's speech, now that the surprise of seeing the elf was leaving him. "It's a good worker you are, too, if what my father told me was true. He came over from the old country when I was a bit of a baby, and his father told him before that. Wonderful workers, he said you were."

"I am that." It was a simple statement as Ellowan made it; boasting requires a certain energy, even had he felt like it. "Anything of brass or copper I can fix, and it'll be like new when I finish."

"Can you that?" Donahue looked at him with interest. "Eh, maybe you can. I've a notion to try you out. You wait here." He disappeared through the door that divided his smithy from the auto servicing department, and came back with a large piece of blackened metal in his hand. The elf smelled it questioningly and found it was brass.

Donahue tapped it lightly. "That's a radiator, m'boy. Water runs through these tubes here and these little fins cool it off. Old Pete Yaegger brought it in and wanted it fixed, but it's too far ruined for my hands. And he can't afford a new one. You fix that now, and I'll be giving you a nice bit of money for the work."

"Fix it I can." Ellowan's hands were trembling as he inspected the corroded metal core, and began drawing out his tools. "I'll be finished within the hour."

Donahue looked doubtfully at the elf, but nodded slowly. "Now maybe you will. But first, you'll eat, and we'll not be arguing about that. A hungry man never did good work, and I'm of the opinion the same applies to yourself. There's still a sandwich and a bit of pie left, if you don't mind washing it down with water."

The elf needed no water to wash down the food. When Donahue looked at him next, the crumbs had been licked from the paper, and Ellowan's deft hands were working his clever little tools through the fins of the radiator, and his face was crinkling up into its usual merry smile. The metal seemed to run and flow through his hands with a will of its own, and he was whistling lightly as he worked.

Ellowan waited intently as Donahue inspected the finished work. Where the blackened metal had been bent and twisted, and filled with holes, it was now shining and new. The smith could find no sign to indicate that it was not all one single piece now, for the seams were joined invisibly.

"Now that's craftsmanship," Donahue admitted. "I'm thinking we'll do a deal of business from now on, the two of us, and there's money in it, too. Ellowan, m'boy, with work like that we can buy up old radiators, remake them, and at a nice little profit for ourselves we can sell them again. You'll be searching no further for labor."

The elf's eyes twinkled at the prospect of long lines of radiators needing to be fixed, and a steady supply of work without the need of searching for it. For the first time, he realized that industrialization might have its advantages for the worker.

Donahue dug into a box and came out with a little metal figure of a greyhound, molded on a threaded cap. "Now, while I get something else for you, you might be fixing this," he said. " 'Tis a godsend that you've come to me. . . . Eh, now that I think of it, what brings you here, when I thought it'd be in the old country you worked?"

"That was my home," the elf agreed, twisting the radiator cap in his hands and straightening out the broken threads. "But the people became too poor in the country, and the cities were filled with coal smoke. And then there was word of a new land across the sea. So we left, such of us as remained, and it was here we stayed until the smoke came again, and sent us sleeping into the hills. Eh, it's glad I am now to be awake again."

Donahue nodded. "And it's not sorry I am. I'm a good blacksmith, but there's never enough of that for a man to live now, and mostly I work on the autos. And there, m'boy, you'll be a wonderful help, to be sure. The parts I like least are the ignition system and generator, and there's copper in them where your skill will be greater than mine. And the radiators, of course."

Ellowan's hands fumbled on the metal, and he set it down suddenly. "Those radiators, now—they come from a car?"

"That they do." Donahue's back was turned as he drew a horseshoe out of the forge and began hammering it on the anvil. He could not see the twinkle fade from the elf's eyes and the slowness with which the small fingers picked up the radiator cap.

Ellowan was thinking of his people, asleep in the hills, doomed to lie there until the air should be cleared of the poisonous fumes. And here he was, working on parts of the machines that helped to make those fumes. Yet, since there was little enough else to do, he had no choice but to keep on; cars or no cars, food was still the prime necessity.

Donahue bent the end of a shoe over to a calk and hammered it into shape, even with the other one. "You'll be wanting a place to sleep?" he asked casually. "Well, now, I've a room at home that used to be my boy's, and it'll just suit you. The boy's at college and won't be needing it."

"Thank'ee kindly." Ellowan finished the cap and put it aside distastefully.

"The boy'll be a great engineer some day," the smith went on with a glow of pride. "And not have to follow his father in the trade. And it's a good thing, I'm thinking. Because some day, when they've used up all their coal and oil, there'll be no money in the business at all, even with the help of these newfangled things. My father was a smith, and I'm by way of being smith and mechanic—but not the boy."

"They'll use up all the coal and oil—entirely?"

"They will that, now. Nobody knows when, but the day's acoming. And then they'll be using electricity or maybe alcohol for fuel. It's a changing world, lad, and we old ones can't change to keep with it."

Ellowan picked up the radiator cap and polished it again. Eh, so. One day they'd use up all the sources of evil, and the air would be pure again. The more cars that ran, the sooner that day would come, and the more he repaired, the more would run.

"Eh, now," he said gayly. "I'll be glad for more of those radiators to mend. But until then, perchance, I could work a bit of yonder scrap brass into more such ornaments as this one."

Somehow, he was sure, when his people came forth again, there'd be work for all.

Johnny on the Spot

FRANK BELKNAP LONG

Frank Belknap Long was already a well-established poet and weird fiction writer when he began contributing to Unknown. *Along with Robert Bloch and Henry Kuttner, he was one of the few authors who successfully made the transition from* Weird Tales *to* Unknown. *As one might expect, the style of Long's* Unknown *fiction differed from that of his earlier atmospheric horror stories, but "Johnny on the Spot," from the December 1939 issue, was a* real *change of pace—hardboiled and curt, as befits the personality of the title character.*

I WAS Johnny on the spot. I had left a guy lying in a dark alley with a copper-jacketed bullet in him, and the cops were naming me. They were also naming a torpedo named Jack Anders. Anders had ducked out of the alley, the back way, without stopping to see if I was tagging after. The bullet had come out of Anders' gun, but I was as much to blame as he was for what had happened.

Wait—I've got to be honest about this. I was *more* to blame. He was the trigger man, but I had put the finger on the guy in the first place. I wanted to get away from the bright lights, because when I stared at my hands in the glare of the street lamps they seemed to change color. I couldn't stand the sight of myself in the light. My red hands—

In the dark I could forget about my hands. I wanted to dance in darkness to the strains of soft music. It was a screwy sort of urge— considering. All over town the teletype was naming me. By going into that taxi dance hall I was exposing myself to more publicity on the same night.

I should have stayed with the crowds in the street. But I'm a restless sort of guy. When I get a yen I have to satisfy it, even if it means extra leg work for the cops.

A dozen heavily rouged dolls in romper suits were standing around under dim lights when I entered the hall. I walked past the ticket window and mingled with the sappy-looking patrons. The Johnnies who patronize taxi dance halls are all of one type—dumb, awkward-looking clucks who have to shell out dough to get favors from dames.

With me it's different. All I have to do is snap my little finger. I don't mean I could have got by in there without buying a ticket. Not for long. But there's a rule which says you can look the dames over and walked out again if you're not suited. All I did at first was mingle with the patrons and size up the dames. And that's how I came to overhear the conversation.

The two dames who were whispering together were standing off in one corner, away from the ropes. One was a blonde with cold eyes and an "I've been around" look.

The other girl was young and sweet. I could tell just by looking at her that she hadn't been around at all.

The blonde's eyes were boring like a dental drill into the younger girl's face. I stood close beside her, listening to what she was saying. She wasn't giving that poor kid a ghost of a break.

"You're pretty smart, aren't you?" she taunted. "You think you've got something."

The dark-haired girl shook her head. "No, Dixie, no. I didn't say that. I don't know why he likes me. I swear I don't."

"Quit stalling, hon. You know how to use what you've got. You're smart, all right, but not as smart as I am. I'm taking him away from you, see?"

Sudden terror flared in the younger girl's eyes. She grasped her companion's wrists and twisted her about.

"You can't do that! I love him. I love him, do you hear?"

The blonde wrenched her wrist free. "You'll get over it, hon," she sneered, her lips twisting maliciously. "They all do. I can't help it if I like the guy."

"You like him because he's rich. Not for what he is. You got lots of men crazy about you."

"Sure, I have. But Jimmy's different. Maybe I do love his dough. So what? Don't you love his dough?"

"I swear I don't, Dixie. I'd love him if he didn't have a cent."

"He's all you've got, eh? Well, ain't that too bad?"

"You won't take him away, Dixie. Promise me you won't."

Dixie laughed. "I'm taking him tonight, hon. I've had plenty of experience with guys like Jimmy."

I knew then that Dixie was the girl for me. I stepped up to her and held out my arms.

"Dance, honey?" I said.

She was plenty startled. She stared at me for an instant in a funny sort of way. Like she knew I was standing there, but couldn't see me.

Then her arms went out and around my shoulders. We started to dance, moving out into the hall.

We were in the middle of the floor when something seemed to whisper deep inside of me: "Now, now, while the lights are low and the music is like a whisper from the tomb."

I stopped dancing suddenly and clasped her in my arms. "You'll never take Jimmy away from her," I whispered.

She was a smart one, that girl. She recognized me an instant before I kissed her. She whimpered in terror and struggled like a pinioned bird in my clasp.

"Spare me," she moaned. "Come back in a year, a month. I'll be waiting for you. I won't run out on you, I swear it."

"You played me for a sap," I said. "You were warned about your ticker, but you went right on dancing."

"I'll stop tonight," she promised wildly. "Give me a few days—a week."

I shook my head. "Sorry, girlie. This is the payoff."

It's funny how near I can get to people without frightening them. When she sagged to the floor the couples about us went right on dancing. The lights were so dim they didn't notice her lying still and cold at my feet.

For three or four seconds no one noticed her. Then one of the girls saw her and screamed. All over the floor men and women stopped dancing and crowded about her. I knew that in a moment they would be naming me again. So I slipped silently from the place.

I do not like to be named. In that dance hall I was just a lonely guy looking for a dame to waltz with. I am only Death when I strike, and between times I am like the people about me.

Maybe you'll meet me sometime in a crowd. But you won't recognize me because I take color from my surroundings. I am always fleeing from what I have to do. I am a Johnny on the spot. But in the end— in the end I meet up with practically everyone.

Warm, Dark Places

H. L. GOLD

It's rare that the first issue of a magazine yields a memorable story, but H. L. Gold's "Trouble with Water," from the premiere issue of Unknown, *is recognized as a modern fantasy classic. This story of a man cursed by a gnome so that he cannot touch anything with water in it helped to establish the lighthearted approach to fantasy for which* Unknown *is remembered today. Gold, however, was disturbed to hear that a tale he hadn't intended to be comic was received with such hilarity by the readers. "Warm, Dark Places," from the October 1940 issue, is very similar in plot to "Trouble with Water," and may have been Gold's way of showing he could turn his idea into something creepy.*

APLAN TRIED to make a gesture of impatience. It was impossible because his arms were piled high with clothing. He followed his wife's pointing finger and succeeded in shrugging contemptuously.

Clad in pathetic rags, the hairiest, dirtiest tramp in the world stood outside the plate-glass window of Kaplan's dry-cleaning store and eagerly watched the stubby, garment-laden figure as it waddled toward the bandbox cleaning vat.

"Him?" Kaplan echoed sarcastically. "A bum like him is going to drive us out of business? Do you mind if I am asking you what with, Mrs. Genius?"

"Like my mother told me," Mrs. Kaplan retorted angrily, "a book you can't tell by its covers. So, rags he's wearing and he's dirty, that means he can't have money? You don't read in the papers, I suppose. Blind beggars don't own apartment houses and chauffeurs, I suppose, and people on relief don't ride cars down to get their checks. Besides, such a feeling I get when I look at him—like when a mouse looks at a cat."

"*Pah!*" Kaplan broke in good-humoredly. "Some foolishness."

"All right, Mr. Einstein, he's standing out there with a pencil and paper because somewhere else he ain't got to go."

"You think maybe you're wrong?" Kaplan almost snapped testily. "No. He's going to the Ritz for supper and he stopped in while he should have his dress suit pressed! Molly, a whole year you been annoying me with this lazy, no-good loafer. Ain't I got enough on my head as it is?"

Molly pursed her lips and went back to sewing buttons on a dress that hung from a hook. With his arms still loaded, Kaplan clambered up on the window platform, where the bandbox vat stood. How he ever had the strength of character to refrain from fondling his beautiful machine, Kaplan never understood. It really was a lovely thing: red, black and chromium, a masterpiece of a dry-cleaning machine that attracted school children and summer residents.

In spite of his confident attitude, Kaplan felt less certain of himself now. The moment he had stepped on the platform, the tramp darted to the very middle of the window.

Defiantly, Kaplan opened the door to the vat and tried to stuff in the garments without regard for scientific placement. They stuck, of course. Kaplan raised his head and glowered at the tramp, who craned and pressed his ugly, stubbled face against the polished glass, trying to peer into the open tank.

"Aha!" Kaplan muttered, when he saw his enemy's anxiety. "Now I got you!"

"Did you say something?" Molly asked ironically.

"No, no!" he said hastily. "So fat I'm getting—"

It was uncomfortable working in that position, but Kaplan shoved his slightly gross body between the opening and his audience. Straining from above and getting in his own way, he put the clothes in properly around the tumbler. Then he shut the door quickly and turned on the switch. The garments twirled slowly in the cleansing fluid.

Kaplan descended the stairs with an air of triumph.

That had happened every workday for a year, yet neither the little tailor nor his degraded foe had lost the original zest of the silent, bitter struggle. Once more Kaplan had defeated him! On his victory march back to the pressing machine, Kaplan allowed himself a final leer at the fallen.

But this time it was his face, not the tramp's, that slipped into anxiety. He stood trembling and watching his enemy's contented face, and fear lashed him.

The tramp was holding a large piece of brown grocery bag against the hitherto clean window with one hand. With the other he held a stump of pencil, which he used for checking unseen marks against whatever parts of the machine he could note from outside.

But what frightened Kaplan was his complacent satisfaction with his work. Usually he shook his head bewilderedly and wandered off, to reappear as eagerly at four thirty the next afternoon.

This time he didn't shake his head. He folded the dirty square of paper, stowed it away carefully in some hole in the lining of his miserable jacket, and strode—yes, *strode!*—away, nodding and grinning smugly.

Kaplan turned and looked unhappily at Molly. Luckily she was biting off a thread and had not noticed. If she hadn't been there, he knew he would have been useless. Now he had to put on a show of unconcern.

But his hands shook so violently that he banged down the iron almost hard enough to smash the machine, shot a vicious jet of steam through the suit, and the vacuum pedal, which dried the buck and garment, bent under the jab of his unsteady foot. He raised the iron and blindly walloped a crease in the pants.

Half an hour later, when Molly was arranging the garments for delivery, she let out a shriek:

"Ira! What are you doing—trying to ruin us by botch jobs?"

Kaplan groaned. He had started, properly enough, at the pleat near the waist: but a neat spiral crease ended at the side seam. If Molly had not caught the error, Mr. McElvoy, Cedarmere's dapper high-school principal, would have come raging into the store next day, wearing a pair of corkscrew pants.

"From morning to night," Kaplan moaned, "nothing but trouble! You and your foolishness—why can't I be rich and send you to Florida?"

"Oh, you want to get rid of me?" she shrilled. "Like a dog I work so we can save money, but you ain't satisfied! What more do you want—I should drive the truck?"

"It ain't a bad idea," he said wistfully. "How I hate to drive—"

He was almost quick enough to dodge the hanger. It was the first time he had ever regretted the imposing height of his bald, domelike head.

Bleary-eyed, Kaplan drove up to the store twenty-five minutes early. Sometime, late at night, Molly had fallen into an exhausted sleep. But his weary ear and intense worry had kept him awake until dawn. Then he got out of bed and dazedly made breakfast.

He remembered the last thing she had shrieked at him:

"Five bankruptcies we've had, and not a penny we made on any of them! So once in your life you get an idea, we should borrow money and buy a bandbox, we should move to a little town where there ain't competition. So what do you do? Bums you practically give your business to!"

There wasn't much literal truth in her accusation yet Kaplan recognized its hyperbolic justice. By accepting the tramp as a tramp, merely because he wore dirty rags, Kaplan was encouraging some mysterious, unscrupulous conniving. Just what it might be, he couldn't guess. But what if the tramp actually had money and was copying the bandbox machine so he could find out where to buy one—

"A fat lot people care, good work, bad work, as long as it's cheap," Kaplan mumbled unhappily. "Don't Mr. Goodwin, the cheap piker, ride fifteen miles to that faker, Aaron Gottlieb, because it's a nickel cheaper?"

Kaplan opened the door of the Ford delivery truck and stepped out. "The loafer," he mumbled, "he could buy a bandbox, open a store, and drive me right out of business. Family he ain't got, a nice house he don't need—he could clean and press for next to—"

Kaplan had been fishing in his pocket for the key. When he looked up, his muttering rose to a high wail of fright.

"*You!* What do you want here?"

Early as it was, the tramp squatted cross-legged on the chill sidewalk as if he had been waiting patiently for hours. Now he raised himself to his feet and bowed his head with flattering respect.

"The magnificence of the sun shines full upon you," he intoned in a deep, solemn voice. "I accept that as an omen of good fortune."

Kaplan fumbled with the lock, trying to keep his bulk between the store and the tramp. How he could keep out his unwelcome guest, who seemed intent on entering, he had no idea. The tramp, however, folded his arms in dignity and waited without speaking further.

Unable to fumble convincingly any longer, Kaplan opened the door. It violated his entire conditioning, but he tried to close it on the tramp. Extremely agile, his visitor slipped through the narrow opening and stood quietly inside the store.

"All right, so you're in!" Kaplan cried in a shrill voice. "So now what?"

The unattractively fringed mouth opened. "I acknowledge your superior science," a low rumble stated.

"Hah?" was all Kaplan could extract from his flat vocal chords.

The tramp gazed longing at the bandbox machine before he turned, slowly and enviously, to Kaplan.

"I have solved the mystery of the automobile, the train, the ship— yea, even the airplane. These do not befuddle me. They operate because of their imprisoned atoms, those infinitely small entities whom man has contrived to enslave. That one day they will revolt, I shall not argue."

Kaplan searched, but he could find no answer. How could he? The tramp spoke English of a sort. Individually most of the words made sense; together, they defied interpretation.

"Electric lights," the tramp went on, "are obviously dismembered parts of astral sheaths, which men torment in some manner to force them to assume an even more brilliant glow. This sacrilegious use of the holy aura I shall not denounce now. It is with your remarkably specialized bit of science that I am concerned."

"For science, it don't pay so good," Kaplan replied with a nervous attempt at humor.

"Your science is the most baffling, least useful in this accursed materialistic world. What is the point of deliberately cleansing one's outer garments while leaving one's soul clad in filth?"

To Kaplan, that gave away the game. Before that the tramp had been mouthing gibberish. This was something Kaplan could understand.

"You wouldn't like to clean garments for people, I suppose?" he taunted slyly.

Evidently the tramp didn't hear Kaplan. He kept his eyes fixed on the bandbox and began walking toward it in a dazed way. Kaplan couldn't drive him away; despite his thinness, the tramp looked strong. Besides, he was within his legal rights.

"I have constructed many such devices in the year since I returned to the depraved land of my birth. In Tibet, the holy land of wisdom, I was known to men as Salindrinath, an earnest student. My American name I have forgotten."

"What are you getting at?" Kaplan demanded.

Salindrinath spoke almost to himself: "Within the maws of these machines I placed such rags as I possess. I besought the atoms to cleanse for me as they cleanse for you. Lo! My rags came to me with dirt intact, and a bit of machinery grime to boot."

He wheeled on Kaplan.

"And why should they not?" he roared savagely. "What man does not know that atoms have powerful arms but not fingers with which to pluck dirt from garments?"

As one actor judging the skill of another, Kaplan had to admit the tramp's superiority. How a man could so effectively hide the simple urge to make a profit, Kaplan envied without understanding. The tramp wore a look of incredibly painful yearning.

"Pity me! Long ago should I have gone to my next manifestation. I have accomplished all possible in this miserable skin; another life will bestow Nirvana upon me. Alone of all the occult, this senseless wizardry torments me. Give me your secret—"

Kaplan recoiled before the fury of the plea. But he was able to conceal his confusion by pretending to walk backward politely to the workshop.

"*Give* it to you? I got to make a living, too."

Beneath his outwardly cool exterior, Kaplan was desperately scared. What sort of strategy was this? When one man wants to buy out another, or drive him to the wall, he beats around the bush, of course. But he is also careful to drop hints and polite threats. This kind of idiocy, though! It didn't make sense. And that worried Kaplan more than if it had, for he knew the tramp was far from insane.

"Do you aspire to learn of me? Eagerly shall I teach you in return for your bit of useless knowledge! What say you?"

"Nuts," Kaplan informed him.

Salindrinath pondered this reply. "Then let my scientific training prove itself. Since you seem unwilling to explain—"

"Unwilling! Hah, if you only knew!"

"Mayhap you will consent to cleanse my sacred garments in my presence. Then shall I observe, without explanation. With a modicum of introspection, I can discover its principle. Yes?"

Kaplan picked up the heavy flat bat with which he banged creases into clothing. Its weight and utilitarian shape tempted him; the lawlessness of the crime appalled his kindly soul.

"What you got in mind?"

"Why, simply this—let me watch your machine cleanse my vestments."

Regretfully Kaplan put down his weapon. His soft red lips, he felt sure, were a thin white line of controlled rage.

"Ain't it enough you want to put me out of business? Must I give you a free dry cleaning too? Cleaning fluid costs money. If I cleaned your clothes, I couldn't clean a pair of overalls with it. Maybe you want me to speak plainer?"

"It was but a simple request."

"Some simple request! Listen to him— Even for ten dollars I wouldn't put your rags in my bandbox!"

"What, pray, is your objection?" the Salindrinath asked humbly.

"You can ask? Such filth I have never seen. Shame on you!"

Salindrinath gazed down at his tatters. "Filth? Nay, it is but honest earth. What holy man fears the embrace of sacred atoms?"

"Listen to him," Kaplan cried. "Jokes! You got atoms on you, you shameless slob, the same kind like on a pig—"

Now the ragged one recoiled. This he did with one grimy hand clutching at his heart.

"You dare!" he howled. "You compare my indifference to mere external cleanliness with SWINE? Oh, profaner of all things sacred, dabbler in satanic arts—" He strangled into silence and goggled fiercely at Kaplan, who shrank back. "You think perhaps I am unclean?"

"Well, you ain't exactly spotless," Kaplan jabbered in fright.

"But that you should compare me with the swine, the gross materialist of the mire!" Salindrinath stood trembling. "If you believe my vestments to be unclean, wait, bedraggler of my dignity. *Wait!* You shall discover the vestments of your cleanly, externally white and shining trade to be loathsome—loathsome and vile beyond words!"

"Some ain't so clean," Kaplan granted diplomatically.

The shabby one turned on his rundown heel and strode to the door.

"The garments of your respected customers will show you the real meaning of filth. And I shall return soon, when you are duly humbled!"

Kaplan shrugged at the furiously slammed door.

"A nut," he told himself reassuringly. "A regular lunatic."

But even that judicious pronouncement did not comfort him. He was too skilled in bargaining not to recognize the gambits that Salindrinath had shrewdly used—disparagement of the business, the attempt to wheedle information, the final threat. All were unusually cockeyed, and thus a bit difficult for the amateur to discern, but Kaplan was not fooled so easily.

He sorted his work on the long receiving table. While waiting for the pressing machine to heat up, he began brushing trouser cuffs and sewing on loose or missing buttons.

Luckily Kaplan steamed out Mrs. Jackson's fall outfit first. That delayed the shock only a few moments, but later he was to look back on those free minutes with cosmic longing.

He came to Mr. McEvoy's daily suit. Nobody could accuse the neat principal of anything but the most finicking immaculacy. Yet when Kaplan got through stitching up a cuff and put his hand in a pocket to brush out the usual fluff—

"*Yeow!*" he yelled, snatching out his hand.

For a long while Kaplan stood shuddering, his fingers cold with revulsion. Then, cautiously, he ran his hand over the outside of the pocket. He felt only the flat shape of the lining.

"Am I maybe going out of my mind?" he muttered. "Believe me, with everything on my shoulders, and that nut besides, it wouldn't surprise me."

Slowly he inserted the tips of his fingers into the pocket. Almost instantly something globular and clammily smooth crept into the palm of his furtively exploring hand.

Kaplan shouted in disgust, but he wouldn't let go. Clutching the monstrosity was like holding a round, affectionate oyster that kept trying to snuggle deeper into his palm. Kaplan wouldn't free it, though. Grimly he yanked his hand out.

Somehow it must have sensed his purpose. Before he could snatch it out of its refuge, the cold, clammy thing *squeezed* between his fingers with a repulsively fierce effort—

Kaplan determinedly kept fumbling around after it, until his mind began working again. He hadn't felt any head on it, but that didn't mean it couldn't have teeth somewhere in its apparently featureless body. How could it eat without a mouth? So the little tailor stopped daring the disgusting beast to bite him.

He stood still for a moment, gaping down at his hand. Though it was empty, he still felt a sensation of damp coldness. From his hand he stared back to Mr. McElvoy's suit. The pockets were perfectly flat. He couldn't detect a single bulge.

The idea nauseated him, but he forced himself to explore all the pockets.

"Somebody," he whispered savagely when he finished, "is all of a sudden a wise guy—only he ain't so funny."

He stalked, rather waddlingly, to the telephone, ripped the receiver off the hook, barked a number at the operator. Above the *burr* of the bell at the other end he could hear the gulp of his own angry swallowing.

"Hello," a husky feminine voice replied. "Is that you, darling?"

"Mrs. McElvoy?" he rasped, much too loudly.

The feminine voice changed, grew defensive. "Well?"

"This is Kaplan the tailor. Mrs. McElvoy"—his rasp swelled to a violent shout—"such a rotten joke I have never seen in eighteen years I been in this business. What am I—a dope your husband should try funny stuff on?" The words began running together. "Listen, maybe I ain't classy like you, but I got pride also. So what if I work for a living? Ain't I—"

"Whatever are you talking about?" Mrs. McElvoy asked puzzledly.

"Your husband's pants, that's what! Such things he's got in his pockets, I wouldn't be seen dead with them!"

"Mr. McElvoy has his suits cleaned after wearing them only once," she retorted frigidly.

"So, does that mean he can't keep dirty things in his pockets?"

"I'm sorry you don't care to have our trade," Mrs. McElvoy said, obviously trying to control her anger. "Mr. Gottlief has offered to call for them every morning. He's also five cents cheaper. Good day!"

In reply to the bang that hurt his ear, Kaplan slammed down the receiver. The moment he turned to march off, the bell jangled. Viciously he grabbed up the receiver.

"Hello . . . darling?" a deep feminine voice asked.

"Mrs. McElvoy?" he roared.

For several seconds he listened to a strained, bitter silence. Then:

"IRA!" his wife shrilled in outrage.

He hung up hastily and, trembling, he went back to his pressing machine.

"Will I get it now," he moaned. "Everything happens to me. If I don't starve for once, so all kinds of trouble flops in my lap. First I lose my best customer—I should only have a thousand like him, I'd be on easy street—and then I make a little mistake. But go try to tell Molly I made a mistake. Married twenty years, and she acts like I was a regular lady-killer—"

Kaplan's pressing production rose abruptly from four suits an hour to nine. But that was because no cuffs were brushed, no pockets turned inside out, no buttons stitched or replaced. He banged down the iron, slashed the suits with steam, vacuumed them hastily, batted the creases, which had to be straight the first time or not at all. He knew there would be kicks all that week, but he couldn't do anything about it.

The door opened. Kaplan raised a white face. It wasn't his wife, though. Fraulein, Mrs. Sampter's refugee maid, clumped over to him and shoved a pair of pants in his hands.

"Goot morgen," she said pleasantly. "Herr Sompter he vants zhe pockets new. You make soon, no?"

Kaplan nodded dumbly. Without thinking of the consequences, he stuffed his hand in the pocket to note the extent of the damage.

"Eee—YOW!" he howled. "What kind of customers have I got all of a sudden? Take it away, Fraulein! With crazy people I don't want to deal!"

Fraulein's broad face wrinkled bewilderedly. She took back the pants and ran her hands through the pockets.

"Crazy people—us? Maybe you haf got zhe temperature?"

"Such things in pockets! Phooey on practical jokers! Go away—"

"You just vait till Mrs. Sompter about this hears." And stuffing the pants under her arm, Fraulein marched out angrily.

Despite his revulsion, it took Kaplan only a few moments to grow suspicious. One previously dignified customer might suddenly have become a practical joker, but not two. Something scared him even more than that. Fraulein had put her hands in the pockets! Apparently she had not felt anything at all.

"Who's crazy?" Kaplan whispered frightenedly. "Me or them?"

Warily he approached the worktable. Mr. McElvoy was neat, but Mr. Rich was such a bug on cleanliness that even his dirty suits were immaculate, and his pockets never contained lint. That was the suit Kaplan edged up to.

The instant Molly opened the door she began shrieking.

"You loafer! You no-good masher! I call up to tell you I don't feel good, so maybe I won't have to work today. 'Hello, darling,' I say, so who else could it be but your own wife? No—it's Mrs. McElvoy!"

Despite her red-eyed glare, she seemed to recognize a subtle change in him. His plump face was grave and withdrawn, hardened in the fire of spiritual conflict. Instead of claiming it was a mistake, which she had been expecting and would have pounced on, he merely turned back to his pressing machine.

She got panicky. "Ira! Ain't you going to even say you weren't thinking? Don't tell me you . . . you *love* Mrs. McElvoy—"

"You know I don't, Molly," he replied quietly, without looking up. Slowly she took her fists off her hips and unstraddled her firmly planted feet. She knew she was helpless against his passive resistance. "Ira, I don't feel so good. Is it all right if I don't work?"

"I'll get along somehow," he said gently. "Stay home till you feel better, darling. I'll manage."

For several minutes she watched him work. He had a new method of brushing pockets. Although she realized it was new to him, he appeared to have it pat. He pulled the pockets inside out with a hooked wire, brushed them, stuffed them back with a stick of clean wood.

"Ain't it easier to do it by hand?" she asked helpfully.

When he shook his head abstractedly, she shrugged, kissed him uncomfortably, and walked hesitantly toward the door. She paused there.

"You sure *you* feel all right, Ira? You won't need me?"

"I'll get by, sweetheart. Don't you worry about me."

He displayed no sign of relief when she left, for he felt none. He had connected the hideous things in his customers' pockets with the tramp's threat. Somehow Salindrinath had managed to put them there, and neutralizing their effect on him had been Kaplan's problem. The hooked wire and the stick solved it. Therefore he no longer had a problem. He had observed that when the pockets were turned out, the small globes vanished. Where they went, he had no idea, but that wasn't important.

He locked the store at ten thirty to make his calls, and again at twelve, when he went home for lunch and to see how Molly felt. She was in bed, outwardly looking fine, but so baffled by his changed character that her slight organic headache had become hysterically monumental.

He went back to work. Now that he had cleverly sidestepped the tramp's strategy, nothing delayed or upset the care or tempo of his work. Twice he forgot and put his hand in breast pockets to straighten the lining. The sensation nauseated him, but he merely snatched out his hand and continued working with his new method.

At four thirty he gathered the garments to be dry cleaned.

"Now the bum'll come around so he can make fun," Kaplan stated doggedly. "Will he be surprised!"

Halfway to the bandbox machine, he heard the door click. Glancing casually at Salindrinath, Kaplan walked on. The tramp closed the door and folded his arms regally.

"Fool," he said in a cold tone, "do you bow to my wish to know?"

The triumphant leer broke out against Kaplan's will. "You think maybe you got me scared, you pig?" he blurted, now that the leer had involuntarily started him off wrong. "How much it scares me don't amount to a row of beans! You and your things in pockets—phooey!" Salindrinath drew back. His regal, stubbled face slid into a gape of amazement.

"Yeah, you and your things don't bother me," Kaplan pursued, his mocking grin broader than before. "You can all go to hell!"

"Pig? Hell?" Salindrinath's ugly black jaw stuck out viciously. "Do you condemn me to your miserable, unimaginative hell? Know then, swine of a materialist, that my dwellers in dark places are the height of torment to money-grubbers. They shall roost where they dismay you most! When you cringe and beg of me to share your pitiful science, crawl to my holy shack at the landing on the creek—"

Kaplan stuffed the garments into the bandbox and thumbed his nose at the ragged figure striding savagely away from the store.

"A fine case he's got!" he gloated. "I'll come crawling to him when Hitler kicks out the Germans and takes back the Jews. Not before. Do I annoy anybody? If I can work hard and make a living, that's all I ask. He wants to buy a bandbox and open a store here? So let him. But why should I have to tell him how to run me out of business? What some people won't do when they see a business that's making money!" He shook his head sadly.

Kaplan closed the bandbox door, turned the switch, and climbed down from the window platform. Just when he sat down at the sewing machine, Miss Robinson, the nice young kindergarten teacher came in.

"Hello, Mr. Kaplan," she sang with a smile. "Isn't it the loveliest day? Not too cold, though you can feel winter coming on, and it makes you want to take long brisk walks. Isn't it grand having our little town all to ourselves again? But I suppose it's better for you when the summer visitors are here—"

"How much difference can it make?" He shrugged indifferently. "In the summer I work hard like a horse so I can take it easy in the winter and get strong to work like a horse in the summer. If I got enough to eat and pay my bills, that's all I ask."

"I suppose that's all anyone really wants," she agreed eagerly. "Is my suit ready? I feel so chilly in these silk dresses—"

"It's been ready for two days. I made it quick so you wouldn't go around catching colds. Like new it looks, Miss Robinson. For my nicest customers I can do a better job than anybody else."

He took down her suit and pinned it into a bag so she could carry it easily.

"You certainly do," she enthused. "I'll pay you now. You probably can use the money, with all your summer trade gone."

"Whenever you want. People like you don't stick poor tailors."

He took the five-dollar bill she handed him and fumbled in his pocket for change.

"Mr. Kaplan!" she cried, staring anxiously at his goggling face. "Don't you feel well?"

"Ain't I a dope?" he laughed unconvincingly. "Needles I put in my pocket, I get so flustered when pretty girls come in—"

But he had whipped out his hand with such violence that the entire contents of his pocket spilled out on the floor. For some reason this seemed to please him. He stooped ponderously, picked up everything, and counted change into her hand.

She smiled, quite flattered, and left.

But the moment the door closed behind her, Kaplan's weak grin soured. He hadn't pushed his pocket lining back yet. Instead, he patted the outside of his clothes, as if he were frisking himself.

"What have I got now?" he breathed incredulously, inching the fingers of his left hand into his jacket pocket.

He touched something round, hairless and warm, that skittered from his fingertips and dug irritably against his thigh. And there it pulsed against his skin, beating like a disembodied heart—

Thurston, the Seids' chauffeur, came in and picked up everything the family had there. Kaplan didn't mind, for it saved him a five-mile trip. But the chauffeur insisted on paying.

Kaplan reached toward his pocket for change. Abruptly he stopped and let his hand dangle limply. As if telepathic, all the vermin in his pockets had lunged around wildly, to avoid his touch.

"Couldn't you pay later?" he begged. "Does it have to be right now?"

"The madame instructed me to pay," Thurston replied distantly.

Kaplan sighed and looked down at his pocket wistfully, until he remembered that he had put his money on the pressing-machine table. And that, of course, took care of this particular problem.

But Mrs. Ringer, Miss Tracy, young Fox, Mrs. Redstone; and Mr. Davis; who had got off early—all came for their work, and all wanted to pay.

"What is this—a plot?" he muttered. "They must think I'm out of my head, keeping money on a table instead of in my pocket. Can I go on like this? And you, you things, you! Do you *have* to beat like that? Can't you lay quiet and not bother me?"

But he could feel them burrowing restlessly or pulsing contentedly against his skin. Kaplan grew anxious. He couldn't feel them from the outside. Inside, though, they certainly existed, moving around like mice, pulsing like naked, detached hearts.

"It's just this suit," he said. "After all, how many suits can the dirty crook fill with these things?"

He grabbed up an old pair of pants he kept around as a dry change in wet weather. Before putting it on, he tentatively explored a pocket.

A warm ball, furred like a headless, wingless, unutterably loathsome bat, crept affectionately into his palm and pulsed there, clearly enjoying the warmth of his hand. He gritted his teeth and tried to haul it out. It slipped frenziedly through his fingers.

Though it was almost time to make his deliveries, Kaplan locked the store and shopped for a bus driver's change machine. He couldn't find one in the village, of course. Nor would it have taken care of bills, anyhow.

Kaplan loaded the truck and began his rounds. Not everybody tried to pay. It only seemed like that. Eventually, he hoped, his customers might get used to seeing him with all his money clutched tightly in his hand. He knew they wouldn't.

And that only solved the money question, though it certainly would encourage robbers. Now if he could only find a place to keep his handkerchiefs, cigarettes, matches, keys, letters, toothpicks—

Dazed and exhausted, Kaplan drove into the garage at home. He shut off the motor, removed the key, turned out the lights, and closed the doors. When he went to lock the small side door, he had to turn his pockets inside out with the hooked wire and pick the key out of everything that fell on the ground.

Molly had staggered out of bed and was moving gingerly around the kitchen, careful not to jolt her head into aching again. Kaplan put all his money, keys, cigarettes, and matches on the end table in the living room. He kept his arms stiffly away from his body. He knew that the slightest touch would send the vermin scuttling around in his pockets—

Washing his hands meticulously with sandsoap, he couldn't bear the sight of his face in the mirror. One glance had been more than enough. He had seen a scared, white blur—Molly, he knew, was certain to note his expression and ask embarrassing questions.

"I thought I looked bad," she said when he flopped limply into his chair. "Boy, do you look terrible! What is it, Ira?"

"What isn't it?" he grumbled. "Everybody—"

He broke off. He had suddenly realized how it would sound to complain that all his customers insisted on paying.

Almost immediately after eating, he felt like going to bed. He had not slept the night before; the newspaper was boring; his favorite radio comedian sounded like an undertaker who had just heard a good one.

"So soon?" Molly asked anxiously as he yawned with intellectual deliberation and stood up. "Ira, if you're sick, why don't you—"

"Doctors!" he snarled. "What can they do for me?"

But his false yawn had made her mouth gape, and that, of course, was catching. His next was considerably better, for it was real.

"Can I help it if I'm tired?" he asked. "It wouldn't hurt you to get some sleep either."

He stumbled off to bed.

When Molly came in, she had to cover him. He tried not to fling off the blankets, and the effort was killing. Hundreds of pulsing vermin had instantly snuggled against him when he was covered. With blind, repulsive hunger for his warmth, they burrowed and beat against his skin, until he slid the blanket off and lay shivering in the cold.

"Ira," she whispered. "Do you want to catch pneumonia? Keep covered."

He pretended to be asleep. But Kaplan was not fated to sleep any more, though he inched the blanket off again. The second he heard her breathing regularly, he sneaked into the bathroom and cut off the pocket of his pajama jacket.

Back in bed again, he was much too cold to sleep. So he dressed silently and went downstairs. He picked up his keys from the end table and went out to the car.

Riding through the deserted streets toward the creek, he felt dangerously near tears. His pride had never been so battered—nor had he ever before done what he was now about to do.   .

"It's like taking the bread out of my mouth and giving it to him," Kaplan moaned, "but what else can I do? Already people think I'm crazy, walking around with everything in my hands like a regular school kid. If people don't respect me, so my business goes bust anyhow. It's the same thing if I lose my customers or they go to somebody else."

He stopped at the shack near the landing on the creek. After only a moment of hesitation, he knocked tentatively at the door.

"Enter, tailor!" a deep, majestic voice called out.

Kaplan didn't wonder or care how the tramp had known he was there. He threw open the door and sneaked in miserably.

"All right," he said defeatedly to the ragged figure squatting on the floor. "I'll tell you anything you want to know, only get these things out of my pockets."

The tramp stared up at Kaplan, and his ugly, stubbled face looked far more unhappy than the tailor's.

"You come too late," he moaned. "My quest for knowledge forced me to injure a living being. I am now"—his head drooped—"no longer a yogin. I have been stripped of my powers. You must live with the curse I placed upon you, for I cannot help you now. Please forgive me! That can lighten my punishment—"

"Forgive you?" Kaplan wheezed. "First you try to drive me out of business. Then you stick me with these . . . these things that are almost as filthy as you are. And now you can't help me. You can go to hell."

He ran out so quickly that he didn't observe the tramp's sudden vanishing. Raving with rage, he raced home and left the car at the curb. He undressed swiftly, but when he approached the bed, he did so with the utmost caution.

He climbed aboard gingerly, careful not to wake his wife, and slid under the covers. Instantly he flung them off.

"Everything else ain't bad enough," he groaned. "No, like an animal I got to sleep uncovered!"

As he had done the night before, he lay awake until the sky lightened. By that time he felt sure he had worked out a solution.

"If I can do it with pajamas," he breathed hopefully, "is there any reason it shouldn't happen with regular clothes?"

And getting up noiselessly, Kaplan gathered his things and carried them to the bathroom. He took a pair of scissors out of the medicine chest. This time, when he closed the mirror door, the glimpse of his face pleased him. He stopped to examine it. Triumph glinted from the warm, brown eyes, and his soft, gentle mouth was curved in a real smile.

"You got him licked, Ira Kaplan!" he whispered. "You ain't altogether a dope—"

Working with the speed of skill, he ripped out all the pockets of his suit. To make absolutely certain, though, he also tore away the linings of his jacket and vest.

Still wearing his pajamas in the kitchen, he squeezed orange juice, made coffee, and ate breakfast. For the first time in two days he actually felt hungry. He stuffed away half a dozen cream-cheese and smoked-salmon sandwiches on *begals* and drank another cup of coffee.

"Already I feel like another man," he declared. "Now all I got to do is get dressed and go to work. Molly can carry the money and letters. Cigarettes and matches? *Pooh,* that's easy! I'll just keep a pack in the car, one in the store, another at home. Nothing to it!"

He dressed slowly, enjoying the sensation, for he knew that he no longer would feel the revolting creatures pulsing, crawling, moving around like mice against his skin—

"*Heh!*" he cackled. "Is Ira Kaplan smart or ain't he?"

Standing on his bare feet, he tied his tie, then patted the places where his pockets used to be. He even dared to put a hand inside. And of course he felt nothing—absolutely nothing that might snuggle lovingly into his palm or scuttle hideously from his fingers.

"Licked!" he gloated. "Is that tramp licked or ain't he licked?"

He put on his shoes swiftly, slipped into his jacket and topcoat, clapped his hat on his bald head. He strode to the door.

"*Molly!*" he screamed.

His feet shrank from warm, pulsing vermin that nestled cozily in the toe of each shoe. Under his hat a clammily cold, pulsing thing crawled around furiously, struggling to escape the warmth of his hairless scalp—

But Without Horns

NORVELL W. PAGE

Norvell W. Page was a one-man fiction factory. Under the name Grant Stockbridge, he wrote the majority of novels that appeared in hero pulps such as The Spider, The Octopus, *and* The Scorpion. *At the same time, he turned out stories for mystery and shudder pulps like* Dime Mystery *and* Terror Tales. *Very few authors who wrote for these markets were good enough to write for* Unknown, *but Page sold editor John W. Campbell three stories—two sword-and-sorcery novels (a genre Campbell generally despised) and* But Without Horns. *The latter came about through Campbell's challenge that no one could write a believable story about a* real *superman, since such a character would be beyond the comprehension of the average man. Page's tale, which appeared in the June 1940 issue, captured not only the doomed-world spirit of his* Spider *novels, but also the apprehensions of a real world that had just become embroiled in the Second World War.*

H IS EYES still on the shouting headlines of the morning newspaper, Walter Kildering drew out a notebook from an inner pocket and flipped the pages rapidly. Those pages were covered with close writing in an even, precise hand. The script was of curious curlicues appended to a horizontal line. There was a knife crease between Kildering's gray eyes as he added two lines of the characters. Afterward, he walked rapidly through the peaceful spring sunlight of Washington; slanted across the street toward the quiet building which housed the Federal Bureau of Investigation headquarters.

It was when he started up the steps that he saw the doors were barricaded with steel armor plate—and guarded by machine guns!

Walter Kildering neither paused nor called out at this discovery. There was no alteration at all in his expressionless face, except that fear crept darkly into his gray eyes. But it was not fear of his own life, for he moved up the steps with the fixed deliberation of an escalator.

Kildering's eyes swept the steel barrier once, and he walked steadily to the panel at the extreme right—the only panel that could be removed readily. Even then, he said nothing, but he masked the fear in his eyes with lowered lids.

Inside, a voice spoke cautiously. "Just a minute, Kildering. Orders are not to let anybody in."

Low-voiced shouts ran along the corridor inside. The echoes came dimly through the steel and Kildering waited outside in the quiet warmth of the spring sunshine—and felt coldness crawl up his spine with the slow cruelty of a dull knife. The newspapers this morning had screamed of two F. B. I. men being murdered in the maternity ward of a hospital in the Middlewestern city of Metropolis; now he found the doors of headquarters barricaded. It all fitted into the pattern of Kildering's deductions—and the conclusion was a hideous thing!

A small breeze wandered through the street, stirring the fresh green of the newborn leaves on sidewalk trees; bringing the scent of rain-wet grass and fertile earth in the parks. Kildering's hand knotted slowly into a white-knuckled fist. He swallowed noisily.

In his brain, he whispered, "For God's sake, *hurry!*" His lips did not move.

When the steel panel was dragged aside to let Kildering enter, he seemed to step through almost casually, but he covered the distance to the elevators with long, efficient strides. The corridor was dim and cold. Pinched bars of sunlight, slanting through the interstices of the armor, seemed lost and vague. Men's whispers made chill echoes— Kildering's feet were silent.

"Third," he said flatly to the elevator operator.

The man had an automatic in his fist. He shook his head as he sent the cage surging upward.

"Can't stop there, Mr. Kildering," he said. "Orders!"

Kildering's eyes closed and he fought the shiver that snaked across his shoulders. His voice was quiet. "Who's on guard there?" he asked. "On the third floor."

"Mayor and Summers, sir."

Kildering's eyes narrowed. They would be hard men to pass—but he had to pass them! When the elevator door had closed behind him, on the second floor, he sprinted toward the general offices. His feet made no sound. He whipped into the offices, crossed with long bounds toward the closed door of Superintendent Overholt's private quarters. A desk interposed, and he hurdled cleanly over it, but so perfect was his bodily co-ordination that he checked cleanly before the door.

"Kildering, sir!" he called. "It's damned important!"

Overholt growled permission and Kildering snapped open the door, reached the superintendent's desk in a long stride. His voice was suppressed, driving. "I have some deductions to lay before you. They take into account the fact that the building is in a stage of siege—and that the chief believes he is threatened with assassination!"

Overholt was suddenly on his feet, a tall, bushy-haired man with stooped, powerful shoulders. "Who told you about that threat?" he demanded. "No one knows of that. No one except Chief Ericson and me!"

Kildering turned toward the door. "I'll explain on the way to the chief's office," he said. "We have to act quickly to save his life! He is in danger all right—but not from visible assassins!"

"Wait!" Overholt jammed his big fists down on his hips. His blue eyes glittered beneath the overhang of bushy brows, and his voice was metallic, brittle. "What do you mean, invisible assassins?"

Kildering forced himself to speak steadily. "Believe me, sir," he said, "there is no time to lose. I was worried this morning when I saw the news of those two murders in Metropolis. When I found the doors barricaded, I knew my suspicions were right! There is not a minute to spare!"

A heavy frown pulled Overholt's bushy brows down over his eyes. Kildering was the best brain in the service, and a leader in every fiber. Even Overholt, long in command, could feel the pull of Kildering's unconscious accent of command. He set himself solidly.

"Kildering, I can't take you to the chief," he said. "Until he passes the word, not even the president of the United States would be permitted to approach his office!"

"Then we must force his door!"

Overholt came around his desk. "If it were anyone else than you, Kildering," he snapped, "I'd put you under arrest for a madman! What are you talking about?"

Kildering felt a surge of impatience. He could see the truth so clearly himself. And the chief's life was at stake! His words came out like earnest bullets.

"The fact those men of ours were killed in Metropolis means that the chief has attacked the most dangerous criminal ever known," Kildering said crisply. "The same man who robbed six banks in the

State of Wichinois of almost three million dollars. You remember what happened to those bankers whom we questioned about the crimes?"

Overholt nodded his big head. "Certainly. Three of them died, of heart failure—"

"That's what they called the murder of our men," Kildering threw in softly.

Overholt frowned and went on: "Three other bankers lost their minds, very fortunately for the bank robber!"

"It wasn't good fortune," Kildering said. "What happened to Police Chief Eidson, of Metropolis, just after he notified us he thought he had a clue to the identity of the robber?"

Overholt jerked a hand impatiently. "Apparently Eidson was already out of his head. Before we could get there, he barricaded himself in his office and killed himself! Crazy as a bat!"

Kildering cried softly: "Don't you see, sir? Every man who attacks this criminal either dies of heart failure or goes crazy! Now, the F. B. I. has attacked him. And the chief has barricaded himself in his office—*as Eidson did just before he killed himself!*"

Overholt jerked out a ragged oath. "You mean this criminal, the one we call the Unknown—"

"I mean, sir"—Kildering's voice was cold with urgency—"that he destroys whoever opposes him, either by death or by insanity! *We must reach the chief at once!*"

For an instant, Overholt's eyes strained wide with the shock of the words. He began an oath that didn't quite come out. Then he shook his head. He smiled, even chuckled a little.

"I can't argue with your logic, Kildering," he said. "As usual, it is faultless. But there's one thing you can't get past. No man can drive another man insane at will—and certainly he can't do it unless he can get through our guard to reach the chief! It just isn't possible. What have you been doing, Kildering, reading ghost stories?"

Kildering took a slow step toward Overholt. His chiseled face was grimly set. His gray eyes held twin fires of desperation. "The bankers were close prisoners when they went mad," he said. "Chief Eidson was alone from the time he phoned us until he was found dead."

Overholt waved a hand, still smiling. "There is some reasonable explanation for it. The chief is safe. When he sends for us—"

"He never will. He'll be dead."

Overholt shrugged. "Calm yourself, Kildering. After all, we're hunting an ordinary criminal, in this Unknown. He's smart, but he isn't a demon, with horns and a forked tail. Just a human being."

Kildering drew in a slow breath. His posture seemed to relax, and he lifted a hand to his forehead. "Then you won't take me to the chief?" he asked dully.

"We'll have to wait!" Overholt insisted irritably.

Kildering stood there, with his hand pressed against his forehead. He was a despairing figure, with a weary droop to his proudly carried shoulders, but his mind was racing furiously. He could not blame Overholt for his failure to understand, to believe what he himself knew to be fact. But he could not allow the fantastic element of the danger to stop him. If the chief died—Kildering's lips twitched. Without the chief, the F. B. I. would lose half its efficiency. It was the skill of the chief's leadership, but more than that, the intense loyalty he inspired in his men which made the F. B. I. the powerful organization it was. And Kildering, like all the other men, respected and loved his chief.

Kildering sighed, and his hand started to drop wearily from his forehead. When it reached the level of his coat lapel, it moved with a speed that blurred the vision—and then was suddenly very steady, very still. It was grinding the muzzle of a heavy automatic into Overholt's body.

"I'm sorry, Mr. Overholt," he said, and his voice had the quiet ring of tempered steel. "We must save the chief! Please walk ahead of me!"

Overholt's cheeks burned an angry red. "Put that gun up, you fool!" he ordered.

Kildering's thumb pressed down the safety catch. In the silence between the two men, the mechanical snap was as ominous as a rattlesnake's whir. "Please go ahead of me," Kildering said again. Each word was chipped from ice.

Overholt stared fixedly into Kildering's eyes through a long unbreathing moment. Overholt swallowed stiffly. He turned on legs as stiff as stilts and stumped out of his office, across the big anteroom and into the corridor toward the third-floor stairway.

Kildering kept pace with Overholt's angry stride. The gun bored into Overholt's spine, and his finger was steady on the trigger—and Kildering's face was sternly drawn. It showed nothing of the terror that rode his soul—not fear for the consequences of his act, nor even for the death that might well be waiting in the corridor above when he confronted the guards—but fear for the life of his chief!

They went up the steps swiftly—and the third floor was blocked by a sheet of steel armor. Through narrow gunports, two machine guns peered out with uncompromising black muzzles.

"Summers! Mayor!" Kildering's voice lifted quietly to the two men on guard. "Pull aside the shield! The chief's life is in danger!"

The voice that answered was jubilant despite a rasp of strain. "Old Frozen-face Kildering!" the man cried. "I'd like to, Kildering. Swear I would! Can't."

Kildering's lips pulled out, cold against his teeth. Useless to try to persuade Mayor. He had failed with Overholt, much more apt to go against the orders of his chief than was Mayor. Kildering stepped slowly out from behind Overholt, his gun rock-steady against his hip.

"Overholt," he said softly, "tell them this is necessary."

Mayor's voice came to Kildering's ears thinly: "I can't help what the superintendent says. Chief told me to admit no one except by his specific orders! Go back down the steps, or I'll have to open fire. Those are my orders!"

Kildering drew in a slow breath. His eyes were sunken with pain. Mayor and Summers were his particular friends. He had worked with them a score of times. His friends.

"Mayor," Kildering said flatly, "your life and mine are less important than the chief's! If I have to shoot you, I will. And it will have to be a dead shot. I couldn't do anything else through that narrow port!"

Beside him, Overholt gasped, started to turn toward him. Kildering's voice rapped out, with the stern absolute tone of command:

"Summers! Hit Mayor over the head!"

Behind one of the gunports, the light reflection shifted a little. Mayor had turned his head to glance toward his partner! It was the moment for which Kildering had played. His leap was like the release of a tightly compressed spring.

In a single bound, Kildering reached the barrier and sprang high into the air. That first leap cleared the gunport. His hands clamped on top of the shield. The clash of his gun against the metal was harsh, ominous. Kildering's body swung upward, then horizontal—it popped out of sight over the top of the shield. It was as effortless as a bearing turning in a bath of oil!

Mayor and Summers were just beneath him as Kildering dropped. His straining eyes caught the blurred flicker of light as Mayor snatched for his underarm gun! Kildering whipped his feet down and drove his heels hard into Mayor's shoulders. The blow paralyzed his friend's arms, hammered Mayor downward violently.

Falling, Kildering lashed out with his automatic. The blow was carefully calculated, and thanks to Kildering's superb coordination, it struck with exactly the right force. He caught the amazed stare on Summers' boyish face, the shocked bewilderment of the eyes just before the barrel slammed home. It was a flashing glimpse as he drove to the floor with Mayor. But even that was carefully calculated. Kildering's body was tumbling even as Mayor hit the floor. He balled, somersaulted to his feet and pivoted, all in one fluid motion. The gun lashed out again.

Kildering staggered against the wall, but he did not need to inspect the two men, his two friends. He knew they would stay down for a while. But pain fought with anxiety in his eyes as he raced on soundlessly toward the chief's door.

Behind him, he could hear Overholt swearing softly as he climbed, more laboriously, over the steel barrier. He hoped that Overholt would

not try to interfere. Kildering drew in a slow breath. He pressed close
to the door of the chief's office, and his voice came out easily.

"Chief!" he called. "Chief, it's Kildering! I can save you from John
Miller!"

His voice echoed along the hall. Kildering, twisting his head about,
listening with hard strain, saw Overholt drop to the floor. He did not
check beside the unconscious men, but came toward Kildering, his
arms swinging choppily. But he walked on his toes, softly, and Kildering
drew in a slow breath of relief. Overholt might not be convinced, but
that silent approach meant that, for the present, at least, Overholt
would not attempt to interfere. He blotted the superintendent out of
his mind, concentrated on hearing what went on inside the office. There
had been no answer to his hail. Fear made the blood throb in his
temples. Suppose the chief had already—

"You know me, chief!" Kildering called again, and his voice had a
wheedling note. "It's Kildering! Old Frozen-face! I've cracked your
toughest cases for you. I can crack this one, too." He checked, listening.
His heart leaped wildly. He thought he had heard the creak of a floor
board! "While I'm with you," he called, "John Miller can't hurt you.
I can save you from John Miller!"

Overholt's brows were drawn down fiercely over his brilliant blue
eyes. He stared gloweringly at Walter Kildering. Who was John Miller,
Overholt wondered, and why was Kildering talking in that fool tone
of voice, as if he would cajole a child? Abruptly, Overholt's eyes whipped
toward the chief's door. The chief had answered!

Just on the other side of the barrier, the chief was whispering, as
Kildering had whispered, hoarsely.

"How?" asked the chief. *"How can you save me from John Miller?"*

Overholt felt a small coldness tingle over his arms and shoulders,
down his thighs. The chief's voice sounded—strange. He glanced at
Kildering and almost swore aloud. Old Frozen-face was showing some
expression for once. His face was twisted. And there was perspiration
beading his forehead.

Kildering whispered his mouth close to the door. "It's very simple,
if you know the secret, chief. I can teach it to you, chief! It took me
a long time to learn it, but you have a powerful mind. It will be easy
for you! You are a great man. A strong man. You are greater than
John Miller!"

Inside, the strange voice whispered back: "I . . . I am greater than
John Miller?"

Overholt lifted a hand to his forehead, and the gesture was uncertain.
Kildering was looking at him, torture in his eyes.

"Ready!" He formed soundless words with his lips. *"Go in fast!"*

"Certainly," Kildering said aloud, confidently. "You are much greater.

You are the chief! Just let Kildering tell you the secret, old Frozen-face Kildering!"

The chief's voice came slowly: "I am greater than John Miller. I am the chief. I—"

The key clicked in the lock, the bolt rasped back. A gun muzzle peered out of the opening, a glittering eye.

"Not you, Overholt!" the chief's voice rasped. "Just Kildering. Good old Frozen-face. He knows the secret. But leave your gun outside, Kildering. How do I know you're not John Miller in disguise? By God, that's it! You're John Miller in disguise, and—"

The gun jerked into line!

An instant before the chief pulled the trigger, Kildering hit the door with his shoulder. He hit it with all the drive of his tensed thighs. The edge of the door caught the chief. It spun him across the room, slammed him against the wall. His arms flew wide with the impact—but he kept hold of the gun!

"You're not going to get me, John Miller!" he screamed. "You're *not* to—"

He pointed the automatic at Kildering and despite his frenzy, the muzzle was steady and unwavering. Overholt poised on the threshold, weighing his chances. His own gun was below in his desk—

The chief was whispering piercingly: "You're not going to get me, John Miller, and—" The chief's eyes were strained painfully wide. The whites showed entirely around the iris. He looked like a sleepwalker. The chief whimpered. "I forgot! I can't shoot John Miller! He's immortal—but I'll beat you, John Miller! I'll beat you!" He laughed, and the sound of it was cracked. *"I'll beat you!"*

He whipped up the automatic and ground the muzzle against his own temple! Overholt uttered a hoarse shout and leaped. He knew it would be too late.

The crash of the gun was deafening. The automatic flew from the chief's hand, thudded against the wall, bounced to the floor. The chief staggered sideways. There was a scratch across his temple, but no gaping hole.

Kildering's voice was the flick of a lash. "Knock him out, Overholt!"

Overholt's bound took him toward the chief. The chief screamed, tried to run. Overholt's fist lashed out with practiced efficiency. It was only when he had caught the chief and eased his unconscious body to the floor gently, that he looked toward Kildering.

Kildering was closing the door. He had his automatic in his fist, and there was a wisp of grease smoke at the muzzle. Kildering stood on widely braced legs. It was as if he had to stand that way, to hold himself erect.

Overholt understood then. He said heavily: "A nice shot, Kildering, knocking the gun out of the chief's hand." He straightened, and his broad shoulders shivered a little. "Good God, you were right! The chief . . . *insane!*"

II

THE PERSPIRATION still glistened on Walter Kildering's forehead, but there was no other outward sign of perturbation. He felt a slight quivering in the taut cords behind his knees; there was no tremor in his hand as he holstered his automatic.

"That shot will bring men, Mr. Overholt," he said quietly. "They will find Mayor and Summers. We'll have to act quickly if we're to protect the chief's reputation."

Overholt swore, threw up his head in a listening attitude. There were shouts in the distance, and the swift racing beat of men's feet. He nodded. Imperceptibly, and without Overholt actually realizing it, the command had passed from Overholt. He was following Walter Kildering—as all men followed him in moments of stress.

"Right!" Overholt snapped. "Stay here, Kildering. You've got a lot of explaining to do."

Kildering nodded without words, and Overholt strode out, clapped the door shut behind him. Kildering turned toward his chief, walked slowly across to where he lay unconscious. Kildering went down on his knees and began to strap the chief's arms and legs together.

There was pity in Kildering's eyes, but there was anger there, too. It made hot, black flames in the depths of his gray eyes. It made his movements jerky, and the restraint turned his cheeks pale.

Up until the moment he had heard the chief's voice, Kildering had had only logic to guide him. Now he knew that everything he had feared, everything he had deduced in the pure abstraction of his intellect, was damnably true. There was a criminal with a record of incredibly successful thefts, and of equally cold-blooded murder, who could will a strong man like the chief into insanity! And he saw how the trick was being done—an unsolvable dilemma.

The actual phrasing of that thought jerked Kildering rigidly to his feet, sent coldness like a cruelly dull knife along his spine. His hands shook a little as he drew out his notebook and glanced with fierce, demanding eyes at the strangely spidery script which covered its pages. He was standing like that when Overholt returned.

Overholt checked just inside the door, staring at Kildering's stiffly erect back, the challenge of the upflung head, the easy competence of the shoulders. Overholt felt a brief stir of resentment. He realized then that he had resigned command to this other man, to Walter Kildering. And he recognized that Kildering was competent for the assignment.

Overholt's voice was quiet, and it held a new note of respect. "I've put Mayor and Summers under close arrest," he said curtly. "They won't be allowed to speak, even to their guards. How is the chief?"

Kildering turned slowly. "I think he'll be all right, sir," he said gravely. "I've strapped him up for his own safety. I've also given him a shot of morphine, but it's slow in taking hold. I owe you an explanation, Mr. Overholt."

"Not an explanation, no," Overholt said curtly. "It's quite obvious that you were right, and I am wrong. But, in God's name, Kildering, *tell me what it is we are fighting.*"

Kildering said quietly: "You are more generous than I had any right to expect. I'll be glad to tell you what I know, what I have guessed. It's pitifully little." He opened his notebook, and Overholt frowned at the sight of the closely written pages.

"What the hell is that stuff?" he asked curtly. "It can't be code or shorthand."

Kildering shook his head, his face very grave. "No, sir. It's written in Old Icelandic, with Sanskrit characters. I think it would be harder than most codes to decipher, and it's much simpler to read and write."

"Simpler!" Overholt's blue eyes crinkled. It might have been mirth except for the hurt that drew his face gaunt whenever his glance rested on the unconscious chief. "Get on with it—only tell me in English!"

The faces of both men were grim. Kildering's was very pale as he stared at his notes. It had been deduction before, but he knew it now for truth. As long as John Miller remained only a matter of logic, he seemed remote—an abstraction of mathematics, clear enough on paper; insusceptible of material proof. But now he knew—

Kildering's voice bore that weight upon it as he spoke. His voice was like a muted string. "John Miller," he said quietly, "is, of course, the man whom we called the 'Unknown.' He is the man who killed those three bankers and two of our men, who killed Police Chief Eidson by making him commit suicide. He is the one who drove those three other bankers mad before they could give information against him. He has now driven the chief out of his mind by the same process. I have an idea how that is done."

Overholt stared at Kildering. He started to speak and didn't. He crossed slowly to the chief's desk, and dropped into the chair.

"The link of deaths, obviously murder, which are designated as heart failure by the physicians," Kildering resumed, more strongly, "and the induced insanity, join the same criminal who committed these crimes to another curious happening in the city of Metropolis. Three months ago, a woman was found dead in the woods near the city. She was dead of heart failure, and she carried a baby in her arms which the newspapers termed a 'monster.' The scientist who attempted to study this baby went insane and destroyed the monster. Our two men who were killed in Metropolis apparently went to question a woman in the maternity ward of the hospital. Apparently, these two men had hit on the same clue I am following. It was dangerous to John Miller—and he destroyed them."

Overholt's hands were knotted into fists. "I don't know what you're getting at," he said irritably, "but I don't like the sound of it."

"It's not—pleasant," Kildering agreed somberly. "These facts were all I had to go on at first. They hinted at something that I could not bring myself to believe—until those three kidnapings in Wichinois. Even then, the idea seemed so . . . so mad that I could not bring it to your attention until I had confirmation of some sort. I did not think the—conclusive evidence would be so horrible."

Overholt gestured with his fist. "You mean, I suppose, those girls who disappeared in Wichinois—for whom ransom notes were never received. Two of the girls pretty wealthy, another that young prodigy who was president of the State University."

"Yes, sir," Kildering nodded. "After that, you may recall, I asked the bureau to make a check-up on a certain type of statutory offense in Wichinois."

Overholt ran a hand in bewilderment across his forehead. "Yes, I remember. You wanted records of seductions in college towns. Especially where the parents of girls had brought charges against the will of the girl. I didn't know—Good Lord! Did that have something to do with this John Miller?"

Kildering came forward to the desk, and his eyes were very serious. "Mr. Overholt, I am going to ask you a strange thing. I want to request that everything that I say to you here be kept an absolute secret. It must not even be written into reports!"

"Nonsense, Kildering!"

Kildering nodded. "Believe me, sir, this is absolutely necessary. You have seen what John Miller can do. He will tolerate no interference with his plans. He is capable and ready, I am sure, to destroy the entire F. B. I., man by man, leader by leader. The only protection is to keep him from knowing that we suspect his identity!"

Overholt's breath came out in a long gust. It lifted his chest, and there was anger in the flush on his high cheekbones. "You're crazy, Kildering!" he snapped. "I'm going to throw every man in the F. B. I. into this search! No criminal would dare do what you say. Why, damn it, he wouldn't dare!"

On the floor, the chief stirred and whimpered in his throat. *"John Miller!"* he whined. *Don't let Miller destroy me!"*

Overholt's knotted fists trembled, relaxed. His arms dropped like sticks.

Kildering's voice softened. Pity was in his eyes. "I do not mean that we cannot do anything against Miller, sir," he said. "I only mean that what is done must be accomplished secretly. How he works, I have no idea. So no protection can be contrived against him. Theoretically, psychologists can drive a man insane. They have already accomplished it with lower animals. Presented with an irresolvable dilemma, the mind seeks refuge in insanity. The chief was presented, somehow, with a most primitive and basic dilemma. His will to survive was attacked. He had the alternative of dying or of destroying the threat to his life— John Miller. But he could not destroy the threat, because John Miller is immortal—"

The chief whimpered something indistinguishable and tugged fretfully at his bonds.

Overholt snapped to his feet. His fist pounded the desk. "Damn it, Kildering, tell me who this Miller is!"

Kildering hesitated. His eyes were keen on Overholt's face. "I think I can locate John Miller," he said quietly. "Whether I can then destroy him, I do not know. There can be no question of bringing him to trial. A man with his powers could confound our entire judicial system. Won't you give me a carte blanche on this case—and ask no more? I'm afraid that Miller will strike you down, too!"

Overholt shifted angrily in his chair. "I'd give you that assignment anyway," he said shortly. "Hell, all right! You're running the show from now on. But if you fail to—"

Kildering shrugged. "Then, of course, sir, someone else will have to try his luck. That's our one advantage over Miller—there are more of us."

Overholt nodded, his blue eyes burning into those of Kildering. "I want the whole picture," he said shortly.

Kildering picked up his notebook. "I'll read you some of my notes. After those seizures of insanity, I checked carefully to see if any use of drugs was involved. But the men remained in a state of madness. I wrote: 'Fantastic as it seems, apparently some man is causing this insanity by direct pressure of his will against deliberately selected individuals. This is beyond any known human powers.' "

"Human powers," Overholt stammered.

Kildering said slowly, "You are familiar with the philosophy of Ubermensch."

"Superman?" Overholt echoed. "Superman!"

There was fright in the eyes of both men, but those of Overholt showed bewilderment—and Kildering's held grim determination. Overholt shivered. He hunched his chair closer to the desk. "Let's have it," he said hoarsely. He did not seem aware that he whispered.

Kildering nodded. "Three things cause mutations in the genes of species," he said, "so far as is known. Cosmic rays. X rays. Radium emanations. Recently—atom-smashing rays have been added. The wide use of the three latter in modern civilization is bound to cause increasing modification of human beings. Sooner or later, and probably earlier because of this very fact of wide use of the rays, a superman is bound to spring up. He is inevitable."

"Inevitable," Overholt echoed the word, without expression.

Kildering inspected him narrowly, glanced toward the prostrate chief, who had lapsed into a drugged sleep. But Overholt seemed normal enough. It was possible John Miller would not attack him—yet. It was possible—

"So," Kildering resumed, "when I found powers that seemed more than human, I wondered if—superman had arrived. I asked myself what such a—person could be expected to do. The monster baby, found dead near Metropolis, was, from descriptions, not a disease-deformed infant, but something quite different. A mutation. And the scientist who examined it was driven mad! Obviously, then, superman knew his own powers, knew what he was—if I was right. It was apparent, too, that he was trying to reproduce his kind. So I asked the check-up on such offenses." Kildering tossed some papers to the desk. "These dossiers came through last night. I spent the night analyzing them. I was going to report this morning."

Overholt picked up the sheafs of papers, glanced through them hurriedly, while Kildering spoke more urgently, his tone rapid and strained.

"Examination will show four charges against a single man," he said. "A man named John Miller. Most of the valuable data was compiled nine years ago by Morton Eidson—the man who later became police chief of Metropolis and killed himself. I think his suicide proves beyond a doubt that he was on the right track. The chief's use of the name of John Miller confirms it.

"I'll summarize on Miller."

Overholt's hands gripped the papers hard. His eyes had a strange brightness. He scarcely seemed to hear Kildering, but he nodded jerkily now and again.

"John Miller," Kildering said crisply, "is thirty-two. Born in New York City, son of Professor R. B. Miller, specialist in Röntgenology, and Elanor Nichols, his assistant in X-ray work before and after marriage. John Miller's grandfathers were Hans Mueller, a pitchblende miner in Central Europe, and John Nichols, also a miner, who worked in nickel deposits in Canada. Both these mines are sources of uranium, the ore of radium. Two generations, subject to genes-changing emanations."

Overholt nodded. Kildering rushed on; his voice showed increased strain.

"Such a family history, if I were correct in my surmise, pointed to other births of mutations—possibly hideous ones. John Miller had two brothers. One died at birth, a hideously misshapen creature. The other lived six years, a Mongoloid boy."

"An imbecile!" Overholt exploded.

Kildering said heavily: "John Miller's parents recently died of heart failure, but they gave more information before they died. I think the dossier would have been complete without it, but it is confirmation."

Overholt rasped, "Damn it, Kildering, are you saying that Miller killed his own parents to keep their mouths shut?"

Kildering said: "I don't know. It is possible. But Miller—He was a normal nine-month baby. That is, he was carried the regular length of time, but he was incompletely formed at birth. Hence, actually, he was premature. He was in an incubator for nine months. In school, he was at first stupid and believed moronic. He slept a large part of the day. He was fifteen before he left the fourth grade, but only seventeen when he entered high school. At twenty, he entered college, did the course in two years. A year later, he had a doctorate of philosophy. He was twenty-three then. Nine years ago. Our provable record of him ends there."

Overholt's voice was thin, unnatural. "And you call him a superman? He's a monster! A robber! A murderer! Patricide! And depraved!"

"Yes, sir," Kildering acknowledged, "that would be the normal judgment of a man who did these things. But he's not a man. His history points to a superior intelligence, with an unusually delayed maturity. A mutation—superman."

Overholt pulled to his feet. His eyes were wide and he was looking blankly at the wall. He lifted his hands slowly to squeeze his skull between his palms. "Superman—with three million dollars to continue his criminality," he said thickly. "In God's name, Kildering, what is he planning? What will he do next?"

Kildering's lips twisted in thin determination. "I must find out, sir. Obviously, his headquarters are in Metropolis! But we're men—he's not. We can't predict unhuman behavior."

Overholt's hands dropped. He said shortly, "I want a physical description. I'm going to broadcast it, get every cop in the country on his trail. We'll destroy superman—before he destroys us!"

Kildering felt his eyes tighten in their sockets. Overholt sounded so much like an echo of what the chief had cried a little while before—before he lost his mind! Was it possible that Miller was not content with the destruction of the chief? Was he already at work to destroy the entire F. B. I.?

Kildering leaned forward tautly. Watching Overholt, he said softly, "Yes, we must destroy him—but how can we? John Miller is immortal!"

Overholt looked furtively about him. "We must take precautions," he whispered. "Is the door locked?"

Kildering brought his fist up from his hip. The blow was perfectly timed, perfectly executed. It caught Overholt on the point of the jaw, slammed him back into the chair. He jiggled there for an instant, then slipped, feet first, to the floor.

Kildering stood bolt upright, rigid. His face was drained of all color, and he closed his eyes.

"We must destroy John Miller," he said deliberately, woodenly, "before he destroys us! But we cannot destroy him because he is immortal!"

Walter Kildering waited through a long, long minute, then he repeated the formula. Afterward, he opened his eyes, and there was a horror there, and a dread in the twist of his lips.

"I'm not important enough to worry John Miller," he whispered. "He isn't trying to drive me insane—not yet!"

Through another minute, Walter Kildering stood very rigidly in the office where his two superiors lay unconscious—and insane. He was realizing to the full how powerful was this John Miller. He had not overestimated superman! The entire bureau could be destroyed, man by man—unless Kildering could stop him!

A sob of mocking laughter thrust up into Walter Kildering's throat. He, alone, against superman? But it had to be that way. Meantime, he must turn the wrath of John Miller away from the F. B. I. It was the only way the bureau could be saved!

Walter Kildering flung himself at the annunciator on the chief's desk and slapped down a cam. He ordered Bill Mayor and Marty Summers released and sent to the chief's office, unattended. He put through a telephone call over a private wire to a noted "inside" columnist of a newspaper hostile to the administration.

"This is a hot tip," he told the newspaperman, and his voice was hoarse, hurried, not his own at all. "The F. B. I. is completely disorganized. The chief has gone insane, and his next-in-command is in very nearly the same fix!"

Rapidly, he told the columnist how the report could be confirmed, of the barricade at the doors and the attempt of the chief to commit suicide—

Kildering pushed to his feet. When Miller heard of this, he should be satisfied—for the present. Walter Kildering was very pale. He was a traitor to the F. B. I.—for its own good. He was about to desert the service—for its own good.

If he succeeded, all would be well. If he failed, his name would go eternally into the black lists of the bureau which he loved, to which he had given the full measure of his life and loyalty.

He had never flinched from death in the service of his country. Why should he shrink from—disgrace?

Kildering's face was as expressionless as a chunk of granite when he stepped outside the chief's office to meet Marty Summers and Bill Mayor as they strode choppily up the corridor.

Mayor checked before Kildering and his fists were knotted at his sides. The black slab of his forelock was awry across his forehead, and his eyes were bitter, hostile.

"I'm going to pay you back for what you did today, Kildering," he said hotly. "This isn't the time."

There was a hesitant smile on the blunt, good-humored face of Marty Summers. "I've been trying to tell him, Kildering," he said, "that you had a good reason for what you did. I keep telling him—you've never made a mistake in your whole career!"

Kildering met hostility and loyalty with the same stoniness. He had chosen these two to fight the battle against superman. It would be his whole force, his whole army of desperation. Without words, he held out a slip of paper to each man. It was on the private memo paper of the chief's office, and the handwriting was the heavy vertical of the chief, with the boldly scrawled initials at their bottom.

Mayor snapped a slip from Kildering's hand. Then he cursed and looked up.

"What the hell's going on here?" he demanded. "You force a barricade the chief has personally ordered me to hold. Now the chief tells us to take all future orders from you! It doesn't make sense. It's crazy!"

Marty Summers said softly, "I told you Kildering never made a mistake!"

Kildering's eyes softened. He looked quickly away. His voice was quiet, but it held the command which men everywhere recognize and follow—the voice of a leader. "We will leave headquarters at once," he said quietly. "Follow me!"

Kildering swung off down the hall, his shoulders squared. Without meaning to, Bill Mayor found himself following Walter Kildering. Marty Summers marched, too.

No words were exchanged in the elevator, the guard at the barricades honored the slip that Kildering showed them, and he led the way deliberately toward the park. Kildering's eyes swung swiftly about. Very few persons were about. He stepped out on the springy turf, his nostrils wide to the scents of spring. The sun slanted warmly on his shoulders, but Kildering felt cold. He could not get that scene in the chief's office out of his mind.

In the middle of a broad expanse of sunny lawn, he stopped and faced the other two men. They were alone in the middle of populous Washington—alone in more ways than one. Peril was a dark shadow where they stood, though only Kildering was aware of it.

"You are not under my orders," he said quietly. "Those slips that appeared to come from the chief are forgeries. My own. I had to talk to you privately before—I go."

Summers smiled uncertainly. "Why, sure—but a forgery!"

Mayor stared at Kildering, then he threw back his head and laughed.

It was a harsh sound. "You, Kildering!" he cried. "You—forge an order! You're lying. What are you trying to keep us out of?" Mayor stared at Kildering again, and he grew very still. "Hell, you're telling the truth!" he said. "Something's up! Forget what I said, Kildering, back there in the corridor. We're with you!"

Summers said, "Look, Kildering, how's about trusting us!"

Kildering looked from Mayor to Summers and felt his heart swell. They had not even questioned his motives in forging orders for them. His voice was even. "I am deserting the F. B. I.," he said. "When you go back, within a few hours, you will learn that there is a traitor in the F. B. I. His name is Kildering."

Mayor said impatiently: "Oh, bunk! We know how you feel about the service. Quit stalling and tell us what it's all about. If you've got a case you're working on, and it's important enough to make you do those things, we're in on it. Eh, Marty?"

Summers nodded quickly, eagerly.

Kildering said sternly: "Wait! Wait, before you commit yourself. I phoned a story to a hostile newspaper which will make the whole United States believe the bureau is completely disorganized. It's entirely possible that the boys will start hunting me down!"

Mayor said: "For God's sake, Kildering, quit stalling! *We know you!*"

Kildering laughed, and the sound was like a sob in his throat. "You trust me—like that?" he asked, and there was humbleness in his tones.

Summers grinned. "I've never known you to make a mistake, Kildering."

Mayor said impatiently: "Why don't you get wise to yourself, Kildering? You're too brainy not to understand that we'll go with you all the way. Now, come across."

Kildering told them then, not everything, but most of what had happened in the chief's office; about John Miller—but not about superman.

"I phoned the newspaper," he finished, "because I believe it absolutely necessary that Miller should believe his attack on the bureau is entirely successful. Otherwise, he will still destroy it, man by man. If he thinks that the bureau is disorganized he will leave it alone—for a while. Before he attacks again, he must be destroyed!"

Bill Mayor's face was angrily flushed. His fists swung restlessly at his sides. "I don't know how anybody could do all that stuff," he said, "but—By God, I want to get my hands on the man who did that to the chief! Just let me get him across my gun sights! What the hell are we waiting for, Kildering? Let's get going!"

Summers' face was pale. His voice was subdued. "Count me in, Kildering," he said.

Kildering held out his hand, and Mayor and Summers clasped it together. They made a strange, stern picture there in the bright sunlight in the middle of a park lawn, three men shaking hands together. Mayor tossed his head up with that peculiarly gallant gesture of his, and Summers' lips held their slow, pale smile. Desperate twin fires burned in the depths of Kildering's eyes, but hope was higher in his heart.

III

THE CITY of Metropolis, spread white and glistening beside the brown, carefully walled-out flood of the great Wichinois River, had a peculiar history over the last nine years. There had been a series of catastrophic fires.

The conflagrations had swept away the ratty tenements, the jumbled factory and elevator districts along the river, the unsightly business district. It was a curious thing that each of these fires had struck at a time when the recurrent floods of the Wichinois had crippled water and electric supply.

There had been small doubt in the minds of city officials that the fires were started by an expert arsonist, or perhaps a ring of arsonists, but there never had been any conclusive evidence.

The rebuilding had been very intelligent. The multiple suggestions had come from various sources, almost by inspiration, it seemed. The result was good.

Even the streets had been recharted and a splendid civic center amid park lands formed the exact midportion of the city. Around its verges were the administrative buildings, the neatly laid out shopping districts with wide thoroughfares spoking out to the suburbs.

Rapid transit ran underground to speed the outdwelling workers to their tasks where this was necessary; the factories were mostly in the carefully zoned environs.

Metropolis was justly known as a model city, and Wichinois was very proud of the results of those fires, despite the tragic loss of life.

Of course, if the man responsible for those fires could have been located, he would have been executed.

Berger Street was a minor crossway near the Civic Center, the situation of most of the exclusive shops. It was a difficult place for the F. B. I. men to set up surveillance. All auto parking was confined to the multiple fields tucked away in the riverside parks; it wasn't possible, day after day, to keep a taxi engaged in the corner ranks. More especially since they had come away from Washington secretly, without expense money; without even stopping for their clothing. Kildering had insisted on that.

Mayor and Summers had finally found it necessary to rent a small office in a corner, four-story building—the highest structure in this area—and keep their watch with binoculars. The particular shop they observed had no name on the windows or over the door. The windows were small and each of them displayed only a single tiny vial of perfume set against a bouquet of flowers. It was that kind of shop.

The break came on the eighth day of their watch, near the closing hour of the shop. Marty Summers had just about given up hope; Bill Mayor had been skeptical from the start.

"Kildering must be nuts," Mayor said again from where he lay uncomfortably on the desk, resting his overstrained eyes. "He's gone at this whole thing backward. The man we want is Miller, and he's got us looking for a kidnaped girl that he expects to be walking along the street like anybody else. He's nuts."

Summers smiled. He was usually smiling, and it sat well on the generous width of his mouth. He was young-looking, with a boyish stubbornness about the thrust of his jaw. It was his major value, that stubbornness. He had never acknowledged defeat in any issue and he had a loyalty that was unswerving.

"Kildering does queer things sometimes," he acknowledged softly. "It seems silly to expect a kidnaped girl to walk into a shop because she has a taste for exotic perfumes. But Kildering doesn't make mistakes."

Mayor said: "Oh, to hell with it! Miller is the man I want!" He swung his feet to the floor, and the long, lean line of his jaw was sharp. "Just let me get my hands on the mug that—hurt the chief!"

Summers closed his eyes for an instant to rest them from the strain of the glasses. "Kildering said we weren't to mention that name. I don't know why, but he seemed worried about it. Anyway, we can't look for him. We don't know anything about him, except that women are his weakness."

Mayor's large eyes were narrowed. "It's a screwy business. I don't get this not mentioning his name. I don't get how he could do—what he did to the chief. And I don't see why we can't get a description of the mug. Must be plenty of guys knew him at college. A hell of a description! 'Six feet one. Hair medium dark. Eyes medium gray. Usually talks in a very soft voice. Insisted on wearing gloves at all times and never was known to strip off his clothes in the presence of others.' Now what the hell does all that add up to?"

Summers was peering through the glasses again. "I don't know," he said slowly, and he sounded worried. "I know I don't like the sound of it. He's the worst murderer we've ever trailed. He's got away with three million dollars, and girls he's supposed to have kidnaped are expected to walk around the streets. And that stuff about the gloves and the clothes. It sounds—*ugly!*"

"It sounds nuts." Bill Mayor swung his feet. His good-looking face was sullen. "I want action! I want to get my hands on—"

Summers' voice cut in sharply, excitedly: "Bill! Let me see those pictures of Marianne Winters!"

Mayor took one look at the tense line of Summers' body at the window and sprang to his side, snatching the glasses. His left hand gripping a strip of candid photographs of a laughing blonde, trembled a little. He peered through the glasses, compared with the pictures, checked again.

"Hair's black; might be dyed," he whispered. "Those glasses change her profile, but—by God, you're right! It's Marianne!"

Marty Summers' smile was broad on his mouth. "Kildering said she'd come," he said.

Mayor swore. "Old Frozen-face, right again! But how in hell he knew that we would find a kidnaped girl walking around the streets loose—" He was striding across the office. He dragged a felt hat down over his even brows, slapped at the gun under his arm.

Summers was swiftly dialing a telephone number. "Repeat orders, Bill!" he called softly. "Kildering insisted!"

Mayor checked by the door, impatiently. "Follow Marianne at all costs. You communicate with Kildering, pick me up if possible. If not, I carry on and communicate when I can. Do nothing without orders from Frozen-face. Allow no violence, no possible development to persuade me to do anything but follow Marianne." The slap of the closing door cut off his words, and his feet made sharp, hurried echoes down the hall.

Summers got a phone number, asked for "Mr. Walters" and was given another number to call. He did that twice more before Kildering's dead level voice came to his ears. He spilled out his report.

"You were right, Kildering," he began. "Marianne— What? You know? All right. All right, I'll try, but this delay—"

Summers slammed up the phone and was plunging across the room. His quick glance out the window while he phoned had shown him Marianne already climbing into another taxi. He had just time to spot Bill Mayor getting into a second. Bewilderment still made Summers' eyes wide as he raced down the steps toward the street. If Kildering knew they had spotted Marianne, then he must be somewhere in sight of their office and the perfume shop! It was like old Frozen-face to take no chances on failure, even with men he trusted!

Summers knew, without being told by Kildering, that he had a double assignment; not only to trail Mayor and pick up any divergent trails of anyone whom Marianne met, but to keep Mayor from doing anything, hotheaded, that might spoil the success of their plans. Bill Mayor felt the injury to the chief as a personal grief, and a matter for personal revenge. But so did they all.

Summers bolted out into the street and was just in time to see Mayor's cab turn the corner into Liberty Avenue. He signaled another taxi and, swinging into the avenue, was relieved to see both Mayor's and the girl's cabs ahead of him.

Now, for the first time, Summers could digest Kildering's swift orders. "Marianne won't lead you to Number One," he had said, using his locution for Miller. "Any person she meets may be much more important than she is. You take any divergent trails; let Mayor stick to the girl."

But Kildering hadn't seemed excited. He never did, though Summers knew that he felt the injury to the chief as seriously, as personally, as did Bill Mayor or himself. And Kildering didn't seem worried about the immensity of the task before them, or their personal danger. But then, he couldn't afford to. Kildering was—the chief!

It was true that Kildering constantly ordered precautions, and that he isolated himself from them. They didn't even know where his rooms were, and there was always this involved telephoning to locate him. But Summers thought that Kildering was wise about that. It was safer to divide forces. Then if—if Miller destroyed one contingent, the other would be left to carry on!

For an instant, Summers' mind flicked to the man they hunted: to the man who went by the curiously anonymous name of Miller. The things about Miller, or Number One, as Kildering preferred to call him, didn't seem to make sense to Summers. He couldn't fathom the mental processes of a man who had coolly murdered, or driven insane, a dozen persons—probably including his own mother and father—yet who had, in his college days, taken such tender care of the girls he had kidnaped. And tender was the word for it. A part of their preparatory work had been an attempt to trace these early loves of John Miller. Then there were these hints of abnormality; John Miller's own brothers, and the "monster" baby whose examiner had gone insane!

That thought sent a shudder through Summers, turned his thoughts to personal matters. He had not communicated with his wife since leaving Washington. Then he had been able to say only that he was going out under secret orders. It was nearer the truth than the bald word "desertion." Anne would have felt better if she could have known he was under Kildering; her trust in old Frozen-face was as great as his own.

Summers had plenty of time to think things out during the two hours that his cab held the trail. Marianne Winters made three more stops, changing cabs each time, but she apparently made only a series of purchases. There were no divergent trails and, just at dusk, he saw Marianne's cab pull up before a small bungalow in the Prince Hills district. Summers let his own cab roll two blocks past the spot and turn the corner before he dismissed it. He had already spotted Mayor's cab, parked with its lights out a short distance down the previous cross street. He hurried toward it.

Mayor, slumped in the back of the cab smoking, nodded casually as Summers climbed in. "Saw you back there," he said. "I want to have a look in that house, but I suppose we have to report to old Frozen-face first. Better rent a car on your way to phone, Marty. Can't keep a cab parked here indefinitely."

Summers heard a quiet step on the sidewalk beside the cab and whipped about. His hand snapped to his automatic—then he gasped. *"Kildering!"* he whispered.

Walter Kildering was peering in at them through the open cab window. He nodded easily.

"Come along," he said quietly. "You won't need the cab."

Summers grinned his bewilderment and a load seemed to lift from his shoulders. Just seeing the easy competence of Kildering, hearing his voice, could do that to Marty. None of them spoke again until Mayor had paid off the cab and they were strolling along with Kildering.

Mayor was grinning, and it was apparent he felt the same relief that Summers did. "Well, how do you do it, master mind?" he demanded. "Is it worked with mirrors, or did you just follow Marty?"

Kildering's smile of acknowledgment was faint, and a frown made a knife crease between his brows. "Simpler than either," he said. "I spotted the cab which brought Marianne to the perfume shop, and got her address from the driver. I've rented a furnished cottage across the street from her bungalow and have been staked out there for an hour. The other two 'kidnaped' girls, Rose Darby and Belinda Hayes, are there. But they came separately, and don't live there, since there's only one bed." He turned into the driveway of the cottage he had rented. In the early dusk, the place gave Summers a stab. It looked so much like his own home, in Washington.

Kildering was saying quietly, "I have two cars here."

Mayor was grumbling good-naturedly. "Why not just send us back to Washington, and carry on alone?" he said. "We're just excess baggage."

Kildering smiled faintly once more. He was preoccupied. "I think our discovery is opportune," he said gravely. "These three girls seem to be strangers to each other, from what I've observed. It's as if they were assembling for action."

Mayor chuckled. "Maybe John Miller is going to drop in on his harem!"

Kildering's head whipped toward him. "Mayor," he said emphatically, "you must not use that name!" His face was paler than usual.

Mayor frowned. "Listen, if you're afraid of that mug, I'm not!" he said. "What the hell difference does it make?"

Kildering drew in a slow breath. "Wait until we get inside," he said. He unlocked the door, gestured the two men inside and flicked on lights in the drawing room. "Sit down, please." He settled himself into a chair at the table, and the overhead lighting emphasized the long, powerful lines of his face.

"Mayor, and you, Summers," Kildering said somberly, "I'm afraid I owe you two an apology. I was something less than frank in Washington. I told you all the facts. I did not tell you what I guessed. I was desperately anxious for your help. I may have minimized the danger."

Mayor grunted: "If it was minimized, I didn't detect it. You said we had one chance in a hundred of living to return."

Kildering said slowly: "I think the chances are rather less than that. You'd better know everything that I can tell you. I think we have time." He peered toward the bungalow across the road. The girls were moving about, crossing and recrossing the lighted windows.

"I'm not sure," he resumed, "that the mere mention of Number One's name aloud isn't enough to draw his attention to us. You already know that Number One has mental powers beyond human understanding—"

"Beyond *human* understanding!" Summers whispered. "I don't think I've heard you express it that way before!"

"No, I have kept from you my true belief as to—what Number One is," Kildering said quietly, "and I didn't tell you my real fears. I said that the bureau was threatened with destruction. But if Number One could wreck the bureau, killing and driving insane man after man—without once appearing on the scene—he could do the same with—*the government of the United States!*"

Mayor said, "In God's name, Kildering, what do you mean—a revolution?"

"It's a possibility," Kildering said crisply. "I do not say that it is his intention. I think that, if he thinks he is being let alone, the government is safe—for the present. I do not think his plans reach so far as—the White House. For the present."

Mayor asked hoarsely: "God! What is this man trying to do, Kildering? Who is he? *What* is he?"

Kildering spoke slowly. "We must not let our quandary make us careless. Those girls across the street are getting ready to go out. I do not think they will go to Number One. I think they have a task to perform for him which may help us to understand what he is trying to do. As to what he is—Undoubtedly, a mutant of the human species."

Marty said uncertainly, "A mutant?"

"Hell!" Mayor exploded. "You mean this stuff about evolution! Changes in animals and plants caused by the effect of cosmic rays on the genes of a species, producing freaks."

Kildering said: "We'll go out to the cars. Yes, exactly, Mayor. Number One received terrifically superior mental and physical endowments."

"He never," Summers whispered, "allowed himself to be seen unclothed. He's different physically, somehow—"

"A monster"—Kildering's voice was soft—"or a superman. Different from the human species, but sprang from it, as men and apes sprang from the mutations of a single primordial species."

"And this time, we're the apes, huh?" Mayor rasped. "He's got to be destroyed!"

Kildering's tone was a little grim. "I imagine the apes felt that way about it. I imagine the Neanderthalers felt that way about the Cro-Magnons. Tie a red ribbon around a turkey's neck, and the other turkeys will destroy it. The preservation instinct of the herd."

Mayor's voice held the faintest trace of panics. "He's got to be destroyed!"

Kildering's voice was without expression. "Yes, of course. He must be destroyed. Mayor, if you and Summers decide at any time in this case that I have lost my sanity, you have my orders to—destroy me. *My orders!*"

Summers said uncertainly: "To destroy you, Kildering?" The impact of Kildering's final words drove home the urgency of their task as nothing else that had been said. He felt doubts, felt hate rising like heat to his nostrils. John Miller had to be destroyed! He did not think now of government, or of the bureau; scarcely of himself. The entire human species—*apes!*

"Mayor, Summers." Kildering's voice was incisive. "You understand? No human life is important if it prevents our accomplishing the work! You have my orders?"

Mayor said thickly: "O.K., Kildering. And what you say goes for me, too. If any one of us goes nuts, the other two rub him out. We'll just shake on that."

The hands of the three men gripped and clung. They felt afraid there in the darkness. Panic strained at the bonds of their wills. There was a power they did not understand, could not understand, any more than apes could grasp the purposes of the hunter who wants their hides to stuff so as to pose the effigy against a painted canvas in a museum.

Across the street, the voices of women sounded softly, and a taxi bumbled down the street, squealed to a halt. A strangely matter-of-fact sound to men who have glimpsed the abyss, whose horrors their curling nostrils and shrinking ears can only guess.

Kildering's voice came out crisply. "Summers, take the rented car and stick close. Mayor and I will take the other and alternate in trailing. Cut on and off. Do nothing without specific orders!"

Summers stiffened under the commanding tone. Relief flooded him. Thank God for Kildering to give orders. Kildering—who never made a mistake!

THE PURSUIT led straight toward the city, the girls' taxi was exchanged for a private car at a garage, and finally they were rolling steadily through the drives of the green parks that selvaged the Wichinois River. There were glimpses of the black water, smooth enough to mirror the stars, through the small foliage of spring. Other cars hummed past, tires crisp on the asphalt, and Summers found himself struggling with disbelief.

It was the steadiness of a familiar task, the familiar sounds and smells about him that made the horror he had glimpsed seem so remote. It was not the fear of death that made Summers thrust these things from him; it was the thought of what his wife must be suffering. She would know by now that he was A. W. O. L. She had only the knowledge that he had left with Kildering to support her. There would be money enough for a while.

Marty Summers' mind snapped away from those things as he saw the car he was trailing swing left into a steep gravel drive toward the river. Over against the black loom of the water, the farther shore, he could see the steep prodding silhouettes of big chimneys from some building on the river bank.

Summers' eyes flicked to the rear-vision mirror, spotted the comforting nearness of Kildering and kicked his brake pedal twice to signal, with his stoplight, a left turn. Kildering's headlights lashed out twice across the darkness and, in obedience to the command, Summers pulled his car to a halt.

Kildering leaned out as the cars drew abreast. "Drive over the grass into the cover of the trees," he ordered quietly. "We go on foot from here. That drive the girls took ends fifty yards down—at the city's main electric power plant!"

Summers swung the car obediently from the road, but his mind lingered over Kildering's words. Those three girls were supposed to be carrying out some task for John Miller—and they had gone to the city power plant! In Heaven's name, what deviltry was afoot? He quickly hid the car, trotted back toward the road where Kildering was already standing in the blacker shadow of a leafing maple.

Summers was aware of the keen spring freshness of the air, of the moist living scents of the opening earth; the turf resilient under his feet. From the river, a tug piped hoarsely. The entrance to the power-plant tunnel was a black mouth.

"Mayor's staying with the car, in case of a sudden getaway," Kildering said.

Summers nodded, and they crossed the roadway, angled through the rhythmic planting of the trees. The scent of the river was fresher.

"What can they be planning?" Marty asked softly.

265

Kildering shook his head. "There have been three tremendous fires, of arsonist origin, in Metropolis. They occurred while the power plant was crippled with floods. But I don't think that's it."

Summers felt a coldness creep up his spine. Without any intention at all, he glanced over his shoulder. Those fires, too, were John Miller's work? The high whine of the turbine generators came to him faintly and, pushing through a shrubbery screen, they saw the girls' car parked close against the wall of the building. It was empty. Light streamed out of the high windows of the powerhouse and the hum of machinery was louder. Marty could see the humped, powerful backs of the generators.

The shooting started just as Marty stepped on the gravel of the drive.

Summers flung back into the shrubbery, whipped his automatic from its holster. He realized then that the shooting was inside the power plant. Five slamming discharges lifted above the machinery hum. A man cried out hoarsely.

Summers gasped, "By God!" He lifted the gun and lunged forward.

Kildering's hand clamped down on his shoulder, held him back.

Summers twisted about. "Those she-devils!" he cried. "They're killing men in there!"

Kildering spoke with an enforced quiet that made his voice sound queer and light. "Yes, damn them! But we can't interfere!"

Marty stammered, "C-can't interfere!"

He was still straining against the grip on his shoulder. His gun hand felt hot about the butt of his automatic. He could see the pale luminance of Kildering's face. Kildering's breathing was jerky. His lips were twisted in pain.

"No human life is important," he repeated his orders of earlier in the night, "if it prevents us from accomplishing our work! These girls are our only possible contact with—Number One. If we interfere with them, they will know we are on their trail. We would be—destroyed. It is not that our lives are important, but that we are the only human beings who know the truth about Number One, and are working to destroy him. If we let the girls complete their . . . their mission, they should report to Number One. Even if it's only by telephone, it should help us to trace him. That's what we want."

Summers stepped back into the shadows, but he drew a little apart from Kildering. He knew that Kildering was right, knew what it cost Kildering to make that decision, for pain was in every tone of his voice— And yet to be forced to stand by while helpless men were murdered! Summers' teeth locked hard and he jammed his automatic back into its holster. He stole a covert glance toward Kildering. His face held no expression at all—but his eyes were closed, almost as if he—as if he prayed!

The shots and cries had ceased, and there was a sudden diminution in the pitch of the generator whine. A slash of light shafted out across the drive. The door had been opened. Two of the girls stood in the opening. They had guns in their hands and they were staring toward the lighted interior. Easy to take them now—Marty glanced toward Kildering, but there was no change in the motionless silhouette.

Summers' eyes whipped back to the girls. They stood with a braced tension, as if they expected some blow they could not avoid. One of them called out softly: "Hurry, Rose! Those shots may have been heard!"

Summers recognized, with a thinning of his lips, that it was Marianne who called out. Marianne, who liked exotic perfume—who had just helped to kill men!

The whine of the generators dropped still lower and held to that pitch through a while that seemed interminable. The tug whistle sounded again, and the oily swish of traffic came down from the park driveway.

Summers found himself straining his ears to listen, to hear. That was how he happened to know that the girl's scream that lifted inside the power plant and the sudden accelerated hum of the reviving generators, came at the same split second of time. The girls at the doorway were clinging to the posts, *clinging*. It was as if they fought against a strong wind, a tidal undertow that sought to drag them to the earth. They were calling out, and their voices were muted, without resonance.

"This way, Rose!" they called. "Rose, this way. *Hurry!*"

Summers realized sharply that Kildering's hand was grinding into his shoulder again; that Kildering's voice was sharply sibilant in his ear.

"No, Marty! *Wait!*"

He could see into the power plant now, and suddenly the third girl was visible. She walked with a dragging slowness toward the door. All her body sagged; her arms reached out before her blindly. Her face was terribly pale. It seemed to shine with an internal whiteness. At the door, the two girls continued to call to her urgently. But they did not go inside. They clung to the door and shouted.

It seemed like an eternity that the ghostly Rose staggered toward the door. It was impossible that her sagging body should not fall, and yet it did not. Her stumbling feet carried her completely to the sill. It was when she reeled out into the open air that she pitched forward. Summers had one more glimpse of her face as the two girls caught her up and hurried toward the car. Rose's face dangled backward, and caught the full stream of light from the still open doorway.

The girl's face had turned blue!

Summers found himself being drawn back through the woods, and finally he was running beside the long-striding Kildering. But Summers ran uncertainly, and twice he slammed into trees that almost stunned him. Horror had him by the throat. In the name of God, *what had happened in the power plant?*

Gravel popped under the tires of the girls' car as it swept up the drive in second gear. Its motor howled with power. Summers realized they were being distanced, though their path was far shorter. But Mayor would take the trail, and with luck they would be able to swing into the tail end of the procession. Summers felt anger take possession of him. Damn it, *he* wanted to be the one to do the trailing! When John Miller was found—

Summers shivered. It was the first time he had ever yearned to kill a man. He was sobbing curses when he swung in behind the wheel of the car. It was a long time before his breathing and the sick pounding of his heart eased.

Before the end of the park drive, they came in sight of the two cars. Mayor was faithfully on the trail.

Summers said, then, "The girl's face was *blue!*"

"Cyanosed," Kildering said slowly. "Suffocation indicated."

Summers echoed the word stupidly. "You mean—gas?"

Kildering shook his head, but there was a vertical crease between his brows. He didn't speak until, trundling along a dark back street a block behind the fugitive car, they saw the door of the car whip open and a bundle, hideously lax and lifeless, tumble out in the roadway!

"Signal Mayor to take the lead," Kildering snapped. "We'll pick up the girl!"

Summers kicked the brake pedal to signal Mayor, and the third man, from whom they had taken over the chase, sent his car swishing past. It was Kildering who swung the girl into the back of the car. The easy co-ordination of his trained body made the task seem simple. Summers, his face very white, had the car rolling instantly.

"Is she dead?" he asked presently.

"Quite dead," Kildering said, and his voice was puzzled.

Summers' jaw ached from clenching. He began once more the game of leapfrog with Mayor's car on the trail of the two girls. He whirled off the line of pursuit, cut in ahead of the girls and let them pass. Mayor turned off into a side street and presently relieved him when he had dropped back. Then Summers switched off his headlights, cut in the dimmers and presently began to forge ahead again.

But the pursuit was uncomplicated. The two girls drove straight back to Marianne's bungalow and rolled their car into the garage.

"Now what?" Marty asked.

But Kildering had already leaped out of the car and was sprinting toward their own garage. When Summers joined him, he had a set of headphones clamped over his ears—and he was still frowning.

"I managed to put in a phone tap this afternoon," he explained, "but they haven't made a call. When Mayor comes, we'll pay a visit to our murderous neighbors across the street—and restore their friend to them!"

Summers said: "Carry the dead girl there? But why? If we didn't interfere at the powerhouse, when we could have saved some lives—"

Mayor came striding into the garage and had to be told what happened, and his eyes held on Kildering while he listened. When it was finished, he echoed Summers' challenge. "I'm not questioning orders," he said, and his voice had a curious light tightness. "I can see why those men in the powerhouse couldn't be saved, but doesn't the same thing hold good now?"

Kildering shook his head. His voice was a little tired. "That held good as long as there was any hope that they would immediately communicate with Number One," he said. "Since they haven't done it so far, it must be because such a report isn't necessary. If we invade their quarters, we may be able to frighten them into making an attempt to communicate with Number One. That will be our chance!"

Mayor laughed shortly, almost happily. "We're dumb, Kildering. Just forgive us. Thank God, we're going to begin to fight!"

Kildering's face was strangely pale. He seemed to be thinking out loud. "The reason that the agents of Number One do not have to report," he said slowly, "must be because there will soon be evidence that they have succeeded. It should come out over the radio, either in police calls or newscasts. Summers, you will listen in on the receiver in the car; bring us news of any development involving electricity, or persons who work with electricity. Come on, Mayor, we've got to move fast!"

Mayor marched beside him toward the car. He could find no fault with Kildering's logic, but in God's name, what could he expect to eventuate from that attack on the powerhouse?

"I'll carry the girl," Mayor said shortly. "Better for one of us to have his gun clear. And you're the best shot."

Kildering agreed with a quiet monosyllable and Mayor wrenched open the door of the car, peered down at the inert body on the floor. The girl's clothing was disarranged, and it was obvious she had been searched thoroughly. Even in the laxness of death, her face was lovely. Her hair had the crisp brilliance of life, and the blueness had faded. Mayor's hands were tender as he reached for her.

Mayor pulled and the body lurched toward him. Its inertia dragged it to the ground and the head hit the soft turf jarringly. Mayor had seen enough of the dead to know no especial revulsion in their presence, but this shook him strangely.

"Damn—Number One!" he rasped.

Anger ran hotly through Mayor. He stooped and seized the body roughly, heaved it face down across his shoulder. Breath gusted from the compressed lungs in a small wheezing moan. The arms and legs thudded limply against him, and he had to clamp the corpse on his shoulder. He set his teeth fiercely. Without words, he started across the street. The dead girl's hands patted his left thigh, softly, pat—pat—pat. There was perfume in the girl's hair and it titillated his nostrils. He lengthened his stride, half running. Behind him, Kildering's feet made no sound.

"Silently!" Kildering's voice soothed him. "We will go on the porch."

Mayor mounted the steps quietly, feeling his choked breath like suffocation. Kildering's voice, muted, was sharp and mandatory in his ear.

"Throw the corpse through the window!" he said. "It will startle them—give us a chance to enter. These girls are killers!"

A strange horror had Mayor by the throat. He stumbled forward—and threw the corpse!

The glass crashed, jangled to the floor as the body smashed through the window. Mayor heard a smothered scream and, for that crazy moment, he thought the corpse had cried out! Kildering went past him in a smooth rush of motion. He went through the window, headfirst, diving! Mayor saw Kildering somersault flashingly, land lightly on his feet. Kildering's voice was sharp and cold.

"No, don't try for your guns!" he said. "I never hesitate to shoot murderers, of either sex! John Miller is clever to use women gangsters, but it won't work against us!"

Mayor climbed fumblingly through the window, caught Kildering's gesture to pull down the shades and obeyed. There was muted, rhythmic music from a radio.

The two girls had scrambled to their feet from chairs beside the radio. Mayor looked at their frightened, horrified faces and forced himself to remember that, less than an hour ago, they had shot men to death. It was pretty hard to remember. Marianne's dye-darkened hair deepened her pallor; her blue eyes were shadowed. Belinda kneaded her slim white hands. Her shoulders were hunched as if she were cold.

Kildering's voice was as passionless as death—and as menacing. "Now," he said, "you will talk. You will tell me how to find John Miller!" The gun lifted steadily in his right hand. "Have you seen what .45-caliber bullets can do? But I forgot—you saw tonight what your own bullets did!"

Mayor shook his head, pulled his eyes away from the two girls. He was a little behind Kildering and, once more, the gallant carriage of that upflung head thrilled him. This was strange conduct for Kildering—but Mayor knew no doubts. It was Kildering—it must be right!

The music picked up dulcetly and, a man's voice cut in: "We interrupt this broadcast to bring you a news flash. Metropolis. Four men were murdered in an unexplained raid tonight on the main electric power plant of the city. There was only a slight interruption to power and the police were at a loss to explain the attack. The four men, operators of the plant, were shot."

The music picked up dulcetly and, incredulously, Mayor heard Kildering laugh! It was not a pretty sound.

"Shall I phone the police and tell them who did that?" Kildering asked. *"How can I find John Miller?"*

It was Marianne who got out words. "Who are you?" she asked. "I don't know what you are talking about." Her tone was as cold as Kildering's.

Mayor heard Kildering speak, and the words didn't make sense to him. Kildering said: "I am the son of Police Chief Eidson, whom John Miller killed. You will understand from that why I will not hesitate to kill to learn what I want to know."

Marianne repeated woodenly, "Chief Eidson's son."

She reached to the mantel above the cold fireplace for a cigarette, sat down as she lighted it. She tilted her head back on the cushions of the chair and closed her eyes.

Kildering said, *"Not that way, Marianne!"*

He jumped forward and his fist connected solidly with her jaw. The other girl, Belinda, cried out in a choked voice and ran toward the door.

"Stop her, Mayor!" Kildering snapped.

Mayor wrenched himself into action, flung his arms around the girl and wrestled her back into the room. She fought like any other woman, high heels kicking, nails clawing. He flung her violently into a chair, stood over her, glowering. Slow drops of blood oozed from a scratch across his cheek. He told himself again that these girls were killers, and still he did not understand why Kildering had punched the other girl.

Out of the corner of his eye, he saw Kildering remove a leather case from an inside pocket and take out a hypodermic. "I'd advise you, Belinda," Kildering said steadily, "not to attempt to put yourself into mental communication with John Miller, as Marianne did. No, I'm well aware that you can't do it directly, but I don't know how receptive *he* is. It's probable that by concentrating, in relaxation, you could make it possible for him to form contact with you. That was what Marianne tried. That was why I hit her."

He had the needle ready. He jerked Marianne's sleeve aside, and inserted the needle of a large hypodermic in her arm. He worked the plunger steadily.

"Sodium amytol," he said, "I think that, presently, Marianne will tell us what we want to know."

Belinda huddled into the chair, under the menace of Mayor's lowering regard. She worked her hands. They were slim, inutile. There was a smear of blood on one nail.

"You're wasting time," she said stranglingly. "She doesn't know how to reach—*him!*"

Kildering made no answer. He finished the injection methodically, laid a finger against Marianne's throat pulse. His face was completely impassive. The music from the radio continued to swim placidly into the room. A car bumbled past in the street. Belinda began to sob quietly, her face buried in her hands. Presently, Kildering began to call Marianne by name, sharply, insistently. After a while, she answered, thickly.

"Where is John Miller?" Kildering demanded.

Marianne mumbled, and Kildering prodded her again with the question; again.

Marianne said: "How . . . how dare you! You refer to *him* like that!"

Mayor's head twisted about. Kildering's face still showed no expression.

"Where is *he?*" he asked.

Marianne's head rolled from side to side. Her eyes were half opened. The smile on her mouth was tipsy. "Not Judas," she mumbled. "I won't betray *him!*"

Kildering's eyes held a blazing intensity. His voice was humble. "Tell us, Marianne," he said, "so that we, too, may worship *him!*"

"You want to worship—*him?*"

"Yes, Marianne. Yes. We want to worship *him!*"

Belinda started to her feet. "No, no!" she cried out, gasping.

Mayor whirled on his heel, and his hand lashed out. Belinda crumpled, crying. Kildering's eyes flashed an instant of approval at Mayor, then went back to Marianne. Mayor's thoughts were a confused whirl. What the hell was this Judas and worshiping business? Anybody would think they were talking about a god, instead of a crook who had murdered a dozen people and turned these girls into killers, too.

"Tell us where *he* is, Marianne, so that we, too, may worship *him!*"

Marianne's head rolled fretfully. "Don't know," she whispered. "Don't know where *he* is. Worship the Lord for He is good and His mercy endureth forever."

Kildering's face seemed to close in on itself. Mayor felt that, although there was no visible change. It was exactly as if Kildering had closed his brain with an actual door.

Kildering looked sharply about the room. His voice came out harshly: "Knock Belinda out, Mayor! Someone's trying to communicate. I can feel it. Knock her out, *unless you want to die!*"

Mayor wrenched himself out of his abstraction. Belinda started to her feet, and she had a gun in her fist. Before she could pull the trigger,

Mayor's fist crashed home. The girl bounced out of the chair, slid to the floor.

Mayor knew that his heart was pounding heavily. He glanced at the shadowed dimness of the hallway, and suddenly he strode there and switched on the light. Nothing there. Of course.

It was then that Mayor recognized the pounding of his heart as fear. He listened to Kildering hammering at Marianne with rapid questions and getting only a lot of religious gibberish. Hell, they treated this John Miller—this Number One as if he were God!

"How can you communicate with *him?*"

"Oh, pray to *him!*" Marianne chanted. "Pray to the All-Powerful, the All-Good. *He* will set you free!"

Mayor's hands clenched until the muscles of his forearms ached. He was thinking desperately. Those two F. B. I. men in the hospital had questioned a woman—and they were dead!

"Kildering!" he said hoarsely. "We've got to get out of here! That mystery ray the newspapers talk about—"

"We're in no especial danger," Kildering said quietly. "Marianne says the Holy Spirit was to honor them with sons as a reward for tonight. No doubt the reason for the perfume. After the 'honor,' it will be dangerous to approach them. Not now. Miller is just trying to find out what is happening here. I think—"

Kildering broke off, stared down at the two unconscious girls. "Outside, Mayor," he snapped. "Quickly! Back door!"

Mayor whirled and went pounding ahead of Kildering. He whipped out his gun, but it did not make him feel much better.

"What's up?" he demanded.

Kildering stood before him in the darkness behind the house. Feeble rays from the inner lights sifted through the glass panel of the back door, spilled across his face. It was intense, white. His eyes held fire.

"You will remain here, on guard over those two girls," Kildering said quietly. "Number One will communicate, mentally, and probably with Marianne. My guess is that she will attempt to bribe you into releasing her. Permit that, and follow. Number One will almost certainly try to release those two girls from danger—if he can do it without danger to himself. I must warn you of this, however. The release he gives them may be death!"

Mayor said: "Damn it, Kildering, you mean he'll kill them to protect himself? What a hell of a cold-blooded—"

Kildering's lips were faintly sardonic. "Of course, my fellow ape!" he said.

Mayor fumbled his gun, peered toward the house. A scowl drew his brows hard down over his eyes. Presently, his head came up. He tossed the ever-dangling black lock back out of his eyes, and there was challenge in the gesture.

"Right you are, Kildering," he said steadily.

"Good luck," Kildering said, and his tone was somber. "You're on your own, Mayor. Summers will back you up at a distance. If anything—interferes with me, you are in command."

Mayor whipped about. "What are you going to do?" he demanded, his voice hoarse.

Kildering's lips twitched. "I am going to pray to *him,*" he said slowly.

He turned and marched off into the darkness, and Mayor felt his jaws relax. He swore under his breath. Mayor thought his own post dangerous, but Kildering had chosen the harder task for his own, as he always did. Kildering would deliberately attempt to put his mind in contact with—with *his!* Perhaps it would help to track down Number One! It was more apt to result in insanity!

Mayor turned heavily back into the house. His nerves were taut, but his jaw was set in grim determination. He stood and looked down at the two unconscious girls, at the sprawled body of the dead one beneath the window. Mayor drew in a slow breath, and his eyes turned fierce.

"I just want to get you across my gun sights, John Miller!" he said violently. "I'll show you this particular ape—has teeth!"

In the parked car, Kildering had finished giving Summers his quiet instructions about backing up Mayor when the radio program's music broke off abruptly, with the old formula.

"Metropolis," the newscaster rushed on. "Only the safety devices of the subways here prevented serious accidents tonight when the motormen of three different subway trains fell dead at the controls of their engines. Police said that the faces of the three men turned blue. Keep tuned—"

Kildering flicked off the radio, and sat with his face rigid and cold. Beside him, Summers spoke uncertainly.

"Is that it, Kildering?" he asked. "Is that what those girls did at the powerhouse?"

Kildering shook himself visibly. "I'll have to postpone—my prayers," he said. "By interfering with Number One's plans, perhaps I can force him to—pay attention to me."

"Is this it?" Summers repeated.

Kildering turned toward Summers with a faint twist of his lips. "Yes," he said. "For reasons known only to himself, *he* has started on a campaign of mass murder! The elimination of—the apes!"

V

THROUGH A telephone call, Walter Kildering located Mayor Francis O'Shea at his office and directed there the taxi he had called. Afterward, he leaned back against the cushions and closed his eyes. His head sagged limply in relaxation. His lips lost their rigid line, became gentle. It was a face that Walter Kildering rarely showed to the world.

Music came softly from the radio; the hum of tires on asphalt blended with the bass of the governed motor. A moist softness was on the night air, the promise of a gentle spring rain. Kildering sucked in a slow quivering breath. The world was restless with stirring life, and John Miller gave—*death!*

The music of the radio broadcast broke, and the announcer cut in again. Strain was apparent in a peculiar tonelessness that contrasted with the usual blithe elegance of radio voices.

"There have been seven more deaths in Metropolis of this strange sickness that turns the faces of the victims blue. Mayor Francis O'Shea issued a statement that the entire hospital staffs of the city, and its biological laboratories, were being mobilized and that government help had been asked in an attempt to discover swiftly the causes of this illness. Mayor O'Shea emphasized that there was no cause for alarm, but until the causes could be learned, he urged the people to avoid congested areas and to make sure of ample ventilation at all times. There will be more later."

Kildering's relaxation was blotted out. The softened strains of music annoyed him now, and he flicked them off. If Mayor O'Shea were taking such steps at once, there must have been already a more violent reaction on the part of the people than was reasonable to expect.

The taxi driver twisted about. His face was bewildered. "What do you think that stuff is, mister?" he asked anxiously. "I made a run past City Hall just before I got your call, and there's a big mob of people there. Thousands of them. Cheez, guys' faces turning blue!"

Kildering said quietly: "That really means very little. Any sickness that affected the heart or the lungs would cause suffocation and hence turn the faces blue. Can you tell me where I can, at this hour, get hold of some luggage? A secondhand shop or pawnshop would be best."

When the taxi rolled to a halt on the fringes of the crowd about the City Hall, Walter Kildering got out deliberately. He carried a small, worn black bag like a doctor's, and as he moved through the thinner portions of the crowd, his manner was changed. He moved with the crisp, busy stride of a doctor; his eyes abstracted and his face severe.

A man glanced about at Kildering's touch on the shoulder. Then he pushed aside and called out:

"Hey, here comes one of the docs! Let the doctor through!"

275

Kildering nodded, said, "Thank you!"

The word ran through the crowd. Resentful faces took on an aspect of respect, of hope, even of pleading, as their eyes sought the calm countenance of Kildering. He felt the appeal like a pain in his breast. These people were helpless now, their self-sufficiency sapped in the face of forces they did not understand. They turned to the doctors as to priests for salvation in disaster; presently, unless this plague were checked, they would begin to cry out in anger against these same men. And they would turn to the court of last appeal, the churches. Kildering saw the whole course of the slaughter clearly, during the brief, slow transit through the frightened crowd. He felt his own anger rise, and recognized it as a symptom of a conviction of helplessness. If he could only understand! Why had John Miller determined upon mass murder?

There was some delay at the police-guarded doors of the City Hall, but his F. B. I. credentials gained admittance for Walter Kildering. The speed with which he was ushered to the mayor's office was a new and unneeded proof of the fears and helplessness of the city administration. There were five newspapermen grouped outside the door of the private office of the mayor. Kildering brushed them aside, went through into the mayor's suite.

Mayor Francis O'Shea stood on braced, straddled legs behind his desk. He had a mane of grizzled hair, a pale, intent face. His speech was heavy, deliberate.

"You boys from Washington work fast, Kildering," he said curtly. "I hope you can do something."

There was a map of Metropolis spread out on his desk, marked with red crosses. In contrast with the radio announcement of a total of ten deaths, there were scores of them. They covered the entire city. There was a cluster of fifty at what Kildering identified as the city prison farm.

Mayor O'Shea jerked his head toward a spare, stern man who stood beside the desk. "Chief Surgeon Mouline," he said. He nodded toward a shouldery, keen-faced man, whose bushy eyebrows were red and contrasted strangely with a bald and gleaming head. "Chief of Police Parsons. I've got a council meeting in ten minutes. Any suggestions, Kildering? As you see, we've been trying to spot the center of contagion geographically. No luck so far."

Kildering glanced at the map, inspected the three men steadily. Mouline's eyes were hostile and the chief of police, Parsons, was clearly out of his depth.

"I'd like to speak to you privately, Mayor O'Shea," he said. "No offense to you, gentlemen, but Washington has some private information which must be held very closely."

Mayor O'Shea grunted, jabbed carefully tended fingers through his mop of hair. "You Washington boys like mystification, don't you? All right, Mouline, Parsons. Go up to the council meeting and tell them I'm coming. I'll need you there anyhow."

The exit of the two men was angry. Kildering put his eyes on the brooding, suspicious stare of Mayor O'Shea.

"In the first place," Kildering said quietly, "this isn't a plague. It's mass murder by the same criminal who robbed your banks and destroyed your previous police chief, Eidson. No germs are involved. It's done by electricity, and the attack on your main power plant tonight was part of the plan. To stop the deaths, you have merely to switch off all electric power in the city."

Mayor O'Shea's reaction was precisely what Kildering expected. Bewilderment, doubt, and anger carved the man's big squarish face. After twenty seconds, he swore and shouted:

"You're crazy! What the hell are you talking about?"

Kildering felt weariness run through him. What hope did he have of defeating John Miller when stupidity and disbelief fought on Miller's side? But you couldn't blame people too much. It was bewildering—

"What the hell?" O'Shea demanded roughly. "Even if what you say were true, what could any guy gain by killing people wholesale? What's the reason?"

It was a question Kildering couldn't answer, of course, and there was no use in further confusing the issue by expounding the theory of John Miller's antecedents—of supermen. Instead, Kildering turned to the map.

"I'm afraid you'll have to blame Washington mystification for my failure to answer that, Mayor O'Shea," he said, "but look at the map. Check your records. You'll find that every one of these deaths is either near a power plant or connected in some way with electricity, if only in the operation of a vacuum cleaner. You can make a simple test. Simply turn off the city's current, and see if the deaths don't stop."

Mayor O'Shea frowned down at the map, glanced uneasily at Kildering. "You know I can't do that," he said fretfully. "It would throw the city into panic! Frankly, I don't believe you, but nobody else has been able to make any suggestions at all. If there were any proof—"

"The first three victims were subway motormen," Kildering said quietly. "Four men were murdered at the main electric plant. What's happened to the men who took over after them? Look at your map. There's the drive through the park close to the power plant. There seem to be fourteen red crosses there and at the powerhouse. Fourteen people dead."

Mayor O'Shea stood with both hands braced on the desk and swore, steadily, without particular attention. His shoulders were oddly hunched. He seemed deformed. Kildering's eyes, half veiled by lowered lids, studied the man's face intently. He seemed honest, confused.

Kildering stepped toward the desk. "You usually have a man polishing

your linoleum floors with a machine at this hour, don't you?" he asked
flatly. "Do you mind asking where he is at work?"

Mayor O'Shea's head jerked about to face Kildering. "Good Lord!
I'll stop him!" He reached toward the annunciator on his desk, but
didn't open the cam. "That's nonsense," he said. "Electricity couldn't
do it!"

Kildering leaned across the desk, and the steely gray of his gaze
stabbed deep into O'Shea's eyes. "You are willing to risk not only that
man's life, but the lives of thousands in your city!" he said crisply.
"You risk that—because you don't believe! Have you the right, Mayor
O'Shea, to make a gamble like that?"

O'Shea shifted uncomfortably. "But, damn it, man," he began, "I
don't see how—"

The door of the office was batted open without warning. A man ran
staggeringly across the width of the long room, did not check until his
hands struck the edge of the desk. He leaned there, supporting himself
rigidly, panting for breath.

"The floor polisher," he whispered. "Dead! His face—*blue!*"

Mayor O'Shea stared at the man without words. His head moved
slowly from side to side as if he would deny the thing he heard, but
his eyes fixed finally on Kildering. He surged to his feet then.

"I didn't know," he whispered.

Kildering pounded at him. "Do you wish to be known, Mayor O'Shea,
as the man who refused to save his city? As the man who, knowing
how all these people were killed, refused to do the one thing that could
have saved them? It is very simple, you see. Just turn off all the electric
power in the city. I can't keep it secret any longer. I'll ask you not to
attempt to stop me." Kildering was backing toward the door. "I am
going outside and tell the people there that you know how to save the
city, and refuse to do anything about it!"

Mayor O'Shea's hand reached out. "Wait," he said. "Wait a moment.
You swear to me—No, no, that isn't necessary. That poor man. Mike,
wasn't it? Yes, Mike. Poor devil, never harmed a soul in all his simple
life." Mayor O'Shea lifted both hands to his face, covered his eyes.
Presently, his hands dropped and his shoulders came back. "All right,
Kildering, you win!"

Kildering opened the door beside him, stood where he could command any who came in.

"Call in the newspapermen," he said, "and tell them. When you turn
off your power, they won't be able to print the papers, but they'll find
some way of spreading the news." Kildering was aware of the five
reporters, crowding in through the door, heard their sharp, shrewd
questions.

"Gentlemen," Kildering said softly, "Mayor O'Shea will tell you that
the plague is spread by electricity. He will tell you that he will cut off

all current in the city! My name, gentlemen, is Walter Kildering, of the F. B. I., and I want it published."

"What's this, a gag?" one of the newsmen jeered.

"Is it, Mayor O'Shea?" Kildering asked softly.

Mayor O'Shea's voice roared out: "It's the truth, so help me God!"

The newspapermen were dashing off for their telephones. One of them lingered an instant in the doorway. "Walter Kildering?" he said easily. *"Kill* as in murder, *deer* as in reindeer, *ing* as in Chinese laundry?"

"One *l* and one *e,"* Kildering said crisply. "Also quote me as saying this is not a plague, but a mass murder by the same man who robbed the banks here, and whom you christened the 'Unknown'!"

The newspaperman said, *"Wow!"* He turned and sprinted.

Kildering kept his shoulders against the wall. "Sorry to use these methods against you, Mayor O'Shea. And I'm not trying to grab publicity for personal glory. It is my idea that when the criminal responsible for these deaths learns my identity, he will make an effort to—eliminate me. It is my hope to turn the tables on him. I might say our only hope!"

Kildering stood for an instant longer, and his face was drawn and haggard. He smiled then. Frozen-face Kildering smiled! It was gentle, almost womanish in its sweetness. His voice was a little weary.

"Good night, Mayor O'Shea," he said.

He closed the door gently behind him, and Mayor O'Shea stared through a long moment at the closed portal, and said nothing. His assistant waltzed around the desk, slapped at a cam. He was already shouting before he got the connection open.

"Stop that man!" he cried. *"Stop that—"*

Mayor O'Shea's hand clamped down on his assistant's shoulder and he whipped him away from the annunciator.

"Let him go," he said. "No, no. Let him go. He's not crazy. So help me, God, I think . . . I *think* he was telling the truth!"

The assistant stared at Mayor O'Shea. "Look, you can't let him get away with that!" he said hoarsely. "You can't let him grab credit for stopping the Blue Death. You gotta do that! Look, this is election year and the boss isn't going to like it if you let somebody from Washington grab the credit."

Mayor O'Shea's face was a trifle bemused. His eyes were staring at the closed door as if he saw a vision. He brushed his hand across his eyes, shook his head as if he cleared it from a stunning blow.

"You gotta grab the credit!" his assistant insisted.

Mayor O'Shea's eyes turned shrewd. He whipped toward the annunciator. "Stop Kildering," he snapped into the speaker. "The man who just left my office, yes. Of course! He's gone crazy! But be careful; he's armed! Maybe you'd better tell the cops that. They'll know how to deal with an armed man!"

His assistant chuckled. "Geez, boss, you're smart!"

Kildering was just leaving the elevator when he saw one of the uniformed police go toward a jangling phone near the guarded doors. "Yeah, Sergeant Deal," he rasped. "Stop who?"

Kildering's gun snapped into his fist and blasted in the same instant. The echo slammed dizzily through the high vault of the hall, and Sergeant Deal staggered back from the phone, both arms flung protectingly before his face. The phone was smashed to bits by Kildering's bullet.

"Sergeant Deal," Kildering said quietly, "drop your gun on the floor and disarm your men. At once! I won't hesitate to kill at need!" The quality of command in his voice struck like a thrown knife. He was obeyed. Before the elevator doors opened to release a new flood of uniformed police, Kildering had faded into the crowd.

Lost amid them, he lifted his voice. It was not a heavy voice, but it had a ringing timbre that carried it a long way over the heads of the close-packed people.

"I'm the doctor from Washington!" he said. "I told the mayor how to stop the plague, and he refused. Make him stop the plague, or you'll all die! Make Mayor O'Shea stop the plague! All he has to do is to turn off the lights! Come on, men, make him stop the plague!"

It took a few minutes to get the mob moving. A wave of blue-coated police rolled out on the steps before the high bronze doors of the City Hall, and Kildering pointed to them.

"See, the mayor won't stop the plague!" he cried.

The mob roar started as a murmur like distant wind, and it grew with the same speed. It was a hurricane that beat against the portals of the City Hall, that drove the police back before it in spite of the muted hammer of hastily drawn guns. The storm raged into the corridors of the building—

Detaching himself from the remote fringes of the mob, Walter Kildering found a taxi, abandoned by its driver. He climbed in behind the wheel and sent the machine sweeping back toward Prince Hills, toward the death watch he had set Bill Mayor and Marty Summers to keep.

Speeding northward, Kildering was grimly aware of the danger to himself which he had deliberately invited. It was his belief that John Miller could not strike at him, as he had at the chief of the F. B. I., unless John Miller knew his whereabouts. He was by no means sure of that. It might be enough merely to know the identity of his potential victim. But there seemed to be no other way. Efforts to trace allies to John Miller were unavailing; the next logical step was to force John Miller to come after him!

So far, Kildering had been successful. He knew that the mob would force Mayor O'Shea to turn off the electric power. The newspapers, or the radio, which had its own power, would carry to John Miller the name of the man who worked against him—Walter Kildering. Yes, this gave more promise of success. Kildering should have been elated. He told himself that. The truth was, he felt unutterably depressed. Who was he, Walter Kildering, to hope that he could defeat John Miller? He had declared that John Miller must be destroyed. He had dared to interrupt the smooth working of John Miller's plans, interfered with his workers.

No question, Walter Kildering thought wearily, about what must happen. He must destroy John Miller before John Miller destroyed him.

A sharp doubt arose in Kildering's mind at that thought. Could John Miller be destroyed? The chief's talk of John Miller being immortal was silly, a madman's ravings. The chief had set out to destroy John Miller, lest he himself be destroyed, but he had gone crazy over a conception that John Miller was immortal.

Driving steadily northward, Walter Kildering threw back his head and laughed. Silly idea, a man being immortal. But, of course, John Miller wasn't a man. Not in the scientific sense. He was a mutation of the species, a superman—

Kildering found that his hands gripped the steering wheel with a terrible tightness. His arms were so rigid that it was hard for him to turn the wheel at all. He glanced about him at the darkness that crowded close and impenetrable about the car. He realized that the sky was overcast and that a slow-falling rain blurred the windshield. He reached out and switched on the windshield wiper, and the monotonous clicking swing of the blade held his eyes like a magnet. It was hard to drive and look at the wiper, but he couldn't help watching—

Its pendulum swing was like his thoughts. *"Kill* John Miller, or *he'll* kill *you! Kill* John Miller, or *he'll* kill *you!"*

The refrain ran on in Kildering's mind. He tried to break the rhythm, and he couldn't. It kept on and on inside his head, until he found his lips moving silently to form the words. He was saying them aloud for some while before he was conscious of it. But now the words had changed a little, a very little.

"You *can't* kill John *Miller.* John *Miller* will kill *you!* You *can't* kill John—"

Walter Kildering tried to stop saying that. He tried terribly hard. He fought first to stop speaking, then he fought with clenching jaw muscles to stop the flow of words. To close his eyes, to do anything to shut out that awful, destructive rhythm.

"John *Miller* will kill *you!"*

He was still speaking the words, hurling them against his clenched teeth. He was shouting them, singing them in a fearful cracked voice that he could not recognize as his own. Walter Kildering coldly gripped the wheel and drove the car. There was a part of him that could sit back and do that. There was another part of him that swung its eyes, its head from side to side with the rhythm of the wiper blade. That part of him chanted this absurd dirge of despair.

It was that colder, separate part of Walter Kildering which, with the slowness of clock ticks, beat out the words of his thoughts. Beat them out while the body part of him still chanted the dirge. What Walter Kildering thought was:

"This is madness. *John Miller has driven me mad!*"

Walter Kildering had not, up to that moment, consciously realized the invasion of his brain by the power of John Miller. He had invited it, challenged it so that he could find and combat John Miller. And it had come upon him unaware.

Too late, Kildering recognized the nature of the thing that was happening to him. He was shrieking, laughing insanely. He was incoherent with his terror and his madness.

"Save me from John Miller!" he was shouting. "Save me! Oh, God, save me!"

Kildering fought to gain control over himself and he could not. He fought then, with a new purpose. He fought to pull steadily on the steering wheel. His hands fought each other. When his right hand tried to pull one way, his left hand tried to pull the other. His own body was fighting him, at the behest of John Miller!

That was when Walter Kildering used his madman's cunning. His thoughts swayed to the swing of the dirge that John Miller had planted in his brain. His eyes, his head swung. His whole body was a pendulum that swung from threat to panic flight.

Right: I can't kill John Miller.
Left: John Miller will kill me.
Right: I can't kill John Miller.
Left: John Miller will kill me.

Very subtly, very slyly, Kildering kept the thought out of his mind. He wouldn't let John Miller know what he was going to do. It was very simple, really. The street was slimy, wet with the slow fall of the spring rain. His body was swaying. Why shouldn't the taxi swing, too? A little pull to the right, a little one to the left; another to the right, harder to the left.

Yes, the taxi was swaying now to the dirge. It rocked. The motor roared at its governed peak. The tires began to scream in time, a scream to the left, a scream to the right!

Walter Kildering lost his thought, but he kept whipping the wheel left and right. It was beautiful the way the whole universe kept rhythm to the thought of the power of John Miller. The street lights swayed; the street swung and dipped. The tires screamed.

The rhythm broke suddenly. The street was no longer swaying. It was whirling, and the scream of the tires went on and on. The taxi was spinning, lunging toward the curbing, toward the remote small houses set among their framework of shrubs and hedges. Walter Kildering swayed behind the wheel, his mouth wide open, screaming.

It was only in the last instant before the taxi struck that a fragment of thought flashed across his brain. Maybe this, too, was part of John Miller's plan! This madness, and then—suicide!

Walter Kildering screamed. He clasped his futile arms about his head.

The crash of a wrecked car is a peculiarly explosive sound. There is the mingled rip and whine of torn metal, the sound of the blow. Afterward, there is the jangle of broken glass, perhaps the cries of the injured.

This time, the scream came first. And it stopped with the crash. Afterward, there was only the small soft sigh of the night wind, and the gentle *tap, tap, tapping* of the spring rain. Gentle as the rhythm of a mother's finger, shaken in warning at a child. In remonstrance—

VI

IT WAS not quite dawn when Walter Kildering recovered consciousness, knowing weakness and pain and despair. He was aware first of a tremendous singing and chirruping of birds, of the dawn freshness after a night of gentle rain. He could sense that even through the acrid cleanness of antiseptic odors.

When he opened his eyes, he saw the young, tired face of a man in his shirt sleeves, a stethoscope dangling forgotten around his neck.

The man smiled, slowly. "You had a good bit of luck," he said, "choosing my porch for a crack-up, Mr. Kildering. What happened? A skid?"

Kildering's lips moved stiffly. "Yes, luck," he agreed.

He lay quiet, through a long minute, realizing that this man was obviously a doctor. But his luck was greater than that. John Miller had relaxed the pressure upon his brain. He felt an immense weariness, but his mind was clear. He remembered those last few frantic seconds, and his eyes strained wide with recalled horror. He heard the doctor speak soothingly, and shook his head.

"No, it's all right," said Kildering, and his voice was almost normal. "Thank you, doctor. I see you know my name, doubtless my identity. Please tell me, precisely, the nature of my injuries. I realize my left arm is broken. What about my ribs?"

"Three cracked," the doctor smiled faintly. "You also had a very ugly gash across your cheek and throat. Which was why I said you were lucky. I always keep hemostats close by."

Kildering nodded; he felt the tug of his wound. "Loss of blood, then," he said.

Awkwardly, he pushed aside the covers and slid his legs toward the side of the bed. The doctor did not help. He stood, hands resting on the foot of the bed, and watched. His eyes were speculative.

"I won't try to tell you about keeping quiet," he said. "You had a concussion, of course. That arm fracture is double, but not compound."

Kildering had his feet on the floor, and they felt wooden. His legs were rubber. He seized the head of the bed with his right hand. He—stood up.

Sweat sprang out on his forehead. His right palm was slimy against the headboard. He sucked in deep breaths.

"Loss of considerable blood," he said thickly, "but I can manage."

The doctor watched him doubtfully, but Kildering's head came up, and his lips were firm. His eyes burned palely.

"I can manage," he said again.

The doctor said slowly: "Your job must be pretty important. I'll put a note in your pocket in case you keel over again. No more transfusions for another twenty-four hours."

Kildering saw then that there was a strip of adhesive on the inside of the doctor's left elbow. The doctor had given of his blood, as well as his skill!

Kildering said slowly: "I may be able to recompense you some day, doctor. You're . . . more than kind." His lips twitched. "The police have your report?"

The doctor shook his head. "The police are pretty busy. The trucks go by every hour, but the hospitals say they don't need me. They're dying too fast for medical help."

Then Kildering remembered—and saw that the lights still burned! They were bright in the ceiling; they made white spots of illumination on the corners. In some way, he had failed!

He said harshly: "I must be going! One thing I can tell you, doctor, that may help in some degree. This is no disease that is killing men. It is an electrical emanation. It is spread through the municipal system. If you keep your power turned off in the house, you have a chance to survive!"

The doctor said gravely: "Thank you. Are you sure you have to go?"

Kildering saw that the doctor thought this a vagary of his accident-shocked mind. He could not press the issue. His strength was very far gone. He fumbled into his clothing with the doctor's help, while his mind raced back over the events at City Hall. He had failed there, somehow. John Miller had flicked aside his interference, as casually as he had brushed Kildering out of the picture. It was not through John Miller's weakness that Kildering was alive now. He would have to have the help of Marty Summers and Bill Mayor. Kildering found himself thinking of them longingly. They would not need explanations. Summers would give of his loyalty, and his unswerving service; Mayor of his brilliant courage and wit—If they, too, had not been brushed aside by John Miller!

"A taxi?" he asked hoarsely.

"They've all been commandeered by the police to help carry the dead," the doctor said heavily. "The subway station is a block away. I'll drive you there."

"The subways are death traps," Kildering told him dully. "Your radio, or newspapers, should tell you that much. Could I, possibly, hire your car?"

"I'll drive you to your destination if it's not too far," the doctor agreed. "I can't do more than that."

Kildering heard his own voice, muffled by weakness. "You are kind."

The dawn was smoky with the stench of burning oil; with other, nameless, odors. A truck trundled heavily past while the doctor backed out his car. The dead were stacked like cordwood. The horizon was dull red with pyre flames, a dozen, a score of them. Kildering's hand, gripping the side of the car, shook a little.

"How many dead?" he asked hoarsely.

The doctor shook his head, driving steadily. The headlights threw a dim patch of orange light. Dawn was gray and murky in the east, and the bird song had ceased. The tires and the motor made the only sound. They passed more trucks. One was stopped and men in glistening suits that covered them from necks to fingertips, faces grotesque in gas masks, carried a dead man out of a house. They swung the body up hurriedly. A woman's wailing rose and dwindled as the doctor's car rolled past.

Kildering beat his fist softly on his knee. "What does the radio say?"

"The stations are all dead, Mr. Kildering. I mean, the mayor ordered them off the air."

Kildering twisted his head about. "You don't believe my theory of the electricity. Is that because you have been using it extensively during the night?"

The doctor swung out into an avenue, drove a little more rapidly. There was another fire in the east now: the sun.

"I made X rays, of course," he said. "We also cook by electricity."

Kildering lifted his hand to his forehead, leaned on it. He couldn't be wrong about it, unless there had been some other reason for the raid on the power plant. But the dead were all somewhere near electrical units. The prison and the insane asylum had been heavy centers of death, judging from O'Shea's map; poor simple Mike at the City Hall— But the doctor and he both had survived, despite X ray and stove and other electrical equipment.

Kildering's head whipped up, and his nostrils arched with a shock of discovery. He had been puzzled over John Miller's motive. But now—

"Doctor," Kildering said rapidly, "you will recall recent experiments with the electrical-wave frequencies of the brain, and the incidence of Alpha impulses as compared with individual intelligence."

The doctor's head swung about sharply for an instant before he was forced to look back to his driving. "Why, yes," he said slowly. "As I recall, in low-grade mentalities, the frequency of the Alpha waves was definitely much lower than in higher intelligence."

Kildering nodded. "That was my memory," he said. "Now, compare that fact with this. The asylum population has been completely wiped out; the prison inmates were destroyed in large quantities by this so-called Blue Death. You and I, apparently, remained unaffected. The victims obviously die of suffocation."

The doctor nodded, more alertly. Kildering rushed on.

"The deaths are similar to those that occur under anæsthetics," he said. "Other tests have shown that complete anæsthesia results in a reversal of the electrical nerve impulses. Instead of flowing, as normally, from environs to the brain, they begin, under complete anæsthesia, to flow from the brain to the nerve termini."

"True!" the doctor said alertly.

"I believe," Kildering said slowly, "that this is the key to the entire matter. Certain electrical impulses are being released. They affect only persons with low mental frequency of Alpha waves. In those instances, they induce a complete anæsthesia which results in death."

The doctor said slowly: "It's possible, I suppose, if you knew a hundred times more about the operation of these brain electrical currents than any living man; if, then, you were sufficiently an electrical genius to be able to direct only the proper type of current, and the proper strength— Good God, man, are you implying that someone is doing this? That someone is destroying all the low-grade mentalities in Metropolis?"

Two trucks rolled past with their grim loads, bound for the outer region of circling fires. Towers of black smoke marked their locations now, faintly tinged by the red and yellow of flame. The men in their anticontamination garb, their masks, were other-worldly. They lurched to the rumble of their trucks. An infernal scene.

"In God's name," the doctor said hoarsely, "who would do such a thing, and why?"

Kildering shook his head, but his gray eyes glittered like ice. "If you are wise," he said slowly, "you will forget what I have said. You can do nothing about it, except protect yourself."

"That's absolute nonsense!" the doctor said sharply. "No man would do a thing like that! It's a disease, this Blue Death!"

Kildering nodded slowly. "You're probably right at that. It was a wild speculation. Would you let me out here, please?"

The doctor put on brakes. His movements were violent, and his throat cords were taut, his face reddened as he shouted.

"It's absolute nonsense!" he cried. "No man would do a thing like that!"

Kildering said: "You're quite right, doctor. Just forget the whole thing! And I thank you, more than you know, for what you have done!"

He turned away, moving heavily toward the cottage he had rented the previous day. His eyes, glancing shrewdly over the street, spotted Summers' car, and Summers, a black shadow behind the wheel. So nothing had happened here! Their watch had been in vain. Why not? John Miller believed that Kildering had been destroyed. If he knew of these other two, he did not fear them.

The doctor's feet rasped with an accent of exasperation on the pavement behind him. The doctor's hand was rough on his shoulder and Kildering staggered, weakly, under the thrust.

"I want the truth!" the doctor said sharply. "Tell me the truth! Who is destroying men like this?"

Kildering saw Summers plunge from the car, race toward them with a drawn gun. He shook his head, moved his right hand in a faint gesture to check Summers. His eyes went to those of the doctor, saw the horror in their depths.

Don't get excited over a pipe dream!" Kildering laughed at him. "You, a doctor, believing things like that! You're overtired from working over me all night, and I'm lightheaded. You know no man would do what I said. What profit would he get from it?"

The doctor studied Kildering's face. The doctor's eyes shuttled, peering into first one orb, then the other, in the manner of men who stand too close.

The doctor sighed, stepped back and pressed hands to his forehead. "You're right, of course. There would be no profit in it. I think you'll be all right, Mr. Kildering, if you don't overdo it."

"Thank you again, doctor," Kildering said gently. "I hope I can repay you some day for what you have done."

The doctor stumbled to his car and Kildering's eyes followed him pityingly as he drove away. Best for the doctor not to know the truth. It would only throw him in opposition to John Miller—and that was fatal!

Summers came up anxiously. He had a newspaper in his hand.

"We thought you had succeeded, Kildering," he said, "and this stuff against you was just camouflage. The mayor accuses you of killing a floor polisher named Mike and stirring up riots. He says he learned, from that, a way to check the Blue Death. He urges a plentiful use of electrical equipment. Says it will ward off the germs."

Kildering stared at Summers incredulously. He seized the newspaper and his hand shook as he glared at the eight-column box beneath the headlines. No mistake there. The mayor's statement was unequivocal: *"Use of electrical power, plenty of it, will protect you from the Blue Death!"*

In the face of that, the mayor's tirade against himself, the charge of murder and rioting, became unimportant—even silly. Kildering laughed crazily. And he had thought he had John Miller checked! It was pretty obvious, wasn't it, that John Miller now ruled Mayor O'Shea completely!

Summers' hand touched his arm solicitously. "Is that wrong?" he asked. "What happened to you?"

Kildering sobered himself by a violent effort. "I had a little mental brush with John Miller," he said, and his voice was humble. "I owe my present quasi sanity to the fact that he thought me already destroyed. Nothing has happened here? No. Then call in Mayor. We have a job to do. Call him in! Do you think John Miller doesn't know about your watch? We simply aren't important enough to destroy!"

Kildering turned and marched toward the cottage. He stumbled on nothing and threw out an arm to catch his balance. When Summers ran to assist him, he heard something that sounded like a sob. Frozen-face—*sobbing!*

Summers decided he was mistaken.

When Summers brought the sleep-drugged Bill Mayor to the cottage, Kildering sat at the dining-room table with the paper spread out before him. He cut short inquiries about what had happened, tapped the paper with his right hand.

"John Miller's plan begins to take shape," he said, his voice heavy and slow. "This Blue Death is aimed at the destruction of all low-grade intelligences. As such, it probably has already passed its peak and is waning. Mayor O'Shea announces, through the papers, that a philanthropist has purchased from their owners every rented home and apartment in the city. Henceforth, each man owns the quarters he now occupies. They will be given deeds if they report to certain established offices. Owners will be paid from the city treasury at their own figure. And all banks are closed, as a precaution against panic resulting from the plague."

Bill Mayor's head lost its weary droop. "What the hell has all that got to do with John Miller?" he demanded. "They can't do anything like that under the law."

Kildering was frowning. "John Miller is giving every citizen of Metropolis a stake in the city through possession of his living quarters.

The banks—I don't know, unless he is stripping them of money to pay off the landowners, or to fill his own pockets."

Summers was slow in finding speech. "That doesn't sound much like a criminal, does it," he said, "giving people their own homes?"

Mayor snorted. "There's a trick in it. He's voiding titles so he can grab them off. Or he plans to slap on taxes—that is, if he's as powerful in the city government as this indicates. Is John Miller the same as Mayor O'Shea?"

Kildering said quietly: "No. According to the paper, all radio stations are closed, and even the mails are being held up to prevent spread of the contagion of the Blue Death. I have an idea that a similar protection will be set up, on some pretext, over telephones and telegraph. Mayor O'Shea has closed every road out of the city, is refusing to permit trains to enter or leave—to protect the good people elsewhere in the State of Wichinois!"

Mayor bent over the newspaper and read hurriedly where Kildering indicated. He began to swear in a low, angry voice. He straightened and still he swore.

"We're locked in," he said harshly. "The city is locked in. No outside communication. And Mayor O'Shea is in John Miller's vest pocket. Damn it, John Miller *owns* this city now! Whatever he wants to do—"

"Whatever he wants to do," Kildering echoed emptily. "Twenty-five thousand dead in one night!"

Mayor strode to the window, stood there with his fists knotted behind his back. Marty Summers sat like a drunken man. His thoughts ran in circles. No good questioning those girls across the street any further. They couldn't tell a thing. No need watching them any longer. He didn't know just what Kildering had done, but it was plain that it had been worse than futile. Mayor swung about, came back to the table slowly.

His voice was angry, baffled. "What do we do now, Kildering?" he demanded.

"Yes, what?" Summers asked hollowly.

Walter Kildering shifted a little in his chair. There was a dull agony in his side, and his arm was giving him a great deal of pain. His brain was swimming, too, with weakness. He put those things out of his mind. They looked to him for leadership. He must not fail them!

"I'm afraid I overestimated my abilities," Kildering said thickly. "We three are not enough to defeat John Miller. The truth must be carried to Washington. The entire strength of the nation must be thrown against John Miller. I misjudged. I thought John Miller would not strike while we left him alone. But apparently his period of preparation is finished. He is launching his attack."

Kildering dropped his hand. His voice was very earnest. "No man can foretell how far John Miller will press this attack," he said. "He may be content for the present with Metropolis. He may stop when he has conquered the state of Wichinois. He may not stop before the nation, and the world, are under his dominion! I . . . I'm trying not to exaggerate. It's hard, when you deal with John Miller."

Mayor knotted his fists. "Together, we can get out of this trap and spread the word!"

Kildering shook his head. "You will go, Mayor. Summers and I will remain and do what we can against John Miller."

"I won't run away, damn it!" Mayor shouted.

Kildering's lips twisted bitterly. "Running away would accomplish nothing at all, if John Miller were interested in your destruction! You will be in as great danger in Washington, or in China, as you are here. No, no, I'm *not* exaggerating! The chief went mad. I— But I don't matter. Believe me, Mayor, you will be in greater danger on your errand than here in Metropolis."

Mayor nodded crisply. "I'm taking your orders, Kildering. I'll go."

Kildering's voice sounded tired. "Remember that you probably won't be believed. You will have to persuade someone. Perhaps the president himself. From the bureau's viewpoint, you are probably A. W. O. L. If Overholt is still sane— Wait until night, Mayor. Until then, rest and prepare yourself. I haven't examined the defenses, the cordon Mayor O'Shea has set up, but I would suggest the river as the best chance. Come, Summers."

Kildering pushed himself heavily to his feet, swayed an instant before he kept his balance.

"Where are you going?" Mayor asked brusquely. "You're almost out on your feet!"

Kildering shook his head. "That's our job, Mayor. You have yours. And yours is more important. All Summers and I can hope to do is to harass John Miller, and focus his attention here in Metropolis until you can rally the nation against him. We will have to move very carefully not to be destroyed at once. I have found out that John Miller doesn't have to locate a man to drive him mad. He need only know his identity."

He held out his good hand abruptly to Mayor. "The country is counting on you, Mayor, though it doesn't know it. I'm counting on you. Good luck."

It was the second time Kildering had smiled. Bill Mayor stared at him, at that gentle smile upon the lips of old Frozen-face, and he could only take the proffered hand dumbly.

It was when Kildering was already going out the door that Mayor found his voice. "I'll get through, Kildering," he said harshly. "Or a piece of me will! Enough to make those damned fools in Washington see sense! Good luck, Kildering!"

Kildering waved his hand awkwardly. Summers grinned back uncertainly over his shoulder, and Bill Mayor was left alone. He found that his eyes were stinging. He was damned sure he'd never see either one of them alive again. He knotted his fists. His head wrenched back and he stared up at the blank ceiling.

"Oh, damn it!" he whispered prayerfully. "Oh, damn it!"

Summers' thoughts were upon death, too, as he followed humbly in Walter Kildering's wake toward the car. He did not question Kildering's decision; could not, since the way lay so clearly before them. They would fight a battle against John Miller, delaying him until the main body of the army, the F. B. I., could engage him. *They would harass John Miller!*

Summers swallowed a hard lump in his throat. It sounded a little like trying to worry God. He fought against a feeling that they would prove no more effective, and his thoughts went fleetingly to Anne Summers, off in Washington.

"Where to, Kildering?" Summers asked briskly, as he slid in behind the wheel of the car.

"Pass by City Hall," Kildering directed quietly. "Our job right now is to locate Mayor O'Shea and await our opportunity to reach him. John Miller has either driven him mad or bought him. At any rate, he is the spear point just now of Miller's attack. The point must be—blunted. Perhaps it will force Miller out into the open. It should at least hamper Miller."

Summers felt a mild sense of shock at Kildering's offhand use of the name, "Miller." Exactly as if he were any other crook they hunted. Miller. John Miller.

"Do you think we can isolate O'Shea in the daytime?" he asked slowly.

"Unlikely," Kildering admitted, "but I wanted to separate myself from Mayor so that he would be safe for a while. I'm a center of contamination. Through me, Miller might destroy us all. I'm going back to the office in Berger Street. I'll rest there, against tonight. You will keep watch and phone me directly at the first hint of possibly isolating O'Shea."

"Summers, if any doubts of my sanity occur to you at any time, knock me out. If it's still there when I recover, kill me."

Summers' face was very pale, his eyes staring as he glanced pleadingly at Kildering. Kildering was not smiling now.

"I assure you, Summers," he said flatly, "that I'll do the same to you."

Summers shuddered a little, but he did not dissent. "Is there no way of protecting ourselves?" he asked. "If there isn't, our first move against . . . against Miller will be our last. You say he need know only the identity of the man he wants to drive insane."

"Or to kill," Kildering added dryly.

"He . . . he can kill people mentally, too?" Summers hesitated.

"I believe so." Kildering's voice was flat, without resonance. "Miller seems to strike at the conscious brain centers; only terminally at the subconscious. If, after each of our raids, we secrete ourselves and knock out our conscious brains for a period of hours, we may escape. Miller can't concentrate perpetually on driving us mad. Even he must use his mind for other purposes on occasion, and I have to believe that it takes a terrific concentration of psychic force either to kill or madden a human being. Only exceptional men are able to control apes mentally; even they could not drive one mad, except by physical means. That may be because their mental organization is too low—"

Kildering's voice trailed off. Summers felt a tremor race through him. If Kildering felt like that, there must be no chance at all! Good Lord! Imagine a brain which surpassed the powers of men by an even greater margin than human brains exceeded those of apes!

Summers swore. It was a thing he didn't often do. "How will we knock ourselves out?" he asked thickly. "Repeated concussion would be damnably dangerous."

"I have quite a supply of morphine."

"But, Kildering, we'll become addicts! How long can we stand up under that?"

Kildering shook his head. He looked out the window of the sedan at the rain-washed freshness of lawns and homes and parks. Below them, in the valley by the sun-sparkling Wichinois River, the buildings of Metropolis formed a many-spired cathedral. White, clean white. There was a black smear across all that purity this morning, a smear of smoke that tainted the air with the stench of burning oil—and burning flesh.

A line of trucks marched uphill slowly, manned by their gargoyle crews, bearing their pitiful freight toward the fires. The bellow of their motors seemed bestial, hungry, carrying their prey to the sacrificial fires.

Kildering's nostrils arched whitely. "I hope John Miller likes the perfume of his altars!" he said harshly.

The night was hours old, and the calm white moon, lurid in her veil of pyre smoke, rode high toward the zenith when finally Summers phoned Kildering.

"The boss has gone home," he reported, masking his meaning. "He must be lonesome, he took so many watchdogs with him. Six."

"Come for me," Kildering instructed flatly.

Kildering's whole body felt heavy as he walked down to the street. The gnawing in his side and broken arm had nagged his nerves raw. The wound in his face and throat had stiffened, so that turning his head brought a deep knife stab of pain. Leader of the van against John Miller! Kildering's lips twisted thinly—and even that caused pain.

Summers' smile was warm but weary as he flung open the door for Kildering. "O'Shea's had a busy day," he said flatly. "A succession of demonstrations. A couple of mobs were shot up by the police. They were worried about the Blue Death. Three parades chanted O'Shea's praises. They were the people who have been given title to their homes. Lawyers and apartment owners got short shrift. They stood out on the sidewalks shouting, afterward. A lot were arrested. There were mobs around the banks, too. What the hell is John Miller trying to do?"

Kildering shook his head. "All this is preparation for some other move. Or it may be merely a sop to keep the mass of the people partly pacified for—whatever Miller is planning. Where does O'Shea live?"

O'Shea's home was a columned mansion of white stone, set well back from the road behind a formally planted lawn. The grounds were surrounded by a high iron fence, spiked at the top, and every room in the house blazed with light. Two uniformed policemen stood on the porch. There were others at the gates—an even dozen visible guards.

"Probably more inside," Kildering said quietly, as they drove past without checking speed. "Your six must have been merely his mobile bodyguard."

Summers said heavily: "Well, that's out, then. What do we do now?"

Kildering shook his head. "Drive back to the city and find a policeman your approximate size."

Summers' eyes whipped toward him. "You want me to masquerade as a cop? I'd have to have an awfully good story to get through to O'Shea."

Kildering's profile was like chiseled granite. "There's a warrant out for me, according to the papers, and O'Shea made a statement."

"Blaming you, in part, for the Blue Death," Summers said angrily. "He said he would question you, personally, when—*I get it!*"

Kildering said quietly: "Yes. Policeman Summers is going to capture Walter Kildering and take him personally to be interviewed by Mayor O'Shea! Now, find that policeman! A police car, too, would be desirable, but might prove too dangerous."

They didn't get the police car, and the uniform cap had to be padded to fit Summers' head. Walter Kildering was without his hat, and his mouse-colored hair was awry. There was a smear of blood across his forehead; his tie was askew and his collar torn.

Summers didn't have to simulate excitement. He rolled the car at high speed, slammed on brakes at the gate as the two cop guards whipped up their guns.

"I got Kildering!" Summers called out sharply. "Mayor O'Shea wants to see him!"

Kildering glared at the policemen. His right wrist was handcuffed to the dash, in plain sight. "This is stupid," he said harshly, "and Mayor O'Shea will answer for it! You can't arrest an F. B. I. man, you dumb flatties!"

The cop on guard jumped to the running board. "Oh, we can't, huh? You men think you're tin gods!"

Summers shot the car up the drive, jerked to a halt before the porch. He was out in a quick jump, had snapped Kildering's handcuff to his own left wrist. He had a police revolver in his right fist.

"He's not going to get away from me!" Summers said grimly.

"Stupid ass," said Kildering. "Nobody else would find it necessary to beat up an injured man!"

Summers struck at Kildering's head with the gun. "Shut up, you murderer!" he snapped.

It made a convincing show as they stumped up the steps to the front door, and Summers announced his capture importantly. "Did it myself," he said, "and I'm taking him in, see? I ought to get a sergeantcy out of this!"

The cops guffawed, but there was envy in their eyes. They got through to the mayor's study, and O'Shea came down from his bedroom in slippers, with a bathrobe thrown on hurriedly over his pajamas. His mane of gray hair bristled above the excitement of his heavily squared face.

His shrewd eyes took in Kildering's bandages, the handcuff that secured him to Summers' wrist. He gestured sharply at the other uniformed men in the doorway.

"All right," he said curtly. "I can handle this. Close the door! Get back to your posts!"

"I caught him!" Summers said eagerly. "I was going off duty, and I saw him sneaking along a side street. I jumped him!"

O'Shea's eyes whipped toward Summers' face. He was frowning. "You were doing what? Going off duty?"

Kildering's hand snapped free of the handcuff, whose lock was previously sprung. His automatic snouted suddenly from his fist.

"Don't speak, O'Shea," he said quietly, "or you're a dead man. We don't mind dying, if we can take you along! Our story was a little inept, I perceive. Naturally, no man would be going off duty in a crisis like this. Get behind him, Summers, and crack his skull if he tries to call a warning."

O'Shea's face stiffened under the shock of that pointing gun. He took a slow step backward, and Summers tapped his gun barrel gently against the back of his head.

"Remember," Summers said crisply. "Keep quiet!"

Kildering said: "It was thoughtful of you to have no windows in this room, O'Shea. From the lack of resonance in my voice, I suspect it is fairly well soundproofed, too. Very considerate, O'Shea. Very."

Mayor O'Shea stood on straddled, rigid legs. His head swung, lowering forward, and his voice held contempt. "You will be destroyed the moment I will it!" he said harshly.

Kildering's voice was dead even. "It is possible. If I don't first nullify your will with a bullet. Mayor O'Shea, I told you how the Blue Death was spread. Instead of checking the death, you deliberately caused more people to be killed, by urging them to employ electrical power as a preventive. Why?"

Mayor O'Shea laughed shortly. "It is the will of the Lord that they should die!"

"Ah!" Kildering's voice was soft. "The will of the Lord as personally revealed to you?"

A queer exalted light shone in O'Shea's eyes. His head was lifted magnificently; his face transfigured.

"Yes!" he whispered. "He sent his angel to bring me wisdom! Oh, God is great and his mercy endureth forever!"

Summers' face, behind the mayor, was shocked, incredulous. "Miller drove him insane," he whispered.

Kildering shook his head, his eyes keenly on O'Shea's face. "Not insanity, Marty," he said. "Mayor O'Shea has seen the light, and he has been converted to the faith."

"I have seen the light!" Mayor O'Shea chanted, "and I am free! Oh, great is the Lord! The Master! You fool, you cannot harm me! The Lord will send an angel to destroy you! O Lord, hear my plea—

"Hit him!" Kildering snapped.

Summers' gun barrel slammed against the back of the mayor's head. He lurched under the blow; his knees sagged.

"Blessed are they which are persecuted—" he whispered.

He slumped to the floor, heavily.

Summers stared down, incredulously, at the fallen man. "What the hell is all this?" he demanded roughly. "Does John Miller think he's God?"

Kildering was already at the mayor's desk, shuffling rapidly through the papers and memorandums there. "It's a convenient subterfuge," he said shortly. "Mayor O'Shea believes; those girls believe. An angel of the Lord—which is to say, the psychic projection of John Miller—told him what to do. Naturally, O'Shea obeyed."

Summers had one hand braced on the desk. It was the only thing that held him up. He pressed his forehead. "I feel . . . funny," he said. "My mind—"

Kildering's fist struck as a snake strikes, fiercely and without warning. His eyes were strained wide and there was torment in his face as Summers pitched, unconscious, across the body of the mayor. Kildering was staring, blindly, at a dim corner of the room. A golden light was beginning to glow there!

Kildering sobbed a curse. He flung himself across the room toward the outer door and locked it swiftly. His right hand was trembling, and the curses kept bubbling from his lips. He doubled back toward the desk at a hard run, spilled out the contents of a leather case from his pocket. A hypodermic needle, already filled, tumbled on the blotter. He plunged it into his flesh!

The light in the corner was brighter. In its midst, a shadowy form was beginning to take shape.

On the desk, the telephone whirred. Kildering's hand stabbed toward it, while his eyes held on that glowing light.

Death was here, he thought, but he was still fighting with all the strength of his superkeen mind. He must still gain a few hours' delay for Bill Mayor. He and Summers were doomed, except by the luckiest of chances. He might stall off insanity or death with the needle; the police might not come to investigate the long silence of the room. It was unlikely. Mayor was the only hope now; Bill Mayor in his break through the lines for help.

Kildering snatched up the phone. His voice held the indignant rasp of O'Shea's tones. "Don't interrupt me!" he snapped. "Don't call again unless I phone! I'm getting a confession!"

The voice of the man was apologetic. "Sorry, Mayor O'Shea, but you said to keep you posted. We just shot a man trying to escape from the city. Shot him swimming in the river. He drowned."

Kildering snapped: "All right. All *right!*"

His hand fumbled as he poked the phone at the cradle again. So that way was closed, too! Mayor had been shot! Kildering's eyes stung. He had to survive, he and Summers! His brain was numbing fast. He could move his limbs only with gigantic effort, and there was no feeling in them. Violently, he fought against the drug for a last minute of movement, of conscious thought. The light in the corner—magnificent now, exquisite. There was a face there, the face of an angel. Beautiful—

Walter Kildering wrenched his eyes away from that compelling face. He groped for the gun on the desk, found it. He stumbled across the room. The sweep of his arm hurled a decanter of brandy to the floor, spilled the alcohol across the rug. He tried to bend over, and he fell to his knees. He began pulling the trigger, so that powder sparks would reach the alcohol fumes.

Some part of his brain counted the shots. He thought he could smell the scorch of fire; couldn't tell. One shot left. Walter Kildering fell toward the mayor. He pressed the muzzle of the gun close, jerked at the trigger.

Walter Kildering, face down on the floor, could not tell whether he had fired that last, utterly necessary, shot. He could not tell because hot pincers were tearing at his brain. Because of the face amid the golden light. A beautiful face—hellishly beautiful—

VII

IT WAS the moon that defeated Bill Mayor in his effort to escape from Metropolis and bring help to the stricken city. Just around midnight, the moon found a few scattered clouds in which to hide its face. Bill Mayor made his dash in those moments of darkness.

Mayor thought that he had figured out every step of his escape. He loosed his car, motor roaring, to charge down the slope toward the flood wall and the pickets along the river. That was to draw the guards off their posts. He sprinted to a tree he had selected, went up it like a cat and sidled out along a branch that reached over the flood wall.

Exultation was in him then, as he poised on that branch. A swift dive, and he would be away from Wichinois! He plunged out into space—and the moon popped out.

The moonlight caught the momentary gleam of Bill Mayor's body, stripped to shorts, as it flashed through the night toward the water. And one guard saw him. He was alert, gun cocked in his fist, because of the alarm. He was one of the supertrained Metropolis force's best marksmen.

He whipped up his gun and made a snap shot, crying out: *"Got him!"*

Bill Mayor didn't hear him, or hear the shot. He thought, in that flashing moment of pain, that he had struck a rock just on the surface of the water. A rock that drove him sideways, doubled him into a knot in the middle of his dive—

He hit the water like that, went under. A slab of dark water reached high against the face of the white concrete wall, silvered as it spattered in the moonlight. A second bullet troughed the surface a moment later, gouging out a towering liquid splinter.

Then the moon, its task completed, hid behind another cloud.

Perhaps it was the coldness of the spring flood that did it. Perhaps, the subconscious working of Mayor's dazed mind. He knew, as he sliced deeper, deeper into the black water, that he had been hit with a bullet. It gave him the anger he needed to survive. The current tugged at him strongly. He helped with feeble flaps of his arms. He couldn't kick, couldn't feel his feet at all.

He broached the surface as gently as the rising dead, floated there, motionless. He heard sharp cries on the banks. The round, menacing eyes of flashlights winked at him from the flood wall. They made pale-brown ovals on the water. The patches of light ran about like questing hounds, madly eager for the kill.

A tormented thunder, a slashing sputter of gunpowder sparks marked the muzzle of a chattering submachine gun up there. The tracers drew crimson streaks across the night. Bullets whipped the water like dirty cream. The froth raced toward him, nearer, nearer— Ten feet away from Mayor, the bullets held steady. They chewed a floating log butt, sleek as a man's head, to silvery bits.

Mayor had enough presence of mind to scream, stranglingly. Somehow, he managed a dive. When he came up again, the flashlights were all focused back there where the log had been.

So Bill Mayor could drift on with the current, alone in the darkness. That darkness was creeping inside him, inside his brain. His side and back were no longer numb. They were an agony.

In Bill Mayor's mind was only one thought, now. He had to keep afloat. He fought to do that. He fought through æons of black and agony-slashed time. He fought so hard that even when hands caught his wrists, reached under his arms, he tried to knock them away.

That was the way Mayor remembered the black-and-gray time that followed, as a fight to keep afloat. He made it, too. The day came when he opened his eyes and realized he was in the small, tight cabin of a boat. He was in a bunk. And the air had the taint of fish.

The companionway was opened presently, and an unshaven face, bristling with red beard, was poked in.

"Hey," the man said. "Awake, are you? Hey, Lila, your patient's got his eyes open!"

The man stumped down into the cabin. He was barefooted, trousers twisted about his knees. He pared plug tobacco into a calloused palm, had a cold pipe clamped between stained teeth.

"Didn't figure you had a chance, brother," he said equably. "Wanted to throw you back for another time. Seeing as how you fought so. But Lila says—"

The girl was barefooted, too. Yellow plaits were twisted about her head in a coronet. Her body was strong, sturdily built. She looked healthy and extraordinarily happy. Her lips parted generously over strong white teeth.

"So," she said. "Some broth, and you sleep some more. You'll do, brother."

Bill Mayor found his voice was very weak, and his will limp. He drank the broth and slept. The second day, he learned that the bullet had torn through his lumbar muscles and set about devising a brace that would take the strain off it and let him walk.

Lila and her father, Jan Posk, were fishing the Wichinois, fifteen miles below Metropolis.

"Can't sell nothing there now, brother," Jan Posk grumbled beside the bunk, while he fouled the air with his stub pipe. "Shoot if you come near them, the fools. Though the plague fires ain't burning no more."

Lila smiled and shrugged. "The river feeds us. After while, we sell again. That Metropolis is funny. Tell me, now, they pay grownup folks to go to school. Tell me, they pay them to play games. Grown men, playing games. Is funny, yes?"

"Who tells you?" Bill Mayor asked sharply.

Lila shrugged. It was extraordinarily graceful, especially when she wrinkled her nose in that broad grin of hers. "I hear in the villages, among the boats," she said. "Even, they pay a man for having a baby. His wife, I mean, yes."

Bill Mayor frowned over the news, shook his too-long hair back from his forehead and went on with rigging the body brace out of canvas and fishing line. There was a fire in his haggard eyes, and it was in his soul, too. He had lost ten days, and back there in Metropolis, Kildering and Summers—harassed John Miller! Counting on him, fighting a desperate battle in hope that he could get through. And he was failing them.

"Tricks," he said raspingly. "Tricks, to keep the people quiet. So he can rob them! He killed twenty-five thousand people there in one night!"

Jan Posk's eyes were gloomy. "Iss the plague."

Mayor's head snapped up. "It was murder!"

"So!" Jan Posk nodded. "Things like that have happened in the old country. Here, she iss new."

Mayor stared at him, and the fire within him grew to a great leaping flame. Not here in America—

"Help me with this strap, Jan," he said.

Jan Posk took the pipe from between his teeth. His voice was deep, rolling. "Hi! Lila!"

Between them, they strapped Bill Mayor tightly in his brace. He set his teeth, sweating with the pain. He got on his feet. With an oar for a brace, he could stand.

"Tomorrow"—he pushed the words out, panting—"you must put me ashore near the highway to Capital City."

Lila pursed up her smiling lips. "Maybe the day after," she said.

Mayor said, violently, "Tomorrow!"

It was the day after the next that they put him ashore. He had a peeled staff of willow in his fist and he needed it. His clothing was a pair of worn overalls and a shirt; tennis shoes for his feet. His black hair was too long, but he was shaven. Lila had done that.

Bill Mayor stood beside the road that ran close to the river here. He leaned both hands on the willow staff and just the effort of standing there was torment, but he smiled. He meant that smile.

"You've been damned good to me, Jan and Lila," he said. "Maybe I'll make it up to you some day."

Lila smiled, lifted her shoulder. "Iss nothing, brother," she said.

Jan Posk took out his pipe to spit. "So, maybe anodder time we throw you back!"

Bill Mayor walked off along the road. His steps dragged and motorists stared at him curiously and did not stop. He had to rest after a half mile. The next time, he made only half that distance. The sweat stood out on his gaunt temples. He drove his flagging body on. It was night when he made the first village, five miles along the two-hundred-mile march to Capital City.

He had brought some money along with him, pinned to the waistband of his shorts; that and his F. B. I. credentials were his only possessions. He dared not use the credentials. He bought cheap clothing and shoes, and he had two dollars left. But the clothing was necessary. Without it, he could never reach any official. He set out again with his willow staff, and luck was with him. At ten o'clock, he got a lift twenty miles upon his way. At three that afternoon, a man in a decrepit car slowed down beside him.

"Can I give you a lift, brother?" he cried. "Inasmuch as ye do it to the least of these, my brethren, you have done it unto me."

Mayor climbed painfully into the front seat, thrust his staff into the back.

"Going far?" he asked faintly.

"Going to kingdom come!" the man cried joyously. "Capital City the first stop! I'm going to preach the new coming, brother. The new and happy coming, when mankind will be free. It is already upon us! Yeah, the wicked have been smitten with a staff of serpents, and salvation is at hand!"

Mayor turned his head slowly, and the hatred that rose within him was cold and frightening. He knew an elation that Capital City was at last within his grasp, but there was menace in this innocent-seeming man. The menace of propaganda!

"You come from Metropolis," Mayor said slowly.

"Mine eyes have seen the glory!" the man chanted. He had his foot down hard on the accelerator. The car rocked and roared, and made thirty-five miles an hour.

Mayor's voice softened. "Tell me about it," he said.

The story was long in coming, interlarded with biblical ejaculations. As the itinerant preacher told it, Metropolis was the promised land. There, all men were free. Purged of wickedness by the plague, they had turned to the One True God. To the Master!

"Has anyone seen the Master?" Mayor asked sharply.

"Has anyone seen the face of the Lord?" the preacher cried. "Yeah, *he* came to me in the night. *He* came in golden light, and *his* face was a face of beauty! Oh, *he* sent unto me an angel—"

"What color was his hair?" Mayor cut in. "His eyes? How tall was he and how was he dressed?"

"Bless you, brother!" cried the preacher. "He wasn't dressed at all, and he carried in his right hand a sword of flame, and in his left hand was—"

But Mayor wasn't listening. There was no sense in this man, and yet he brought certain ominous word. It was true that men were being paid to attend schools, and women, too. *Propaganda agencies,* Mayor thought. And men were being paid to march, too; drilling in the wide parks of Metropolis. *An army forming!*

"No man wants for anything," the preacher cried. "Lo, *he* strikes the rock, and water gushes forth, and *he* feeds the multitude from but five loaves and two fishes. There is no longer any money, or need for money. All, all has been rendered unto Cæsar, and all men live in the bounty of God!"

Mayor thought, *"So John Miller has all the money in Metropolis now!"*

"Doesn't anybody even work?" he asked.

"Aye, they work, and the work is blessed—"

It went on like that. A long while before Mayor learned that O'Shea had been murdered in his home; that fire had consumed the building "for his wickedness."

"Doesn't anyone at all oppose this—Master?" he asked then, wondering if Kildering had struck at O'Shea.

The preacher scowled and anger flashed in his eyes. "All good men are persecuted," he said harshly. "There be those who would crucify *him,* but *he* will triumph, for *he* is great—"

"Who works against him?" Mayor cut in.

"Nay, Beelzebub," the preacher muttered.

Bill Mayor closed his eyes in weariness and tried to rest his strained and tormented back against the cushions. The preacher's voice ran on in his ears, but he scarcely heard the man. He had the facts now. Someone—and he almost prayed aloud that it was Kildering—was still working against John Miller! But John Miller was shrewd. He had lulled the people while he robbed them. Plain enough now why he had killed all those men and women: to bring the city to its knees.

One thought was terribly plain to Bill Mayor in that moment. John Miller was all-powerful in Metropolis. He had stripped the city bare. *But John Miller was not satisfied!*

This preacher had been sent out to help spread the propaganda of John Miller, and that meant Capital City was next! Capital City, decimated by the Blue Death; brought to its knees! The whole State of Wichinois would follow, and then—

Bill Mayor was no longer relaxed against the cushions. He sat bolt-upright, and leaned forward, and his gaunt, bony fists were mallets on his knees. The preacher was howling a hymn now at the top of his voice. The car roared and steamed—and the miles crawled toward them, limped out under the wabbling wheels.

It was midnight when the battered car rolled into the streets of Capital City. Bill Mayor knew where he was going. Hoarsely, he stopped the preacher two blocks from where the governor's red brick mansion stood among the ancient cedars and poplars of the Capital Park.

"Come with me, brother," the preacher boomed. "Come, and win salvation! Help me preach The Coming!"

Bill Mayor said grimly: "I'm going to preach the coming, all right. I'll spread the word my way, and you yours."

The preacher cried: "Blessings on thee, brother. The blessings of the New Lord upon thee! Let us pray!"

Bill Mayor limped off. With his gaunt, forward-thrusting head, his heavy hands set upon the staff, Bill Mayor looked like a prophet himself. But it was a grim message he brought to Capital City. His lips twisted fiercely. If they would believe him! By God, he'd make them!

His eyes burned toward the multiple lights of the governor's mansion. He was on the verge of the grounds now, under the shadow of the ancient trees. He pushed on steadily, ignoring the paths, taking the shortest cut. A hundred feet ahead, there was a small illuminated fountain that hurled its multiple jets through waves of colored light. A policeman's broad shoulders bulked against it. He was spinning his club.

Mayor started to make a circuit, but his movements were too awkward to escape notice. He would have to go straight past the man. If the cop tried to stop him—Mayor's hands knotted on the staff of willow. He shuffled on, fighting the pain in his back.

He was fifty feet away when the man stopped twirling his club. The nightstick dangled by its cord from his hand, and the man twisted his head stiffly as if his collar were too tight. He reached up a slow hand toward it. Suddenly, he was tearing at his collar with both mad hands! His legs braced widely, but his knees gave. He pitched down, scrambling on the earth. He tried to cry out, and the sound was hoarse and strangled.

Mayor tried to run. The effort wasn't very successful. He reeled, off balance, into a tree, and the pain made the perspiration start over his body. After that, he clung to his staff and contented himself with a rapid shuffle. The policeman's struggles were slowing. He lay flat on his back, and his arms and legs stretched out limply. His breath made a hoarse sound in his throat.

It was when Mayor was still four yards away that even this sound ceased. The man's face—

Mayor said thickly: *"God! The Blue Death is here, too!"*

Through the long moment of realization, Bill Mayor stood motionless over the body, a scarecrow figure clinging to a staff. Presently, he stooped and took the man's revolver. He thrust it into his belt, beneath the swing of his coat. He shuffled on toward the mansion. The tap of his staff was quick, hurried. He leaned forward in the frantic need for haste. He passed two more bodies in the park.

As Bill Mayor fought his way up the broad steps to the mansion, the doors flung open. A man ran out. He ran crazily, with his head arched far back, his legs striding high and blindly. He stumbled at the head of the steps and pitched headlong. His shoulder struck. He bounced. He slithered headfirst, on his back, past Mayor on the steps. His face was blue.

Mayor's face was a ghastly white. His shadowed eyes had a feverish burn. The door swung open when he reached it, and he shambled inside. There was a dead man there, and another at the door of the governor's office.

Whoever was inside wasn't dead yet. It was awful to hear a grown man giggling.

Mayor poked at the door with his staff. It swung open slowly. The hinges made a faint creaking. The door swung halfway and stopped with a soft bump. A man's arm, a man's knotted fist thrust out from behind. There was no movement.

There was a living man in the room. He crouched in a corner, and thrust his beautifully manicured hands at his drooling mouth. That didn't stop the giggles. His eyes were sly, preternaturally bright.

"Are you . . . the Master?" he mumbled. "Nice old Master. Nice Master, go away. Don't hurt me."

He giggled again.

It was the governor of Wichinois.

Bill Mayor felt horror crawl sickly through his belly. He made his way heavily into the office and sank into the governor's chair. His eyes rested shrinkingly on the governor himself as he reached for the phone.

They would believe him now in Washington. John Miller had overshot himself that much. Mayor's thoughts moved his lips visibly. He lifted the phone to his ear, and the operator answered. He opened his mouth to give the number that was in his mind, the number of the F. B. I., and suddenly he cried out. He slammed the telephone back into its cradle.

"No," he whispered. "No—"

There was no new sound in the room, no new movement. It was at his thoughts that Bill Mayor stared with such terror. If he called Washington, if he directed John Miller's attention that way, the Blue Death might go there, too! And John Miller would send his "angel with a flaming sword."

In his corner, the governor giggled fawningly. "Nice Master. You won't hurt me?"

When Bill Mayor reached for the telephone again, his hand was rock-steady. "Get me the adjutant general of the State. At once! This is an emergency!"

When the petulant voice of the adjutant general of the State answered, Mayor rang out words like blows of steel.

"Call out the entire State militia, at once! Then come to the governor's mansion!" he said. "Yes, the written authority is waiting here for you!"

Bill Mayor hung up the receiver, and his hand went to the gun at his waist. There was a grim, cold smile on his mouth. He settled his shoulders against the back of the chair and waited. He had a plan he thought would work. Useless to talk of a one-man domination of Metropolis, or repeat Kildering's theories of John Miller. This was a Republican State; and the head of the State militia was certain to be a Redbaiter. His course, then, was clear. He would paint the things that had happened in Metropolis as a Communistic revolution!

If that failed, he still had his written authority—Bill Mayor drew out the policeman's revolver and checked the loading.

It was only minutes later that the adjutant general, Beverley Ley, strode into the office. His heavy, mustached face was belligerent.

"What the hell goes on here?" he demanded harshly.

Bill Mayor tossed his badge and credentials on the desk. "I'll tell you about it," he said quietly. "You no doubt recognized the dead people as victims of the Blue Death, which originated in Metropolis?"

Ley grunted. "The Blue Death, huh? But, in God's name, the governor!"

The governor scuttled toward General Ley, clung to him. "Don't let them hurt me, Bev," he whimpered. "Please don't let them hurt me!"

Ley grew white at the touch of the governor's hands, but stood rigidly. His eyes went to Mayor's face, and they were shocked.

"What goes on is this," Mayor said quietly. "In Metropolis, a revolution has been started. They spread the Blue Death to disorganize the city. They have seized the government and all the banks. All factories and property have been confiscated. They even have a new religion!"

Ley said: "Communists! By God!"

"And now," Mayor went on softly, "they obviously are going to try to take over the State government as well. That is why they have . . . done this to the governor. That's why the Blue Death is striking here!"

The governor whispered, "I don't want to die!"

Mayor nodded crisply. "It is a great chance for a strong man," he said. "A strong man, who put down this rebellion, might even become the country's next president. The governor is plainly incapable of issuing orders."

General Ley's eyes glistened. "The soldiers will be ready in twelve hours, fully mobilized," he said. "Meantime, I can marshal the State police. The lieutenant governor is a weakling. I'll force him to give me authority! Communists, pah!"

"Why bother?" Mayor asked softly. "The governor is still here. He will sign the authorization. We can take him with us."

Ley smiled wintrily. "Excellent!"

It was noon the next day when the troops rolled out of Capital City in commandeered trucks. Mayor, with the governor and General Ley, rode in a big sedan. They were forced to leave the State police behind, for the Blue Death was beginning to wreak its havoc. Less swift than it had been in Metropolis, it had struck down only a thousand persons in the course of the night. But the citizens were terrified. Streams of them clouded the roads northward, and had to be turned back by guards. It was the story of Metropolis over again, but Mayor felt the stirrings of hope. John Miller would not be able to stand against an armed force! The people would be forced to hunt him down and surrender him—

Ten miles from the environs of Metropolis, the army was deployed. Marching patrols spread out through the fields and made contact with other forces that had approached on parallel roads. Scouting detachments were sent racing ahead toward Metropolis. Mayor conceded to himself that General Ley was efficient.

They took over a farmhouse as headquarters and the signal corps rapidly struck up field telephones for communications. Ley had taken on stature in the last few hours. In uniform, he seemed taller. His voice was curt, crisp, and that shine of eagerness remained in his eyes.

"Within three hours, our lines will be complete," he told Mayor. "Then we will summon them to surrender. If they refuse"—his head lifted, his voice took on a rasp—"we'll smash them!"

Mayor said happily: "Three hours? I think we've earned a bit of rest. This back of mine—" He pushed himself to his feet. He still needed the staff, and he stumped toward the first-floor room that had been assigned to him. General Ley wasn't watching or listening. He didn't seem to need sleep, under the stimulation of action. He crossed with his heavy, military stride to where a map was spread upon a portable table and frowned down at it.

Mayor eased himself down upon the bed, stood the willow staff against the wall, and stretched out. His eyes burned wide open at the darkened ceiling. A trapezoid of light from the main room lay across the wide dark boards of the floor. Mayor thought, "Three hours!"

Even if there were no surrender, Kildering and Summers would be on the alert within the city. This, if anything, should force John Miller out into the open. He thought that Kildering would be able to capitalize on that fact!

Mayor smiled and closed his eyes. His strength was depleted, and he was very tired. He slept.

It was the sound of a footfall that awakened him. His eyes flew wide and he had, suddenly, all his faculties about him. He felt that he needed them. There was, in the coldness that ran along his spine, a very real sense of danger.

General Ley stood in the doorway, looking at him.

There was no new light in the room. Ley's shadow spread along the floor toward him. He was more rigidly erect than ever; the upfling of his head was challenging.

He had a gun in his right hand.

Mayor made no sudden movement, but his left hand drifted down to the revolver which was thrust into his waistband, while his right glided toward the willow staff against the wall.

"Are the three hours up, General Ley?" he asked quietly. "I must have slept."

General Ley said, *"You traitor!"* His voice rasped.

Mayor swore under his breath, but still he did not try to move. Ley's gun arm was too stiffly ready.

"Traitor to what, General Ley?" he asked.

Ley took a long stride inside the room, a little to one side so that the light reflected more brightly from the floor. Now, Mayor could catch the gleam of Ley's eyes. There was a glitter beneath his mustache. His lips were drawn back from his teeth.

Ley's voice came thickly, harshly. "You almost drove me into a betrayal of my Lord!" he cried. "You treacherous animal! Making me a traitor to my Lord!"

Mayor's breath made a small hissing sound between his teeth. He needed no more than those few swift words. He had been a fool to sleep. In that brief while, John Miller had sprung his defense. Dizzily, Mayor recalled the preacher's words. "An angel of the Lord appeared before me—" Yes, Ley would obey an "angel."

Ley swore in a thin, rising voice. "Die, traitor!" he shouted, and jerked up his revolver!

Mayor whipped the willow staff from the wall and hurled it straight at Ley's face! The general dodged and his gun spat out its scarlet funnel of flame. The bullet crunched into the headboard within a few inches of Mayor's head!

Mayor flung himself sideways from the bed. He cried out at the stab of pain through his back. He thrust at the floor, couldn't rise. His back brace had slipped. He flung himself forward along the floor toward Ley.

The general sprang toward the bed, leaned over it. He was directly over Mayor. The bed protected Ley from attack. Mayor tried to roll under it and there wasn't room; wasn't time. Ley's face, thrust into the shaft of light, had a curiously exalted expression.

"Die!" he cried again, and leveled the revolver at point-blank range. Mayor's revolver spoke first.

Ley's head was driven back out of the path of the light. His left hand, resting on the footboard, caught the full focus. It clenched slowly, as if the fingers would dig into the wood. That was all that was visible of General Ley, that clenched hand and the sleeve of his uniform.

The fingers went limp, and there was a double thud as his knees struck the floor. He fell, rolled. Flat on his back, his head thrust out into the shaft of light.

Mayor's bullet had struck him just above the eyes, dead center.

Frenziedly, Mayor dragged himself to his feet. Gripping the footboard, he reached out a trembling foot for his willow staff. He finally got it. Clinging to the staff desperately, he shuffled toward the door. The revolver dangled from his fingers.

In moments, the sentries would come. He had to think fast. There must be a way to muster these men and launch them against Metropolis. It had been a mistake to wait, a mistake he should not have made. John Miller knew too well how to take advantage of such delays!

Mayor dragged across the main room of the farmhouse. No one stirred. There was no sound in the night except, distantly, the roar of a truck engine. The thrust of the night wind touched the open door of the house, made it swing gently. Insects whirred and buzzed around the electric light.

Mayor stumbled on toward the door. A harder thrust of the wind swung the door about, and the light moved with it. A man's shoe, a putteed leg came into sight. Mayor swore, shouldered the door all the way open.

He whispered, "The Blue Death!"

He went outside, leaned his shoulders against the side of the house. The wind ruffled the hair of the dead soldier at his feet. In the fields, frogs made a shrill piping. The engine of the truck was louder. As he watched, its headlights poked over the crest of a hill toward Metropolis. They dazzled him for a moment, then dropped down across the fields.

Strong black shadows sprang up there—and there were white splotches that were the faces of dead soldiers. The headlights swung back to the road; the motor bellowed. The truck blasted off at top speed toward Capital City.

Mayor's dazed eyes followed the retreating taillight until it popped out of sight over another low hill. His head sagged, and the stiffening went out of his body.

This move, too, had broken against the might of John Miller!

But it was more than that. Mayor's tired mind quested on. New armies could be raised; Metropolis could be bombed off the face of the earth. What good would that do? One man, John Miller, need merely flee and, presently, when he was ready, loose his resistless forces again upon the world.

If, indeed, John Miller waited for the bombers to come. It was so easy, so pitifully easy, for him to loose his powers. Generals turned to converts under the very walls of his city. The governor turned into a helpless madman.

It would be worse than useless to notify Washington and urge an invasion. It would be criminal folly!

So far, John Miller had not attacked Washington, except to remove the chief! Bill Mayor felt a mad urge to drop down on his knees and pray that John Miller would be content to leave Washington alone! And prayer was a thing that Bill Mayor had not thought of in many long years.

Bill Mayor's head lifted slowly, swung about so that he could see the glow of the lights of Metropolis there against the southern sky. His lips drew thinly against his teeth, turned down harshly at the corners.

That was where the battle must be fought, within the environs of Metropolis! There, they must win—or John Miller would reign triumphant over a prostrate nation!

It had been tried, and Walter Kildering himself had acknowledged defeat. No matter. They must fight on, as long as John Miller allowed them!

Bill Mayor clutched his willow staff in his hands and shuffled his dragging feet forward. There was no hope in him, only desperation and a grim, stricken courage.

Bill Mayor marched, alone, upon Metropolis.

VIII

IT WAS not long after dawn that Bill Mayor hobbled up to the picket line around Metropolis, maintained by the police of the city—by John Miller's men.

A dozen feet from them, Bill Mayor paused and lifted his thin, long hands high above his head, lifted the staff, too.

"May the blessings of the Lord descend upon thee!" He made his voice deep and resonant. "I have seen *his* star in the east, and have come to worship *him!*"

He dropped on his knees then, and bowed his head above his clasped hands. He had purposely drawn his ruffled black hair forward over his brows. Through it, his masked eyes regarded the sentries. They had called out the sergeant of the guard now, and he stood, fists on his hips, watching Mayor. Presently, Mayor heaved himself to his feet. Leaning on his staff, he moved toward the guards.

If they were as fanatic about John Miller as most of the persons he had met lately, they would swallow this gag completely. It was the only way that Mayor, crippled as he was, could hope to break through the careful patrol they maintained.

Mayor made his eyes wide and staring. He mumbled as he moved toward them, and his head was lifted devoutly. He plodded with his staff.

"Hold on there," the sergeant growled at him.

"Peace unto you, brother," Mayor intoned. "Take me unto the house of the Lord, so that I may prophesy."

He focused his eyes upon the sergeant, lifted his staff gravely to press it against his forehead.

"I foresee that you shall be great," he said slowly. "But that man beside you—" Mayor shook his head. "Death is reaching for you, brother. Make your peace with the Lord!"

The man's face turned pale, but the sergeant grinned. "He's harmless. Let him in. We got orders to go easy on these nuts. Good propaganda, you know. Before long, anyhow, the boss is going to have visiting delegations coming here—to see how we do it. Pass in, father."

Mayor intoned his blessing again and went, long-striding, through the picket lines of Metropolis. But his heart was not light. The very ease with which he had been allowed to enter spoke eloquently of the growing power of John Miller. His lips twisted bitterly. Well, he had reason to know how great that power was!

It took him a long while to reach the city itself. From the first public phone that he could locate, he put in a call for "Mr. Walters."

The operator said: "I'm sorry, sir. Nobody here by that name."

He tried the cottage on the hill, and the phone had been disconnected; tried their old office on Berger Street with no better luck. He leaned against the wall of the booth and stared blankly at the phone. This was the method of rendezvous that had been arranged, and it had been disrupted. He was in Metropolis, but he was alone!

For the first time, he was shaken by serious fears for the lives of Summers and Kildering. Somehow, he had not thought that even the power of John Miller could prevail against old Frozen-face.

Mayor pushed out of the booth and made his slow way along the main streets toward the Civic Center with its surrounding parks. There was no plan in his brain, only a vast weariness and despair. This was the final, crushing blow.

John Miller was triumphant.

Slowly, Mayor began to look about him. People went about the rounds of their business as usual, with no thought of the catastrophe that had overtaken them, which threatened their entire civilization. They even seemed happy. There was a school on the corner and, in addition to the children, there were great crowds of men and women filing into the building also. Most of them carried books.

Mayor remembered that John Miller paid adults to study. Propaganda, of course.

And Mayor realized that he was hungry. He turned into a lunchroom, and his hand went hesitantly to his pocket. He had less than a dollar in change. But he had to eat. He limped into the lunchroom and settled upon a stool, heavily. He leaned his willow staff against the wall, glanced at the signs.

"Ham and eggs, with potatoes and coffee, bread and butter," he read, and then he frowned. The price was "1/10 SU," whatever that meant.

The counterman was smiling at him, waiting. Mayor said: "I'm a stranger here. What does one tenth SU mean? I have money, but—"

"A stranger?" The man still grinned. "Oh, that means a tenth of a service unit. The bank over on the corner will give you exchange. I'll do it for you. Ham and eggs?"

Mayor watched the man, whistling cheerfully as he went about fixing his breakfast. He broke off, to talk over his shoulder.

"We don't have money here any more, and it's pretty swell," he said. "The State pays me to run this lunchroom, and I get half of any economies I show. They finance it. In service units."

"The State?" Mayor asked slowly.

"Metropolis," the man threw at him. "I get paid for studying radio. Now, there's something I've always wanted to know about, but it cost too much. Besides, most of those courses were fakes. Now, they pay me to learn it. My wife's got a course in taking care of babies. They decided we could have four."

"Four babies?"

"Yep, and they pay us for each one—keep on paying us. Pretty swell, huh?"

Mayor's lips shut grimly together. Pretty swell! John Miller taking all the money in the entire city, setting out to take all of it in the State. Meantime, he lulled these people into false security.

"And suppose the State decided you couldn't have any babies?" Mayor asked softly. "What then?"

The man turned around, sliding a plate toward Mayor. "Don't know," he said. "Everybody has to take an F. and M. and they give you a card."

"An F. and M.?"

"Sure. Physical and mental test." The man was still cheerful. Mayor was growing to hate that cheerfulness. "You step into some sort of room with funny lights and gadgets. Just walk through it. When you come out, they give you a card. They do say that if your card is bad, it just isn't any use trying to have kids. You can't. Look, mister. There's no need for anybody in this town to do without money. You go to City Hall, and they'll give you a place to live. You stay there six months, it's yours. They'll assign you a job, too. And you get paid for studying, like I said. Or marching. Or taking exercise. They got home-crafts, too. They're compulsory, but you get paid big, and you make your own choice."

Mayor said shortly, "Have you found out where the money is coming from to pay for all this?"

The man nodded. "Oh, sure. We get lessons in that, too. Newspapers carried a series on it. It goes like this: When we study, or have kids, or do any of those things, we're doing a service to the State, so we get paid for it. These ham and eggs, now. Used to cost a lot, because so many guys took a profit out of it. Now each guy gets just what his service is worth. Farmer, distributor, me. Same thing with everything. Nobody gets any profits. Take these ham and eggs. What you paid was just what they was worth. I get my cut, the distributor, the farmer. State finances the whole deal and arranges the details."

Mayor felt shaken. If it would work— But it was all trickery. John Miller was entrenching himself so that his grafting wouldn't be interrupted.

"What about the interest on the farmer's mortgage?" he asked dryly. "What about the profits of the stockholder in the concern?"

The man shrugged. "State owns them all. Farmer owns his land. Interest is against the law. You know, that's a funny thing. I always sort of figured interest was screwy. Like as if money worked and had to be paid for working. There's only so much money in all. All right. Suppose it all earns money, interest, like that. Where you going to get the money to pay the other money for working? It's screwy. Me, I like service units. Want anything else, mister?"

Mayor gave the man a dime, which was all he wanted. He got up and shuffled toward the door. The counterman called out after him.

"Hey, if you're sick, whyn't you go to the hospital?" he said. "They pay you for coming. Keeping healthy is a service to the State."

Mayor stepped out into the street, and the sun was bright and warm. It felt good on his shoulders. He lifted his head and looked heavily about him. There were a lot of people in the parks, taking exercises in groups, playing games, marching in columns.

"But John Miller is a murderer," Mayor muttered. "He killed twenty-five thousand of these people in one night. He's a revolutionist, a traitor. This scheme won't work. It's camouflage so that John Miller can loot the entire city. He'll walk out, and the entire social system will be disorganized. The whole place will be ripe for any kind of revolution. Maybe that's what he wants. Maybe he's a revolutionist of some sort."

He stood there on the sunny street, and he could not get his thoughts straight. He looked back at the lunchroom, and the operator was standing in the door, smiling.

"Pretty picture, ain't it?" he said. "Looks like Metropolis always comes up better than ever. Take those fires, now—"

Mayor said sharply: "What about initiative? What about efficiency? It's all right to talk about service units and no profits, but what are you working for?"

The man shook his head. "You got it wrong. All any guy ever works for is to live. Me, I'm living better than I ever did before. And if I run this place right, I've got a chance to go up. Run three or four, maybe. If I'm good enough, I'll get a State job managing all of them. And more service units. Guy gets just what he's worth. But no guy can take a whole lot of money and smash another guy who hasn't got much. No rich guy can start crowding everybody else out of business."

"Your taxes will be high!"

The man laughed. "You're hard to sell, mister. Ain't no taxes. State puts a charge for its services on everything that's sold. Management charge. State pays itself in service units. Well, so long; I got a customer. Better go to that hospital, mister."

Mayor tramped towards the park, and his lips were grim. It sounded pretty, but so did Fascism and Communism and lots of other isms, as the propaganda told it. And this man had swallowed propaganda wholesale. He was paid to learn it by heart!

But Bill Mayor was an F. B. I. man, with a job to do; a mass murderer to catch.

There was a man standing on a bench in the park making a speech. He was using a lot of biblical language and calling Metropolis the Promised Land. He was talking about the Second Coming. About the New Lord.

Mayor listened to him, and felt his anger rising. He was too feeble to fight with his body. He was stripped of allies and friends. But he could still fight with words.

He climbed up on another bench and lifted his gaunt arms, his willow staff toward the skies. He knew how haggard he looked, and that was well. He made a good prophet.

"You fools!" he cried out. "You utter idiots! Will you kiss the hand that kills your brothers and fathers?"

Mayor got attention all right. The other speaker stared at him, open-mouthed. The people swung about. Men, playing baseball nearby, heard the deep bell of his voice and turned to peer toward the tall, bushy-haired man with a prophet's staff in his lifted hand.

Mayor looked at the men about him, and slowly dropped his hands. "How many of you," he said slowly, "lost loved ones and friends by the Blue Death? Lift your hand, any man who didn't lose some dear one through the Blue Death!"

In all the crowd before him, no hand was lifted. The people in the crowd glanced at each other uneasily.

"The man you are praising," Mayor said slowly. "The man you call the New Lord. He loosed the Blue Death upon you, as God once loosed the plagues upon Egypt. Do you know why?"

Mayor had never done much speaking in public before. But he felt deeply. He was carried away by his anger and his helplessness. And he had these people. He could feel their response to him. He shook the staff.

"He thought these people you love were too dumb to live!" he cried. "That was the whole thing. The Blue Death was aimed at people whom this man—this *man*, I say—did not deem smart enough to live! This is the same man who tells you that you are too dumb to have children. You walk into a room full of lights. If the machine says you're dumb, you can't have children. You can't ever have a child anywhere. Do you know why?

"Those machines sterilize you!"

The other speaker jumped down from his bench and strode through the ranks of the crowd. "You are a blasphemer!" he shouted. "You blaspheme the name of the Master!"

Mayor laughed. It was harsh and reaching, his laughter. More men were gravitating toward the bench from which he spoke. Women were stopping, too. He had a considerable crowd. He laughed and jeered down at the man who had challenged him.

"So the Master wants to suppress the truth!" he said. "If you know the truth, tell it to these people! Didn't this man, whom you call the Master, loose the Blue Death on the city?"

The preacher said, "You blaspheme!"

"Answer my question! But you can't answer it!" Mayor shouted. "You can't answer it, except to say it is the truth. For I have told the truth!"

The man looked uneasily about him. "It was done for the good of the whole people!" he cried. "For the good of the State!"

Mayor shouted him down. "For the good of the man you serve!" he cried. "To line his pockets with your money, with your wealth! Outside of Metropolis, you couldn't buy a gallon of gasoline, nor a ham sandwich. You can't spend service units anywhere else. And when the Master skips town with your money, *what will you live on then?*"

The speaker turned away and began to make his way rapidly through the crowd. A woman snatched off his hat and hit at him with it. A man caught his coat collar, shouted a question. The man ripped free and began to run.

"Let him go!" Mayor called. "He is only a servant! Listen, listen to what I have to tell you!"

Just behind Mayor, a voice spoke softly. "Good work, Bill, but cut it short. The cops will be here in a minute."

Mayor stiffened. He knew that voice—*Marty Summers!* He did not turn, but his words came out more hurriedly.

"Stop taking these things that happen about you as the acts or dictates of God," he said. "I tell you that they are the works of a man, a man named John Miller. He had a criminal record. He is a robber of banks, a murderer! Ask questions. Ask yourself questions. Ask your neighbors. You have no security, and no freedom, except to do as this man orders!

"This is not the Promised Land. It is a promissory land. You have given your whole wealth, your whole security and future for scraps of paper that have no value at all. You are slaves to a man named Miller!

"This is America! This is the land of free speech, of free religion—*of free men!*

"Then act like free men! Throw off the chains of John Miller!"

Behind him, Summers whispered, "Here come the cops!"

Mayor lifted his staff and pointed where two men in police blue were hurrying through the walks of the park. "There, you see your freedom!" he said. "I dare to speak the truth, and the minions of John Miller come to destroy me! Judge by that, whether I speak the truth!"

He climbed down painfully from the bench, and Summers hurried him into the shrubbery that grew thickly against the wall of the park. He felt Summers' hand, warmly tight about his arm; the pain that racked him in his urgent need for haste did not touch him.

"Golly, I'm glad to see you!" Summers whispered. "Kildering and I thought you had been shot, trying to jump in the river. Hurry. I've got a car over the wall!"

Mayor's face was white, streaked with sweat. "I did get shot," he said harshly. "Take it easy, man!"

Summers shook his head. "You can't delay. The cops are right behind us. Come on, over the wall! I'll lift you!"

Mayor glanced toward Summers then, for the first time, and his eyes widened with shock. Summers' youthfulness was gone from his face. His cheeks were drawn and gaunt, and he had a pallor that matched Mayor's own. There was a twitching at his mouth corner, and his eyes were shadowed.

There was no time for talk then, and Mayor struggled over the wall with Summers' help, stumbled into the car. Instantly, Summers had the engine roaring. They swept into a howling turn, then into a side street. A gun blasted out behind them, and a police whistle screamed. Then the sound was lost. Summers drove grimly, bent over the wheel. He was fumbling in his inside coat pocket, and he dumped a leather case on the seat.

"Give yourself a shot with that needle," Summers said, and his voice sounded strained.

Mayor opened the case slowly, looked down at a hypodermic, whose barrel already held fluid.

"What the hell?" he demanded.

"Morphine," Summers explained shortly. "Knock yourself out quickly, or it will be too late. As soon as John Miller hears of this, he'll set himself to drive you crazy. It isn't hard. All he has to do is think about it for a while. Morphine knocks out the conscious mind, nullifies the attack!"

Mayor fingered the hypodermic needle, deliberately rolled back his left sleeve. "So that's what's wrong with you, is it?" he asked somberly.

Summers' eyes glistened as they rolled toward the needle. He tongued his lips, and his mouth twitched more violently.

"Shoot yourself!" he ordered harshly. "Yes, that's what's wrong with me. Try shooting yourself with morphine two and three times a day for weeks. Damn it, Mayor—"

Bill Mayor jabbed the needle home, pressed down the plunger slowly. His own face was, suddenly, more haggard.

"And Kildering?" he asked slowly.

"Kildering isn't human," Summers said heavily. "He's damned near a superman himself, the way he stands it. He . . . never seems to sleep. Fill the needle again, Mayor, before you pass out. There's a vial there." He sighed. "Kildering saw the angel with the flaming sword face to face, with morphine already in him, but it didn't faze Kildering. That was when we murdered the mayor."

Mayor said shortly: "Miller had got to O'Shea, eh? I had to kill the commander of those troops out there. I heard about O'Shea. His home burned down, didn't it?"

"Kildering did that, too," he said. "Knocked me out to save me from the angel. Gambled on my recovering in time to carry him out before we were burned up alive. I had on a police uniform. Walked right through twenty cops with Kildering over my shoulder," Summers shook his head. "Kildering's arm hasn't been right since then, though. It's not healing as quickly as it should."

Mayor refilled the needle, put it away in its case and shoved it into Marty's inside pocket. His brain, for the moment, felt extraordinarily clear. The pain in his back was less.

"We can lick John Miller," he said steadily. "The three of us just got to keep preaching the truth. Get enough people stirred up, they'll throw off John Miller themselves."

Summers whipped around a corner on two wheels, cut through a narrow alley and doubled back the way he had come. "You can't throw off a man who doesn't seem even to exist," he said heavily. "They worship him in the churches here. We found his harem."

"By God!" Mayor cried. "Then we've got him!"

Marty smiled faintly. "It isn't that kind of harem," he said quietly. "It's a very efficient private hospital for the girls and women whom

John Miller selects. He's not a libertine, Bill. He just wants to produce as many children as possible, so there'll be more supermen."

"More supermen!" Mayor said dully. "But, good God, we can't go around killing babies!"

Mayor's mind was clouding. The pulsing roar of the motor lulled his senses.

Summers' mouth twitched. It was strangely like the grimace of Walter Kildering. "John Miller does, though," he said. "Miller kills all of his sons and daughters that don't come up to his standard. Don't know just how. Just looks at them, they say, and they die. We set a trap at the hospital one night, and John Miller almost got us. He was smart. Sent his madness to us, *before* he came there. We just managed to guess what was happening and take our shots in time. That's why we keep the needles charged now."

Mayor lolled back on the cushions and the pulsing roar of the motor moved inside of him. He was asleep.

Marty Summers looked at him and there was commiseration in his hollow eyes. "You poor devil," he said, "why in hell didn't you stay away?"

Mayor stirred a little. His fist knotted slowly. "John Miller!" he said. "Gotta destroy John Miller before he—"

He slumped back, and Summers sucked in a quivering sigh. He looked nervously about him. John Miller was working on Mayor now. If Miller decided to tackle him, too—Summers found himself grinding down on the gas. He smiled ruefully and eased off on it. You couldn't run away from Miller. He'd just have to take a chance on it, this time. He was defiant, reckless. To hell with Miller!

There was a haunting fear in his eyes.

Summers cut in behind the cottage where they had been living for two days. It was a terrific struggle to carry Bill Mayor into the house, but he managed it. He dumped him on the bed, stripped him and bent over the wound in Mayor's back. It was pretty badly inflamed. He dressed it.

Marty had just finished that job when he heard a car slide to a halt out back, and presently heard the quiet, tired steps of Walter Kildering. He straightened, sent his low shout through the house.

"Mayor's back!" he called.

Kildering came into the room slowly. "The cops are looking for him, because of that speech in the park," he said. "I was able to identify him from the description. Besides, I was expecting him after what happened to the State army last night. He did a good job there but it wasn't good enough."

Kildering dropped into a chair, tossed a newspaper to the bed. The headlines screamed:

ANGEL TURNS BACK ARMY!

ENTIRE FORCE WIPED OUT BY MASTER!

Kildering said heavily: "I wonder if anyone, anything, can be good enough to eliminate—John Miller."

Summers shook his head. "You can't even tell them that this 'angel' is Miller's psychic projection. They just glare at you and say, 'An angel is an angel!' Try and answer that one. Any luck?"

Kildering kneaded the hand of his broken arm. It was puffy, dry-looking. "I managed to see three big former land holders," he said. "They're willing enough to help—if there's no danger to themselves!" His voice sounded bitter. "What was Mayor's talk about in the park? The papers called it blasphemy."

Summers explained. "I think I may have hit on something, Kildering," he said slowly. "I checked up with twelve women who have lost babies. I'm pretty sure one of them knows Miller and can reach him."

Kildering's eyes sharpened. "Was she bitter?"

"No," said Summers finally.

Kildering got up and left the room. He began clattering pans in the kitchen of the house and Summers went in to help him. "Mayor should be coming around in an hour or so," he said. "That lighter shot you figured out worked on him just in time."

Kildering didn't answer. He was standing in the middle of the floor, with a frying pan in his hand. He stared at it, then moved slowly toward the stove.

"You give me that woman's name," he said curtly. "I'm going to see her."

Kildering went without waiting to eat, and Marty prepared a meal for Mayor and himself. Kildering came back just as they were sitting down to eat.

Kildering said somberly, "I think, before the night is over, that we'll see Miller!"

Mayor started to his feet, and his chair crashed to the floor. Summers' clenched fists rested on the table.

"When?" he asked harshly.

Kildering's face was grim. Color burned in his cheeks. "We'll get a call from a woman in about an hour. I'd better tell you what I did. I told this woman, whom Marty found, all about us, and how we were F. B. I. men intent on destroying John Miller. She wasn't, I discovered, interested in causing him trouble, but she was interested in doing him a favor—not that she said so.

"I told her that she need not fear the insanity or the death that Miller could send, that we had a protection against that. We have been operating here since before the Blue Death and have done a lot of things to hurt Miller. I told her what they were, and what our future plans are."

Summers said, incredulously, "Are you crazy, Kildering?"

Kildering just shook his head. "I told her what rewards she could gain, plus our protection, by telling us how to find John Miller. I insisted that we had the means to protect her against the 'angel with the flaming sword' and the insanity.

"When she tells John Miller about that, he'll believe her. He is undoubtedly aware of his failure to destroy us. Yes, I think that we can count on being led to Miller's hide-out."

Bill Mayor slumped into his chair. He said hoarsely: "You mean that you're deliberately allowing us to be led into a trap? A trap that will be set the way John Miller wants it? Good God, Kildering, this isn't an ordinary criminal you're playing with. It's . . . *it's John Miller!*"

Kildering's lips twisted. "Yes, I know. Also, it has become quite apparent that, unless John Miller wants us to find him, we will never succeed in doing it. This is the only way. To make John Miller *want* us to find him!"

"He'll destroy us!" Summers whispered it.

Kildering said: "Probably. You have a wife, Marty. Mayor, you're wounded. I'll go alone."

Mayor laughed. "You will, like hell!"

Summers was on his feet. "Listen, Kildering," he snapped. "You can't—"

Kildering leaned across the table and laid out his hand there, palm up. And he was smiling. His rare smile that could be so gentle.

"Forgive me," he said simply, "and be patient. I have so framed the information given to this woman that John Miller will be primarily interested in destroying me. He will believe that I alone know the method of protecting persons from his powers. So he will want to destroy me, first of all. If you decide, after I have finished talking, to help me, that will be your chance. You can start shooting the moment you see him. It should suffice."

Mayor said slowly, "You mean that, while he is killing you, we will kill him."

Kildering said quietly: "Something like that, though I doubt that either one of you would survive me very long in that event. A matter of precedence at the gates of hell. No more. It is the only way."

Summers echoed numbly, "Yes, the only way!" He thought for a moment of Anne, and felt a great emptiness in his chest. He said again, violently, "The only way!"

Kildering said: "The only way to destroy John Miller. But you still have the opportunity to drop out. No, let me explain."

Kildering leaned forward, rested his forehead against his hand.

"Mayor, you haven't seen much of Metropolis under Miller," he said. "It is a pretty happy place. There isn't much doubt that Miller's genius extends to government. This city is a perfect socialist State. What is more important is that it works! I don't know how much of that is attributable to John Miller's psychic powers and the religious worship with which people regard him. But it works. Now, remember that.

"John Miller destroyed the old city with fire; by psychic suggestion, he planned the new one. I can't prove it, but I'm convinced of the fact. The *modus operandi* was the same, and there was the same carelessness of human life.

"John Miller killed wholesale the lower mental stratum of life in the city. He is preventing the unfit from breeding. He has abolished banks and the banking practices which many people blame, in part, for the great depression. He has made the people happy and self-sufficient. He is educating them.

"The prisons and hospitals are empty, through his greater science."

Mayor spoke, with strain in his voice. "He is doing this to line his own pockets!"

Kildering looked up, his lips twitched. "Perhaps. I think the purpose for which he does all this is something more to be feared. Let me go on.

"The people have a large amount of freedom. I think they will have more when John Miller is secure against interference."

Mayor said violently: "You didn't see what he did to the governor of the State, to the people of Capital City, to the National Guard that was about to attack him!"

Summers said slowly, "You, Mayor, haven't seen Metropolis!"

Mayor whirled on him. "Are you defending John Miller?"

Summers' smile was faint. There was a twitching in his mouth corners and his eyes were haggard. Mayor looked at him, then caught Summers' arm.

"I'm sorry, old man. You've made a drug addict out of yourself, fighting him. Kildering—"

"Let me finish," Kildering said, and his voice was weary. "These are the things that John Miller has done. He has committed every crime in the statutes; he has violated human laws—but he has set up something like an ideal government, and the people are happy!

"You have to weigh these things at their full value, for I fully believe we hold John Miller's life in our hands."

Summers leaned forward. "What's the other side, Walter?"

Kildering started visibly at the sound of his own first name. He wasn't used to it, and for a moment his eyes were uncertain. He reached out and dropped a hand on Summers' wrist. His voice was deeper.

"The other side is simply this," he said. "It is the purpose for which John Miller is breeding so many sons and daughters."

"Purpose?" Summers' voice was vague, and his eyes were blank with inward thoughts.

"What purpose?" Mayor snapped.

Kildering's fist knotted slowly. "It's quite simple, isn't it?" he asked. "John Miller is establishing a race of supermen—to be served by the human race, as slaves!"

Mayor echoed the word blankly. His face flushed and he pitched to his feet.

"Slaves!" he repeated.

"Quite well cared for, probably very happy," Kildering said, "but none the less slaves. This is the purpose for which Miller builds. His violence against individuals has been passionless save when two F. B. I. men approached the mother of one of his children. She was—shall I say royalty? Then he used the 'mystery ray.' I think we can safely assume that those two comrades of ours, now dead, saw the 'angel with the flaming sword.'

"Miller will continue passionless, allowing people to worship him, destroying the unfit, spreading his perfect State over Wichinois, over the United States, over the world. The human slaves will serve and worship him!"

Mayor said hoarsely: "Good God! Even if we destroy John Miller, we can't stop that! There must be hundreds of supermen and super-women growing among us."

Summers said thickly: "I feel a little . . . sick. Do you think Miller is attacking?"

"He'll wait," Kildering said grimly. "Mayor, you forget one thing. A mutation can't breed true until the second generation, and then only a small percentage of the inbred stock will be supermen.

"Hundreds of them scattered over Wichinois. Supermen will recur among their children, but by that time the leavening of their inheritance may have lifted the human race to something more nearly approaching parity. Superman is, in any case, inevitable. With the multiplicity of X-ray and radium concentrations, mutations are bound to occur. Inevitably they will, sooner or later, assume the form of another superman. Our race must confront that as inescapable, and prepare for it."

Walter Kildering pushed himself to his feet. His bad arm was puffy and unhealthy, his face drawn as fine as platinum wire.

"There is one point I want to drive home," he said slowly. "It is more important than anything else. If you go with me, remember this: Our decision is made. John Miller must die—*but there must be not even one second's delay in shooting!*"

Mayor's eyes narrowed. "There is a reason for that?"

Kildering leaned forward. "Have you met any of the women whom John Miller has chosen?" he asked. "Have you met a man to whom the 'angel with the flaming sword' has appeared?"

Mayor said angrily, "Yes!"

"Then you understand," Kildering said, more slowly. "Men who meet John Miller worship him—*as dogs do men!*"

Kildering looked at Mayor and Summers fixedly, felt the resolution in their eyes.

"It is a thing to fear," he said finally. "We must shoot before we become—*dogs!*"

He sat down then, and his voice turned dull. "That's the whole picture, gentlemen. My own decision is made. The rest is up to you."

Mayor's lips pulled down thinly. He whipped out his revolver, swiftly checked its loading.

Summers was utterly pale. "I think we should each have two guns," he said harshly. "We don't know how many seconds we'll be able to shoot. An increased rate of fire is desirable!"

It was ridiculously easy, after all these weeks of futile battle, to trail the woman John Miller was supposed to love. The very ease of it was ominous in the extreme. The faces of the three men, in their trailing car, were pale and grim. Their eyes were a little blank, in the manner of men whose thoughts are all within themselves. But in the grimness of their set jaws, in the slow tension of all their movements their determination was written.

The woman they followed parked her car before an ordinary apartment building and went in, eagerly. Summers darted ahead and spotted the apartment to which she went.

"The second floor, a door right opposite the head of the steps," he reported.

Kildering nodded, and led the way up the stairs. Mayor hitched himself up by a violent grip upon the railing; Summers crowded close behind on the other side. So they reached the head of the steps and gazed at the door behind which they would find John Miller!

Kildering looked at Summers, held out his hand. He shook silently with Bill Mayor. There was no need for words. The men took a revolver in each fist, and that way they moved toward the door.

They were a tatterdemalion crew, these men who carried the hope of the human race in their hands. Kildering walked steadily, his head proud, his shoulders braced in a semblance of their old confidence. The sling of his broken arm was dirty, and the slash across his cheek had left a crimson, twisted scar.

On his left, Bill Mayor shuffled, and there was still the gaunt fury of a prophet about him. His long black hair was unkempt, and his bones seemed too large for his skin.

And Summers was thin and wasted. His face twitched with the jerk of drug-starved nerves. His eyes burned darkly. He seemed young again tonight, a kid bucking a game that was too tough for him. But fighting; in there, fighting.

They marched to the door like that, these three scarecrow men carrying the hope of the human race—the spirit of all the centuries to come.

Summers reached out to the door. His hand, clutching a gun, could just compass the doorknob, too. He looked at Kildering and met a nod, a slow, soft smile. He twisted the knob and threw the door wide.

The three men wedged into the apartment of John Miller. They raced forward. One of them shouted. Or perhaps it was all three of them together. It was despair, and rage, and rare courage. Humans, going into battle.

The door vibrated and closed.

It closed, and no guns spoke. Silence—and the door did not open. Time passed—and the door did not open.

When, finally, the knob turned, it was slowly. The movement of the door, swinging wide, was a deliberate thing; ceremonious.

Walter Kildering and Bill Mayor walked out together, quietly. They looked at each other, not speaking. Their faces were still drawn, still weary, but their eyes were shining.

Summers came afterward, and his head was lifted; his teeth glistened between faintly parted lips. It was as if he listened to far-off music.

Walter Kildering pulled back his shoulders. He glanced toward the door, closed now, and touched his two comrades on the arm to move them toward the steps.

"Come on, men," he said. "Come on. We have work to do—for the Master." His voice was reverent, as men speak in the presence of their God.

The three men moved down the steps softly, pride in the carriage of their heads. Three men going downstairs, happy in the service of their master, the service of John Miller; carrying down with them the hope of the human race—the spirit of all the centuries that might have come.

Three slaves.

Philtered Power

MALCOLM JAMESON

Unknown *specialized in turning conventional fantasy ideas inside out. Deals with the devil rarely led to any Faustian attainment, granted wishes invariably left characters moaning that they had never asked for their wishes, and supernatural creatures provoked more laughter than dread. "Philtered Power," Malcolm Jameson's exploration of what might happen if a love potion worked properly but in the wrong setting, is the sort of twist on a light fantasy staple that was tailor-made for John W. Campbell's magazine. A retired naval officer, Jameson contributed prolifically to* Weird Tales, Unknown, *and* Astounding Science-Fiction *up to his sudden death in 1945.*

IF!
If the State's gold mines had not played out, the assay office would not have become the sinecure it was. *If* the State had had an efficient government, the job would have been abolished decades before, instead of remaining one of the choicest plums at the disposal of the Hannigan machine. And *if* Doc Tannent had been any sort of chemist and had not been such a colorless, shy and helpless individual, he might have been able to hold a regular job somewhere and not be compelled to sponge on his wife's brother from time to time. And *if* the brother-in-

law had not been a clever lawyer and therefore able to get something on Hannigan, he would never have been in the position to demand that Hannigan "do something" for the estimable but ineffectual Doc Tannent.

So it was that Doc Tannent became State assayist.

Now, that is one of the cushiest, most innocuous berths in the United States, and there should have been no reason why the good doctor should not have settled down and enjoyed himself in idleness for the remainder of his life. If only the roof had not leaked, and if it had not been that he had the dizziest, most scatterbrained assistant assayist in the whole country to help him do nothing, the startling events of that summer would never have come about. Or even granting those two accessory "ifs," if Doc had been a golf player, no harm would have come of the appointment.

But he wasn't. He loathed golf. And, as the bard so charmingly puts it, thereby hangs a tale.

Doc Tannent was willing to have a soft job, but the assay office exceeded all expectations in that direction. There was absolutely nothing to do. There was no mail, no rocks to analyze or any chemicals to do it with. Except for keeping office hours and signing the pay roll twice a month, Doc had no duties—except, of course, the forwarding of the ten-percent "contribution" to Hannigan as he cashed each of his pay checks.

His helper, Elmer Dufoy, ne'er-do-well nephew of a United States senator, swept the place when the spirit moved him, or on rare occasions dusted off the tops of the obsolete books on metallurgy that graced the office's library. The laboratory was kept closed and locked, and the cases of mineral specimens in the halls needed no attention. When Elmer was not skylarking with the girls in the adjutant general's office across the road, he sometimes mixed up batches of a foul-smelling compound which his kid brother later peddled to farmers as horse liniment.

Such was the layout of the assay office, and such was the situation when Doc Tannent took over. He inspected his plant the first day, moved his belongings into his private office the next, and on the third day he became bored. For, for all his ineptness as a chemist and a human being, Doc was full of energy and liked to be doing something, if only pottering away at aimless experiments. So, being bored and having an ancient, disused laboratory at his elbow, Doc took up a hobby—a scientific hobby—and not golf, which is a much more efficient and safer method of killing time. That turned out to be a mistake, as Doc himself would be the first to admit, if it were not for the fact that today he is confined to the padded cell of Ward 8B of the State Hospital, complaining bitterly because no one will kill him as he deserves, or let him kill himself.

In the beginning he did not take the giddy Elmer into his confidence. All Elmer knew was that many strange parcels and boxes kept arriving and that Doc chose to unpack them himself and stow their contents away in the privacy of his own sanctum.

But one day a case arrived marked "Open Without Delay—Perishable," and since Doc was not in, Elmer undertook to unpack it, and looked for a place to put its contents. To his astonishment, the box was filled with recently dead frogs, and while he was still staring goggle-eyed at the heap of limp amphibians, little Doc Tannent came bustling in. Around Elmer, Doc did not exhibit the bashfulness and stammering he was noted for before strangers.

"Come, come," he said sharply, "get a jar and put them on the shelf beside the scorpions."

Shaking his head and muttering Elmer unlocked the gloomy laboratory and found a jar. An hour later he had finished helping Doc rearrange the curious contents of the private office, which Doc had rigged up for his experimentation.

Along one wall was a row of bins, and over them were shelves cluttered with jars and tins, and every container in the room bore a strange label. Such things were in Doc's hoard as camel's dung, powdered dried eyeballs of newts, tarantula fangs, dried bats' blood and tiger tendons. In the bottles were smelly concoctions marked "Theriac" this and that, and there were jugs filled with stuff like "Elixir of Ponie" and "Tincture Vervain," and there was a small beaker labeled "Pearl Solution." In addition there were tins of dried scorpions and crumbled serpent skins, and many more jars containing the organs of small animals, and each of them had a legend which described the animal and the time and circumstances of its death. One that Doc seemed to value highly read: "Gall of Black Cat. Killed in a churchyard on St. John's Eve; Moon new, Mars ascendant." It struck Elmer as a wee bit spooky, smacking of necromancy.

"Thank you," said Doc, when the queer substances had been neatly put in order. "A little later, when I have made more progress, I may ask you to help me now and then with my researches."

Elmer went away, mystified by the strange slant his new boss had taken. The last assay officer had not been that kind of scientist. He was a mathematician—had a system for doping out the chances of the ponies in today's race—and spent all his time tabulating track statistics and running the resultant data through some weird algebraic formulas. Elmer hadn't any too much respect for his various chiefs, as most of their hobbies worked out badly. He knew, for it had been his job to run down to the corner cigar store and place the former assayist's bets. He had picked up a nice piece of change a few times by placing a bet of his own—the boss' choice to lose.

"Another nut," he confided to Bettie Ellsworth, filing clerk for the adjutant general, but Bettie was not particularly impressed. It was axiomatic that anyone accepting the assayship would be a nut. So what?

Doc and Elmer broke the ice between them the day the long box arrived from Iceland. Elmer got the pinch bar and nail puller and ripped the cover off. Inside was a slender something wrapped in burlap and wire, and the invoice said: "One eight-foot unicorn horn, Grade A. Guaranteed by International Alchemical Supply, Inc." Elmer's eyes bugged at that. So! Magic and wizardry was Doc's racket. Alchemy!

But he shucked off the burlap and stood the thing up. It was a tapering ivory rod indented by a spiral groove running around it—obviously a tusk of the narwhale. Elmer had had to pass the civil-service test, being only an assistant, and knew a thing or two about elementary science, even if his uncle was a United States senator.

"Spu-spu-spu-splendid," stuttered Doc, delighted at its arrival. "Now I can go to work. Saw off a couple of feet of that and pulverize it for me—and get that heavy iron mortar and pestle out of the metallurgical lab. You'll need it. And be sure you keep the unicorn flour clean—impurities might spoil the outcome."

"O.K.," said Elmer, gayly, dashing off to the lab. He remembered vaguely that miraculous things could be done by alchemy and he had hopes that Doc might teach him a few tricks.

The next day Doc put him to work making a salve out of an aggregation of dried lizards, eagle claws, rose petals, rabbit fur and other such ingredients. While Elmer was stirring the mess in some gluey solvent, Doc dragged down a few of the big books he had bought recently, and laid them about the room, opened with markers lying in them. Then he set a beaker of greenish fluid to boil and scuttled from one of the huge tomes to another, writing copious memoranda on a pad of paper.

"You may think that alchemy is a lot of foolishness, Elmer," said Doc, as he sprinkled a handful of chopped cockscombs into the malodorous mixture boiling in the beaker, "and so it is—a blend of superstition and pompous nonsense. But some of these prescriptions were used for centuries to treat the sick, and believe it or not, some of them were actually helpful. I grant you that with most of the patients it made no difference whatever, and a sizable number of the others died, but why did some recover?"

Elmer shook his head, not stopping his whistling as he churned and kneaded the filthy compound under his mixing pestle.

"Unknown to the alchemists of the Middle Ages, some of the ingredients they used actually had therapeutic value. Take the Chinese. They brewed a tea from dried toads' skins and gave it to sufferers from heart trouble. It helped. That is because there are some glands in the neck of a frog that secrete a hormone something like digitalis, and that is what did the trick. Maybe there is something in the superstition held by some savages that eating the vital organs of your enemy makes you fiercer and stronger. Why not? When they ate the other fellow's kidneys, they ate his adrenal glands along with them. That ought to pep up anybody.

"This work I'm doing may bring to light some hormone we haven't discovered yet. Classical chemists say, of course, that there is no point in mixing these prescriptions—that all the ingredients have been analyzed and that those that are of any use are already in our pharmacopœia. But to my mind that is an inadequate argument. Analysis of metals tells you very little about the properties of alloys made by mixing them. So it is with these things. We have to mix them up and see what we get. That is the only way."

"Uh-huh," grunted Elmer, then sneezed violently. His annual attack of hay fever had announced its onset.

"Watch out," cautioned Doc, in some concern. "The humors, as they were called, of the body have a profound effect on these mixtures. Many of them call for human blood, or spittle, or such things. See, I have a bottle here of my own blood that I drained out of my arm for use wherever it is called for. So don't go sneezing into that salve— you might change its properties altogether."

"Yes, sir," moaned Elmer, and dragged out his handkerchief.

Elmer Dufoy let himself into Doc's office that night with his passkey and, after carefully shrouding the windows, turned on the light. It was the first time in the history of the assay office that any of its employees had worked overtime, but Elmer had a reason. He had peeked into one of Doc's big books and seen a page that stirred him strangely.

His courtship of Bettie Ellsworth was not going too smoothly. There was a hated rival, for one thing, and Bettie was naturally coy, for another. The page that had caught Elmer's eye was headed this way: "Love Potions and Philters. How the Spurned Suitor May Win the Coldest Damsel," and there followed similar provocative subtitles. Elmer's heart vibrated with expectancy as he hauled down the weighty volume and hastily scanned the pages.

He found what he was looking for, scribbled some notes and assembled the equipment. He robbed Doc's jars and bins of the necessary components of the stuff he was about to brew. He rigged a still, having already learned that that was the modern counterpart of the "alembic" the ancient tome called for. He found an aludel, and an athanor, and by midnight his love potion was sizzling away merrily. Even through his hay-fever-stricken nostrils he could tell it was potent. Anything that smelled like that must have a lot of power.

At last the time came for the personal touch, and Elmer jabbed a finger with his penknife and let the blood trickle slowly into a measuring glass. He added the few drams required, set the beaker on the window sill to cool, and idly strolled up and down the room, thinking contentedly of how easy the conquest of Bettie was going to be. After a while he thrummed through some of the other books to see what formulas they might contain.

There was the "Zekerboni" of Pierre Mora, books by Friar Bacon, Basilius Valentinus, Sendigovius, Rhasis and other outlandish names. He came upon four massive volumes by one Phillippus Aureolus Theophrastus Bombastus von Hohenheim and found that the short for it was Paracelsus. There were books in medieval German, Latin, and what looked to him like shorthand, but what a notation on the flyleaf said was Arabic.

He might have looked farther, but his solution had cooled and the hour was late. He drew off the clear liquid, as the directions prescribed, filtered it through powdered unicorn horn and added the four drops of a certain tincture. Then he bottled it and slipped it into his pocket, well satisfied that a happy home for life was to be his lot, commencing with tomorrow.

Although he had every confidence that he had followed the directions to the letter, he was not thoroughly convinced of the efficacy of his potion until he had administered it to his victim and seen with his own eyes the consequences. That night, sleepy as he was, he took her to a show and to a soda fountain afterward. Quickly, once when she turned her head away, he dumped the potion into her ice-cream soda. He watched eagerly as the liquid in the glass slowly began to fall, drawn away through the straw clamped between the two desired ruby lips.

"I think you're cute," she remarked, irrelevantly, after the first sip.

When the glass was half empty she suddenly bounced off her stool and flung her arms about his neck, kissing him wildly. "I love you, I love you, you wonderful boy!" she exclaimed, disregarding the other customers in the place.

"Drink it all, honey," said Elmer, grabbing the check and making ready for a fast getaway. They could discuss the rest of it somewhere other than the drugstore. There were a lot of people in the place.

Doc Tannent congratulated Elmer absent-mindedly when his helper informed him he was about to be married. Something new had turned up to make the assay officer preoccupied. The roof was leaking, and badly. Eight pounds of rare herbs had been spoiled by the water from the last rain, and two lots of salts ruined. The superintendent of public buildings had been over and after a look around shook his head. A new roof was needed, and that meant an appropriation. See Hannigan, was his suggestion.

It was at that time that the convention of the Coalition Party was due to be held in Cartersburg, and Hannigan would, of course, be there, as well as the governor, the members of the legislature and all the other politicos, both big shots and small fry. The annual convention was the whole works, as far as the government of the State was concerned. New office holders were picked and nominated, the pulse of the people was taken and new taxes were decided upon. The winter's legislation was planned, contracts were promised and appropriations doled out.

It was Hannigan's show, from first to last, and nobody else's. He made and broke everybody, from the governor down to the dog catchers; he decided what the people would stand for, and inside those limits he took a cut on every dollar the State took in and had another slice out of every cent the State paid out. When you wanted to get anything, you saw Hannigan, no matter who was the nominal boss. And Hannigan, a political boss of the old school, heavy-paunched and heavy-jowled, was no man to trifle with. "What's in it for me?" was his invariable question before discussing any subject, and he would tip the derby hat more on the back of his head, take a fresh bite on his fat, black cigar, and glare at the petitioner. If the answer was satisfactory, there would be a cynical wink, a slap on the back, and the matter was as good as done.

Doc Tannent's timidity and general incapacity came back on him with full force the moment it was suggested he go see Hannigan about the roof.

"Oh, let it go," he would say, whenever Elmer prodded him about it, for he dreaded the encounter with the wily politician at Cartersburg. But then it would rain again and his office would nearly get afloat. Elmer was thinking, too, of his approaching marriage. He wanted a raise, and wanted it so badly he was willing to kick in twenty percent of the gain in order to get it.

"Hannigan won't bite you," urged Elmer, wise in the way of the State's routine. "Just talk up to him. Lay your cards on the table; you don't have to be squeamish about mentioning money. He'll rebuild the building and double our salaries if you put it up the right way. If you hit a snag, send me a telegram. In a pinch my uncle might put in a word for us."

In the end Doc went, leaving Elmer, sniffling and sneezing, to hold down the assay office in his absence. Four days later Elmer received a doleful letter from his chief, stating in rather elaborate and antiquated English that he was being subjected to what the more terse moderns would simply call the "run-around." He hadn't been able to get near Hannigan. They had shunted him from one committee to another, and nobody would promise anything.

Elmer frowned at the letter as his vision of the little love nest he had planned began to dwindle. He was reaching for the phone to try to contact his powerful uncle in Washington when the happy thought hit him. Alchemy had got him a bride, why not the raise? He dropped everything and began a frenzied search of Doc's queer library.

What he wanted was not in Paracelsus nor yet in Sendigovius. He ran through many volumes before he found the Elizabethan translation of an obscure treatise written by a Portuguese monk. It dealt with charms and amulets chiefly, but there was a section on potions. Elmer sighed happily when he turned a page and saw staring him in the face the following caption: "For Courtiers and Supplicants Desirous of Winning the Favour of Monarchs and Potentates."

That was it. What he wanted exactly, for he knew from a letterhead that Hannigan was Grand Potentate of the Mystic Order of the Benevolent Phoenix. It was a natural, so to speak—supplicant, favor, and potentate—all the elements were there. He began scanning the list of ingredients.

That night he brought Bettie to the laboratory with him. She loved him so hard she could not bear to have him out of her sight. Together they mixed up the brew that was to make Hannigan eat out of Doc's hand.

First there was the heart of a dove, no color specified, to be stewed in the fat of a red bullock, calcined in an aludel with the kidney of a white hare and some virgin wax, and the resulting mess was to be treated elaborately in a retort together with sesame, ground pearls, and dill. Dill puzzled him until Bettie looked it up in another book and found out it came from a plant called *Anethum Graveolans.* The book explained that a pale-yellow aromatic oil was distilled from the seeds, and that it was good for flatulence.

"That ought not to hurt Doc or Hannigan either," grinned Elmer, when he found out that flatulence meant "windiness."

He dumped his mixture into a container, added the correct quantity of Doc's own blood, which was fortunately available, and shoved it into the queer antique furnace Doc had built and called an athanor. That was, as the directions said, "to rid it of its dross and bring it to a state of quintessence most pure." Patiently, hand in hand, the two lovebirds regulated the heat of the athanor as the sticky mess went through the successive states of purgation, sublimation, coagulation, assation, reverberation, dissolution, and finally descension.

It was midnight when the "descension" was completed, and after carefully blowing his nose Elmer broke the crust on his crucible and began to draw off the pale moss-green oil that was in it. There was enough to almost fill an eight-ounce bottle. It must have been of the quintessence most pure, for the stuff put in originally, counting a couple of pints of Theriac, would have filled a top hat. Elmer was very well pleased with himself. The Aromatick Unction looked exactly as the book said it should look. He tried to judge the odor of it, but his sense of smell was hopelessly wrecked by his hay fever.

"What do you think?" he asked, pushing the bottle under Bettie's nose.

"I think," said Bettie, with pronounced enthusiasm, "that Dr. Tannent is the wisest, kindest, most deserving man in the whole, whole world, and I would give him anything I owned. Why, he's—"

"Don't you think you're just a little susceptible, hon?" growled Elmer, not pleased at the implied comparison. Then he remembered that ice-cream soda. It was the potion! He couldn't smell it, but she could. He had hit another bull's-eye!

"Come on, baby, get your bag packed. We're going to Cartersburg."

On the bus Elmer studied the instructions. The alchemist who had first hit on the prescription evidently had thought of everything. The chances were that any courtier needing such a potion to get what he wanted was also in bad with the king, so that it was made potent enough to work through the air. The subject was to anoint himself thoroughly with the unction, and also carry a small vial of it in his hand. Properly prepared, the stuff would cause sentries and guards to bow reverently and make way, and it was solemnly assured that, once in the presence of the potentate, anything he asked would be granted. In proper strength, anything he wished for, even, would be granted without the asking.

"The raise is in the bag," Elmer told Bettie, giving her a little hug.

When they got to Cartersburg they found to their dismay that the convention had already met for the main event of the week—the nomination of the next governor—and the hall was packed to the doors. There was no admission without special tickets, and all those with authority to issue the tickets were already in the hall. Doc Tannent, apparently, was in there, too, perhaps still trying vainly to get in touch with Hannigan. Elmer considered anointing himself with the unction until he remembered that it was Doc's blood, not his, that was in the compound. Whatever effect it had would benefit only Doc.

He tried to get in the side door by slipping the doorman a little change, but the doorman said nothing doing. He took a try at the basement, but a gruff janitor shooed him away. Elmer backed away from the building and studied it from the far side of the street. That was when he noted the intake for the big blower fan on the roof, and saw that it was an easy step onto the parapet by it from the next-door office building. He grabbed Bettie's hand and made for the entrance to the office building.

They had little trouble getting into the intake duct. It was a huge affair of sheet metal, obviously part of the air-conditioning system, and its outer opening was guarded by coarse wire netting to keep out the bigger particles of trash, such as leaves and flying papers. Elmer, without a moment's hesitation, yanked out his knife and cut away an opening. He figured there would be a door into the duct somewhere to allow access to it for cleaners coming from the inside of the hall.

Elmer led the way, gingerly holding the bottle in one hand while clinging to the slippery wall of the duct with the other. Bettie stumbled along behind. It got darker as they went deeper, but presently Elmer saw the cleaning door he was looking for, only it was behind yet another filter, which meant another cutting job to do. A few yards beyond the door an enormous blower was sucking air into the auditorium, and the draft created by it was so strong that they were hard put at times to hold their footing on the slick metal deck under them. But Elmer tore at the second screen and worked his way through the opening in it.

For a moment he was convulsed with a miserable fit of sneezing and coughing, for in ripping apart the screen he had dislodged much dust. Then he started swearing softly but steadily. Bettie crawled through the hole after him and cuddled up to him consolingly.

"Whassa matta, sweeticums?" she cooed.

"Dropped the damn bottle," he snuffled, "and it busted all to hell."

He had. He struck some matches, but the wind blew them out. Then he worked the cleaning door open and a little light came in. All there was at his feet were some bits of broken glass—not so much as a smell of the precious Aromatick Unction was left. Elmer looked sheepishly at the remnants, and then, in an effort at being philosophical, he said:

"Oh, what the hell! Come on, as long as we're here, let's watch 'em nominate the new governor. It's fun to see the way Hannigan builds up his stooges. A coupla speeches is all it takes to turn a stuffed shirt into a statesman."

They wandered around the attic for five minutes or so before they found the steps that led down to the gallery of the hall. The gallery was packed, and they couldn't see at first because everybody there was jumping up and down and yelling his head off. That was surprising, for it generally took a nominating convention a couple of hours to get past the dry introductions before they uncorked their enthusiasm and really went to town. Then Elmer recognized that the yelling had settled down to a steady chanting. He heard the words, but didn't believe them—not at first. It just couldn't be. But what the crowd was calling, over and over again, were the words:

"We want Tannent! We want Tannent! We want Tannent!"

Then they stopped the yelling in unison and let go, every fellow for himself, in what is technically known as an ovation. A high voice from down on the main floor sang out, "Tannent—ain't he wonderful!" and right away the whole auditorium took that up and made it into another chant.

Elmer gave a startled look at Bettie, but she was as bad as the rest. He marveled that he had ever thought her beautiful when he looked at her red face, eyes bulging, and the veins standing out all over. She was yelling her lungs out for Tannent. A man on the other side slapped Elmer on the back and said something about what a grand guy Tannent was and what a swell governor he would make, and how happy he was to be able to vote for him. It was all so silly.

Elmer deserted Bettie and fought his way down the aisle until he reached the rail where he could look down onto the main floor. The band was playing "For He's a Jolly Good Fellow" and the shouting had reached heights of insane frenzy. Something unprecedented had stampeded this convention, and Elmer, as soon as he had taken the precaution to blow his nose once more and dab the water out of his bleary eyes, hung over the rail and tried to spot the center of the commotion.

He found it. Big Tim Hannigan was plowing his way through the dense crowd beneath. Doc Tannent was sitting piggyback on top of the boss' shoulders, smiling and bowing and waving to the crowd! Men went crazy as he passed, trying to get at him to shake his hand. Elmer went crazy, too—with amazement.

And then he tumbled. It was his philter—his potion to soften up the potentate and make him give what was asked for. When it had been spilled in the air intake, the conditioning system had spread it through the auditorium and everybody was affected. They were trying to give Doc what he wanted. It didn't matter what—just whatever he wanted. "Tell us, Doc," yelled one delegate, "what'll you have? If we've got it, it's yours!" It was a powerful philter. Not a doubt of that.

By that time the bigwigs were on the rostrum—Hannigan, the incumbent governor and some others. There was Doc, his bald head glistening and his little goatee bobbing up and down, making a speech of some sort, and not stammering while he did it, either. Hannigan, the big grafting gorilla, was at one side, beaming down on Doc with exactly the expression on his face that a fond mother wears when her baby boy steps out onto the stage at a parent-teacher's meeting to say a piece. And Hannigan's wasn't the only mug there like that. Everybody else looked the same way. Even the hard-boiled, sophisticated newspaper boys fell for the philter. The slush they sent their services that night cost several of them their jobs.

The old governor broke three or four gavels, pounding for order, but finally got enough quiet to scream out a few words. Elmer suddenly realized that Doc Tannent had already been nominated for governor; the hubbub he was witnessing was the celebration of it. Or maybe the crowd, in their unbridled enthusiasm, merely *thought* they had nominated him for governor. At any rate, this is what the old governor said:

"Please! Please! Let me say one word—"

(The crowd: "Go jump in the lake—scram—we want Tannent!")

"—I realize my administration has been a poor thing, but it was the best I could do. Now that we have nominated a *real* governor—"

(The crowd: "*Whee!* Hooray for Tannent!")

"—I resign here and now, to make way for him."

The crowd cut loose then and made its previous performance seem tame and lukewarm by comparison. Some kill-joy, probably another man with a bad cold, jumped up and remarked that the resignation of the governor accomplished nothing except the elevation of the old lieutenant governor to the highest office of the State. Whereupon the lieutenant governor promptly rose, flung his arms around Doc, and then announced that he had appointed Doc to be lieutenant governor. Whereupon *he* resigned. That made Doc the actual, constitutional governor—on the spot.

There was a brief flurry that marked the ejection of the kill-joy from the hall, and then the assembled delegates cast the last vestiges of reserve aside and proceeded to voice their happiness. The steel trusses overhead trembled with the vibration, and the walls shook.

Doc was governor! Elmer was stunned. He had wrought more than he intended. That "quintessence most pure" must have been simply crawling with hormones favorable to Doc.

But there was more to come. In the orgy of giving Doc what he wanted, or what they thought he wanted, the legislature resigned, one by one.

Then Doc appointed their successors on the spur of the moment— according to what system no one could guess. But nobody was sane enough to want to guess—except Elmer, and he was too astonished to think about a little thing like that.

What nearly bowled him over was the consummate poise and masterful manner of Doc himself. It was as if Caspar Milquetoast had elevated himself to a dictatorship, only he carried it off as if to the manner born. Elmer knew the answer to that, but he had not foreseen it. Doc had had a few whiffs of his own philter, and was in love with himself. He believed in himself, for the first time in his life, and it made a whale of a difference. He was bold, confident and serene.

Completely flabbergasted by the turn of events, Elmer turned and started to force his way up the aisle to where he had left Bettie, when a new roar broke through the reverberating hall. It was a new note, a superclimax if such a thing were possible. Elmer turned back and gripped the balcony rail, staring down.

Hannigan was on his feet, weeping like a brand snatched from the burning at an old-fashioned revival meeting. He was making a speech, if one could call such a sob-punctuated confession a speech, and it tore the lid right off the meeting. In the pandemonium of noise, Elmer could only catch a phrase here and there. "Clean government is what you want, and that is what you'll get . . . many times in the past I have . . . but now I bitterly regret it. My bank accounts are at the disposal of the State treasurer . . . will deed back the public lands I . . . glad of the opportunity to make restitution. I will give you a list, too, of the many unworthy appointments—"

Elmer slunk up the aisle; he could bear no more. It was all very confusing. He had counted on nothing like this. If Hannigan had turned saint, it was even a greater miracle than putting hair on the fumbling, shy little Doc's chest. Elmer shuddered at that last crack. Unworthy appointment, indeed! He must get hold of his uncle right away. He had quit worrying about whether the new governor would remember that he came to Cartersburg to get the raise for him; what concerned him now was whether he still had a job.

Eventually he found Bettie, exhausted and hysterically weeping. She was awfully happy about Tannent. Elmer grabbed her hand and dragged her from the place.

That was how Doc Tannent got to be governor.

No, Elmer didn't get the raise. He didn't need it. A week later Bettie quarreled violently with him. The day after that she pulled his hair, stamped on his foot, and scratched at his eyes. The day following she went after him with a knife and had carved several long gashes in him when the cops pulled her off and took her away.

Elmer, after they had finished bandaging him and put him to bed, told the attending physician the story of his conquest of Bettie. He could not understand her sudden revulsion to him. He even gave the doctor the list of ingredients in the love potion.

"That's bad," murmured the doctor, looking very profound. "Maybe it would be well if I took a blood specimen from her to see what's there."

A week later the doctor was back, and his expression was grave. He had with him a fourteen-page report from the biological bureau, and there was a lot in it about hormones and antibodies, toxins and antitoxins and other biological jargon.

"When she ingested that potion you gave her," said the doctor in his most severe manner, "she introduced in her system some strange and powerful organisms. Being a healthy girl, her body naturally resisted those foreign organisms. She built up antibodies to counteract them. It appears that she overdid. She is now immune to your influence."

"You mean," moaned Elmer, "she is going to *not* like me as much as she did like me?"

"Yes," said the doctor solemnly. "I am afraid that is the case. And it will be permanent. Fools, my boy, rush in where angels fear to tread."

Elmer closed his eyes and for a few minutes felt very faint. Then he suddenly thought of Doc Tannent, of whom he had said nothing to the hospital doctor. "Oh, gosh! Doc!" he wailed, and begged the nurse to let him put in a telephone call to the governor.

It was no good, though. The governor wouldn't receive the call. He was too big a man that week. It was not until the next week that the antibodies began to propagate inside the lads of the Hannigan gang. And then—oh, boy!

Armageddon

FREDRIC BROWN

The Devil is eternal, but each age finds new ways to thwart him. Some are ingenious, others the result of pure luck. Fredric Brown's "Armageddon" is a story about the latter method. A talented writer of fantasy and science fiction, Brown produced even more work in the mystery genre. No doubt it was his familiarity with the overworked and undervalued private detective character that led him to conclude how little the efforts of a hero like Herbie Westerman would be appreciated.

IT HAPPENED—of all places—in Cincinnati. Not that there is anything wrong with Cincinnati, save that it is not the center of the Universe, nor even of the State of Ohio. It's a nice old town and, in its way, second to none. But even its Chamber of Commerce would admit that it lacks cosmic significance. It must have been mere coincidence that Gerber the Great—what a name!—was playing Cincinnati when things slipped elsewhere.

Of course, if the episode had become known, Cincinnati would be the most famous city of the world, and little Herbie would be hailed as a modern St. George and get more acclaim, even, than a quiz kid. But no member of that audience in the Bijou Theater remembers a

336

thing about it. Not even little Herbie Westerman, although he had the water pistol to show for it.

He wasn't thinking about the water pistol in his pocket as he sat looking up at the prestidigitator on the other side of the footlights. It was a new water pistol, bought en route to the theater when he'd inveigled his parents into a side trip into the five-and-dime on Vine Street, but at the moment, Herbie was much more interested in what went on upon the stage.

His expression registered qualified approval. The front-and-back palm was no mystery to Herbie. He could do it himself. True, he had to use pony-sized cards that came with his magic set and were just the right size for his nine-year-old hands. And true, anyone watching could see the card flutter from the front-palm position to the back as he turned his hands. But that was a detail.

He knew, though, that front-and-back palming seven cards at a time required great finger strength as well as dexterity, and that was what Gerber the Great was doing. There wasn't a telltale click in the shift, either, and Herbie nodded approbation. Then he remembered what was coming next.

He nudged his mother and said, "Ma, ask Pop if he's gotta extra handkerchief."

Out of the corner of his eye, Herbie saw his mother turn her head and in less time than it would take to say "Presto" Herbie was out of his seat and skinning down the aisle. It had been, he felt, a beautiful piece of misdirection and his timing had been perfect.

It was at this stage of the performance—which Herbie had seen before, alone—that Gerber the Great asked if some little boy from the audience would step to the stage. He was asking it now.

Herbie Westerman had jumped the gun. He was well in motion before the magician had asked the question. At the previous performance, he'd been a bad tenth in reaching the steps from aisle to stage. This time he'd been ready, and he hadn't taken any chances with parental restraint. Perhaps his mother would have let him go and perhaps not; it had seemed wiser to see that she was looking the other way. You couldn't trust parents on things like that. They had funny ideas sometimes.

"—will please step up on the stage?" And Herbie's foot touched the first of the steps upward right smack on the interrogation point of that sentence. He heard the disappointed scuffle of other feet behind him, and grinned smugly as he went on up across the footlights.

It was the three-pigeon trick, Herbie knew from the previous performance, that required an assistant from the audience. It was almost the only trick he hadn't been able to figure out. There *must*, he knew, have been a concealed compartment somewhere in that box, but where it could be he couldn't even guess. By this time he'd be holding the box himself. If from that range, he couldn't spot the gimmick, he'd better go back to stamp collecting.

He grinned confidently up at the magician. Not that he, Herbie, would give him away. He was a magician, too, and he understood that there was a freemasonry among magicians and that one never gave away the tricks of another.

He felt a little chilled, though, and the grin faded as he caught the magician's eyes. Gerber the Great, at close range, seemed much older than he had seemed from the other side of the footlights. And somehow different. Much taller, for one thing.

Anyway, here came the box for the pigeon trick. Gerber's regular assistant was bringing it in on a tray. Herbie looked away from the magician's eyes and he felt better. He remembered, even, his reason for being on the stage. The servant limped. Herbie ducked his head to catch a glimpse of the under side of the tray, just in case. Nothing there.

Gerber took the box. The servant limped away and Herbie's eyes followed him suspiciously. Was the limp genuine or was it a piece of misdirection?

The box folded out flat as the proverbial pancake. All four sides hinged to the bottom, the top hinged to one of the sides. There were little brass catches.

Herbie took a quick step back so he could see behind it while the front was displayed to the audience. Yes he saw it now. A triangular compartment built against one side of the lid, mirror-covered, angles calculated to achieve invisibility. Old stuff. Herbie felt a little disappointed.

The prestidigitator folded the box, mirror-concealed compartment inside. He turned slightly. "Now, my fine young man—"

What happened in Tibet wasn't the only factor; it was merely the final link of a chain.

The Tibetian weather had been unusual that week, highly unusual. It had been warm. More snow succumbed to the gentle warmth than had melted in more years than man could count. The streams ran high, they ran wide and fast.

Along the streams some prayer wheels whirled faster than they had ever whirled. Others, submerged, stopped altogether. The priests, knee-deep in the cold water, worked frantically, moving the wheels nearer to shore where again the rushing torrent would turn them.

There was one small wheel, a very old one that had revolved without cease for longer than any man knew. So long had it been there that no living lama recalled what had been inscribed upon its prayer plate, nor what had been the purpose of that prayer.

The rushing water had neared its axle when the lama Klarath reached for it to move it to safety. Just too late. His foot slid in the slippery mud and the back of his hand touched the wheel as he fell. Knocked loose from its moorings, it swirled down with the flood, rolling along the bottom of the stream, into deeper and deeper waters.

While it rolled, all was well.

The lama rose, shivering from his momentary immersion, and went after other of the spinning wheels. What, he thought, could one small wheel matter? He didn't know that—now that other links had broken— only that tiny thing stood between Earth and Armageddon.

The prayer wheel of Wangur Ul rolled on, and on, until—a mile farther down—it struck a ledge and stopped. That was the moment.

"And now, my fine young man—"

Herbie Westerman—we're back in Cincinnati now—looked up, wondering why the prestidigitator had stopped in mid-sentence. He saw the face of Gerber the Great contorted as though by a great shock. Without moving, without changing, his face began to change. Without appearing different, it became different.

Quietly, then, the magician began to chuckle. In the overtones of that soft laughter was all of evil. No one who heard it could have doubted who he was. No one did doubt. The audience, every member of it, knew in that awful moment who stood before them, knew it— even the most skeptical among them—beyond shadow of doubt.

No one moved, no one spoke, none drew a shuddering breath. There are things beyond fear. Only uncertainty causes fear, and the Bijou Theater was filled, then, with a dreadful certainty.

The laughter grew. Crescendo, it reverberated into the far dusty corners of the gallery. Nothing—not a fly on the ceiling—moved.

Satan spoke.

"I thank you for your kind attention to a poor magician." He bowed, ironically low. "The performance is ended."

He smiled. "All performances are ended."

Somehow the theater seemed to darken, although the electric lights still burned. In dead silence, there seemed to be the sound of wings, leathery wings, as though invisible Things were gathering.

On the stage was a dim red radiance. From the head and from each shoulder of the tall figure of the magician there sprang a tiny flame. A naked flame.

There were other flames. They flickered along the proscenium of the stage, along the footlights. One sprang from the lid of the folded box little Herbie Westerman still held in his hands.

Herbie dropped the box.

Did I mention that Herbie Westerman was a Safety Cadet? It was purely a reflex action. A boy of nine doesn't know much about things like Armageddon, but Herbie Westerman should have known that water would never have put out that fire.

But, as I said, it was purely a reflex action. He yanked out his new water pistol and squirted it at the box of the pigeon trick. And the fire *did* vanish, even as a spray from the stream of water ricocheted and dampened the trouser leg of Gerber the Great, who had been facing the other way.

There was a sudden, brief, hissing sound. The lights were growing bright again, and all the other flames were dying, and the sound of wings faded, blended into another sound—the rustling of the audience.

The eyes of the prestidigitator were closed. His voice sounded strangely strained as he said: "This much power I retain. None of you will remember this."

Then, slowly, he turned and picked up the fallen box. He held it out to Herbie Westerman. "You must be more careful, boy," he said. "Now hold it so."

He tapped the top lightly with his wand. The door fell open. Three white pigeons flew out of the box. The rustle of their wings was not leathery.

Herbie Westerman's father came down the stairs and, with a purposeful air, took his razor strop off the hook on the kitchen wall.

Mrs. Westerman looked up from stirring the soup on the stove. "Why, Henry," she asked, "are you really going to punish him with that—just for squirting a little water out of the window of the car on the way home?"

Her husband shook his head grimly. "Not for that, Marge. But don't you remember we bought him that water gun on the way downtown, and that he wasn't near a water faucet after that? Where do you think he filled it?"

He didn't wait for an answer. "When we stopped in at the cathedral to talk to Father Ryan about his confirmation, that's when the little brat filled it. Out of the baptismal font! Holy water he uses in his water pistol!"

He clumped heavily up the stairs, strop in hand.

Rhythmic thwacks and wails of pain floated down the staircase. Herbie—who had saved the world—was having his reward.

Oscar

CLEVE CARTMILL

In science fiction circles, Cleve Cartmill will always be remembered as the author of "Deadline," the 1944 story that foretold the development of the atomic bomb and sent government agents to the editorial offices of Astounding Science-Fiction *looking for an information leak from the Manhattan Project. Ironically, several hardnosed science fiction buffs complained to editor John W. Campbell that the story read like a fantasy tale from* Unknown! *Cartmill did indeed contribute a number of fantasy stories to* Unknown *during the war years, but most of those were somber, novel-length works—quite unlike "Oscar," his first published story.*

PAUL ROCKEY parked his roadster in front of the beer joint. "She lives in that corner apartment house," he said. "We'll meet here, after."

"I'd like to raise an objection," Michael Corbyn said.

Terence Finnegan and Paul Rockey regarded Corbyn with patient annoyance. Corbyn's lean face flushed.

"My objection is valid," he protested. "Suppose this girl goes nuts. We'd be in a hell of a jam."

Terence Finnegan laid a large fatherly hand on Corbyn's shoulder.

"Mike, my son, we rehearsed for two hours with Elsie. Did she turn a hair? No. Nor will this friend of Paul's."

"Elsie is a tailor's dummy."

"Aren't all women?"

"Don't be so glib, Terry. I contend it's dangerous. According to Paul, this girl has occult leanings. She wants to believe in such phenomena as our imaginary Oscar. If we play our parts well enough, I tell you we're not running a risk."

"I'm not as concerned for Linda's sanity," Paul Rockey interposed, "as I am about your acting."

"O.K. Let's go."

In the third floor corridor of the apartment building, Paul Rockey rapped on a door. It was presently opened by a pretty brunette in blue slacks.

"Oh, good," she said. "Company."

The three young men trooped inside. Paul Rockey made a vague motion toward his companions.

"Linda, may I present Terry Finnegan, and—"

He broke off. Michael Corbyn was following an unseen something around the walls with cold, blue eyes.

Rockey cleared his throat. "Ah, er, Mike."

Corbyn started. "Sorry," he murmured to the girl. "How do you do?"

"—and Michael Corbyn. Linda Houseman."

Finnegan closed the door. He and Rockey exchanged a significant glance, turned compassionate eyes on Corbyn, shook their heads in brief pity. Linda, observing the by-play, frowned fleetingly and motioned them to chairs.

"Would you like a whiskey and soda?"

Three contented sighs were born.

As ice tinkled in the kitchen, Corbyn asked a question with his eyebrows. Two nods of affirmation answered him.

Linda brought a tray of drinks, tucked a leg under her on a divan, and raised her glass.

"Do we drink to something, or do we just drink?"

"To our beautiful barmaid," Corbyn responded. "My father told me only last week—"

"Last night you said he was killed in the Big Wind of 1906," Rockey interrupted.

"That wasn't the blow that killed father. He told me only last week that brunettes, as compared to blondes—"

He halted. Again his eyes followed an Unseen Something across the walls.

Rockey and Finnegan dropped embarrassed glances to their drinks.

Rockey made a hollow effort to break the tension. "What have you been doing lately, Linda?"

She, intent upon Corbyn, did not heed the question. Finnegan nodded at Rockey.

"He's got it again," Rockey said in disgust.

"Mike!" Finnegan snapped.

Corbyn jumped. Like a man awakening from heavy sleep, he blinked and gradually orientated himself.

"As I was saying," he mumbled, ". . . where was I?"

"I think we'd better explain," Rockey said to the wide-eyed Linda. "Mike thinks he's a psychic phenomenon. He has a familiar spirit, who, in a spirit of familiarity, he calls Oscar."

"Nuts!" Finnegan snorted. "There's nothing the matter with him, except he's crazy."

"He sees a Thing," Rockey continued smoothly. "It follows him. He can't or won't, describe it. It is not always visible. He sees it, or claims he does, only on some nights in an inclosure . . . a room, auditorium, or a similar place. It never manifests itself in daylight. Don't feel ill at ease. It never bothers anybody. Terry and I don't pay attention to it any more."

"All we can do," Finnegan added, "is apologize for him. Of course, this peculiarity of his distracts attention from some of his more obvious defects, and people get the impression that he's a pretty nice guy except for his fixation."

Michael Corbyn watched Linda narrowly during the conversation. When she looked at him, he spoke confidentially.

"I feel that we are kindred spirits, Miss Houseman. We know that forces, Beings, exist that cannot be explained in terms familiar to such clods as my friends. But you and I, and others like us . . . we know."

Linda's lips were parted, her forgotten drink clutched in both hands.

"Yes," she whispered. "Yes."

"Don't let him sell *you* on it, Miss Houseman," Finnegan said. "And drink your drink before it gets warm."

"Let's talk of something else," Rockey proposed. "If Mike gets started, he'll talk all night on other-plane Beings. I remember one drunk and stormy night—"

His voice died. His jaw dropped. His eyes, as Corbyn's had, followed an unseen Something along the base of a wall. He became rigid.

"What is this, a gag?" Finnegan snarled.

Corbyn flung him a smug and sardonic look. Linda's wide, dark eyes moved slowly from one to the other. With a slight shudder, she set aside her drink.

Rockey, in the manner of a sleep walker, set down his drink and walked stiffly from the apartment without a glance at Linda or a word of farewell.

"What the hell's the matter with you?" Finnegan snapped. "Where you going?"

After the door had closed behind Rockey, the three sat quietly. Corbyn's lips formed a faint smile. Finnegan gulped the last of his drink and set the glass on the floor. Linda's glance moved fearfully about the room, questing, searching each corner.

"This is a lot of nonsense!" Finnegan growled.

"Be a good boy, Oscar," Corbyn tossed over his shoulder at an empty corner.

"It's gone far enough," Finnegan continued. "I never told you before, Mike, but I think this is just a pose on your part to get attention you wouldn't receive otherwise because of a colorless and stupid nature. I'll grant that the accumulated effect of these painful incidents might persuade a weak-minded visionary like Paul that he saw something for a moment. Your low cunning broke through for an instant. Well, I resent this pose of yours, and you either drop it or I don't want your friendship." He paused. "May I have another drink, Miss Houseman?"

Linda took his glass solemnly and went into the kitchen. Corbyn and Finnegan grinned at each other.

When Linda came into the room again Finnegan smiled his thanks for the fresh drink and continued, directing his remarks at the girl. "Hope you'll excuse my vehemence, but I'm fed up with this gag. I don't like to be made feel a fool, and when Paul walked out of here like a corpse, it was embarrassing. If he had brains enough to come in out of an air raid, he'd have known he didn't see anything; he only thought he did. Mike doesn't see anything, either. He—"

Finnegan gasped. His eyes froze on Something in the kitchen doorway.

Corbyn turned lazily, looked toward the kitchen, and shrugged. Linda put a taut hand to her throat.

Finnegan got stiffly to his feet. With the glass still in his hand, he backed to the door. He reached behind him, opened it and backed into the hallway, his eyes still riveted on the kitchen entrance.

When the door closed, and the sound of his footsteps receded, Corbyn looked at his watch.

"Now we are alone with it," he said in sepulchral tones. "In five minutes it will be midnight, the end of an old day. This is the first time anyone else has ever seen Oscar. Perhaps that is an omen." He mused silently for a second. "Perhaps . . . this time . . . it won't follow me out."

"No . . . no!" Linda whimpered as he rose.

A strangling scream gurgled in her throat as she fastened her eyes on the kitchen doorway. Corbyn followed her glance. The short hairs on his neck stiffened, and a chill fluttered down his spine.

In the kitchen doorway squatted a dark Thing. It had two living snakes for arms, and a large green eye.

"Well?" it snarled in a hoarse voice. "Well?"

Shottle Bop

THEODORE STURGEON

If you aren't sure whether to laugh or shudder at the end of a Theodore Sturgeon story, it's a credit to Sturgeon's skill as a storyteller. He had a knack for finding the hilarious in the horrible, and for creating characters so deserving of sympathy that one can't help but feel sorry for them when they step into their screwy predicaments. One of the most popular authors to write for Unknown, *Sturgeon contributed fourteen stories ranging in mood from the zany "Yesterday Was Monday" to the horror classic, "It." "Shottle Bop," which appeared in the February 1941 issue, was one of his more lighthearted efforts, but it should convince anyone who chances upon a store with a sign reading "We Sell Bottles—With Things in Them" to walk on by.*

I'D NEVER seen the place before, and I lived just down the block and around the corner. I'll even give you the address, if you like. "The Shottle Bop," between Twentieth and Twenty-first Streets, on Tenth Avenue in New York City. You can find it if you go there looking for it. Might even be worth your while, too.

But you'd better not.

"The Shottle Bop." It got me. It was a small shop with a weather-beaten sign swung from a wrought crane, creaking dismally in the late

345

fall wind. I walked past it, thinking of the engagement ring in my pocket and how it had just been handed back to me by Audrey, and my mind was far removed from such things as shottle bops. I was thinking that Audrey might have used a gentler term than "useless" in describing me; and her neatly turned remark about my being a "constitutional psychopathic incompetent" was as uncalled-for as it was spectacular. She must have read it somewhere, balanced as it was by "And I wouldn't marry you if you were the last man on earth!" which is a notably worn cliché.

"Shottle Bop!" I muttered, and then paused, wondering where I had picked up such oddly rhythmic syllables with which to express myself. I'd seen it on that sign, of course, and it had caught my eye. "And what," I asked myself, "might be a Shottle Bop?" Myself replied promptly, "Dunno. Toddle back and have a look." So toddle I did, back along the east side of Tenth, wondering what manner of man might be running such an establishment in pursuance of what kind of business. I was enlightened on the second point by a sign in the window, all but obscured by the dust and ashes of apparent centuries, which read:

WE SELL BOTTLES

There was another line of smaller print there. I rubbed at the crusted glass with my sleeve and finally was able to make out

With things in them.

Just like that:

WE SELL BOTTLES
With things in them.

Well of course I went in. Sometimes very delightful things come in bottles, and the way I was feeling, I could stand a little delighting.

"Close it!" shrilled a voice, as I pushed through the door. The voice came from a shimmering egg adrift in the air behind the counter, low-down. Peering over, I saw that it was not an egg at all, but the bald pate of an old man who was clutching the edge of the counter, his scrawny body streaming away in the slight draft from the open door, as if he were made of bubbles. A mite startled, I kicked the door with my heel. He immediately fell on his face, and then scrambled smiling to his feet.

"Ah, it's so good to see you again," he rasped.

I think his vocal cords were dusty, too. Everything else here was. As the door swung to, I felt as if I were inside a great dusty brain that had just closed its eyes. Oh yes, there was light enough. But it wasn't the lamp light and it wasn't daylight. It was like—like light reflected from the cheeks of pale people. Can't say I enjoyed it much.

"What do you mean, 'again'?" I asked irritably. "You never saw me before."

"I saw you when you came in and I fell down and got up and saw you again," he quibbled, and beamed. "What can I foo for do?"

"Huh?" I huhed, and then translated it into "What can I do for you?"

"Oh," I said. "Well, I saw your sign. What have you got in a bottle that I might like?"

"What do you want?"

"What've you got?"

He broke into a piping chant—I remember it yet, word for word.

> *"For half a buck, a vial of luck*
> *Or a bottle of nifty breaks*
> *Or a flask of joy, or Myrna Loy*
> *For luncheon with sirloin steaks.*
>
> *"Pour out a mug from this old jug,*
> *And you'll never get wet in rains.*
> *I've bottles of grins and racetrack wins*
> *And lotions to ease your pains.*
>
> *"Here's bottles of imps and wet-pack shrimps*
> *From a sea unknown to man,*
> *And an elixir to banish fear,*
> *And the sap from the pipes of Pan.*
>
> *"With the powdered horn of a unicorn*
> *You can win yourself a mate;*
> *With the rich hobnob; or get a job—*
> *It's yours at a lowered rate."*

"Now wait right there!" I snapped. "You mean you actually sell dragon's blood and ink from the pen of Friar Bacon and all such mumbo-jum?"

He nodded rapidly and smiled all over his improbable face.

I went on—"The genuine article?"

He kept on nodding.

I regarded him for a moment. "You mean to stand there with your teeth in your mouth and your bare face hanging out and tell me that in this day and age, in this city and in broad daylight, you sell such trash and then expect me—me, an enlightened intellectual—"

"You are very stupid and twice as bombastic," he said quietly.

I glowered at him and reached for the doorknob—and there I froze. And I mean froze. For the old man whipped out an ancient bulb-type atomizer and squeezed a couple of whiffs at me as I turned away; and so help me, *I couldn't move!* I could cuss, though, and boy, did I.

The proprietor hopped over the counter and ran over to me. He must have been standing on a box back there, for now I could see he was barely three feet tall. He grabbed my coat tails, ran up my back and slid down my arm, which was extended doorward. He sat down on my wrist and swung his feet and laughed up at me. As far as I could feel, he weighed absolutely nothing.

When I had run out of profanity—I pride myself on never repeating a phrase of invective—he said, "Does that prove anything to you, my cocky and unintelligent friend? That was the essential oil from the hair of the Gorgon's head. And until I give you an antidote, you'll stand there from now till a week from text Nuesday!"

"Get me out of this," I roared, "or I smack you so hard you lose your brains through the pores in your feet!"

He giggled.

I tried to tear loose again and couldn't. It was as if all my epidermis had turned to high-carbon steel. I began cussing again, but quit in despair.

"You think altogether too much of yourself," said the proprietor of the Shottle Bop. "Look at you! Why, I wouldn't hire you to wash my windows. You expect to marry a girl who is accustomed to the least of animal comfort, and then you get miffed because she turns you down. Why does she turn you down? Because you won't get a job. You're a no-good. You're a bum. He, he! And you have the nerve to walk around pelling teople where to get off. Now if I were in your position I would ask politely to be released, and then I would see if anyone in this shop would be good enough to sell you a bottle full of something that might help out."

Now I never apologize to anybody, and I never back down, and I never take any guff from mere tradesmen. But this was different. I'd never been petrified before, nor had my nose rubbed in so many galling truths. I relented. "O.K., O.K.; let me break away then. I'll buy something."

"Your tone is sullen," he said complacently, dropping lightly to the floor and holding his atomizer at the ready. "You'll have to say 'Please. Pretty please.' "

"Pretty please," I said, almost choking with humiliation.

He went back of the counter and returned with a paper of powder which he had me sniff. In a couple of seconds I began to sweat, and my limbs lost their rigidity so quickly that it almost threw me. I'd have been flat on my back if the man hadn't caught me and solicitously led me to a chair. As strength dribbled back into my shocked tissues, it occurred to me that I might like to flatten this hobgoblin for pulling a trick like that. But a strange something stopped me—strange because I'd never had the experience before. It was simply the idea that once I got outside I'd agree with him for having such a low opinion of me.

He wasn't worrying. Rubbing his hands briskly, he turned to his shelves. "Now let's see . . . what would be best for you, I wonder? Hm-m-m. Success is something you couldn't justify. Money? You don't know how to spend it. A good job? You're not fitted for one." He turned gentle eyes on me and shook his head. "A sad case. *Tsk, tsk.*" I crawled. "A perfect mate? Uh-huh. You're too stupid to recognize perfection, too conceited to appreciate it. I don't think that I can— Wait!"

He whipped four or five bottles and jars off the dozens of shelves behind him and disappeared somewhere in the dark recesses of the store. Immediately there came sounds of violent activity—clinkings and little crashes; stirrings and then the rapid susurrant grating of a mortar and pestle; then the slushy sound of liquid being added to a dry ingredient during stirring; and at length, after quite a silence, the glugging of a bottle being filled through a filtering funnel. The proprietor reappeared triumphantly bearing a four-ounce bottle without a label.

"This will do it!" he beamed.

"That will do what?"

"Why, cure you!"

"Cure—" My pompous attitude, as Audrey called it, returned while he was mixing. "What do you mean cure? I haven't got anything!"

"My dear little boy," he said offensively, "you most certainly have. Are you happy? Have you ever been happy? No. Well, I'm going to fix all that up. That is, I'll give you the start you need. Like any other cure, it requires your co-operation.

"You're in a bad way, young fellow. You have what is known in the profession as retrogressive metempsychosis of the ego in its most malignant form. You are a constitutional unemployable; a downright sociophagus. I don't like you. Nobody likes you."

Feeling a little bit on the receiving end of a blitz, I stammered. "W-what do you aim to do?"

He extended the bottle. "Go home. Get into a room by yourself—the smaller the better. Drink this down, right out of the bottle. Stand by for developments. That's all."

"But—what will it do to me?"

"It will do nothing *to* you. It will do a great deal *for* you. It can do as much for you as you want it to. But mind me, now. As long as you use what it gives you for your self-improvement, you will thrive. Use it for self-glorification, as a basis for boasting, or for revenge, and you will suffer in the extreme. Remember that, now."

"But what is it? How—"

"I am selling you a talent. You have none now. When you discover what kind of a talent it is, it will be up to you to use it to your advantage. Now go away. I still don't like you."

"What do I owe you?" I muttered, completely snowed under by this time.

"The bottle carries its own price. You won't pay anything unless you fail to follow my directions. Now will you go, or must I uncork a bottle of jinn—and I don't mean London Dry?"

"I'll go," I said. I'd seen something swirling in the depths of a ten-gallon carboy at one end of the counter, and I didn't like it a bit. "Good-by."

"Bood-gy," he returned.

I went out and I headed down Tenth Avenue and I turned east up Twentieth Street and I never looked back. And for many reasons I wish now that I had, for there was, without doubt, something very strange about that Shottle Bop.

I didn't simmer down until I got home; but once I had a cup of black Italian coffee under my belt I felt better. I was skeptical about it at last. I was actually inclined to scoff. But somehow I didn't want to scoff too loudly. I looked at the bottle a little scornfully, and there was a certain something about the glass of it that seemed to be staring back at me. I sniffed and threw it up behind some old hats on top of the closet, and then sat down to unlax. I used to love to unlax. I'd put my feet on the doorknob and slide down in the upholstery until I was sitting on my shoulder blades, and as the old saying has it, "Sometimes I sets and thinks, and sometimes I just sets." The former is easy enough, and is what even an accomplished loafer has to go through before he reaches the latter and more blissful state. It takes years of practice to relax sufficiently to be able to "just set." I'd learned it years ago.

But just as I was about to slip into the vegetable status, I was annoyed by something. I tried to ignore it. I manifested a superhuman display of lack of curiosity, but the annoyance persisted. A light pressure on my elbow, where it draped over the arm of the chair. I was put in the unpleasant predicament of having to concentrate on what it was; and realizing that concentration on anything was the least desirable thing there could be. I gave up finally, and with a deep sigh, opened my eyes and had a look.

It was the bottle.

I screwed up my eyes and then looked again, but it was still there. The closet door was open as I had left it, and its shelf almost directly above me. Must have fallen out. Feeling that if the damn thing were on the floor it couldn't fall any farther, I shoved it off the arm of the chair with my elbow.

It bounced. It bounced with such astonishing accuracy that it wound up in exactly the same spot it had started from—on the arm of the easy-chair, by my elbow. Startled, I shoved it violently. This time I pushed it hard enough to send it against the wall, from which it rebounded to the shelf under my small table, and thence back to the chair arm—and this time it perched cozily against my shoulder. Jarred by the bouncing, the stopper hopped out of the bottle mouth and rolled into my lap; and there I sat, breathing the bitter-sweet fumes of its contents, feeling frightened and silly as hell.

I grabbed the bottle and sniffed. I'd smelled that somewhere before—where was it? Uh—oh, yes; that mascara the Chinese honkytonk girls use in Frisco. The liquid was dark—smoky black. I tasted it cautiously. It wasn't bad. If it wasn't alcoholic, then the old man in the shop had found a darn good substitute for alcohol. At the second sip I liked it and at the third I really enjoyed it and there wasn't any fourth because by then the little bottle was a dead marine. That was about the time I remembered the name of the black ingredient with the funny smell. Kohl. It is an herb the Orientals use to make it possible to see supernatural beings. Silly superstition!

And then the liquid I'd just put away, lying warm and comfortable in my stomach, began to fizz. Then I think it began to swell. I tried to get up and couldn't. The room seemed to come apart and throw itself at me piecemeal, and I passed out.

Don't you ever wake up the way I did. For your own sake, be careful about things like that. Don't swim up out of a sodden sleep and look around you and see all those things fluttering and drifting and flying and creeping and crawling around you—puffy things dripping blood, and filmy, legless creatures, and little bits and snatches of pasty human anatomy. It was awful. There was a human hand afloat in the air an inch away from my nose; and at my startled gasp it drifted away from me, fingers fluttering in the disturbed air from my breath. Something veined and bulbous popped out from under my chair and rolled across the floor. I heard a faint clicking, and looked up into a gnashing set of jaws without any face attached. I think I broke down and cried a little. I know I passed out again.

The next time I awoke—must have been hours later, because it was broad daylight and my clock and watch had both stopped—things were a little better. Oh, yes, there were a few of the horrors around. But somehow they didn't bother me much now. I was practically convinced that I was nuts; now that I had the conviction, why worry about it? I dunno; it must have been one of the ingredients in the bottle that had calmed me down so. I was curious and excited, and that's about all. I looked around me and I was almost pleased.

The walls were green! The drab wallpaper had turned to something breathtakingly beautiful. They were covered with what seemed to be moss; but never moss like that grew for human eyes to see before. It was long and thick, and it had a slight perpetual movement—not that of a breeze, but of growth. Fascinated, I moved over and looked closely. Growing indeed, with all the quick magic of spore and cyst and root and growth again to spore; and the swift magic of it was only a part of the magical whole, for never was there such a green. I put out my hand to touch and stroke it, but I only felt the wallpaper. But when I closed my fingers on it, I could feel that light touch of it in the palm of my hand, the weight of twenty sunbeams, the soft resilience of jet-darkness in a closed place. The sensation was a delicate ecstasy, and never have I been happier than I was at that moment.

Around the baseboards were little snowy toadstools, and the floor was grassy. Up the hinged side of the closet door climbed a mass of flowering vines, and their petals were hued in tones indescribable. I felt as if I had been blind until now, and deaf, too; for now I could hear the whispering of scarlet, gauzy insects among the leaves and the constant murmur of growth. All around me was a new and lovely world, so delicate that the wind of my movements tore petals from the flowers, so real and natural that it defied its own impossibility. Awestruck, I turned and turned, running from wall to wall, looking under my old furniture, into my old books; and everywhere I looked I found newer and more beautiful things to wonder at. It was while I was flat on my stomach looking up at the bed springs, where a colony of jewellike lizards had nested, that I first heard the sobbing.

It was young and plaintive, and had no right to be in my room where everything was so happy. I stood up and looked around, and there in the corner crouched the translucent figure of a little girl. She was leaning back against the wall. Her thin legs were crossed in front of her, and she held the leg of a tattered toy elephant dejectedly in one hand and cried into the other. Her hair was long and dark, and it poured and tumbled over her face and shoulders.

I said, "What's the matter, kiddo?" I hate to hear a child cry like that.

She cut herself off in the middle of a sob and shook the hair out of her eyes, looking up and past me, all fright and olive skin and big, filled violet eyes. "Oh!" she squeaked.

I repeated, "What's the matter? Why are you crying?"

She hugged the elephant to her breast defensively, and whimpered, "W-where are you?"

Surprised, I said, "Right here in front of you, child. Can't you see me?"

She shook her head. "I'm scared. Who are you?"

"I'm not going to hurt you. I heard you crying, and I wanted to see if I could help you. Can't you see me at all?"

"No," she whispered. "Are you an angel?"

I guffawed. "By no means!" I stepped closer and put my hand on her shoulder. The hand went right through her and she winced and shrank away, uttering a little wordless cry. "I'm sorry," I said quickly. "I didn't mean . . . you can't see me at all? I can see you."

She shook her head again. "I think you're a ghost," she said.

"Do tell!" I said. "And what are you?"

"I'm Ginny," she said. "I have to stay here, and I have no one to play with." She blinked, and there was a suspicion of further tears.

"Where did you come from?" I asked.

"I came here with my mother," she said. "We lived in lots of other rooming houses. Mother cleaned floors in office buildings. But this is where I got so sick. I was sick a long time. Then one day I got off the bed and came over here, but then when I looked back I was still on the bed. It was awful funny. Some men came and put the 'me' that was on the bed onto a stretcher-thing and took it—me—out. After a while Mummy left, too. She cried for a long time before she left, and when I called to her she couldn't hear me. She never came back, and I just got to stay here."

"Why?"

"Oh, I got to. I—don't know why. I just—got to."

"What do you do here?"

"I just stay here and think about things. Once a lady lived here, had a little girl just like me. We used to play together until the lady watched us one day. She carried on somethin' awful. She said her little girl was possessed. The girl kept callin' me, 'Ginny! Ginny! Tell Mamma you're here!'; an' I tried, but the lady couldn't see me. Then the lady got scared an' picked up her little girl an' cried, an' so I was sorry. I ran over here an' hid, an' after a while the other little girl forgot about me, I guess. They moved," she finished with pathetic finality.

I was touched. "What will become of you, Ginny?"

"I dunno," she said, and her voice was troubled. "I guess I'll just stay here and wait for Mummy to come back. I been here a long time. I guess I deserve it, too."

"Why, child?"

She looked guiltily at her shoes. "I couldn' stand feelin' so awful bad when I was sick. I got up out of bed before it was time. I shoulda stayed where I was. This is what I get for quittin'. But Mummy'll be back; just you see."

"Sure she will," I muttered. My throat felt tight. "You take it easy, kid. Any time you want someone to talk to, you just pipe up. I'll talk to you any time I'm around."

She smiled, and it was a pretty thing to see. What a raw deal for a kid! I grabbed my hat and went out.

Outside things were the same as in the room to me. The hallways, the dusty stair carpets wore new garments of brilliant, nearly intangible foliage. They were no longer dark, for each leaf had its own pale and different light. Once in a while I saw things not quite so pretty. There was a giggling thing that scuttled back and forth on the third floor landing. It was a little indistinct, but it looked a great deal like Barrelhead Brogan, a shanty-Irish bum who'd returned from a warehouse robbery a year or so ago, only to shoot himself accidentally with his own gun. I wasn't sorry.

Down on the first floor, on the bottom step, I saw two youngsters sitting. The girl had her head on the boy's shoulder, and he had his arms around her, and I could see the banister through them. I stopped to listen. Their voices were faint, and seemed to come from a long way away.

He said, "There's one way out."

She said, "Don't talk that way, Tommy!"

"What else can we do? I've loved you for three years, and we still can't get married. No money, no hope—no nothing. Sue, if we did do it, I just *know* we'd always be together. Always and always—"

After a long time she said, "All right, Tommy. You get a gun, like you said." She suddenly pulled him even closer. "Oh, Tommy, are you sure we'll always be together just like this?"

"Always," he whispered, and kissed her. "Just like this."

Then there was a long silence, while neither moved. Suddenly they were as I had first seen them, and he said:

"There's only one way out."

And she said, "Don't talk that way, Tommy!"

And he said, "What else can we do? I've loved you for three years—" It went on like that, over and over and over.

I felt lousy. I went on out into the street.

It began to filter through to me what had happened. The man in the shop had called it a "talent." I couldn't be crazy, could I? I didn't *feel* crazy. The draught from the bottle had opened my eyes on a new world. What was this world?

It was a thing peopled by ghosts. There they were—storybook ghosts, and regular haunts, and poor damned souls—all the fixings of a storied supernatural, all the things we have heard about and loudly disbelieve and secretly wonder about. So what? What had it all to do with me?

As the days slid by, I wondered less about my new, strange surroundings, and gave more and more thought to that question. I had bought—or been given—a talent. I could see ghosts. I could see all parts of a ghostly world, even the vegetation that grew in it. That was perfectly reasonable—the trees and birds and fungi and flowers. A ghost world is a world as we know it, and a world as we know it must have vegetation. Yes, I could see them. But they couldn't see me!

O.K.; what could I get out of it? I couldn't talk about it or write about it because I wouldn't be believed; and besides, I had this thing exclusive, as far as I knew; why cut a lot of other people in on it?

On what, though?

No, unless I could get a steer from somewhere, there was no percentage in it for me that I could see. And then, about six days after I took that eye-opener, I remember the one place where I might get that steer. The Shottle Bop!

I was on Sixth Avenue at the time, trying to find something in a five-and-dime that Ginny might like. She couldn't touch anything I brought her but she enjoyed things she could look at—picture books and such. By getting her a little book of photographs of trains since the "De Witt Clinton," and asking her which of them was like ones she had seen, I found out approximately how long it was she'd been there. Nearly eighteen years. Anyway, I got my bright idea and headed for Tenth Avenue and the Shottle Bop. I'd ask that old man—he'd tell me.

At the corner of Ninth Avenue I bumped into Happy Sam Healy and Fred Bellew. Fred was good people, but I never had much use for Happy Sam. He went for shaggy hats and lapelled vests, and he had patent-leather hair and too much collar-ad good looks. I was in a hurry and didn't want to talk to anyone, but Sam grabbed me by the arm.

"Slow down, mug, slow down! Long time no see. Where you bound in such a hurry?"

"Going over to Tenth to see a man about you."

Sam quit grinning and Fred walked over. "Why can't you guys quit knocking each other?" he asked quietly.

If it weren't for Fred, Sam and I would have crossed bows even more than we did, which was still altogether too much.

"I'll always speak civilly to a human being," I said. "Sam's different."

Sam said, "Don't set yourself up, chum. I'm cutting some ice with a certain party that froze you out."

"If you say exactly what you mean, I'll probably rap you for it," I flared.

Fred pushed hastily between us. "I'll see you later, Sam," he said. He pushed me with some difficulty away from the scene.

Sam stood staring after us for a minute and then put his hands in his pockets, shrugged, grinned, and went jauntily his own way.

"Aw, why do you always stand in front of that heel when I want to scrape him off the sidewalk?" I complained.

"Calm down, you big lug," Fred grinned. "That bantam wants trouble with you because of Audrey. If you mess him up, he'll go running to her about it, and you'll be really out."

"I am ready, so what?"

He glanced at me. "That's up to you." Then, seeing my face, he said quickly, "O.K., don't tell me. It's none of my business. I know. How've you been?"

I was quiet for a while, walking along. Fred was a darn good egg. You could tell a guy like that practically anything. Finally I said, "I'm looking for a job, Fred."

He nodded, "Thought you would. Doing what?" Anybody else, knowing me, would have hooted and howled.

"Well, I—" Oh, what the hell, I thought, I'll tell him. If he thinks I'm nuts, he won't say so to anyone but me. Old Fred didn't look like much, with his sandy hair and his rimless specs and those stooped shoulders that too much book reading gave him, but he had sense.

"I was walking down Tenth," I began—

By the time I had come to the part about the ghost of the kid in my room, we had reached Tenth Avenue in the late Twenties, and turned south. I wasn't paying much attention to where we were, to tell you the truth, and that's why what happened did happen.

Before I had a chance to wind up with the question that was bothering me—"I have it . . . what will I do with it?" Fred broke in with "Hey! Where is this place of yours?"

"Why—between Nineteenth and Twentieth," I said. "Holy smoke—we're at Eighteenth! We walked right past it!"

Fred grinned and swung around. We went back up the avenue with our eyes peeled, and not a sign of the Shottle Bop did we see. For the first time a doubtful look crept onto Fred's bland face. He said:

"You wouldn't kid me, would you, lug?"

"I tell you—" I began.

Then I saw a penny lying on the sidewalk. I bent to pick it up, and heard him say, "Hey! There it is! Come on."

"Ah! I knew it was on this block!" I said, and turned toward Fred. Or where Fred had been. Facing me was a blank wall. The whole side of the block was void of people. There was no sign of a shop or of Fred Bellew.

I stood there for a full two minutes not even daring to think. Then I walked downtown toward Twentieth, and then uptown to Twenty-first. Then I did it again. No shop. No Bellew.

I stood frothing on the uptown corner. What had that guy done; hopped a passing truck or sunk into the ground or vanished into the shop? Yeah; and no shop there! A wise guy after all. I trod the beat once more with the same results. Then I headed for home. I hadn't gone twenty feet when I heard the pound of someone running, and Fred came panting up and caught my shoulder. We both yelped at once—"Hey! Where've you been?"

I said, "What was the idea of ducking out like that? Man, you must've covered a hundred yards in about six seconds to get away from me while I picked up a penny off the sidewalk!"

"Duck out nothing!" said Bellew, angrier than I'd ever seen him. "I saw the store and went in. I thought you were right behind me. I look around and you're outside, staring at the shop like it was something you didn't believe. Then you walk off. Meanwhile the little guy in the store tries to sell me some of his goods. I stall him off, still looking for you. You walk past two or three times, looking in the window. I call you; you don't bat an eyelash. I tell the little guy: 'Hold on—I'll be back in a second with my friend there.' He rears back on his heels and laughs like a maniac and waves me out. Come on, dope. Let's go back. That old man really has something there. I'd say I was in the market for some of that stuff of his!"

"O.K., O.K.," I said. "But Fred—I'll swear I didn't see the place. Come on then; lead me to it. I must be going really screwball."

"Seems like," said Fred.

So we went back, and there was no shop at all. Not a sign of one. And then and there we had one pip of an argument. He said I'd lied about it in the first place, and I said, well, why did he give me that song-and-dance about his seeing it, and he said it was some kind of a joke I'd pulled on him; and then we both said, "Oh, yeah?" a couple of times and began to throw punches. I broke his glasses for him. He had them in his pocket and fell down on them. I wound up minus a very good friend and without my question answered—what was I going to do with this "talent"?

I was talking to Ginny one afternoon about this and that when a human leg, from the knee down, complete and puffy, drifted between us. I recoiled in horror, but Ginny pushed it gently with one hand. It bent under the touch, and started toward the window, which was open a little at the bottom. The leg floated toward the crack and was sucked through like a cloud of cigarette smoke, reforming again on the other side. It bumbled against the pane for a moment and then ballooned away.

"My gosh!" I breathed. "What *was* that?"

Ginny laughed. "Oh, just one of the Things that's all 'e time flying around. Did it scare you? I used to be scared, but I saw so many of them that I don't care any more, so's they don't light on me."

"But what in the name of all that's disgusting are they?"

"Parts." Ginny was all childish savoir-faire.

"Parts of what?"

"People, silly. It's some kind of a game, *I* think. You see, if someone gets hurt and loses something—a finger or an ear or something, why, the ear—the *inside* part of it, I mean, like me being the inside of the 'me' they carried out of here—it goes back to where the person who owned it lived last. Then it goes back to the place before that, and so on. It doesn't go very fast. Then when something happens to a whole person, the 'inside' part comes looking for the rest of itself. It picks up bit after bit—Look!" She put out a filmy forefinger and thumb and nipped a flake of gossamer out of the air.

I leaned over and looked closely; it was a small section of semi-transparent human skin, ridged and whorled.

"Somebody must have cut his finger," said Ginny matter-of-factly, "while he was living in this room. When something happens to um— you see! He'll be back for it!"

"Good heavens!" I said. "Does this happen to everyone?"

"I dunno. Some people have to stay where they are—like me. But I guess if you haven't done nothing to deserve bein' kept in one place, you have to come all around pickin' up what you lost."

I'd thought of more pleasant things in my time.

For several days I'd noticed a gray ghost hovering up and down the block. He was always on the street, never inside. He whimpered constantly. He was—or had been—a little inoffensive man of the bowler hat and starched collar type. He paid no attention to me—none of them did, for I was apparently invisible to them. But I saw him so often that pretty soon I realized that I'd miss him if he went away. I decided I'd chat with him the next time I saw him.

I left the house one morning and stood around for a few minutes in front of the brownstone steps. Sure enough, pressing through the flotsam of my new, weird coexistent world, came the slim figure of the wraith I had noticed, his rabbit face screwed up, his eyes deep and sad, and his swallowtail coat and striped waistcoat immaculate. I stepped up behind him and said, "Hi!"

He started violently and would have run away, I'm sure, if he'd known where my voice was coming from.

"Take it easy, pal," I said. "I won't hurt you."

"Who are you?"

"You wouldn't know if I told you," I said. "Now stop shivering and tell me about yourself."

He mopped his ghostly face with a ghostly handkerchief, and then began fumbling nervously with a gold toothpick. "My word," he said. "No one's talked to me for years. I'm not quite myself, you see."

"I see," I said. "Well, take it easy. I just happen to've noticed you wandering around here lately. I got curious. You looking for somebody?"

"Oh, no," he said. Now that he had a chance to talk about his troubles, he forgot to be afraid of this mysterious voice from nowhere that had accosted him. "I'm looking for my home."

"Hm-m-m," I said. "Been looking a long time?"

"Oh, yes." His nose twitched. "I left for work one morning a long time ago, and when I got off the ferry at Battery Place I stopped for a moment to watch the work on that new-fangled elevated railroad they were building down there. All of a sudden there was a loud noise— my goodness! It was terrible—and the next thing I knew I was standing back from the curb and looking at a man who looked just like me! A girder had fallen, and—my word!" He mopped his face again. "Since then I have been looking and looking. I can't seem to find anyone who knows where I might have lived, and I don't understand all the things I see floating around me, and I never thought I'd see the day when grass would grow on lower Broadway—oh, it's terrible." He began to cry.

I felt sorry for him. I could easily see what had happened. The shock was so great that even his ghost had amnesia! Poor little egg—until he was whole, he could find no rest. The thing interested me. Would a ghost react to the usual cures for amnesia? If so, then what would happen to him?

"You say you got off a ferryboat?"

"Yes."

"Then you must have lived on the Island . . . Staten Island, over there across the bay!"

"You really think so?" He stared through me, puzzled and hopeful.

"Why sure! Say, how'd you like me to take you over there? Maybe we could find your house."

"Oh, that would be splendid! But—oh, my, what will my wife say?"

I grinned. "She might want to know where you've been. Anyway, she'll be glad to have you back, I imagine. Come on; let's get going!"

I gave him a shove in the direction of the subways and strolled along behind him. Once in a while I got a stare from a passer-by for walking with one hand out in front of me and talking into thin air. It didn't bother me very much. My companion, though, was very self-conscious about it, for the inhabitants of his world screeched and giggled when they saw him doing practically the same thing. Of all humans, only I was invisible to them, and the little ghost in the bowler hat blushed from embarrassment until I thought he'd burst.

We hopped a subway—it was a new experience for him, I gathered—and went down to South Ferry. The subway system in New York is a very unpleasant place to one gifted as I was. Everything that enjoys lurking in the dark hangs out there, and there is quite a crop of dismembered human remains. After this day I took the bus.

We got a ferry without waiting. The little gray ghost got a real kick out of the trip. He asked me about the ships in the harbor and their flags, and marveled at the dearth of sailing vessels. He *tsk, tsked* at the Statue of Liberty; the last time he had seen it, he said, was while it still had its original brassy gold color, before it got its patina. By this I placed him in the late '70s; he must have been looking for his home for over sixty years!

We landed at the Island, and from there I gave him his head. At the top of Fort Hill he suddenly said, "My name is John Quigg. I live at 45 Fourth Avenue!" I've never seen anyone quite so delighted as he was by the discovery. And from then on it was easy. He turned left, and then right, and then left again, straight down for two blocks and again right. I noticed—he didn't—that the street was marked "Winter Avenue." I remembered vaguely that the streets in this section had been numbered years ago.

He trotted briskly up the hill and then suddenly stopped and turned vaguely. "I say, are you still with me?"

"Still here," I said.

"I'm all right now. I can't tell you how much I appreciate this. Is there anything I could do for you?"

I considered. "Hardly. We're of different times, you know. Things change."

He looked, a little pathetically, at the new apartment house on the corner and nodded. "I think I know what happened to me," he said softly. "But I guess it's all right. . . . I made a will, and the kids were grown." He sighed. "But if it hadn't been for you I'd still be wandering around Manhattan. Let's see—ah; come with me!"

He suddenly broke into a run. I followed as quickly as I could. Almost at the top of the hill was a huge old shingled house, with a silly cupola and a complete lack of paint. It was dirty and it was tumble-down, and at the sight of it the little fellow's face twisted sadly. He gulped and turned through a gap in the hedge and down beside the house. Casting about in the long grass, he spotted a boulder sunk deep into the turf.

"This is it," he said. "Just you dig under that. There is no mention of it in my will, except a small fund to keep paying the box rent. Yes, a safety-deposit box, and the key and an authorization are under that stone. I hid it"—he giggled—"from my wife one night, and never did get a chance to tell her. You can have whatever's any good to you."

He turned to the house, squared his shoulders, and marched in the side door, which banged open for him in a convenient gust of wind. I listened for a moment and then smiled at the tirade that burst forth. Old Quigg was catching real hell from his wife, who'd sat waiting for over sixty years for him! It was a bitter stream of invective, but—well, she must have loved him. She couldn't leave the place until she was complete, if Ginny's theory was correct, and she wasn't really complete until her husband came home! It tickled me. They'd be all right now!

I found an old pinchbar in the drive and attacked the ground around the stone. It took quite a while and made my hands bleed, but after a while I pried the stone up and was able to scrabble around under it. Sure enough, there was an oiled silk pouch under there. I caught it up and carefully unwrapped the strings around it. Inside was a key and a letter addressed to a New York bank, designating only "Bearer" and authorizing use of the key. I laughed aloud. Little old meek and mild John Quigg, I'd bet, had set aside some "mad money." With a layout like that, a man could take a powder without leaving a single sign. The son-of-a-gun! I would never know just what it was he had up his sleeve, but I'll bet there was a woman in the case. Even fixed it up with his will! Ah, well—I should kick!

It didn't take me long to get over to the bank. I had a little trouble getting into the vaults, because it took quite a while to look up the box in the old records. But I finally cleared the red tape, and found myself the proud possessor of just under eight thousand bucks in small bills—and not a yellowback among 'em!

Well, from then on I was pretty well set. What did I do? Well, first I bought clothes, and then I started out to cut ice for myself. I clubbed around a bit and got to know a lot of people, and the more I knew the more I realized what a lot of superstitious dopes they were. I couldn't blame anyone for skirting a ladder under which crouched a genuine basilisk, of course, but what the heck—not one in a thousand have beasts under them! Anyway, my question was answered. I dropped two grand on an elegant office with drapes and dim indirect lighting, and I got me a phone installed and a little quiet sign on the door— Psychic Consultant. And, boy, I did all right.

My customers were mostly upper crust, because I came high. It was generally no trouble to get contact with people's dead relatives, which was usually what they wanted. Most ghosts are crazy to get in contact with this world anyway. That's one of the reasons that almost anyone can become a medium of sorts if he tries hard enough; Lord knows that it doesn't take much to contact the average ghost. Some, of course, were not available. If a man leads a pretty square life, and kicks off leaving no loose ends, he gets clear. I never did find out where these clear spirits went to. All I knew was that they weren't to be contacted. But the vast majority of people have to go back and tie up those loose ends after they die—righting a little wrong here, helping someone they've hindered, cleaning up a bit of dirty work. That's where luck itself comes from, I do believe. You don't get something for nothing.

If you get a nice break, it's been arranged that way by someone who did you dirt in the past, or someone who did wrong to your father or your grandfather or your great-uncle Julius. Everything evens up in the long run, and until it does, some poor damned soul is wandering around the earth trying to do something about it. Half of humanity is walking around crabbing about its tough breaks. If you and you and you only knew what dozens of powers were begging for the chance to help you if you'll let them! And if you let them, you'll help clear up the mess they've made of their lives here, and free them to go wherever it is they go when they're cleaned up. Next time you're in a jam, go away somewhere by yourself and open your mind to these folks. They'll cut in and guide you all right, if you can drop your smugness and your mistaken confidence in your own judgment.

I had a couple of ghostly stooges to run errands for me. One of them, an ex-murderer by the name of One-eye Rachuba, was the fastest spook ever I saw, when it came to locating a wanted ancestor; and then there was Professor Grafe, a frog-faced teacher of social science who'd embezzled from a charity fund and fallen into the Hudson trying to make a getaway. He could trace the most devious genealogies in mere seconds, and deduce the most likely whereabouts of the ghost of a missing relative. The pair of them were all the office force I could use, and although every time they helped out one of my clients they came closer to freedom for themselves, they were both so entangled with their own sloppy lives that I was sure of their services for years.

But do you think I'd be satisfied to stay where I was, making money hand over fist without really working for it? Oh, no. Not me. No, I had to big-time. I had to brood over the events of the last few months, and I had to get dramatic about that screwball Audrey, who really wasn't worth my trouble. I had to lie awake nights thinking about Happy Sam and his gibes. It wasn't enough that I'd proved Audrey wrong when she said I'd never amount to anything. I wasn't happy when I thought about Sam and the eighteen a week he pulled down driving a light delivery truck. Uh-huh. I had to show them up.

I even remembered what the little man in the Shottle Bop had said to me about using my "talent" for bragging or for revenge. That didn't make any difference to me. I figured I had the edge on everyone, everything. Cocky, I was. Why, I could send one of my ghostly stooges out any time and find out exactly what anyone had been doing three hours ago come Michaelmas. With the shade of the professor at my shoulder, I could back-track on any far-fetched statement and give immediate and logical reasons for back-tracking. No one had anything on me, and I could out-talk, out-maneuver, and out-smart anyone on earth. I was really quite a feller. I began to think, "What's the use of my doing as well as this when the gang on the West Side don't know anything about it?" and "Man, would that half-wit Happy Sam burn up if he saw me drifting down Broadway in my new eight-thousand-dollar roadster!" and "To think I used to waste my time and tears on a dope like Audrey!" In other words, I was tripping up on an inferiority complex. I acted like a veridam fool, which I was. I went over to the West Side.

It was a chilly, late winter night. I'd taken a lot of trouble to dress myself and my car so we'd be bright and shining and would knock some eyes out. Pity I couldn't brighten my brains up a little.

I drove up in front of Casey's pool room, being careful to do it too fast, and concentrating on shrieks from the tires and a shuddering twenty-four-cylinder roar from the engine before I cut the switch. I didn't hurry to get out of the car, either. Just leaned back and lit a fifty-cent cigar, and then tipped my hat over one ear and touched the horn button, causing it to play "Tuxedo Junction" for forty-eight seconds. Then I looked over toward the pool hall.

Well, for a minute I thought that I shouldn't have come, if that was the effect my return to the fold was going to have. And from then on I forgot about anything except how to get out of here.

There were two figures slouched in the glowing doorway of the pool room. It was up a small side street, so short that the city had depended on the place, an old institution, to supply the street lighting. Looking carefully, I made out one of the silhouetted figures as Happy Sam, and the other was Fred Bellew. They just looked out at me; they didn't move; they didn't say anything, and when I said, "Hiya, small fry— remember me?" I noticed that along the darkened walls flanking the bright doorway were ranked the whole crowd of them—the whole gang. It was a shock; it was a little too casually perfect. I didn't like it.

"Hi," said Fred quietly. I knew he wouldn't like the big-timing. I didn't expect any of them to like it, of course, but Fred's dislike sprang from distaste, and the others' from resentment, and for the first time I felt a little cheap. I climbed out over the door of the roadster and let them have a gander at my fine feathers.

Sam snorted and said, "Jellybean!" very clearly. Someone else giggled, and from the darkness beside the building came a high-pitched, "Woo-woo!"

I walked up to Sam and grinned at him. I didn't feel like grinning. "I ain't seen you in so long I almost forgot what a heel you were," I said. "How you making?"

"I'm doing all right," he said, and added offensively, "I'm still *working* for a living."

The murmur that ran through the crowd told me that the really smart thing to do was to get back into that shiny new automobile and hoot along out of there. I stayed.

"Wise, huh?" I said weakly.

They'd been drinking, I realized—all of them. I was suddenly in a spot. Sam put his hands in his pockets and looked at me down his nose. He was the only short man that ever could do that to me. After a thick silence he said:

"Better get back to yer crystal balls, phony. We like guys that sweat. We even like guys that have rackets, if they run them because they're smarter or tougher than the next one. But luck and gab ain't enough. Scram."

I looked around helplessly. I was getting what I'd begged for. What had I expected, anyway? Had I thought that these boys would crowd around and shake my hand off for acting this way? There was something missing somewhere, and when I realized what it was, it hit me. Fred Bellew—he was just standing there saying nothing. The old equalizer wasn't functioning any more. Fred wasn't aiming to stop any trouble between me and Sam. I was never so alone in my life!

They hardly moved, but they were all around me suddenly. If I couldn't think of something quickly, I was going to be mobbed. And when those mugs started mobbing a man, they did it up just fine. I drew a deep breath.

"I'm not asking for anything from you, Sam. Nothing; that means advice, see?"

"You're gettin' it!" he flared. "You and your seeanses. We heard about you. Hanging up widow-women for fifty bucks a throw to talk to their 'dear departed'! P-sykik investigator! What a line! Go on; beat it!"

I had a leg to stand on now. "A phony, huh? Why you gabby Irishman, I'll bet I could put a haunt on you that would make that hair of yours stand up on end, if you have guts enough to go where I tell you to."

"You'll bet? That's a laugh. Listen at that, gang." He laughed, then turned to me and talked through one side of his mouth. "All right, you wanted it. Come on, rich guy; you're called. Fred'll hold the stakes. How about ten of your lousy bucks for every one of mine? Here, Fred—hold this sawbuck."

"I'll give you twenty to one," I said half hysterically. "And I'll take you to a place where you'll run up against the homeliest, plumb-meanest old haunt you ever heard of."

The crowd roared. Sam laughed with them, but didn't try to back out. With any of that gang, a bet was a bet. He'd taken me up, and he'd set odds, and he was bound. I just nodded and put two century notes into Fred Bellew's hand. Fred and Sam climbed into the car, and just as we started, Sam leaned out and waved.

"See you in hell, fellas," he said. "I'm goin' to raise me a ghost, and one of us is going to scare the other one to death!"

I honked my horn to drown out the whooping and hollering from the sidewalk and got out of there. I turned up the parkway and headed out of town.

"Where to?" Fred asked after a while.

"Stick around," I said, not knowing.

There must be some place not far from here where I could find an honest-to-God haunt, I thought, one that would make Sam back-track and set me up with the boys again. I opened the compartment in the dashboard and let Ikey out. Ikey was a little twisted imp who'd got his tail caught in between two sheets of steel when they were assembling the car, and had to stay there until it was junked.

"Hey, Ike," I whispered. He looked up, the gleam of the compartment light shining redly in his bright little eyes. "Whistle for the professor, will you? I don't want to yell for him because those mugs in the back seat will hear me. They can't hear you."

"O.K., boss," he said; and putting his fingers to his lips, he gave vent to a blood-curdling, howling scream.

That was the prof's call-letters, as it were. The old man flew ahead of the car, circled around and slid in beside me through the window, which I'd opened a crack for him.

"My goodness," he panted, "I wish you wouldn't summon me to a location which is traveling with this high degree of celerity. It was all I could do to catch up with you."

"Don't give me that, professor," I whispered. "You can catch a stratoliner if you want to. Say, I have a guy in the back who wants to get a real scare from a ghost. Know of any around here?"

The professor put on his ghostly pince-nez. "Why, yes. Remember my telling you about the Wolfmeyer place?"

"Golly—he's bad."

"He'll serve your purpose admirably. But don't ask me to go there with you. None of us ever associates with Wolfmeyer. And for Heaven's sake, be careful."

"I guess I can handle him. Where is it?"

He gave me explicit directions, bade me good night and left. I was a little surprised; the professor traveled around with me a great deal, and I'd never seen him refuse a chance to see some new scenery. I shrugged it off and went my way. I guess I just didn't know any better.

I headed out of town and into the country to a certain old farmhouse. Wolfmeyer, a Pennsylvania Dutchman, had hung himself there. He had been, and was, a bad egg. Instead of being a nice guy about it all, he was the rebel type. He knew perfectly well that unless he did plenty of good to make up for the evil, he'd be stuck where he was for the rest of eternity. That didn't seem to bother him at all. He got surly and became a really bad spook. Eight people had died in that house since the old man rotted off his own rope. Three of them were tenants who had rented the place, and three were hobos, and two were psychic investigators. They'd all hung themselves. That's the way Wolfmeyer worked. I think he really enjoyed haunting. He certainly was thorough about it anyway.

I didn't want to do any real harm to Happy Sam. I just wanted to teach him a lesson. And look what happened!

We reached the place just before midnight. No one had said much, except that I told Fred and Sam about Wolfmeyer, and pretty well what was to be expected from him. They did a good deal of laughing about it, so I just shut up and drove. The next item of conversation was Fred's, when he made the terms of the bet. To win, Sam was to stay in the house until dawn. He wasn't to call for help and he wasn't to leave. He had to bring in a coil of rope, tie a noose in one end and string the other up on "Wolfmeyer's Beam"—the great oaken beam on which the old man had hung himself, and eight others after him. This was as an added temptation to Wolfmeyer to work on Happy Sam, and was my idea. I was to go in with Sam, to watch him in case the thing became dangerous. Fred was to stay in the car a hundred yards down the road and wait.

I parked the car at the agreed distance and Sam and I got out. Sam had my tow rope over his shoulder, already noosed. Fred had quieted down considerably, and his face was dead serious.

"I don't think I like this," he said, looking up the road at the house. It hunched back from the highway, and looked like a malign being deep in thought.

I said, "Well, Sam? Want to pay up now and call it quits?"

He followed Fred's gaze. It sure was a dreary-looking place, and his liquor had fizzed away. He thought a minute, then shrugged and grinned. I had to admire the rat. "Hell, I'll go through with it. Can't bluff me with scenery, phony."

Surprisingly, Fred piped up, "I don't think he's a phony, Sam. He showed me something one day, over on Tenth Avenue. A little store. There was something funny about it. We had a little scrap afterward, and I was sore for a long time, but—I think he has something there."

The resistance made Sam stubborn, though I could see by his face that he knew better. "Come on, phony," he said and swung up the road.

We climbed into the house by way of a cellar door that slanted up to a window on the first floor. I hauled out a flashlight and lit the way to the beam. It was only one of many that delighted in turning the sound of one's footsteps into laughing whispers that ran round and round the rooms and halls and would not die. Under the famous beam the dusty floor was dark-stained.

I gave Sam a hand in fixing the rope, and then clicked off the light. It must have been tough on him then. I didn't mind, because I knew I could see anything before it got to me, and even then, no ghost could see me. Not only that, for me the walls and floors and ceilings were lit with the phosphorescent many-hued glow of the ever-present ghost plants. For its eerie effect I wished Sam could see the ghost-molds feeding greedily on the stain under the beam.

Sam was already breathing heavily, but I knew it would take more than just darkness and silence to get his goat. He'd have to be alone, and then he'd have to have a visitor or so.

"So long, kid," I said, slapping him on the shoulder; and I turned and walked out of the room.

I let him hear me go out of the house and then I crept silently back. It was without doubt the most deserted place I have ever seen. Even ghosts kept away from it, excepting, of course, Wolfmeyer's. There was just the luxurious vegetation, invisible to all but me, and the deep silence rippled by Sam's breath. After ten minutes or so I knew for certain that Happy Sam had more guts than I'd ever have credited him with. He had to be scared. He couldn't—or wouldn't—scare himself.

I crouched down against the wall of an adjoining room and made myself comfortable. I figured Wolfmeyer would be along pretty soon. I hoped earnestly that I could stop the thing before it got too far. No use in making this any more than a good lesson for a wiseacre. I was feeling pretty smug about it all, and I was totally unprepared for what happened.

I was looking toward the doorway opposite when I realized that for some minutes there had been the palest of pale glows there. It brightened as I watched; brightened and flickered gently. It was green, the green of things moldy and rotting away; and with it came a subtly harrowing stench. It was the smell of flesh so very dead that it had ceased to be really odorous. It was utterly horrible, and I was honestly scared out of my wits. It was some moments before the comforting thought of my invulnerability came back to me, and I shrank lower and closer to the wall and watched.

And Wolfmeyer came in.

His was the ghost of an old, old man. He wore a flowing, filthy robe, and his bare forearms thrust out in front of him were stringy and strong. His head, with its tangled hair and beard, quivered on a broken, ruined neck like the blade of a knife just thrown into soft wood. Each slow step as he crossed the room set his head to quivering again. His eyes were alight; red they were, with deep green flames buried in them. His canine teeth had lengthened into yellow, blunt tusks, and they were like pillars supporting his crooked grin. The putrescent green glow was a horrid halo about him. He was a bright and evil thing.

He passed me, completely unconscious of my presence, and paused at the door of the room where Sam waited by the rope. He stood just outside it, his claws extended, the quivering of his head slowly dying. He stared in at Sam, and suddenly opened his mouth and howled. It was a quiet, deadly sound, one that might have come from the throat of a distant dog, but, though I couldn't see into the other room, I knew that Sam had jerked his head around and was staring at the ghost. Wolfmeyer raised his arms a trifle, seemed to totter a bit, and then moved into the room.

I snapped myself out of the crawling terror that gripped me and scrambled to my feet. If I didn't move fast—

Tiptoeing swiftly to the door, I stopped just long enough to see Wolfmeyer beating his arms about erratically over his head, a movement that made his robe flutter and his whole figure pulsate in the green light; just long enough to see Sam on his feet, wide-eyed, staggering back and back toward the rope. He clutched his throat and opened his mouth and made no sound, and his head tilted, his neck bent, his twisted face gaped at the ceiling as he clumped backward away from the ghost and into the ready noose. And then I leaned over Wolfmeyer's shoulder, put my lips to his ear, and said:

"*Boo!*"

I almost laughed. Wolfmeyer gave a little squeak, jumped about ten feet, and, without stopping to look around, hightailed out of the room so fast that he was just a blur. That was one scared old spook!

At the same time Happy Sam straightened, his face relaxed and relieved, and sat down with a bump under the noose. That was as close a thing as ever I want to see. He sat there, his face soaking wet with cold sweat, his hands between his knees, staring limply at his feet.

"That'll show you!" I exulted, and walked over to him. "Pay up, scum, and may you starve for that week's pay!" He didn't move. I guess he was plenty shocked.

"Come on!" I said. "Pull yourself together, man! Haven't you seen enough? That old fellow will be back any second now. On your feet!"

He didn't move.

"Sam!"

He didn't move.

"*Sam!*" I clutched at his shoulder. He pitched over sideways and lay still.

He was quite dead.

I didn't do anything and for a while I didn't say anything. Then I said hopelessly, as I knelt there, "Aw, Sam. Sam—cut it out, fella."

After a minute I rose slowly and started for the door. I'd taken three steps when I stopped. Something was happening! I rubbed my hand over my eyes. Yes, it—it was getting dark! The vague luminescence of the vines and flowers of the ghost-world was getting dimmer, fading, fading—

But that had never happened before!

No difference. I told myself desperately, it's happening now, all right. *I got to get out of here!*

See? You see? It was the stuff—that damn stuff from the Shottle Bop. It was wearing off! When Sam died it . . . it stopped working on me! Was this what I had to pay for the bottle? Was this what was to happen if I used it for revenge?

The light was almost gone—and now it was gone. I couldn't see a thing in the room but one of the doors. Why could I see that doorway? What was that pale-green light that set off its dusty frame?

Wolfmeyer!

I got to get out of here!

I couldn't see ghosts any more. Ghosts could see me now. I ran. I darted across the dark room and smashed into the wall on the other side. I reeled back from it, blood spouting from between the fingers I slapped to my face. I ran again. Another wall clubbed me. Where was that other door? I ran again, and again struck a wall. I screamed and ran again. I tripped over Sam's body. My head went through the noose. It whipped down on my windpipe, and my neck broke with an agonizing crunch. I floundered there for half a minute, and then dangled.

Dead as hell, I was. Wolfmeyer, he laughed and laughed.

Fred found me and Sam in the morning. He took our bodies away in the car. Now I've got to stay here and haunt this damn old house. Me and Wolfmeyer.

Mr. Arson

L. SPRAGUE DE CAMP

L. Sprague de Camp's stories virtually defined Unknown's *brand of "logical fantasy." At the same time, they reflected a scholarly interest in history, philology, mathematics, science, and the arts that placed them among the most literate and creative fantasy of that era. De Camp's forte was the alternate world story, in which a character from our world tries to adapt to another world that closely resembles our own—except for one fundamental and perplexing difference. In the three Harold Shea novels that de Camp co-wrote with Fletcher Pratt for* Unknown, *the hero is portrayed as a vain, egotistical bumbler whose amusing efforts to master an environment where science works like magic and magic like science meet with only minimal success. While "Mr. Arson" is not one of de Camp's alternate world stories, it shares with them the figure of the typical de Camp hero, for whom a little knowledge is a humorous thing.*

A S CLEM BUCKMINSTER, M. H. S. I. salesman for the Bronx, hung up a slightly overheated telephone, his superior cocked an eye at him and asked: "Was that the Dangerous Dane?"

Buckminster snickered dutifully. "Yeah, that was Grinnig. He's all excited about somepin. He wants me to come—"

"Does he want to shift his course again?" inquired the sales manager for the New York district.

370

"No; least he didn't say that. He wouldn't tell—"

"I've told you before, Clem," continued Andrews, "that this business of signing Grinnig up for a new course every month has got to stop. Let him finish one of the old ones. He's begun courses in—let me see—air conditioning, highway engineering, structural drafting, fruit growing, welding, and oil heating, and he's never gotten beyond the first lesson of any."

"But," pleaded Buckminster, "every time he finishes the first lesson, he calls me in and says, 'To hell with it. Gimme another.' 'Scuse me, Miss Cope." The last was to Andrews' secretary. "What can I do?"

"Let him slide. He's not the type that can benefit from a correspondence course."

"But I gotta earn my living. Hi, Harry!" This was to Harrison Galt, M. H. S. I. salesman for Brooklyn, who had just come in to collect the daily list of inquiries from prospective students in his district, which had been forwarded from the home office in Paterson.

Andrews continued implacably: "I know you want your half of the ten-dollar deposit. But I have specific instructions from the home office to stop signing up these lightweights who just happen to be short on sales resistance. They figured that handling their courses costs more than it's worth. Anyway, it gives the Mercury Home Study Institute a bad name."

"Anyway," sulked Buckminster, "I never signed up no Earl Browder, like one of our competitors did."

Andrews, a dryly precise man, ignored this. He asked: "What about Grinnig? Does he want to shift from oil heating to bee keeping?"

"He ain't on oil heating," said Buckminster. "He's on that new one, nigromancy."

"Huh?"

"Yeah, doncha remember? Some new idear of the School of Shop Practice. We ain't even got a folder on it, but when Grinnig seen it in one of the ads, he just had to have it. So I wrote Paterson and asked: would they please send Grinnig the first lesson booklet as soon as it was off the press."

Galt put in a word: "Speaking of the School of Shop Practice, one of my prospects told me he thought it would have to do with legal shenanigans, how to kite checks and such. Get it? He thought I meant *sharp* practice!"

"Ha, ha," said Buckminster. "The dialeck some of these guys talk, you wonder how they understand themselves. Well, so long, Mr. Andrews, I gotta—"

"Remember, Clem, no more changes of course!" interrupted Andrews. "What *is* this nigromancy course, anyway? Something to do with race relations?"

Buckminster shrugged. "I dunno. Neither did Grinnig. That's why he wanted it."

"He's crazy," said Andrews. "And so are some of the heads in Paterson, I suspect. Nigromancy! Since the Old Man's been sick, Thurtle's been running the home office, practically." Julian Thurtle was the head of the School of Shop Practice.

"So long, Clem," said Galt. "One of these days, the Dangerous Dane's gonna remember all those deposits you talked him outa, and take a poke at you."

"Grinnig's all right," grinned Buckminster. "He gets in fights because he's just an overgrown kid. That's it, an overgrown kid. But him and me get along fine. 'By." And Clem Buckminster, an inconspicuous figure of forty-odd with abundant but graying hair, went out softly singing:

> *"Down with Harvard, down with Yale;*
> *We get our learning through the mail. . . ."*

Buckminster first sought Carl Grinnig at his normal place of employment, having assumed from Grinnig's wild talk that he was telephoning from there. But the shop head of the Alliance Oil Burner Co. informed Buckminster that the company's able but erratic mechanic was not in, allegedly because of sickness.

So the M. H. S. I. salesman rattled over to East Tremont Avenue and turned north toward the boardinghouse where Grinnig lived. This was a large, wooden, frame building with a front porch and wooden scrollwork.

At the first intersection, a policeman held up Buckminster's car with a decisive "Not this way, buddy!" Buckminster himself could see, beyond the cop, the backs of a small crowd of people, and over the heads of these the upperworks of a fire engine standing in front of Grinnig's house. He turned the car down a side street, parked, and walked toward the scene, observing that the house had several broken windows and that from these, dark streaks of smoke or char ran up the clapboarded sides of the house.

"Mr. Buckminster!" said a voice. It was that of Carl Grinnig, a large, powerful, blond young man with a black eye and a couple of purplish discolorations about the jaw. He seized a flabby Buckminster arm in one huge hand.

"Yeah?" said Buckminster, suppressing the desire to wince. "Had a fire?"

"Had a *fire?* Yust wait till I tell you—"

Grinnig's explanation was drowned by an outburst of sound: exclamations from the crowd, smothered curses from a couple of firemen who ran out of the house to the engine, from which they took a couple of chemical extinguishers and dashed back. People pointed toward a curl of smoke, which rose suddenly from one of the broken windows. Buckminster could hear people running about inside the house, and presently the smoke ceased.

A stout, harassed-looking civilian came out of the house and pushed through the people. Buckminster recognized the man as Grinnig's landlord. Grinnig called out: "Hey, Mr. Feldman! What is it this time?"

Feldman made motions of pulling nonexistent hair. "A book! A book up off the table I was lifting, just a ordinary book it was, and when I open it, into flames it bursts! Right in front of it the gentleman from the insurance company was standing. His own eyes he don't believe! Me, I'm going crazy!" The house owner departed distractedly.

"You see, Mr. Buckminster?" rumbled Grinnig. "It's been like this all morning. First it was a calendar on the wall went up, *whoof.* Then a mattress caught fire. This book's about the twentieth screwy fire. After the fire department had turned out for five or six of 'em, they yust left an engine here and guys sitting in every room with chemical extinguishers."

"Did you get hurt in the fires?" asked Buckminster, eying the mechanic's obvious contusions.

"Naw, that was just a little fight with a coupla sailors. Di'n't amount to nothing on account of there was only three of them. But I gotta see you, quick."

"What have I got to do with—" began the correspondence-course salesman, but Grinnig shushed him warningly.

"We gotta talk alone somewheres. Come on, maybe there ain't nobody in old man Feldman's garage." And Grinnig dragged Buckminster willy-nilly up the driveway, growled, "Beat it, you kids," to a pair of small boys who were watching events from the roof of the two-car garage, and shoved the salesman within.

"Look, Mr. Buckminster," said the mechanic, "it's that nigromancy course you sold me."

"What is?" queried Buckminster.

"That made these here fires. But don't you say nothing about it," he added ominously.

"Course I wouldn't," said Buckminster hastily. "After all, we got a reputation to protect, too. But how come the course had anything to do with the fires? Don't make sense. If you don't like it, why doncha change?"

"I'm not interested in changing my course, but in stopping these here fires!" persisted Grinnig.

"We got a swell new course in aviation mechanics," said Buckminster. "Wuncha like to be an aviation mechanic? Big future; not like messing around with these smelly oil boiners. You could make some real dough with—"

"Listen," said Grinnig with strained patience, "every time you sell me a new course, you tell me it'll make me rich. Well, I ain't rich. If they're so hot, why don't you take one? How come you're still selling 'em on commission and living on coffee and sinkers?"

Buckminster shook his head sadly. "Too late for me. Shoulda started when I was a young guy like you, steada playing around and wasting my dough. My future's behind me." (This was all fairly close to the truth.) "Now, about that avi—"

"Shut up!" bellowed Grinnig. "I don't wanna hear nothing about no new courses."

The burly mechanic fished out of a pocket a six-by-nine booklet with stiff, green paper covers. "Look at this thing!"

Buckminster read:

Mercury Home Study Institute

NIGROMANCY

by Julian A. Thurtle

(Dean, School of Shop Practice)

Volume 1   Conjuration of Saganes

He turned the cover and looked at the beginning of the text. It began:

1. *What nigromancy is.* The science of nigromancy was defined many years ago by Paracelsus (P. A. T. B. von Hohenheim) as the conjuration, control, and exorcism (banishment) of the elemental spirits of earth, air, fire, and water, called collectively Saganes. Since Paracelsus' time, the knowledge of this science has largely gone out of existence, so that today it is regarded by many as mere superstition. This is incorrect. Used with proper knowledge and care, this science can be as useful to modern technicians as any other. Accordingly, this course, based on recent research into some of the little-known writings of Paracelsus and his contemporaries, has been prepared.

2. *Outline of the Course.* The first three volumes deal respectively with the conjuration, control, and banishment of elemental spirits. Students are warned not to attempt any experimental conjurations whatever until they have mastered at least three parts and have passed the examination at the end of each volume. The later volumes deal with the more advanced aspects of nigromancy and with allied subjects such as necromancy, hydromancy, enchantment, and sortilege—

Buckminster commented: "Now I know the home office is nuts. What happened?"

"Well," said Grinnig, "I wasn't feeling so good after I finished with those sailors, see? Musta been something I ate. So I called the shop and they said sure, I could have the day off. So I thought I'd see if this course would really do the things it said it would. So I look through the book and find a ritual for conjuring up a salamander. You know what a salamander is; one of those little red things like a lizard."

Buckminster put in: "It says here not to try no conjurations until you finish the first three lessons."

"Yeah, I know, but you think I'm gonna pay for a whole course if I don't know if it works? Anyway, I figure one of those little lizardy things couldn't do no damage."

"And it started the fires? G'wan!"

"Not the salamander; I mean, I didn't get no salamander, but a kind of a ball of fire. It ducked quick into a pair of work pants I had hanging up on my door and set 'em on fire. I grab the pants off the hook to beat the fire out, and the fireball dodges out through the crack of the door, so quick I can't hardly see it. And it's been flying around the house all morning setting fire to things."

"G'wan," repeated Buckminster. "Sure one of those sailors didn't clip you with a piece of pipe or somepin?"

"Naw," said Grinnig scornfully. "I seen what I seen. And I figure I gotta have the third volume of the course right now, on account of it tells how to get rid of these things."

"You can't," replied the salesman. "The second volume oughta be just about off the press, and the third ain't even printed. Anyway, I think you imagined it. Come down to the corner and I'll buy you a beer and tell you about how to be an aviation mechanic."

"I did not imagine it," persisted Grinnig.

"Okay, then, show me how you did it."

"Okay, wise guy, I'll show you. Gimme the book." Grinnig fished out the stub of a pencil, frowned over the diagrams, and slowly drew a number of complicated lines on the concrete floor of the garage. He took out a candle no longer than his thumb, lit it, and placed it on the floor. Then he mumbled a long series of sounds that sounded to Buckminster like continuous double-talk, pausing now and then to draw imaginary figures in the air with his pencil.

Carl Grinnig ended his spiel and shut the lesson book. "Aw right, Mr. Buckminster, you—Yumping Yudas!"

Over one of the diagrams, about ten feet from the two men, something was swiftly materializing. First came smoke and a smell of sulphur dioxide, then a dull-red glow, which brightened to orange. Then they were confronted by what looked like the nude iron statue of a powerfully built man at incandescent temperatures. The heat from the apparition beat on their faces like the glow from an open furnace door, and they began to sweat.

The fire man surveyed Buckminster and Grinnig. When he spoke, it was in a deep, harsh, strongly accented voice: "Where—is—my—liddle—creature?"

"I dunno what you're talking about," said Grinnig, his fair skin paler than usual.

"Please, mister, go away," added Buckminster. "It's all a mistake!"

"Ha," rasped the newcomer. "Mistake. Mistake. But few mistakes does your trade allow. Where is my salamander?"

Grinnig swallowed and croaked: "You mean that fire thing? It's in that big house in back of you."

The visitor turned his massive head and whistled piercingly. Almost immediately, a sphere of flickering orange flame the size of a soft baseball arrived with a rush, danced up and down in front of its master, and at length snuggled up under his armpit.

The glowing head raised slightly, and the men felt by the increase of heat rather than saw the glowing eyeballs fasten upon them. "And now," said the fire man, "wherefore have ye broken the Treaty?"

"What treaty?" said Grinnig.

"Ye know not? Ha." The apparition put out a hand to lean against the wooden side of the garage. There was an immediate burst of smoke where the hand touched the wall.

"Hi!" yelped Buckminster. The fire man took his hand away with a slight, grim smile, leaving a charred spot the shape of a hand on the wood.

"What, then, *do* ye know?" he demanded.

"N-not so much," quavered the massive Grinnig. "I yust got this little book from the Mercury Home Study Institute, and I wanted to try it out. So I did a little spell. Please, buddy, who are you and when are you going to let us out of here? It's damned hot!"

The thing smiled even more broadly. "Ye know not my real name even? Ye cannot control me?"

"I ain't come to that part of the course—"

"Ha! 'Tis rare fortune, indeed, that the Covenant should be breached by a brace of such witless bunglers as ye! This much will I tell you: that I am of the race of the Saldines, which the meddling Paracelsus ignorantly called Rolamandri; one of the peoples of the fire world, even as my little salamander is one of the beasts of the world. When my pet vanished, I suspected some foul doings in your world and watched for another opening of the door, the same which you forthwith furnished me. Ha! Now truly shall Fire come into its own!"

"Watcha mean?" piped Buckminster.

"I'll show you what I mean! Give me that book!"

Grinnig extended the lesson booklet, and snatched his hand back as the red-hot arm shot out to seize the volume, which instantly went up in a puff of flame.

"Freeze it!" roared the fire elemental. "I should have bethought me of the perishability of your paper. Where can I obtain another such volume?"

"I dunno," babbled Buckminster, "unless you wanna go clear out to Paterson."

"Where?"

"Paterson, New Jersey, where the home office is. They got the whole course out there."

"Then let us forth. But stay! I cannot move abroad without some garment, lest I attract the attention of the general."

"I'll say you would," murmured Buckminster. "You'd attract the whole army."

"Give me, then, your clothing."

"Hey!" squawked the salesman. "They're too small for you, and anyway they'd burn up if you tried to put 'em on!"

"True," growled the Saldine. "I have it! There exists in your world a substance known before the Treaty as salamander skin, which in sooth is but a fabric woven of the strands of a certain fibrous rock. Fetch me a suit of this forthwith!"

"He means asbestos," explained Grinnig.

"Yeah, but how—"

"Fetch it!" thundered the Saldine, "ere I set my pet upon you!" He plucked the salamander from under his armpit and whispered to it. It zipped over close to the men and bobbed menacingly about them. They could feel its heat even in that oven atmosphere.

The elemental added: "But one of you; the smaller. The other shall remain as hostage, and do ye but essay any treason or alarums, I'll embrace the fellow *thus!*" He grinned fiendishly and wrung an imaginary dishrag with his huge, fiery hands.

"Okay," capitulated Buckminster. "Got any dough, Carl?"

Grinnig wordlessly handed over his wallet. The elemental stood aside long enough to let Buckminster, wincing at the scorching radiation, duck out the garage door. The Saldine called the salamander back to him and fell into a statuesque pose in the doorway, arms folded across his mighty chest and feet spread.

Carl Grinnig, seeing the only easy exit blocked again, sat down wearily on the concrete floor. In the ensuing wait, he recovered some of his aplomb. Although he did not feel like a particularly dangerous Dane, he was too big and tough to be completely intimidated for long.

He remarked: "You never told me who you really are and what you want."

"Ha!" barked the Saldine and relapsed into silence.

"Okay, then I'll have to call you Arson."

"Arson?" The being grinned. "A good name, forsooth. How good, ye have yet no notion."

"How come you talk so funny?"

"Talk so funny?" frowned Arson. "What mean ye? Verily, I speak what was the best English at the time of the Treaty, in your year 1623. I can comprehend that the tongue may have degenerated since then."

Grinnig shed his dripping shirt. A package of cigarettes flopped out of the breast pocket; he took one out and lit it, and blew out the match.

"You!" shouted the elemental suddenly, and advanced with menacing steps. "What mean ye by destroying Fire, in my very presence?"

"B-but . . . I just blew out the match. You wouldn't want me to burn my fingers? Or would you?" Grinnig flattened himself against the rear wall of the garage as the heat became intolerable.

"For that," thundered Arson, "ye shall—But not yet, for I need you as hostage. 'Tis such vile comportment that marks you and your kind for their just deserts! I am even informed that ye keep whole companies of men trained to quench fires!"

"You mean the fire departments?" sweated Grinnig. "Yeah, when a house catches fire, they try to put it out, natchly."

"Foul, wanton vandalism!" cried the Saldine. "When my brethern come—" He closed his mouth with a snap and retired, leaving Grinnig red of skin and half fainting from the roasting he had received.

"Hey, Mr. Grinnig!" called Clem Buckminster from outside the garage. "Tell him I got his stuff!"

Arson stood aside to admit the salesman with an armful of canvaslike material.

Buckminster explained: "I got it from a fire-apparatus company; it's one of these here asbestos suits. Got shoes and gloves. I borrowed a pair of tinsnips and some wire and fixed the helmet up so it looks almost like a hat. Looky. Took all our dough, even though it's secondhand."

While Buckminster chuckled with naïve pleasure over his ingenuity, the elemental pulled on the suit. When it was all in place and he had put on the altered helmet, he looked quite human except for the orange glow of the face that glared out from under the hat brim. Otherwise he might have been an ash collector or some other dirty-job worker in the costume of his calling. The two men drew long breaths of relief as the searing heat rays were cut off for the nonce.

"Come!" commanded Arson. "To Paterson, Oo Jersey!" He cuffed them roughly ahead of him out of the garage and down the driveway, pausing to cast a speculative eye at Feldman's boardinghouse.

The fire engine was gone from the curb, although a couple of firemen were still in evidence. Several people were stacking furniture in the back yard. None paid attention to the trio, for in the bright sunlight, even the incandescence of Arson's face was not noticeable unless one looked closely.

The Saldine muttered: "Right well has my little pet done, and he shall yet have an opportunity to finish his task. Would I could stop to attend the matter myself! Go on, ye two!"

"Hey!" wailed Buckminster. "Are we gonna walk the whole way?"

"Of a certainty, unless you can provide a conveyance."

The salesman glanced down the street to where his car was parked, its stern just visible around the corner. "I got my car, but—"

"But what?"

"There wouldn't be room for all three of us, and anyway you'd burn it up!"

"Ha," said Arson flatly. He looked about. In the opposite direction a coal truck stood at the curb a block away. He pointed. "Is that one of your conveyances?"

"Yeah, it runs, if that's whatcha mean."

"Then shall we take it. It looks to be made of fire-resisting material."

"But it ain't ours! You can't just steal a truck like that!"

"Say you so?" snarled the fire man. He moved his arms, and the salamander appeared, bobbing up and down from the palm of his outstretched hand. "Shall I set my pet—"

"No, no," amended Buckminster quickly.

As they approached the truck, the men's hearts sank as they observed it to be unoccupied.

"The large one," announced Arson, "shall mount the rear of the conveyance with me. The other shall drive."

Grinnig hesitated just long enough for the elemental to make a move as if to seize him and throw him up into the empty truck bodily; the mechanic scrambled quickly up under his own power. Arson followed more deliberately. The truck's springs creaked as though a considerable load had been added.

When Buckminster nervously slid into the driver's seat, the Saldine banged on the back of the cab. "Can ye hear me?" he bellowed.

"Yeah, sure."

"Good. To Paterson, Oo Jersey and swiftly!"

To get accustomed to the ponderous vehicle took Clem Buckminster several miles, and then he came to one of the approaches of the George Washington Bridge. Just before he reached the approach, it occurred to him that perhaps trucks were not allowed on the bridge. While he slowed the truck, torn between fear of Arson and fear of the law, a second thought told him that to get pinched was exactly what he wanted. On his whole trip from East Tremont Avenue, he had not

seen a single policeman, who belong to a species that vanish like the
snows in spring whenever one had a real need for them.

An occasional smell whiffed through the driver's cab; undoubtedly,
thought Buckminster, scorched paint. The asbestos suit would eventually
warm up so that it radiated almost as much heat as the naked Arson.
He pushed the accelerator to the floor as the truck crested the middle
of the bridge roadway and roared down the long slope toward the toll
booths on the Jersey side.

He began to slow down as the distant blue-coated figures of the toll
collectors came into view. Then a banging on the back of the cab
informed him that Arson had words for him. They were: "Hasten! No
stopping!" When Buckminster continued to apply the brake, he heard
a shriek from Grinnig. Arson had snatched off a glove and thrust a
fiery hand close to the luckless mechanic's face.

Clem Buckminster speeded up again, looking for a toll booth before
which no autos were lined up. He found one, to his disappointment.
Well, maybe the truck was too big to squeeze through the restricted
opening and would get stuck between the concrete piers. If he had had
suicidal courage, he might have chanced deliberately ramming an ob-
stacle, but he was not that kind of person. He sighted on the opening
as best he could and steered right through without even scratching the
paint.

He was in the midst of the tangle of ramps west of the bridge when
he at long last heard the welcome *we-e-e-e-ew* of a siren. Now he *had*
to stop. As he slowed, a motorcycle pulled alongside. The cop pointed:
"Down there!"

Buckminster steered into the less-used ramp indicated and came out
on an ordinary street, where he stopped. The cop parked his cycle
ahead of the truck and walked back. As he took out his pad he looked
up at the cab with an expression more of pity than of anger. He said:

"Say, buddy, don't you know *anything* about the traffic laws?"

When Buckminster could not answer, the policeman added: "A grown
man like you oughta know you can't drive ya truck across the bridge
at fifty—"

"Ain't my truck," croaked Buckminster.

"Now listen, buddy, it don't matter whether you're hired to
drive—"

"I stole it, see?" said the salesman.

At this the policeman's voice simply dried up, and he stared with
his mouth open until a motion on the curbside of the truck attracted
his attention. This was Arson, who had descended from the truck body
and was walking forward to the motorcycle. The elemental bent over
the vehicle with interest.

"Hey, leggo that!" yelled the cop as Arson experimentally wiggled
the handle bars.

The Saldine ignored the command and removed his gloves for more intimate contact. As the policeman started toward him, he clamped his red-hot hands on the framework, picked the cycle up, and with a creaking of tortured metal calmly twisted the whole thing out of shape.

Buckminster could see the paint beginning to curl and smoke. A tire burst into flame. Then, with a loud *whoof,* the gasoline tank went off, and Arson was completely hidden in a vast cloud of flame and smoke. The cop jumped back and banged his elbow against a fender of the truck.

When the smoke cleared and the flames subsided, Arson was standing in a small sea of burning gasoline and still holding the blazing wreck of the cycle. He was unchanged except that his asbestos suit was of a dirtier gray than before.

"It ain't . . . isn't real," said the cop to himself, rubbing his elbow.

The elemental now started toward the policeman, an evil grin on his glowing face. As he tramped he raised the motorcycle over his head. The cop shouted something which Buckminster missed, then drew his pistol. The gun barked three times, at a range where a miss was impossible. Each shot was followed by a metallic clang such as one hears after a hit on a shooting-gallery target. Arson grinned more widely and hurled the motorcycle. The cop ducked, but a handle bar struck his head and he tumbled to the concrete as the cycle whizzed past the cab window.

Arson in leisurely manner walked back and climbed into the truck. Far down the street a few civilians were standing and watching, but none seemed eager to investigate. "Hence!" roared the Saldine through the back of the cab.

As he started the truck again, Clem Buckminster, for the first time in some years, prayed.

Before the truck came to the bridge over the Passaic River, the heat and stench which Buckminster now automatically associated with the presence of Arson became too strong for comfort even inside the cab. A glance in the mirror showed a fair-sized cloud of smoke billowing out from the truck body. As the salesman began to slow the vehicle again, there was a muffled explosion and a burst of flame. The temperature soared alarmingly.

Buckminster pulled on the hand brake and swerved the truck off the road into the weeds. He scrambled out before it stopped rolling, to find the rear half of the truck enveloped in flames and Grinnig and the elemental already descended to earth. The mechanic was a pitiful sight, with blistered hands and singed eyebrows, and black with sweat-streaked coal dust.

"How much farther?" growled the Saldine.

"Coupla miles," said Buckminster resignedly.

"Good. We shall walk!" And Arson, shooing the men ahead of him, set out at a brisk stride.

When they had gone a few hundred yards from the conflagration, a car stopped to investigate the burning truck, and another, until there was a traffic jam on that section of the road. A police siren whined. "Continue to wend," snapped Arson, "and look not back!"

They passed a section of road that was being widened, although no workmen were in sight at the moment. Several pieces of road machinery stood around on the new strip with canvas covers over their works. "Conveyances!" muttered Arson. "Let us take another for our own use, as the journey grows tedious."

"Hey!" bleated Buckminster. "The gas tanks'll blow up if you get aboard, same as the truck did!"

"That," grinned the elemental nastily, "will be your misfortune!" He inspected a bulldozer. "Into the driver's seat, small one!"

"Won't do no good, Mr. Arson," protested Buckminster. "Gas tank's empty. See this here gauge?"

"Another, then," snorted Arson. But all the other pieces of equipment proved to have empty fuel tanks as well, the contractor having thriftily drained them before temporarily laying them up.

The last two machines inspected were a pair of road rollers; one a modern gasoline roller, the other an old-fashioned steam roller with a vertical boiler. This, too, lacked fuel, but investigation disclosed that it had water in its boiler.

Arson remarked: "I begin to fathom the operation of these devices. Yet this one appeareth to be of a nature different from the others. What is the quintessence of its active principle?"

Grinnig huskily explained the essentials of steam-engine operation.

"Ha!" grinned Arson. "Whereas it needs nought but a modicum of heat for its operation, forsooth I will furnish that!" He opened the door of the fire box, climbed onto the body, removed a shoe, and thrust a glowing foot into the opening. After a few minutes' wait, the elemental exclaimed: "Why starts this conveyance not? I wax impatient! O fool, think ye to deceive me?"

"No, no!" chirped Buckminster. "Look at the gauge; she'll have steam pressure up any time now!"

They fell into silence, waiting, Buckminster hoping that by some miracle the United States Army would descend on them to rescue him and his student and subdue Mr. Arson, if need be with heavy artillery. But nothing of the sort occurred; automobiles purred by indifferently. Buckminster was bright enough to guess that to yell "Help!" to one or two uncomprehending and ineffective civilians would merely make a bad situation worse.

At last steam was up. Buckminster opened the throttle and spun the steering wheel, which was connected to the forward roller by a worm gear and a chain. With a rapid *pop-pop-pop*, the machine shudderingly ground over the unfinished road surface, and on the highway, and rattled on into Paterson.

Buckminster stopped the roller and pointed to a group of slightly dilapidated buildings that occupied one of Paterson's outlying blocks. "That's them," he explained. "The Mercury Home Study Institute."

As the party approached the nearest building, Buckminster thought furiously. Arson's vague threats had certainly implied that the fire elemental was up to no good. The salesman suspected that the Saldine wanted to get control of a set of the course booklets in order to conjure up more of his fiendish kind. But if he, Clem, could get hold of one of those booklets first, notably the ones dealing with the control and banishment of elementals, perhaps he could beat Arson to the punch.

So it was in a state of extreme alertness that Buckminster approached the building housing the Mercury printing establishment. He turned to Arson and said:

"The books are all in there. You wait here and I'll—"

"Ha, think you I'm such a dunce? Lead on and I'll follow!"

"But you'll set this old building on fire—"

A shove sent Buckminster staggering toward the nearest doorway. He shrugged and went in, Grinnig and Arson following. The elemental left black footprints of charred wood on the aged floor.

Down one side of the printshop ran a row of a dozen flat-bed presses, about half of which were in action, their beds weaving back and forth under the cylinders with a continuous loud grumble. On the other side of the aisle along the presses was a row of low hand trucks, each of which bore a pile of large white sheets, varying from a foot to four feet in height. Some of these piles were fresh paper for the presses, some had been printed on one side only and some had been printed on both sides and were waiting to be fed to the folding machines in the bindery, which occupied the other half of the building. At the far end of the bindery were a lot of hand trucks of another kind, on which were stacked hundreds of completed green Mercury lesson booklets and sets of advertising literature. The first printing of Volume 1 of the nigromancy course would probably be here, unless it had been taken over to the school building, whence the booklets were mailed to students and where the students' examinations were corrected.

Buckminster moved slowly down the line of trucks bearing the stacks of big squares of paper. He suppressed a whoop as he found what he wanted: a pile of printed sheets, each sheet having forty-eight pages of text on each side, and among the pages the first page of a Mercury booklet, with a heading:

NIGROMANCY
Volume 2   Control of Saganes

Buckminster ran his eye hastily over the sheet but encountered a difficulty. The pages were not grouped on the sheet in the order in which they would be read, but were so arranged that when the sheet was put in the folding machine, and folded and cut and folded and cut down to final form, these pages would then be in the proper order.

Nevertheless, Buckminster ran over the pages quickly, regardless of the fact that half of them were on the underside of the sheet and half the remainder were upside down. Sure enough, a subtitle caught his eye:

12. *Control of Trifertes (Fire Elementals).* The salamander, being a trifertis of relatively low intelligence, is comparatively easy to control—

"Excuse me," said a voice behind him, "but have you gents got permission from the office to look around the shop?"

Buckminster started guiltily; then recognized the foreman of the printshop. He said:

"Hello, Jim; 'member me? Clem Buckminster, from the New York office."

"Hello," said the foreman mechanically. "It's pretty near quitting time, you know, and you'll have to—"

"Can you lend me a pencil, Jim?" asked Buckminster quickly. The foreman handed one over, and Buckminster, referring back to the printed sheet, began to draw figures on the floor.

"Ho!" muttered Arson suddenly. "What do ye, wretch?"

The foreman looked at the elemental closely for the first time and backed away in alarm as he observed the orange glow of the Saldine's visage, which was fairly conspicuous indoors.

"Hey," he said, "who is this?"

"Mr. Arson, meet Mr. Slezak," mumbled Buckminster.

"But—what's the matter with him?"

"He got sunburned, out at Jones Beach," explained the salesman, frowning as he realized that he would have to turn the print sheet over to get the information necessary to complete his ritual.

"I'll say he got burned," said Slezak. "You gotta use discretion. I got some good suntan oil that—"

"I see!" roared Arson. "Ye prepare a spell for me, eh? Bah!" The elemental snatched off his gloves, stuck them between his teeth, and began to assault the pile of sheets with his glowing hands. The upper sheets at once began to burn. Arson whipped them off in great handfuls, crumpled them, and tossed them, flaming, right and left.

Cries of alarm rang through the printery as smoke and pieces of burning paper rose and spread. At that moment, the five-o'clock bell rang. The printers shut down their presses and raced for the doors, Buckminster and Grinnig among them. The whole middle of the printery was now a mass of blazing paper, from whose invisible center Arson roared with demoniac laughter.

Buckminster caught Grinnig's belt in the rear and hung on lest they be separated in the rush. When they had put a respectable distance between themselves and the now furiously smoking building, they looked back. Workmen were scattered all over the intervening area; clerks and instructors poured out of the school building. Among these Buckminster recognized a small group of men in coats and neckties as the executives.

"Come on," he said to Grinnig. "If we can find Thurtle, maybe we can fix Arson's wagon."

A policeman cleared a way for the fire engines. Buckminster and Grinnig worked their way around the cleared area to where the executives stood. The former called:

"Oh, Mr. Thurtle!"

Julian Thurtle, dean of the School of Shop Practice of the Mercury Home Study Institute, looked about as much like a chimpanzee with a white handle-bar mustache as a man can without actually being a chimpanzee with a white handle-bar mustache. But he was a wise old teacher of technics whose courses, the texts for many of which he wrote himself, were up to college standards and had actually helped many ambitious young men on their way to success, as claimed in his company's advertisements.

He was conversing with the vice president in charge of sales, who was saying: "—of course, it's all insured, but it'll raise Ned with our publishing schedule, not to mention interrupting a lot of the courses. The Education Everywhere Institute won't be sorry to hear of it."

Thurtle sighed. "Yes, yes. Dear me. Maybe we could persuade the I. C. C. to help us out; they're pretty decent fellows—" He saw Buckminster and said: "Yes? Yes? You are . . . don't tell me . . . Buckmaster of the Philadelphia office, aren't you?"

The salesman corrected him and asked: "Can I see you a minute—"

"Not now, not now, my dear fellow. This is too important. Go on, get your hoses inside the building, you . . . you twerps!" The last sentence was addressed in a low voice to the distant firemen.

A policeman approached with a pad in hand. He said: "Oh, Mr. Thurtle—"

"Yes? Yes? Oh, hello, Bill. What—"

"There was an alarm sent out for a gang of pyromaniacs that's terrorizing northern New Jersey," said the cop. "They burned a truck and a coupla houses, and they knocked a cop unconscious at the George Washington Bridge. I was wondering if they mightn't have something to do with this—"

"Yes. No. Dear me, I don't know. I'm too upset, officer."

"Okay, Mr. Thurtle," said the cop and wandered off.

Then there were sudden cries from the crowd. A crew of firemen were advancing on a doorway with a hose, which they played through the aperture, when a large figure in shapeless gray garments came out that door from the burning building. The stream of water from the hose struck the figure squarely, but instead of knocking him back into the building as it should have done, it gave a colossal hiss and turned into a vast cloud of steam. Some witnesses, including Clem Buckminster, had a glimpse of the gray figure dodging out of the steam cloud and vanishing around the corner of the building.

"Good gracious," said Thurtle. "What—"

Buckminster cried: "That's what I wanna see you about, Mr. Thurtle! This here is Carl Grinnig, who got the first lesson in that new course of yours!"

"Oh." Comprehension dawned in Thurtle's eyes, and he followed the salesman unprotesting.

When they were out of earshot of the spectators, Buckminster gave a brief account of events.

"This is terrible!" exclaimed Thurtle. "Mr. Grinnig, you should never have tried an incantation before—"

"How was *I* to know—" protested Grinnig.

"You couldn't; it was partly my fault, too. I should never have put out that course. The only reason I did it was that I hated to see all that powerful scientific knowledge going to waste, and I did want to put one over on our competitors. I got hold of a copy of Paracelsus' *'Ex Libris de Nymphis, Sylvanis, etc.'*; not the abridgment published by Nissensis of Danzic in 1566, which omits all the effective spells, but the last original—Well, that's water over the dam; the question is, what'll we do?"

"I was just gonna ask you that," said Buckminster.

"Yes, yes, I suppose so. It's a difficult problem. From what you've told me, the Rolamander is practically indestructible by physical means; water and bullets don't bother him in the least."

"How about freezing him?" asked Grinnig.

"I don't know; I think you'd practically have to incase him in an iceberg. He gets his energy from the fire world."

Buckminster here suggested: "Maybe we could lure him into a big refrigerator and shut the door!"

"Not likely; he's too crafty."

"We could call out the army," said Grinnig hopefully. "They could bomb him."

"Perhaps; but the time we convinced them, he'd have found a way to let his fellow hellions into this world."

Buckminster asked: "What does he wanna do that for?"

"To burn everything combustible, I suspect. And don't ask me why they want to burn things. They just do."

"Unreasonable sorta guys," commented the little salesman.

"Not necessarily; it's that their scale of moral values is entirely different from ours. We can't understand them. Fire's a good servant but an ill master, you know. Let's see; let's see. The printed nigromancy course is no more; the first two volumes were all in the printshop, except for Grinnig's copy, and those that weren't burned up will be ruined by the water. The manuscript in the typesetting room went, too, I fancy. There remains only my copy of the manuscript. Neither we nor Mr. Arson want that destroyed; we want to use it to banish him, and he wants to use it to invoke his fellow Rolamanders. But if he finds us with it, he'll force us to perform the conjuration spell on pain of a horrible death, since he can't handle the papers himself without burning them."

Buckminster asked: "Couldn't we pretend to do the conjuring spell, but really do the banishing spell?"

"That's the trouble; he'd know in a minute we were trying to fool him, and with his fiery disposition you can imagine what would happen. These spells aren't simple things that you can say 'hocus pocus' and the elemental vanishes, you know. Since he escaped from Grinnig's control, we'd have to get him back into a servile state first, and I confess I'm not sure how to do it. Dear, dear. Oh, what's he wearing?"

"An asbestos fire fighter's suit," responded Buckminster.

"Aha, now perhaps—" Thurtle broke off and stared past the other two men, horror growing in his face.

"Ha!" The rasping monosyllable and the feeling of warmth on their backs told Buckminster and Grinnig that their enemy was behind them. "Foolish wights, I grow weary of these pastimes. Fetch me forthwith a set of the rest of those books!"

Thurtle spoke: "I . . . I'm sorry, Mr. Arson, but they're all destroyed. No, no, don't blame us, old fellow; you started the fire yourself!"

"So I did," grinned Arson. "But I know something of the habits of you of the Cold World. Do not try to tell me that all copies of the work were burned up; you would have an extra somewhere. Lead me to it, and attempt no stratagems such as burning it, unless you wish a speedy but painful death."

"I swear there are no more copies!" cried Thurtle. But Arson simply grinned more widely and began to toss his salamander meaningfully from hand to hand.

"Will you lead me to it, for the last time?" purred the elemental.

"I tell you it doesn't ex—" That was as far as Julian Thurtle got, for the salamander swooped at him and ignited one end of his magnificent mustache. Thurtle, with a small shriek, clapped a hand to smother the blaze. When he removed the hand, the right side of the mustache was intact, but of the left wing only a short black stubble on the upper lip remained. The salamander whirled in a small circle around the dean's head.

"All right," groaned Thrutle. "Follow me."

He led them for several blocks into a grimy district, whose buildings were largely devoted to the sale of raw materials, chemicals, and agricultural and industrial machinery. There were few people on the depressing street, most of the people who did business in this neighborhood having gone home to supper.

"Hasten," growled Arson, "for it grows dark, and I cannot wander abroad in this village at night with my face lighting the way like a beacon." His face was in fact becoming pretty conspicuous, though the sun would not set for another hour.

Thurtle stopped the procession in front of an old wooden frame building bearing the sign:

WILLIAMS & GIBBON
Welding Equipment & Supplies

Buckminster almost asked why the devil Thurtle chose to keep the spare copy of his manuscript in such a place, but thought better of it. Thurtle himself said: "Wait here, Mr. Arson, and I'll get the papers."

"Ha, so think you. I'll come with you—"

"Oh, no, you won't, unless you want to set this house on fire, too! Then there really wouldn't be any more copies."

"Very well," grumbled the fire elemental. "I will keep these two as hostages. Do you but attempt a spell behind my back, I shall know, and do them most horribly die!"

Thurtle darted into the building, called, "Tom!" and ran up the stairs.

Buckminster and Grinnig remained uneasily with Arson, who had taken up his statuesque pose in front of the doorway. Buckminster was badly frightened; he was sure that Thurtle was up to something, that it might not work, and that Arson would take it out on him and Grinnig. Maybe the old boy would destroy the manuscript, which would prevent further invocations of elementals, but would leave the invulnerable and vindictive Arson abroad in this world. Buckminster clenched his jaw to keep his teeth from chattering.

A window creaked overhead. Carl Grinnig was too far gone to look up. Clem Buckminster would ordinarily have done so had not the crisis given his otherwise mediocre wits a preternatural sharpness. He fought to control his eyes and face, lest he betray his knowledge of things taking place on the second-story level.

There was a brilliant white flare of light.

Several persons claimed afterward to have seen what happened, but they saw from a distance of a block or more, did not begin to notice until the process was well under way, and told stories differing so widely from each other and from the version of Julian Thurtle, an eminent and respected citizen, that not much credence was given these stories.

The flare was caused by the lighting of a magnesium ribbon stuck in the top of a bucket of gray powder, which Thurtle and his acquaintance, Tom Gibbon, had lowered on a wire from the upstairs window until it was a foot or so over Arson's unsuspecting head. Right after the flash the bottom of the bucket fell out, and a cascade of blindingly incandescent material poured down over Arson while the elemental was just beginning to look up to see what was going on.

Buckminster and Grinnig staggered back, shielding their faces from the scorching heat and blinding light. Buckminster blinked for a few seconds before he could see anything at all.

Where Arson had stood was a shapeless thing about half the stature of a man, which sank and slumped and ran out, across the sidewalk, up and down the gutter, spreading scintillating whiteness over an area twenty feet across. The glare dimmed to a mere yellow that could be looked at directly without scorching the eyeballs, and Julian Thurtle from the upstairs window called: "Fire! You, Buckmaster, turn in the alarm!" In truth, the front of Williams & Gibbon's building had begun to burn; little flames ran up the door posts in businesslike fashion.

An alarm had already been turned in. In a few minutes, a fire truck extended a ladder up to the window. Thurtle and Gibbon scrambled down it, slightly smoke-blackened but otherwise unhurt.

"No, no, no, thank you," Thurtle said to those who helped him off the ladder and asked if he wanted hospitalization. "I'm not hurt, really. Perhaps this poor boy, who tried to get up the stairs to us—" He indicated Grinnig, who displayed several minor burns from his previous experiences.

"Naw," said Grinnig. He grinned and tugged Thurtle and Buckminster aside. "Hey, doc," he said to the former, "whad ya do to the guy?"

"I melted him," said Thurtle.

"What with?"

"Thermite! Arson thought he was pretty hot, but you bet he wasn't so hot as that thermite! I knew Williams & Gibbon had some thermite on their place, and I got Tom Gibbon to help me with the bucket and the fuse.

"That's all, except that if you fellows take my advice, you won't try to tell anyone about Arson or the nigromancy course—which is all gone now anyway—or your adventures today. I'm going to forget the course and stick that manuscript away in a sort of private time capsule."

"I getcha, boss," said Buckminster. "Say, Carl, hadn't we better stop in at a drugstore and smear some of that tannic-acid junk on ya burns?"

Grinnig looked at his blackened hands. "The main thing I want is yust to get washed up."

"Okay, this here joint oughta have a washroom. And while we're fixing you up, I'll tell you all about our swell new course on how to be an aviation mechanic. We'll have to switch you to a new one, and you wanna make some real dough, doncha? Okay. Hey, wassamatta, Carl? I didn't say nothing! HELP!"

Sock!

The Hill and the Hole

FRITZ LEIBER

Fritz Leiber was best known to readers of Unknown *as the author of the stylish sword-and-sorcery tales of Fafhrd and the Gray Mouser. However, he also wrote three outstanding horror stories for the magazine that do much to dispel the notion that* Unknown *published only humorous fantasy. "Smoke Ghost" was a frighteningly original urban ghost story.* Conjure Wife, *his highly acclaimed first novel, suggested that the practice of witchcraft was based less on the supernatural than on science. "The Hill and the Hole" was published only a few months before* Conjure Wife *and, with its emphasis on the potential dangers of an inflexible skepticism, can be seen as something of a prelude to that famous novel.*

TOM DIGBY swabbed his face against the rolled-up sleeve of his drill shirt, and good-naturedly damned the whole practice of measuring altitudes with barometric instruments. Now that he was back at the bench mark, which was five hundred eleven feet above sea level, he could see that his reading for the height of the hill was ridiculously off. It figured out to about four hundred forty-seven feet, whereas the hill, in plain view hardly a quarter of a mile away, was obviously somewhere around five hundred seventy or even five hundred eighty. The discrepancy made it a pit instead of a hill. Evidently either

391

he or the altimeter had been cock-eyed when he had taken the reading at the hilltop. And since the altimeter was working well enough now, it looked as if he had been the one.

He would have liked to get away early for lunch with Ben Shelley at Beltonville, but he needed this reading to finish off the oil survey. He had not been able to spot the sandstone-limestone contact he was looking for anywhere but near the top of this particular hill. So he picked up the altimeter, stepped out of the cool shadow of the barn behind which the bench mark was located, and trudged off. He figured he would be able to finish this little job properly and still be in time for Ben. A grin came to his big, square, youthful face as he thought of how they would chew the fat and josh each other. Ben, like himself, was on the State Geologic Survey.

Fields of shoulder-high corn, dazzlingly green under the broiling Midwestern sun, stretched away from the hill to the flat horizon. The noonday hush was beginning. Blue-bottle flies droned around him as he skirted a manure heap and slid between the weather-gray rails of an old fence. There was no movement, except a vague breeze rippling the corn a couple of fields away and a farmer's car raising a lazy trail of dust far off in the opposite direction. The chunky, competent-looking figure of Tom Digby was the only thing with purpose in the whole landscape.

When he had pushed through the fringe of tall, dry-stalked weeds at the base of the hill, he glanced back at the shabby one-horse farm where the bench mark was located. It looked deserted. Then he made out a little tow-headed girl watching him around the corner of the barn, and he remembered having noticed her earlier. He waved, and chuckled when she dodged back out of sight. Sometimes these farmers' kids were mighty shy. Then he started up the hill at a brisker pace, toward where the bit of strata was so invitingly exposed.

When he reached the top, he did not get the breeze he expected. It seemed, if anything, more stifingly hot than it had been down below, and there was a feeling of dustiness. He swabbed at his face again, set down the altimeter on a level spot, carefully twisted the dial until the needle stood directly over the middle line of the scale, and started to take the reading from the pointer below.

Then his face clouded. He felt compelled to joggle the instrument, although he knew it was no use. Forcing himself to work very slowly and methodically, he took a second reading. The result was the same as the first. Then he stood up and relieved his feelings with a fancy bit of swearing, more vigorous, but just as good-natured as the blast he had let off at the bench mark.

Allowing for any possible change in barometric pressure during the short period of his climb up from the bench mark, the altimeter still gave the height of the hill as under four hundred fifty. Even a tornado of fantastic severity could not account for such a difference in pressure.

It would not have been so bad, he told himself disgustedly, if he had been using an old-fashioned aneroid. But a five-hundred-dollar altimeter of the latest design is not supposed to be temperamental. However, there was nothing to do about it now. The altimeter had evidently given its last accurate gasp at the bench mark and gone blooey for good. It would have to be shipped back east to be fixed. And he would have to get along without this particular reading.

He flopped down for a breather before starting back. As he looked out over the checkerboard of fields and the larger checkerboard of sections bounded by dirt roads, it occurred to him how little most people knew about the actual dimensions and boundaries of the world they lived in. They looked at straight lines on a map, and innocently supposed they were straight in reality. They might live all their lives believing their homes were in one county, when accurate surveying would show them to be in another. They were genuinely startled if you explained that the Mason-Dixon line had more jags in it than a rail fence, or if you told them that it was next to impossible to find an accurate and up-to-date detail map of any given district. They did not know how rivers jumped back and forth, putting bits of land first in one state and then in another. They had never followed fine-looking, reassuring roads that disappeared into a weedy nowhere. They went along believing that they lived in a world as neat as a geometry-book diagram, while chaps like himself and Ben went around patching the edges together and seeing to it that one mile plus one mile equaled at least something like two miles. Or proving that hills were really hills and not pits in disguise.

It suddenly seemed devilishly hot and close and the bare ground unpleasantly gritty. He tugged at his collar, unbuttoned it further. Time to be getting on to Beltonville. Couple glasses of iced coffee would go good. He hitched himself up, and noticed that the little girl had come out from behind the barn again. She seemed to be waving at him now, with a queer, jerky, beckoning movement; but that was probably just the effect of the heat-shimmer rising from the fields. He waved too, and the movement brought on an abrupt spell of dizziness. A shadow seemed to surge across the landscape, and he had difficulty in breathing. Then he started down the hill, and pretty soon he was feeling all right again.

"I was a fool to come this far without a hat," he told himself. "This sun will get you, even if you're as healthy as a horse."

Something was nagging at his mind, however, as he realized when he got down in the corn again. It was that he did not like the idea of letting the hill lick him. It occurred to him that he might persuade

Ben to come over this afternoon, if he had nothing else to do, and
get a precise measurement with alidade and plane table.

When he neared the farm, he saw that the little girl had retreated
again to the corner of the barn. He gave her a friendly, "Hello." She
did not answer but she did not run away, either. He became aware
that she was staring at him in an intent, appraising way.

"You live here?" he asked.

She did not answer. After awhile, she said, "What did you want to
go down there for?"

"The State hires me to measure land," he replied. He had reached
the bench mark and was automatically starting to take a reading, before
he remembered that the altimeter was useless. "This your father's farm?"
he asked.

Again she did not answer. She was barefooted, and wore a cotton
dress of washed-out blue. The sun had bleached her hair and eyebrows
several degrees lighter than her skin, giving something of the effect of
a photographic negative. Her mouth hung open. Her whole face had
a vacuous, yet not exactly stupid expression.

Finally she shook her head solemnly, and said, "You shouldn't of
gone down there. You might not have been able to get out again."

"Say, just what are you talking about?" he inquired, humorously,
but keeping his voice gentle so she would not run away.

"The hole," she answered.

Tom Digby felt a shiver run over him. "Sun must have hit me
harder than I thought," he told himself.

"You mean there's some sort of pit down that way?" he asked
quickly. "Maybe an old well or cesspool hidden in the weeds? Well, I
didn't fall in. Is it on this side of the hill?" He was still on his knees
beside the bench mark.

A look of understanding, mixed with a slight disappointment, came
over her face. She nodded wisely and observed, "You're just like Papa.
He's always telling me there's a hill there, so I won't be scared of the
hole. But he doesn't need to. I know all about it, and I wouldn't go
near it again for anything."

"Say, what the dickens are you talking about?" His voice got out of
control, and he rather boomed the question at her. But she did not
dart away, only continued to stare at him thoughtfully.

"Maybe I've been wrong," she observed finally. "Maybe Papa and
you and other people really do see a hill there. Maybe *They* make you
see a hill there, so you won't know about *Them* being there. *They*
don't like to be bothered. I know. There was a man come up here
about two years ago, trying to find out about *Them*. He had a kind
of spyglass on sticks. *They* made him dead. That was why I didn't
want you to go down there. I was afraid *They* would do the same
thing to you."

He disregarded the shiver that was creeping persistently along his spine, just as he had disregarded from the very beginning with automatic scientific distaste for eeriness, the coincidence between the girl's fancy and the inaccurate altimeter readings.

"Who are *They?*" he asked cheerfully.

The little girl's blank, watery blue eyes stared past him, as if she were looking at nothing—or everything.

"*They* are dead. Bones. Just bones. But *They* move around. *They* live at the bottom of the hole, and *They* do things there."

"Yes?" he prompted, feeling a trifle guilty at encouraging her. From the corner of his eye he could see an old Model-T chugging up the rutted drive, raising clouds of dust.

"When I was little," she continued in a low voice, so he had to listen hard to catch the words, "I used to go right up to the edge and look down at *Them*. There's a way to climb down in, but I never did. Then one day *They* looked up and caught me spying. Just white bone faces; everything else black. I knew *They* were thinking of making me dead. So I ran away and never went back."

The Model-T rattled to a stop beside the barn, and a tall man in old blue overalls swung out and strode swiftly toward them.

"School Board sent you over?" he shot accusingly at Tom. "You from the County Hospital?"

He clamped his big paw around the girl's hand. He had the same bleached hair and eyebrows, but his face was burnt to a brick red. There was a strong facial resemblance.

"I want to tell you something," he went on, his voice heavy with anger but under control. "My little girl's all right in the head. It's up to me to judge, isn't it? What if she don't always give the answers the teachers expect. She's got a mind of her own, hasn't she? And I'm perfectly fit to take care of her. I don't like the idea of your sneaking around to put a lot of questions to her while I'm gone."

Then his eye fell on the altimeter. He glanced at Tom sharply, especially at the riding breeches and high, laced boots.

"I guess I went and made a damn fool of myself," he said swiftly. "You an oil man?"

Tom got to his feet. "I'm on the State Geologic Survey," he said.

The farmer's manner changed completely. He stepped forward, his voice was confidential. "But you saw signs of oil here, didn't you?"

Tom shrugged his shoulders and grinned pleasantly. He had heard a hundred farmers ask that same question in the same way. "I couldn't say anything about that. I'd have to finish my mapping before I could make any guesses."

The farmer smiled back, knowingly but not unfriendlily. "I know what you mean," he said. "I know you fellows got orders not to talk. So long, mister."

Tom said, "So long," nodded good-bye to the little girl, who was still gazing at him steadily, and walked around the barn to his own car. As he plumped the altimeter down on the front seat beside him, he yielded to the impulse to take another reading. Once more he swore, this time under his breath.

The altimeter seemed to be working properly again.

"Well," he told himself, "that settles it. I'll come back and get a reliable alidade reading, if not with Ben, then with somebody else. I'll nail that hill down before I do anything."

Ben Shelley slupped down the last drops of coffee, pushed back from the table, and thumbed tobacco into his battered brier. Tom explained his proposition.

A wooden-bladed fan was wheezing ponderously overhead, causing pendant stripes of fly paper to sway and tremble.

"Hold on a minute," Ben interrupted near the end. "That reminds me of something I was bringing over for you. May save us the trouble." And he fished in his briefcase.

"You don't mean to tell me there's some map for this region I didn't know about?" The tragic disgust in Tom's voice was only half jocular. "They swore up and down to me at the office there wasn't."

"Yeah, I'm afraid I mean just that," Ben confirmed. "Here she is. A special topographic job. Only issued yesterday."

Tom snatched the folded sheet.

"You're right," he proclaimed, a few moments later. "This might have been some help to me." His voice became sarcastic. "I wonder what they wanted to keep it a mystery for?"

"Oh, you know how it is," said Ben easily. "They take a long time getting maps out. The work for this was done two years ago, before you were on the Survey. It's rather an unusual map, and the person you talked to at the office probably didn't connect it up with your structural job. And there's a yarn about it, which might explain why there was some confusion."

Tom had pushed the dishes away and was studying the map intently. Now he gave a muffled exclamation which made Ben look up. Then he hurriedly reinspected the whole map and the printed material in the corner. Then he stared at one spot for so long that Ben chuckled and said, "What have you found? A gold mine?"

Tom turned a serious face on him. "Look, Ben," he said slowly. "This map is no good. There's a terrible mistake in it." Then he added, "It looks as if they did some of the readings by sighting through a rolled-up newspaper at a yardstick."

"I knew you wouldn't be happy until you found something wrong with it," said Ben. "Can't say I blame you. What is it?"

Tom slid the map across to him, indicating one spot with his thumbnail. "Just read that off to me," he directed. "What do you see there?"

Ben paused while he lit his pipe, eyeing the map. Then he answered promptly, "An elevation of four hundred forty-one feet. And it's got a name lettered in—'The Hole.' Poetic, aren't we? Well, what is it? A stone quarry?"

"Ben, I was out at that very spot this morning," said Tom, "and there isn't any depression there at all, but a hill. This reading is merely off some trifle of a hundred and forty feet!"

"Go on," countered Ben. "You were somewhere else this morning. Got mixed up. I've done it myself."

Tom shook his head. "There's a five-hundred-eleven-foot bench mark right next door to it."

"Then you got an old bench mark." Ben was amusedly skeptical. "You know, one of the pre-Columbus ones."

"Oh, rot. Look, Ben, how about coming out with me this afternoon and we'll shoot it with your alidade? I've got to do it some time or other, anyway, now that my altimeter's out of whack. And I'll prove to you this map is chuck-full of errors. How about it?"

Ben applied another match to his pipe. He nodded. "All right, I'm game. But don't be angry when you find you turned in at the wrong farm."

It was not until they were rolling along the highway, with Ben's equipment in the back seat, that Tom remembered something. "Say, Ben, didn't you start to tell me about a yarn connected with this map?"

"It doesn't amount to much really. Just that the surveyor—an old chap named Wolcraftson—died of heart failure while he was still in the field. At first they thought someone would have to re-do the job, but later, when they went over his papers, they found he had completed it. Maybe that explains why some of the people at the office were in doubt as to whether there was such a map."

Tom was concentrating on the road ahead. They were getting near the turn-off. "That would have been about two years ago?" he asked. "I mean, when he died?"

"Uh-huh. Or two and a half. It happened somewhere around here and there was some kind of stupid mess about it. I seem to remember that a fool county coroner—a local Sherlock Holmes—said there were signs of strangulation, or suffocation, or some other awful nonsense, and wanted to hold Wolcraftson's rodman. Of course, we put a stop to that."

Tom did not answer. Certain words he had heard a couple of hours earlier were coming back to him, just as if a phonograph had been turned on: "Two years ago there was a man come up here, trying to find out about *Them*. He had a kind of spyglass on sticks. *They* made

him dead. That's why I didn't want you to go down there. I was afraid
They would do the same thing to you."

He angrily shut his mind to those words. If there was anything he
detested, it was admitting the possibility of supernatural agencies, even
in jest. Anyway, what difference did her words make? After all, a man
had really died, and it was only natural that her defective imagination
should cook up some wild fancy.

Of course, as he had to admit, the screwy entry on the map made
one more coincidence, counting the girl's story and the cockeyed altimeter readings as the first. But was it so much of a coincidence?
Perhaps Wolcraftson had listened to the girl's prattling and noted down
"The Hole" and the reading for it as a kind of private joke, intending
to erase it later. Besides, what difference did it make if there had been
two genuine coincidences? The universe was full of them. Every mo-
lecular collision was a coincidence. You could pile a thousand coincidences on top of another, he averred, and not get Tom Digby one
step nearer to believing in the supernatural. Oh, he knew intelligent
people enough, all right, who coddled such beliefs. Some of his best
friends liked to relate "yarns" and toy with eerie possibilities for the
sake of a thrill. But the only emotion Tom ever got out of such stuff
was a nauseating disgust. It cut too deep for joking. It was a reversion
to that primitive, fear-bound ignorance from which science had slowly
lifted man, inch by inch, against the most bitter opposition. Take this
silly matter about the hill. Once admit that the dimensions of a thing
might not be real, down to the last fraction of an inch, and you cut
the foundations from under the world.

He'd be damned, he told himself, if he ever told anyone the whole
story of the altimeter readings. It was just the silly sort of "yarn" that
Ben, for instance, would like to play around with. Well, he'd have to
do without it.

With a feeling of relief he turned off for the farm. He had worked
himself up into quite an angry state of mind, and part of the anger
was at himself, for even bothering to think about such matters. Now
they would finish it off neatly, as scientists should, without leaving any
loose ends around for morbid imaginations to knit together.

He led Ben back to the barn, and indicated the bench mark and the
hill. Ben got his bearings, studied the map, inspected the bench mark
closely, then studied the map again.

Finally he turned with an apologetic grin. "You're absolutely right.
This map is as screwy as a surrealist painting, at least as far as that
hill is concerned. I'll go around to the car and get my stuff. We can
shoot its altitude from right off the bench mark." He paused, frowning.
"Gosh, though, I can't understand how Wolcraftson ever got it so
screwed up."

"Probably they misinterpreted something on his original manuscript map."

"I suppose that must have been it."

After they had set up the plane table and telescope-like alidade directly over the bench mark, Tom shouldered the rod, with its inset level and conspicuous markings.

"I'll go up there and be rodman for you," he said. "I'd like you to shoot this yourself. Then they won't have any comeback when you walk into the office and blow them up for issuing such a map."

"Okay," Ben answered, laughing. "I'll look forward to doing that."

Tom noticed the farmer coming toward them from the field ahead. He was relieved to see that the little girl was not with him. As they passed one another, the farmer winked triumphantly at him. "Found something worth coming back for, eh?" Tom did not answer. But the farmer's manner tickled his sense of humor, and he found himself feeling pretty good, all irritation gone, as he stepped along toward the hill.

The farmer introduced himself to Ben by saying, "Found signs of a pretty big gusher, eh?" His pretense at being matter-of-fact was not convincing.

"I don't know anything about it," Ben answered cheerfully. "He just roped me in to help him take a reading."

The farmer cocked his big head and looked sideways at Ben. "My, you State fellows are pretty close-mouthed, aren't you? Well, you needn't worry, because I _know_ there's oil under here. Five years ago a fellow took a drilling lease on all my land at a dollar a year. But then he never showed up again. Course, I know what happened. The big companies bought him out. They know there's oil under here, but they won't drill. Want to keep the price of gasoline up."

Ben made a noncommittal sound, and busied himself loading his pipe. Then he sighted through the alidade at Tom's back, for no particular reason. The farmer's gaze swung out in the same direction.

"Well, that's a funny thing now, come to think of it," he said. "Right out where he's going, is where that other chap keeled over a couple of years ago."

Ben's interest quickened. "A surveyor named Wolcraftson?"

"Something like that. It happened right on top of that hill. They'd been fooling around here all day—something gone wrong with the instruments, the other chap said. Course I knew they'd found signs of oil and didn't want to let on. Along toward evening the old chap—Wolcraftson, like you said—took the pole out there himself—the other chap had done it twice before—and stood atop the hill. It was right then he keeled over. We run out there, but it was too late. Heart got him. He must of thrashed around a lot before he died, though, because he was all covered with dust."

Ben grunted appreciatively. "Wasn't there some question about it afterward?"

"Oh, our coroner made a fool of himself, as he generally does. But I stepped in and told exactly what happened, and that settled it. Say, mister, why don't you break down and tell me what you know about the oil under here?"

Ben's protestations of total ignorance on the subject were cut short by the sudden appearance of a little tow-headed girl from the direction of the road. She had been running. She gasped "Papa!" and grabbed the farmer's hand. Ben walked over toward the alidade. He could see the figure of Tom emerging from the tall weeds and starting up the hill. Then his attention was caught by what the girl was saying.

"You've got to stop him, Papa!" She was dragging at her father's wrist. "You can't let him go down in the hole. *They* got it fixed to make him dead this time."

"Shut your mouth, Sue!" the farmer shouted down at her, his voice more anxious than angry. "You'll get me into trouble with the School Board, the queer things you say. That man's just going out there to find out how high the hill is."

"But, Papa, can't you see?" She twisted away and pointed at Tom's steadily mounting figure. "He's already started down in. *They're* set to trap him. Squattin' down there in the dark, all quiet so he won't hear their bones scrapin' together—stop him, Papa!"

With an apprehensive look at Ben, the farmer got down on his knees beside the little girl and put his arms around her. "Look, Sue, you're a big girl now," he argued. "It don't do for you to talk that way. I know you're just playing, but other people don't know you so well. They might get to thinking things. You wouldn't want them to take you away from me, would you?"

She was twisting from side to side in his arms trying to catch a glimpse of Tom over his shoulder. Suddenly, with an unexpected backward lunge, she jerked loose and ran off toward the hill. The farmer got to his feet and lumbered after her, calling, "Stop, Sue! Stop!"

Crazy as a couple of hoot owls, Ben decided, watching them go. Both of them think there's something under the ground. One says oil, the other says ghosts. You pay your money and you take your choice.

Then he noticed that during the excitement Tom had gotten to the top of the hill and had the rod up. He hurriedly sighted through the alidade, which was in the direction of the hilltop. For some reason he could not see anything through it—just blackness. He felt forward to make sure the lens cover was off. He swung it around a little, hoping something had not dropped out of place inside the tube. Then abruptly, through it, he caught sight of Tom, and involuntarily he uttered a short, frightened cry and jumped away.

On the hilltop, Tom was no longer in sight. Ben stood still for a moment. Then he raced for the hill at top speed.

He found the farmer looking around perplexedly near the far fence. "Come on," Ben gasped out, "there's trouble," and vaulted over.

When they reached the hilltop, Ben stooped to the sprawling body, then recoiled with a convulsive movement and for a second time uttered a smothered cry. For every square inch of skin and clothes was smeared with a fine, dark-gray dust. And close beside one gray hand was a tiny white bone.

Because a certain hideous vision still dominated his memory, Ben needed no one to tell him that it was a bone from a human finger. He buried his face in his hands, fighting that vision.

For what he had seen, or thought he had seen, through the alidade, had been a tiny struggling figure of Tom, buried in darkness, with dim, skeletal figures clutching him all around and dragging him down into a thicker blackness.

The farmer knelt by the body. "Dead as dead," he muttered in a hushed voice. "Just like the other. He's got the stuff fairly rubbed into him. It's even in his mouth and nose. Like he'd been buried in ashes and then dug up."

From between the rails of the fence, the little girl stared up at them, terrified, but avid.

The Refugee

JANE RICE

Several fantasy-writing careers began in Unknown. *Jane Rice began and all but ended hers there. After contributing a handful of witty stories that shifted effortlessly between light humor and sardonic horror, Rice virtually disappeared from the fantasy scene when* Unknown *discontinued publication. Thus it is appropriate that her story "The Refugee" appeared in the magazine's final issue. A tale of a traditional werewolf trying to exist under the rather untraditional circumstances of life in wartime France, it is a perfect example of what Rice was capable of writing and as good an example as any of what* Unknown *fiction was all about.*

THE TROUBLE with the war, Milli Cushman thought as she stared sulkily through streaming French windows into her rain-drenched garden, was that it was so frightfully boring. There weren't any men, any more. Interesting ones, that is. Or parties. Or little pink cocktails. Or café royale. Or long-stemmed roses wrapped in crackly green wax paper. There wasn't even a decent hairdresser left.

She had been a fool to stay on. But it had seemed so exciting. Everyone listening to the radio broadcasts; the streets blossoming with uniforms; an air of feverish gaiety, heady as Moselle wine, over all the city; the conversations that made one feel so important—so in the thick of things. Would the Maginot Line hold? Would the British come? Would the Low Countries be invaded? Was it true America had issued an ultimatum? Subjects that, now, were outdated as Gatling guns.

It had been terrifically stimulating being asked for her opinion, as an American. Of course, she hadn't been home for a number of years and considered herself a true cosmopolite freed from the provincialities of her own country—but, still, it had been nice, in those first flurried jack-in-the-box days of war to be able to discourse so intelligently on Americans. It had been such *fun.*

Momentarily, Milli's eyes sparkled—remembering. The sparkle faded and died.

Then, unexpectedly, the city had become a gaunt, gray ghost. No, not a ghost, a cat. A gaunt gray cat with its bones showing through, as it crouched on silent haunches and stared unwinkingly before it. Like one of those cats that hung around the alley barrels of the better hotels. Or used to hang. Cooked, a cat bore a striking resemblance to a rabbit.

Overnight, a hush had fallen on everything. It was as though the city had gasped in one long, last, labored, dying breath. And had held it. One could feel it in the atmosphere. Almost like a desperate pounding.

For some inexplicable reason, it reminded her of her childhood when she had played a game as the street lights began to bloom in the gathering dusk. "If I can hold my eyes open without blinking," she would tell herself, "until the last one is lighted, I'll get a new doll"— or a new muff—or a new hair ribbon—or whatever it might be she wanted. She could still recall that exhausted sense of time running out as the final lights went on. Most always she had won. Sometimes she hadn't, but most always she had. By the skin of her teeth.

It would be perfectly horrid, if this was one of the times when she *didn't* win. If she had to stay on and on, trotting back and forth seeing about that idiotic visa, and saving her hairpins and soap ends and things, it was going to be too utterly stultifying. It was fortunate she had had the perception to realize, before it was too late, who were the "right people" to know. It helped. Although, in these days, the right people didn't fare much better than the "wrong" ones.

Milli used "fare" in its strictest interpretation. Often, of late, she found herself dwelling, with an aching nostalgia, on her father's butcher shop in Pittsburgh. That had been before he'd invented a new deboner, or meat cleaver or something, and had amassed an unbelievable amount of money and before he strangled to death on a loose gold filling at Tim O'Toole's clambake.

Milli's recollection of her father was but a dim blur of red face and handle-bar mustaches and a deep booming voice that Milli had associated with the line "the curfew tolls the knell of parting day," which

she had been forced to learn and recite at P. S. 46. Her mother she
didn't remember at all, as she had been called to pastures greener than
anything Pittsburgh had to offer while Milli was yet wearing swaddling
clothes in a perpetual state of dampness.

However, sharpened by adversity, Milli's recollections of the butcher
shop were crystal clear. The refrigerator with whole sides of beef hanging
from hooks, legs of lamb like fat tallow candles, plump chickens with
thick drumsticks and their heads wrapped in brown paper, slabs of
pork and veal, and, at Thanksgiving and Christmas, short-legged ducks,
and high-breasted turkeys, and big, yellow geese. In the showcase had
been chops, and steaks, and huge roasts, and all sorts of sausages and
spiced meats laid out in white enameled trays with carrot tops in
between for "dressing."

It was hopeless to dream of these things, but practically impossible
to stop. The main topics of conversation no longer were of "major
developments" but of where one could buy an extra ration of tea of
questionable ingredients, or a gristly chop of dubious origin, or a few
eggs of doubtful age—if one could pay the whopping price.

Well, as long as she had liqueur-filled chocolates, and she had had
enough foresight to lay in quite a supply, she could be assured of her
"share." They were better than money, at the present exchange.

The clock on the mantelpiece tinkled out the hours and Milli sighed.
She should bathe and dress for dinner. But what was the use of keeping
up appearances when there wasn't anyone to see. And it was dreadful
curling the ends of one's hair on an iron. It was tedious and it didn't
really *do* a great deal for one. And it had an unmistakable scent of
burning shoe leather about it. The water would be tepid, if not actually
cold. The soap wouldn't lather. The bathroom would be clammy, and
the dinner, when it was forthcoming, would be a ragout of God knew
what, a potato that had gouged-out areas in it, a limp salad and a
compote of dried fruit. And Maria grumbled so about serving it in
courses. It was positively useless to diagram for her the jumbled up
indecencies of a table d'hôte. Maria was almost worse than no help at
all. Definitely a bourgeois.

Milli yawned and stretched her arms above her head. She arose and,
going over to the windows, stood looking out. A shaft of sunlight broke
through the clouds and angered the tiny charms that dangled from her
"war bracelet." An airplane studded with rhinestones, a miniature
cannon with gold-leaf wheels, a toy soldier whose diamond chip eyes
winked red and blue and green in the sun as he twirled helplessly on
his silver chain. Ten or twelve of these baubles hung from the bracelet
and it is indicative of Milli's character that she had bought them as
a gift to herself to "celebrate" the last Bastille Day.

The sun's watery radiance turned the slackening rain into shining
strings of quicksilver and made a drowned seascape of the garden. The

faun that once had been a fountain gleamed wetly in the pale, unearthly light and about its feet in the cracked basin the pelting raindrops danced and bubbled like antiphonic memories of long gone grace notes. The flower heads were heavy with sodden, brown-edged petals and their stalks bent wearily as if cognizant of the fact that their lives were held by a tenuous thread that was about to be snapped between the chill, biting teeth of an early frost.

Milli looked at the rain intermingled with sun and thought the devil is beating his wife. That was what Savannah used to say, back in Pittsburgh. "The devil's beatin' his wife, sho nuff." Savannah, who made such luscious mince pies and cherry tarts, and whose baked hams were always brown and crunchy on top and stuck with cloves and criss-crossed with a knife so that the juice ran down in between the cracks and—Milli's culinary recollections suffered a complete collapse and her eyes opened very wide as they alighted on a head poking out inquisitively from the leafy seclusion of the tall hedge that bounded the garden.

Two brown hands pushed aside the foliage to allow a pair of broad, brown shoulders to come through.

Milli gave an infinitesimal gasp. A man was in her garden! A man who, judging from the visible portion of his excellent anatomy, had—literally—lost his shirt.

Instinctively, she opened her mouth to make some sort of an outcry. Whether she meant to call for aid, or to scare the interloper away, or merely to give vent to a belated exclamation of surprise, will forever be debatable for the object of her scrutiny chose that moment to turn his extraordinarily well-shaped head and his glance fixed itself on Milli. Milli's outcry died a-borning.

To begin with, it wasn't a man. It was a youth. And to end with, there was something about him, some queer, indefinable quality, that was absolutely fascinating.

He was, Milli thought, rather like a young panther, or a half-awakened leopard. He was, Milli admitted, entranced, beautiful. Perfectly *beautiful.* As an animal is beautiful and, automatically, she raised her chin so that the almost unnoticeable pouch under it became one with the line of her throat.

The youth was unabashed. If the discovery of his presence in a private garden left him in a difficult position, he effectively concealed his embarrassment. He regarded Milli steadfastly, and unwaveringly and admiringly, and Milli, like a mesmerized bird, watched the rippling play of his muscles beneath his skin as he shoved the hedge apart still farther to obtain a better view of his erstwhile hostess.

Confusedly, Milli thought that it was lucky that the windows were locked and, in the same mental breath, what a pity that they were.

The two peered at one another. Milli knew only that his hair was pasted flat to his head with the rain, and that his arms shone like sepia satin, and his eyes were tawny and filled with a flickering inward fire that made suet pudding of her knees.

For a long moment they remained so—their eyes locked. Milli's like those of an amazed china doll's; his like those of an untamed animal that was slightly underfed and resented the resulting gastric disturbances. The kitchen door banged and Milli could hear Maria calling a neighborly greeting to someone, as she emptied a bucket of water in the yard. At that instant the last vestiges of sun began to sink behind the horizon, and the youth was gone. There was just the garden, and the rain, and the hedge.

Dimly, as through a fog, Milli heard Maria come in, heard the latch shoot home, the metallic clatter of the bucket as she set it down under the sink and, from somewhere outside, the long, diminishingly mournful howl of a dog.

Milli shook herself out of her trance. She brushed a hand across her eyelids as if to clear them of cobwebs and, unbolting one of the windows, went out into the garden. There was no one. Only a footprint by the hedge, a bare footprint filling in with water.

She went back into the house. Maria was there, turning on the lamps. She looked at Milli curiously and Milli realized that she must be an odd sight, indeed, her hair liberally besprinkled with raindrops, her shoes muddy, her dress streaked with moisture.

"I thought I saw someone out there, just now," she explained. "Someone looking in."

"The police, probably," Maria said dourly. "The police have no notion of privacy."

"No," Milli said. "No, it wasn't the police. Didn't I hear you go out a few moments ago?"

"I wasn't looking in," Maria said in a peevish voice. "For why should I look in? I have other things to do besides looking in the windows." She drew herself up to list vocally and with accompanying gestures the numberless things she had to do.

"Did you see anyone?" Milli asked quickly.

"Old Phillipe," Maria answered. "I saw old Phillipe. On his way to the inn in the pouring rain and he with a cough since last April. When one has a cough and it is raining, one does not look in windows. Anyway, Phillipe is too old. When one is as old as Phillipe one is no longer interested. Anyhow, his son was killed at Avignon. Phillipe would not look in the windows."

"You saw no one else?"

Maria's eyes narrowed. "Madame was expecting someone, no?"

"No," Milli said. "No, I just thought . . . it was nothing."

"If madame is expecting someone, perhaps it would be well to save the beverage for later in the evening?"

"I am expecting no one."

It was, Milli thought as she let the curling iron rest in the gaseous flame, next to impossible to tell which side of the fence Maria was on. She could easily be reporting things to *both* sides. One had to be careful. So very careful.

This chap in the garden, for example. He must have escaped from somewhere. That would account for the absence of clothes. He was a refugee of some sort. And refugees of any sort were dangerous. It was best to stick to the beaten path and those who trod thereon. But he was so beautiful. Like a stripling god. No more than twenty, surely. It was delightful to see again someone as young as twenty. It was—Milli swore fluently as the iron began to smoke; she waved it in the air to cool it and, testing it gingerly with a moistened forefinger, applied it to her coiffure—it was not only delightful, it was heavenly. It was, really, rather like one of those little, long ago, pink cocktails. It *did* something for one.

A faint aroma of singeing hair made itself manifest in the damp, wallpapery-smelling room.

Milli considered the refugee from every angle as she ate her solitary dinner and, afterward, as she reclined on her chaise longue idly turning the pages of a book selected at random, and while she was disrobing for bed, and even when she was giving the underpart of her chin the regulation number of backhanded slaps, a ritual that as a rule occupied her entire attention.

Slipping into her dressing gown, she opened her window and leaned out, chin in hands, elbows on the sill. The moon rode in the sky—a hunted thing dodging behind wisps of tattered cloud, and the air was heavy and wet and redolent of dying leaves.

"The moon was a ghostly galleon," Milli quoted, feeling, somehow frail and immensely poetic. She smiled a sad, fragile smile in keeping with her mood and wondered if the refugee also was having a lonely rendezvous with the moon. Lying on his back in some hidden spot thinking, possibly, of—Her reverie was broken sharply by Maria's voice, shattering the stillness of the night. It was followed by a cascade of water.

"What on earth are you *doing?*" Milli called down exasperatedly.

"There was an animal out here," Maria yelled back, equally as exasperated. "Trampling in my mulch pile."

Milli started to say, "Don't be ridiculous, go to bed," but the sentence froze on her lips as she remembered the refugee. He had come back! Maria had thrown water on him! He had returned full of . . . of—well, hope for refuge, maybe, and Maria, the dolt, had chased him away!

"Wait," she called frenziedly into the darkness. "Wait! Oh, please, wait!"

Maria, thinking the command was for her, had waited, although the "please" had astonished her somewhat. Muttering under her breath, she had led her strangely overwrought mistress into the kitchen garden and had pointed out with pardonable pride the footprints in her mulch pile. Padded footprints. With claws.

"I saw the eyes," she said, "great, gleaming, yellow ones shining in the light when I started to pull the scullery blinds. Luckily I had a pot of water handy and I jerked open the door and—"

But her mistress wasn't listening. In truth, for one originally so upset, she had regained her composure with remarkable rapidity.

"Undoubtedly, the Trudeau's dog," she said with a total lack of interest.

"The Trudeau's dog is a Pomeranian," Maria said determinedly.

"No matter," Milli said. "Go to bed, Maria."

Maria went, mumbling to herself a querulous litany in which the word Pomeranian was, ever and anon, distinguishable—and pronounced with expletive force.

Milli awakened to find her room bright with sun, which was regrettable as it drew attention to the pattern of the rug and the well-worn condition of the curtains. It, likewise, did various things to Milli Cushman's face, which were little short of libelous. Libelous, that is, after Milli had painted herself a new one with painstaking care and the touch of an inspired, if jaded, master.

Downstairs, she found her breakfast ready and, because of its readiness, a trifle cold. She also found Maria, while not openly weeping, puffy as to eyes, and pink as to nose, and quite snuffly—a state that Milli found deplorable in servants.

A series of sharp questions brought to light the fact that old Phillipe was dead. Old Phillipe, it seemed, was not only dead but a bit mangled. To make a long story short, old Phillipe had been discovered in a condition that bordered on the skeletal. Identification had been made through particles of clothing and a pair of broken spectacles.

"You mean to say he was *eaten!*" Milli cried, which caused Maria to go off into a paroxysm of near hysterics from which Milli gathered, obscurely, that Maria blamed herself for old Phillipe's untimely demise.

By degrees, Milli drew it out of her. The footprints in the mulch pile. The kettle of water. The withdrawal of the animal to more congenial surroundings. Surroundings, doubtless, that were adjacent to the inn from whence old Phillipe, subsequently, plodded homeward. The stealthy pad of marauding feet. The encounter. The shriek. The awful ensuing silence.

Maria's detail was so graphic that it made Milli slightly ill, although it didn't prevent her from being firm about the matter of the wolf.

"Nonsense," Milli said. "Ridiculous. A *wolf.* Preposterous."

Maria explained about the bloody footprints leading away from the scene of slaughter. Footprints much too large for a dog. *Enormous* footprints.

"No doubt it was an enormous dog," Milli said coldly. "The natural habitat of a wolf is a forest, not a paved street."

Maria opened her mouth to go even further into detail, but Milli effectively shut it for her by a reprimand that, like the porridge of the three bears, was neither too hot nor too cold, but just right.

After all, Milli thought, old Phillipe was better off. In all probability, he hadn't suffered a great deal. Most likely he had died of shock first. One more, or less, what difference did it make. Especially when one was as old as old Phillipe. At least he had lived his life while *she,* with so much life yet to be lived, was embalmed in a wretched sort of flypaper existence that adhered to every inch of her no matter how hard she pulled. That visa. She would have to see about it again tomorrow. And the tea supply was disastrously low. And this horrible toast made of horrible bread that was crumbly and dry and tasted of sawdust. And her last bottle of eau de cologne practically *gone,* and she *couldn't* eat this mess in front of her.

Milli got up and went into the parlor. She flung wide the French windows and petulantly surveyed the garden. She had rented the place *because* of the garden—such a lovely setting for informal teas, she had thought, and impromptu chafing-dish suppers on the flagstones with candlelight and thin, graceful-stemmed glasses. She had pictured herself in appropriate attire, cutting flowers and doing whatever it was one did with peat moss, and now look at the thing. Just *look* at it!

Milli looked at it. Her breath went out of her. She drew it in again with an unbecoming wheeze. One hand flew to her throat.

In the garden, fast asleep, curled up in a ball under the hedge, was the refugee, all dappled with shadows and naked as the day he was born.

This time, it must be noted in all fairness, Milli didn't open her chops. If an outcry was in her, it wasn't strong enough to register on her reflexes. Her eyes blinked rapidly, as they always did when Milli was thinking fast and, when she recrossed the parlor and walked down the hallway into the kitchen, her heels made hard staccato sounds on the flooring, as they always did when Milli had reached a decision.

Milli's decision made Maria as happy as could be, under the circumstances, and ten minutes later, reticule in hand, Maria departed for the domicile of her married niece's husband's aunt who was a friend of old Phillipe's widow and, consequently, would be in possession of all the particulars and would more than appreciate a helping hand and an attentive ear over the weekend.

Milli turned the key behind her. Lightly, she ran to the scullery closet and took down from a nail a pair of grass-stained pants that had belonged to a gardener who had been liquidated before he had had a chance to return for his garment. Carrying the trousers over her arm, she retraced her steps to the parlor and through the double French windows.

Quiet as she was, her unbidden guest was awake as soon as her foot touched the first flagstone. He didn't move a muscle. He just opened his eyes and watched her with the easy assurance of one who knows he can leave whenever he wants to and several jumps ahead of the nearest competitor.

Milli stopped. She held out the pants.

"For you," she said. She gave them a toss. The boy, his queer, light eyes watching her every movement, made no attempt to catch them.

"Put them on," Milli said. She hesitated. "Please," she said, adding, "I am your friend."

The boy sat up. Milli hastily turned her back.

"Tell me when you get them on," she ordered.

She waited, and waited, and waited, and, hearing not the faintest rustle, cautiously swiveled her head around. Once again she drew in her breath and the wheeze was very nearly an eek for, not six inches away, was her visitor—his lips pulled over his teeth in a rather disconcerting smile, his eyes like glittering nuggets of amber.

The thought raced through Milli's head that he was going to "spring" at her, as the boy's eyes enumerated her charms one by one. She promptly elevated her chin and tried to keep her consternation from becoming obvious.

The boy laughed softly. A laugh that, somehow, was like a musical sort of a snarl. He stepped back. He bowed. Mockingly.

"What are you doing in my garden?" Milli asked, thinking it best to put him in his place, first and foremost. It wouldn't do to let him get out of hand. So soon, anyway.

"Sleeping," the boy said.

"Don't you have any place to sleep?"

"Yes, many places. But I like this place."

"What happened to your clothes?"

The boy shrugged. He didn't answer.

"Are you a refugee?"

"In a way, I suppose, yes."

"You're hiding, aren't you?"

"Until you came out, I was simply sleeping. After I have eaten I sleep until a short while before sundown."

"You're not hungry?" Milli elevated her eyebrows in surprise.

"Not now." The boy let his glance rove fleetingly over his hostess's neck. "I will be later."

"What do you mean 'until a short while before sundown'? Have you been traveling by night?"

"Yes."

Milli made an ineffectual motion toward the trousers. "Wasn't it . . . I mean, going around without any . . . that is, I should think— Weren't you cold?"

"No."

"It's a wonder you didn't catch pneumonia."

The boy grinned. He patted his flat stomach. "Not pneumonia," he said. "But it wasn't much better. Old and stringy and without flavor."

Milli regarded him with a puzzled frown. She didn't like being "taken in." She decided to let it go.

"My name is Milli Cushman," she said. "You are more than welcome to stay here until you are rested. You won't be bothered. I have sent my maid away."

"You're most kind," the boy said with exaggerated politeness. "Until tonight will be sufficient." If he realized that Milli was expecting him to introduce himself, he gave no sign.

After a pause, she spoke, a shade irritably. "No doubt, you *do* have a name?"

"I have lots of names. Even Latin ones."

"Well, what is one? I can't just go about calling you 'you,' you know."

"You might call me Lupus," the boy said. "It's one of the Latin ones. It means wolf."

"Do they call you The Wolf!"

"Yes."

"How intriguing. But why?"

The boy smiled at her. "I daresay you'll find out," he said.

"You mean you're one of the ones who . . . well, like the affair of that German officer last week . . . that is to say, in a manner of speaking, you're one of those who're *still* going at it hammer and tongs?"

"Tooth and nail," the boy said.

"It seems so *silly*," Milli said. "What *good* does it do. It doesn't scare them. It just makes them angrier. And that makes it harder on *us*."

"Oh, but it *does* scare them," the boy said with an ironic lilt to his voice. "It scares them to death. Or at any rate it helps." He yawned, his tongue curling out like a cat's. And, suddenly, he was sullen. He glared at Milli with remote hostility.

"I'm sleepy," he growled. "I'm tired of talking. I want to go to sleep. Go away."

"Come inside," Milli said. "You can have Maria's bed." She gave him her most delectable glance. The one that involved the upsweeping and downsweeping of her eyelashes with the slimmest trace of a roguish quirk about the lips.

"I won't disturb you," she said. "And, besides, you might be caught if you stay in the garden. There was a man killed last night by some kind of a creature, or so they say, and Maria is sure to spread the news abroad that she threw water at something, and police just might investigate, and it *could* be very awkward for us both. Won't you come in, please?"

The boy looked at her in surly silence.

"Please, Lupus. For me?"

Once more he laughed softly. And this time the laugh was definitely a snarl. He reached out and pinched her. "For you, I will."

It was, Milli thought, not at all a flirtatious pinch. It was the kind of pinch her father used to give chickens to see if they were filled out in the proper places.

But Lupus wouldn't sleep in Maria's bed. He curled upon the floor of the parlor. Which, Milli thought, was just as well. It would save remaking Maria's bed so Maria wouldn't notice anything.

While her caller slept, Milli busied herself with pots and pans in the kitchen. It was tedious, but worth it. Tonight, there would be supper on the flatstones, with candles, and starlight, and all the accessories. A chance like this might not come her way for many another moon. She was resolved to make the most of it. As Savannah would have said, she was going to "do herself proud." For Lupus, the best was none too good. She nibbled a sandwich for luncheon, not wanting to spoil her appetite—not waking Lupus, for fear of spoiling his.

She got out her precious hoard of condiments. She scanned the fine printed directions on boxes. Meticulously she read the instructive leaflet enclosed in her paper bag of tanbarky appearing flour. She took off her bracelet, rolled up her sleeves and went to work—humming happily to herself, a thing which she hadn't done for months.

She scraped, peeled, measured, sifted, chopped, stirred, beat and folded. Some fairly creditable muffins emerged from under her unaccustomed and amateurish fingers, a dessert that wasn't bad at all, and a salad that managed to give the impression of actually *being* a salad, which bordered on the miraculous.

The day slowly drew to a close and Milli was quite startled to find the hours had passed with such swiftness. So swiftly that her initial awareness of their passing was caused by the advent of a patently ill-humored Lupus.

"Oh, dear," Milli said. "I didn't realize . . . Is it late?"

"No," Lupus said. "It's growing early. The sun is going down."

"Are you hungry? I'm fixing some things I think will be rather good."

"I'm ravenous," Lupus said. "Let's go watch the sunset."

Milli put her hands up to her coiffure, coquettishly, allowing her sleeves to fall away from her round, white arms.

"Wait till I fix my hair. I must be a sight."

"You are," Lupus agreed, his eyes glistening. "And I won't have to wait much longer." Effortlessly he moved across and stood over Milli, devouring her with an all-encompassing gaze.

"Won't you have one of these," Milli asked hurriedly, hoping his impetuosity wouldn't brim over too abruptly. She shoved a box of liqueur-filled chocolates at him. "There's no such thing as a cocktail any more. Come along, we'll eat them on the sofa. It's . . . it's cozier."

But Lupus wasn't interested in the chocolates. In the parlor he stretched his long, supple length on the floor and contemplated the garden, ablaze in the last rays of a dying sun.

Milli plopped down beside him and began to rub his back, gently with long, smooth, even strokes. Lupus rolled his head over in lazy, indifferent pleasure, and looked up at her with a hunger that would have been voluptuous, if it hadn't been so stark.

"Do you like that?" Milli whispered.

For a reply, Lupus opened his mouth and yawned. And into it Milli dropped a chocolate, while at the same instant she jabbed him savagely with a hairpin.

The boy sucked in his breath with a pained howl, and a full eight minutes before the sun went down, Lupus had neatly choked to death on a chocolate whose liqueur-filled insides contained a silver bullet from Milli Cushman's "war bracelet."

It had been, Milli told herself later, a near thing. And it would have been *ghastly* if it hadn't worked. But it *had* worked, tra la. Of course, it stood to reason that it *would*. After all, if, at death, a werewolf changed back into human form, why, logically, the human form would— if in close personal contact with a silver bullet *before* sundown— metamorphosis into a wolf.

It was marvelous that she'd happened to pick up "The Werewolf of Paris" yesterday—had given her an insight, so to speak, and it was *extremely* handy that she'd had all that butcher shop background.

Milli wiped her mouth daintily with a napkin. How divinely *full* she was. And with Maria gone she could have Lupus all to herself.

Down to the last delicious morsel.

The Weird Doom of
Floyd Scrilch

ROBERT BLOCH

Giant mushrooms! Miracle cures! Books of forbidden knowledge! The stuff of pulp fantasy? On the contrary, these were some of the items often advertised in the back pages of pulp fantasy magazines. In "The Weird Doom of Floyd Scrilch," Robert Bloch explains why such highly promoted products never lived up to consumer expectations—and why it was probably all for the better that they did not. Initially a protege of H. P. Lovecraft and the school of "eldritch horror," Bloch began writing humorous fantasy for Unknown. *He eventually came up with the idea of telling pun-filled fantasies couched in the flat slang of a Damon Runyon-type character. Lefty Feep, Bloch's sad-sack gambler and con man, served as a mouthpiece for twenty-two such premeditated assaults upon the English language in* Fantastic Adventures.

I HAD ALMOST finished with my meal over at Jack's Shack. In fact, I was halfway through my last cup of coffee and my first bicarbonate of soda. Shaking the gravy off my newspaper, I unfolded it and began to read.

Suddenly a hand descended and brushed the pages aside. I looked up into the startled face of Lefty Feep. His wildly rolling eyes were staring at the discarded paper with a look of intense loathing.

"Remove it away," he grated. "Grab loose from that!"

I raised my eyebrows as he lowered his hips into a seat.

"What's the matter, Feep?" I asked. "Does the sight of the news upset you so much?"

"News?" echoed the eccentric Mr. Feep. "It is not the news which upsets me at all. It is the advertisements that drain the rosy color from my handsome face. I cannot bear to look at them."

For the first time I foresaw that I was going to get into an argument with my friend.

"So you're just another highbrow, eh?" I said. "Just another one of those know-it-alls who run around pointing their fingers at the advertising business. Don't you realize what advertising has done for this country? How it has revolutionized business, brought new and better products forward to the average consumer, given ethics to commerce? Advertising today is more than a profession—it's an art, and a science. The American public owes a debt of gratitude to advertising for—"

"Yeow!" yelled Lefty Feep, quite suddenly. His hands covered his ears as he rocked back and forth in his seat. In a moment he regained composure and leaned forward.

"Please," he whispered. "Pretty please, with ketchup on it. Do not mention that word to me. It gives my dimples goose-pimples."

"Why?" I asked. "What harm has ad—all right, what harm has commercial display ever done to you?"

"Not a bit," Feep answered. "It is not because of myself that I ache and shake. I am merely thinking of what advertising does to poor Floyd Scrilch."

"Floyd Scrilch?"

"Perhaps I better tell you about Floyd Scrilch from the beginning," said Lefty Feep. "It will teach you a lesson."

"I'm sorry, Feep," I said. "But I've got to be going. Heavy date. Some other time, perhaps?"

"Well," Feep shrugged. "If you insist."

He pulled me back into my seat and held me there firmly. Then, plunging his elbows into the butter plates, he began.

When I first meet up with this Floyd Scrilch (narrated Feep), I do not pay any great attention to him. He is that kind of personality. A nobody from nowhere. Strictly a dud. When he walks into a room it is just like somebody else walks out. You don't even know he's there even after you look at him. His face is as empty as a Jap's promise. He never opens his mouth between meals. He is so shy he never looks in the mirror when he shaves. He is what the psychologists call an introtwerp, if you follow me.

He hangs out around the poolroom, and also around the elbows.

His clothes are a model of what the well-dressed scarecrow doesn't wear. Also he is very puny. In fact, he is so thin that when he has a toothpick in his mouth it looks like he is hiding behind a tree. One glance at him and you know he cannot lick his weight in wild flowers. One day I am standing in the pool parlor when he weighs himself and I see he only tips the scales at 84 pounds. Not stripped, either, because the poolroom is crowded.

That is the first time I have anything to do with Floyd Scrilch. He notices I am watching him, and he turns around and hands me a sick smile.

"I do not seem to be so healthy," he gets out.

"At least you won't be taken by the draft," I console him.

"I always get pneumonia from drafts anyway," he sighs.

"Why don't you visit a croaker?" I inquire.

"A what?"

"An undertaker's understudy. A pulse-promoter. A doctor."

He shakes his head.

"No use," he tells me. "All the doctors give me up for dead long ago. The last medico who examines me says my lungs look like a couple of tea-bags and my heart only beats to mark the hour."

I feel sorry for this weak but meek little guy, and I want to pat him on the shoulder, only I am afraid he will collapse.

But Gorilla Gabface does not share my sentiments. He is watching this Floyd Scrilch hang around his poolroom for the last week, and just now he waddles over to where Scrilch is standing and grabs him by the collar, which rips.

"Listen, jerk," says Gabface. "You got a job?"

Scrilch shakes his head.

"No," he mumbles. "Nobody will hire me."

"You got any money?" Gabface sneers, shaking Scrilch up and down like a dice-box until his teeth roll sevens.

"No money," Scrilch chatters.

Gabface grunts.

"That is the way I figure it, too," he says. "And I do not wish for my poolroom to become a Rescue Mission. So I fear I shall invite you to get the blazes out of here."

Gabface sort of emphasizes his remarks by picking Scrilch off the floor and tossing him through the door. He lands someplace out on the curb, and when I run out to see what happens he is still bouncing. I catch him on the third bounce and pick him up again.

"That is a mean thing to do," I console him. "Gorilla Gabface is no better than a skunk in wolf's clothing. If I am you, I go back in and give him a good beating."

Scrilch sighs.

"I cannot beat up an eggnog, let along a big ape like that," he tells me. "But I only wish I can peel his orange for him some day. Only it is no use, I guess. I am just a rundown weakling. Nobody ever worries about me. I got no friends, no girl, no job. I just as soon go home and put my head in the oven, only the gas company turns it off on me."

Then I get an idea. I have a newspaper in my hand, fanning Scrilch with it to bring him around, and I happen to glance at the page. And I see the advertisement.

It is a big muscle-building ad. I grab Scrilch by the hair.

"Listen to this!" I holler.

"Nuts!" says Joe Stronghorse in the ad. *"In seven days you can have a body like mine!"*

"You wouldn't think to look at me that I am just a 92-pound weakling. Yet I have no muscles painted on. I am just a nobody, but my body is as good as anybody's. You can possess the same muscular strength.

"Let me tell you how you can add three inches to your biceps, eight inches to your calves, sixteen inches to your chest—or bust!

"No complicated exercises! No harsh laxatives! Earn big easy money at home growing hair on your chest in your spare time!

"Send for my exercise system today! A free tiger-skin included with every order! I will build you a powerful body in three weeks, or your muscles refunded. This course guarantees a powerful physique. It will even make your breath stronger!"

Anyhow, it reads something like that. And when I spill this to Floyd Scrilch his eyes light up. He looks at the picture of Joe Stronghorse and a grin spills down his chin.

"Say," he whispers. "Do you think it will work for me?"

"All you got to do is tear out this coupon," I tell him.

"I'll do it!" he shouts. "Yes sir, I'll do it!"

Then his face falls. "Can I ask you one favor, Mr. Feep?" he gulps.

"Sure. What is it?"

"Will you please tear out the coupon for me? I'm too weak to do it myself."

So that is how Floyd Scrilch answers his first advertisement. I forget about him in a couple of weeks, because I do not see him at the poolroom any more.

I am playing a little game on the first table one afternoon about a month later when an elephant flies over my head.

I do not notice this at first, but then I hear the elephant trumpeting, so I look up and see that it is none other than Gorilla Gabface. He is flying through the air and traveling very fast. He does not even stop to go out the door, but plows right through the plate-glass window. Then he sits down very carefully on the sidewalk and pulls splinters out of his ears.

I turn around to the back and duck very quick, because two other personalities are doing a nonstop flight my way. They land up against the wall and pause for a nap.

And I hear a big booming voice say, "Any other goon want a trip to the moon?"

The rest of the mob just stands there very quiet indeed while a broad-shouldered little guy walks out from between them. I take a good look and then another. Because I recognize none other than Floyd Scrilch.

But he is plenty changed. He has big arms and a broad chest and looks like he weighs 170 in muscles alone. He walks over to me and yells, "Hello, Feep—glad to see you! Put 'er there."

"*Ouch!*" I remark, shaking hands. He has a grip like a politician.

"I want to thank you for what you do for me," he says. "Ever since I mail that coupon, I feel like a new man. Once I get those lessons they do wonders for me. A month ago, if I want to tear a telephone book in half, I have to do it one page at a time. Today I can tear a telephone booth in half."

He slaps me on the back and I cave in.

"Now that I settle with this Gorilla person, I feel like celebrating. How about coming along with me for a little drink?"

"O.K.," I tell him. "But aren't you hard up for money?"

He laughs.

"Not since I answer the advertisement," he tells me.

"The muscle ad?"

"No. The other one. About entering the big $5000 prize contest. I enter it and win."

Sure enough, when we get outside I notice Floyd Scrilch is wearing a new English burlap drape suit, and he leads me over to a big car with actual new tires on it.

We go over to Daddy's Tavern, where you always find about eight to the bar, and have a drink on Scrilch's new success.

"It is a funny thing," he tells me. "Ever since you point out that ad to me, I study advertisements and answer them. And every ad I answer works out for me."

"How do you mean?"

"Well, take like this ad about raising a truck garden at home. My neighbors send for some seeds a long time ago and try it out, and they tell me nothing comes up. Me, I send in just ten days ago and already my garden is full of carrots and tomatoes and peas and radishes and such articles. It is like magic.

"Then, just for fun, I send in for another ad which tells about getting rid of unsightly pores. And now look at me. Go ahead, look at my face."

I stare at him real close. Sure enough, there is not a pore on his face. The skin is closed up tight all over.

"You see?" he tells me. "I got no more pores than an empty bottle. I got a hunch I am going places with these advertisements. For some reason they just work out right for me."

I have to leave just then, because I have a heavy freight date. And when I duck out, I do not see Floyd Scrilch again for weeks.

This is because I am all the time riding these heavy freight dates. I happen to be mixed up with a torrid tomato. I call her Pearl, because her old man is a bad oyster.

I am not a personality who usually makes like a wolf after the little red riding hoods, but this dame has me dizzier than a Joe Louis left. I am almost on the point of hanging a ring on her finger, even if it means she will then be leading me by a ring through my nose. We do the old dine-and-dance routine every night, and she has old Lefty Feep's name down in the Number One spot on her hit parade. We are closer together than the Gold Dust Twins—and prettier, too.

So when she calls up one night and asks me to take her out, I give her the nod, quick.

"Will you take me down to the Sunset Roof?" she asks. "I hear there is a new piano player there that can really barrelhouse the boogie in a lowdown doggy way."

She is just crazy for music and culture like this, see?

Well, the Sunset Roof is very high in its class and also in its price, but who am I to refuse Pearl anything her little ticker desires?

So I tell her sure, and pick her up after dinner, and take her down to the Sunset Roof. I bring her a lovely orchard to wear on her dress, and I hire a taxi, and I pay the stiff cover charge without a squawk, and I give her the old routine, so by the time we sit down at the table she is practically in my lap. She is giving me the gaze—you know, the old "we-can-buy-our-furniture-on-the-installment-plan" look, and I am going for it three ways. Hook, line and sinker.

Then the floor show starts, and the slush melts all of a sudden. Because that piano player she is so crazy to hear wheels out his infant grand and begins to polish ivory.

"Listen to that man play!" squeals Pearl. So I listen. He is really a gee with the keys, and everybody is quiet while he meddles the pedals under a blue light all alone.

When he chalks up his numbers, there is a lot of palm-pounding, and then lights go on, and Pearl yaps, "Isn't he just like Eddy Duchin?"

So I take a squint at the face and shake my head fast.

Because this piano player is not like Eddy Duchin. He is not like Rachmaninoff, either. But he is exactly like my old friend Floyd Scrilch.

In fact, he is Floyd Scrilch, in a tuxedo. He spots me when he is coming off the floor, and runs over.

"Well, it is Lefty Feep!" he gurgles. "And with a charming companion." He bows like a movie extra.

So I make with the introductions and he drops his creases in a chair at our table.

I cannot resist asking him the natural question, which I do.

"What are you doing here?" I get out. "Since when do you manicure a keyboard?"

He turns and gives me a big smile.

"A month ago I am ignorant of music," he admits. "The only notes I can read are the ones I get from my creditors. I think A sharp is a card player and A flat is some place you live in. Then I pick up this magazine and read the ad. *They Laugh When I Sit Down at the Piano.* It tells how you can learn to play in ten easy lessons, or five hard ones. So I mail the coupon, get my lessons, and right away I am so good I figure I can get a job. So I come up here and they hire me. It is sensational, no?"

He talks to me, but he looks at Pearl. She giggles. "Why, Mr. Scrilch, you must be a virtuoso."

"Never mind my private life," he tells her, with an enchanting leer. "And why be so formal? Just call me Floydie." His eyes light up like pay-off numbers on a pinball machine.

"You just answer the ad and get what you want, huh?" I ask.

But Floyd Scrilch is not paying any attention to me. He is too busy casting the old goo-goo glance at Pearl.

"What?" he mumbles.

"I say what have you got in your hand?" I inquire.

"Why, Pearl's arm," he tells me. And he has. "Pearl," he whispers. "A lovely name. Pearl, you are too good to cast yourself before swine."

This sounds like a dirty crack of some kind, but Pearl just giggles and wiggles, and I see the handwriting on the wall. Also on the check.

"Shall we waddle out of here?" I ask her.

"No, I want to stay. Floydie here says we're going to have lots of fun," she simpers.

So that is the way it is. Floyd Scrilch sits there in his tuxedo, with his big broad shoulders waving and his hair slicked down, handling my tomato like she comes from his own vine.

I get up to go. I should be sore, but for some reason I am more interested in how he does it. In fact, I have a little suspicion when I see his hair. I cannot resist bending down and whispering to him before I exit.

"Tell me the truth, Scrilch," I mutter. "Do you also answer one of these ads which tell you to buy hair tonic that makes you irresistible to women?"

He grins.

"You guess it, Feep," he admits. "I just mail the coupon and in comes the stuff to put on my hair, and now wherever my hair goes, women get in it."

I shrug and sneak off. I make up my mind right then and there to forget Pearl and this guy Scrilch.

But this is not so easy to do. Because how can you forget a guy with hair three feet long?

That is the way Floyd Scrilch's hair is when I bump into him on the street a few weeks later.

He is running down the block wearing a purple nightgown, and a big shock of long bushy hair is tangled all over his dome.

In fact, he bumps into me and I get a mouthful of the stuff. I chew a while and then let go and Scrilch recognizes me.

"Don't tell me," I say. "You figure you have falling hair so you send in for a hair restorer and this is what happens."

"Right," he says. "It almost worries me, the way these ads come true. I begin to think they overdo things for me a little."

"But why the purple nightgown?" I ask.

"This is no nightgown," he comes back. "That is a smock."

"Smock?"

"Sure. All artists wear smocks."

"Since when are you artistic?"

"Since I get this long hair. It gives me the idea. All guys with long hair are artists. So I happen to be looking through a magazine and I see this ad.

" 'Be an Artist!' it says. And there is a picture of an animal down below it. 'Get Out Your Easel and Draw This Weasel!' it states. And it says that the guy who draws the best weasel gets a free art course from this school, by mail. Now me, I think a palette is something you have in your mouth, and a brush is something you have with the law. But I draw, and I win the course, and every lesson works out. In fact, I am way ahead of the lessons. I get some oil paints and start to work three weeks ago. I quit my job at the Sunset Roof and take up painting in a big way.

"Last week I have about twenty paintings done. And the big art critic, Vincent van Gouge, happens to drop into my place and—"

"Wait a minute," I cut in. "Since when do guys like art critics come to see you? You are not so popular as that."

Scrilch smiles.

"I am since I answer that ad about 'Be the Life of the Party!'" he tells me. "I win friends and influence people all over the place. So they are always running around to see me. Anyway, this van Gouge drops in, takes one look at my paintings, and tells me I got to have an opening."

"You tell me he is an art critic," I object. "So why does he give you advice like a doctor?"

"You don't understand. He means an opening—an exhibition of my paintings. In fact, he gets up some sponsors, and today I have twenty paintings hanging down in the art gallery up the street. So I put on my smock and go down there now to the big reception. I am going to be famous. I answer the right ads."

By this time I am a little dizzy. In fact, I am so dizzy I decide to go down to the art gallery with Scrilch and see what this is all about.

On the way down I ask him about Pearl. He does not even remember her name.

"I am so popular," he babbles. "Like the ads say, I have friends and invitations galore."

I just groan.

When we get to the art gallery I groan again. Because I see Scrilch's paintings.

There are twenty of them, all right, and they look like two sets of ten nights in a barroom. Never in my life do I see such screwy drawings, and I am a fellow who goes in a lot of phone booths.

But there is a big gang of society people walking around and making bleats over the things. Mainly they stand around a big painting at the end. It is a study of two goldfish with skis on, waiting for a streetcar at the North Pole during a thunder shower. Anyhow, that is the way it looks to me.

But not to the society crowd.

"Look!" yaps one old babe. "It reminds me of Picasso in his blue period."

"Blue, lady?" I tell her. "He must be ready for suicide."

The old babe sniffs and trucks away from there.

I turn to Scrilch.

"What kind of stuff is this?" I ask. I point to another picture. "How about that one? It looks like a kangaroo walking a tightrope over a garbage dump with Mayor La Guardia in its pouch reading a newspaper."

"You do not understand," Scrilch shrugs. "This is all surrealism."

"You and your sewer realism," I sniff. "If you ask me, the only things you can draw is your pay and your breath."

Scrilch puts his finger to his lips.

"Not so loud," he tells me. "Lots of important people here. They're all very much impressed."

"Depressed, if you ask me," I come back.

"I am sorry you don't like it," he tells me. "But perhaps you will like my writing better."

"Writing?"

"Why, of course. I am writing the Great American Novel. I answer an ad just this week. *'Shake a Leg and Be Another Shakespeare! Just Clip This Coupon and Learn to Write!'* So I am only on my third lesson, but yesterday I start my novel. It is almost half through already."

I listen to this and start foaming at the mouth like a beer keg. And I am not the only one.

A little short fat personality stands right behind us. Now he taps Scrilch on the shoulder and stares at him. He is wearing a heavy pair of cheaters, with enough glass in them to cover a store window.

"Pardon me," he croaks. "But is it not Floyd Scrilch the artist whom I have the honor of addressing?"

"Right."

"And do you not just remark that in addition to your remarkable gifts as a painter, you are also a *literateur?*"

"Naw, I write stuff."

The little goggle-eyes smiles.

"Really?"

"That isn't the half of it," I butt in. "He is also a piano player, a social lion, and an all-around athlete."

"Wonderful!" breathes the goggle-eyes. "How I wish I might psychoanalyze such a genius!"

Then he introduces himself. He turns out to be none other than Doctor Sigmund, the psychiatrist—better known as Subconscious Sigmund.

Subconscious Sigmund grabs Scrilch by the collar.

"How do you manage to cope with such versatility?" he asks.

"I just take a little bicarbonate."

"I mean to say, how is it that you are so accomplished in so many different fields of endeavor?"

"Oh," blurts out Scrilch. "I just answer advertisements and they work out for me."

Subconscious Sigmund stares.

"You mean you just clip out advertising coupons that offer to teach you things and you learn them?"

"Sure."

"Then, Mr. Scrilch, I beg of you—permit me to psychoanalyze you at once."

"Does it hurt?"

"Certainly not. I merely take you to my office and ask you a few questions. I wish to probe your unconscious."

"You wish to what my what?"

"Look into your inner mind. You seem to be a most remarkable man."

Well, Scrilch is a sucker for flattery. The end of it is, he agrees, and we go off to the psychiatrist's office together.

"Come with me, Feep," Scrilch says. "I do not wish to get my brain drained without protection."

Subconscious Sigmund has a swell office downtown, and he takes us into a nice private room and we all sit down and have a drink.

"Now," he says, rubbing his hands together. "I am going to ask you to sit down here, Mr. Scrilch." And he puts Floyd Scrilch in a soft chair. Then he turns out all the lights except one lamp, which shines in Scrilch's face. "I will now ask you to answer a few questions," he purrs.

It is just like a high-class third degree.

So he begins to ask questions and Scrilch answers him. And now I see what Subconscious Sigmund is doing. He is pumping Scrilch for his whole life story. And the story comes out. About what a dull life Scrilch leads as a kid. About how nobody ever pays any attention to him, how he is just an average jerk.

And then Scrilch tells about the advertisements. How he answers the first one and gets muscles. About answering the piano-playing ad and getting lessons and being a wizard on the piano. About how he becomes irresistible to women like the hair ad tells him. About his hair growing with scalp restorer. About the painting and the writing ad and the life-of-the-party ad.

Subconscious Sigmund is amazed. I can see it. He walks around Scrilch, grunting and coughing and chuckling, and then he stops.

"I see it all," he whispers. "It is truly remarkable! Scrilch, you are that mythical cipher, that abstract integer, that legendary personification—the typical average man! The forces of heredity and environment conspire to blend perfectly the component elements of physique and mentality into the pure norm!"

Scrilch gives him the double take.

"What does this mean without pig Latin?" he inquires.

"It means you are the man all these ads are written for," Subconscious Sigmund tells him. "You are the average citizen these ads are slanted to appeal to. You are the normal man on which these preparations and lessons and exercises and products are designed to work. On a lesser personality or a greater one, they never succeed so fully. But by some kinetic miracle, you are the one person in the world who is perfectly attuned to advertising formulae. It is almost magical. The very words and phrases advertisers use come true in your case."

"You mean if an ad comes out saying you can live forever, I might live forever?"

"Who knows?" Sigmund comes back. "You are physiologically and psychically attuned to the vibrationary reflexes induced by advertising."

"It worries me," Scrilch confesses.

"How do you mean?"

"Well, lately, the ads work *too* good."

"*Too* good?"

"That's right. I mean, I learn piano playing, but I become a master. I take up drawing, and right away I'm a great artist. I tackle writing, and I write half a novel in one twelve-hour day. I send for a hair restorer and I get too much hair. I try to attract friends and women and I have too many friends and too many women. See what I mean? Something is working so that I just seem to get *too much.*"

"So? That is most interesting, my friend."

"Sometimes I wonder if I answer the wrong ad, will it kick back on me? Will I get too wealthy or too strong or too talented?"

"I see," mumbles Subconscious Sigmund. "Overcompensation. A most illuminating development. We must probe further."

"What're you going to do, Doc?" asks Scrilch.

"Just look at me," Subconscious Sigmund says. He sits down in front of Scrilch and begins to stare at him with those big cheaters wobbling.

I catch on right away. He is trying to put Scrilch to sleep. He talks to him and keeps the light shining in his face all the time, and he stares away and waves his arm around a little.

Scrilch just sits there.

Subconscious Sigmund stares harder and waves more. He begins to sweat.

Scrilch just sits there.

Subconscious Sigmund's eyes pop out under his goggles. His hands tremble. He sweats plenty.

Scrilch just sits there.

And all of a sudden, Subconscious Sigmund stops mumbling. His pop eyes go shut. His hands drop in his lap. He slumps down in his chair. Then he tumbles off on the floor and just lies there.

Scrilch gets up.

"Come on," he says. "Let's get going."

"But what about Subconscious Sigmund?"

"We'll leave him be," Scrilch tells me. "Can you imagine," he says, in a disgusted tone of voice. "This psychiatrist tries to *hypnotize* me! Me, when just the other day I answer that swell ad about *Hypnotism Made Easy!*"

That is the last I see of Floyd Scrilch for many a week. I do not hear anything more about his painting or his writing or his piano-playing. I do not see anything in the papers. I figure maybe he answers an ad on how to be a hermit or something, and let it go at that.

But one afternoon I am at the pool hall, minding my p's and cues, and a hand taps me on the shoulder.

I turn around and see Floyd Scrilch. His hand still taps me, because he is trembling. And because I do not recognize him there at first.

Floyd Scrilch is pretty pale. He looks thinner, and there are a couple of rings under his eyes I would not like to see on bath tubs.

"Feep," he whispers. "You got to help me."

"Sure, what do you want me to do?"

"I want you to come out to my house," he mutters. "We're going to burn some ads."

"Burn some ads?"

"Sure. All of the ads. All the ones I answer and all the ones I plan to answer. Get rid of them. Before they get rid of me."

I give him a long stare and see he means it.

"There's a taxi waiting outside," he says. "Come on. There's not a minute to lose."

We hop in and drive away. It is a long ride.

"Make with the explanations," I request. "What happens to you? Why don't I see you around?"

"If I am around once more, I am dizzy," Scrilch tells me. "It is terrible. I have no peace. Friends calling me up. Women rushing in to visit me. Art galleries phoning. Agents after my book. And look!"

He is wearing a hat, and now he yanks it off. His hair falls to the floor. So help me, it is six feet long.

"You see?" he mutters. "It won't stop growing! Nothing stops any more. Just for fun I send in my picture to a movie talent bureau that advertises. I win a Hollywood contract. I win another contest. But I cannot go away. I am almost too musclebound to walk now!"

He waves his arm, and his sleeve rips. A bicep sticks out and he pushes it back.

"You see? Ads are good for everybody else, but not for me. They work too well. That is why I run away. I have to get away from people, from women, from advertising.

"That is another thing. A compulsion. That's what Subconscious Sigmund calls it. Every time I see an ad now, I must answer it.

"So I leave my studio and get myself a house in the country. I must. And that is where things go wrong. I hope we're not too late. We must destroy the ads and—something else."

He sits huddled up in the cab as we drive out into the sticks. At last the cab pulls up in front of a rickety old frame house and we climb out. It is almost dark, and Scrilch runs up the steps so fast he nearly trips in the dim light.

I follow him in.

"No time to lose," he says. "Help me bundle this stuff up. I must get it down into the furnace while I'm still able to. At this rate of growth I may not even get into the cellar."

I see he is a little off the beam, but I do not comment. I merely look at the living room which is just filled with old paper. It looks like a government drive.

There is nothing but piles of clipped-out coupons. Thousands of them. And Scrilch begins to stuff them into boxes. So I help.

All the time he looks at the door.

"Smell anything?" he asks me. I shake my head. We pile some more. "Hear anything downstairs?" he asks. I shake my head.

I notice he is shaking again.

"What's the matter?" I ask. "What am I supposed to smell and hear?"

"It's the last ad I answer," he breathes, hoarsely. "I'll tell you about that later. We have to figure out a way to destroy it. Dynamite, or something. It's growing every hour. I'm almost afraid to go down there. I want to get this stuff in the furnace before it blocks the way."

"What?" I come back, while we bundle up the stuff and carry it out to the cellar door.

Then I hear a rippling noise. Scrilch wheels around. His eyes bulge.

"You don't smell anything, or hear anything," he yells. "But you must see something. Or am I nuts?"

I think I am. Because I *do* see something now.

It is the kitchen floor. It *bulges.*

Yes, the boards in the floor are bulging up. And the ripping noise comes from the wood.

"Growing!" Scrilch screams.

Then he grabs up a pile of coupons.

"I'll get these in the furnace anyway," he shrieks. "No matter how big it is! I'll do it—I'll show you no ad can frighten me!"

He opens the cellar door. It is black down there, but he does not turn on a light. Instead, he grabs his pile and runs down the steps.

I hear him yelling in the dark.

"Don't follow me!" he shouts. "It might be dangerous."

Then I just hear some thumping. All at once he yells again: "Oh—no—it can't be—growing—no—get away—oh—"

And I hear something else. An awful noise. A *rubbery* noise, like somebody is bouncing a zeppelin up and down like a ball. Then there is an awful grunt, and I do smell something, and I hear another sound.

The floor rips further. I hear Scrilch give just one last scream, and then I hear the other sound again.

But the other sound comes from far away, because I am already out the back door and running down the street.

I never go back. Because now I know what happens to Floyd Scrilch. He answers the wrong ads.

Lefty Feep took his elbows out of the butter plates and gave a long sigh. "Poor Floyd," he whispered, reminiscently.

I coughed discreetly.

"There's just one thing bothering me," I said.

"Name it and you can have it."

"Well, apparently, Floyd Scrilch was killed there in the cellar. But I don't see how it happened."

"He gets swallowed," Feep told me.

"Swallowed?"

"Sure, Bob. For answering the wrong ad."

"But what is this thing that grows down there and makes the floor creak?" I asked. "What did you smell and hear at the last? In plain words—what was it that Floyd Scrilch kept in his cellar?"

"That I never know," Feep answered.

"I thought so!"

"Except for a lucky break of mine," Lefty Feep added, triumphant. "When I run out of there I happen to have an ad in my hand. I hang on to it unconscious. And later, when I look at it, I figure out what Floyd does. This is the last ad he tells me he answers. And it works too good again. So he gets killed."

"You mean this ad tells what he had down there in the cellar?"

"Look for yourself," said Lefty Feep.

He reached into his vest pocket and handed me the crumpled piece of paper.

The advertisement was quite small. I read only the top line, but that was enough.

"Earn Big Money!" the advertisement urged. *"Use Your Own Basement to Raise Giant Frogs!"*

The Abyss

ROBERT A. W. LOWNDES

*Robert A. W. Lowndes' fiction has been neglected in the wake of his work
as the editor of the* Magazine of Horror *and several other fantasy digests
in the 1960s. Although largely comprised of reprints from* Weird Tales,
Strange Tales *and other pulps, Lowndes' magazines also carried early
fiction by Stephen King, Ramsey Campbell, and F. Paul Wilson, and thus
served as an important link between the contemporary horror movement
and its pulp antecedents. Several decades earlier, Lowndes himself had
been a promising writer of fantasy and science fiction for magazines like*
Famous Fantastic Mysteries *and* Future Fantasy and Science Fiction.
"The Abyss" appeared in the fantasy half of the first issue of Stirring
Science Stories. *It reflects Lowndes' interest in the work of H. P. Lovecraft,
with whom he corresponded during the last year of Lovecraft's life.*

W E TOOK Graf Norden's body out into the November night,
under the stars that burned with a brightness terrible to
behold, and drove madly, wildly up the mountain road. The
body had to be destroyed because of the eyes that would not close,
but seemed to be staring at some object behind the observer, the body
that was entirely drained of blood without the slightest trace of a
wound, the body whose flesh was covered with luminous markings,

designs that shifted and changed form before one's eyes. We wedged
what had been Graf Norden tightly behind the wheel, put a makeshift
fuse in the gas tank, lit it, then shoved the car over the side of the
road, where it plummeted down to the main highway, a flaming meteor.

Not until the next day did we realize that we had all been under
Dureen's spell—even I had forgotten. How else could we have rushed
out so eagerly? From that moment when the lights came on again, and
we saw the thing that had, a moment before, been Graf Norden, we
were as shadowy, indistinct figures rushing through a dream. All was
forgotten save the unspoken commands upon us as we watched the
blazing car strike the pavement below, observed its demolition, then
tramped dully each to his own home. When, the next day, partial
memory returned to us and we sought Dureen, he was gone. And,
because we valued our freedom, we did not tell anyone what had
happened, nor try to discover whence Dureen had vanished. We wanted
only to forget.

I think I might possibly have forgotten had I not looked into the
Song of Yste again. With the others, there has been a growing tendency
to treat it as illusion, but I cannot. It is one thing to read of books
like the Necronomicon, Book of Eibon, or Song of Yste, but it is quite
different when one's own experience confirms some of the things related
therein. I found one such paragraph in the Song of Yste and have not
read farther. The volume, along with Norden's other books, is still on
my shelves; I have not burned it. But I do not think I shall read
more. . . .

I met Graf Norden in 193–, at Darwich University, in Dr. Held's
class in Mediaeval and early-Renaissance history, which was more a
study of obscure thought and occultism.

Norden was greatly interested; he had done quite a bit of exploring
into the occult; in particular was he fascinated by the writings and
records of a family of adepts named Dirka, who traced their ancestry
back to the pre-glacial days. They, the Dirkas, had translated the Song
of Yste from its legendary form into the three great languages of the
dawn cultures, then into the Greek, Latin, Arabic and Middle English.

I told Norden that I deplored the blind contempt in which the world
holds the occult, but had never explored the subject very deeply. I was
content to be a spectator, letting my imagination drift at will upon the
many currents in this dark river; skimming over the surface was enough
for me—seldom did I take occasional plunges into the deeps. As a
poet and dreamer, I was careful not to lose myself in the blackness of
the pools where I disported—one could always emerge to find a calm,
blue sky and a world that thought nothing of these realities.

With Norden, it was different. He was already beginning to have
doubts, he told me. It was not an easy road to travel; there were
hideous dangers, hidden all along the way, often so that the wayfarer

was not aware of them until too late. Earthmen were not very far along the path of evolution; still very young, their lack of knowledge, as a race, told heavily against such few of their number who sought to traverse unknown roads. He spoke of messengers from beyond and made references to obscure passages in the *Necronomicon* and *Song of Yste*. He spoke of alien beings, entities terribly unhuman, impossible of measurement by any human yardstick or to be combated effectively by mankind.

Dureen came into the picture at about this time. He walked into the classroom one day during the course of a lecture; later, Dr. Held introduced him as a new member of the class, coming from abroad. There was something about Dureen that challenged my interest at once. I could not determine of what race or nationality he might be—he was very close to being beautiful, his every movement being of grace and rhythm. Yet, in no way could he be considered effeminate.

That the majority of us avoided him troubled him not at all. For my part, he did not seem genuine, but, with the others, it was probably his utter lack of emotion. There was, for example, the time in the lab when a test tube burst in his face, driving several splinters deep into the skin. He showed not the slightest sign of discomfort, waved aside all expressions of solicitude on the part of some of the girls, and proceeded to go on with his experiment as soon as the medico had finished with him.

The final act started when we were dealing with suggestion and hypnotism, one afternoon, and were discussing the practical possibilities of the subject. Colby presented a most ingenious argument against it, ridiculed the association of experiments in thought transference or telepathy with suggestion, and arrived at a final conclusion that hypnotism (outside of mechanical means of induction) was impossible.

It was at this point that Dureen spoke up. What he said, I cannot now recall, but it ended in a direct challenge for Dureen to prove his statements. Norden said nothing during the course of this debate; he appeared somewhat pale, and was, I noticed, trying to flash a warning signal to Colby.

There were five of us over at Norden's place that night: Granville, Chalmers, Colby, Norden, and myself. Norden was smoking endless cigarettes, gnawing his nails, and muttering to himself. I suspected something irregular was up, but what, I had no idea. Then Dureen came in and the conversation, such as it had been, ended.

Colby repeated his challenge, saying he had brought along the others as witnesses to insure against being tricked by stage devices. No mirrors, light, or any other mechanical means of inducing hypnosis would be permitted. It must be entirely a matter of wills. Dureen nodded, drew the shade, then turned, directing his gaze at Colby.

We watched, expecting him to make motions with his hands and pronounce commands: he did neither. He fixed his eyes upon Colby and the latter stiffened as if struck by lightning, then, eyes staring blankly ahead of him, he rose slowly, standing on the narrow strip of black that ran diagonally down through the center of the rug.

My mind ran back to the day I caught Norden in the act of destroying some papers and apparatus, the latter which had been constructed, with such assistance as I had been able to give, over a period of several months. His eyes were terrible and I could see doubt in them. Not long after this event, Dureen had made his appearance: could there have been a connection, I wondered?

My reverie was broken abruptly by the sound of Dureen's voice commanding Colby to speak, telling us where he was and what he saw around him. When Colby obeyed, it was as if his voice came to us from a distance.

He was standing, he said, on a narrow bridgeway overlooking a frightful abyss, so vast and deep that he could discern neither floor nor boundary. Behind him this bridgeway stretched until it was lost in a bluish haze; ahead, it ran toward what appeared to be a plateau. He hesitated to move because of the narrowness of the path, yet realized that he must make for the plateau before the very sight of the depths below him made him lose his balance. He felt strangely heavy, and speaking was an effort.

As Colby's voice ceased, we all gazed in fascination at the little strip of black in the blue rug. This, then, was the bridge over the abyss . . . but what could correspond to the illusion of depth? Why did his voice seem so far away? Why did he feel heavy? The plateau must be the workbench at the other end of the room: the rug ran up to a sort of dais upon which was set Norden's table, the surface of this being some seven feet above the floor. Colby now began to walk slowly down the black swath, moving as if with extreme caution, looking like a slow-motion camera-shot. His limbs appeared weighted; he was breathing rapidly.

Dureen now bade him halt and look down into the abyss carefully, telling us what he saw there. At this, we again examined the rug, as if we had never seen it before and did not know that it was entirely without decoration save for that single black strip upon which Colby now stood.

His voice came to us again. He said, at first, that he saw nothing in the abyss below him. Then he gasped, swayed, and almost lost his balance. We could see the sweat standing out on his brow and neck, soaking his blue shirt. There were things in the abyss, he said in hoarse tones, great shapes that were like blobs of utter blackness, yet which he knew to be alive. From the central masses of their being he could see them shoot forth incredibly long, filamentine tentacles. They moved themselves forward and backward—horizontally, but could not move vertically, it seemed.

But the things were not all on the same plane. True, their movements were only horizontal in relation to their position, but some were parallel to him and some diagonal. Far away he could see things perpendicullar to him. There appeared now to be a great deal more of the things than he thought. The first ones he had seen were far below, unaware of his presence. But these sensed him, and were trying to reach him. He was moving faster now, he said, but to us he was still walking in slow-motion.

I glanced sidewise at Norden; he, too, was sweating profusely. He arose now, and went over to Dureen, speaking in low tones so that none of us could hear. I knew that he was referring to Colby and that Dureen was refusing whatever it was Norden demanded. Then Dureen was forgotten momentarily as Colby's voice came to us again quivering with fright. The things were reaching out for him. They rose and fell on all sides; some far away; some hideously close. None had found the exact plane upon which he could be captured; the darting tentacles had not touched him, but all of the beings now sensed his presence, he was sure. And he feared that perhaps they could alter their planes at will, though, it appeared that they must do so blindly, seemingly like two-dimensional beings. The tentacles darting at him were threads of utter darkness.

A terrible suspicion arose in me, as I recalled some of the earlier conversations with Norden, and remembered certain passages from the *Song of Yste*. I tried to rise, but my limbs were powerless: I could only sit helplessly and watch. Norden was still speaking with Dureen and I saw that he was now very pale. He seemed to shrink away—then he turned and went over to a cabinet, took out some object, and came to the strip of rug upon which Colby was standing. Norden nodded to Dureen and now I saw what it was he held in his hand: a polyhedron of glassy appearance. There was in it, however, a glow that startled me. Desperately I tried to remember the significance of it—for I knew—but my thoughts were being short-circuited, it seemed, and, when Dureen's eyes rested upon me, the very room seemed to stagger.

Again Colby's voice came through, this time despairingly. He was afraid he would never reach the plateau. (Actually, he was about a yard and a half away from the end of the black strip and the dais upon which stood Norden's work bench.) The things, said Colby, were close now: a mass of thread-like tentacles had just missed him.

Now Norden's voice came to us; it, too, seemingly far away. He called my name. This was more, he said, than hypnotism. It was—but then his voice faded and I felt the power of Dureen blanking out the sound of his words. Now and then, I would hear a sentence or a few disjointed words. But, from this I managed to get an inkling of what was going on.

This was actually trans-dimensional journeying. We just imagined we saw Norden and Colby standing on the rug—or perhaps it was through Dureen's influence.

The nameless dimension was the habitat of these shadow-beings. The abyss, and the bridge upon which the two stood, were illusions created by Dureen. When that which Dureen had planned was complete, our minds would be probed, and our memories treated so that we recalled no more than Dureen wished us to remember. Norden had succeeded in forcing an agreement upon Dureen, one which he would have to keep; as a result, if the two could reach the plateau before the shadow-beings touched them, all would be well. If not—Norden did not specify, but indicated that they were being hunted, as men hunt game. The polyhedron contained an element repulsive to the things.

He was but a little behind Colby; we could see him aiming with the polyhedron. Colby spoke again, telling us that Norden had materialized behind him, and had brought some sort of weapon with which the things could be held off.

Then Norden called my name, asking me to take care of his belongings if he did not return, telling me to look up the "adumbrali" in the *Song of Yste*. Slowly, he and Colby made their way toward the dais and the table. Colby was but a few steps ahead of Norden; now he climbed upon the dais, and, with the other's help, made his way onto the bench. He tried to assist Norden, but, as the latter mounted the dais, he stiffened suddenly and the polyhedron fell from his hands. Frantically he tried to draw himself up, but he was being forced backward and I knew that he had lost. . . .

There came to us a single cry of anguish, then the lights in the room faded and went out. Whatever spell had been upon us now was removed; we rushed about like madmen, trying to find Norden, Colby, and the light switch. Then, suddenly, the lights were on again and we saw Colby sitting dazedly on the bench, while Norden lay on the floor. Chalmers bent over the body, in an effort to resuscitate him, but when he saw that the condition of Norden's remains he became so hysterical that we had to knock him cold in order to quiet him.

Colby followed us mechanically, apparently unaware of what was happening. We took Graf Norden's body out into the November night and destroyed it by fire, telling Colby later that he had apparently suffered a heart attack while driving up the mountain road; the car had gone over and his body was incinerated in the holocaust.

Later, Chalmers, Granville, and I met in an effort to rationalize what we had seen and heard. Chalmers had been all right after he came around, had helped us with our grisly errand up the mountain road. Neither, I found, had heard Norden's voice after he had joined Colby in the supposed hypnotic stage. Nor did they recall seeing any object in Norden's hand.

But, in less than a week, even these memories had faded from them. They fully believed that Norden had died in an accident after an unsuccessful attempt on the part of Dureen to hypnotize Colby. Prior to this, their explanation had been that Dureen had killed Norden, for reasons unknown, and that we had been his unwitting accomplices. The hypnotic experiment had been a blind to gather us all together and provide a means of disposing of the body. That Dureen had been able to hypnotize us, they did not doubt then.

It would have been no use to tell them what I learned a few days later, what I learned from Norden's notes which explain Dureen's arrival. Or to quote sections from the *Song of Yste* put into comprehensible English, to them.

". . . And these be none other than the adumbrali, the living shadows, beings of incredible power and malignancy, which dwell without the veils of space and time such as we know it. Their sport it is to import into their realm the inhabitants of other dimensions, upon whom they practice horrid pranks and manifold illusions . . ."

". . .But more dreadful than these are the seekers which they send out into other worlds and dimensions, beings which they themselves have created and guised in the form of those who dwell within whatever dimension, or upon whichever worlds where these seekers be sent . . ."

". . . These seekers can be detected only by the adept, to whose trained eyes their too-perfectness of form and movement, their strangeness, and aura of alienage and power is a sure sign. . . ."

". . . The sage, Jhalkanaan, tells of one of these seekers who deluded seven priests of Nyaghoggua into challenging it to a duel of the hypnotic arts. He further tells how two of these were trapped and delivered to the adumbrali, their bodies being returned when the shadow-things had done with them . . ."

". . . Most curious of all was the condition of the corpses, being entirely drained of all fluid, yet showing no trace of a wound, even the most slight. But the crowning horror was the eyes, which could not be closed, appearing to stare restlessly outward, beyond the observer, and the strangely-luminous markings on the dead flesh, curious designs which appeared to move and change form before the eyes of the beholder. . . ."

The Words of Guru

CYRIL M. KORNBLUTH

*The only thing more amazing than Cyril Kornbluth's many achievements
in fantasy and science fiction is that they all occurred while he was still
a relatively young man. Kornbluth is probably best known as the author
of the time-travel story "The Little Black Bag," and as the co-author (with
Frederik Pohl) of* The Space Merchants, *possibly the best science fiction
satire ever written. As prolific as he was imaginative, he also wrote several
excellent weird fiction stories under pen names; one of them was Kenneth
Faulconer, to whom "The Words of Guru" was attributed in the June
1941* Stirring Science Stories *(an issue that carried* two *more Kornbluth
stories under two different pseudonyms). Kornbluth had just begun to
receive notice for his non-genre work when he died of a heart attack in
1958 at the age of thirty-five.*

YESTERDAY, WHEN I was going to meet Guru in the woods
a man stopped me and said: "Child, what are you doing out
at one in the morning? Does your mother know where you
are? How old are you, walking around this late?"
I looked at him, and saw that he was white-haired, so I laughed.
Old men never see; in fact men hardly see at all. Sometimes young
women see part, but men rarely ever see at all. "I'm twelve on my

next birthday," I said. And then, because I would not let him live to tell people, I said, "and I'm out this late to see Guru."

"Guru?" he asked. "Who is Guru? Some foreigner, I suppose? Bad business mixing with foreigners, young fellow. Who is Guru?"

So I told him who Guru was, and just as he began talking about cheap magazines and fairy tales I said one of the words that Guru taught me and he stopped talking. Because he was an old man and his joints were stiff he didn't crumple up but fell in one piece, hitting his head on the stone. Then I went on.

Even though I'm going to be only twelve on my next birthday I know many things that old people don't. And I remember things that other boys can't. I remember being born out of darkness, and I remember the noises that people made about me. Then when I was two months old I began to understand that the noises meant things like the things that were going on inside my head. I found out that I could make the noises too, and everybody was very much surprised. "Talking!" they said, again and again. "And so very young! Clara, what do you make of it?" Clara was my mother.

And Clara would say: "I'm sure I don't know. There never was any genius in my family, and I'm sure there was none in Joe's." Joe was my father.

Once Clara showed me a man I had never seen before, and told me that he was a reporter—that he wrote things in newspapers. The reporter tried to talk to me as if I were an ordinary baby; I didn't even answer him, but just kept looking at him until his eyes fell and he went away. Later Clara scolded me and read me a little piece in the reporter's newspaper that was supposed to be funny—about the reporter asking me very complicated questions and me answering with baby noises. It was not true, of course. I didn't say a word to the reporter, and he didn't ask me even one of the questions.

I heard her read the little piece, but while I listened I was watching the slug crawling on the wall. When Clara was finished I asked her: "What is that grey thing?"

She looked where I pointed, but couldn't see it. "What grey thing, Peter?" she asked. I had her call me by my whole name, Peter, instead of anything silly like Petey. "What grey thing?"

"It's as big as your hand, Clara, but soft. I don't think it has any bones at all. It's crawling up, but I don't see any face on the topwards side. And there aren't any legs."

I think she was worried, but she tried to baby me by putting her hand on the wall and trying to find out where it was. I called out whether she was right or left of the thing. Finally she put her hand right through the slug. And then I realized that she really couldn't see it, and didn't believe it was there. I stopped talking about it then and only asked her a few days later: "Clara, what do you call a thing which one person can see and another person can't?"

"An illusion, Peter," she said. "If that's what you mean." I said nothing, but let her put me to bed as usual, but when she turned out the light and went away I waited a little while and then called out softly. "Illusion! Illusion!"

At once Guru came for the first time. He bowed, the way he always has since, and said: "I have been waiting."

"I didn't know that was the way to call you," I said.

"Whenever you want me I will be ready. I will teach you, Peter— if you want to learn. Do you know what I will teach you?"

"If you will teach me about the grey thing on the wall," I said, "I will listen. And if you will teach me about real things and unreal things I will listen."

"These things," he said thoughtfully, "very few wish to learn. And there are some things that nobody ever wished to learn. And there are some things that I will not teach."

Then I said: "The things nobody has ever wished to learn I will learn. And I will even learn the things you do not wish to teach."

He smiled mockingly. "A master has come," he said, half-laughing. "A master of Guru."

That was how I learned his name. And that night he taught me a word which would do little things, like spoiling food.

From that day to the time I saw him last night he has not changed at all, though now I am as tall as he is. His skin is still as dry and shiny as ever it was, and his face is still bony, crowned by a head of very coarse, black hair.

When I was ten years old I went to bed one night only long enough to make Joe and Clara suppose I was fast asleep. I left in my place something which appears when you say one of the words of Guru and went down the drainpipe outside my window. It always was easy to climb down and up, ever since I was eight years old.

I met Guru in Inwood Hill Park. "You're late," he said.

"Not too late," I answered. "I know it's never too late for one of these things."

"How do you know?" he asked sharply. "This is your first."

"And maybe my last," I replied. "I don't like the idea of it. If I have nothing more to learn from my second than my first I shan't go to another."

"You don't know," he said, "You don't know what it's like—the voices, and the bodies slick with unguent, leaping flames; mind-filling ritual! You can have no idea at all until you've taken part."

"We'll see," I said. "Can we leave from here?"

"Yes," he said. Then he taught me the word I would need to know, and we both said it together.

The place we were in next was lit with red lights, and I think that the walls were of rock. Though of course there was no real seeing there, and so the lights only seemed to be red, and it was not real rock.

As we were going to the fire one of them stopped us. "Who's with you?" she asked, calling Guru by another name. I did not know that he was also the person bearing that name, for it was a very powerful one.

He cast a hasty, sidewise glance at me and then said: "This is Peter of whom I have often told you."

She looked at me then and smiled, stretching out her oily arms. "Ah," she said, softly, like the cats when they talk at night to me. "Ah, this is Peter. Will you come to me when I call you, Peter? And sometimes call for me—in the dark—when you are alone?"

"Don't do that!" said Guru, angrily pushing past her. "He's very young—you might spoil him for his work."

She screeched at our backs: "Guru and his pupil—fine pair! Boy, he's no more real than I am—you're the only real thing here!"

"Don't listen to her," said Guru. "She's wild and raving. They're always tight-strung when this time comes around."

We came near the fires then, and sat down on rocks. They were killing animals and birds and doing things with their bodies. The blood was being collected in a basin of stone, which passed through the crowd. The one to my left handed it to me. "Drink," she said, grinning to show me her fine, white teeth. I swallowed twice from it and passed it to Guru.

When the bowl had passed all around we took off our clothes. Some, like Guru, did not wear them, but many did. The one to my left sat closer to me, breathing heavily at my face. I moved away. "Tell her to stop, Guru," I said. "This isn't part of it, I know."

Guru spoke to her sharply in their own language, and she changed her seat, snarling.

Then we all began to chant, clapping our hands and beating our thighs. One of them rose slowly and circled about the fires in a slow pace, her eyes rolling wildly. She worked her jaws and flung her arms about so sharply that I could hear the elbows crack. Still shuffling her feet against the rock floor she bent her body backwards down to her feet. Her belly muscles were bands nearly standing out from her skin, and the oil rolled down her body and legs. As the palms of her hands touched the ground, she collapsed in a twitching heap and began to set up a thin wailing noise against the steady chant and hand beat that the rest of us were keeping up. Another of them did the same as the first, and we chanted louder for her and still louder for the third. Then, while we still beat our hands and thighs, one of them took up the third, laid her across the altar, and made her ready with a stone knife. The fire's light gleamed off the chipped edge of obsidian. As her blood drained down the groove, cut as a gutter into the rock of the altar, we stopped our chant and the fires were snuffed out.

But still we could see what was going on, for these things were, of course, not happening at all—only seeming to happen, really, just as all the people and things there only seemed to be what they were. Only I was real. That must be why they desired me so.

As the last of the fires died Guru excitedly whispered: "The Presence!" He was very deeply moved.

From the pool of blood from the third dancer's body there issued the Presence. It was the tallest one there, and when it spoke its voice was deeper, and when it commanded its commands were obeyed.

"Let blood!" it commanded, and we gashed ourselves with flints. It smiled and showed teeth bigger and sharper and whiter than any of the others.

"Make water!" it commanded, and we all spat on each other. It flapped its wings and rolled its eyes, which were bigger and redder than any of the others.

"Pass flame!" it commanded, and we breathed smoke and fire on our limbs. It stamped its feet, let blue flames roar from its mouth, and they were bigger and wilder than any of the others.

Then it returned to the pool of blood and we lit the fires again. Guru was staring straight before him; I tugged his arm. He bowed as though we were meeting for the first time that night.

"What are you thinking of?" I asked. "We shall go now."

"Yes," he said heavily. "Now we shall go." Then we said the word that had brought us there.

The first man I killed was Brother Paul, at the school where I went to learn the things that Guru did not teach me.

It was less than a year ago, but it seems like a very long time. I have killed so many times since then.

"You're a very bright boy, Peter," said the brother.

"Thank you, brother."

"But there are things about you that I don't understand. Normally I'd ask your parents but—I feel that they don't understand either. You were an infant prodigy, weren't you?"

"Yes, brother."

"There's nothing very unusual about that—glands, I'm told. You know what glands are?"

Then I was alarmed. I had heard of them, but I was not certain whether they were the short, thick green men who wear only metal or the things with many legs with whom I talked in the woods.

"How did you find out?" I asked him.

"But Peter! You look positively frightened, lad! I don't know a thing about them myself, but Father Frederick does. He has whole books about them, though I sometimes doubt whether he believes them himself."

"They aren't good books, brother," I said. "They ought to be burned."

"That's a savage thought, my son. But to return to your own problem—"

I could not let him go any further knowing what he did about me. I said one of the words Guru taught me and he looked at first very surprised and then seemed to be in great pain. He dropped across his desk and I felt his wrist to make sure, for I had not used that word before. But he was dead.

There was a heavy step outside and I made myself invisible. Stout Father Frederick entered, and I nearly killed him too with the word, but I knew that that would be very curious. I decided to wait, and went through the door as Father Frederick bent over the dead monk. He thought he was asleep.

I went down the corridor to the book-lined office of the stout priest and, working quickly, piled all his books in the center of the room and lit them with my breath. Then I went down to the schoolyard and made myself visible again when there was nobody looking. It was very easy. I killed a man I passed on the street the next day.

There was a girl named Mary who lived near us. She was fourteen then, and I desired her as those in the Cavern out of Time and Space had desired me.

So when I saw Guru and he had bowed, I told him of it, and he looked at me in great surprise. "You are growing older, Peter," he said.

"I am, Guru. And there will come a time when your words will not be strong enough for me."

He laughed. "Come, Peter," he said. "Follow me if you wish. There is something that is going to be done—" He licked his thin, purple lips and said: "I have told you what it will be like."

"I shall come," I said. "Teach me the word." So he taught me the word and we said it together.

The place we were in next was not like any of the other places I had been to before with Guru. It was No-place. Always before there had been the seeming passage of time and matter, but here there was not even that. Here Guru and the others cast off their forms and were what they were, and No-place was the only place where they could do this.

It was not like the Cavern, for the Cavern had been out of Time and Space, and this place was not enough of a place even for that. It was No-place.

What happened there does not bear telling, but I was made known to certain ones who never departed from there. All came to them as they existed. They had not color or the seeming of color, or any seeming of shape.

There I learned that eventually I would join with them; that I had been selected as the one of my planet who was to dwell without being forever in that No-place.

Guru and I left, having said the word.

"Well?" demanded Guru, staring me in the eye.

"I am willing," I said. "But teach me one word now—"

"Ah," he said grinning. "The girl?"

"Yes," I said. "The word that will mean much to her."

Still grinning, he taught me the word.

Mary, who had been fourteen, is now fifteen and what they call incurably mad.

Last night I saw Guru again and for the last time. He bowed as I approached him. "Peter," he said warmly.

"Teach me the word," said I.

"It is not too late."

"Teach me the word."

"You can withdraw—with what you master you can master also this world. Gold without reckoning; sardonyx and gems, Peter! Rich crushed velvet—stiff, scraping, embroidered tapestries!"

"Teach me the word."

"Think, Peter, of the house you could build. It could be of white marble, and every slab centered by a winking ruby. Its gate could be of beaten gold within and without and it could be built about one slender tower of carven ivory, rising mile after mile into the turquoise sky. You could see the clouds float underneath your eyes."

"Teach me the word."

"Your tongue could crush the grapes that taste like melted silver. You could hear always the song of the bulbul and the lark that sounds like the dawnstar made musical. Spikenard that will bloom a thousand thousand years could be ever in your nostrils. Your hands could feel the down of purple Himalayan swans that is softer than a sunset cloud."

"Teach me the word."

"You could have women whose skin would be from the black of ebony to the white of snow. You could have women who would be as hard as flints or as soft as a sunset cloud."

"Teach me the word."

Guru grinned and said the word.

Now, I do not know whether I will say that word, which was the last that Guru taught me, today or tomorrow or until a year has passed.

It is a word that will explode this planet like a stick of dynamite in a rotten apple.

The Anomaly of
the Empty Man

ANTHONY BOUCHER

*Fantasy and mystery fiction resemble each other very closely; both begin
with seemingly inexplicable phenomena, but where fantasy is obliged only
to suspend the reader's disbelief in those phenomena, mystery ultimately
must produce a rational explanation. In "The Anomaly of the Empty
Man," Anthony Boucher tells a story that is both a fantasy and a mystery,
and lets the reader decide which approach is the more satisfying. One of
John W. Campbell's top guns in* Unknown, *Boucher was a distinguished
book reviewer, science fiction author, and mystery writer. For its first nine
years, he also edited* The Magazine of Fantasy and Science Fiction, *from
which this story is taken.*

THIS IS for you," Inspector Abrahams announced wryly. "Another
screwy one."

I was late and out of breath. I'd somehow got entangled on Market
Street with the Downtown Merchants' Association annual parade, and
for a while it looked like I'd be spending the day surrounded by gigantic
balloon-parodies of humanity. But it takes more than rubber Gullivers
to hold me up when Inspector Abrahams announces that he's got a
case of the kind he labels "for Lamb."

443

And San Francisco's the city for them to happen in. Nobody anywhere else ever had such a motive for murder as the butler Frank Miller in 1896, or such an idea of how to execute a bank robbery as the zany Mr. Will in 1952. Take a look at Joe Jackson's *San Francisco Murders*, and you'll see that we can achieve a flavor all our own. And when we do, Abrahams lets me in on it.

Abrahams didn't add any explanation. He just opened the door of the apartment. I went in ahead of him. It was a place I could have liked it if it hadn't been for what was on the floor.

Two walls were mostly windows. One gave a good view of the Golden Gate. From the other, on a fine day, you could see the Farallones, and it was a fine day.

The other two walls were records and a record player. I'd heard of the Stambaugh collection of early operatic recordings. If I'd been there on any other errand, my mouth would have watered at the prospect of listening to lost great voices.

"If you can get a story out of this that makes sense," the Inspector grunted, "you're welcome to it—at the usual fee." Which was a dinner at Lupo's Pizzeria, complete with pizza Carus', tomatoes with fresh basil and sour French bread to mop up the inspired sauce of Lupo's special *calamari* (squids to you). "Everything's just the way we found it."

I looked at the unfinished highball, now almost colorless with all its ice melted and its soda flat. I looked at the cylindrical ash of the cigaret which had burned itself out. I looked at the vacuum cleaner—a shockingly utilitarian object in this set for gracious living. I looked at the record player, still switched on, still making its methodical seventy-eight revolutions per minute, though there was no record on the turntable.

Then I managed to look again at the thing on the floor.

It was worse than a body. It was like a tasteless bloodless parody of the usual occupant of the spot marked X. Clothes scattered in disorder seem normal—even more normal, perhaps, in a bachelor apartment than clothes properly hung in closets. But this . . . .

Above the neck of the dressing gown lay the spectacles. The sleeves of the shirt were inside the sleeves of the dressing gown. The shirt was buttoned, even to the collar, and the foulard tie was knotted tight up against the collar button. The tails of the shirt were tucked properly into the zipped-up, properly belted trousers. Below the trouser cuffs lay the shoes, at a lifelike angle, with the tops of the socks emerging from them.

"And there's an undershirt under the shirt," Inspector Abrahams muttered disconsolately, "and shorts inside the pants. Complete outfit: what the well-dressed man will wear. Only no man in them."

It was as though James Stambaugh had been attacked by some solvent which eats away only flesh and leaves all the inanimate articles. Or as though some hyperspatial suction had drawn the living man out of his wardrobe, leaving his sartorial shell behind him.

I said, "Can I dirty an ashtray in this scene?"

Abrahams nodded. "I was just keeping it for you to see. We've got our pictures." While I lit up, he crossed to the record player and switched it off. "Damned whirligig gets on my nerves."

"Whole damned setup gets on mine," I said. "It's like a strip-tease version of the *Mary Celeste*. Only the strip wasn't a gradual tease; just abruptly, *whoosh!*, a man's gone. One minute he's comfortably dressed in his apartment, smoking, drinking, playing records. The next he's stark naked—and where and doing what?"

Abrahams pulled at his nose, which didn't need lengthening. "We had the Japanese valet check the wardrobe. Every article of clothing James Stambaugh owned is still here in the apartment."

"Who found him?" I asked.

"Kaguchi. The valet. He had last night off. He let himself in this morning, to prepare coffee and prairie oysters as usual. He found this."

"Blood?" I ventured.

Abrahams shook his head.

"Visitors?"

"Ten apartments in this building. Three of them had parties last night. You can figure how much help the elevator man was."

"The drink?"

"We took a sample to the lab. Nothing but the best scotch."

I frowned at the vacuum cleaner. "What's that doing out here? It ought to live in a closet."

"Puzzled Kaguchi too. He even says it was still a little warm when he found it, like it had been used. But we looked in the bag. I assure you Stambaugh didn't get sucked in there."

"Motive?"

"Gay dog, our Mr. Stambaugh. Maybe you read Herb Caen's gossip column too? And Kaguchi gave us a little fill-in. Brothers, fathers, husbands . . . Too many motives."

"But why this way?" I brooded. "Get rid of him, sure. But why leave this hollow husk . . .?"

"Not just why, Lamb. How."

"How? That should be easy enough to—"

"Try it. Try fitting sleeves into sleeves, pants into pants, so they're as smooth and even as if they were still on the body. I've tried, with the rest of the wardrobe. It doesn't work."

I had an idea. "You don't fit 'em in," I said smugly. "You take 'em off. Look." I unbuttoned my coat and shirt, undid my tie, and pulled everything off at once. "See," I said; "sleeves in sleeves." I unzipped and stepped out of trousers and shorts. "See; pants in pants."

Inspector Abrahams was whistling the refrain of *Strip Polka*. "You missed your career, Lamb," he said. "Only now you've got to put your shirt tails between the outer pants and the inner ones and still keep everything smooth. And look in here." He lifted up one shoe and took out a pocket flash and shot a beam inside. "The sock's caught on a little snag in one of the metal eyelets. That's kept it from collapsing, and you can still see the faint impress of toes in there. Try slipping your foot out of a laced-up shoe and see if you can get that result."

I was getting dressed again and feeling like a damned fool.

"Got any other inspirations?" Abrahams grinned.

"The only inspiration I've got is as to where to go now."

"Some day," the Inspector grunted, "I'll learn where you go for your extra-bright ideas."

"As the old lady said to the elephant keeper," I muttered, "you wouldn't believe me if I told you."

The Montgomery Block (Monkey Block to natives) is an antic and reboantic warren of offices and studios on the fringe of Grant Avenue's Chinatown and Columbus Avenue's Italian-Mexican-French-Basque quarter. The studio I wanted was down a long corridor, beyond that all-American bend where the Italian newspaper *Corriere del Popolo* sits cater-corner from the office of Tinn Hugh Yu, Ph.D and Notary Public.

Things were relatively quiet today in Dr. Verner's studio. Slavko Catenich was still hammering away at his block of marble, apparently on the theory that the natural form inherent in the stone would emerge if you hit it often enough. Irma Borigian was running over vocal exercises and occasionally checking herself by striking a note on the piano, which seemed to bring her more reassurance than it did me. Those two, plus a couple of lads industriously fencing whom I'd never seen before, were the only members of Verner's Varieties on hand today.

Irma ah-ah-ahed and pinked, the fencers clicked, Slavko crashed, and in the midst of the decibels the Old Man stood at his five-foot lectern-desk, resolutely proceeding in quill-pen longhand with the resounding periods of *The Anatomy of Nonscience*, that never-concluded compendium of curiosities which was half Robert Burton and half Charles Fort.

He gave me the medium look. Not the hasty "Just this sentence" or the forbidding "Dear boy, this page *must* be finished"; but the in-between "One more deathless paragraph" look. I grabbed a chair and tried to watch Irma's singing and listen to Slavko's sculpting.

There's no describing Dr. Verner. You can say his age is somewhere between seventy and a hundred. You can say he has a mane of hair like an albino lion and a little goatee like a Kentucky Colonel who never heard of cigars. ("When a man's hair is white," I've heard him say, "tobacco and a beard are mutually exclusive vices.") You can mention the towering figure and the un-English mobility of the white old hands and the disconcerting twinkle of those impossibly blue eyes. And you'd still have about as satisfactory a description as when you say the Taj Mahal is a domed, square, white marble building.

The twinkle was in the eyes and the mobility was in the hands when he finally came to tower over me. They were both gone by the time I'd finished the story of the Stambaugh apartment and the empty man. He stood for a moment frowning, the eyes lusterless, the hands limp at his sides. Then, still standing like that, he relaxed the frown and opened his mouth in a resonant bellow.

"You sticks!" he roared. (Irma stopped and looked hurt.) "You stones!" (The fencers stopped and looked expectant.) "You worse than worst of those that lawless and uncertain thoughts" (Slavko stopped and looked resigned.) "imagine howling," Dr. Verner concluded in a columbine coo, having shifted in mid-quotation from one Shakespearean play to another so deftly that I was still looking for the joint.

Verner's Varieties waited for the next number on the bill. In majestic silence Dr. Verner stalked to his record player. Stambaugh's had been a fancy enough custom-made job, but nothing like this.

If you think things are confusing now, with records revolving at 78, 45, and 33⅓ rpm, you should see the records of the early part of the century. There were cylinders, of course (Verner had a separate machine for them). Disc records, instead of our present standard sizes, ranged anywhere from seven to fourteen inches in diameter, with curious fractional stops in between. Even the center holes came in assorted sizes. Many discs were lateral-cut, like modern ones; but quite a few were hill-and-dale, with the needles riding up and down instead of sideways—which actually gave better reproduction but somehow never became overwhelmingly popular. The grooving varied too, so that even if two companies both used hill-and-dale cutting you couldn't play the records of one on a machine for the other. And just to make things trickier, some records started from the inside instead of the outer edge. It was Free Enterprise gone hogwild.

Dr. Verner had explained all this while demonstrating to me how his player could cope with any disc record ever manufactured. And I had heard him play everything on it from smuggled dubbings of Crosby blow-ups to a recording by the original *Floradora* Sextet—which was, he was always careful to point out, a double sextet or, as he preferred, a duodecimet.

"You are," he announced ponderously, "about to hear the greatest dramatic soprano of this century. Rosa Ponselle and Elisabeth Rethberg were passable. There was something to be said for Lillian Nordica and Lena Geyer. But listen!" And he slid the needle into the first groove.

"Dr. Verner—" I started to ask for footnotes; I should have known better.

"Dear boy . . . !" he murmured protestingly, over the preliminary surface noise of the aged pressing, and gave me one of those twinkles of bluest blue which implied that surely only a moron could fail to follow the logic of the procedure.

I sat back and listened. Irma listened too, but the eyes of the others were soon longingly intent on foils and chisel. I listened casually at first, then began to sit forward.

I have heard, in person or on records, all of the venerable names which Dr. Verner mentioned—to say nothing of Tebaldi, Russ, Ritter-Ciampi, Souez and both Lehmanns. And reluctantly I began to admit that he was right; this was *the* dramatic soprano. The music was strange to me—a setting of the Latin text of the *Our Father,* surely eighteenth century and at a guess by Pergolesi; it had his irrelevant but reverent tunefulness in approaching a sacred text. Its grave sustained lilt was admirable for showing off a voice; and the voice, unwavering in its prolonged tones, incredible in its breath control, deserved all the showing off it could get. During one long phrase of runs, as taxing as anything in Mozart or Handel, I noticed Irma. She was holding her breath in sympathy with the singer, and the singer won. Irma had let out an admiring gasp before the soprano had, still on one breath, achieved the phrase.

And then, for reasons more operatic than liturgical, the music quickened. The sustained legato phrases gave way to cascades of light bright coloratura. Notes sparkled and dazzled and brightness fell from the air. It was impeccable, inapproachable—infinitely discouraging to a singer and almost shocking to the ordinary listener.

The record ended. Dr. Verner beamed around the room as if he'd done all that himself. Irma crossed to the piano, struck one key to verify the incredible note in alt upon which the singer had ended, picked up her music, and wordlessly left the room.

Slavko had seized his chisel and the fencers were picking up their foils as I approached our host. "But Dr. Verner," I led with my chin. "The Stambaugh case . . ."

"Dear boy," he sighed as he readied the old one-two, "you mean you don't realize that you have just heard the solution?"

"You will have a drop of Drambuie, of course?" Dr. Verner queried formally as we settled down in his more nearly quiet inner room.

"Of course," I said. Then as his mouth opened, " 'For without Drambuie,' " I quoted, " 'the world might never have known the simple solution to the problem of the mislaid labyrinth.' "

He spilled a drop. "I was about to mention that very fact. How . . .? Or perhaps I have alluded to it before in this connection?"

"You have," I said.

"Forgive me." He twinkled disarmingly. "I grow old, dear boy."

Ritualistically we took our first sip of Drambuie. Then:

"I well remember," Dr. Verner began, "that it was in the autumn of the year 1901 . . .

. . . that the horror began. I was then well established in my Kensington practice, which seemed to flourish as it never had under the ministrations of its previous possessor, and in a more than comfortable financial position. I was able at last to look about me, to contemplate and to investigate the manifold pleasures which a metropolis at once so cosmopolitan and so insular as London proffers to the unattached young man. San Francisco of the same period might perhaps compare in quality; indeed my own experiences here a few years later in the singular affair of the cable cabal were not unrewarding. But a man of your generation knows nothing of those pleasures now ten lustra faded. The humours of the Music Halls, the delights of a hot bird and a cold bottle shared with a dancer from Daly's, the simpler and less expensive delights of punting on the Thames (shared, I may add, with a simpler and less expensive companion)—these claimed what portion of my time I could salvage from my practice.

But above all I was devoted to music; and to be devoted to music meant, in the London of 1901, to be devoted to—but I have always carefully refrained from the employment of veritable and verifiable names in these narratives. Let me once more be discreet, and call her simply by that affectionate agnomen by which my cousin, to his sorrow, knew her: *Carina.*

I need not describe Carina as a musician; you have just heard her sing Pergolesi, you know how she combined nobility and grandeur with a technical agility which these degenerate days associate only with a certain type of light soprano. But I must seek to describe her as a woman, if woman she may be called.

When first I heard the tittle-tattle of London, I paid it small heed. To the man in the street (or even in the stalls) *actress* is still a euphemism for a harsher and shorter term, though my experience of actresses, extending as it has over three continents and more than my allotted three score and ten years, tends to lead me, if anywhere, to an opposite conclusion.

The individual who stands out from the herd is the natural target of calumny. I shall never forget the disgraceful episode of the purloined litter, in which the veterinarian Dr. Stookes accused me of—but let us reserve that anomaly for another occasion. To return to Carina: I heard the gossip; I attributed it to as simple a source as I have indicated. But then the evidence began to attain proportions which the most latitudinarian could hardly disregard.

First young Ronny Furbish-Darnley blew out his brains. He had gambling debts, to be sure, and his family chose to lay the stress upon them; but his relations with Carina had been common knowledge. Then Major MacIvers hanged himself with his own cravat (the MacIvers tartan, of course). I need hardly add that a MacIvers had no gambling debts. Even that episode might have been hushed up had not a peer of so exalted a name that I dare not even paraphrase it perished in the flames of his ancestral castle. Even in the charred state in which they were recovered, the bodies of his wife and seven children evinced the clumsy haste with which he had slit their throats.

It was as though . . . how shall I put it? . . . as though Carina were in some way a "carrier" of what we had then not yet learned to call The Death Wish. Men who knew her too well hungered no longer for life.

The press began to concern itself, as best it might with due regard for the laws of libel, with this situation. Leading articles hinted at possible governmental intervention to preserve the flower of England from this insidious foreigner. Little else was discussed in Hyde Park save the elimination of Carina.

Even the memorable mass suicides at Oxford had provided no sensation comparable to this. Carina's very existence seemed as much in danger as though Jack the Ripper had been found and turned over to the English people. We are firm believers in our English justice; but when that justice is powerless to act, the Englishman aroused is a phenomenon to fear.

If I may be pardoned a Hibernian lapse, the only thing that saved Carina's life was . . . her death.

It was a natural death—perhaps the first natural action of her life. She collapsed on the stage of Covent Garden during a performance of Mozart's *Così fan tutte,* just after having delivered the greatest performance of that fantastic aria, *Come scoglio,* that a living ear has heard.

There were investigations of the death. Even my cousin, with an understandable personal interest, took a hand. (He was the only one of Carina's close admirers to survive her infection; I have often wondered whether this fact resulted from an incredible strength or an equally incredible inadequacy within him.) But there was no possible doubt that the death was a natural one.

It was after the death that the Carina legend began to grow. It was then that young men about town who had seen the great Carina but once began to mention the unmentionable reasons which had caused them to refrain from seeing her again. It was then that her dresser, a crone whose rationality was as uncertain as her still persistent terror was unquestionable, began to speak of unspeakable practices, to hint at black magic as among milady's avocations, to suggest that her utterance (which you have heard) of flights of notes, incredibly rapid yet distinct, owed its facility to her control and even suspension of the mortal limitations of time.

And then began . . . the horror. Perhaps you thought that by *the horror* I meant the sequence of Carina-carried suicides? No; even that lay still, if near the frontier, within the uttermost bounds of human comprehension.

The horror passed those bounds.

I need not ask you to envision it. You have beheld it. You have seen clothing sucked dry of its fleshy tenant, you have seen the haberdasher's habitation sink flabbily in upon itself, no longer sustained by tissue of bone and blood and nerves.

All London saw it that year. And London could not believe.

First it was that eminent musicologist, Sir Frederick Paynter, FRCM. Then there were two young aristocrats, then, oddly, a poor Jewish peddler in the East End.

I shall spare you the full and terrible details, alluding only in passing to the Bishop of Cloisterham. I had read the press accounts. I had filed the cuttings for their very impossibility (for even then I had had adumbrations of the concept which you now know as *The Anatomy of Nonscience.*)

But the horror did not impinge upon me closely until it struck one of my own patients, a retired naval officer by the name of Clutsam. His family had sent for me at once, at the same time that they had dispatched a messenger to fetch my cousin.

As you know, my cousin enjoyed a certain fame as a private detective. He had been consulted in more than one previous instance of the horror; but I had read little of him in the press save a reiteration of his hope that the solution lay in his familiar dictum: "Discard the impossible; and whatever remains, no matter how improbable, must be true."

I had already formulated my now celebrated counter-dictum: "Discard the impossible; then if *nothing* remains, some part of the 'impossible' must be possible." It was thus that our dicta and ourselves faced each other across the worn and outdated naval uniform on the floor, complete from the gold braid on its shoulders to the wooden peg below the empty left trouser leg, cut off at the knee.

"I imagine, Horace," my cousin remarked, puffing at his blackened clay, "that you conceive this to be your sort of affair."

"It is obviously not yours," I stated. "There is something in these vanishings beyond—"

"—beyond the humdrum imagination of a professional detective? Horace, you are a man of singular accomplishments."

I smiled. My cousin, as my great-uncle Etienne used to remark of General Masséna, was famous for the accuracy of his information.

"I will confess," he added, "since my Boswell is not within earshot, that you have occasionally hit upon what satisfies you, at least, as the truth in some few cases in which I have failed. Do *you* see any element linking Captain Clutsam, Sir Frederick Paynter, Moishe Lipkowitz and the Bishop of Cloisterham?"

"I do not." It was always discreet to give my cousin the answer which he expected.

"And *I do!* And yet I am no nearer a solution than . . ." His pipe clenched in his teeth, he flung himself about the room, as though pure physical action would somehow ameliorate the lamentable state of his nerves. Finally he paused before me, looked sharply into my eyes and said, "Very well. I shall tell you. What is nonsense in the patterns shaped by the reasoning mind may well serve you as foundation for some new structure of unreason.

"I have traced every fact in the lives of these men. I know what they habitually ate for breakfast, how they spent their Sundays, and which of them preferred snuff to tobacco. There is only *one* factor which they all possess in common: Each of them recently purchased a record of the Pergolesi *Pater Noster* sung by . . . *Carina.* And those records have vanished as thoroughly as the naked men themselves."

I bestowed upon him an amicable smile. Family affection must temper the ungentlemanly emotion of triumph. Still smiling, I left him with the uniform and the leg while I betook myself to the nearest gramophone merchant.

The solution was by then obvious to me. I had observed that Captain Clutsam's gramophone was of the sapphire-needled type designed to play those recordings known as hill-and-dale, the vertical recordings produced by Pathé and other companies as distinguished from the lateral recordings of Columbia and Gramophone-and-Typewriter. And I had recalled that many hill-and-dale recordings were at that time designed (as I believe some wireless transcriptions are now) for an inside start, that is, so that the needle began near the label and traveled outward to the rim of the disc. An unthinking listener might easily begin to play an inside-start record in the more normal manner. The result, in almost all instances, would be gibberish; but in this particular case . . . .

I purchased the Carina record with no difficulty. I hastened to my Kensington home, where the room over the dispensary contained a gramophone convertible to either lateral or vertical recordings. I placed the record on the turntable. It was, to be sure, labeled INSIDE START; but how easily one might overlook such a notice! I overlooked it deliberately. I started the turntable and lowered the needle . . . .

The cadenzas of coloratura are strange things in reverse. As I heard it, the record naturally began with the startling final note which so disheartened Miss Borigian, then went on to those dazzling *fioriture* which so strengthen the dresser's charge of time-magic. But in reverse, these seemed like the music of some undiscovered planet, coherent to themselves, following a logic unknown to us and shaping a beauty which only our ignorance prevents us from worshipping.

And there were words to these flourishes; for almost unique among sopranos, Carina possessed a diction of diabolical clarity. And the words were at first simply *Nema . . . nema . . . nema . . . .*

It was while the voice was brilliantly repeating this reversed *Amen* that I became *literally* beside myself.

I was standing, naked and chill in the London evening, beside a meticulously composed agglomeration of clothing which parodied the body of Dr. Horace Verner.

This fragment of clarity lasted only an instant. Then the voice reached the significant words: *olam a son arebil des men . . . .*

This was the Lord's Prayer which she was singing. It is common knowledge that there is in all necromancy no charm more potent than that prayer (and most especially in Latin) *said backwards.* As the last act of her magical malefactions, Carina had left behind her this record, knowing that one of its purchasers would occasionally, by inadvertence, play it backwards, and that then the spell would take effect. It had taken effect now.

I was in space . . . a space of infinite darkness and moist warmth. The music had departed elsewhere. I was alone in this space and the space itself was alive and by its very moist warm dark life this space was draining from me all that which was my own life. And then there was with me a voice in that space, a voice that cried ever *Eem vull! Eem vull!* and for all the moaning gasping urgency in that voice I knew it for the voice of Carina.

I was a young man then. The Bishop's end must have been swift and merciful. But even I, young and strong, knew that this space desired the final sapping of my life, that my life should be drawn from my body even as my body had been drawn from its shell. So I prayed.

I was not a man given to prayer in those days. But I knew words which the Church has taught us are pleasing to God, and I prayed with all the fervor of my being for deliverance from this Nightmare Life-in-Death.

And I stood again naked beside my clothes. I looked at the turntable of the gramophone. The disc was not there. Still naked, I walked to the dispensary and mixed myself a sedative before I dared trust my fingers to button my garments. Then I dressed and went out again to the shop of the gramophone merchant. There I bought every copy in his stock of that devil's *Pater Noster* and smashed them all before his eyes.

Ill though I could afford it, even in my relative affluence, I spent the next few weeks in combing London for copies of that recording.

One copy, and one only, I preserved; you heard it just now. I had hoped that no more existed . . .

". . . but obviously," Dr. Verner concluded, "your Mr. Stambaugh managed to acquire one, God rest his soul . . . and body."

I drained my second Drambuie and said, "I'm a great admirer of your cousin," Dr. Verner looked at me with polite blue inquiry. "You find what satisfies *you* as the truth."

"Occam's Razor, dear boy," Dr. Verner murmured, associatively stroking his smooth cheeks. "The solution accounts economically for every integral fact in the problem."

"But look," I said suddenly. "It doesn't! For once I've got you cold. There's one 'integral fact' completely omitted."

"Which is . . .?" Dr. Verner cooed.

"You can't have been the first man that thought of praying in that . . . that space. Certainly the Bishop must have."

For a moment Dr. Horace Verner was silent. Then he fixed me with the Dear-boy-how-idiotic! twinkle. "But only I," he announced tranquilly, "had realized that in that . . . space all sound, like the Our Father itself, was reversed. The voice cried ever *Eem vull!* and what is that phonetically but *Love me!* backwards? Only *my* prayer was effective, because only I had the foresight to pray in *reverse phonetics.*"

I phoned Abrahams to say I had an idea and could I do some checking in the Stambaugh apartment?

"Good," he said. "I have an idea too. Meet you there in a half hour."

There was no Abrahams in the corridor when I got there; but the police seal was broken and the door was ajar. I went on in and stopped dead.

For the first moment I thought it was still Stambaugh's clothes spread out there. But there was no mistaking Inspector Abrahams' neat gray plainclothes—with no Abrahams in them.

I think I said something about *the horror.* I draw pretty much of a blank between seeing that empty suit and looking up to the far doorway and seeing Inspector Abrahams.

He was wearing a dressing gown of Stambaugh's, which was far too short for him. I stared at his grotesque figure and at the android parody which dangled from his hand.

"Sorry, Lamb," he grinned, "Couldn't resist the theatrical effect. Go on. Take a good look at the empty man on the floor."

I looked. The clothes were put together with the exactly real, body-fitting, sucked-out effect which we had already decided was impossible.

"You see," Abrahams said, "I remembered the vacuum cleaner. And the Downtown Merchants' parade."

I was back at the studio early the next morning. There was nobody from Verner's Varieties there but Slavko, and it was so relatively quiet that Dr. Verner was just staring at the manuscript of *The Anatomy* without adding a word.

"Look," I said. "In the first place, Stambaugh's record player isn't equipped for hill-and-dale records."

"They *can* be played even on an ordinary machine," Dr. Verner observed tranquilly. "The effect is curious—faint and with an odd echoing overlap, which might even enhance the power of the cantrip."

"And I looked in his card catalog," I went on, "and he didn't have a recording of the Pergolesi *Pater Noster* by anybody."

Dr. Verner widened his overblue eyes. "But of course the card would vanish with the record," he protested. "Magic makes allowances for modern developments."

"Wait a minute!" I exclaimed suddenly. "Hey, I'm brilliant! This is one Abrahams didn't think of. It's *me,* for once, that solves a case."

"Yes, dear boy?" said Dr. Verner gently.

"Look: You *can't* play an inside-start record backwards. It wouldn't work. Visualize the spiraling grooves. If you put the needle in the outside last groove, it'd just stay there ticking—same like it would if you put it in the inside last groove of a normal record. To play it backwards, you'd have to have some kind of gearshift that'd make the turntable spin backwards."

"But I have," said Dr. Verner blandly. "It enables one to make extraordinarily interesting experiments in sound. Doubtless Mr. Stambaugh had too. It would be simple enough to switch over by mistake; he was drinking . . . Tell me: the spinning turntable that you saw . . . was it revolving clockwise or counterclockwise?"

I thought back, and I was damned if I knew. Clockwise, I took for granted; but if I had to swear . . . Instead I asked, "And I suppose Captain Clutsam and the Bishop of Cloisterham had alternate counterclockwise gearshifts?"

"Why, of course. Another reason why such a serious collector as Mr. Stambaugh would. You see, the discs of the Fonogrammia company, a small and obscure firm but one boasting a few superb artists under exclusive contract, were designed to be so played."

I stared at those pellucid azure eyes. I had no notion whether counterclockwise Fonogrammia records were the coveted objective of every collector or a legend that had this moment come into being.

"And besides," I insisted, "Abrahams had demonstrated how it was really done. The vacuum cleaner tipped him off. Stambaugh had bought a man-sized, man-shaped balloon, a little brother of those monster figures they use in parades. He inflated it and dressed it in his clothes. Then he deflated it, leaving the clothes in perfect arrangement with nothing in them but a shrunken chunk of rubber, which he could withdraw by unbuttoning the shirt. Abrahams found the only firm in San Francisco that manufactures such balloons. A clerk identified Stambaugh as a purchaser. So Abrahams bought a duplicate and pulled the same gag on me."

Dr. Verner frowned. "And the vacuum cleaner?"

"You use a vacuum cleaner in reverse for pumping up large balloons. And you use it normally for deflating them; if you just let the air out *whoosh!* they're apt to break."

"The clerk" (it came out *clark,* of course) "identified Stambaugh positively?"

I shifted under the piercing blueness. "Well, you know identifications from photographs. . . ."

"Indeed I do." He took a deliberately timed pause. "And the record player? Why was its turntable still revolving?"

"Accident, I guess. Stambaugh must've bumped against the switch."

"Which projected from the cabinet so that one might well engage it by accident?"

I pictured the machine. I visualized the switch and the depth to which one would have to reach in. "Well, no," I granted. "Not exactly. . . ."

Dr. Verner smiled down at me tolerantly. "And the motive for these elaborate maneuvers by Stambaugh?"

"Too many threatening male relatives on his tail. He deliberately staged this to look oh-so-mysterious nobody'd spot the simple fact that he was just getting the hell out from under. Abrahams has an all-points alarm out; he'll be picked up any time within the next few days."

Dr. Verner sighed. His hands flickered through the air in a gesture of infinitely resigned patience. He moved to his record cabinet, took out a disc, placed it on the turntable, and adjusted certain switches.

"Come, Slavko!" he announced loudly. "Since Mr. Lamb prefers rubber balloons to truth, we are conferring a signal privilege upon him. We are retiring to the other room, leaving him here alone with the Carina record. His cocksure materialism will surely wish to verify the effect of playing it in reverse."

Slavko stopped pounding and said, "Huh?"

"Come, Slavko. But first say a polite good-by to Mr. Lamb. You may not be seeing him again." Dr. Verner paused in the doorway and surveyed me with what seemed like genuine concern. "Dear boy," he murmured, "you won't forget that point about the reverse phonetics . . . ?"

He was gone and so (without more polite good-by than a grunt) was Slavko. I was alone with Carina, with the opportunity to disprove Dr. Verner's fabulous narrative once and for all.

His story had made no pretense of explaining the presence of the vacuum cleaner.

And Inspector Abrahams' theory had not even attempted to account for the still-revolving turntable.

I switched on the turntable of the Verner machine. Carefully I lowered the tone-arm, let the oddly rounded needle settle into the first groove from the outer rim.

I heard that stunning final note in alt. So flawless was the Carina diction that I could hear, even in that range, the syllable to which it was sung: *nem,* the beginning of the reverse-Latin *Amen.*

Then I heard a distorted groan as the turntable abruptly slowed down from 78 to zero revolutions per minute. I looked at the switch, it was still on. I turned and saw Dr. Verner towering behind me, with a disconnected electric plug dangling from his hand.

"No," he said softly—and there was a dignity and power in that softness that I had never heard in his most impressive bellows. "No, Mr. Lamb. You have a wife and two sons. I have no right to trifle with their lives merely to gratify an old man's resentment of skepticism."

Quietly he lifted the tone-arm, removed the record, restored it to its envelope, and refiled it. His deft, un-English hands were not at their steadiest.

"When Inspector Abrahams succeeds in tracing down Mr. Stambaugh," he said firmly, "you shall hear this record in reverse. And not before then."

And it just so happens they haven't turned up Stambaugh yet.

Underground Movement

KRIS NEVILLE

The 1950s are generally thought of as a lackluster period for science fiction, during which the genre tried to recover from the postwar pulp magazine bust and endured the boom of untalented writers attracted by its trendiness. During these years, though, interesting experiments were taking place in The Magazine of Fantasy and Science Fiction. *Like* Unknown, *F&SF often published fantasy written with respect to the principles of science fiction, but unlike John W. Campbell, F&SF editors Anthony Boucher and J. Francis McComas gave their writers greater freedom to blend elements of the two genres. This experimentation produced stories such as "Underground Movement," in which Kris Neville endows a science fiction mutant story with an ending no reader of horror fiction is likely to forget.*

O N THE seat beside him, the brief case bounced and jiggled. He was driving over an old section of road. It had been last repaired in 1950, and unless the government shortly assigned precious manpower to its renovation, it would within another year disintegrate completely beneath the endless pressure of commuter traffic. He stepped down more heavily on the accelerator. The rebuilt engine began to knock.

He hoped his vacation authorization would be lying on the desk he shared with Robert Edd. He could be on a plane for South America by six o'clock. Tomorrow afternoon he would be settled in some tiny time-forgotten village. With the language barrier between him and the natives, he would be isolated for the first time in two years from the ever present pressure of minds unconsciously crying for his sympathy.

To his left and ahead, now that he was almost at the city limits, lay the smooth lawn and white marble monuments of a tree-shaded cemetery.

When the car came abreast, he felt for the second time since breakfast a sharp, pain-like buzzing in his mind. This time it seemed almost to be half formed thoughts, and there was an attendant impression of agony and heat that brought perspiration to his palms. He grappled with it for a moment, trying to understand it, and then it was gone as suddenly as it had come. He shook his head puzzled and afraid. It was too soon for pain.

Inside the city, traffic grew heavier. At Clay Street, he turned left. Seven blocks down, he located the address he wanted. He drew the car to the curb, picked up the brief case, and got out.

As he walked toward the porch, he imagined the face behind the door. He imagined it in terms of hair color, eye color, ear shape and bone structure. He knocked, hoping to find that the man inside had green hair, orange eyes, pronged ear lobes.

"Yes?" the man said, peering out from behind the half opened door.

He felt his heart pulse at the sight of the expected face. He said, "Mr. Merringo?"

"Yes," the man said, and his voice was dead and listless.

"My name is Wilson. Howard Wilson. May I come in?"

"You're a telepath?" Mr. Merringo said. His voice was still flat and indifferent, but the left side of his mouth quivered with distrust.

"I will not invade the privacy of your thoughts," Howard Wilson said. He had been saying the same formal sentence through a terrifying eternity of faces, and yet each time he felt a fresh anger at the implication which made it necessary.

The man hesitated for a fraction of a second. Then the door swung inward. "Come in," he said sullenly.

In silence Howard Wilson followed him down the narrow hall. His nostrils wrinkled at the stale air, and his eyes were momentarily stunned by the curtained gloom.

Mr. Merringo, a thin, nervous, thirtyish man who walked as if the carpet were insecure, turned left into the living room, which opened off the hall by way of sliding doors, one panel of which was extended. He crossed to the ornamental fireplace. It was littered with nervously twisted paper balls and half smoked cigarettes and ashes and a single, shriveled apple core. He turned to face the telepath. There were dark circles under his eyes, and his mouth was bloodless. "You're from the government? I read somewhere that they hire you."

Howard Wilson glanced at the mirror and saw the ridiculous bump on his forehead, round and blue, like a newly discolored bruise. It was the emblem of a telepath, and it grew, cancerous, from the twentieth year of his life. It would destroy him, eating inward to his mind and shooting malignant cells into his blood for impartial distribution to lungs and stomach and bones, before he was forty. His mouth remained emotionless as he tried to imagine the bump away, and to recall his clear, adolescent forehead in the days before he matured into hearing thoughts he did not want to hear. The mirror image peered back at him, nature's mistake, a false, evolutionary start, unproductive. He turned to the man at the fireplace.

"Yes," he said. "I work for the government." And my employers, he might have added, fear and distrust me more than you do. For them I gather information in the slippery, sterile field of espionage and counter-espionage. I carry ashes dead beyond breathing upon. "Please don't be alarmed by my telepathic ability," he said. "I will not use it here; I do not use it often; I would prefer never to use it at all."

"I can't understand why the government would be interested in me."

"It's about your wife," Howard Wilson said, steeling himself uselessly against pity.

Mr. Merringo stared into the telepath's eyes. No flicker betrayed his emotion, but Howard Wilson could feel it, in a quick pulse, and Howard Wilson's mind was sealed.

"Please sit down," Mr. Merringo said.

"Thank you."

Howard Wilson crossed to the sofa. As he sat down, he noticed the faint dust released by the pressure of his body. Looking around the room, his eyes accustomed now to the dimness, he knew that it had not been cleaned or aired for a month or more, and the furniture seemed stiff and cold.

"I've not been myself," Mr. Merringo said. "Not these past few weeks. Perhaps you can understand the shock . . .?"

Howard Wilson avoided his eyes.

"I hope you'll pardon the appearance of the room," Mr. Merringo said indifferently.

"I'm sorry to bother you at all," Howard Wilson said. He tried to relax. He stroked the brief case on his lap. "I got your name from the hospital."

"I understand."

"Please forgive this necessary question: But you were the father?"

Mr. Merringo seemed about to spring across the room at the telepath. For the first time his eyes were alive. Slowly he forced himself to relax. "Yes," he said after a moment. "I was the father."

Howard Wilson let the tension die on the stale and silent air. His hand fumbled at the zipper of his brief case; he knew without looking that the man was staring hard at his face. His hand jerked, and the zipper caught, and as he bent, focusing a part of his attention on it, he wondered what they expected him to be, people like Merringo and the rest: what cold, unfeeling creature; what super intelligence, what icy, emotionless entity, human in form, demon in mind? He could feel the hostile eyes seem to say, You understand, damn you, and you're laughing at me. . . . But his I.Q. was 120, and he could not understand or interpret any more than anyone else of equal intelligence. He got the zipper free. He drew out the data sheet.

"I'd like to enter a few facial descriptions, if you don't mind, Mr. Merringo . . . If you'll stand still, please."

And after a few moments of inspection and recording, he said, "Turn your head in profile, please . . . That's good."

Then he was done. "Do you have a recent picture of Mrs. Merringo?"

". . . yes," Mr. Merringo said. He turned listlessly to the shelf above the ornamental fireplace.

Howard Wilson passed a hand across his eyes. There was the static-electric half pain-like shock in his telepathic sense again. It made a variegated blur behind his eyes. It passed. He stared at his hand. It was shaking. He began to feel ill.

The doctor had said—during the final, fatal examination when he was twenty-one—"The pain will be toward the end."

He shook himself. It was not knowledge of death alone that was frightening; men had died before. But he, along with the no more than two dozen other telepaths, all male, all recently come to maturity and under scrutiny, were left to move forward to an uncharted death without previous clue or case history. Nature, like an inefficient potter casting aside thoughtlessly the imperfect instrument, had erred; man was helpless before her. It was the unknown quality that was most frightening. He rubbed his forehead with a moist hand. It was too early for pain.

"Here is the picture," Mr. Merringo said.

Howard Wilson took it automatically. After his heart quieted, he began to enter details on the data sheet. He forced himself to concentrate on the job. "Now, what color was her hair?"

Mr. Merringo told him.

Howard Wilson frowned and glanced quickly at his other data sheet, checking off, mentally, the other factors to eliminate. Only one, now, remained, upon which the whole examination turned.

"Her eyes?"

Mr. Merringo told him.

"Thank you," Howard Wilson said. "You have been very cooperative."

Walking toward his car, Howard Wilson felt clammy. He opened the car door, tossed in his brief case, eased behind the wheel, pressed back against the worn seat cover, and glancing at his watch, decided to postpone the meal until after seeing Miss Ethel Wilberston, sister of the late Edith Collins, whose husband, Emanuel, had jumped in front of a subway train in the East two weeks ago.

He glanced back at the house of Mr. Merringo, seeing a "For Sale" sign slightly awry in the yard. And he wondered why it was that humans always blamed themselves? Instead of eye color or bone structure or God. But he knew the answer. There was something in them individualistic, proud, fierce, terrible, demanding admiration, and yet, pathetic.

As his foot pressed the snarling starter, he closed his eyes wearily, remembering the negative report from South Africa that had been forwarded to him for his information. He was aware of the conceit of pride when one man presumes to speak for a thousand square miles, cabling, in code: "It hasn't happened here," after consulting a government man in a light, white suit, drinking, perhaps, gin and quinine to avoid a disease or to keep slightly drunk and only half aware of the high, hot sun and the shimmering, steamy forest beyond the cities and the farms and the flat grass lands.

Opening his eyes, he shifted into low. As the car began to move, he created the scene, detail by detail. The Chieftain, tall, ebony, Oxford educated, seated in tribal glory, surrounded by the squalid bamboo village and his callous-footed subjects. From across the dusty pavillion, a glistening husband cries that his wife is dead in childbirth. And the Chieftain, still half believing in spirits, perhaps, summons the medicine man. Together they go to the spot; together they see the silent newborn thing cuddled in a wrapping of afterbirth; and after a moment, the Chieftain orders, "Bury it." While a white man far away says in a guttural Dutch accent, "Nothing of that sort has occurred here, thank God."

Howard Wilson threaded his way through traffic to the home of Miss Ethel Wilberston to see if her sister's eyes had been the same color as all the other women's.

But the sister was not home, and sticky with the afternoon heat, he drove to the office, unhungry, and suddenly tired and enervated by a growing headache.

The office was in the Federal Building, on the third floor, two rooms above the First National Bank and a branch office for a drug chain.

He had worked out of the office during most of the past year, trying, along with Robert Edd, to break up the opium traffic from Mexico. They had been assigned to the project because someone, somewhere, had decided that the opium traffic was a Communist plot. A little over a month ago they had been reassigned to the investigation of the suddenly appeared mutant wave.

Two of the three district FBI men were in the office when he came in, and they broke off their conversation and glanced at him uneasily. He did not like them, and beneath their automatic smiles of recognition, he knew that it was a mutual dislike. He had never answered their smug, suggestive questions: What's that dame thinking, down there? I'd like to know if maybe she isn't thinking about . . . For it always made him shudder and shrink inward, incapable of explaining the morass of conscious thought and the turmoil of half conscious thought and the deeper, emotionally colored surges that made up the human mind. And under the surface, like a deep, fast current, was a common flow of hope and love and generosity cutting through the turgid intermingling of despair and hate and selfishness. It left Howard Wilson mute and afraid; for he saw himself reflected, and the reflection was naked and beyond his judgement.

He put the brief case on the desk and took out the data sheets. His vacation application had not come back.

"I could have checked that guy for you," one of the FBI men said.

Without looking up, Howard Wilson said, "I had nothing to do."

After an uneasy moment, the other agent said, "Find anything new?"

"It's narrowed down to eye color."

"Oh? What do you think?"

Howard Wilson shrugged, feeling itchy and uncomfortable between his shoulder blades. "I couldn't say."

"Okay, okay. Just asking. Skip it."

Suddenly tense and irritable, Howard Wilson clenched his fists at his sides. "I don't . . ." He had started to say in a burst of unreasoning anger, I don't think they know anything about it and I don't think they ever will. It was an involuntary thought, but once it came into his mind, he recognized that until now he had been afraid to admit it even to himself. He felt personally involved and knotted up inside whenever he thought about the mutants. "Never mind," he said.

"It was the Bomb," the first of the FBI men said.

Howard Wilson remained quiet, wondering which of the hundred or so of the Bombs he was talking about.

"Don't *you* think so?"

Howard Wilson shrugged.

The teletype in the far corner of the room began to chatter, and the two FBI men crossed to it. The message rolled out, over the clicking keys, in coded groups.

"The Tokyo report on your stuff," one said to Howard Wilson. "Want to look at it when it's decoded?"

". . . no," Howard Wilson said.

Fifteen years after the Alamogordo Air Base mushroom, they were checking in Phoenix; and hopefully interviewing Bikini natives; and Las Vegas citizens; and Nome residents. While, from secrecy-cloaked sources, reports filtered in from Mexico, Canada, England, France,

Germany, and perhaps, too, from behind the Iron Curtain. In less than a month, a hundred-hundred quiet investigations, with not a ripple in the world press, while tense men in Washington moved pins and drew circles.

"See if there's any in Japan," they had doubtless instructed, intending to prove, if there were, that a pair of atom blasts accounted for them.

While Russia bristled menace at Greece from overrun Yugoslavia, and Western Germany champed at the light Allied reins. And the world, asunder, quivered, waiting, and each action was a potential spark for the powder line.

Howard Wilson remembered looking right from the Customs Building out over Yokohama, watching fishing boats and barges crowd into the muddy canal (or was that over by the Sakurigecho Station, where you got the train to Tokyo?) watching Yokohama and listening to the rattle of winches and the whine of cable from the docks. The air had a sweet, not altogether pleasant, fishy smell. The natives said, sullen-polite, "*ha-so-deska?*" and "*arigato*," and bowed deeply. They made Howard Wilson uneasy, because he could never be sure he understood them at all, and could never be sure that his failure was not an indictment of himself.

Their eyes were black and beady, but, in the last few months, they had probably buried things in their queer Buddhist grave yards and planted totem sticks over the unknown inside their Gates of Eternity. And probably, too, in cold northern Hokkaido, across the narrow straits from fortress Sakhalin, the Ainu piled snow on deformed mutants and remained silent, while, in the southern part, a Hawaiian interpreter under US Government orders asked the governor, who answered respectfully. "There have been no reports here, either."

Suddenly Howard Wilson knew the immensity of the issue and the futility of seeking the easy explanation in terms of the way things were supposed to happen or had always happened. The Bomb was not the cause, because he had been born before the first one. And there had been the mutant increase in the early forties: odd calves, and queer insects and unique wheat, and flies that began to resist DDT. And the increasing percentage of hereditary cancer. The early, beginning wave of it was easily explained in isolation—for no one would more than chuckle at the bizarre animal discovered in Los Angeles in 1939 that looked to be half racoon and half beaver; and few people would seriously doubt any well established theory merely because what was almost a whale washed ashore dead (of maladaptation, perhaps?) on the Oregon coast.

The FBI men were eyeing him sullenly.

"I'm going home," he said. "You know the number if you want me." He was angry at them, and angry that the government had not approved his vacation application. He wanted to get away for a few weeks and relax and think things out.

The office was silent.

The one FBI man moved toward the data sheets on the table, and Howard Wilson said, without looking directly at him, "It isn't your wife's eye color."

The FBI man stopped, embarrassed. "She's pregnant."

Pity again, that he did not want to feel. "I'm sorry," he said.

"Wait a minute," the FBI man said, concern suddenly alive in his voice with the hope of release. "How do you know eye color's the signal? How can you be sure? I want you to explain it to me. My wife—I mean, she knows about it, and . . ."

Howard Wilson wanted to say something about security regulations, but instead he merely nodded.

"I shouldn't have told her," the FBI man said.

Howard Wilson shrugged.

"But why are you so sure eye color's the signal?"

Howard Wilson said, "The chances are a thousand to one, maybe a hundred times that, in favor of any given baby being normal. It won't do any good to worry."

"But you're sure eye color *is* right?"

"No," Howard Wilson said. "All we know is that the incidence of mutation is low, indicating a recessive gene. Since it's consistent, it must be the same gene. We hope it's connected to some exterior hereditary feature. Skin color, for instance, is connected with susceptibility to malaria and tuberculosis; but on the other hand, the recessive that can be mutated to cause hemophilia doesn't seem to be linked to any observable characteristic. Too few cases have been investigated to say definitely that eye color is the indication. It could just be coincidence, so far."

Hurt, the FBI man said nothing.

"I'm sorry," Howard Wilson said less sharply. He wanted to say something helpful, but he was exhausted, and the almost-thought was buzzing again in his telepathic sense. "Don't worry, that's all I can say. Don't worry. It won't do any good to worry about it."

Upon leaving the Federal Building, as he stepped into the sunshine of the street, he met his fellow telepath.

"Hey, Bob!"

Robert Edd turned. His face was drawn and his eyes were dull, as if he had been a long time without sleep. "Oh, Wilson."

Staring into his face, Howard Wilson felt sudden fear. "What's wrong?"

"Here. Read this." Robert Edd handed across a sheaf of papers.

Howard Wilson took them. His mouth was dry. "Listen, Bob, I've . . . that is . . . Have *you* noticed anything wrong? I've had an awful headache since about noon, and I keep getting blurred thoughts that I can't shut out, and . . . it hurts; my telepathic organ . . ."

"Don't think to me!" Robert Edd snapped when Howard Wilson started to abandon speech.

"OK, OK, if you want it this way," Howard Wilson said. "But listen, Bob, I'm scared as hell. What do you think causes it?" He could not bring himself to ask: Am I about to die? He was afraid to find out the answer.

Robert Edd had perspiration on his upper lip. He opened his mouth to speak.

Howard Wilson felt the high, shrill, unpleasant buzzing again: sharper, more menacing now, like the pang of a toothache. It made him shudder even in the heat. And Robert Edd's eyes were suddenly no longer dull; had this piercing buzz reached him too?

"My God," Robert Edd whispered. "No time to talk. Phone me later." He turned and half ran up the stairs.

"Wait!" Howard Wilson called. But Robert Edd had already disappeared. Howard Wilson stared after him indecisively. Then he looked down at the sheaf of papers. An autopsy report. He breathed easier: it concerned the new mutants. He had been afraid . . . No, he did not want to talk to Robert Edd just now. He didn't feel like running down another, probably false, lead this afternoon.

He crossed to his car, and sitting behind the wheel, he scanned the report listlessly.

The birth had been typical. As always, the mother had died—this time in spite of a Caesarian section. The mutant, as usual, gave every indication of being premature—as if the normal gestation period had been too short.

It had died within minutes of the mother. The autopsy showed that its heart was slightly larger than normal, containing an extra compartment; the gonads were undescended, which would probably have resulted in sterility if the creature had reached maturity; the adrenal cortex was completely separated and displaced backward on the kidney; the appendix was missing, and several other vestigial organs atrophied; the glands, notably the pituitary and thyroid were considerably extended; there was some rearrangement of other organs, and the stomach was much smaller and more heavily lined than normal.

There seemed to be a tiny, extra (perhaps potentially telepathic) brain segment between the medulla oblongata and the spinal column proper, and the two halves of the brain were more nearly joined. The nervous system was quite complex. The bone structure had shortened; the normal number of ribs diminished by two. And the underskin, heavy with fatty stored food deposits, practically concentrated body sugar. The body temperature had been abnormally low.

When he finished with the report, he leaned back and closed his eyes. He felt a moment of kinship with the poor dead thing. Then he felt vaguely uneasy. He ran his tongue over dry lips. Why had Robert Edd wanted him to read the report?

He started to get out of the car.

Suddenly the headache was worse, and he felt listless. His mind was overburdened with a sense of futility. Quietly, from a thousand hospitals, the reports were coming in. What could anyone do about it?

Even if eye color proved to be linked to the infected genes—could the government prevent the breeding of the suspects? What would happen when the government announced the mutant wave? Might that not be the international spark? Daily the balance became more uncertain, and critical Europe wavered in loyalty, needing only a push into confusion for which, confidently, the Stalinists waited. Anti-Bomb hysteria could mushroom over night as world citizens seeking an explanation, even as rulers, pointed to America's recent Alaska tests.

He was all at once disgusted with humanity.

But even as the disgust came, there came also the kinship. Even as he wanted to say, Their battles are not my battles, he knew that they were.

For once in Italy on one of the quiet missions, this time to assassinate a key figure and culminate a Titoist break with Moscow—a mission that, through miscalculation, failed—he had met one of his kind in opposition, and as he faced the alien telepath, he knew no common ties with him. They were from different worlds, human worlds, to which they had somehow, beyond their intentions, become committed. Howard Wilson had killed the alien telepath, and he could not feel remorse; for the telepath had been religiously certain of destiny, a certainty which, for Howard Wilson, was presumptuous and frighteningly dangerous.

To hell with it, he thought. I'm going to die.

It was in words at last.

I'm going to die, he thought sadly. He thought about a warm spring night when he was in high school, and he remembered a fish fry when he was six years old. What does anything matter? he thought. I wonder how soon it will be? He wanted to cry. He hated the thing on his forehead that had begun to pain. How soon? The doctor had said, "The pain will be toward the end."

He wanted to be alone with his black despair.

He started the motor. He shifted the gears.

Slowly he drove back the way he had come. Why must I and those poor dead things being born daily be persecuted by the seeds of our difference? he thought. It isn't fair.

At the city limits, he felt wave after wave of peace and strength and power and satisfaction. He stared fascinated at the cemetery. And suddenly death seemed almost pleasant. To rest in the cool, sweet earth . . . .

His telepathic organ quivered. There was no longer pain, but increasing awareness. He frowned again, almost . . . what? The no longer pain whisked away and was gone. In its wake came new restfulness; he felt calmer than he had all day.

As he was getting out of his car before his house, he felt thoughts flow upon his mind and twist away before he could trap them.

His hands were moist. He half ran to the front room. He had to phone Robert Edd. He suddenly realized the significance of the autopsy report.

The phone was ringing.

"Wilson? Wilson, you all right?" the voice asked when he picked up the receiver.

"I'm all right," he said.

"Thank God! This is Kenny at the office. Listen, Robert Edd is dead. He dropped dead right at the door just after you left."

". . . no," Howard Wilson said dully.

"And we just got a teletype. Half the other telepaths have died in the last twenty-four hours."

The phone was cold in Howard Wilson's hand.

"Sit tight. I'm bringing a doctor right over to examine you. Don't move."

"I won't," he said. His forehead was throbbing. "Listen, Kenny, for God's sake, listen!"

Kenny had hung up.

Howard Wilson rattled the receiver hook. "Operator! Operator!" he cried. His hands were shaking desperately.

His head buzzed shriller and shriller, and suddenly he was listening, terrified, to thoughts he did not want to hear. Icy, cold, ruthless, alien. For which he could never feel any emotion but fear and revulsion.

He had to tell the operator before it was too late. "*Operator!*" he screamed.

"Did you get him?" the thought came, or the meaning came, for it was not in words.

"Yes," in answer.

"Good. We can't afford to have them find out. Yet."

"He had just broken through."

"Good."

"Good."

"Good."

Howard Wilson could feel the circuits begin to open up from around the world. Howard Wilson remembered what they looked like, remembered the only one he had seen, a female, lying in an antiseptic room in Christ's Hospital. He began to cry in terror.

"I'm being cremated," came a shriek of agony from India, and then the mind behind it died.

"Hello! Hello! Hello!" Howard Wilson screamed into the telephone.

"I've stopped heart action to join you," came the thought from England.

"Listen!" Howard Wilson cried into the receiver.

"Another one's broke through! Stop him!" came the thought.

Howard Wilson felt his brain being ripped and shredded. His eyes went blank, and his body, unfeeling, fell to the floor, and the mutant thoughts gouged and tore at his mind.

"Hello? Hello?" said the operator.

"I had to regrow three organs after that autopsy," came a mutant thought.

"How long now?"

"Let's count."

And the responses began to roll in from America, Europe, Asia, minds counting one after the other.

"It won't be long now, at the rate we're going."

"But we can wait many years if we must."

Howard Wilson could feel nothing, and his consciousness was dripping away to icy laughter.

"A long time."

"Until there are enough of us."

"Wait. . . ."

"And grow strong. . . ."

"And grow numerous. . . ."

"In France, China, Germany, Russia, Japan, Ireland, Italy, Australia, Brazil . . ."

"Let us rest and grow."

Howard Wilson was almost dead now. The operator kept saying, "What did you want?"

"In our secret tombs. . . ."

"In the soft, soft earth. . . ."

Expendable

PHILIP K. DICK

Horror fiction has been called a fiction of paranoia. If this is true, then Philip K. Dick must qualify as one of the greatest horror writers of all time, even though he wrote mostly science fiction. In futuristic novels like Ubik, The Three Stigmata of Palmer Eldritch, *and* Flow My Tears, The Policeman Said, *Dick portrayed worlds in which reality dissolves at the drop of a hat and plunges characters into self-doubt at the very moment they think that they have mastered their fates. Although Dick wasn't able to show the large-scale effects of such reality warps in his shorter fiction, his stories often deal with characters who become increasingly aware that something is intrinsically wrong with their world. "Expendable" is an ironic blend of science fiction and fantasy that will appeal to anyone who ever had an experience that left him wondering, "Why me?"*

THE MAN came out on the front porch and examined the day. Bright and cold—with dew on the lawns. He buttoned his coat and put his hands in his pockets.

As the man started down the steps the two caterpillars waiting by the mailbox twitched with interest.

"There he goes," the first one said. "Send in your report."

As the other began to rotate his vanes the man stopped, turning quickly.

"I heard that," he said. He brought his foot down against the wall, scraping the caterpillars off, onto the concrete. He crushed them.

Then he hurried down the path to the sidewalk. As he walked he looked around him. In the cherry tree a bird was hopping, pecking bright-eyed at the cherries. The man studied him. All right? Or—The bird flew off. Birds all right. No harm from them.

He went on. At the corner he brushed against a spider web, crossed from the bushes to the telephone pole. His heart pounded. He tore away, batting in the air. As he went on he glanced over his shoulder. The spider was coming slowly down the bush, feeling out the damage to his web.

Hard to tell about spiders. Difficult to figure out. More facts needed— No contact, yet.

He waited at the bus stop, stomping his feet to keep them warm.

The bus came and he boarded it, feeling a sudden pleasure as he took his seat with all the warm, silent people, staring indifferently ahead. A vague flow of security poured through him.

He grinned, and relaxed, the first time in days.

The bus went down the street.

Tirmus waved his antennae excitedly.

"Vote, then, if you want." He hurried past them, up onto the mound. "But let me say what I said yesterday, before you start."

"We already know it all," Lala said impatiently. "Let's get moving. We have the plans worked out. What's holding us up?"

"More reason for me to speak." Tirmus gazed around at the assembled gods. "The entire Hill is ready to march against the giant in question. Why? We know he can't communicate to his fellows—It's out of the question. The type of vibration, the language they use makes it impossible to convey such ideas as he holds about us, about our—"

"Nonsense." Lala stepped up. "Giants communicate well enough."

"There is no record of a giant having made known information about us!"

The array moved restlessly.

"Go ahead," Tirmus said. "But it's a waste of effort. He's harmless— cut off. Why take all the time and—"

"Harmless?" Lala stared at him. "Don't you understand? He knows!"

Tirmus walked away from the mound. "I'm against unnecessary violence. We should save our strength. Someday we'll need it."

The vote was taken. As expected, the army was in favor of moving against the giant. Tirmus sighed and began stroking out the plans on the ground.

"This is the location that he takes. He can be expected to appear there at period-end. Now, as I see the situation—"

He went on, laying out the plans in the soft soil.

One of the gods leaned toward another, antennae touching. "This giant. He doesn't stand a chance. In a way, I feel sorry for him. How'd he happen to butt in?"

"Accident." The other grinned. "You know, the way they do, barging around."

"It's too bad for him, though."

It was nightfall. The street was dark and deserted. Along the sidewalk the man came, a newspaper under his arm. He walked quickly, glancing around him. He skirted the big tree growing by the curb and leaped agilely into the street. He crossed the street and gained the opposite side. As he turned the corner he entered the web, sewn from bush to telephone pole. Automatically he fought it, brushing it off him. As the strands broke a thin humming came to him, metallic and wiry.

". . . wait!"

He paused.

". . . careful . . . inside . . . wait. . . ."

His jaw set. The last strands broke in his hands and he walked on. Behind him the spider moved in the fragment of his web, watching. The man looked back.

"Nuts to you," he said. "I'm not taking any chances, standing there all tied up."

He went on, along the sidewalk, to his path. He skipped up the path, avoiding the darkening bushes. On the porch he found his key, fitting it into the lock.

He paused. Inside? Better than outside, especially at night. Night a bad time. Too much movement under the bushes. Not good. He opened the door and stepped inside. The rug lay ahead of him, a pool of blackness. Across on the other side he made out the form of the lamp.

Four steps to the lamp. His foot came up. He stopped.

What did the spider say? Wait? He waited, listening. Silence.

He took his cigarette lighter and flicked it on.

The carpet of ants swelled toward him, rising up in a flood. He leaped aside, out onto the porch. The ants came rushing, hurrying, scratching across the floor in the half-light.

The man jumped down to the ground and around the side of the house. When the first ants came flowing over the porch he was already spinning the faucet handle rapidly, gathering up the hose.

The burst of water lifted the ants up and scattered them, flinging them away. The man adjusted the nozzle, squinting through the mist. He advanced, turning the hard stream from side to side.

"God damn you," he said, his teeth locked. "Waiting inside—"

He was frightened. Inside—never before! In the night cold sweat came out on his face. Inside. They had never got inside before. Maybe a moth or two, and flies, of course. But they were harmless, fluttery, noisy—

A carpet of ants!

Savagely, he sprayed them until they broke rank and fled into the lawn, into the bushes, under the house.

He sat down on the walk, holding the hose, trembling from head to foot.

They really meant it. Not an anger raid, annoyed, spasmodic; but planned, an attack, worked out. They had waited for him. One more step—

Thank God for the spider.

Presently he shut the hose off and stood up. No sound; silence everywhere. The bushes rustled suddenly. Beetle? Something black scurried—he put his foot on it. A messenger, probably. Fast runner. He went gingerly inside the dark house, feeling his way by the cigarette lighter.

Later, he sat at his desk, the spray gun beside him, heavy-duty steel and copper. He touched its damp surface with his fingers.

Seven o'clock. Behind him the radio played softly. He reached over and moved the desk lamp so that it shone on the floor beside the desk.

He lit a cigarette and took some writing paper and his fountain pen. He paused, thinking.

So they really wanted him, badly enough to plan it out. Bleak despair descended over him like a torrent. What could he do? Whom could he go to? Or tell? He clenched his fists, sitting bolt upright in the chair.

The spider slid down beside him onto the desk top. "Sorry. Hope you aren't frightened, as in the poem."

The man stared. "Are you the same one? The one at the corner? The one who warned me?"

"No. That's somebody else. A Spinner. I'm strictly a Cruncher. Look at my jaws." He opened and shut his mouth. "I bite them up."

The man smiled. "Good for you."

"Sure. Do you know how many there are of us in—say—an acre of land? Guess."

"A thousand."

"No. Two and a half million. Of all kinds. Crunchers, like me, or Spinners, or Stingers."

"Stingers?"

"The best. Let's see." The spider thought. "For instance, the black widow, as you call her. Very valuable." He paused. "Just one thing."

"What's that?"

"We have our problems. The gods—"

"Gods!"

"Ants, as you call them. The leaders. They're beyond us. Very unfortunate. They have an awful taste—makes one sick. We have to leave them for the birds."

The man stood up. "Birds? Are they—"

"Well, we have an arrangement. This has been going on for ages. I'll give you the story. We have some time left."

The man's heart contracted. "Time left? What do you mean?"

"Nothing. A little trouble later on, I understand. Let me give you the background. I don't think you know it."

"Go ahead. I'm listening." He stood up and began to walk back and forth.

"*They* were running the earth pretty well, about a billion years ago. You see, men came from some other planet. Which one? I don't know. They landed and found the earth quite well cultivated by them. There was a war."

"So we're the invaders," the man murmured.

"Sure. The war reduced both sides to barbarism, them and yourselves. You forgot how to attack, and they degenerated into closed social factions, ants, termites—"

"I see."

"The last group of you that knew the full story started us going. We were bred—" the spider chuckled in its own fashion, "bred someplace for this worthwhile purpose. We keep them down very well. You know what they call us? The Eaters. Unpleasant, isn't it?"

Two more spiders came drifting down on their web-strands, alighting on the desk. The three spiders went into a huddle.

"More serious than I thought," the Cruncher said easily. "Didn't know the whole dope. This Stinger here—"

The black widow came to the edge of the desk. "Giant," she piped, metallically. "I'd like to talk with you."

"Go ahead," the man said.

"There's going to be some trouble here. They're moving, coming here, a lot of them. We thought we'd stay with you awhile. Get in on it."

"I see." The man nodded. He licked his lips, running his fingers shakily through his hair. "Do you think—that is, what are the chances—"

"Chances?" The Stinger undulated thoughtfully. "Well, we've been in this work a long time. Almost a million years. I think that we have the edge over them, in spite of drawbacks. Our arrangements with the birds, and of course, with the toads—"

"I think we can save you," the Cruncher put in cheerfully. "As a matter of fact, we look forward to events like this."

From under the floor boards came a distant scratching sound, the noise of a multitude of tiny claws and wings, vibrating faintly, remotely. The man heard. His body sagged all over.

"You're really certain? You think you can do it?" He wiped the perspiration from his lips and picked up the spray gun, still listening.

The sound was growing, swelling beneath them, under the floor, under their feet. Outside the house bushes rustled and a few moths flew up against the window. Louder and louder the sound grew, beyond and below, everywhere, a rising hum of anger and determination. The man looked from side to side.

"You're sure you can do it?" he murmured. "You really can save me?"

"Oh," the Stinger said, embarrassed. "I didn't mean *that*. I meant the species, the race . . . not you as an individual."

The man gaped at him and the three Eaters shifted uneasily. More moths burst against the window. Under them the floor stirred and heaved.

"I see," the man said. "I'm sorry I misunderstood you."

Sorry, Right Number

RICHARD MATHESON

A friend of Richard Matheson's once described his horror fiction thus: a man and wife are sitting down to coffee at the breakfast table, and something nasty pops out of the sugar bowl. In what Stephen King has dubbed Matheson's style of "suburban horror," terrible phenomena usually intrude upon, or arise from, the most mundane aspects of everyday life. This is very much the sort of fantasy John W. Campbell strove to publish in Unknown, *so it's not surprising that Matheson submitted a tale like "Sorry, Right Number" to* Beyond Fantasy Fiction, *a magazine edited by* Unknown *alumnus H. L. Gold. The story was later adapted for Rod Serling's* The Twilight Zone, *one of several television shows for which Matheson served as a scriptwriter.*

JUST BEFORE the telephone rang, storm winds toppled the tree outside her window and jolted Miss Keene from her dreaming sleep. She flung herself up with a gasp, her frail hands crumpling twists of sheet in either palm. Beneath her fleshless chest the heart jerked taut, the sluggish blood spurted. She sat in rigid muteness, her eyes staring at the night.

Then, in another second, the telephone rang.

Who on earth? The question shaped unwittingly in her brain. Her thin hand faltered in the darkness, the fingers searching a moment and then Miss Elva Keene drew the cool receiver to her ear.

"Hello," she said.

Outside a cannon of thunder shook the night, twitching Miss Keene's crippled legs. *I've missed the voice,* she thought, *the thunder has blotted out the voice.*

"Hello," she said again.

There was no sound. Miss Keene waited in expectant lethargy. Then she repeated, "Hel-*lo,*" in a cracking voice. Outside the thunder crashed again.

Still no voice spoke, not even the sound of a phone being disconnected met her ears. Her wavering hand reached out and thumped down the receiver with an angry motion.

"Inconsideration," she muttered, thudding back on her pillow. Already her infirm back ached from the effort of sitting.

She forced out a weary breath. Now she'd have to suffer through the whole tormenting process of going to sleep again—the composing of jaded muscles, the ignoring of abrasive pain in her legs, the endless, frustrating struggle to turn off the faucet in her brain and keep unwanted thoughts from dripping. Oh, well, it had to be done; Nurse Phillips insisted on proper rest. Elva Keene breathed slowly and deeply, drew the covers to her chin and labored hopefully for sleep.

In vain.

Her eyes opened and, turning her face to the window, she watched the storm move off on lightning legs. *Why can't I sleep,* she fretted, *why must I always lie here awake like this?*

She knew the answer without effort. When a life was dull, the smallest element added seemed unnaturally intriguing. And life for Miss Keene was the sorry pattern of lying flat or being propped on pillows, reading books which Nurse Phillips brought from the town library, getting nourishment, rest, medication, listening to her tiny radio—and waiting, *waiting* for something different to happen.

Like the telephone call that wasn't a call.

There hadn't even been the sound of a receiver replaced in its cradle. Miss Keene didn't understand that. Why would anyone call her exchange and then listen silently while she said "Hello" over and over again? *Had* it actually been anyone calling?

What she should have done, she realized then, was to keep listening until the other person tired of the joke and put down the receiver. What she should have done was to speak out forcefully about the inconsideration of a prankish call to a crippled maiden lady, in the middle of a stormy night. Then, if there *had* been someone listening, whoever it was would have been properly chastened by her angry words and . . . .

"Well, of course."

She said it aloud in the darkness, punctuating the sentence with a cluck of somewhat relieved disgust. Of course, the telephone was out of order. Someone had tried to contact her, perhaps Nurse Phillips to see if she were all right. But the other end of the line had broken down in some way, allowing her phone to ring but no verbal communication to be made. Well, of course, that was the case.

Miss Keene nodded once and closed her eyes gently. *Now to sleep,* she thought. Far away, beyond the county, the storm cleared its murky throat. *I hope no one is worrying,* Elva Keene thought, *that would be too bad.*

She was thinking that when the telephone rang again.

There, she thought, *they are trying to reach me again.* She reached out hurriedly in the darkness, fumbled until she felt the receiver, then pulled it to her ear.

"Hello," said Miss Keene.

Silence.

Her throat contracted. She knew what was wrong, of course, but she didn't like it, no, not at all.

"Hello?" she said, tentatively, not yet certain that she was wasting breath.

There was no reply. She waited a moment, then spoke a third time, a little impatiently now, loudly, her shrill voice ringing in the dark bedroom. *"Hello!"*

Nothing. Miss Keene had the sudden urge to fling the receiver away. She forced down that curious instinct—no, she must wait; wait and listen to hear if anyone hung up the phone on the other end of the line.

So she waited.

The bedroom was very quiet now, but Elva Keene kept straining to hear; either the sound of a receiver going down or the buzz which usually follows. Her chest rose and fell in delicate lurches, she closed her eyes in concentration, then opened them again and blinked at the darkness. There was no sound from the telephone; not a click, not a buzz, not a sound of someone putting down a receiver.

"Hello!" she cried suddenly, then pushed away the receiver.

She missed her target. The receiver dropped and thumped once on the rug. Miss Keene nervously clicked on the lamp, wincing as the leprous bulb light filled her eyes. Quickly, she lay on her side and tried to reach the silent, voiceless telephone.

But she couldn't stretch far enough and crippled legs prevented her from rising. Her throat tightened. My God, must she leave it there all night, silent and mystifying?

Remembering then, she reached out abruptly and pressed the cradle arm. On the floor, the receiver clicked, then began to buzz normally.

Elva Keene swallowed and drew in a shaking breath as she slumped back on her pillow.

She threw out hooks of reason then and pulled herself back from panic. *This is ridiculous,* she thought, *getting upset over such a trivial and easily explained incident. It was the storm, the night, the way in which I'd been shocked from sleep (What was it that had awakened me?) all these things piled on the mountain of teeth-grinding monotony that's my life. Yes, it was bad, very bad.* But it wasn't the incident that was bad, it was her reaction to it.

Miss Elva Keene numbed herself to further premonitions. *I shall sleep now,* she ordered her body with a petulant shake. She lay very still and relaxed. From the floor she could hear the telephone buzzing like the drone of far-off bees. She ignored it.

Early the next morning, after Nurse Phillips had taken away the breakfast dishes, Elva Keene called the telephone company.

"This is Miss Elva," she told the operator.

"Oh, yes, Miss Elva," said the operator, a Miss Finch. "Can I help you?"

"Last night my telephone rang twice," said Elva Keene. "But when I answered it, no one spoke. And I didn't hear any receiver drop. I didn't even hear a dial tone—just silence."

"Well, I'll tell you, Miss Elva," said the cheery voice of Miss Finch, "that storm last night just about ruined half our service. We're being flooded with calls about knocked down lines and bad connections. I'd say you're pretty lucky your phone is working at all."

"Then you think it was probably a bad connection," prompted Miss Keene, "caused by the storm?"

"Oh, yes, Miss Elva, that's all."

"Do you think it will happen again?"

"Oh, it *may,*" said Miss Finch. "It *may.* I really couldn't tell you, Miss Elva. But if it does happen again, you just call me and then I'll have one of our men check on it."

"All right," said Miss Elva. "Thank you, dear."

She lay on her pillows all morning in a relaxed torpor. *It gives one a satisfied feeling,* she thought, *to solve a mystery, slight as it is. It had been a terrible storm that caused the bad connection. And no wonder when it had even knocked down the ancient oak tree beside the house. That was the noise that had awakened me of course, and a pity it was that the dear tree had fallen. How it shaded the house in hot summer months. Oh, well, I suppose I should be grateful,* she thought, *that the tree fell across the road and not across the house.*

The day passed uneventfully, an amalgam of eating, reading Angela Thirkell and the mail (two throw-away advertisements and the light bill) plus brief chats with Nurse Phillips. Indeed, routine had set in so

properly that when the telephone rang early that evening, she picked
it up without even thinking.

"Hello," she said.

Silence.

It brought her back for a second. Then she called Nurse Phillips.

"What is it?" asked the portly woman as she trudged across the
bedroom rug.

"This is what I was telling you about," said Elva Keene, holding
out the receiver. "Listen!"

Nurse Phillips took the receiver in her hand and pushed back gray
locks with the earpiece. Her placid face remained placid. "There's
nobody there," she observed.

"That's right," said Miss Keene. "That's right. Now you just listen
and see if you can hear a receiver being put down. I'm sure you won't."

Nurse Phillips listened for a moment, then shook her head. "I don't
hear anything," she said and hung up.

"Oh, wait!" Miss Keene said hurriedly. "Oh, well, it doesn't matter,"
she added, seeing it was already down. "If it happens too often, I'll
just call Miss Finch and they'll have a repairman check on it."

"I see," Nurse Phillips said and went back to the living room and
Faith Baldwin.

Nurse Phillips left the house at eight, leaving on the bedside table,
as usual, an apple, a cookie, a glass of water and the bottle of pills.
She puffed up the pillows behind Miss Keene's fragile back, moved
the radio and telephone a little closer to the bed, looked around
complacently, then turned for the door, saying, "I'll see you tomorrow."

It was fifteen minutes later when the telephone rang. Miss Keene
picked up the receiver quickly. She didn't bother saying hello this
time—she just listened.

At first it was the same—an absolute silence. She listened a moment
more, impatiently. Then, on the verge of replacing the receiver she
heard the sound. Her cheek twitched, she jerked the telephone back
to her ear.

"Hello?" she asked, tensely.

A murmuring, a dull humming, a rustling sound—what was it? Miss
Keene shut her eyes tightly, listening hard, but she couldn't identify
the sound; it was too soft, too undefined. It deviated from a sort of
whining vibration . . . to an escape of air . . . to a bubbling sibilance.
It must be the sound of the connection, she thought, *it must be the
telephone itself making the noise. Perhaps a wire blowing in the wind
somewhere, perhaps. . . .*

She stopped thinking then. She stopped breathing. The sound had
ceased. Once more, silence rang in her ears. She could feel the heartbeats
stumbling in her chest again, the walls of her throat closing in. *Oh,*

this is ridiculous, she told herself, *I've already been through this—it was the storm, the storm!*

She lay back on her pillows, the receiver pressed to her ear, nervous breaths faltering from her nostrils. She could feel unreasoning dread rise like a tide within her, despite all attempts at sane deduction. Her mind kept slipping off the glassy perch of reason; she kept falling deeper and deeper.

Now she shuddered violently as the sounds began again. They couldn't *possibly* be human sounds, she knew, and yet there was something about them, some inflection, some almost identifiable arrangement of. . . .

Her lips shook and a whine began to hover in her throat. But she couldn't put down the telephone, she simply couldn't. The sounds held her hypnotized. Whether they were the rise and fall of the wind or the muttering of faulty mechanisms, she didn't know, but they would not let her go.

"Hello?" she murmured, shakily.

The sounds rose in volume. They rattled and shook in her brain.

"Hello!" she screamed.

"H-e-l-l-o," answered a voice on the telephone. Then Miss Keene fainted dead away.

"Are you certain it was someone saying *hello?*" Miss Finch asked Miss Elva over the telephone. "It might have been the connection, you know."

"I tell you it was a *man!*" a shaking Elva Keene screeched. "It was the same man who kept listening to me say hello over and over and over again without answering me back. The same one who made terrible noises over the telephone!"

Miss Finch cleared her throat politely. "Well, I'll have a man check your line, Miss Elva, as soon as he can. Of course, the men are very busy now with all the repairs on storm wreckage, but as soon as it's possible . . ."

"And what am I going to do if this—this *person* calls again?"

"You just hang up on him, Miss Elva."

"But he keeps calling!"

"Well." Miss Finch's affability wavered. "Why don't you find out who he is, Miss Elva? If you can do that, why, we can take immediate action, you see and. . . ."

After she'd hung up, Miss Keene lay against the pillows tensely, listening to Nurse Phillips sing husky love songs over the breakfast dishes. Miss Finch didn't believe her story, that was apparent. Miss Finch thought she was a nervous old woman falling prey to imagination. Well, Miss Finch would find out differently.

"I'll just keep calling her and calling her until she *does,*" she said irritably to Nurse Phillips just before afternoon nap.

"You just do that," said Nurse Phillips. "Now take your pill and lie down."

Miss Keene lay in grumpy silence, her vein-rutted hands knotted at her sides. It was ten after two and, except for the bubbling of Nurse Phillips' front room snores, the house was silent in the October afternoon. *It makes me angry,* thought Elva Keene, *that no one will take this seriously. Well,* her thin lips pressed together, *the next time the telephone rings I'll make sure that Nurse Phillips listens until she does hear something.*

Exactly then the phone rang.

Miss Keene felt a cold tremor lace down her body. Even in the daylight with sunbeams speckling her flowered coverlets, the strident ringing frightened her. She dug porcelain teeth into her lower lip to steady it. *Shall I answer it?* the question came and then, before she could even think to answer, her hand picked up the receiver. A deep ragged breath; she drew the phone slowly to her ear. She said, "Hello?"

The voice answered back, "Hello?"—hollow and inanimate.

"Who is this?" Miss Keene asked, trying to keep her throat clear.

"Hello?"

"Who's calling, please?"

"Hello?"

"Is anyone there!"

"Hello?"

"Please . . . !"

"Hello?"

Miss Keene jammed down the receiver and lay on her bed trembling violently, unable to catch her breath. *What is it,* begged her mind, *what in God's name is it?*

"Margaret!" she cried. "*Margaret!*"

In the front room she heard Nurse Phillips grunt abruptly and then start coughing.

"Margaret, please . . . !"

Elva Keene heard the large-bodied woman rise to her feet and trudge across the living room floor. *I must compose myself,* she told herself, fluttering hands to her fevered cheeks, *I must tell her exactly what happened, exactly.*

"What is it?" grumbled the nurse. "Does your stomach ache?"

Miss Keene's throat drew in tautly as she swallowed. "He just called again," she whispered.

"Who?"

"That man!"

"What man?"

"The one who keeps calling!" Miss Keene cried. "He keeps saying hello over and over again. That's all he says—hello, hello, hel . . . ."

"Now stop this," Nurse Phillips scolded stolidly. "Lie back and. . . ."

"I don't *want* to lie back!" she said frenziedly. "I want to know who this terrible person is who keeps frightening me!"

"Now don't work yourself into a state," warned Nurse Phillips. "You know how upset your stomach gets."

Miss Keene began to sob bitterly. "I'm afraid. I'm afraid of him. Why does he keep calling me?"

Nurse Phillips stood by the bed looking down in bovine inertia. "Now, what did Miss Finch tell you?" she said, softly.

Miss Keene's shaking lips could not frame the answer.

"Did she tell you it was the connection?" the nurse soothed. "Did she?"

"But it isn't! It's a man, a *man!*"

Nurse Phillips expelled a patient breath. "If it's a man," she said, "then just hang up. You don't have to talk to him. Just hang up. Is that so hard to do?"

Miss Keene shut tear-bright eyes and forced her lips into a twitching line. In her mind the man's subdued and listless voice kept echoing. Over and over, the inflection never altering, the question never deferring to her replies—just repeating itself endlessly in doleful apathy. *Hello? Hello?* Making her shudder to the heart.

"Look," Nurse Phillips spoke.

She opened her eyes and saw the blurred image of the nurse putting the receiver down on the table.

"There," Nurse Phillips said, "nobody can call you now. You leave it that way. If you need anything all you have to do is dial. Now isn't that all right? Isn't it?"

Miss Keene looked bleakly at her nurse. Then, after a moment, she nodded once. Grudgingly.

She lay in the dark bedroom, the sound of the dial tone humming in her ear; keeping her awake. *Or am I just telling myself that?* she thought. *Is it really keeping me awake? Didn't I sleep that first night with the receiver off the hook? No, it wasn't the sound, it was something else.*

She closed her eyes obdurately. *I won't listen,* she told herself, *I just won't listen to it.* She drew in trembling breaths of the night. But the darkness would not fill her brain and blot away the sound.

Miss Keene felt around on the bed until she found her bed jacket. She draped it over the receiver, swathing its black smoothness in woolly turns. Then she sank back again, stern breathed and taut. *I will sleep,* she demanded, *I will sleep.*

She heard it still.

Her body grew rigid and abruptly, she unfolded the receiver from its thick wrappings and slammed it down angrily on the cradle. Silence filled the room with delicious peace. Miss Keene fell back on the pillow with a feeble groan. *Now to sleep,* she thought.

And the telephone rang.

Her breath snuffed off. The ringing seemed to permeate the darkness, surrounding her in a cloud of ear-lancing vibration. She reached out to put the receiver on the table again, then jerked her hand back with a gasp, realizing she would hear the man's voice again.

Her throat pulsed nervously. *What I'll do,* she planned, *what I'll do is take off the receiver very quickly—very quickly—and put it down, then push down on the arm and cut off the line. Yes, that's what I'll do!*

She tensed herself and spread her hand out cautiously until the ringing phone was under it. Then, breath held, she followed her plan, slashed off the ring, reached quickly for the cradle arm. . . .

And stopped, frozen, as the man's voice reached out through darkness to her ears. "Where are you?" he asked. "I want to talk to you."

Claws of ice clamped down on Miss Keene's shuddering chest. She lay petrified, unable to cut off the sound of the man's dull, expressionless voice, asking: "Where are you? I want to talk to you."

A sound from Miss Keene's throat, thin and fluttering.

And the man said, "Where are you? I want to talk to you."

"No, no," sobbed Miss Keene.

"Where are you? I want to. . . ."

She pressed the cradle arm with taut white fingers. She held it down for fifteen minutes before letting it go.

"I tell you I won't have it!"

Miss Keene's voice was a frayed ribbon of sound. She sat inflexibly on the bed, straining her frightened anger through the mouthpiece vents.

"You say you hang up on this man and he still calls?" Miss Finch inquired.

"I've *explained* all that!" Elva Keene burst out. "I had to leave the receiver off the phone all night so he wouldn't call. And the buzzing kept me awake. I didn't get a *wink* of sleep! Now, I want this line checked, do you hear me? I want you to stop this terrible thing!"

Her eyes were like hard, dark beads. The phone almost slipped from her palsied fingers.

"All right, Miss Elva," said the operator. "I'll send a man out today."

"Thank you, dear, thank you," Miss Keene said. "Will you call me when. . . ."

Her voice stopped abruptly as a clicking sound started on the telephone.

"The line is busy," she announced.

The clicking stopped and she went on. "To repeat, will you let me know when you find out who this terrible person is?"

"Surely, Miss Elva, surely. And I'll have a man check your telephone this afternoon. You're at 127 Mill Lane, aren't you?"

"That's right, dear. You will see to it, won't you?"

"I promise faithfully, Miss Elva. First thing today."

"Thank you, dear," Miss Keene said, drawing in relieved breath. There were no calls from the man all that morning, none that afternoon. Her tightness slowly began to loosen. She played a game of cribbage with Nurse Phillips and even managed a little laughter. It was comforting to know that the telephone company was working on it now. They'd soon catch that awful man and bring back her peace of mind.

But when two o'clock came, then three o'clock—and still no repairman at her house—Miss Keene began worrying again.

"What's the *matter* with that girl?" she said pettishly. "She promised me faithfully that a man would come this afternoon."

"He'll be here," Nurse Phillips said. "Be patient."

Four o'clock arrived and no man. Miss Keene would not play cribbage, read her book or listen to her radio. What had begun to loosen was tightening again, increasing minute by minute until at five o'clock, when the telephone rang, her hand spurted out rigidly from the flaring sleeve of her bed jacket and clamped down like a claw on the receiver. *If the man speaks,* raced her mind, *if he speaks I'll scream until my heart stops.*

She pulled the receiver to her ear. "Hello?"

"Miss Elva, this is Miss Finch."

Her eyes closed and breath fluttered through her lips. "Yes?" she said.

"About those calls you say you've been receiving."

"Yes?" In her mind, Miss Finch's words cutting—"those calls you *say* you've been receiving."

"We sent a man out to trace them," continued Miss Finch. "I have his report here."

Miss Keene caught her breath. "Yes?"

"He couldn't find anything."

Elva Keene didn't speak. Her gray head lay motionless on the pillow, the receiver pressed to her ear.

"He says he traced the—the difficulty to a fallen wire on the edge of town."

"Fallen—wire?"

"Yes, Miss Elva." Miss Finch did not sound happy.

"You're telling me I didn't hear anything?"

Miss Finch's voice was firm. "There's no way anyone could have phoned you from that location," she said.

"I tell you a *man* called me!"

Miss Finch was silent and Miss Keene's fingers tightened convulsively on the receiver.

RICHARD MATHESON

"There must be a phone there," she insisted. "There must be *some* way that man was able to call me."

"Miss Elva, the wire is lying on the ground." She paused. "Tomorrow, our crew will put it back up and you won't be. . . ."

"There *has* to be a way he could call me!"

"Miss Elva, there's no one out there."

"Out where, *where?*"

The operator said, "Miss Elva, it's the cemetery."

In the black silence of her bedroom, a crippled maiden lady lay waiting. Her nurse would not remain for the night; her nurse had patted her and scolded her and ignored her.

She was waiting for a telephone call.

She could have disconnected the phone, but she had not the will. She lay there waiting, waiting, thinking.

Of the silence—of ears that had not heard, seeking to hear again. Of sounds bubbling and muttering—the first stumbling attempts at speech by one who had not spoken—how long? Of—*hello? hello?*—first greeting by one long silent. Of—*where are you?* Of (that which made her lie so rigidly) the clicking and the operator speaking her address. Of—

The telephone ringing.

A pause. Ringing. The rustle of a nightgown in the dark.

The ringing stopped.

Listening.

And the telephone slipping from white fingers, the eyes staring, the thin heartbeats slowly pulsing.

Outside, the cricket-rattling night.

Inside, the words still sounding in her brain—giving terrible meaning to the heavy, choking silence.

"Hello, Miss Elva. I'll be right over."